Labour
of Love

Labour
of Love

James Eden

Arcadian Lifestyle

Arcadian Lifestyle Publications is an affiliate of
The Arcadian Group S.A., Case Postale 431, 1211 Geneva 12, Switzerland
Copyright © Arcadian Lifestyle Publications 2017

Database right Arcadian Lifestyle Publications (maker)

First published 2017

ISBN 9781941634394

Designed and typeset by Megan Sheer

Printed in Great Britain by CPI UK,
141–143 Shoreditch High Street, London, E1 6JE

Typeset in Monotype Arcadian Bembo and Stempel Garamond

Although based on the author's experiences, it should be noted that this book is
a work of fiction presented entirely for entertainment purposes. The author and
publisher are not offering professional service advice. The stories and their characters
and entities are fictional. Any likeness to actual persons, whether in terms of
character profiles or names, either living or dead, is strictly coincidental.

I dedicate this this novel to my impossible dream.

Foreword

Ever since I can remember, it has been my dream to establish, in our family home, a collection of galleries that would reflect the decorative tastes of different cultures. I was born in a castle with thirty rooms, and as a child I would roam the narrow, winding corridors, imagining the aesthetic delights I could create behind each closed door. Back then, my experience of the world was limited, as were my ideas. I imagined that instead of our traditional dining room we could create a baroque French area; instead of a regular old living room we could create a grand, Art Deco American salon; instead of a regular bathroom we could create a wood-panelled Scandinavian space. As I grew older and I began to travel the world, the germ of this idea sprouted into something altogether more ambitious – I decided that I wanted to create a home the rooms of which could be turned into galleries representing different time periods and civilisations throughout history.

As such, I began to dream of rooms tiled from floor to ceiling with Phoenician mosaics, Cordoba leather and Byzantine pietra dura, rooms in which I could also gather objects from around the world to document that particular civilisation's culture and history. From this grand design came something even more important – I realised that in undertaking this project, I could examine the influences of both Eastern and Western civilisations upon one another.

Of course, such a project is beyond the financial reach of most people – myself included – but I realised that I could at least create a handful of galleries as a testament to my dream. It took a while to get my family to come around to the idea of redecorating our apartment in such an outlandish way, but once they gave their reluctant assent, we set about redesigning the spaces. The task required hundreds of man hours – millions of days would have been necessary for the complete fulfilment of my dream – and we assembled the best team of traditional artisans from around the world to assist us in our endeavour; from Arabian pearl carvers to American illustrators; from Chinese lacquer experts to Spanish leatherworkers. Each of the five ambitious galleries we set about creating together had one common denominator – a huge amount of work. I had to dedicate an enormous amount of my own time to the project, and in the process I started to become an expert in mosaics, trompe l'oeil decoration, frescoes, murals and gilding. I began to realise that this decorative process would come at a large cost : my business and my social life would begin to suffer. My life was hijacked by the project, and my attention consumed by it. The endeavour was fraught with so much drama, so much conflict and such passion that I realised that, once the dust settled, it would make for an enthralling novel, which would represent the fulfilment of my dream.

At this stage, I would like to extend profound thanks to my friends and colleagues at Arcadian Lifestyle, who have been of great help to me in putting together this novel.

Chapter One

Jemme Mafeze walked through the dusty streets of Istanbul back to the family home. He was hot and tired after kicking a ball around with his friends after school, and stopped at a street vendor to buy a glass of fresh orange juice. The man's cart was piled high with bright oranges and he squeezed them into a glass for Jemme with a practiced hand. Jemme finished, paid the man a handful of lira, returned the glass and made his way home. As he neared the house, as usual there was a hubbub of activity at the front. In the middle of the melee was Grandma. Slim and elegant with a shock of silver hair, she was highly respected within the community. The house was always filled with visitors who had come to ask her advice on everything from the social to the spiritual as well as those who just came to enjoy a small glass of mint tea, sweetened with honey, whilst they listened to her stories. As well as being a centre of the community, Grandma was a cornerstone of Jemme's life. She was a remarkable and compelling woman, who despite being well into her eighties, had the strength and energy of a woman half her age. She had lived in the same house all her life and was part of the fabric of the city, as strong and permanent as the great dome of Hagia Sophia. Like many of Istanbul's great dowagers, she had seen great change – she had experienced the city's splendid highs and desperate lows. She had seen the fall of the Empire and the rise of the Republic and the sorrow of innumerable wars. She was written into the city's history and it was written into her eyes. There was a depth to them which can only be achieved through great wisdom. For the young Jemme, it was impossible to imagine anyone wiser and more knowledgeable. He looked on at the house as the crowd drifted inside to make their way to the *haremlik*, the exclusive social preserve of the women.

Jemme scurried inside, keen to be inside the cool, tiled courtyard of his home and to splash water from its fountain on his face. In many ways, his was an idyllic childhood and he had everything a young boy could dream of. His school was large and full of friends. It encouraged sports and had large fields for the purposes, perfect for the lively young Jemme to burn off some of his energy with classmates, before collapsing in the shade of the cedar trees which picked out the borders of the field. He enjoyed his lessons too, especially history, and would listen enraptured as his teachers told the story of his city. All children have active imaginations, but Jemme's was exceptionally vivid, and when his teachers described the riches and power of the Ottoman Empire, to Jemme it was as if he was there. He could see the palaces and the great libraries as if he was wandering through them, wondering at their beautiful decorations, running his small hands over their silks and breathing in their spices. His memory was as sharp as his imagination, and everything he heard would be first visualised and then memorised, stored for night time when he would play the scenes over and over in his head. Literature lessons also appealed to him; the malleability of words meant that they were raw material to be turned into whatever their creator desired – a haunting poem, a romantic letter, a fiery polemic. Words anchored the abstract and committed it to paper. Once written, something became someone's property, and, if carefully preserved could become history. One could segue seamlessly into the other, a cross-over evident in the works of great men such as Herodotus, Procopius and Abu Ja'far Muhammad ibn Jarir al-Tabari. His enthusiasm was equal to that of his teacher, and if it had not been for the regular interruption of games and friends, Jemme could have lost himself for days, reading his way into the rich tradition not just of his homeland, but of the Western world too.

Jemme looked up from the fountain; the last of the women had gone inside and he traipsed his way across the courtyard with its black and white tiles forming spirals of interlocking geometric shapes. The bedrooms of the house all sat around the central courtyard and Jemme had his own room, with a high ceiling and soft muslin curtains which billowed gently when caught by an afternoon breeze. Jemme flung his satchel into his room and set off to find his mother, who greeted him with a kiss on the forehead. 'You're just in time for supper,' she said, smoothing down his hair, 'your cousins are here too,' she added as Jemme ran off to the table. In addition to his grandmother's visitors, there was a near constant stream of people coming in and out of the home. Cousins, neighbours, relatives, business partners, there was always someone to entertain, to show around, break bread, or exchange stories with. Best of all was when Jemme's cousins visited, or grown-up visitors bought their children with them. They would run around the courtyard, chasing each other and kicking a football, much to the consternation of Jemme's mother, who wondered at the fact they had any windows left at all. Jemme's mother could often be found in the kitchen, sometimes with her sisters who were regular visitors. They would spend hours patiently preparing delicious little *mezze*, some of which would be set out in bright small dishes on the supper table, ready for when Jemme returned from school, and his father from work, and some would be stored under a seal of olive oil in tall glass jars. On occasion there would be huge amounts of milk from the market to make yoghurt. They would diligently stir it until it thickened and then store it in smooth maple jars. A voile cloth would be dampened and stretched across the top, tied into place and then the jars placed on a shelf in the cool pantry.

Jemme raced in to join his cousins who were already in the *qaa*, a highly decorated reception room. The floor was elaborately mosaicked and the sherds of tiles dazzled in the light. Carved wooden occasional furniture filled the room, although none was used during supper time. Meals were taken from a low table with a large brass top. Everyone sat cross-legged, supported by cushions in rich colours, hand embroidered with gold thread. In times past, families would have eaten with their hands from a large communal dish. Now a mixture of cutlery and hands was used, although the idea of a communal dish was still present, as meals were served 'family style' in which a dish or a platter heaped with food would be set down and everyone would help himself, transferring his own portion to his own, smaller plate. As they ate, Jemme and his cousins chattered excitedly. Despite the fact they lived only a short walk away, they always behaved as if they had been separated for months and, bursting with excitement, would talk over each other, stopping only to wolf down fresh *dolmas* or take spoonfuls of *tabbouleh*. Jemme's mother looked on at them from the doorway and smiled. Her son looked a lot like his cousins, with a thick crop of dark hair and an olive complexion. However, he was instantly recognisable by his sartorial flair. Even at a young age, he was rarely out of a suit. Despite the fact that it was often worn with shorts (although admittedly they were held up with braces) he would, unfailingly, wear his blazer. Made by the family tailor, it was a smaller version of a suit jacket of his father's and Jemme wore it with all the solemnity and pride becoming of a five-year-old. After supper, Jemme's mother cleared the table whilst Jemme and his cousins continued to play until it was time for them to leave. As with most evenings, before retiring to bed, Jemme walked softly over to his grandmother's area of the house. He teetered at the threshold, craning his neck to see inside. Satisfied that her visitors had left and she was now alone, he burst into the room. Grandma seemed to have a sixth sense for this kind of thing, and despite the fact that he had crept as quietly as possible she anticipated him, sweeping him up into a great hug as he ran into the room. As with most days, Jemme would ask her questions about her visitors, intrigued as much by the grand ladies in all their finery as the Sufi dancers in their white robes. Grandma would tell him all about the gifts they had brought with them, as she rearranged the room after an afternoon's entertaining, readjusting the cushions and airing the seat covers until everything looked as perfect as it always did. As she fiddled with flowers in a vase, she told Jemme of the presents she had received today – tea from England, stuffed dates and a basket of fresh apricots, soft and golden. These gifts were received with a genuine gratitude, but Grandma was far from materialistic and also had a deep sense of duty. Most ended up in the hands of the needy and the hungry and Grandma would pile them up at the end of a day's visits, ready to distribute the next day. When she had finished tidying up, she would settle down and Jemme would come over and sit next to her; if he was tired he would lay his head in her lap and she would gently stroke his hair as she told him a story. With the perfect mix of fantasy and history, for Jemme, no day felt complete unless it ended with one of Grandma's stories.

When not at school Jemme could often be found running through the narrow streets of Istanbul with his friends. It was a splendid backdrop for a childhood, and as they ran and tussled and played, they did so in front of the proud edifices of the old Empire. To the visitor, at times it seems as if there is nothing in Istanbul that is without embellishment. From the low tables and stalls grounded in the chaos of the *souk* to the dizzying heights of the spires, towers and minarets in the city's skies, everything appears to be made more beautiful, with iznik tiles, glass beads and tiny slivers of mirror which gleam and glitter in the Turkish sun. As an adult these would become some of Jemme's most cherished memories and throughout his many travels, occasionally something would catch his eye and nostalgia would wash over him as he remembered the bright spools of silk, the shouts of the carpet sellers and the precarious stacks of pottery in the market. As a child however, it seemed the most natural thing in the world that the steps up and down which he chased his friends should be marble, and the places he dived behind to catch his breath should be the giant columns of ornately decorated mosques. He did not think to imagine a place less steeped in history than his own and so as a child could not imagine the unlovely concrete sprawl of the Eastern Bloc, rising in prominence at the time, following Soviet dissolution. For now, everything in the city fed the little boy's imagination. At every corner there was a treat for the senses; the cries of the Muezzin echoed down the ancient alleyways, much as he imagined the battle cries of the knights in the Fourth Crusade did. As the sound bounced from the walls he imagined the terror his city's historic inhabitants would have felt, as the clashing of shield and sword and the crackling of fire filled these same streets. Gazing out across the sparkling Bosphorous, he could almost see the Venetian armada amassing there, swelling in number before finally attacking and its men scaling the city walls and clashing with the Varangian Guard. The calls to prayer mixed with the shouts of traders, each touting his wares as the best, the freshest, the most exotic. They competed with each other, and against the sound of music from musicians, who would set up on a street corner with an upturned hat in front of them, hoping for silver coins from passers-by. The sound of the *kemençe,* the *zurna, ney* and *davul* all mixed with the sizzling of juicy shish kebabs, being cooked by the roadside, and the air hung thick with a heady mix of grilled meat, roasting coffee beans and syrupy *mu'assel* emerging in billowing clouds from the *narguile,* smoked by gnarled old men who sat amongst the business of the bazaar and watched the world go by.

Istanbul was a playground, rich with delights and waiting to be explored. The school holidays seemed to stretch endlessly, offering unlimited possibilities for young children. Jemme and his friends would walk through the spice bazaar, the ground dusty with spilled cinnamon and cardamom and the air spicy and sweet. Chattering excitedly, they would reach the end of the market and dive their way around the crowds to emerge outside Haci Bakir, the home of *luqum,* or Turkish Delight. Originally made of molasses -- until the Europeans introduced sugar -- the delicious sweet has been produced at this shop, where it was also said to have been invented, since 1771. Spilling into the shop, coins hot in their hands, they would crowd around the polished wooden counter and agonise over choosing between the different brightly coloured sweets kept piled up under glass domes. Finally emerging, with coins gone and replaced by small brown paper bags, they would indulge in their treats, well worth a whole week's pocket money, and savour the delicate tastes of pistachio, rose water and lemon.

For one glorious week in the summer, Jemme's family would take the short ferry ride in the Sea of Marmara to the *Prens Adaları*, the Prince's Islands. They would stay in the same grand old hotel on the largest island, Büyükada, that they had been staying on for as long as Jemme could remember and whose every nook and cranny he knew like the back of his hand. The hotel was on a wide, airy boulevard and stood between equally grand town houses, each with creamy faces and shutters picked out in various bright colours. The kindly staff knew the family well, and Jemme was a particular favourite, with his unbridled enthusiasm for everything.

The beach was just a few moments' walk from the hotel, or even less for the little Jemme, who would dash full pelt towards it, his parents beseeching him to calm down and trying in vain to remind him that the sea would always be there. Once there, the spits of fine white sand provided excellent building materials for budding young castle-builders, and the calm waters were perfect for small swimmers. Once he had braved the icy plunge for the first time and grown used to it, Jemme would swim happily in the sparkling sea, scooping up armfuls of seaweed to decorate his castle with and playing with the tiny, harmless jellyfish. Whilst his exhausted parents lay on the warm sand, his ever-energetic grandma would keep a watchful eye on the young boy. She was particularly attentive when supervising his sandcastle building, challenging him on his decisions and encouraging him to extend, enlarge and think beyond the capacities of his little bucket. She took it all rather seriously, and under her auspices, and occasionally with her help too, Jemme would produce something really quite impressive, each year bigger and more ambitious than the last. Finally, when both Grandma and Jemme were satisfied, she would settle down on the sand, and sit cross-legged, back bolt upright. She would begin to tell Jemme another story, and Jemme, finally worn-out from the day's efforts would lie back in the last of the afternoon sun and listen gratefully.

She would tell him the history of the island and its place as a refuge throughout the Byzantine Christian period. She would tell him of the empresses who had sought sanctuary in its convent, of Euphrosyne in the eighth and ninth centuries, who lived there until she was able to return to court to be the bride of the Emperor. 'What happened to her, Grandma?' the young Jemme would ask. Grandma's eyes twinkled with delight. Despite his young age, her grandson's love of history and story-telling nearly matched her own.

'Well, her husband died and his son, Theophilos, succeeded him.' she replied, 'She held a bride-show for him and picked the best lady there to be his wife. Her name was Theodora.'

Jemme nodded as sagely as he could, before pausing and asking as casually as possible, 'What's a bride-show, Grandma?' Grandma never patronised him in her answers. She was happy for him to ask as many questions as he could; indeed she encouraged it. She felt that children could only learn properly through being inquisitive and seeking to learn more about the world around them from the people in it. She never adapted her stories for children either. She told them as they were, as she had been telling them for years, whether the audience was a group of professors, a couple of teenagers or one small grandson, sleepy in the holiday sunshine.

'A bride-show,' she responded, 'was a tradition amongst the Byzantine emperors and the Russian tsars. The most beautiful women from the best families would gather and the ruler would choose his new bride from amongst them. That's how Peter the Great's mother married her husband.' She told him of the great religious turmoil and debate within Byzantium at the time between the Iconodules and the Iconoclasts, the latter of whom wished for the destruction of the icons, under the leadership of Emperor Leo III in the eighth century. Theodora was a great Iconodule, she said, and set about preserving and restoring the ancient Icons, keeping some in her imperial chambers in the palace. Jemme, for whom the beautiful golden paintings held a mystical fascination, listened, rapt. Grandma told him about other empresses who had been exiled there over the ages, of Theophano in the tenth century -- a beautiful but dangerous empress who initially sought asylum in Hagia Sophia before being removed and sent to the island. She told him of Anna Delassene in the eleventh century who guarded the empire whilst her son was at war, patronised literary figures and was renowned for her dignity and poise. She too found herself in exile on the island, having been accused of treason following a lost battle with the Seljuks. Jemme, by this point completely under the spell of the story, would listen carefully, soaking in every detail, no matter how small. He was satisfied by the neatness of the history; he liked the fact that landscape and buildings around him were the physical embodiment of this story and provided a link back to the past. Not just one event either, but a series of historical encounters and experiences, played out in the same place, creating a continuous thread that he could be a part of himself, if he chose. By this point the sun would have set and Jemme would have tired himself out. Docile and content, his grateful parents would scoop him up and take him back to the hotel for a huge Turkish supper with baskets piled up with pide flatbreads, bowls of chopped green parsley and creamy *cacık* and platters of *İskender kebap*. These summers were filled with outdoor adventures, good food, clean air, but most of all, stories. Exploring the sounds and coves carved out by the Marmara, Grandma would tell Jemme how Trotsky lived on the island in the early thirties, following his own exile from Russia. He spent his four years there writing his autobiography. Again, Jemme felt the pull of the historical thread, only this time, to his intense fascination, the source of continuity was living and breathing and in front of him. His grandmother had seen so much within her lifetime, that she herself was the source of history. She was alive when Belarusians had fled during the Russian Civil War and settled on the island, and she was just a short boat ride away when the famous Trotsky had been working on his *History of the Russian Revolution*, protected from the White Army in Istanbul by loyal supporters. The fact that Grandma could remember something Jemme had learned about in history classes was mind-boggling. If her grandmother was here too, imagine what they could remember between them! Two elderly women sitting together would be able to recall over a hundred years' of history between them, just through personal experience. Jemme couldn't quite get his head around the concept, but he played with it for weeks. Not that Grandma could be considered an elderly lady. During their walks she was not short of breath for a moment; in fact it was sometimes Jemme who was left behind, scrambling up a rocky path, which she had just ascended with the greatest of ease and grace. Walking past *İsa Tepesi*, Jemme caught up with Grandma, slipped his hand into hers and asked her, 'Why is it called Jesus Hill?' Grandma would smile in the small way she always did when he asked questions. 'Look up, Jemme,' she said. Jemme followed the direction of her slender finger and squinted against the sunshine. Rising above the treeline he could just make out the top of a stone building.

'What's that?'

'That's the Hristos Monastery.'

'What does Hristos mean?'

'It's Greek, Χριστός, it means Christ – that's a Christian monastery. There are lots of religious buildings on this island. Do you remember the church with the domed bell tower we passed a while back?'

Jemme thought back to the whitewashed walls of the church they had walked past about half an hour ago and nodded.

'Well, that's Ayia Yorgi. We've also seen Ayios Dimitrios and the Hamidiye Mosque, all on this short walk. I remember Abdul Hamid II building that mosque,' Grandma added as they paused in the shade cast by a plant with thick, waxy green leaves. They both looked out over the sea in silence for a moment. 'Do you know what a microcosm is Jemme?' Grandma asked, turning to her grandson. Jemme shook his head. 'It's a tiny world – a miniature version of something much bigger. I often think that this island is a microcosm of how the world could be; for such a small place, it's multicultural with everyone living equally and side by side. There are Armenian churches, Greek Orthodox churches, a monastery, a synagogue and a mosque all so close to each other. The people live in harmony and instead of resenting each other's differences, they have learned from them to improve all of their lives. Did you know this island is famous for its beautiful buildings? Well, look at all the wonderful houses we see on the way to the hotel. They display so many different influences and individually are very pleasing, but when seen in a terraced row they're really quite remarkable. Their differences enrich them, and standing shoulder to shoulder they are even more beautiful than when they're apart – just like the people here. If we could all live in such harmony, imagine what we could achieve as a civilisation!' she sighed imperceptibly. Jemme knew that she had seen a great deal in her long life, but these were all quite weighty concepts for a young boy on holiday. Nevertheless, the idea of different people influencing each other with their customs and ideas stuck with him and he started looking for evidence of this influence, on his future walks with Grandma. Grandma had a wonderfully cheerful disposition though, and was never one to dwell on the world's ills, especially when she could be teaching someone else of its great wonders. Gathering herself, she turned to Jemme with a bright smile and a twinkle in her eye. 'Let's race down to the beach,' she declared, and was off before Jemme had had a chance to take her seriously.

In this way the summers of Jemme's childhood were filled with delight. He learned to connect history with the world around him, to hang the past onto physical pegs he found in the present. Whilst his classmates often found history one of the most boring subjects, rigidly academic and conceptual, he saw it as the greatest story of all, a way of explaining why things were the way they were. Grandma was quick to capitalise on this interest and foster it wherever possible. Having caught Jemme's imagination with stories of Büyükada that summer, she followed it up with a trip to the Istanbul Archaeology Museum, once they had returned. There she showed him 'The Treasure of Büyükada' which had been found in the Greek Cemetery in 1930. There, in the glass case in front of Jemme were 207 coins stamped with the insignia of King Phillip II, the father of Alexander the Great. This treasure would have been kept safe, hundreds of years ago, held onto tightly and then traded in shops and marketplaces of the fourth century BC for goods and produce. Each individual coin was an artefact of the past, guarded by its different owners until they all found their way into the soil. It was unbelievable to think that the little objects in the sterile case in front of him were such tokens of the past. However, it appealed to his ever-lively imagination to try to connect them to their original context and imagine how things might have been. What did people look like? What clothes were they wearing? What did they eat? He screwed his face up as he peered into the case, but the coins were giving away no secrets, he would have to rely on his imagination instead. He concentrated hard and forced ghostly apparitions to seep out of the coins. The shadowy figure of a Greek soldier appeared, with his curled hair and curled beard; he recognised him from a poster of a mosaic on his classroom wall. Had he been paid with the coins? Focussing on the others and trying with all his might to unlock their secrets, he was able to make a poorly-formed city appear from another, maybe somewhere this soldier had lived or fought battles. In any case he recognised it from a story Grandma had once told and he had stored all the details at the time in the back of his mind. Her description was only fleeting though, which probably explained the lack of detail in the image in front of him. Despite all his best efforts, he was unable to conjure anything else out of the coins. He could have imagined anything he wanted – dragons, camel-riding bandits and the ilk, but he wanted his picture to be more accurate than that. Jemme wanted to see the people to whom the coins had belonged and the places where they'd been. He wanted to see Thracians, Scythians and voyages across the Adriatic, Aegea, Eurydice and Thermopylae. In a way, he just didn't know that that was what he wanted to see. However he certainly was aware that he would only be able to furnish his understanding and imagination accurately and properly through further study at school, and through greater understanding of the stories he heard. Comprehension could only be based on experience, and this hardened his resolve to study hard at school and deepened his thirst for further stories. There was no greater ambition for the young boy than the perfect realisation of a story.

Chapter Two

'Where are we going, Grandma?' Jemme panted a little as he skipped to keep up with his grandmother. She smiled down at him, 'Never you mind *where* we're going, young man, just look at what we're seeing on the way there,' she said, barely breaking her stride. In Istanbul Lily was known for her walking. She was a firm believer that exercise was vital for a healthy mind as well as a healthy body and had been relying on her own two legs for years. Born before the advent of the motorcar, she viewed these luxury objects, which had been arriving in Istanbul to great excitement, with a certain degree of suspicion; there was something honest about getting somewhere under your own steam, something which made the journey worthwhile and these new contraptions were bound to make people lazy and dependent on machines. Besides, when one was rushing around all over the place, one missed the most important part of the journey. Beautiful buildings went past in a blur, and, behind glass, the car's passengers were insulated from the unique smells different journeys offered: sizzling meat, wet grasses – the senses brought experiences alive and cars numbed all of the things which Lily valued most about travelling.

By now they had reached the Fatih district. Slowing a little so that Jemme could draw parallel with her, Lily pointed to her left.

'Do you know what this building is, Jemme?' The small boy followed her finger to the complex, a pile of domes and roofs which jutted out at different angles and at different heights. The bricks were worn and weeds poked their way up between the flagstones of the path. The whole thing had an air of faded glory about it, something which was once great but had been left to crumble. Jemme looked at it inquisitively, sure that it held secrets. 'No, Grandma, what is it?' he asked. They paused for a moment and Lily took Jemme's hand, leading him up to the buildings.

'This is Zeyrek Camii, Jemme.'

'It's huge, Grandma! I think it's the biggest building I've ever seen – is it bigger than Hagia Sophia?'

Lily smiled, 'It is big, you're right. In fact it's one of our most important religious buildings after Hagia Sophia. Every building tells a story, Jemme, even modern ones and I wanted you to see this one for yourself.'

Jemme looked up at his grandmother, squinting against the sun. He wanted to say something knowledgeable, but couldn't think of anything. He screwed up his face in concentration. Grandma laughed at his efforts; he needn't have worried, Grandma made everyone feel like an equal in her company and she had always treated Jemme as a grown-up.

'I would have compared it to Hagia Sophia myself too,' she said generously. Jemme beamed, pleased, 'I don't think there are two finer examples of Byzantine architecture in the whole of Istanbul,' she continued. 'In fact, they have something else in common: both buildings started out as Christian churches and then became mosques,'

'Is that part of the story, Grandma?'

'Yes, it is, although only a small part. When a building is as old as this, it tells more than its own story. It tells the story of people who visited it, as well as the story of the city it's in.'

Jemme looked intrigued, 'Where does this story start?'

'Well, with this church it started all the way back in the twelfth century. The Byzantine Empress Eirene Komnena built a monastery dedicated to Christ Pantokrator. She built all sorts of buildings: – a church, a library and a hospital too; but that was just the beginning of the story. After she died, her husband, the emperor, built another church and a chapel filled with shrines.' She pointed at the chapel building, which had long since been turned into a mausoleum, entombing various Byzantine dignitaries. Jemme nodded his understanding and Lily continued, 'Well, lots of other people have used this place; after the Fourth Crusade, the Venetian clergy used the complex as a monastery again, and then it was used as an imperial palace by the last Latin Emperor, Baldwin II.'

Jemme's brow unknotted a little. The Crusades were one of his favourite subjects at school and it was pleasing to be able to ground this story somewhere, in a framework he already knew. 'What next?' he asked.

'Well, after the fall of Constantinople, it was converted into a *medrese*, a place of learning, which the Ottomans named after a teacher there – Molla Zeyrek.'

Jemme began to look confused again. He was turning things over furiously in his mind, but the term he had a problem with most was 'the fall of Constantinople' – how could a city have fallen? He lived in modern-day Constantinople, he knew that; he went to school there, he played there. Some buildings had certainly fallen down and there were some shabby parts too, but the whole city falling down?

'Grandma...' he began as casually as he could, 'tell me some more about the fall of Constantinople.'

'Let's save that for another day – that's a very big story,' said Lily with a twinkle in her eye, 'Come on, let's have a quick explore, then we'd better get going.'

Together they wandered around the complex, Lily running her hands over the thick, buttress-like walls of the buildings with their brick facades worn smooth.

'These walls are much thicker than you'd find in other buildings, Jemme,' she told the boy, who was squatting down to investigate a sleepy lizard. 'Look, this is recessed brick – it's typical of the middle Byzantine period and it's about three times as thick as a normal wall. Even if you knew none of the history of this building, this small detail here would tell you a great deal. '

Jemme squinted up at her, 'You mean you can tell the age of a building without learning its story – just by looking at it?'

'Of course! Look over there – you see these domes? They sit on apses with seven sides. If they were from the Early Byzantine Period they would be sitting on five-sided apses.'

Jemme looked up at the domes, which, with their worn edges looked like mounds of dough against the bright sunlight. He was intrigued that Grandma could unlock the building's secrets that easily. Before he had time to ponder on this any more, Grandma took his hand, 'Come on!' she said breezily, 'We'll be late.'

He picked up the pace and trotted back to the main path with her.

About ten minutes later, the sea was in full view. The scimitar-shaped Golden Horn formed a deep natural harbour and had been the naval base of the Byzantine Empire. It shimmered with history, but Lily decided to save that lesson for another day too. 'You see Jemme?' she looked down without breaking stride, 'Look how much we would have missed out on if we'd come by car!'

'Yes, Grandma,' Jemme nodded emphatically as they turned down a residential street. They drew up to a house with a buttercup yellow front door, on which Lily rapped smartly.

An elderly lady dressed in white linen opened the door. Her face was tanned and as creased as a walnut. Although she was significantly younger than Lily, she looked decades older. Nevertheless, she possessed some of the grace and poise of Jemme's grandmother, which gave her the same ageless quality. When she saw who her two visitors were, she broke out into smiles,

'Come in, come in!' she said warmly

Lily bent to kiss her on the cheek, 'Thank you, Souraya,' she said, 'You remember my grandson Jemme?'

'But of course, of course! My, how you've grown!'

Jemme flushed slightly and muttered his *salamat* as he entered the welcome coolness of the hallway.

Souraya looked amused and responded, '*Marhaba*, Jemme,' as earnestly as she could. About half an hour later, Jemme was sat cross-legged on a floor cushion, nearing the bottom of a bowl of pistachio ice cream. Snatches of the ladies' conversation drifted across to him, and he listened contentedly. He often accompanied Grandma on these trips to see her friends and enjoyed hearing their discussions almost as much as when he was the centre of attention. The visits were always pleasurable. Grandma would try and vary the walk there to show him a part of town he didn't know, or an interesting side street. Sometimes they would cut through beautiful parks, sometimes walk along the seafront. They always seemed to encounter someone Lily knew as well, from local dignitaries to leather cutters in the market. They would stop to exchange greetings and Jemme enjoyed hearing the stories from all these different people too. In his short life he had already encountered people from all backgrounds, professions and levels of society. They always showed an interest in him, sometimes giving him a ripe peach, or a promise to introduce him to a young son of a similar age. The people Grandma regularly called on were becoming as familiar as friends to Jemme and he was as comfortable in their houses as his own. He enjoyed sitting in their *liwans*, taking in the difference in the décor and wondering how he would decorate his own home when he grew up. He sat and listened as Grandma and her friends discussed all sorts of things – politics, religion, the city, charity work and sometimes just reminiscing about the past. Sometimes he would try and keep up, sometimes he would just allow the words to wash over him, appreciating their rich sounds and the wise, animated faces in front of him who spoke them.

Visits such as the one to Souraya were perhaps his favourite of all. For Souraya was a Sufi friend of Grandma's, and Jemme was fascinated by the Sufis. Putting his spoon down as silently as he could, he picked up his cushion and moved closer to them. They were discussing the origins of Sufism, and he listened as closely as he could. When there was a lull in the conversation he thought it was time to speak up,

'Grandma, Maimy Souraya, what does *Sufi* actually mean? I mean, I know that you are Sufis and that the religion is Sufi, but I didn't think it was a religion? You still go to the mosque; where does it fit in?'

Lily gestured to Souraya, who turned on her cushion, to give Jemme her full attention. 'Well Jemme, those are all very interesting questions. Let's start with the name. You are almost right – it is called *Sufism*, whilst practitioners are called *Sūfīs* –'

'Where does the name come from?' Jemme interrupted, faltering slightly towards the end – he had got a little carried away and hadn't meant to cut Souraya off.

Souraya smiled reassuringly, 'Well, that's another good question Jemme. To be honest I can't say for certain, and this is something Sheikha Lily and I have disagreed on in the past. She believes it comes from *sūf*, the wool used in the distinctive coats early Sufis wore. I follow Abū Rayhān al-Bīrūnī.' She saw

Jemme's puzzled look, 'He was a great Iranian scholar,' she explained, 'from mediaeval times. He said that the word came from the Greek *sophia*, meaning "knowledge", something which I feel is closer to actually describing Sufism. Of course there are those who think it comes from the word *safã*, meaning pure, and those who think it comes from the *ahl as-suffah* who were the impoverished companions of Muhammad and regularly practiced *dhikr* together. To some extents it doesn't matter, as all of these represent a part of Sufism – the *dhikr*, the impoverished life, the purity. But I don't think I'm explaining myself properly.' She looked down at Jemme, who looked none the wiser and was starting to toy with his spoon, 'All of these things are at the heart of Sufism,' she continued, 'which is at once at the heart of Islam, but also esoteric to it. It is a very hard concept to understand, so perhaps it would help if your grandmother told you a little about the history.'

She raised her eyebrows at Lily who nodded and continued, 'Well, Sufism is about pursuing the perfect understanding of, and unity with, the divinity -- through your own experiences. That is why there are so many different elements to Sufi practice. They all help the Sufi along his or her path. You've seen many of these practices already Jemme, but perhaps they would mean a little more to you if you understood their background. Sufism began with Mohammad and there has been an unbroken line of mysticism ever since: the *silsilah*. That is why it is so important that the teacher himself must have received the *ijazah* from another master, otherwise the line is broken and the continuity lost. Do you understand?'

Jemme nodded slowly, he liked the idea of there being something so ancient which he couldn't even see. It was an idea which reached back and made a connection with the past. Through his grandmother and her friends, he had a link to the very first Sufis. He started to listen, but he had already heard many of the stories and drifted off in thought. Sufism was a big part of Grandma's life and Jemme always enjoyed being around her and her Sufi friends. Their conversations were fascinating; full of references to ancient scholars and mystics and there was something ennobling about seeing so many wise people sitting together discussing important matters – it almost felt as if it would rub off on him somehow. However, more than being a Sufi, Grandma was a Dervish too. Dervishes shared the same aims as Sufis, but as members of the Mevlevi order, their practices in achieving an elevated state of consciousness differed. They practiced asceticism, just as Christian mendicant friars or Hindu sadhus. Many people in Istanbul were Dervishes, as the Mevlevi order was based in Konya. It was founded there by Jalāl ad-Dīn Muhammad Balkhī a thirteenth century Persian poet, jurist, theologian and mystic. His shrine in Konya was a great pilgrimage site and Grandma herself had been many times. In the past, Sufis had often gathered in special lodges, or *zaouia* to practice. Jemme wasn't sure if

Grandma had ever been to such a place, but he doubted she needed to, so frequent were the gatherings that she held at their house. Dervishes would come from all over Istanbul to practice *sema*. At first, Jemme was intrigued by these strange visitors, with their black overcoats, tall camel-hair hats and white garments. He would watch them disappear into the *majlis* with Grandma and wonder what on earth they could be up to, especially when he heard the strange sounds emanating out afterwards. Then, as time went by, he began to talk to them and ask them questions. He learned that the overcoat was called a *khirqa* and that it was symbolically removed before practice began, to signify the starting of a new life. He learned that the hat was called a *sikke* and that it represented the tombstone of the ego, whilst the wide white skirt (the *tennure*) represented the shroud of the ego. He wasn't quite sure what the ego was, or why Grandma should be gathering these people together to kill it, but as time went on and he grew up, he asked more and learned more. Now he often sat with Grandma and her friends, and had become as well-versed in the practice as someone four times his age.

First, the Sufis would gather. They would exchange greetings and pleasantries and then gradually the conversation would die down as they prepared their minds for more spiritual matters. There were three principal ways in which Sufis could progress on the path to achieving divine communion, or *fillah*; they were: *dhikr, muraqaba* and visitation. The first was the most impressive to non-Sufis and the one Jemme understood the most. 'Dhikr helps us to remember God' one of Grandma's friends, Fasialoo, had once explained to him, 'The Qur'an refers to Mohammed as the embodiment of the *dhikr* of God.' Jemme had nodded sagely, but hadn't really understood the concept at all. It was only through witnessing multiple Sufi rituals that he had begun to realise what Fasialoo had been trying to explain. The *dhikr* was expressed in a number of different ways, mostly through ritualised ceremonies or *semas*. These could involve recitation of the names of God, instrumental music, singing, dance, incense, ecstasy and perhaps most impressive of all, the whirling of the Mevlevi order. Jemme couldn't remember the first time he had actually seen the Dervishes whirling and twirling, but it was a sight that never failed to fill him with astonishment and a feeling he couldn't quite put his finger on. Whatever it was, it made a deep and long-lasting impression on him. The twirling usually occurred after the invocation of the names of God; the white-clad Sufis would gather, the low hum of their voices still reverberating around the room. They would begin to move in a great circle around the room, the soft thud of their bare feet on the tiled floor pulsing rhythmically. The *dhikr* sheikh would stand in the corner and they would pass by him three times, each time exchanging greetings. Then the whirling would begin. With the left foot remaining in constant contact with the floor, they would twirl and whirl, pivoting off the right through a full three hundred and sixty degrees. As they became faster and faster, their robes flowed and billowed until the dervishes themselves appeared to turn into a blur, and the robes seemed to blend into one huge piece of fabric, waving and pulsing, and filling the whole room. The rhythmic sounds, the ocean of white cloth and the sight of the dervishes turning around and around was captivating and mesmerising. Many who have seen it describe even the act of observing the ceremony as a meditative experience. Although Jemme was a little too young to understand such things properly, the spirituality of the event was palpable and made a deep impression on him. There was no mistaking the look of intense concentration on the dervishes' faces, and he felt privileged to have attended such a private ceremony.

Back in the house, Jemme's thoughts were interrupted by a rasping laugh. Souraya was wheezing slightly and wiping tears from her eyes. Lily saw him watching and waved him over with one hand. She swept him up in a tight hug that knocked the breath out of him, 'Grandma!' he protested. Souraya smiled affectionately.

'Oh your grandmother does make me laugh, little one!' she said, 'We were remembering things from the past, when we were both much younger – old stories.'

Jemme looked up from under Grandma's arm, 'Old stories, Maimy Souraya?'

'Yes, old, old stories;' she emphasised, 'we were reminiscing about the Karagöz and Hacivat and the shadow puppets of our youth.' She broke off into another wheezy chuckle. Jemme looked confused.

'Oh dear,' Grandma sighed, laughing herself, 'I think it's time we got you home, Jemme; it's getting dark, and you need to be up nice and early tomorrow if you're to be ready for when your cousins visit.' She turned to Souraya, 'Thank you for your hospitality, my dear friend. It is always a pleasure to see you.

'Marhaba, Sheika Lily,' Souraya replied, 'the pleasure is all mine. Please, come back and see me soon.'

By the time they left the house, the sky had turned to a deep, indigo blue and the city had undergone its daily transformation. Just as alive by night as by day, everything about it seemed different. The light cast from the streetlamps, with their rose-glass panels, lit up things ignored during the day and cast familiar daytime landmarks into shadows, which strained and stretched shapes. The smells, sounds and colours changed too; the market thronged with women buying large sacks of flour and great bunches of herbs for the evening meal; street vendors began to prepare their own feasts; fresh waves of buskers, hawkers and peddlers arrived and men gathered on street corners before setting off together for a session in the coffee house. Coffee and tobacco were entrenched in Turkish culture, and were inseparable from hospitality and socialising. The coffee house was the centre of the male social world, and as important to Jemme's father and his father's friends as Grandma's Sufi meetings were to her. It was more than just a place to drink coffee, it was a forum for story-telling, an opportunity to catch up, to enjoy music, play backgammon, read books, smoke nargile and, of course, drink coffee. The thick, dark, Turkish coffee was served very hot in small quantities, and accompanied by a tall glass of cold water. The dense coffee was almost syrupy in texture, and incredibly strong, both in flavour and caffeine. Anyone who had not drunk it before soon understood what the glass of water was for.

They walked past the door of a coffee house left ajar, and Jemme caught the sound of laughter drifting out of the thick fug of smoke created by the sticky nargile tobaccos.

'Do you see how bright the stars are, Jemme?' Grandma asked, pointing up.

Jemme looked up at the sky, which was now completely black, save for what looked like hundreds of pinprick holes of brilliant white, 'Yes, Grandma,' he replied.

'Well, when I was a girl, before all these electric lights were installed, they were even brighter. Can you imagine such a thing? Things change so quickly these days; when I was your age, if someone had told me that within my lifetime the stars would have dulled and faded I would never have believed them; the stars which have shone over our city for thousands of years!' She looked momentarily sad. Jemme slipped a hand into hers. He knew that Grandma was a clever woman and didn't fear change like some of the elderly around her. However, he was wise enough to know that it saddened her when change and progress meant the loss of something which was dear to her.

She squeezed his hand and looked down brightly, 'Do you know what the Ancient Egyptians believed about the night, Jemme?'

Normally Jemme hated admitting that he didn't know things, but he was too pleased that Grandma had flicked back to story-telling form for it to matter.

'They believed that Ra was the sun god. He had the head of a falcon –'

Jemme interrupted her, 'The head of a falcon, Grandma? AND the body of a man?!' he found the whole thing rather funny.

'Yes, Jemme, plenty of Egyptian gods and goddesses were mixes of animals and people, they had lion heads, jackal heads, even a snake instead of a head.' Jemme giggled and Grandma waited until he had finished, 'Anyway, during the day Ra was a living god, and his sun burnt brightly; but every evening he died and his sun slowly faded until there was nothing, no light in the sky at all. Each morning he would be born again as a small boy. He would be a fully grown adult by midday, when his sun was strongest and then an old man by the time he died again in the evening.'

Jemme started giggling again, and Grandma looked at him questioningly, 'Sorry, Grandma, it just sounds silly to me. How could they believe that the sun was a man with a bird's head and that he died every day? That's just silly.'

Grandma looked stern. She had a very expressive face and there was usually a trace of laughter in it somewhere, whether in the wrinkles around her eyes or hidden in the creases at the side of her mouth. Now she looked completely serious.

'Jemme, listen to me. It is very important that you respect people's beliefs, even if you don't agree with them. Everyone has the right to religion, and to believe in whatever they please. When people stop respecting this, that is what divides us, not difference in belief. Tolerance and respect are two of the most important things in the world, Jemme, I want you to remember that always.'

Jemme nodded solemnly. Grandma still looked serious, but now she started to look slightly wistful too, 'So many of our problems could be solved through dialogue and understanding,' she continued, 'and so much of our conflict arises from misunderstanding and fear. But these are weighty subjects to be bringing up. I just want you to remember that other people's beliefs must be respected. That is the most important thing.'

Jemme nodded again, 'Yes, Grandma, I do. I do understand, I mean. I do respect other people too, I was just being silly' he said, trying to sound as grown up as possible. 'What was Maimy Souraya saying about Carragus and Hakvit?' he asked, keen to change the subject. Grandma started laughing again as she remembered her conversation of earlier.

'Don't worry, sweetheart, I'm not laughing at you, although they're called Karagöz and Hacivat! They were the best shadow puppets in the whole of the Ottoman Empire. Ramadan was the season of puppet theatre, and we would go and watch the shows after the daily *iftar*. The story is hundreds of years old, Jemme but it's still very funny. It used to be the most popular form of entertainment before the silent pictures came in. In fact, one of my best friends, from when I was a little girl, grew up to be a master puppet animator.'

By this time they had left the market, the people had thinned out and the streets grew quieter. They arrived back at the house, and Grandma led James across the courtyard to his room. She opened the door softly and ushered him in, turning the lamp on for him and drawing back the covers. They had done a lot of walking, and Jemme was certainly tired, but as inviting as the bed looked, he was loathe to be parted from Grandma. Apart from anything else, he didn't feel that they had finished the story-telling for the day. He wanted to hear about Karagöz; was he a boy or a girl? Was he even a person? Who was Hacivat? Were they friends? Husband and wife? He hated only hearing half the story; he liked feeling like he could repeat the story himself, as if it was one of his own. But the bed did look so soft and comfortable, and his legs were so weary... his eyes were growing heavy and his protests to Grandma became increasingly mumbled, 'But.....Grandma.... I...'

'I know, I know,' Lily soothed, as she deftly scooped him into the bed, in such a way he barely noticed.

'I wanted....to know,' Jemme muttered, struggling to keep his eyes open.

'Goodnight, Jemme,' Lily said, switching off the light, 'I had a lovely day with you today, and I'm looking forward to another walk again soon.'

Jemme's eyes were now firmly shut, and he had abandoned any effort at protest. He just about managed to murmur something that sounded like, 'Goodnight Grandma,' before he drifted off to a deep sleep, resolving that he would ask his mother if he could move his bed into Grandma's room for a little bit.

* * * *

Jama had indulged her son's request, and allowed him to move his bed, although she had been quick to point out that it was just a temporary treat. She knew that he would have to grow up some day, and didn't want to start to infantilise him. However, for the moment she was pleased with her choice, as she could see how much pleasure it was bringing both of them. Lily was always cheery and positive, but she had had even more of a spring in her step of late. Similarly, Jama was astonished at her small son's capacity for learning. His teachers had told her how well he did in school; how attentive he was and what excellent questions he asked. It was his ability to continue learning once he left school that surprised her. Whilst his classmates were keen to run out of the school gates and play as soon as lessons ended, Jemme looked forward to his grandmother telling him more tales from her life, or describing to him ancient civilisations, far off places and lives of great scholars and poets. He seemed to absorb all the details, sponge-like, and retain them too. Since moving into Grandma's room, he had come bounding into the kitchen at regular intervals, relaying to his mother all the tales he had just heard. She had already heard of the adventures of Alexander the Great, the prowess of Hannibal and the great lion hunts of Ashur Banipal. There was something so engaging about his enthusiasm. She would have worried that he was becoming too bookish, and too withdrawn from his friends, more content to spend time with his grandmother than his contemporaries, but the opposite seemed to be true. He was an incredibly active child and loved running round, and any kind of sport he could be involved in, especially when it involved his friends. He had shown a flair for volleyball at school and as it was an easy-enough game to set up, the courtyard was often filled with a throng of small boys, all shrieking and trying to get a ball over the central net her husband would put up for them. She loved to watch him play, although always slightly nervous about her windows when the boys were in a particularly exuberant mood. She looked up at him now, talking to his cousins in the courtyard. They were throwing pebbles into the different coloured tiles, then collecting them and re-throwing them in some sort of game they seemed to have invented. Whatever it was, they were having a great deal of fun. She sighed happily. She was pleased that her first child was such a happy, well-adjusted boy. She had only been young when she had married, and was just eighteen when Jemme was born, so everything had been a steep learning curve for her. She was proud of how she had coped though, proud of her son and how he had developed. He was shaping up to be a fine young man; she just wished he had some brothers or sisters too.

In the courtyard, Jemme was finishing his game. It had evolved over the course of the morning; until the rules had become so complicated he wasn't sure any of them understood them any more. He was enjoying being with his cousins though, so it didn't really matter. In fact, he was enjoying life in general at the moment. His teacher had told him that as soon as he was old enough, he was almost guaranteed a place in the school's volleyball team; he was getting to hear even more of Grandma's stories, but most excitingly of all, this month he was joining the Scouts. He couldn't wait; his older cousins were Scouts, and some of his neighbours too, and Jemme had always been in awe of them when he was younger. They seemed so grown up to him then, and so impressive when they went off in their smart khaki uniforms. He heard stories of what they got up to as well; camping trips, canoeing, discovery adventures and even trips to far off places, and all whilst surrounded by their friends. It sounded like the most exciting thing he could imagine, and he couldn't wait. Of course, he already felt like he had been on many adventures already. Grandma had been teaching him so many things, and she described them so vividly, it was impossible not to get sucked in and feel as if you were within the story, watching the other characters around you. Most recently, he felt like he had seen the Hittites, racing past in their highly engineered chariots. He found the civilisation fascinating: they had been so close to where he was now, yet it was a completely different land. The borders didn't exist like they did now, and so the countries were different shapes and sizes. It was strange to think of Turkey being in the same place, but not yet being Turkey. The names of the places were so romantic and appealing though: *Anatolia, Mesopotamia, Qadesh*. He found the Battle of Qadesh particularly satisfying; he was now learning so much that his knowledge started to overlap and the coming together of the Ancient Egyptians and the Hittites in this furious battle represented just such an occasion. He was able to understand the battle from both sides and realised how much this changed his view of the proceedings. Perhaps this was what Grandma was actually trying to teach him and not about Ramesses' fight with Muwatilli on the Orontes River.

It was incredible too, to learn about something, so ancient, which left traces perceptible today. The Hittites lived so long ago that trying to comprehend such a chronology stretched Jemme's imagination. They hadn't just lived in a different time, they'd lived in a different age too, something Grandma called The Bronze Age. Despite the fact that their adventures happened such a long time ago, their stories had been captured and preserved all the way until today. They'd been written on tablets, using cuneiform letters. That was another word Jemme liked – *cuneiform*. He liked the way it sounded and what it meant too. For this was the first, and best, step to preserving stories. It was all very well handing them down from generation to generation, and this was an important tradition, but what if there was a break in the chain? What if someone didn't have children to tell stories too? What if they died before they had a chance? What if they forgot important details? Important pieces of history could be lost forever. Cuneiform letters represented the way a spoken language could turn into a textual one, and Jemme was old enough to realise what a significant step this was. The great libraries of the world were filled with the voices of ancient peoples, scholars and poets, captured and stored for future writers, scientists and researchers. It was something he could think about for hours at a time, and he looked forward to building his own collection of writings when he was older. He would bring together the preserved stories of his favourite authors, about his favourite civilisations, in one beautiful library like his father owned and like the great library of Alexandria that his grandmother had told him about.

After their great chariot battle at Qadesh, the Hittites outlined the terms of a peace treaty on a silver tablet. Grandma said that it was the earliest international peace treaty ever discovered, and might even have been the first. This was something else that provided a link back to the modern day. Jemme was intrigued by the fact that the big, important, international treaties, which his father read of in the newspapers, all stemmed from this one small tablet. Grandma said that it was such a perfect example that modern versions followed the same formula and very little had changed in all that time. Jemme liked the idea of precedent, and the first time something happened. It was all very well to take the world around you as it came, but people often forgot that everything had to start at some point. It was his lesson on the Babylonians that started him thinking about this. His teacher taught the class about Hammurabi, whom he called 'the first lawyer'. It was strange to think that there had been no lawyers before him, when law today was such an ancient and respected profession. Jemme learned that Hammurabi's portrait hung in the offices of government buildings throughout the world, and that his famous set of laws, Hammurabi's Code, had been found within Grandma's lifetime. They were carved into a *stele,* which his teacher explained meant a large stone pillar. He told the class that it was at least double their height, and Jemme could imagine how imposing it must have been for the Babylonians to have all their laws written out on such a large structure. The top of the stele showed Hammurabi himself, being given the laws by one of the Babylonian gods, which reminded Jemme of the story of Moses receiving the Jewish laws from God too. The class agreed that it was exciting to be able to see the actual image of an historic character they were learning about; they could see Hammurabi through the carver's eyes and see how he had been the great lawmaker over a thousand years ago.

Jemme collected up the pebbles they had been playing with, and made a neat little cairn with them at the side of the courtyard. It was a good game, and he would play it again; if he could remember the rules that was. His cousins looked at him expectantly,

'Well? What shall we do now?'

Jemme thought for a while. It was beginning to get a little cold outside, and the light was fading too much for any further games. He looked over and saw his mother lighting the lamps in the *majlis*. It looked cosy and inviting. He had an idea. Turning to his cousins, he said: 'How about a story?'

Chapter Three

Life with the Scouts was suiting Jemme very well. He had been a member for about three months now, and loved everything about it. His troop met every Thursday after school had finished, in a special Scout building. He loved the fact that it was just for them. The walls were covered in certificates, boasting various members' prowess in camp-craft or sports. Proudly framed photographs showed troops over the years beaming out of the black and white murkiness in front of recognisable landmarks and attractions. The adventures were one of the things that Jemme was looking forward to most. There was one coming up at the end of the summer, although the Scout Leader hadn't decided where yet. He looked over the photos and the handwritten labels underneath them, on yellowed paper, curling at the edges: *Troop XII – Prague, Troop XIV – Budapest, Troop XX – Vienna*. He already knew these places from Grandma's stories and from school too, but they still seemed hundreds of miles away. He knew people did things differently there, looked different, ate different food and talked in a different language and he was thrilled at the prospect that he might be plunged into that environment soon.

For now he had learned how to tie a reef knot, a clove hitch and a single sheet bend. He could just about manage a fisherman's bend, although he didn't know how it would hold up on an actual boat. He could pitch a tent, lay a fire and keep it going once it was lit. He was learning to identify the different types of bird and had duly noted egrets, grebes and cormorants in his small notebook. He was hoping to spot a petrel soon, and a pink-footed goose would put him well on the way to getting his birdwatcher's badge. He enjoyed the practical, hands-on nature of Scouting activities. Much as he adored storytelling, it was a very sedentary activity. It was easy to disappear into your own imagination, but in Scouts, everything learned was practiced straight away. It helped you remember much better and there was something very satisfying about whittling a stick or planting a sapling. Perhaps one of the best things about Scouts was the new friends he was making. So far, his friends were only from school or related to him, as well as all of Grandma's friends, obviously. He was now meeting people of all ages, who went to all the different schools of the city. They were a mixed bunch: quiet Walli, who seemed so pale compared to the rest of them; mischievous Akaljat, whose parents had come over from the Punjab when he was just a baby; Rafi who had recently arrived from Armenia, to name but a few. All were about the same age as Jemme; they had started Scouts at the same time and sat wide-eyed at the first meeting, as in awe of the older boys as they were of the adventures ahead of them.

The other big change in Jemme's life was that his mother was now pregnant. He had only found out recently, and he had mixed feelings about it. Whilst a little brother or sister could be a playmate and a new source of fun, he was rather used to being the only child in the house. He didn't like the idea that he would have to share his mother or father, and especially not his grandmother, with anyone else. Lots of his new Scout friends had younger brothers and sisters, and they seemed to get along just fine, but he resolved to decide about it later. His mother had told him that there would be plenty of time before the baby was born and for now he wanted to think only about his Scouting adventures. He couldn't wait until he was one of the boys in the black and white photographs, beaming proudly back at the camera from some far off location. He packed the last of the things that were out, into the cupboard, and waited for the Scout Master to dismiss them all for the evening. Normally he hung around for as long as possible, or went off with a big group of friends. Today however, he couldn't wait to get back. His father had been away on a business trip for three weeks and Jemme had missed him terribly. His father was often away, and although it meant that his return was hugely exciting and included lots of presents, it never made up for him having to go. Jemme rushed back to the house through the park, skirting the edge of the marketplace and taking a short cut across the square.

Arriving back at home, breathless with anticipation, he could see instantly that his father was already back. Cases, trunks and paper packages were piled up inside the courtyard and relatives were flocking in and out of the kitchen, helping with the preparations for the big welcome back meal that evening. Jemme darted past aunties, struggling with large saucepans and huge piles of supplies. With their shouts still ringing in his ears he burst into the *majlis* where his father was gently embracing his pregnant wife. At the sound of Jemme's running feet, Wadeah turned around, 'Come here!' he boomed, sweeping his son up into a big bear hug.

As an adult, Jemme would always be surprised by how small his father was. He wasn't more than average height, but to Jemme in his childhood he had seemed like a giant – tall, broad and with a deep, rich voice. With his dark hair and light skin, he was often mistaken for an Italian, but he was as Turkish as they came, from generations of prominent Istanbulites. Any son of Lily's was bound to be a respected figure in the community.

'Baba! You're squashing me!' Jemme protested as he wriggled free.

Wadeah laughed and ruffled his hair, 'Sorry, little one! I'm just so pleased to see you and be back with my family again,' he pointed the last in his wife's direction and looked meaningfully at her belly. Jemme noticed, but decided to change the subject straight away,

'How was it, Baba? How was it?' he asked, tugging at the bottom of his father's smart blazer, his 'work outfit' as he called it. He looked up; his father looked tired. Although he wore a broad smile on his face and seemed relaxed, Jemme knew his face so well that he could instantly detect changes in it. He knew its contours like a map, and as a toddler had traced the lines of it with his pudgy hands whenever his father heaved him up onto his lap. He could see that there were more lines around his father's eyes than normal and that, although he was tanned, he seemed paler underneath it. He didn't understand why his father had to go away to work, when so many people worked here in Istanbul, even the most important ones. His father always seemed to come back tired, and the places he went to were so far away. Surely it would make sense for him to do all his work from home? Wadeah interrupted his train of thought with a stifled yawn,

'It was excellent, thank you Jemme. I did lots of deals, saw lots of things... bought lots of presents...' he looked slyly at his son who was now paying him his full attention.

'Presents, Baba?' he ventured casually. Wadeah threw back his head and laughed again. He tossed his work blazer onto a nearby bench, undid the top button of his primrose shirt and gathered his family in for another hug,

'Come on, let's go and eat some of that delicious food, I can smell my sister's cooking and I'll tell you all about it.'

Over a magnificent supper, Jemme sat by his father's side and drank in everything he said. Most of it was about business, which Wadeah was discussing with his brothers. Leather was a family business, and generations of Mafezes had built up the empire. Wadeah was in charge and had been responsible for a huge expansion, particularly into Western Europe. However, the others were all involved somehow, from bookkeeping to meeting visiting merchants. For most it was a family commitment, which supplemented their work in other areas. However, for Wadeah it was his life. He had worked hard to grow the family business, update it and prepare it for the modern world. Things were very different to when his great great great grandfather first began trading pelts. Now Wadeah oversaw a large warehouse where the skins were prepared, and another where they were crusted, as well as a tannery too. He would organise large shipments of skins – mostly cow hides, but often kid too and sometimes even mutton. These would be prepared by an army of workers in the first warehouse. They would be variously soaked, limed, bated, bleached and pickled until only the skin was left. However, when it dried out, this would become as stiff as a board; little use in making fine shoes or for ladies' bags. In order for it to become the soft, supple material artisans, cobblers and craftsmen used, it first needed to undergo the tanning process. Lots of specialist equipment was used and the hide was put inside what looked like a giant revolving drum. The drum slowly rotated, tumbling the hides around in the tanning liquor. Once they emerged, they were ready for crusting and would be sent to the last of the warehouses. Here they would be neutralised, split, dyed, stripped, fixed, set, dried, softened and buffed. By the end, there would be a stack of leathers, beautifully coloured, finished and conditioned, ready for sending out to buyers across the world.

The leather industry in Istanbul had developed hugely within Wadeah's lifetime and undergone something of a boom. The city was now divided into organised leather industrial zones, and competition was stiffer than it ever had been. He was not worried however; the family's name carried a great deal of weight, as did the reputation of the leather itself. Whilst many of the new companies vying for business had only been around for a few years, leatherworking was in his blood. He had grown up watching his father work, and had continued this work for all of his adult life. His competition were former carpet-weavers, stall-vendors and tradesmen, all keen to try their hand at this profitable rising industry. This was their downfall though; whilst new methods had offered the opportunity to increase production and lower costs, his experience allowed him to sift through these developments, and only adopt the ones which would be profitable to his business. A perfect example was the new advances in tanning. Others had embraced the chemicals, mass-produced in the Far East and shipped over in bulk. They speeded up the tanning process, allowing more leathers to be wrung through the drum in a day's work. However, whilst on the surface they seemed to be a progressive innovation, Wadeah knew better. He knew that the chemicals produced leather of inferior quality. It gave the appearance of being ready, but often it had not had enough time to tan. It wouldn't be as soft, and without the proper treatment, the patina would crack at some point in the future, ruining the texture and maybe the item into which the leather had been fashioned too. In addition to that, these new chemicals were noxious: they were toxic to deal with, smelled awful and created contaminated water. He would never abandon the traditional methods handed down for generations. The materials used were all organic, safe and sustainable, and the leather he produced was the best for miles around. Before it was shipped off to fill orders it was graded, according to its shape, texture and overall quality. This was Jemme's favourite stage; his school was very close to the crusting factory and sometimes after lessons he would walk down. His father sat in his great chair, behind his big desk, poring over plans, letters and notes. Jemme would bounce in and take up his seat on the opposite side of the desk. Facing Wadeah, the chair was obviously intended for meetings and clients, and Jemmes' legs didn't even touch the floor. He would kick them freely and fiddle with the ornate paperweights on the edge of the desk, asking questions and chattering away until Wadeah would tell him to go and sort stock in the storeroom next door. This was the final stage for all the skins, stored and stacked neatly in a cool, narrow room. Wooden shelves and dividers separated the skins which had already been sorted, and made it almost like a library of leather. At the end of the long row were the piles of unsorted skins, and whenever he started distracting his father in his office, Jemme was always tasked with sorting through them. It was a job he enjoyed, even though he knew others saw it as a chore. He liked the attention to detail it involved and the fact that it involved him as well. His decisions, although small, were important, and linked him into the same industry as his father, his uncles and his ancestors. He would drag a selection of skins up the shelved aisle, into the middle of the floor and sit cross-legged in front of them. They were to be graded from one to four. One was the category for the highest quality skins. They had to be flawless, as these were the ones which were sent to the *haute couturiers* of Paris and Italy. Only the very best would do, as the Mafeze reputation would be damaged if anything subpar was sent. Jemme always checked he was extra, specially sure about these ones, running his palms over the smooth surfaces again and again, checking for imperfections, nicks and lumps. After the highest grade, grade two leathers still had to be of a fine quality. These were mostly sent to high-end clothes manufacturers in Italy; it was important that they were of an excellent quality too, and grade twos pretty much comprised leather that should have been grade one but for some small problem. Grade three was used for luggage, and so could afford to be a little coarser, although the material Wadeah classed as grade three was comparable to some of the highest quality leather that was being turned out of the newer factories. Lastly, grade four was the poorest quality. Sometimes the leather itself looked good, but the skin would have large holes in it, restricting how it could be cut and what it could be used for. This was mostly sold locally and used for shoes, covering books and everything in between. Jemme prided himself on his ability to grade the leather and liked to imagine the skins he had handled being sent to important men far away. One of Wadeah's greatest achievements was expanding the empire into Europe. There was a constant demand for leather from the fashion industries there, and he had cultivated a network of contacts which had served the business very well indeed. This last trip had been to meet another potential client in Venice. As always, he had gone with samples, testimonials and prices. His brothers were eager to hear if he had come back with results.

Leaning across the table to take another warm *pide* from the basket, one of Jemme's uncles said, 'So, come on, brother Wadeah! Tell us – did you get it?!'

Wadeah smiled at his brother, 'Yusouf! I have done nothing but travel – can a man not enjoy a supper with his family without having to talk business?!'

'He's teasing you,' Satir piped up, 'we all know you, Wadeah, you love to talk shop. Come on, stop the suspense! How did it go?'

Wadeah shook his head in mock sorrow, 'All I want to do,' he said, looking down, 'is to eat a simple *börek* with my brothers and sisters and – ' he was drowned out by shouts of protests. 'Alright, alright,' he said, looking up with a smile, 'since I can see that I'm not going to be able to eat until I tell you, I may as well.' He paused for dramatic effect, which he would have prolonged if he hadn't seen his sister, Varda rolling her eyes at him, 'I got the deal!' he said with a flourish. Much cheering ensued and Varda poured a new round of mint tea for everyone. The general chatter resumed with the sisters fussing about whether or not they had made enough *mezze* and the brothers clamouring for every detail of the deal – did the new Italian contact drive a hard bargain? Had they had to negotiate on the price? How many skins would he want? How often? Wadeah became engrossed in conversation with them and Jemme tried to keep up. Jama watched from the other side of the table, smiling quietly to herself. She had never known her husband not to get a deal. He always returned from a trip exhausted, but successful. She wished he didn't have to travel so much, and hoped he did less when the new baby arrived, but she could see how much he loved the thrill of it all.

After supper, the aunts began to clear away the dishes, overseen by Jama. Jemme followed his father and uncles into the *Selamlik*, the male area of the house. Having discussed the business deal exhaustively, they now wanted to know everything about Venice. Wadeah was by far and away the best travelled of all of them, and, like their mother, he knew how to tell a good story. Jemme was entranced by his tale of a whole city where the streets were made of water and everybody had to cross small bridges to get around, or use special boats with flat bottoms which were propelled by a man with a pole. He listened to his father talk about the mask shops, with their fantastical creations, made for the *Carnevale* during which the resplendent wearer would be bedecked in golden brocade and wrapped in a velvet cloak. It seemed like a mystical place, where legend collided with fantasy in the dimly lit backstreets, lined with historic buildings, many of which had housed famous artists and musicians.

'Ah, you've finished,' said Wadeah, looking up as the ladies entered. 'Just in time. I have something for you – for this room, in fact,' he directed to his wife. Jama broke into a girlish grin and chided him for bringing presents back every single time he went away. She did a poor job of hiding her excitement though, which soon turned into intrigue as her husband dragged a large, oddly shaped parcel in front of her. Wrapped up in brown paper, it had made an odd noise as he pulled it across the floor and all sorts of strange lumps protruded from it. Jama gently began to unpack the paper covering it.

'Come on!' everyone shouted at her impatiently, 'We want to see what it is!'

Smiling, she began to tear at the paper. However, where most people would have ripped it off in frenzy, she couldn't bring herself not to be gentle. It was a good thing too, as the object gradually emerged from the folds of packing to gasps of admiration. As the last of the paper was taken away, a beautiful glass chandelier was revealed.

'Do you like it?' Wadeah asked, 'I brought it from Murano; it's for this room. I bought it from an artisanal workshop on an island. The men who made it were brothers and their family have been glassworkers for hundreds of years.'

Jama listened, raptly. 'It's beautiful,' she said simple, 'thank you.'

As everyone murmured their agreement, Jemme couldn't take his eyes off the object. He had seen chandeliers before, but nothing like this one. The lamps in the *majlis* gave it a soft, luminous beauty, picking out the coloured beads, delicate shapes and complex branches. Although he had heard the clunking noise it had made, Jemme couldn't believe that something which looked so fragile could be so heavy and solid. It looked as if a spider had crawled around, spinning it out of fine gossamer, and leaving something delicate and shimmering behind. A large, fluted goblet at the top hid the chain and was surrounded by a ring of small flowers, all deftly created from pale peach-coloured glass. Tendrils of glass curled out from under them and rose up, curving in symmetrically around them. Another tier below that bore different coloured flowers, and thicker branches rose out from around and next to them. Each branch ended in a different coloured flower – every single one made of glass. The tiers became progressively bigger and the branches progressively thicker. Towards the bottom of the chandelier, the thickest supported further ornaments. Hanging from glass rings looped around the branches were further flowers, as well as pears and rounded apples. The detail in the finish was remarkable, and they looked like perfect glass miniatures. As he moved around it, the light played and changed with the shapes, and different angles made different patterns in the glass appear. Jemme was stunned by the object and couldn't stop staring at it.

'You wouldn't believe the factory!' he heard his father say, 'It was absolutely filled with things like this. The brothers were so interesting too. I think this was the nicest and the best for this room, but it was by no means the biggest – they had some which were over six feet tall! Six feet! Can you imagine that, little one – a chandelier bigger than your father!' He ruffled Jemme's hair and everyone laughed as they saw the look of concentration and wonder on Jemme's face.

'Why do you like it so much?' one of his uncles asked, 'Children aren't interested in art! They only like playing outside, eating and getting in my way when I'm in the market.'

Everyone laughed, but Jemme was still transfixed by the chandelier. It had awakened something in him he didn't quite understand. He had seen pretty things before, but never anything that was so beautiful it stopped him in his tracks. He couldn't even begin to imagine what a bigger version would look like, and less so one that was bigger than his father. There was something more to the object in front of him though, something which appealed to him more than just its beauty. It seemed exotic somehow, like it was vested with the mystery and romance of the place it had come from, with its watery streets and strange boats. The colours used, and the patterns wrought from the shimmering glass, were completely foreign and new; and yet, there was something recognisable and familiar about the whole thing. The fruits were similar to those painted on the walls of homes throughout Turkey. In fact, painting fruit onto things was one of the easiest ways to decorate things which were drab and boring, and such examples could be found all over the city. It was almost like the makers of this chandelier had seen these paintings and copied them in glass. He heard laughter again and looked up; everyone was still staring at him,

'I think your gift is a hit with one person at least, Wadeah!' Uncle Faisaloo said, 'Jemme, why don't you tear yourself away from that thing and come and tell us about Scouts? Did you know that I was a Scout once?'

Jemme went over to the rest of the family, and began to talk about Scouts, school and everything he had been up to. He hadn't forgotten about the chandelier though, and once everyone had left and his father was sitting back, relaxing with a tea, he approached him,

'Baba, tell me about the place you bought the chandelier. Was it really an island?'

Wadeah drew him on to his lap. He was exhausted, but he always had time to tell his son a story, 'Yes it was, Jemme. It's called Murano and it's known as the glass-blowing island. There was a time when the best glass in the world came from this one island. Venetian glass was a byword for quality and luxury, much as I hope my leather is today.'

'But I thought you said it came from Murano, Baba?'

'Murano is in Venice, Jemme; it's one of many islands there. The canals divide up the land and the whole city sits on the edge of a lagoon. Wherever you are, you're likely to be on an island. Some of them are big and are full of houses and churches and museums and some of them are very tiny. All of them are beautiful though. The Venetians have a special relationship with the water because it's been their life source for so long. The boats are how they get around, but also what made the city rich. They could transport all sorts of goods around between the rich merchants, and Venetians have been masters of ship building for over a thousand years.'

'A thousand years, Baba?! When were ships invented?'

'Ships have existed for much longer than that, Jemme! Before man was even living in houses, he was building boats and ships. By the time the Venetians came along, the ship had had time to develop quite a bit! Even in the seventh century, craftsmen were leaving Venice to go abroad and learn ship-building techniques in Dalmatia and Istria. But I'm digressing: you should ask your grandmother about this, she knows a great deal about Venice. Anyway, Murano is just one of these islands and they've been making glass there for eight hundred years, if you can believe such a thing.'

'Is everyone there father and son, like the men you met?

'Well, not quite – a lot can change in eight hundred years. There are still families there who have been involved in the business since the thirteenth century though. They're very protective of their art and their heritage. Glassmaking is a skill, Jemme, and it must be learned from a master. These families did not want just anyone to learn how to produce the same beautiful objects as them – the secret of his trade is one of the most important things to a master craftsman. So, they kept it in the family, amongst those they could trust, and that's how the secrets were preserved and the craft handed down the generations.'

Jemme nodded sagely.

'In fact, even today you can only learn the skills if you are apprentice to a master craftsman. Back in its heyday, they were so protective of the industry that if you left the island you were instantly branded a traitor.'

'Is it a big island?'

'No, not at all; certainly not if you are going to be living there for your whole life. But then, glassmaking was a way of life for these people and being known as a traitor would mean your life was not very pleasant, so this would be enough to keep you there, even if nothing else.'

'Why would you put something which was so important on an island that's not even very big?'

'That's actually a very good question, because there actually was a reason they did this. Glassmaking is dangerous – it needs lots of furnaces, which are like really hot fires and these burn throughout the day. The Venetians were terrified of fire spreading in their city, and so they moved anything risky out of the city centre and into the lagoon islands, which are the furthest away.'

'But would it matter if there was fire, when you said there was so much water in the streets?'

Wadeah laughed, 'You are a logical little thing. It might be easier to put out, but the buildings there are packed so close together and there's lots of wood in them too. It would be quite quick for fire to spread. Also, the houses are filled with wonderful treasures – silks and tapestries and all sorts, many of them very old. I suppose the Venetians are just protective of their city. Also, there's more to it than that. By putting everyone with special skills in one place, they were able to control their monopoly on glass.'

'What's a monopoly Baba?' asked Jemme, whose head by now had sunk into his father's chest and whose eyes were growing heavy.

'It just means that you're the only one who makes something; a bit like you're in charge of it. For example, in the fourteenth century every single mirror in Europe had been produced by Venice…. Jemme?' Wadeah looked down at his son. He had been astounded by that fact when the Italian brothers he met had told him it, and he thought it was just the type of thing to capture Jemme's imagination. Jemme, however, was fast asleep.

Travel-weary and exhausted by the frenetic chatter of the evening, Wadeah himself was soon asleep. The next day he awoke to a household already full of activity. His sisters were cleaning and sweeping after last night's feast, and one of his brothers was attempting to hang the chandelier, balancing rather precariously on a step ladder. Wadeah decided it was best to leave them to their own devices, and made his way to the kitchen. Jama was already setting dishes onto the table, leaning over the roundness of her belly. Baskets of warm *pide* and bowlfuls of creamy yoghurt sat with small dishes of spices and fiercely salty olives. Breakfast in Italy hadn't been nearly as good, as Wadeah remembered. It lacked a certain exoticism and he had missed being able to sprinkle a handful of fragrant *zatar* on his yoghurt, and the thick honey he smeared over the fresh bread, both of which he did now with relish. He heard the door behind him open and a small face appeared,

'Shouldn't you be in school, young man?' he asked his son.

Jemme laughed, 'Baba! It's a Saturday!'

'Oh, Jemme, I'm sorry – I completely lose track of time when I'm travelling,' Wadeah replied.

Jemme hopped up onto his chair and popped an olive in his mouth, wincing slightly at its salty bite.

'Plate, Jemme!' his mother chided. Turning to her husband she looked a little beseeching, 'I suppose that the fact it's the weekend doesn't really make a difference? You'll still be working?'

Wadeah sighed, 'I'm sorry, I just need to finish everything I started with the deal. I won't be long, I promise, and I'll work from my study here.' He cracked a grin, 'then I want to hear all about what you've been up to and how you are doing. Both of you,' he added placing a hand on Jama's belly. She looked appeased and smiled, 'Of course. I'll bring you through some coffee later on.'

'Can I help, Baba?' Jemme asked.

'Of course! Where would I be without my little secretary!' Wadeah said, as he helped himself to the last piece of bread.

Shortly afterwards, Jemme sat in his father's study. It was smaller than his proper offices, and wasn't just used for work. Sometimes his father would come in here to read, or just for some quiet relaxation. A large bookcase displayed a small part of his book collection, with its neat rows of volumes, all bound in Moroccan red leather, their titles picked out on the spines in gold. A comfortable chair sat behind a heavy walnut desk, which Jemme's mother lovingly polished with beeswax every month. Jemme loved this room. Everything in it represented his father, from the small bronze figurines, to the gramophone player in the corner.

It was a smart, grown-up room, full of personal touches. There was always a different smell in here to the rest of the house; a sort of woody smell which hung in the air and mixed with leather and the special shaving soap his father used.

Wadeah settled himself into his chair, and pulled a large ledger towards himself. He flicked through it, frowning slightly with concentration. When he had found the page he wanted, he marked his place in the column with one finger and reached into the bottom drawer of the desk.

'Here,' he said, holding it out to Jemme, 'I bought this recently. Why don't you have a look through it, and find some space on the shelves for it when you've finished?'

Jemme took the book and sat on his favourite cushion in the corner of the room. He carefully opened the front cover, and began to look through. It was a book on the history of leather production, but the text was quite dense and difficult to follow. There were some marvellous sketches and prints though, and he looked at them closely for a while. The function of some was obvious and he had seen them before: a swivel-knife to cut designs into the surface of the leather, various punches and hammers and things his father called 'awls', but he thought looked more like screwdrivers. However, at the bottom of one page there was a picture of something he didn't recognise. It appeared to be a large block of wood with various patterns on the front of it. They looked like flowers and broad leaves, and the whole thing looked like something which would be part of an architect's tool-kit, not a leather-maker's. He looked up. Although Wadeah's brow was furrowed in concentration, he never really minded being interrupted.

'Baba, what's this?' Jemme asked, as he climbed off the cushion and made his way over to the desk, with the book stretched out in front of him. Wadeah put his finger down again to mark his place and looked up.

'What's what, my son?' he asked. Jemme held the book up for him to look at and he glanced at the object quickly. 'That's a mould, Jemme, it's used by craftsmen in Córdoba to shape wet leather. It would have taken someone a long time to carve that,' he added before looking back down to his ledger.

'To shape it into what Baba?' Jemme asked, 'a bag? Why don't you do that?' He paused for a second before adding, 'Where's Córdoba?'

Wadeah sighed slightly. He marked his place in the margin with a pencil, and sat back in his chair, 'Why do you have to ask so many questions Jemme?! Córdoba is in southern Spain. It's very famous for its leather production, and has been for nearly a thousand years. That mould in the book is used to make Cordovan brocade, which is one of their specialities. It's very beautiful – I gave a piece to your Uncle Satir for his birthday last year if you remember?' Jemme shook his head.

'What is it though, Baba? The brocade I mean. What do you mean, "it's one of their specialities?"'

'This is why it's impossible to get anything done when you're around, Jemme! Answering one question leads to about three more!' He saw the expression on his son's face, 'It's fine though, I don't mind, I'd nearly finished anyway. Why don't you come over here and I'll tell you all about it.'

Jemme went back and grabbed his cushion, dragging it to the other side of the desk so he could listen to his father. Wadeah shut the ledger book, turned his chair round and began.

'Well son, leather brocade is something they traditionally make in Córdoba. It's a bit like having a tapestry. It includes some kind of picture or pattern and you hang it on the wall. The more beautiful and detailed the piece, the more luxurious the home it's likely to be in. That's what the mould is for. It textures the leather and gives it the shape of the patterns carved into the block. I wish it did make it in to the shape of a bag; that would certainly help my business a great deal! Rather, it shows the shapes of leaves, or flowers, or maybe even animals. They're quite often painted over the top and sometimes they're gilded too. Those are the best examples but, of course, the amount of gilding depends on how wealthy you are. They've been making things like this in Córdoba since the ninth century, although these hangings aren't as popular as they were. They take a long time to make and people's tastes have changed. You find silk being used instead, a lot more nowadays. For people who've worked in the industry, or anyone who has an interest in that kind of history, a well-made Cordovan brocade is really something quite special though. That's why your Uncle Satir was so pleased with his. Does that answer everything?' He looked down teasingly.

'Yes, Baba. Although I still want to know what you meant when you said it was "one of their specialities."'

Wadeah smiled, 'I thought you might,' he said, 'I just meant that over the course of a thousand years, no one town is ever famous for just one thing. Craft changes with people's tastes, and as technique develops. Over the course of time you come into contact with different influences as different craftsmen visit, or perhaps your country is invaded by another. With a history as long and rich as Córdoba's, the craft industry was bound to change a great deal. When you say "Córdoba leather" to someone now, it will mean a different thing, depending on which period of its history they're most familiar with. To some people it will just mean leather of high quality which has been vegetable tanned to a dark maroon colour. The skin is usually taken from the middle layer, so it's extra-fine and extremely durable. Some people will think of the brocades I just told you about, although that technique isn't just restricted to wall hangings. You can find it covering wooden furniture, like chests or even chairs, on screen panels, table-tops, mirror frames, on headboards, pretty much anywhere you can think of that provides a surface for decoration. That doesn't mean it was easy to get hold of, or even cheap. Like I said, the mould takes a long time to carve, and must be done by hand. The painting and the gilding are also done by specialist craftsmen, and it takes a long time. However, that's not the end of it. Some people will think of Córdoba leather as the soft, kid leather used to make delicate articles, such as fine ladies' gloves. These were so important in polite society that fashionable ladies would go to great lengths to buy a pair better than any of their friends'. They were even sold with perfumed fingers, and sometimes they were so delicate and fine that the lady wouldn't actually wear them, but tuck them under her belt so that all her friends could see them. Can you imagine such a thing?'

Jemme giggled a little, 'No, Baba, but I can't imagine one city producing leather for a thousand years either.'

'Well, as I said, Córdoba has a very long history, which has involved many people and places you might already know of. For example, I know your Grandmother was telling you about the Umayyads recently; do you remember?'

Jemme nodded, 'She told me about their fight with the Abbasids and about how their empire was five million square miles,' he said proudly.

'Exactly, although it wasn't an empire exactly; it was a caliphate. An empire is ruled over by an emperor and a caliphate is ruled over by a caliph. There were some great Umayyad caliphs you might have heard of: Omar ben Abdul Aziz who was just and loyal to his people, and al-Walid, the great patron of the arts and architecture.' He looked questioningly at Jemme.

'I haven't heard of either of them, Baba.'

'Well, no matter; you will in time. Your mother was telling me that you have been learning about the Abbasids at school?'

Again, Jemme nodded.

'Well, their stories are intertwined. The Abbasids were very powerful. They ruled the Islamic Empire for a long time. In fact, power was only formally transferred from them to the Ottomans in 1519 and then the Ottomans ruled for a long time too – your grandmother was born whilst they were still in power. The Abbasid's capital was in Damascus, and had been from the eighth century. However, they had to overthrow someone else to get that city as their capital, and that someone else was Abd al-Rahman I and his family. They were Umayyads and were forced into exile as the Abbasid power grew and grew. Abd al-Rahman wandered though the Middle East and the Maghreb for a long time, until he sailed to al-Andalus. That was to be the beginning of his success and the first step in establishing his own caliphate.'

'Where is al-Andalus Baba? Is it in the Middle East?' Jemme asked.

'Today it's mostly called Andalucía and it's in southern Spain,' Wadeah explained. Jemme nodded. He had definitely heard of Andalucía.

'You're right to ask though; the name does make it sound as if it would be found around here. That's what I was talking about earlier. The influences different people and peoples leave on a place stick to it and become part of that place's own story. So it was with the Umayyads, as you'll see. They left their trace even from the beginning. Do you know what *al-Andalus* means?'

Jemme thought for a moment. 'I think so. Is if from the Qur'an?'

'Yes, it is. It's one of the layers of Paradise. Andalucía is very beautiful with clear waters, lush grasses and beautiful sunshine. One day I shall take you there and you will see for yourself. It is a little like Paradise. It certainly must have seemed that way to Abd al-Rahman, after all his years in exile. There were people there who were his allies and gave him their support straight away. Of course, it wasn't easy and he had to fight many battles, some of them just small skirmishes, but some of them very big indeed. Eventually though, he won control of the whole region, including the city of Córdoba. He was able to unite the whole of al-Andalus under his rule, making himself very powerful and the promoting the Umayyad caliphate in the process – something the Abbasids back in Baghdad weren't too happy about.'

'Did they do anything?'

'Yes, they did. They sent an army over to try to topple Abd al-Rahman and the Umayyads, but by then they were too powerful, and the Abbasid army met with a rather sticky end. There were other small rebellions after that, but not so many to distract Abd al-Rahman from all his reforms and building projects. He began work on the Great Mosque and the city went from strength to strength, enjoying good relations with the Christian kings to the north and the Berber tribes of North Africa to the south. Under the Umayyad Caliphs, Córdoba became the cultural capital of all of al-Andalus, with ancient Greek texts being translated into Latin, Hebrew and Arabic –'

'Why, Baba? Why would you want to translate something into all three, I mean?'

'Do you know who speaks those languages Jemme?'

'What do you mean?'

'Each one is the official language of a different religion. Can you name them for me?'

'Well, Arabic is spoken by Muslims and Hebrew is spoken by Jews.'

'Good,' Wadeah prompted as Jemme screwed his face up whilst he deliberated on the third.

'I don't know who speaks Latin though.'

'I suppose that's a bit of a trick question. No one really speaks Latin these days, but it's a very important language to the Christian religion. Lots of their worship is conducted in Latin, and it is the language of some of their most sacred texts. Anyway, the reason these works were being translated is because these three religions – Muslims, Christians and Jews lived together in Córdoba. That's what made it such a great intellectual centre: instead of fighting, everyone lived peacefully together and shared their knowledge. Córdoba became renowned for its culture and learning, full of scholars, philosophers and scientists. Whilst the arts and learning were being cultivated, all the time the Great Mosque was being built. It attracted artisans and craftsmen from around the world, who came to work on it and be part of such an ambitious project. They brought with them their own practices, which mixed with those of the people already there. Do you see, Jemme? What makes a city great isn't necessarily the citizens, it's the way they work together. If everyone contributes something they're good at, then you find you have a vast pool of skills and expertise. If people are willing to work in co-operation, then that's when something becomes greater than the sum of its parts. If fourteen people all contributing a skill have learned their skill in different places, then the combined force of all their different skills is better than if fourteen people individually contributed their skills. Do you understand what I'm trying to say? I'm afraid I'm not explaining myself very well.'

Jemme nodded readily. The concept was not a new one to him, and it was one of Grandma's favourite themes. Many of her stories were told specifically to illustrate this point. She was always pointing out examples of different cultures, races and religions working together for the common good. She seemed to have examples from every era and every corner of the world. It was only through working in harmony that humanity can achieve great things, she would always tell Jemme sagaciously. By contrast she had lots of examples of ambitions frustrated, and half-finished projects, all through people refusing to co-operate. Plenty of great buildings lay unfinished because people had mistrusted their neighbours, instead of working with them.

'Anyway,' Wadeah continued, 'like I said, craftsmen came from all over to work on the mosque and brought with them all sorts of skills – marble cutting, sculpting, gilding to name but a few. They brought new craft influences to the workshops surrounding the mosque, and new cultural influences to the city when they settled there to live. Perhaps the most influential of all were the leather-makers from Damascus, which is what led us to this in the first place. As you know, Damascus already had a booming leather trade. The strength of the sun there is great for drying leather, and there's a ready supply of water too. These Damascene men took with them their specialist skills, which had been honed and developed over generations to be amongst the best in the world. They settled in the city and taught their skills to other people, mixing their influence with the practices they found there already. That's how Córdoba learned her leather-craft, which grew and developed to become the best in the world, some would say. Its reputation is certainly strong, even today.'

'Is the mosque still there today?'

'Sort of. The building is very much still there, but it's not a mosque anymore.'

'What is it instead?'

'It's a cathedral. You find that situation a lot in this region. These buildings are very old, and over the course of their history caliphates have risen and fallen, Christian kings have invaded and been fought back, and reconquistas have tried to assert their power. The building is a backdrop to all of these power struggles and its function reflects whoever is most powerful at the time. If a king or a caliph conquers a city, then changing the function of its biggest, most impressive and iconic building to reflect his own tastes and beliefs is quite a symbolic act – it makes a big statement. Do you see?'

'Yes, Baba. So, who turned it into a cathedral?'

'Well, in this instance it was King Ferdinand, but in a way he was only bringing it back to its original function. Abd al-Rahman didn't start building it from scratch. It was originally a Christian church for St Vincent. Abd al-Rahman expanded it and various Umayyad caliphs added domes and minarets, and developed the mihrab. Each new part reflected the fashions and technologies of its time, and so the building today tells a tremendous story – it's a construct of its own history and all the more beautiful for it. Once it was turned into a cathedral, lots more work was done and they were still building and developing it as late as the eighteenth century. I have a book on it somewhere with some beautiful illustrations. Would you like to see?'

'Yes please, Baba,' Jemme responded enthusiastically.

Wadeah crossed over to the bookshelf and ran his finger along the spines of the books, as he searched for the one he wanted. 'Aha! Here it is,' he said as he pulled out a thick volume with *Historia de la Catedral de Córdoba* printed in bold lettering. He leafed through for a while until he came to a double-page spread, which bore a large photograph of the cathedral-mosque's interior. He held it open for Jemme to see. 'Look, this is just some of the decoration you can find there.'

Jemme stared at the photograph for a while. There was so much to take in – it didn't seem as if there was a single square inch of surface which had been left undecorated in some way. One whole side of the mosque seemed impenetrably thick with columns and arcades, with arches of bold red and white voussoirs springing from the top, linking them all together. Smooth columns of jasper, onyx and aubergine-coloured marble rose from the floor, creating a forest of stone so large it disappeared into murky shadows. Their capitals were heavily embellished with leaves, palm fronds, clover and grapes. Elsewhere, intricate ribbon work twisted and interwove with the honeycombed carvings atop other columns. Each cornice bore beautiful golden calligraphy and each door was carved with geometric designs which tessellated and repeated, creating further patterns as they spread, giving the impression of endless decoration. Every time Jemme focussed his attention on one small area, something else would catch his eye and he would realise that there was another large area of splendid decoration he had not even seen yet.

'It's beautiful, Baba,' he breathed.

'It is, isn't it?' his father replied. 'Here, look at this,' he said, turning the page, and then turning the book around again to face Jemme. The next page bore another glossy photo of a different area of the mosque. Jemme looked at it for a moment. Although some of the features looked familiar to him, he couldn't identify its place within the mosque.

'This whole room, believe it or not, is the mihrab,' Wadeah explained.

Jemme was astonished. The mihrab was usually no more than a niche which showed the direction of Mecca, so that worshippers would know how to orientate themselves when they prayed. This, however, was a room in its own right. It was elaborately decorated with marble and mosaics, with inscriptions and scrolling flora. Jemme slowly took in all the detail. He didn't know if he was more impressed by its beauty or its sheer size.

Wadeah smiled at his concentration. 'The size isn't the only unusual thing about this mihrab though, son,' he said.

'No, Baba?' Jemme asked

'No. Tell me, Jemme, which direction would you expect it to be facing?'

Jemme paused, it seemed like a trick question, 'Towards Mecca?' he ventured. Everyone knew that all mihrabs showed the *qibla* – the direction of the Kaaba in Mecca. That was the whole point of the mihrab: it showed Muslims how to pray facing Mecca. He had known that for as long as he could remember, and he didn't understand why this one would be any different.

'You're right,' Wadeah said, 'you would assume it was facing Mecca. However, this one faces south.'

Jemme was intrigued. 'Why, Baba?'

'It's a good question. To be honest I'm not sure: there are several different theories, but no one can agree on which one is right. Some people think it points to the place at which Abd al-Rahman landed, when he arrived in southern Spain. I suppose it would make sense – after all his years in exile he might have wanted to commemorate the beginning of his new life in some way. However, something bothers me about the idea. I suppose it's the fact that it would be a colossal act of egotism on Abd al-Rahman's part, and I prefer to think of him as a more noble caliph than that. Although, I suppose that constructing something so grand as the Córdoba mosque isn't possible without some degree of ego.'

'What are the other theories?' Jemme asked.

'Well, some people think that it faces towards Damascus, recognising Abd al-Rahman's years in exile. I don't know how likely that is, and again, I struggle to believe that he would do something like that. I suppose the most likely explanation is the most obvious: he was influenced by the foundations of the old church. You remember that I told you there was a church there before the mosque?'

Jemme nodded.

'Well, I think that he was constricted by the orientation of the existing foundations. When he started the building project he was adapting and converting what was already there; he didn't build brand new parts until later. I think that this bit was just facing in the wrong direction. Incidentally, do you know how Christians position their churches?'

Jemme thought about it for a bit, 'I don't think so, Baba. I suppose that it's not towards Mecca?'

Wadeah smiled. 'No, it's not! In general, their churches face the East, where the sun rises. It's because it represents Christ rising again, and it's a piece of symbolism which is very important to them. It's not really relevant to this, but I thought you might find it interesting – I know how you love these little facts.'

'It is interesting, Baba, especially because the mosque is now a church again. I suppose that everything is the right way round now?'

'Actually, that's not really the case. It was a mosque for such a long time that that's what it became in essence. It was developed and adapted and decorated to such an extent that the original church was no more than a ghost – a shell the mosque had long since broken out of. When it was later converted back into a cathedral, the Christians faced the same problems as the Muslims had done all those years beforehand when confronted with a church. It's such an interesting place now – it's really two buildings in one, both of which have been sacred to different people, and reflect the beliefs and decorative ideologies of those who have worshipped there over the ages. We really must visit at some point; it's somewhere I'd like you to see. Of course –' he added as an after thought, 'I suppose the interesting thing is the fact that its conversion into a cathedral probably saved the whole building. There's no way the Spanish Inquisition would have left it untouched, and so by changing its present, King Ferdinand helped save its past. Not that he had intended to do so – the Spanish Inquisition were rather ferocious to put it mildly, but that's a much bigger story!'

Jemme looked up expectantly.

'Certainly not! That would take me all day to explain and I've already become sidetracked enough as it is! I've enjoyed talking to you, Jemme, but I really must finish these accounts; otherwise I won't be able to get on. Why don't you keep hold of that book for a while? It's full of photographs and pictures and I'm sure it will give you more of an idea of what the mosque looks like than me explaining it to you ever could.'

He closed the book and handed it over to Jemme who held out both hands to receive it. Making his way back to his corner of the room, he settled down and drank in every detail in the pictures, tracing columns, apses and arches with his finger. Back behind the desk, Wadeah was also settling back in to his own book, tracing the columns with the chewed end of a pencil, as he muttered numbers and sums under his breath, utterly engrossed. To an outsider it would have been difficult to determine who was enjoying himself more.

✼ ✼ ✼ ✼

After his father had told him about Córdoba, it had occupied Jemme's mind for a while. Over the next few days, every time he saw a furled leaf it would remind him of the delicate wooden carvings he had seen in the photos; each time a piece of marble caught the sun, he couldn't help but think of the curious forest of marble within the mosque-cathedral. What would it be like, he wondered, to be inside somewhere that was so big it felt like being outside? When he relayed his father's stories to her, Grandma had added that it was only a little smaller than the great basilica of St Peter in Rome. Jemme had seen enough pictures of St Peter's to know how big it seemed, and heard enough reverential discussion of it to be impressed by the comparison. However, something more urgent was also currently occupying him. His Scout Master had announced the destination for the troop's next trip. His very first adventure was to be to Venice! He hadn't believed his ears when he first heard it – he was going to get to see the places his father had just been telling him of; the strange glass island, the streets made of water, the big squares and the funny boats. He was so excited he could barely contain himself. He just had a few weeks to prepare; his mother had already bought him a brand new suitcase and two new Scouting jumpers. She had put the suitcase in a spare room and piled the jumpers neatly on the bed. The pile was gradually growing as Jama added batches of freshly laundered shirts and khaki shorts. Every so often Jemme would put his head around the door and eye the pile of possessions on the bed, nodding to himself when he was satisfied. His parents were finding these serious little stock-takes very amusing; last time his mother had caught him counting his socks and looking through the pile of vests, she couldn't help but let out a small giggle, 'You can be such a solemn little thing sometimes!' she said as she stroked his hair. Jemme looked wounded, 'Come now, I'm only joking.' she said and chucked him under the chin, 'Take that look off your face – it makes you look too serious for a boy your age. Look, there is plenty of time until you leave, and I promise I won't let you go until I'm certain that you have everything you could possibly need with you. I know going away on your own for the first time is scary, as well as exciting, but there will be plenty of grown-ups there too and they'll be able to help you with anything you need.'

Jemme's face softened a little and he was visibly placated.

'Your cousins have just arrived,' Jama told him, 'why don't you go and play with them in the courtyard and leave all the grown-up worrying to me?'

'Go!' she prompted laughingly, but Jemme was already halfway there before she had even finished saying, 'Make sure you tie your shoelaces!'

One hour later, Jemme and his cousins were crowding round his mother in the kitchen, whilst she prepared them a jug of refreshing cordial. Kicking a ball around had been thirsty work, but it had also made Jemme forget all about packing. Although he would never admit it, he was a little nervous about the trip. He had been on holidays and gone exploring all over Istanbul, but he had always been accompanied by Grandma or his parents. He was excited about Venice, and the chance to do something so grown up, but there was no denying it was a little intimidating – it was his first real taste of responsibility. However, he trusted his mother absolutely, and if she said everything would be alright then he knew it would. All he needed to do now was absorb as many stories from Grandma as he could, before he left. He wanted to know everything she did about Venice and Italy; he didn't want to miss out on anything whilst he was there and thought that this was probably the best way to prepare. Grandma agreed wholeheartedly, but had told him that there wasn't time to hear *everything* about Italy. Besides, she had said, if he knew everything before he went, then there wouldn't be any surprises when he got there. It hadn't dented her enthusiasm for sharing her knowledge with him though, and Jemme had already learned that the old name for Venice was *Serenissima* – the most serene. Grandma had told him that it related to the city's great beauty, but also its status as a republic, ruled over by someone called a *Doge*. She had promised to explain more, and Jemme was keen to understand how all the pieces of the puzzle fitted together. Right now, he was more than happy to play with his cousins, who were finishing their cordial and holding their glasses up for more.

He could hear his mother laughing, 'No more! You boys shouldn't have drunk it so quickly!'

'But it's so good!' they beseeched, looking pleadingly.

Jemme knew that his mother could never deny anyone anything, and he knew that his cousins knew that too – it was written all over their mischievous faces.

True to form, Jama soon relented, 'Go on then, just a little bit, but next time it's water for all of you.'

'Thank you,' they all said in chorus and greedily drank down the glasses she had just poured. Suitably refreshed, they all went back into the courtyard and played Jemme's pebble game until it was time for the cousins to go home.

'Bye-bye Jemme!' they called from the other side of the gates.

'See you tomorrow!' Jemme shouted back as he went back inside to find his mother.

'Did you have fun?' she smiled down at him.

Jemme looked up at her for a while. She was always calm, but there seemed to be something extra peaceful about her – she almost seemed to be glowing.

'You look serene, Mama,' he said.

'Serene?! Thank you sweetheart, where on earth did you learn that word?'

'Grandma taught it to me.'

'Of course, why did I even ask? Well, it's very fitting, Jemme. I feel quite serene. Would you like to know why?'

Jemme nodded readily.

'Even better than that, you can feel why.'

Jemme looked confused as his mother took his hand. She placed it on the side of the large bump which had replaced her slim stomach. 'Do you feel that?' she asked him.

Jemme furrowed up his face in concentration for a while. Then, sure enough, he felt something. There was a sharp movement beneath his hand which caused him to withdraw it in alarm. However, there was nothing underneath, just the smooth cotton of his mother's dress.

'What was that?' he asked.

'That was your little brother or sister, kicking,' his mother explained.

Jemme stared at her wide-eyed for a while. He was still getting used to the idea of having a smaller sibling, but had assumed it was a long way off. He couldn't believe that it was already big enough to be able to kick his hand, and from inside his mother's stomach too. It had been at the back of his mind for a few weeks, and now he realised he was going to have to think about it some more before the baby arrived. Furrowing his brow he pondered the little kick. Suddenly he broke out into a smile.

'He can play football with me when he's born!' he said, adding, 'or she,' quickly.

That evening Grandma tucked Jemme into bed. His mother was still allowing him to sleep in Lily's room, and so shortly after she had pulled the covers up and kissed his forehead, Jemme's grandmother got into her own bed. She had barely pulled her own covers up when Jemme piped up, 'Grandma?'

'Yes, my love?'

'Will you finish telling me about the Doge?'

'Do I have a choice…?' Lily teased.

'Please?' Jemme wheedled slightly.

'Of course, of course, but then you must promise to go to sleep. I am planning a very long walk for tomorrow and I need all the sleep I can get!'

'I promise.'

'Well, that sounds like a deal. Where would you like me to start?'

'You had told me all about the Republic, and that the head of it all was called the Doge.'

'Ah yes; well remembered. Well, as I told you, Venice was and is a very important city, but I'm not going to tell you why – I think you'll only really learn it properly by discovering the reason whilst you're there. Anyway, it was more than just a city, it was a city state. Today you think of it as being within Italy, but up until the eighteenth century it existed in its own right. For over a thousand years it was a republic, controlling its own great riches, with its own distinctive art and decoration, its own culture – even its own language. It's similar to Italian, but you can still see the difference. Even today you'll find signs in Venetian rather than Italian. A republic as wealthy and complex as Venice needed a special type of ruler, and that person became known as the Doge.'

'What does "Doge" mean, Grandma?'

'Some people translate it as "duke", but it's better not to translate it at all. It's a special title which just refers to this particular position, and I always think it's better to use the proper terms for things.'

'Doge,' Jemme turned the word over. 'Dooooooge,' he repeated, drawing it out.

'The Venetian word was "Doxe", but that's a lot more difficult to say, so we'll stick to Doge for now,' Grandma continued. 'The Doge was hugely powerful, although completely accountable for all his actions. In fact, after his death, a commission analysed all his acts and if they decided that he had not acted in the people's best interests then his estate could be fined. That's another interesting fact about the Doge – he tended to rule for his lifetime, and a new Doge would only be elected on the death of the old one.'

'Like a king?'

'A bit like a king, yes. However, the next Doge wouldn't necessarily be the son of the old Doge. The position tended to be shared around the wealthy families of Venice, but there was actually a law in place to prevent it becoming a hereditary title.'

Jemme nodded furiously. He wasn't quite sure what the word 'hereditary' meant, but he was determined not to let on.

'So, how did they choose the next Doge, Grandma?' he asked cautiously.

'Well, instead of it passing from father to son, the position was elected. It wasn't as simple as that though. The Venetian ruling classes were very wary of one person being able to gain too much influence, so they introduced a very complicated system to make sure that didn't happen. Are you sure you want to hear about it?'

'Yes please, Grandma.'

'Very well. First of all you should know that the most important group in Venetian politics were known as the Great Council. They were a bit like the parliament, or the senate. Although the Doge was the head of state, they chose the Doge and they had the power to remove him from office too. Secondly, I should explain sortition to you, as that's a big part of the process. Have you covered it in school?'

'Not yet, Grandma.'

'A great shame. It is the bedrock of democracy and has been used from Ancient Athens to modern-day America. I hope that your teachers explains it at some point. It is important to learn these things. Anyway, it is very simple. It involves a large group of people drawing lots to determine who amongst them will be the decision makers. It is a very fair system, but it is only the beginning of this story. After the death of a Doge, the first step in the selection process was to choose thirty members from the council. This is the first instance of sortition, do you see?'

'Yes, Grandma.'

'Well, after that, the thirty drew lots until they were reduced to nine. Then the nine chose forty people. Then, those forty people drew lots until they were reduced to twelve. Then those twelve people chose twenty-five people. Are you following me so far?'

'I think so.'

'It's not over yet! Those twenty-five people drew lots until they were reduced to nine again and they then elected forty-five people. The forty-five people drew lots until they were only eleven and then those eleven chose forty-one people. Finally, those forty-one people were the ones who actually chose the next Doge.'

'Wow!'

'I know – isn't it lucky they only had to do it once the Doge had died? Can you imagine if they had to undergo this process once every five years? Although it's complicated, at least it ensures fairness, and I suppose it shows how advanced the Venetians were in terms of politics and democracy. Once the Doge had been presented to the people, he was installed in the Doge's Palace, which still stands today. I'm very excited you're going to get to see it at such a young age. It's a very beautiful building, not to mention incredibly old. I hope you'll appreciate it a little more, knowing how seriously the role was taken by its former inhabitants. I have some illustrated books on Venice which I'll get out for you tomorrow. We can have a look and see if there are any portraits of the Venetian Doges – I'm sure you'd like to see what they looked like before you visit what used to be their home!'

'Yes I would, thank you. What did they wear, Grandma, if they weren't kings? Did that mean they couldn't have a crown?'

'I suppose they could have worn a crown if they'd wanted to, but in reality they wore a special sort of hat. It's completely unique to Venice and quite distinctive. It was very stiff and rose up at the back into a sort of blunt horn. Once you've seen a picture of it, you'll recognise it in all the portraits. It was made of brocade, and sometimes had gold detailing too. Venice is full of decoration and rich trimmings, as you'll see when you get there. It's only fitting that that was reflected in the head of state's dress. He even wore golden slippers to match his golden robes, and must have been quite a sight.'

'He sounds quite Eastern, Grandma.'

'Well, it's funny you should say that, because that's a very big part of Venetian history. I think that's another part of the story I'll leave for you to discover whilst you're there; you'll find that Venice's history criss-crosses with that of many cities from the East and I think you'll recognise some things which might surprise you. That's all I'll say for now,' Lily said with a twinkle in her eye.

Jemme knew better than to push her, but he wasn't quite ready for their conversation to end.

'Tell me more about the Doge, Grandma.'

'There's a lot to tell Jemme! There were many different Doges, spanning many centuries and the rise and fall of Venice's fortunes. I think the best way for you to learn most of these things is by actually going and taking in what you see. So much of education is based in experience.' She saw the look on his face and relented slightly.

'But, I will definitely tell you a little more before we both go to sleep. Let me think, what would be most interesting to you? I could tell you about the Ducal Procession, the state galley, or the ceremonial marriage to the sea, but you can only pick one.'

'The marriage to the sea!'

'I thought you would be intrigued by that! It also involves the state galley a little bit, so you get another story for free. The marriage to the sea was one of the Doge's most important ceremonial roles. It happened for an entire millennium, and even had its own name – *La Sensa*; it's exactly as it sounds, and was an actual marriage between La Serenissima and the Adriatic Sea –'

'But why ,Grandma?'

'Patience, young man – I'm getting there. The sea was, and is, hugely important to Venice. The city's fortunes were tied to the sea, for reasons that will be obvious when you get there. The sea had the ability to bring Venice great riches and wealth when it was calm, but also cause very great problems when it was not. The fate of Venetian maritime wealth and the cultural riches it brought the city were completely tied up with the behaviour of the sea. The ceremony was a way of demonstrating the close bond between the citizens and the water, with the hope that it would prove auspicious for the coming year.'

'So how did it work?'

'That's where the state galley comes in, or *Bucentaur*, to give it its proper name. It was like a magnificent floating palace, and was the official vessel of the Doge. On the day of the wedding, which was always Ascension Day, the Doge and his retinue would board Bucentaur and sail out of the Lido into the Adriatic, with a regatta of smaller boats following. With great ceremony, the Doge would produce a gold ring, which had been consecrated by the city's priests. He would recite a Latin prayer out loud and then toss the ring into the sea, showing that Venice was one with the water, dominant of the seas, yet also dependent on them. One year, the Pope himself even attended, and removed a ring from his own finger and handed it to the Doge, who threw it into the sea. It must have been quite a spectacle, with all the city's patrician classes decked out in their finest robes and music playing from the different boats.'

'Does it not happen any more, Grandma?'

'Not properly, no. The republic does not exist anymore and there is no longer a Doge. Not only that, but the galley was completely destroyed by Napoleon, and a new one was never built. I believe that there is still some sort of ceremony in which the mayor throws a ring, but it would be a shadow of its former self and mostly for the tourists.'

'That's such a shame,' Jemme said, looking a little sad.

'I know, although, one can never cling on to the past to the detriment of the future. If things didn't evolve and change during our time, then we wouldn't be able to contribute anything to the history of the cities we live in. We just wouldn't be part of their stories. It's not as if any of Venice's glorious past has been forgotten. There are countless fine paintings which record its beauty and ceremony; some of them are amongst the most famous in Western Europe in fact. You'll see when you get there, the history of the place is written across its fabric. Everything in it seems to tell a story and they haven't faded in modern times. In fact, if anything, they seem more fabulous by comparison. But I digress. You, my young grandson, have had your story and I must go to sleep! Good night, Jemme.'

'Good night, Grandma,' Jemme replied, as Lily turned off the light. Within minutes he could hear his Grandmother's breath become shallow as she drifted into sleep. He closed his eyes, but was a long way from sleep. Ancient galleys sailed across his mind, full of men in strange brocade hats throwing golden rings from the decks. The more he thought about it, the more excited he became to see this wonderful and mysterious new place.

* * * *

Finally, the day of the big adventure had arrived. Jemme's smart new suitcase stood in the hallway, bulging a little at the clasps. His mother had to enlist his father's help to close it in the end, as the piles of clothes and kit on the bed had grown so large that it didn't seem physically possible the case would close over the top of them all, once inside. Jemme could barely lift it, but he didn't need to worry; Wadeah was accompanying him to the drop-off point, where all the Scouts were meeting ahead of their long journey. Then, the Scout Master would take over, making sure that all the bags were loaded onto the coach and checking the boys on and off every time they stopped. Jemme was happy with the plan, and any residual anxiety he might have felt had melted into excitement as soon as he had woken up that morning. He had said his goodbyes at home, and hugged his grandmother and tried to hug his mother too, but her belly was now so big he couldn't get his arms around her. She kissed him on his forehead and looked tearful as she told him to behave himself, and do whatever the Scout Master told him. His grandmother had looked almost as excited as Jemme and had reminded him to ask questions and see as much as he could. Then, his father had picked the case up with one hand and extended the other to Jemme. He had slipped his small hand into his father's and they were off. As they walked along he chattered non-stop, telling his father about all the things he would see. Soon the bleached wooden exterior of the Scout hut hove into view and it was time to say goodbye to his father too. Wadeah leant down to his level and gripped him in a tight hug. 'Good luck, son,' he said into his ear, then embraced him again. He straightened up, handed Jemme's case to the Scout Master, turned to wave again and left. Suddenly Jemme felt as if the adventure had begun in earnest. He looked around him. There were several boys his age, looking a little bereft as they too waved goodbye to parents, whilst some older-looking ones stood around and chatted, looking far more at ease with the situation. He spotted his friends Walli and Rafi and went over.

'Hello! Isn't this exciting?'

Walli nodded, but didn't look convinced, whilst Rafi broke out into a wide smile, 'Definitely! My uncle gave me a book about Venice; there are so many things I'm looking forward to seeing!' he said.

'Me too,' nodded Jemme enthusiastically as the Scout Master ushered them onto the coach. They ran to the back and were able to grab the only place with three seats together. Walli sat between them, and within about five minutes of their enthusing and cajoling he looked just as excited as the other two. After an hour or so the Scout Master walked down the aisle of the coach, checking that everyone was alright. He laughed as he reached them.

'You three are going to wear yourselves out if you keep chattering like that! We've got a very, very long journey ahead of us, so I'd advise you to settle down for a little bit.'

They had soon talked themselves out, and sat back, watching the scenery gradually change. They stopped for breaks several times and it seemed that every time they did, they were in a different country. After a while all the countries seemed to merge into one – Bulgaria with the strange writing on its road signs; Yugoslavia, which the Scout Master informed them was at the crossroads of Europe; Croatia where they stopped for a strange dinner of *riblja* – a sort of spicy fish stew. As dusk fell, they gradually drifted off to sleep, awaking only when they hit a bump. as Slovenia slowly slipped past them, arriving at the Italian border just after dawn.

One by one the boys stirred to life, waking each other with excitement when they could see Italy spread before them. To one side the glittering Adriatic swam into view every time they rounded a corner, whilst lush fields dotted with laurel trees extended outwards as far as the eye could see on the other. Occasionally they could catch sight of a purplish slick in the far distance, which the Scout Master informed them was the edge of the Dolomites. Gradually the coast became a constant view, only to give way to clumps of marshy land which broke into small lagoons. Various exciting sounding places went past – Trieste, Cervignano and Santo Stino, until, finally, they had arrived.

✳   ✳   ✳   ✳

Over a thousand miles later, the Scouts poured out of the coach into the bright early morning sunshine. As they rubbed the drowsiness from their eyes, the Scout Master began to organise them into a crocodile to walk to their hostel. There were general murmurings of approval as they got their first proper look at Venice. Jemme was wide-eyed; he couldn't believe what he could see before him. The streets really were made of water. It wasn't just that a small stream ran down the middle of the road – there was no road; just a seamless carpet of water from one building to the next. Anyone opening the front door to their house would step out into nothing but water. A network of tiny bridges jumped over the maze of canals, connecting strips of towpath and pavement. He was soon glad of the Scout Master; he'd never seen a place so confusing. Every time they turned a corner another set of waterways and bridges would fan out in front of them. Jemme kept expecting to get to the end and reach dry, solid land, but they just discovered more and more strips of dark water. After ten minutes of walking, he had completely lost track of the direction they had come from, and indeed the direction in which they were heading. He started to look up from the canals to the buildings crouching over them. They seemed to grow up out of the water, standing tall and terraced, and boxing in the canals. There was something compelling about them; to start with, Jemme was surprised at how shabby they seemed. He was expecting rows of smart marbled grandeur, but these houses looked like they'd seen better days. However, in a way it added to their beauty. They weren't dilapidated by any means, and the slightly run-down look gave them an air of mystery. The wear on plaster embellishments only served to give them further character, and make Jemme wonder what stories they held – who had fitted them? Somebody who wanted to make his house look impressive, obviously. 'I wonder if people were impressed,' he thought to himself. The path they were walking on suddenly emerged into a square, or *piazza*, as the Scout Master called it. A fountain sat in the middle, and a church took up one whole side of the square. As the bell tolled, cassocked priests scuttled inside, disturbing the sparrows who were pecking around the stone steps, looking for crumbs.

'Look at their hats!' Walli said, pointing at the strange black caps on their heads. They were roughly square, with three peaks which rose from the side and gathered in together at the top. On some this was finished off with a sort of pom-pom. They all agreed they had never seen anything like it before.

'We're nearly there, boys,' the Scout Master called back to them as they reached the edge of the square and once again found themselves in a narrow alleyway. Just as soon as they had entered it in single file, they found it coming to an end, and one by one the entire Scout troop emerged with gasps of surprise. Towards the back of the queue, Jemme and his friends grew impatient as they heard others exclaiming at what they were seeing. When it was finally their turn, and they found themselves in the sunshine again, they were not disappointed at what lay in front of them. They found themselves standing at the side of the biggest canal yet. An unbroken line of buildings stood on both sides, some marble, some brick, some even looked wooden. Some were palatial, some were tall and some just seemed to be filling the small gap between their much grander neighbours. By now, the city was definitely awake and the day was underway. The canal was an absolute hive of activity, thronged with every type of boat imaginable. They raced alongside each other, crossed each other's paths, moored up and cast away from the front of buildings, always within a hair's breadth of each other, but never once colliding, as if in some choreographed dance. Large canoes, heading towards a market, bore boxes of fresh fruit, bulging hessian sacks with vegetables protruding from the top and crates of what looked like shellfish. Tiny boats, which looked barely big enough for their solitary steersman, teetered impossibly with parcels, whilst passengers sat in incredibly ornate slim-line boats which appeared to be controlled from the back by a man with a large pole. There was so much noise and bustle, and the air was rich with a sing-song language none of them had ever heard before. The men delivering packets and parcels shouted to the waiting recipients in docking areas; the drivers of grubby-looking refuse barges joked with each other, and shouts rang out from the market-place as people called out their wares. There seemed to be buskers and hawkers everywhere, singing, reading poetry and playing musical instruments. It was as chaotic as the souk in Istanbul, but in a completely different way.

'This is the Canal Grande,' the Scout Master told them. 'It's the main canal here,' he added rather needlessly. It was perfectly obvious that this was the artery of the whole city. The buildings, people and activities contained in this one small space provided more to look at than some whole towns could during an entire week.

They stood for a while, soaking up the atmosphere. Jemme could see what Grandma meant about not yearning after the past; this was a busy city which was very much alive, rather than a museum town which existed solely to promote its past. He scanned the line of buildings on the opposite side of the canal. They were well adapted to their watery surroundings. Each had a portico area for docking boats; in some this was finished with rounded arches, creating an airy central section for the building. Some of the buildings had arched windows on the first floor too, echoing those of the portico; some facades were entirely decorated with different coloured marbles, all inlaid so that it seemed as if the colours had been painted on. Some were decorated with plaster friezes, so delicate it looked as if lace had somehow been suspended on the front of the building, and some of the flat roofs had been finished with fretwork that looked more like a sugar confection than plasterwork. It was a mix of decoration Jemme had never experienced before. Even things which initially looked familiar were skewed and transformed into shapes and colours he didn't recognise. As he stared at the buildings, the city continued around him, a swirl of new colours, sounds and smells. It was almost overwhelming.

The Scout Master started to lead them along the banks of the Canal Grande and Jemme stumbled behind the others, completely caught up in his own reverie. He vaguely heard the Scout Master pointing out the colourfully striped poles sticking out of the water – they were mooring posts, he thought he said, and the colours identified which of the hotels they belonged to. After a few hundred yards they reached a platform which looked like it was floating on the water. A small booth sat above it on the bank with a smartly painted sign reading 'GIUDECCA'.

'This is ours, boys; come on – I can see the boat coming in,' the Scout Master urged. He bought their tickets as the boys climbed down the steps onto the platform. As Jemme neared the bottom of the steps, he was snapped from his day-dreaming with a nasty shock. He could have sworn the ground had moved in front of his very eyes. He looked around at the others, but no one seemed to have noticed anything. Tentatively he put his foot down – there it was again! The entire surface on which he was standing had lurched forwards. He edged his way over to the others and peered cautiously at the approaching boat. As it neared them the ground they stood on began to pitch increasingly. Suddenly he understood. He had been right, it *was* floating on water. The Scout Master explained that these boats, or *vaporetti,* were the only form of public transport, and Jemme realised that he was standing on the equivalent of a train platform. *How funny,* he thought to himself as he boarded the boat. He couldn't imagine trying to get onto a train when the station platform was shifting beneath his feet. They had barely sat down when the boat chugged off again. It was crammed full of people, just as a train would be at that time in the morning. The younger boys looked up at the adults standing around them. They seemed to be a mixed crowd, mostly comprising suit-wearing professionals, probably on their way to work. Some men were wearing a uniform that Jemme didn't recognise, and one person wore paint-spattered overalls and carried a canvas tool bag. Some of them were talking in the fascinating sing-song language Jemme had heard earlier. The vowels were very long and people seemed to roll the words extravagantly in their mouths.

After about two minutes the boat stopped and the configuration of passengers changed. The man with the tool bag got off and some girls holding violin cases got on. A man in a suit stood up to give an elderly lady his seat. Jemme looked on, fascinated, as the events all unfolded in this utterly foreign language. This was the first time in his life he hadn't been able to understand what those around him were saying, and it was a very strange experience. After another few stops and only around ten minutes later the vaporetto reached its final stop, the Giudecca island. The island was long and thin and had a skyline peppered with church spires. A large dock ran the length of the waterfront and they walked along it until they came to the hostel. A former corn-house, it was a large building of warm red brick with big, old windows. The boys found their way to their dormitories, with Walli and Rafi helping Jemme drag his case along. After a late breakfast and a roll call, the Scout Master was ready to lead them out again. This time the vaparetto was not so packed, and they were able to look at the view as it progressed up the Canal Grande. There were so many things they had missed out on, during the squash of the first journey. Jemme couldn't believe he hadn't seen those highest buildings: tall, and thin, they stuck up through the skyline like red and orange pencils. They had pointed, pyramid-like roofs and small glassless windows near the top. The Scout Master explained that they were called *campaniles* and that they were the bell towers for the churches they sat next to. The small windows were for the bells, he said, and every time a peal was rung, people would have had to climb up a spiral staircase inside the tower, all the way to the top. Apparently some towers were open to the public and he was going to see if he could find one for the Scouts to climb. In any case, they were about to see perhaps the most famous campanile in the world, he told them. As the vaparetto neared the small alighting platform, the top of the bell tower he had pointed to grew larger and a green pyramid spire came into view, topped by a gold weathervane. The tower was of dark red brick, save for a large stripe of white, just below the spire. As it grew larger, they could see that it was a marble section of arches, which apparently encased the belfry itself. Once back on firm ground, the Scout Master assured them they were about to see something really special.

'This,' he said, dramatically gesturing with his arm, 'is St Mark's Square.'

The boys let forth a chorus of approving noises. There, in the corner of the square stood the tower they had seen from the distance. It was an impressive sight, soaring up three hundred feet into the air. A gentle breeze span its weathervane, which glinted as it caught the sun. The detail on the marble arches was visible, even from the ground. However, few of them were looking at the tower. The building to its side, although considerably shorter, was utterly arresting.

'Wow,' Jemme could hear Walli exclaim next to him. He nodded slowly, as he surveyed the building's spires and domes

'This is the Basilica of St Mark, or, as the Italians call it, the *Basilico di San Marco*, the Scout Master told them, ignoring some passing girls who tittered at his pronunciation.

'I've arranged a tour for the inside,' he continued, 'but we have about ten minutes to look around outside first.'

'Come on, let's go,' said Rafi turning to Jemme and Walli.

They didn't need much prompting, and all three of them moved towards the Basilica. The square was busy with both people and pigeons, and with their chins up to look at the amazing roof of the building, a string of Italian exclamations followed the boys as people swerved out of their paths.

'It looks like something from a fairy story,' said Jemme as they drew level with the giant brass front door.

'I know what you mean,' said Rafi looking up. Marble angels seemed to trumpet visitors inside, whilst a gold winged lion stood guard against an indigo backdrop, starred with silver. Above the door a gilded mosaic clung to the curves of the portico and depicted the Basilica itself. Everywhere they looked, there was something new to see, some statuary, gilding, mosaicking or marblework. Jemme drank in as much as he could. It seemed so mystical and he was anxious not to miss anything or forget anything he'd seen. The more he looked, however, and discovered new decorations and architectural detailing, the more it struck a chord with him somewhere. There was an ineffable air of familiarity about the place. He didn't know if it was the large onion shaped domes, the marble columns or the building's piers and arches, but there was definitely something he felt he had seen before. He shrugged it off, *maybe he had seen a photo in one of the books he had looked at*, he thought to himself as they made their way inside for the tour.

If any of the boys had failed to be impressed by the outside, then the inside was unanimously greeted with a sharp intake of breath.

'It often has that effect!' a heavily accented voice announced. The man who had just appeared announced himself as their tour guide.

'In fact, for about a thousand years, this church has had the nickname *Chiesa d'Oro*, which means "Church of Gold".' he added.

The Scouts could see why. It seemed as if the entire ceiling was made of gold. It spread across the capitals of the columns, ran up inside the cupolas and flowed over the tops of the arches. It was hard to imagine anything more opulent. The sea of gold was interrupted only by paintings of saints, their richly coloured robes picked out in glossy tempera.

'The ceiling certainly is beautiful,' their guide continued, 'but I always think it is a great shame it detracts from the floor.'

Almost as one they all looked down. He was right – the floor was a work of art and would have been the focal piece in any other building. It was a carpet of interweaving geometric designs and depictions of animals, all rendered in mosaic form using tiny coloured tiles. With the guide leading the way, they moved through the interior, stopping first at the Presbytery.

'Note the red marble columns,' he told them, which they duly did. He pointed out the statues on top of them, which he told them were some of the best examples of fourteenth-century Gothic sculpture. Marble banisters supported bronze statues leading up to the high altar.

'You see how much there is, just in this small space?' asked the tour guide.

They murmured in agreement.

'I'm afraid it would take me all year to show you everything in here, but I can tell you've already got a feel for its ability to awe. I'll give you a short tour of the most impressive parts, and tell you a bit of our city's history along the way.'

They shuffled after him, looking at every marble carving and gilded mosaic he pointed out. He was obviously enjoying his hushed audience, and waxed lyrical about the church's symbolism. He told them that its richness and splendour captured part of what Venice was like at the height of its glories. He told them that this church, more than any other, enshrined the city's history. It was a showcase for centuries of prosperity, multiculturalism, and cultural and artistic achievement.

'Throughout the republic, Venice was a sphere of influence,' he told them, 'it was a small and unique world in which architects, merchants, artists and diplomats gathered, to name but a few. It became a hotbed of creativity, fuelled by its maritime and silk wealth. It did more than merely fund what you see, this money profoundly influenced it too, in a way that it couldn't in other great cities of Western Europe. Do any of you know what I could mean?'

A sea of blank faces looked back at him.

'Well, do you know where much of Venice's wealth came from?'

'The sea?' asked one Scout.

'Yes, it wouldn't have been possible without the sea, but there was one product in particular which brought with it all sorts of exotic influences. Think about it, I've already given you the answer.'

Silence pervaded for a little while whilst they thought back over what he had said. Eventually one Scout remembered.

'Silk?'

'*Fantastico*! Exactly; well done. I don't know what you've learned so far about the Silk Route?' Again his look was returned by blank faces, although it appeared to have rung a bell with some of the older boys.

'I see. Well, again, I could take all year describing it to you, so I'll just give you a quick summary: silk was integral to the success of this city, financially and culturally. Do any of you know where silk comes from traditionally?'

'China,' someone replied.

'Bravo. The silk would start its life in China, far from here. It undertook a very long journey to get here, both across land and sea. Picture in your minds how far China is from Italy, and how many different countries must be crossed to get here. Think about your own journey here and how many different countries you passed through. Well, imagine if you had had to ride here on horse back, or lead camels carrying boxes full of silk. Can you think how long that would have taken you?'

They shook their heads.

'Well, thinking about how many countries you would cross, and how slowly you would be travelling, imagine how you would pick up different influences along the way. As different merchants and traders would join you along the route, they would bring with them all sorts of new practices.'

'Like what?' asked Walli, prompting Rafi to elbow him in the ribs.

'No, it's a good question,' the tour guide replied. 'It could be anything; maybe a new style of cooking, a different set of folk tales or a new set of tools for working silk. All of them would have enriched the caravan in some way, and as more people brought more learning and innovation with them, together they became greater than the sum of their parts. The different influences only led to more innovation and a unique culture.'

Just like Grandma always says, thought Jemme to himself, as he recognised one of Lily's favourite topics appearing.

'The caravan would travel from the Far East all the way here, picking up new ideas and learning as it went. You could think of it almost like a snowball, growing as it moved. By the time it arrived here it was more than just a delivery of silk, it was something much more special. This city became a repository for all these different influences, and they continued growing and evolving long after the merchants had left. In fact, some of the merchants stayed here, so the city continued to evolve with all of their different influences. You can see them everywhere you look in the city. It's a unique expression of East/West influence, and all the more beautiful for it. You might have recognised certain Eastern elements in this basilica already. Are there any parts which remind you of things you have seen where you come from?'

Jemme thought for a while. There certainly had been something familiar about the exterior, he just couldn't put his finger on what. The tour guide hadn't waited for an answer, 'This place is full of Eastern influences, both in terms of structure and decoration,' he continued, 'I thought it might look familiar to some of you from the outside. Those domes are classically Byzantine, it's as if they have been taken straight out of the Byzantine Empire.'

Almost everyone had heard of the Byzantine Empire, but they hadn't quite put the pieces together yet. Their Scout Master helped them out, 'Think about the capital of the Byzantine Empire boys,' he prompted, 'it was Constantinople. You all know what it's called today!'

Of course, Jemme thought to himself, Istanbul – his home city. He thought back to the bowl-shaped domes on the outside. They were just like those you found around Istanbul. Even Hagia Sophia bore domes of a similar shape. In fact the golden mosaics in Hagia Sophia, and the style of painting on them, were almost exactly the same as the ones they had all been marvelling over here. He started to see what the guide meant when he was talking about influence and building something that was greater than its individual pieces. This basilica incorporated some of the best elements from structures he already knew and combined them with features and designs he'd never come across before. He began to think about how that idea could be applied to things other than a building and realised how big its implications were. He followed the rest of the tour with a renewed perspective, constantly looking out for things he recognised.

Once they had climbed into one of the upper balconies, the tour guide gathered them around a set of four large bronze horses. They were incredibly lifelike: the sculptor seemed to have caught them mid-action, with manes slightly tousled and nostrils flared; one of them champed and pulled back his lips, revealing large teeth. Jemme was astonished to discover that they were nearly two thousand years old. The guide told them that the collection were known at the 'Triumphal Quadriga' and that they spent a large part of their life on display at the Hippodrome of Constantinople. At the beginning of the day, Jemme would have been surprised to hear that too, but now he was beginning to see the link between his city and this far away place. As the guide told them that the horses had been looted during the Fourth Crusade, he started to see what Grandma had meant when she had told him that Venice's story interwove with others he already knew. This was furthered when he learned that Napoleon had removed them to display them on the Arc de Triomphe in Paris, during the eighteenth century. He thought about all the different episodes in history these horses had been part of, and realised that Venice could be a positive treasure chest of artefacts and ornaments which had been variously looted and returned, traversing time and continents and stringing together different historical events in a unique way. By the time they finally turned in that evening, Venice had already made a deep and long-lasting impression on him

✻   ✻   ✻   ✻

The trip continued to be a source of education for Jemme. He carefully stored up each sight, mentally recording the details so that he could relay them to his grandmother and mother when he returned home. It was difficult to keep them separate in his mind, and despite his best efforts, after a while one canal blurred into another. He couldn't remember which churches he had seen certain paintings in and he started to forget how many squares they had visited. The major sights, however, were seared into his memory. He didn't think he could ever forget the bustle of the Grand Canal, the splendour of St Mark's or the elegance of the Ca' d'Oro, which they had visited on the third day.

On the last day, they returned to St Mark's Square. Their last tour was to be of the Doge's Palace, bringing their trip full circle. Jemme was especially excited to look around, after all he had heard from Grandma about its former occupants and the power they wielded. It fronted onto the canal and so he had already seen the outside a few times, but he had not yet had the opportunity to look at it properly. He stood now, taking it in: the top of the building looked solid and imposing. Its pink and white façade gave it an air of opulence, but what was really catching his eye was the way in which this heavy slab appeared to sit on top of two layers of spindly marble arches. He had no idea how they could support the Palace, they looked so thin and brittle. The arches in the second layer were especially narrow, and yet they seemed to be bearing the weight of the entire palace. His thoughts were interrupted by Walli, tugging on his elbow.

'Isn't that the man from the hostel?' he asked. Jemme looked over and recognised the man who had greeted them from behind reception every day.

'Yes, it is – I wonder why he's here.' The man had obviously run to get there as he was red-faced and out of breath.

'*Signore*!' he gasped at the Scout Master, '*Telegramma, telegramma*!' he said as he waved a small slip of paper at the rather confused looking Scout Master, who managed a '*Grazie*,' before the man had run off again. Jemme and Walli eyed him curiously as the Scout Master read whatever was written on the paper and then broke into a smile

'Mafeze!' he called, 'It's a telegram from your father. Congratulations, you are now a big brother!'

Chapter Four

Jemme sat on the edge of his bed in Grandma's room. The last few days had gone in a blur, and he was tired. In a short space of time his world had been turned upside down, his horizons broadened and his family grown. He lay backwards as he tried to straighten out the jumble of recent memories. The Doge's Palace, which had been held in anticipation for so long, had seemed to blur out of focus as Jemme had attempted to keep up with the rest of the group. As the Scout Master pointed out various oil paintings, antique furniture and sculptures, the palace had seemed to swirl around Jemme, in a haze of pinks and whites. His mind was hot with a thousand different thoughts, as he tried to absorb the news about his new brother or sister. He stood rooted to the spot whilst he thought about his mother, hundreds of miles away in Turkey. He could picture her lying in bed with the new baby and his father standing proudly over them – a small vignette of domestic perfection. And yet, he wasn't there. It was the first time he had left home and the first time he had experienced being excluded from something. He didn't know how he felt about it, and was only roused from his thoughts by Rafi tugging on his sleeve.

'Come on!' he hissed.

Jemme looked up. The rest of the party were way ahead and looking out of one of the curiously shaped windows, as the Scout Master explained something. Jemme trotted along with Rafi and caught up with them. The rest of the trip had passed in a similar way, with Jemme drifting off into thought, only rousing when one of his friends poked him, or shook him. He had fallen into a deep and grateful sleep on the bus back, completely oblivious to the European countries slipping past the windows, which had been such a source of excitement on the outward-bound journey.

He thought about when he had finally arrived home. His father had come to meet him at the Scout Hut, as a coach emptied its contents of sleepy Scouts. Jemme had been awake for a while and had been staring stolidly out of the window, trying to prepare himself for what lay ahead. Before he had time to gather his thoughts, he was being ushered off the bus.

'Jemme!' he heard Wadeah's deep boom. He had looked up and seen his father's face – so familiar, so redolent of home. There was a new look to it – a sort of happiness which almost glowed. Jemme was reminded of his mother's face during her pregnancy. Before he had had time to ponder on it any further, he had the breath knocked out of him in one of his father's large bear-hugs. As he felt himself squeezed close to his father's chest, wrapped tightly in his arms, a strange sense of calm spread over him. He realised that everything was going to be alright.

'I am so pleased to see you, son!' Wadeah said.

'Put me down, Baba!' Jemme gasped.

'Sorry,' Wadeah put him back on the ground, tousled his hair and grabbed his suitcase.

'My! I had forgotten how heavy this was. Come, let's go! Are you ready to meet your baby sister?'

'Sister?'

'Yes, she's waiting for you at home – we all are.'

Jemme had followed his father, trepidation turning into excitement with every step. He realised that this new sister had made him into a big brother. He was coming back home an intrepid explorer – a travelling man. He would be able to tell her all of his adventures and she would look up to him as much as he looked up to Grandma.

Home had been bursting at the seams with well-wishers, baskets of fruit and huge bunches of flowers. As his father led him through the corridors to his mother's room, he had had to pick his way over piles of hand-crocheted blankets, duck around baskets of flannel towels, and what seemed like yards and yards of baby things. Everyone they had passed had made some comment – telling him how lucky he was, pressing chunks of crumbly halva on him and telling him how beautiful his sister was. As he ran the gauntlet of chin-chucking and cheek-pinching people, the corridor to his mother's room seemed to grow and grow.

Finally he had reached his mother. Lying on the bed and cradling the new child in her arms, she was a central point of serenity, amongst all the activity and hubbub. Jemme looked at her for a moment. She reminded him of some of the paintings he had seen in Venice. Calm, collected and staring at her child with love and devotion, she seemed just like the lady painted by a famous artist whose name Jemme couldn't remember. The Scout Master had called him something like 'Bellini', but Jemme wasn't sure.

'Go on,' his father had encouraged him, gently pushing him into the room.

Jemme had remembered the softness of the whole scene – the smooth cotton covers of his mother's bed and the soft feel of the shawl, which she unwrapped from one of her own shoulders to bundle Jemme in.

'Jemme, my love, how was Venice?'

'It was amazing, Mama, I want to go back already!'

'I'm so pleased, sweetheart,' Jama murmured, looking down at the small bundle in her arms.

'Jemme, I'd like you to meet Astarté,' she said, smoothing down a small curl on the baby's forehead. Jemme leaned forward, trying to take in the baby's small face. She was the colour of caramel, with tiny curls of brown hair. He couldn't believe how small everything about her was – her nose was no bigger than one of the buttons on his best coat, and her little mouth looked like one of the tiny rosebuds his mother kept in a jar in the kitchen to decorate cakes for festivals. Her eyes were closed, and she looked completely peaceful. Jemme contemplated her face a little while longer and then slowly, and with great solemnity, leaned forward and kissed her on the forehead. He looked up at his mother – the corners of her mouth were twitching slightly.

'I knew you two would get along,' she said, just as Astarté opened her eyes. The baby stared up curiously at Jemme. 'See, she likes you already!'

Jemme ran over these details again and again in his mind, as he lay on his own bed. He thought about Astarté's eyes – they sat in her face like two chips of Onyx, and seemed just as serious and inquisitive as Jemme's own. He remembered his instant fascination with her, and seemingly hers with him too. His mother had told him to hold his finger out, and Astarté had closed her small hand around it, as if grabbing at a thick branch. He stared at the ceiling as he thought and didn't notice the door opening. Grandma made her way softly over the bed and sat down next to him. Jemme sat bolt upright with a start.

'I'm sorry, I didn't mean to startle you, Jemme. I've just come to see if you're alright. It's been a lot to take in for you, I'm sure.'

'I'm alright, Grandma, I'm just tired.'

'I'm not surprised, you've been quite the little traveller recently. I'm keen to hear even more about your trip, but in the meantime I thought I might tell you a little bit about your sister's name. In all this melee, I don't think anyone's stopped to explain it to you.'

Jemme thought about it. He hadn't really considered it before,

'Is there a reason for her name, Grandma?'

'Of course there is! Names are very important, Jemme. They always have been; it's what we use to identify everything and everyone. Think about this city – how would you describe its streets, its hills and its mosques without names? Their names all mean something and they've changed over time to reflect the qualities of a place and to convey some of its beauty. Think about the poetry of the "Golden Horn"; the name describes the place so perfectly – its shape, its glorious beauty. You wouldn't understand any of that if I just described it as a "watery inlet" would you?'

Jemme thought about it and shook his head, 'I suppose not, Grandma.'

'Well, the same is true with people – parents spend a long time thinking about what to call their child; in fact some people believe that the name itself will determine the child's future qualities. The ancients certainly believed that saying a God's name invoked some of his magic.'

'Which ancients, Grandma?'

'Well, it was quite a commonly held belief in ancient times. In Persia and in Mesopotamia, people believed that names held a power in themselves – the more powerful the person being named was, the more significant the act of saying their name was. So you see, it's something that is worth thinking about. People are often too accepting of the obvious and that which is in front of them, so they never stop to question it. The incurious pass by rich mines of information, merely because they are looking the other way. Theirs must be such empty lives – not like you of course!' she smiled at Jemme who by now was sitting cross-legged and giving her his full attention.

'You're the most curious little boy I've ever come across,' she continued, 'which is why I thought you'd be interested in the name Astarté.'

'I am, Grandma,' Jemme replied eagerly. His interest, so easily piqued, would rarely subside until he was completely satisfied. 'What does it mean?'

'Well, in this case it doesn't mean anything as such,' Lily explained, 'but rather, it's the name of a very ancient goddess.'

'A goddess? What's she a goddess of?' asked Jemme, intrigued.

'She's usually associated with fertility and war,' Lily replied, 'but she's been worshipped for thousands of years by many different societies, each of whom interpreted her slightly differently. You find this a lot with important figures – they're adopted and then adapted by different religions. There's often an exchange of ideas when people come into contact with each other: on trade routes, in meetings at borders and so on; it all helps with the diffusion of new ideas. When one culture recognises that a particular figure is important to their neighbours, they sometimes incorporate him or her into their own beliefs. Do you remember our conversation about Yaḥyā ibn Zakarīyā?'

Jemme thought back to their conversation of a few weeks ago. Grandma had explained that the Islamic prophet Yaḥyā was revered by the Christians as John the Baptist. He remembered being intrigued that there was common ground between what people often described as two completely different religions. 'I remember, Grandma,' he said.

'Good, I thought you might. Well, it's the same with Astarté. There were places dedicated to her worship at Sidon, Tyre and Byblos. As her cult spread geographically, she was adopted by different peoples too. Once a temple was built for her at Eryx in Sicily the Romans discovered her and adopted her as Venus. The Greeks themselves had already been worshipping her as Aphrodite. So, you see – one goddess had spread across so many different civilisations: Phoenicians, Persians, Romans, Greeks – and it all started not far from here. It's as I always tell you, Jemme, we are blessed to live in the cradle of culture and civilisation. Think how much sprang from these lands of ours – how many civilisations, great governors and famous diplomats. Many countries think of history as being exclusively their own, but if you dig a little deeper, it is all interwoven with the civilisations and peoples of the Levant. Look at this – ' she fished a small pocket book from her skirts, 'I was just using this to show your mother how the Romans imagined Astarté looking.' The cover of the book was worn soft and the edges battered and folded. As she held it in her palm it fell open at a particular page, one evidently looked at more than the others.

'Do you see this coin?' Grandma asked, pointing at two round black and white photos next to each other. Jemme nodded.

'Well, this was found at Sidon. Astarté is on the reverse. Look – she's very beautiful and her large eyes look full of wisdom; but, the best part is the obverse. She's pictured on the opposite side of a coin to Julia Maesa!'

Jemme frowned slightly. He wanted to share Grandma's enthusiasm, but didn't quite know who she was talking about. With her sharp reflexes, Lily picked up on this instantly.

'We have already talked about her younger sister, Julia Domna – they were both very important women in the Roman Empire. They were powerful and respected empresses and significant historical figures. Most interestingly, they were from Homs – not very far away from here at all. This is what I'm talking about. Many people who think about the Roman Empire, forget, or don't know, how deep its connections to Syria were. They think of it as being exclusively Italian history, and of the story as belonging to the Italians only. But I digress – I always do when I'm talking to you, little one! Anyway, I hope I've given you an idea of the background to your new sister's name.'

Jemme nodded, 'You have, Grandma. Do you have any other pictures of her?'

Lily shook her head, 'Not on me, no, but I can tell you what her symbols were.'

'Symbols, Grandma?'

'Gods and Goddesses are often associated with different symbols – their symbols are carved in temples, painted above them in pictures and woven into the garments of priests. In Astarté's case, she is shown variously as a lion, horse, sphinx and dove. All very good things to be associated with, I think you'll agree.'

Jemme nodded slowly, he had no idea there could be such depth to a name. It hadn't even entered his mind that there could be symbols associated with a name, let alone that there could be a bunch so diverse, so rich in their symbology. He wondered if his name could be traced out in pictures or evoke the qualities of an ancient god. Before he could put any of his questions to Grandma she had sprang up,

'Come on!' she said enthusiastically, with an energy belying her age, 'Let's have some supper, then I think you've earned a story.'

Jemme couldn't argue with that and slid off the bed, trotting after Lily's springy step.

It seemed that each visitor had brought a bowl of food with them too, and the kitchen was filled with brightly painted china dishes and platters, teetering with sweets, and goods baked, stuffed, fried and grilled.

'My, hasn't everyone been kind!' Lily said, smacking her lips enthusiastically.

She pulled platters and plates from the side, setting Jemme up at the table with a plate and a fork. As they tucked into hunks of *çökelek*, a spicy cheese, and smothered *pekmez*, mulberry molasses, on to bread, Lily began to ask questions about Venice. Between mouthfuls, Jemme began to answer, until he was chattering freely. Lily listened attentively, nodding and spooning more *hummous* onto his plate. By the time they returned to the room, Jemme felt he would be incapable of eating or talking ever again. He sank heavily into bed, and gratefully wriggled under the covers. He managed, however, to summon enough energy to remind Grandma about her promise of a story.

Lily laughed, 'I knew you wouldn't forget – of course, my love. Now, you can choose: Charlemagne and his game of chess, François I of France and the Field of the Cloth of Gold or the adventures of Hulagu Khan.'

Jemme thought for a while; he was torn between the cloth of gold and the game of chess, but he was pretty sure he could wrangle a second story out of Grandma, so he said, 'The game of chess please,' with a certain nonchalance.

'Very well. I think you will like this story. It's woven from many different historical threads, and I think you'll recognise certain parts of it. The story begins in the Frankish kingdom with Charlemagne – Charles the Great. He had expanded his empire within Europe, pushing the borders upwards and outwards and gobbling up whole countries as he did so. He galloped across France and swept up parts of Italy. By the time of his death, he had spread his kingdom out across most of western Europe. It had become the Carolingian Empire, and he was its great emperor. His sword never slept in his hand, and she too, became legendary. Her name was "Joyeuse" and she's talked about in epic poetry as if she too was a character in battle scenes, standing proud beside her owner.

'Of course, the borders of the countries Charlemagne took weren't where they are now, and indeed the countries of Europe as you know them didn't even exist. Instead, they were known by their old names – Frisia, Septimania, Neustria, Aquitaine and Lombardy, to name but a few. They were so culturally diverse too: the people of Saxony wore thick woollen cloaks and lived at the foot of the mountains, whilst the people of Gascony fished and made brandy, in a hilly, sunny landscape. Charlemagne became a great reformer, many call his changes the beginning of the Carolingian Renaissance. He reformed and improved many things – monetary systems, government, education, the military, the church and, of course, culture. So many parts of European history were touched by Charlemagne – even the writing script used in manuscripts. He has left his presence in the annals, the legal tracts and the churches of Europe, and he has left his image in popular myth and folklore too. However, this harks back to what I was saying about shared history. Although Charlemagne was a mighty ruler in Europe, and all but founded modern-day France and Germany, his story is not just theirs. Rather, it overlaps with a different story. During all this time, there was another, equally powerful and intelligent ruler. His name was Haroun al-Rashid, and he was the fifth Abbasid Caliph. He was resourceful and clever – a great military leader, but also a great scholar. During his rule, Baghdad flourished, and was the most splendid city of the East. Art, music, science and learning all prospered.

'This could so easily be a tale of two rulers – two separate powerful men, who kept to their Eastern and Western spheres, each suspicious of the other. In fact, it began that way. The lower part of Charlemagne's empire was designed to be a buffer zone. The Spanish Marches became a defensive barricade between the Moors in Al-Andalus and the Carolingian kingdom. However, both men were wise enough to realise that walls made their kingdoms smaller, and international peace enlarged their outlooks. Diplomacy is a fine art and the hallmark of a great ruler. Both Charlemagne and Haroun al-Rashid were accomplished diplomats, and began a process of diplomacy and exchange which brought their two cultures together, enriching each of them in different ways. They sent envoys and ambassadors to each other's palaces, laden with gifts and professions of friendship.'

'What kind of gifts, Grandma?' Jemme wondered. What could be given to a man who ruled such a large empire? Surely he must already have everything he needed?

'All sorts of things. Don't forget, these weren't presents such as you might receive on your birthday or during Eid. These were important pieces, carefully selected by each man to showcase the power and prowess of their empires. If you were going to take someone, in a different city, a bag of Turkish Delight from Haci Bakir, then you would make sure that you chose the best squares – the biggest and most colourful, wouldn't you?'

'I suppose so, Grandma.'

'Well, it was the same with Charlemagne and Haroun al-Rashid. When Haroun al-Rashid's emissaries made the journey to Aachen in 802, he wanted to take with him the very best of the riches and technology of the Arab world. Whether or not he wanted to show Charlemagne the follies of his buffer zone, he certainly went about it in the right way. They took with them chests of fine silks, exotic perfumes and balsams and a brass candelabra. They were all special products from Haroun's caliphate, and unlike anything which would have been seen in the Carolingian empire.'

'Would the silk have come from China, Grandma?'

'Excellent question Jemme! I see you're using your knowledge from Venice already. Yes, it almost certainly would have come from China. Think about the closeness of the Middle East and the Far East, as opposed to Western Europe and the Far East. Silk was much more accessible to those halfway up the route, but to those beyond the end of it, in Frisia, Saxony and Neustria, it would have had an even greater shimmer of luxury. Rare goods were even more of a symbol of power and status in the past than they are now. But that's not everything Haroun al-Rachid sent. He also sent a water-clock, and if you hold on a moment, I will tell you exactly what it looked like.'

Jemme looked intrigued – he had no idea what a 'water-clock' was, and even less how Grandma would know 'exactly' what one looked like. Lily half-turned in her chair and scanned the bookcase behind her, selecting a book. There was almost a carelessness about the act, as if she knew the bookcase so well that it had ceased to be a separate object. Rather than study it, she seemed attuned to it. She was the same when she was looking for the passage she wanted inside the book, leafing through with a certain languid assuredness, as if she had been studying the words the book contained all her life. Instead of searching for the passage, it was as if she was merely going through the motions of turning the pages, until she arrived at exactly where she knew it was going to be all along. She looked up at Jemme.

'Here: Charlemagne's biographer was a man called Einhard and he knew the emperor for all of his life. He wrote down exactly what he saw when the clock arrived,' Lily held the book up and read: '.. a marvellous mechanical contraption, in which the course of the twelve hours moved according to a water clock, with as many brazen little balls, which fell down on the hour and through their fall made a cymbal ring underneath. On this clock there were also twelve horsemen who at the end of each hour stepped out of twelve windows, closing the previously open windows by their movements.'

She looked up, 'Isn't that remarkable? Can you imagine seeing such a thing for the first time, and how impressed you would be?'

Jemme shook his head as he contemplated a clock which managed to include horsemen, water and 'brazen' balls,

'What's "brazen", Grandma?' he asked suddenly.

'It's just an old fashioned way of saying bronze,' Lily replied.

Jemme still couldn't picture the item, even though he had an incredibly active imagination.

'Is there a picture in your book, Grandma?'

'No, unfortunately not. I have seen sketches of it though, and it's really quite wonderful. I will look out for one for you. In the meantime, I'm sure it will be lots of fun to imagine how it might look. And-' she had a slight glint in her eye,'whilst you're imagining that, you should also picture another of Haroun al-Rashid's gifts, and almost certainly his biggest one.'

'Bigger than the water-clock?!'

Lily looked a little mischievous, 'Bigger in size certainly. I don't think you'll be able to guess though..... it was an elephant!'

'An elephant!' Jemme squealed.

'Yes!' Lily laughed at his pleasure, 'His name was Abul-Abbas apparently. Can you imagine how out of place the poor thing must have looked in rainy France? Think about Charlemagne's courtiers too – they would have been terrified!' She chuckled, 'But I forgot one of the gifts – the one I promised when you chose this story. In addition to all these things, Haroun al-Rashid also sent a beautiful chess set, with a set of chess men, intricately carved from ivory, to sit on the squares. It was a very generous series of gifts, and one that could not have failed to make an impression. Imagine how Charlemagne would have felt – the Arab peoples to his south had just been a far-off idea before, they didn't have anything to do with him and he was happy to leave them alone as long as they didn't invade his lands. Now, here were these extravagant and exotic gifts, from a man he suddenly realised could be his ally.'

Jemme thought about it. It seemed strange that two powerful and beautiful spheres could be so self-contained, and yet so ultimately contiguous. All it needed was for one person within one sphere to establish a connection with one person in another, and the two could meld together, creating something more beautiful and more powerful. He found the idea fascinating – people could be neighbours and not talk to each other, he knew that, and his mother was always telling him it was 'a great shame.' However, he had never thought of *peoples* being neighbours and not talking to each other. That was surely an even greater shame. He burrowed deep into his own thoughts as he tried to work out who could be introduced to whom, for mutual benefit. He realised that he didn't really know that much about where different countries actually were. He was so used to discussing their histories with Grandma, and hearing their ancient names, that he probably wouldn't deal with a modern-day map as well in the same way he could a ninth-century atlas, or a Renaissance-era plan of the seas. He couldn't stop pondering on the matter, teasing it in different directions, and seeing if it would yield any further information for him. He felt that there was so much potential within this concept, but he had no idea how to go about unlocking it.

'Are you alright, little one? You've gone very quiet, and you haven't even asked me what Charlemagne sent Haroun al-Rashid in return.'

'Oh yes,' Jemme muttered.

'He sent him Spanish horses, brightly coloured cloaks from Frisia and a whole pack of hunting dogs,' Lily said softly, wrapping up the story. 'Now, I think that's a good place to stop for this evening.'

Jemme didn't even answer. All thoughts of drawing a second story out of Grandma were completely forgotten as he lay back in bed. He closed his eyes when Lily turned the light out, but he didn't sleep instantly, despite how tired he was. He could not stop thinking about what Grandma had said, and about the connection between Haroun al-Rashid and Charlemagne. Grandma had been right – the fabric of the story pulled together several different threads he recognised. It was so rare that all the stories and bits of history he had learned wove together in such a way. There was the Silk Route he had learned of in Venice, the great Caliph and the great Emperor, both from completely separate areas of history – the Carolingians and the Abbasids. Yet, they were all connected. The ideas turned in circles in his head; he kept coming back to the orbs, sitting perfectly next to each other – touching even, yet perfectly retaining their shape and integrity. As he focussed on them, they too began to spin and drop, just like the brazen balls in Charlemagne's clock. Elephants marched across his mind, leading great caravans of noble men wearing brightly coloured cloaks. They trampled through a field made of gold and, as he drifted into sleep, his visions became increasingly vivid. The elephants started to be ridden by ivory chessmen and were being chased by hunting dogs. Before he knew it, Jemme was in a deep state of sleep. However, his dreaming had not stopped, but rather the visions flowed and melded with each other, becoming increasingly colourful and vivid as they swirled around him. Just as it was starting to become heady and overwhelming, suddenly the elephants of the caravan began to fade. Their dusty greys became mottled as they blurred out of focus. Jemme reached towards them, but grabbed a handful of air. He swiped again, but this time the elephants and their riders had completely disappeared, like a shimmering mirage in the oasis. The colours around him ebbed away, as if an unseen artist was washing off his palette. The brilliant cloaks of the noblemen dribbled into a murky nothingness and, before he knew it, Jemme was in complete darkness. Just as suddenly, he felt the darkness behind him give way and he was aware of a falling sensation. He reached out and flapped his arms, but he was definitely tumbling, and yet, as he realised this, he experienced no fear, just a mild sense of curiosity.

His fall appeared to be completely outside time. Even as he felt the wind whooshing up around his ears, hot as from a horse's nostril, he could not say when he first began falling. It could have been a mere split-second ago or it could have been a whole hour ago. He tried to readjust his eyes to the dark, but there was nothing there. He could not even project anything onto it from his imagination. It was the purest form of nothingness he had ever experienced: a total and complete privation of anything sensory. All of a sudden his fall came to an end, and he felt himself land with a thump. He was completely unhurt, in fact it seemed like the kind of landing one might have merely from toppling backwards whilst sitting cross-legged on the ground. He picked himself up and looked up. He was still in this odd sphere of darkness, but for one thing. In front of him rose a beautiful palace. It was like no other he had ever seen and yet parts of it seemed vaguely familiar. He walked towards it, craning his neck to take in its highest parts. As he stared, the different shapes and features of the building shifted and moved in front of him, but without ever once cracking the palace's smooth façade. He continued approaching it, tilting his head further back as he got closer. He started to recognise various elements of the building; there were the pink arches of the Doge's Palace in Venice, perching on top of this palace like spun sugar. He scrutinised them for a moment. *How strange to see them here again*, he thought to himself. As he looked further up, he noticed that the palace was flanked by green capped minarets, which soared up to an impossible height. He frowned – had they been there a minute ago? They seemed to be growing even taller as he looked at them and suddenly he recognised them: they were the towers from his very own Hagia Sophia, so often called the most beautiful building in the world, by Istanbulites. The more he stared at the palace in front of him, the more its features seemed to veritably jump out at him, as if longing to be recognised. There were cornices from Bavarian castles he had seen pictures of in history books; over there were the corbles and battlements, exactly as Grandma had recently described those of Hever Castle in England. He looked down and saw that amongst this architectural miscellany an open door beckoned. He could have sworn there was not a door when he had approached the building, not least an open one. He made his way inside and found himself at the beginning of a long corridor which did not seem to lead anywhere. It stretched into its own vanishing point and as much as he strained his eyes it was impossible to gain any idea of direction or depth. In fact, the more he attempted to visualise the end of the corridor, the more disorientated he became. Despite the alien setting, he had a strange sense of purpose – almost as if it was his pre-ordained destiny to walk along the corridor. With barely a hint of trepidation, he took his first step. As he moved forward, it seemed as if the corridor was expanding and contracting in front of his very eyes. He had no idea how long he would have to walk along it before he found something. Indeed, after a few steps, he began to lose any sense of time and distance altogether. He looked curiously at the walls on either side of him as he moved forward. Just like the corridor, they appeared to be moving. None of the planes within the palace remained constantly flat, despite giving the illusion of doing so. Rather, they were in perpetual movement, shifting before his very eyes. Gradually he started to notice they bore decorations. Intricate geometric patterns swept and spiralled across them, reminding him of a cross between Latinate mosaics and the beautiful Islamic art which had decorated his childhood. Just like the walls it sat on, the décor did not remain static. Instead, patterns moved and melded into each other, leaving trails of radiant colour behind them, tracing their trajectory. It was utterly mesmerising and he focussed on the intricate patterns, allowing his feet to blindly carry him forward. He was surprised when the patterns suddenly held still for a moment, and seemed to come to an end. He was even more surprised when this solid stopping point seemed to indicate a shape. He stopped walking and turned himself fully towards the wall to inspect the definite object in front of him. It seemed to be an immutable hub in a sea of moving colour. He leant forwards and touched it. It felt solid and unyielding beneath his fingers. He pushed it again, just to make sure. There was a soft clicking sound and it moved forwards. Suddenly he realised that it was another door, although this time it was tiny, especially in comparison to the giant entranceway to the palace. He crouched down and peered through. There was nothing but a cool darkness. The same feeling of what he was *supposed* to do surged through him again and he realised that this was the next stage of the adventure – he was meant to go through the door. Crouching down on all fours he crawled through.

Standing up on the other side he found himself in a completely different environment to the shifting, eidetic corridor. Here, he appeared to be outside. He looked behind him at the small door he had just crawled through and saw that it looked completely different from the other side. The door itself seemed huge, as large as two men standing on each others' shoulders. It was set into a large gate, which reminded him vaguely of the *pilons* of the Ancient Egyptians' temples. The gate was completely covered in tiles, glazed to become a rich, glossy mazarine. Ribbons of flowers ran along the gate and on top of them marched ceramic figures of animals. Jemme recognised golden lions, and the creature known as *auroch* which Grandma had told him of. It was the huge ancestor of the domestic cow, and it loomed large with proud horns and a tail carried high. Turning away from the gate he looked around himself. Even though he was outside, he still appeared to be within a room. Whilst there was sand beneath his feet and sky above him, he could clearly see four walls bordering the area – containing this piece of outdoors inside. The piece of sky was bright blue and the sand he stood on felt hot, even through his shoes. Despite the arid landscape, lush ferns clung to rocky cairns, and a sea of glossy green acanthus knots spread out to one side. A stone seat sat amongst the rocky outcrops and, as Jemme looked at it, it seemed to develop and flourish until it seemed to be a grand throne, with rich decorations running down each leg. He saw a footstool push itself out of the ground like a mushroom, and when he looked up he saw a man sitting on the throne, resting his feet upon the stool. The man's beard was black as a smudge of ink, and echoed his heavy brows. He seemed to be engrossed in a tablet he was holding in his hands. Apparently it bore some text as his eyes flickered across it, as if reading from a book. He turned to his side where an assistant had appeared, to hand him a stylus. Suddenly Jemme recognised the figure. He had seen this precise scene, cast in stone. The man was none other than Hammurabi, exactly as he was depicted in the stele Jemme had seen at school. The tablet must have been his legal code, and Hammurabi seemed particularly preoccupied with it. He finished with the stylus and handed it back to his assistant, whereupon they both began to grow dimmer. As they did, the door on the wall to the side of them bloomed larger, and Jemme understood again that he was meant to go through it. He walked through the sand, feeling its resistance against his shoes, and savouring the feel of the sun on his skin. By the time he reached the door, Hammurabi and his assistant were almost gone, with only their faint outline left – as if Jemme was looking at their reflection in a shard of glass. The door was bigger than it had been, but he still needed to bend down on all fours to open it. The handle turned with a soft click and he prepared to crawl through it. Looking behind him, the sand and the ferns had already shrunk away from him, as if they were the tide, pulling back towards the centre of the room.

He stood up on the other side of the door and again, realised he was in an oddly liminal place, at once inside and outside. It was just as bright and sunny as the previous room, but this time there was grass underfoot, rather than sand. As he surveyed his surroundings, he suddenly was aware of a *WHOOSH*. He ducked as quickly as possible as an arrow flew over his head and disappeared into the nothingness behind him. As soon as he had stood up again, he felt the ground beneath his feet begin to tremble. The distant rumble grew closer and closer and again, he was forced to jump out of the way as he felt another giant *WHOOSH*, this time as something charged past him. He looked after it, and recognised it as the back of a disappearing chariot. When he looked back into the room, it had already become populated with what appeared to be a pitched battle. Arrows hurtled through the air, as fast as the men standing on the chariots could draw them. The chariots themselves seemed small, with only enough room for a couple of men to stand on the platform at the back. As he studied the scene in front of him, he realised that the chariots were divided into two distinct groups. On one side they seemed much faster and lighter; there were only two men on the platform and the chariot seemed to dart around corners with great alacrity and deftness. What's more, they seemed to have devised a system in which one man held the reigns of the charging horses, and one focussed solely on firing his bow. It was an interesting looking weapon. Every time one of their chariots thundered past him, Jemme caught a glimpse of it. It seemed to have been pieced together from many different types of material, including what looked like bone or horn, and wood too. By contrast, the other chariots seemed heavier and clunkier. The men who stood on the platforms looked different, with different colourings and bushier hair. There were also three of them to each chariot, which seemed to slow the cumbersome vehicles even more. Jemme couldn't see properly, but their bows appeared to be carved from a single piece of wood and didn't fire nearly as far, or as fast, as the other men's. It was hard to keep up with what was going on, as he was constantly ducking and jumping. He didn't know if he could actually be hurt by any of the battle; although everything so far had been completely out of the parameters of his own perception, it had been oddly lucid at the same time. He decided it was best not to try to find out, and kept himself as out of the way as possible. He watched the thrust of the battle for some time. It was hard to focus on individual soldiers, as the massed ranks of chariotry were so large, they almost looked a black cloud of swarming wasps. In spite of that, it soon became obvious who was going to win. After his experience in the first room, Jemme was not surprised when this scene too started to fade. The sunlight glinting from spears grew duller, and the clash of metal and frantic whinnying of horses faded too. Like an old hand, Jemme made his way to the next door, dropping to his hands and knees straight away to crawl through. This time he found himself in a completely different enclosure. He was definitely indoors, in an opulent-looking room with sumptuous gilding and rich velvet furnishings. The room was filled with men, sitting in wooden chairs and talking amongst themselves. On closer inspection, the chairs appeared to be inlaid with mother-of-pearl and small pieces of ivory, reflecting the beautiful geometric patterns Jemme had seen on the walls of the corridor. He tried to listen to what the men were saying, but he could not understand the language they were talking. They nodded their heads sagely and appeared to pass documents between themselves. Behind them a window looked out onto what appeared to be a bustling market. Jemme walked around the circle of men and looked through the window. There was something odd about it; although it seemed to be a portal into a world of activity, the people he could see through it were completely static, as if they had been frozen at the height of their activity. As he neared it, he realised that the people had never been active – they were completely two dimensional and painted onto the wall. He suddenly realised: this was the trompe l'oeil work he had first experienced in Venice. In fact, the scene depicted on the wall looked familiar, with its bridges and distinctive flat-bottomed boats. He scrutinised it a moment longer before thinking of something. He slowly turned and looked back at the men behind him. They were still talking amongst themselves with the utmost formality and gravity. He took a moment to absorb their hats and cloaks, and the finery of their costumes, right down to their exquisite shoes. He had seen each and every one of them before, although never such a vivid representation of them. Some he had seen in paintings in Venice, some he had seen in books, bearing photographs of paintings in Venice, and art galleries around the world. Each one of them was an ambassador, but from different eras, as could be seen in their clothes. They talked amongst themselves as if they were contemporaries, yet there were centuries between some of them. Jemme studied their faces closely. It was interesting to see them in a new dimension and he started to recognise them as individuals, rather than as a group. One in particular took his eye and he stared openly at him for a while. The man was completely oblivious to his presence, and continued to talk in low, lilting tones. Jemme was sure he knew his name and stretched his memory as much as he could.

'Teldi!' he suddenly said aloud, 'Francesco Teldi.' The man did not look up and carried on talking with those sat around him. It was all coming back to Jemme now; this man had been described in detail by the Scout Master when they were in Venice. His portrait had hung on the wall of one of the galleries they had visited, showing a fair man with hooded eyes dressed in the black cape and hat of the city's patrician classes. Jemme looked at him now, exactly as he was in the portrait, he thought to himself. He racked his brains, trying to think what else he could remember about Teldi. He knew he was from the sixteenth century, but he was sure that there was something more. He looked around at the other men, trying to glean any information to prompt his memory, then looked back to Teldi. Someone new had sat next to him and Teldi seemed to know him. The new man looked distinctly Middle Eastern, and wore green robes, trimmed with gold. Perched on his head was a pink turban, of unexpectedly large proportions. Their body language appeared gracious, and Teldi was speaking to the new man in a different language, which he appeared to understand. Suddenly it all began to fall into place – there *was* something more about Teldi. He had appeared in not one, but two paintings Jemme had seen; the Scout Master had pointed out Francesco Teldi in the procession of Venetian ambassadors who had been sent to Damascus, in a famous painting by an artist called Bellini. Jemme remembered looking at the huge canvas, and recognising the distinctly Levantine background of the painting. There were minarets, cupolas, a courtyard and an iwan, all awash with the sable colourings of the buildings from home. He remembered the small knot of black-clothed Venetians, looking distinctly drab amongst the colourfully-clad Mamluks with their exotic turbans. The Scout Master had explained that the painting was important because it was the first proper, accurate portrayal of the East, from an outsider. It would appear that this Bellini was a Venetian artist, and extremely influential in terms of the art which was being produced there at the time. Jemme vaguely recalled the Scout Master saying something about Bellini leaving an important legacy, and being a major part of Venetian cultural history. It certainly seemed this way, now that Jemme could see the fleshed-out characters of his paintings before his very eyes. As he looked at them he could remember the figures in their turbans, the camel laden with packages, the mosque in the background, the citadel and the lush gardens. How exciting and different Damascus must have looked to these men, when compared with their watery home, Jemme mused to himself. He looked around at the group, and determined to see if he could recognise any other figures.

As he moved amongst them, unseen and unheeded, he couldn't help marvelling at such an assemblage of ambassadors. Not only did they come from many different eras, but there were also many men here who were not Venetian. Perhaps they're part of an ambassadorial exchange, Jemme thought to himself. He remembered numerous teachers, and Grandma, telling him that the swapping of emissaries and ambassadors was a key part of diplomatic strategy. He wondered where all the other men had come from, as he walked to the corner to investigate some other goings-on. Two men who appeared to be Venetian were carefully taking things out of a wooden case. One man was showing the objects to the other, who was nodding and saying something about each one, before helping gently pack them into a much larger crate, which seemed to be filled with straw. Jemme peered over at the objects they were taking out. It seemed to be a mix of things – delicate pieces of glass, chunks of amber and spools of silk. When he thought about it, these seemed to be all the things he first remembered Venice being famous for. He wondered why they would be packing such treasures up, and inspected the large crate. Neatly painted on one side were some very regal looking insignia with the words Henry VIII Rex underneath. The symbol itself was a large red rose with five petals. A green leaf could be seen in between each petal, and a small white rose sat at its centre. The whole heraldic achievement was topped by a golden crown, and looked very impressive. Jemme didn't know who 'Rex' was, but he had certainly heard of Henry VIII. They must be preparing gifts to take to him, he thought, silently admonishing himself for not realising that the rich Tudor court of Henry VIII would have been an obvious destination for Venetian ambassadors. He continued his tour around the room, marvelling at not only the costumes, but the luxurious objects the men were handling. From the smallest trinkets to the most lavishly decorated manuscripts, everything seemed to represent the best that a place had to offer, whether tokens to represent the finery of Venice abroad, or emblems of other countries' technological and cultural prowess, which returning ambassadors had brought back with them.

It was odd though, he thought to himself, that these men all seemed to be able to talk to each other. In a room full of strangers from time, he seemed to be the only one who was unable to interact with the scene in some way. Despite the fact some of these men would have been long-dead before their interlocutors were even born, they seemed to be well-acquainted and not in the least bit perturbed by their anachronistic companions or surroundings. 'Why can't I join in?' Jemme asked out loud. Still no-one paid him any attention. The more he thought about it, the stranger it all seemed. It was the first time he'd stopped to question his environment, since arriving in this odd world. He didn't even know where he was, let alone why *he* was the ghost in a room full of men straight from paintings and history books. How would he know what to do next? How would he even find his way out of this place, if he didn't even know how he'd got here to begin with? In the other rooms, the scenes had started to fade, and he had somehow known that it was time to move on, but in this one the figures before him remained real and vivid. It was he who was trapped, he who was the one no one could see, the ghost at the feast. He was no longer certain of his reality, no longer sure what existed and what was a construct of his own imagination. Was it possible for him to become lost within his own mind? He tried to think about it as logically as he could, but there were no solid facts or objects for him to peg his thoughts on to. There was no possible way of triangulating his experience, or his journey. He vaguely wondered if he was in some sort of dreamscape, rather than lucid reality; but if that was true then whose was he in? Could it even be possible to be self-critical within one's own dream? As he furrowed his brow, he started to realise that his surroundings might be more problematic than he had realised. He heard a soft thump behind him and looked round. The Mamluk ambassador's turban had fallen off backwards, but he hadn't seemed to notice. On a whim, Jemme leant down and picked it up. It felt solid in his hands, and he was relieved by its tangibility, as if it somehow affirmed his own existence. If anything, the images in this room were growing stronger, rather than fading away. Without thinking, he reached up and put it on his own head. The ambassador was a much larger man, and it instantly fell down over Jemme's eyes, completely blacking out all light. He tried to pull it up, but it suddenly felt heavy. Furthermore, despite the fact it had fallen because it was too large, it now seemed to fit snugly around his eyes. He could no longer see or hear anything of the room around him; no matter how much he pulled at the turban and tried to wriggle free of it, he was lost inside another world of darkness. He blinked, but he could no longer tell if his eyes were open or shut; he had lost all sensory perception, in this return to the black nothingness he had experienced earlier. The only thing he could feel was the soft fabric of the turban around his face.

Soon he became aware of another sensation. He could have sworn he could hear something, some sort of noise. He strained his ears and was sure that he heard it again – a sort of elongated muffled hum. There it was again! He tried to analyse it; it wasn't a hum, it was something more than that. It almost sounded like a word. It was getting louder too and clearer. Finally he could make out a long open vowel sound, with a soft finish. He listened again, 'eeeeeeemmmmmm' – it was becoming more distinct. As it became clearer, there was some sort of coloured vowel sound which gave shape to the noise, almost a 'dj' sound, 'djeeeemmmmmm'. Finally, he recognised his own name being called, 'Jeemmmee, Jemmmee!' How did anyone here know his name? Who was calling him? The voice was too far away for him to recognise, but by now there was no mistaking; it was definitely his name. It became shorter and closer to him, 'Jemme! Jemme!' Suddenly the total blackness in which he'd been immersed was pierced. Light flooded in as the voice became crystal clear, 'Jemme!' It was Grandma! But what was she doing here? As the blackness faded into nothing, he realised that his eyes were shut and opened them straight away. He found himself lying down, looking up Grandma. He sat bolt upright, 'But, this is...' he trailed off, confused. 'Where are....why...' he tried again.

'Don't worry, sweetheart,' Lily soothed. 'I think you were having quite a dream; you'd worked your way under the covers, and were muttering something with the pillow completely covering your face.'

'The turban!' Jemme explained.

Lily looked pensive, 'Everything's OK, my love; you're back in your room. There's nothing to be scared of.'

'I'm not scared, Grandma,' Jemme said, as everything started to become clear, 'but I think I've just had the most amazing dream anyone's ever had!'

'That anyone's *ever* had?' Lily looked amused

'Truly, Grandma – it was all so real. There were so many people there!'

Lily placed Jemme's pillow back onto the bed. 'Well, I don't think it looks like either of us are going to get much more sleep this evening. Why don't I go and make us some jasmine tea, and you can tell me all about it? I'm keen to hear all about the world's most amazing dream,' she said with a twinkle in her eye.

✻ ✻ ✻ ✻

Jemme sat cross-legged on his bed, leaning against the wall. He blew across his tea, and with one hand wiped the remaining sleep from his eyes. He now felt fully alert and assured of himself. He knew he was back in his room and that this was reality. Yet somehow his dream visions were just as clear as they had been when he had been wandering amongst them. Despite the shift in the paradigm of reality, he refused to accept his visions as fantasy.

'It was just as if I was there, Grandma,' he explained. 'It was so much more than a dream. I could feel things and I could think things too. I can even remember it all now – every last bit!'

Grandma looked thoughtful, 'Tell me again about the things you saw.'

Jemme didn't even need to think twice, he had instant and perfect recall, 'Once I'd got inside the palace I followed a corridor. The corridor itself was very strange and it didn't seem to have a beginning or an end. It was decorated, but the decorations shifted around – much like the corridor itself actually. Then, I found a door and I went through it – but I had to crawl. When I got inside, I found Hammurabi sitting on a magnificent throne, made of stone, but highly decorated.'

'How did you know he was Hammurabi?' Lily asked. Compared to her grandson's enthusiastic recounting of his experience, her speech sounded slow – almost laboured.

'I recognised him from when we studied him at school,' Jemme replied as if it was an obvious answer.

'I see. But what was he doing, where was he? I'm trying to work out how he fits into things; dreams are very interesting. If we interpret them correctly, then they can tell us all sorts of things that our waking mind keeps hidden from us.'

'But that's just it, Grandma, nothing had anything to do with anything else. Everything was all self contained and separate – because of the doors.' Jemme started to sound impatient. Lily started to say something about doors and perception, but thought better of it and just repeated, 'Tell me what he was doing.'

'Well, he had an assistant with him, and they were both looking at his legal code. Hammurabi was adding to it and his assistant was helping him write. But the best part is that the legal code Hammurabi was holding is the very one I recognised him from! We saw a poster of it at school, and there's an engraving of him at the top. Do you see? There were so many different layers! There were so many different versions of him!'

Lily nodded, 'I see,' she said again, 'This is all very interesting indeed. Where was Hammurabi?'

'I think he was in Babylon. It was dry and desert-like but at the same time there were lots of plants which were very lush and green. Oh, and I've just remembered, there was something else. Once I'd got into Babylon, I looked behind me and there was a magnificent blue gate framing the door I'd just come through. I didn't recognise it at all.'

'What did it look like?'

'Well, it was blue, like I said, and there were lots of pictures of lions and suns and the aurochs you told me about.'

Lily inhaled sharply, 'But Jemme, I know exactly what you're describing! That's the Ishtar Gate! It used to be one of the gates into the inner city of Babylon, and at one point it was thought of as one of the wonders of the ancient world. I'm just astounded, because I didn't think we'd ever discussed it.'

'Discussed what Grandma?'

'I mean, I didn't think I'd ever told you about the gate. I remember thinking about it specifically yesterday. I thought you'd be interested to hear all about it, but I only realised I hadn't described it to you, after you'd gone to sleep last night.'

Jemme momentarily slowed the pace of his story, 'Why did you think I'd be interested in it, Grandma?' he asked, taking a sip of jasmine tea.

'It's all to do with what we were talking about last night – about your new sister.'

'My sister?'

'Yes, remember we were discussing her name?

Jemme nodded slowly, it seemed like a lifetime ago.

'Well, I was telling you about Astarté, Venus and Aphrodite being all one and the same goddess. After you'd fallen asleep, I started to wonder if there were any other civilisations who'd had a variation of the same goddess, and then I remembered the Babylonians. Well, it's all very complicated and I don't want to interrupt your story, so I won't go into it, but there was a large amount of cross-over between the Assyrian and Babylonian gods and goddesses. In fact Hammurabi himself developed a number of different theories and practices. Anyway, without going into too much detail, the Assyrians and Babylonians believed that there were five different planets, and a god or goddess was attributed to each one. The one which the Romans called Venus, the Babylonians called Ishtar. So you see, it all leads back to the same thing.'

'I do see, Grandma,' replied Jemme, warming to his sister's name more and more.

'The thing that is puzzling me though is whether you had heard of this gate before. I know I certainly didn't discuss it with you. Think carefully, Jemme; can you remember anyone else mentioning it to you?'

Jemme didn't need to think for long, 'No, Grandma. I would have remembered something like that. Besides, everything else I saw in the dream I recognised straight away, and if I knew what the gate was then I wouldn't have needed to ask you about it.'

'Interesting, very interesting,' Lily murmured. 'Do go on, I'm so enjoying hearing about what you saw.'

Jemme picked up the pace again, and told his grandmother about every single thing he had seen. Details tumbled over each other in his rush to explain each little part. Lily sat, rapt, and took it all in. She was particularly taken with his description of the chariot battle, and kept asking him to repeat different details. She seemed astonished by each one, from the types of bow Jemme described, 'Composite,' she explained, to the lighter chariots.

'Do you know what this battle was, Jemme?' she asked.

Jemme shook his head. 'I'm not too certain, Grandma, but I know I've heard about it before, I just couldn't remember its name.'

'Was it near a river?' Lily asked, as if double checking something.

'Yes, it was. In fact, it was in a field right next to a river.'

'I thought as much. That river was the Orontes and that battle was the Battle of Qadesh – probably the greatest chariot battle in history.'

'There were a lot of chariots.'

Lily laughed, 'I can imagine there were. The thing that keeps surprising me is the amount of detail, not just that you can remember, but that you saw in the first place. I know you've learned a bit about this battle, but I doubt you would have learned the details about weapons they used and the specific type of chariots they used too. It's astonishing, it really is. Do you know who it was who had the lighter chariots you described?'

'I'm not sure, they definitely looked different to the men with the heavy chariots though.'

'I expect they would have done. They were the Egyptians – the ones with the nippy little chariots I mean. Their leader was Ramesses II. I think we've talked about him before; he's known as Ramesses the Great and he might be the most famous and most highly regarded of all the pharaohs.'

'Wasn't he the one with the beautiful wife?'

'Yes, that's right – her name was Nerfertiti, and she was thought of as one of the most beautiful queens of Egypt. But, back to the battle: Ramesses was fighting the Hittites and they were led by Muwatalli III. It all happened quite early on in Ramesses's reign, and I think the victory really shaped his legacy as a great ruler.'

'What was special about Muwatalli?' Jemme asked.

'To be honest, I don't know much about him. Ramesses is such a large historical character that he tends to eclipse those he fought. They become part of his story of victory, rather than having their own stand-alone histories. Apart from its relevance to Ramesses's empire, the other really interesting thing about the battle is the outcome.'

'Did the Egyptians win?'

'They did, and that's interesting in terms of Egyptian history, but there's something else too: the peace treaty.'

'I don't understand, Grandma.'

'There's a set form to battles. It's not just people running at each other with bows and spears, there are conventions that have to be obeyed, it's almost like etiquette.'

'Really?'

'Absolutely. It's even more the case during mediaeval times; the knights had very strong notions of chivalry and courtly manners, even when they were fighting to the death. One of the most formulaic elements of all battles is the very last part, it's almost the coda to the whole performance: the peace treaty. In battles throughout history, one of the first things the victor does, even whilst the wounded are still lying on the battle field, is draw up the terms of the peace treaty. Its format is pretty rigid and it has been for a very long time. It is the formal end of the war and gives the guidelines for how both sides will conduct themselves during peace time.'

'What sort of guidelines?'

'Everything you can think of, from what to do with hostages to deciding on borders and territories. They're all rigorously laid-out and strictly adhered to. It's an interesting enough subject to study in itself if you're looking at military history, but the most interesting part is the fact that they all follow after this one seminal treaty which is over three thousand years old. And you've come the closest to seeing the actual battle which gave rise to it, for some three millennia!'

'I suppose so,' Jemme said. He hadn't stopped to think that he might be standing in a position of privilege. Perhaps no one else had dreamed these things, or perhaps no one else had dreamed them with the same degree of clarity he had. He hadn't realised how many different tissues there were to each scene and how they interwove with his own life and setting. 'How did they draw up the treaty if it was so long ago, Grandma?' he suddenly asked.

'Well, that's an interesting matter too,' Lily replied. 'Whilst there were certainly copies carved into stone, as you would expect, the Egyptians' copy of the text was carved into a silver plaque, which they then took back to Egypt and used as the exemplar when constructing the great temple of Karnak. It's interesting from another aspect too, because whilst the Egyptian copy was carved in hieroglyphs, the Hittite copy was carved in Akkadian, written using cuneiform lettering. Because both copies survive, we have a cypher – a sort of linguistic key to help us understand both ancient languages.'

'What's "cuneiform", Grandma?'

'It's a very early form of writing, but I don't want to get into that now. I do want to hear the rest of your stories, but I thought you'd be interested to know that a large chunk of the surviving treaty is right here in Istanbul. It's in the Archaeology Museum – I'll take you there tomorrow if you like.'

Jemme looked pleased, and finished the last of his jasmine tea.

'Now, tell me about everything else you saw,' Lily encouraged.

Jemme sat up as he took up the tale again. Grandma listened attentively as he told her all about the ambassadors he had seen, from all ages and countries, all gathered in one room. She seemed particularly interested in the box which two of them had been packing together, and impressed by the fact that Jemme had read the recipient's name from the side of the box.

'I haven't told you much about Henry VIII,' she said, 'but he's a fascinating character and an important figure too – not just in English history, but in European history too. Do you know what the symbol you saw was?'

'The rose?'

'Yes, the double rose – had you ever seen it before?'

Jemme shook his head.

'It's often called "the Tudor Rose" Grandma explained, 'and even today the English prize it as a symbol – it appears in their courts, on their ceremonial uniforms and even on their coins. It's an emblem of power through unity; it represents two different, powerful families united.'

'English families, Grandma?'

'Yes, English families, but with connections and marriages which reached throughout Europe and the West. One family, the Yorks, is represented by the white rose, and the other, the Lancasters, is shown by the red rose. Those were their symbols separately, and they fought for thirty years in the Wars of the Roses.'

Jemme giggled.

'They weren't actually fighting with the flowers,' Grandma chided.

'Sorry,'

'Anyway, the wars were only decisively ended when Henry VII beat Richard III in a famous battle called the Battle of Bosworth. Henry was from the Lancasters and Richard was from the House of York. Once Henry had won, he made peace even more assured by marrying Elizabeth of York. Marriage alliances were very important in those times. In fact, at some points all of Europe was tied together with interconnecting marriages and allegiances; but, going back to the battle, the most obvious way to show the people that the families were united, and the country was under a strong leadership, was to create a new symbol and associate it with positions of public office, civic buildings and so on. It creates a powerful message and is instantly identifiable. That's what you saw on the case, although, again, I'm curious about how you could have seen it and remembered it so clearly with no previous exposure to it.'

'I don't think I'd even heard of Henry VII before, Grandma, let alone his rose.'

'Henry VII was Henry VIII's father, my love, but the rose symbol is so widely known, perhaps you'd seen it somewhere in a book and not remembered…' she trailed off, 'but then again, dreams are such powerful things. For as long as we have been sentient, they have fascinated mankind; and all sorts of cultures react differently to them and how they interpret them. Some think they are guides and contain hidden messages, some alter their waking activity to try to influence the nature or intensity of their dreams. For example, there is a traditional ceremony in Judaism called *Hatavat Halom,* in which a specially appointed individual can disturb the sleeper in certain ways to stimulate or suppress different elements of the dream. There's such a rich culture and tradition surrounding dreams and the dreamer, not to mention scholarship. Respected academics have spent their entire lives studying dreams, to try to understand them and what they mean – from a scientific as well as spiritual point of view. Personally, I refuse to believe that they are without meaning. The images you see are sometimes so vivid, there is no way of distinguishing them from reality. Something so powerful should not just be discarded as soon as the dreamer wakes and transfers to a different reality. I always try to remember my dreams, and spend a long time thinking them over and wondering *why* I dreamed such a thing. Some peoples have believed that dreams were controlled or given by spirits, and shamans could channel the images. I'm not sure what I think about that, but if there is no external source, then it means the dreams must have been created by my own mind, and that's hugely important. There must have been something which my mind was trying to tell me, and I would only listen when I was in a deep state of sleep. The ego often clouds things, Jemme; it distracts you and prevents you from listening to your true thoughts. That's why Sufis work so much on breaking down the ego, so we can achieve a higher level of understanding. But, for now, I think it's important that we think very carefully about this most interesting dream of yours. I'm sure we will be able to unlock some sort of meaning from it. One of the things which is most interesting me is the sense of purpose you say you felt. That must be relevant somehow – you have such a lively imagination and I'm sure your mind was trying to use your imagination to tell you something. Or even show you something.'

After her long speech, Lily suddenly looked tired, as if she was feeling the physical effect of handling such weighty concepts. Jemme too felt as if the air around them was thick with ideas and unanswered questions. He had only just started to realise that the dream had relevance, and now the prospect that it could be showing or telling him something opened up a whole new level of questions and complex thoughts. He turned the images over and over in his head, trying to shine light on them from different angles and perspectives. He wondered if they would fade with time, and disappear before he had started to understand them properly, just as some of them had started fading within the dream itself. He resolved to retain them in his consciousness for as long as possible, and gently packed them away into a corner of his mind, with as much care as he had seen the Venetian ambassadors pack away the precious gifts for Henry VIII.

Chapter Five

Nearly two decades had passed since the first time Jemme had had his dream. Over the years he had found his sleeping self in the palace many times. However, no two visions had ever been the same. Sometimes the dream seemed much shorter; sometimes it seemed to stretch indefinitely. During the dream, at no point did he ever stop to question whether he was dreaming or not; as far as he was concerned, his reality was intrinsically connected with his environment. When he found himself in the palace, in that moment, it was just as real as his life in Istanbul. Other things had changed more dramatically however. Sometimes when he went into the rooms, he would find completely new civilisations behind the doors. Often he recognised them, from his recent study or conversations with Grandma. However, sometimes they would seem completely new to him. He would recognise small elements – ceremonial robes, the language engraved into the walls and so on, but he would not be able to identify the civilisation. It would play on his mind for days, and he would doggedly chase through volumes of history trying to trace his dream civilisation. Often Grandma was able to help, but sometimes it would take months of almost-forensic study to identify the people he had seen. Once he had opened the door and found himself looking onto an ocean of long ships. He had not recognised the seamen on them, nor the funny writing on their sides. There was precious little to go on, and he had spent about three months piecing everything back together. First he had trawled through books on the history of ships. He was able to come up with a pretty broad identification straight away: the ship was a galley. However, it was another few weeks before he had been able to narrow it down. He skimmed through pictures of merchant vessels with their square-rigged sails, and flicked through endless descriptions of oar locations and hull-construction methods. Eventually he found a pen and ink drawing of the exact ship he had seen in his dream. He read that it was called a 'Bireme', from its Greek name. However, the galley had not been devised by the Greeks, but rather the Phoenicians, a maritime people who dominated the Mediterranean from 1500-300 BC. It was under their auspices that a second row of oarsmen was added, on a higher deck – something which had revolutionised shipbuilding at the time. He read about their language, and how they had developed one of the first alphabets to transmit it. By the end of his search, he knew that their capital could be found at Byblos, and that they held the monopoly on trade of the purple dye derived from the Murex snail, which was so highly prized by the Greeks. So it was that Jemme's knowledge grew and grew. Sometimes he recognised the civilisation instantly, but there had been a particular element which was new to him – a character, an object or an inscription. These were investigated with the same assiduous attention as his hunts for whole civilisations. He never worked out how it was he could see these things so clearly, when he had no prior knowledge of them, but it didn't concern him. What really mattered was using his conscious mind to investigate the imaginings of his unconscious mind.

Other things had changed too over the years. Although still tanned, with a thick head of dark hair, Jemme had certainly grown up. Active throughout his life, in his adolescence he had played sport wholeheartedly and this could be seen in his muscular frame now. He was definitely an attractive man, and did himself no disservice in the way he dressed. Just as in childhood, he was always impeccably turned out and, as had been his habit since he was five years old, every outfit featured a pair of braces. He usually wore a pinstripe suit, and the girls in his office would always giggle whenever his jacket flapped open and flashed his snappy red or purple braces. Jemme did not mind in the slightest – if truth be known, he probably played up to it a little. It fitted in well with his office persona: smart and authoritative, but with a playful streak. He had become well-known for his matching silk tie and pocket square, and no suit was complete without a pair of Church's shoes worn over the top of a pair of Marcoliani socks.

Several major things had also changed in his life. He had swapped the dust and romance of Istanbul for the chic streets of well-heeled Paris. His work had brought him here, and although he had initially found it hard to adjust, his naturally gregarious personality had helped integrate him and he was now a permanent fixture. Further trips with the Scouts, as well as a few independent ventures when he was a bit older, meant that he was very well travelled for someone of his age. It wasn't that his horizons had been narrow when he had arrived in Paris, it was more that Turkey was woven into the fabric of his childhood and to leave its beautiful mosques and colourful bazaars had been a wrench. He'd also been a little taken aback when first arriving in this new city. He was used to strangers being friendly, open and welcoming. He would never have eschewed conversation just because he didn't yet know someone. After all, all of one's friends began as strangers at some point. However, here people were often cold, to the point of being standoffish. Back at home, he had been accustomed to going into shops, looking at the bales of fresh produce on offer and having a long conversation with the owner. Maybe he would hear an amusing story about the proprietor's nephew, maybe receive a piece of wisdom about the size of aubergines that year; such little exchanges were what made one feel a part of a city. Here attempts to spark up chatter with shop owners were greeted with a wary mistrust, and browsing in a shop with no intention to buy could be met with outright hostility. He missed the casualness of such interactions, and longed for the chats which came with picking up a piece of fresh watermelon from the market on a hot day, or a paper bag of pistachios from a street-side vendor to munch on his way home. However, he had adapted well, and people had begun to warm to his sunny attitude. Concierges and café owners around his home now recognised him, and he was soon on nodding terms with most. This had developed, until he found that he was now the one sharing small stories and bits of gossip. Moving to Paris had been like putting on someone else's glove. However, he had pushed and wriggled and adapted until now it fitted him well. It was still someone else's, but for now it was comfortable enough.

Jemme's lifestyle was definitely comfortable too. His career in banking had gone from strength to strength, and he now found himself heading an entire bank with some four hundred employees, almost unprecedented at his age. It had been a hard slog to get there, but he had relished the challenge, and was proud of how he had pushed and stretched himself. In many ways, his family had been surprised by his choice of career and, to a certain extent, Jemme himself had been too. However, it pulled together so many things which interested him; there were the academic, methodical angles, in which he carefully and exhaustively researched all aspects of a deal; then there was the logical way in which it was put together, as if he was building something concrete, brick by brick. For as long as he could remember, he had always tackled problems in the same studious way; something which had garnered much gentle teasing when he was younger. There were other things which appealed to him though; he had recently branched out into foreign exchange trading in which two currencies were pitted against each other. It had meant that he spent a great deal of time telephoning people in different countries, and he loved the small talk which had been involved and the insight he got into the lives of different people in different cultures. There was a creative element to all of this too, and the truly successful were the ones who were able to think laterally and approach deals and problems from innovative and new angles. Jemme surpassed even his own expectations, and his great trading success had propelled his career into the stratosphere. It had given him the lifestyle to go with his station too, and he now found himself living in a beautiful *appartement* on the exclusive Avenue Foch. A clutch of highly polished cars sat in his garage, just waiting for him to drive them. Although he had increasingly less leisure time these days, no matter how busy he was he still managed to spend a couple of hours in his Mercedes or his Daimler. There was nothing quite like zipping down the Champs-Elysees with the roof down, and the wind whipping through your hair, to make you feel like you'd made it in the world. He was greatly enjoying his new life and all the trappings it brought. However, there were also simpler pleasures in Paris, and ones which reminded him of home too. He enjoyed being able to get up in the morning and jog down to the Bois de Boulogne. It was a simple, honest pleasure, and one which never failed to delight. As he ran through the ancient oakland, he thought of all the history which grew through the park as much of the roots of the trees. The area was over a thousand years old, and originally belonged to the abbey at St Denis. It had grown over the years, morphing into a thick forest which was a hideout for thieves during the Hundred Years' War. Each time he pounded its tarmac paths, Jemme felt that he was somehow tapping himself into the history of this remarkable space. As he ran through the thicket of trees, he remembered how Henry IV had planted thousands of mulberry trees there, in the hope of beginning a great Parisian silk industry. It was impossible not to connect with the history of a place, particularly a beautiful one such as this. As he ran, Jemme could feel the hornbeam and beech leaves rustle with stories, and the cedar and chestnut murmur tales of ages past and battles lost. It was a very basic pleasure which somehow kept him grounded in this strange new world he had entered. He tried to run nine kilometres about three times a week. It was a wonderful catharsis, and as he engaged in such a primal activity he could feel all the worries of his new world dropping away from him.

Whilst there were certainly many worries and stresses, there were many positive aspects to life in Paris too. Perhaps the most positive, and certainly the most beautiful, was Jemme's new girlfriend. Hil was everything he could have hoped for. She was intelligent, graceful and utterly enchanting, not to mention incredibly beautiful. Jemme had been captivated by her the moment he had first set eyes on her, around two years before at a New Year's Eve party in London – in Chelsea to be precise. From afar, there had been something enticing about the way she moved, as if everything was tied into one single, elegant action. She seemed completely attuned with her own body and comfortable within it. As much as Jemme had tried not to stare, he had found it incredibly difficult to look elsewhere. He had taken her for dinner the very next day and tried to get to know her. It hadn't been difficult: Hil, or to give her her full name, Hilyana Radison, was disarmingly open, warm and engaging. They had dinner in a restaurant in South-West London, and they had talked easily and without reservation late into the night. She was wholly without pretence, and there was still a naïve quality to her which was unshakable, regardless of her surroundings. Perhaps this was due to her rather conservative upbringing in Ireland. She had attended a convent school for some thirteen years, and whilst by no means prudish, certain behavioural tropes had become ingrained in her personality. She was modest to a fault, and had a strong sense of justice and fairness. She was the most considerate person Jemme had ever met, and was always putting others first. It was just the way she thought – it wouldn't even have occurred to her to think of her needs before those of other people; this kindness made Jemme feel instantly protective of her. He could see that it would be easy for others to take advantage of her good nature, and he could sometimes feel himself slipping into an almost guardian-like role around her. It was impossible not to – there was just something about her that made him want to preserve her exactly as she was, as if she perfectly embodied an innocence and virtue which had been long since lost in parts of Paris. Jemme sometimes felt that he would give anything to protect that purity, and prevent anything or anyone besmirching it.

Hil had integrated seamlessly with every part of his life. Her presence could definitely be felt within the flat on Avenue Foch. It was a curious *coin* – a melting pot of different influences and tastes. The framework of the flat was quintessentially French. Its beautiful original mouldings and cornices were as crisp as the day they had first been installed. The large sash windows, the high ceilings and the parquet floor conveyed some of the regal splendour of Versailles, and anchored the flat in its context. However, within this French *cadre* was a shifting picture of Eastern exoticism. Each room testified to the origins of the flat's owner. Jemme had painstakingly imported hand-crafted Levantine furniture from the workshops of Istanbul. He had spared no time or expense in sourcing the perfect *divan* and the gold-embroidered upholstery to go with it. Each object within the flat had been carefully thought about, and was a product of planning and genuine desire rather than anything opportunistic. Jemme had also brought over some pieces from the house in Istanbul; an occasional table which had spent his childhood in the *liwan* of his parent's house, now sat in his own *salon*. Its form was familiar and comforting, and every time he passed it, it elicited an ineffable feeling of happiness and contentment as it evoked various childhood memories. The silver coffee set in the kitchen played a similar role, and although he hardly ever used it, every time he was near it, he could have sworn that he smelled strong, syrupy, thick, Turkish coffee and the voice of his father in the coffee house rang in his ears. The trinkets with which he had surrounded himself brought him a great deal of joy, and a feeling of belonging. The flat felt like a transitional space; it was neither Turkey nor France, it was his own little kingdom and he adored it. Hil's influence had gradually crept in, and in many ways it was she who prevented it from turning into an Aladdin's den of Eastern treasures. At first she had brought small objects with her, sometimes as gifts and sometimes her own possessions which she had left behind: a cashmere shawl over the arm of the settee, an arrangement of peacock feathers in a rather plain vase. They added a certain softness to the place, which was undeniably feminine but welcome nonetheless. Over time her influence had become greater. She had suggested that Jemme started to acquire French antiques for the flat. It would be in keeping with the building's age, she said, and it would be a lovely thing to do together. Jemme had always had a passion for antiques and collectables, whether in furniture, painting or manuscript form. However, when he had first arrived in Paris he had been too busy to begin any large-scale acquisitions. Together with Hil he had leafed through catalogues, attended auctions and raised his hand in sales, keeping his nerve right until the end, even when the nail-biting tension became unbearable. He put just as much effort into his auction going as he had into sourcing his furniture, and he thoroughly enjoyed it. He felt that the thrill was comparable to chasing a great deal: a mix of painstaking research, knowledge of a particular sector, the courage of your convictions, guts and a certain amount of bravado were vital in beating off opponents. There was nothing quite like the feeling of bringing home a carefully packaged brown paper parcel from Sotheby's, after a three-month chase, and he relished every moment of it. Whilst he certainly bought things at auction on his own, his favourites were the pieces he had bought with Hil. They reminded him of their time together – the planning, the sale and the celebration dinner he always took her for afterwards, as they giggled like children, giddy with their success. Jemme felt as if the flat was emblematic of his life; each seemed to become more complete and more comfortable as Hil became a bigger feature in both.

Jemme reflected on this fact as he walked to work. He tried to take a different route each day, for no other reason than the fact that he enjoyed the variety. He hated the idea of routine, and did all he could to eschew it. Sometimes it was just little things, like varying the way he walked to the bakery, or which suit he wore on a Monday, but they were all important to him in their individual ways. It bordered on the obsessive; even if something took him well out of his way, cost him more or took him much longer, he would religiously follow through with it. He didn't quite know where this impulse came from. When he was in a self-analytical mood, he would ponder whether it stemmed from a fear that routine breeds stasis and thus stagnation. He felt that if he became too comfortable in his habits, it could dull his instincts. The ability to think on his feet, and wits as sharp as hunting knives, were vital to his success. Sometimes however, he thought it was more to do with his childhood. He remembered his long walks with Grandma and how, for her, the journey was more important than the destination. She would vary the route every single time, no matter how infinitesimal the change. On this particular day in Paris, he skirted down a small alleyway and cut across the edge of the park. Spring was on its way and the ground felt crisp underfoot. It raised a murmur of excitement within him – he had great plans for the summer. He had been planning a trip back to Turkey for a while, and he was very much hoping that a certain someone might accompany him.

Although the sun shone, it was still a cold morning, and as he rounded the corner, a warm smell of coffee and freshly-baked croissants hung thick on the sharp air. He smiled to himself as he thought back to the smell of mint tea and grilling meat he would have encountered in Turkey. A few moments later he was walking up the steps to the bank. The building had an impressive Restoration period façade with a brass banister running up the side of the stone steps. The same unseen hands who were responsible for keeping the windows spotlessly clean must have been in charge of polishing the banister to within an inch of its life, for it never looked anything other than smart and shipshape. As with every day, after exchanging pleasantries with the staff he encountered on the way in, Jemme would go straight to his office on the fourth floor where he would find Dieter Dietz waiting for him. Dieter Dietz was a man of impeccable manners, faultless professionalism and totally indispensable. Sometimes Jemme wondered how he had managed before Dieter was hired. To try to summarise his role would be to do his work a disservice. In fact Dieter himself would have found the very proposition anathema. Universally known as 'DD', he was an urbane German gentleman. A polished, classical education in Berlin had put him in possession of a clutch of languages, and the apparent ability to converse with anyone. Jemme had long stopped being surprised when he heard DD answer the phone in a language he had never heard before, let alone heard DD speak. No one was sure how old DD was, and he would have found it highly indecorous to be asked the question, and more so to actually disclose his age. However, most people within the bank put his age at about forty-five. Jemme secretly thought he had always been in his mid-forties; the idea of DD as a louche teenager or a petulant child was faintly ridiculous. Like Jemme, DD was always impeccably dressed. However, there was a distinct lack of flair in his attire. Whilst Jemme's sartorial exuberance sometimes made him look like some sort of exotic bird, DD made a point of being understated yet elegant. He had a thick head of salt and pepper hair, which matched his habitual two colours: black and white. Today he was being a little adventurous and was sporting a grey waistcoat, with the bulge of his favourite fob watch just visible in the pocket.

'Good morning, Sir,' he greeted Jemme as soon he entered.

'Hullo, DD! Hope all's well,' Jemme replied breezily.

'Most well, thank you, Sir. If you would permit me to cut straight to business, I believe that we will be able to fit everything in before your meeting.'

'My meeting?'

'Yes, Sir, your 9.40.'

'Ah yes. Thank you.'

DD answered with a slight inclination of his head. Jemme settled into the chair behind his large mahogany desk, and let DD talk. He listened attentively, as DD ran through yesterday's performance figures, briefed him on upcoming events and major trades for the day ahead and prepared him for the imminent meeting. Although it was a thorough and serious delivery, Jemme never found it difficult to concentrate on what DD was saying. In his own way he was engaging and could captivate people's attention for as long as he needed to. Once he had finished speaking, DD laid out all the relevant documents on Jemme's desk, and double-checked if there was anything else he needed before leaving for his own office, just outside Jemme's.

Looking down at the documents in front of him and running over DD's points, Jemme felt completely prepared for the day ahead. No matter how many appointments, phone calls and important meetings he had, DD was always able to compartmentalise the whole day in advance for him. It always seemed manageable and accessible. It freed Jemme to focus all his energies on whichever subject was in hand. Often DD sat in on the meetings, and would prepare invaluable documents afterwards, full of key points which Jemme might not have had time to absorb during his sometimes heated discussions with trading partners. As he flicked through the sheaf of papers headed 'stock options', he wondered whether DD could be described as his male secretary. 'That's just one of his many hats,' he decided, 'and what formal hats they would be!' he added to himself, and smiled slightly at the thought of DD wearing an old fashioned stove-pipe top hat. Working his way through the stock options, he absent-mindedly imagined DD wearing a variety of different hats. There was his secretarial hat of course, but that was somehow inadequate. It was more of a personal assistant hat; then of course there was his role as a driver – that couldn't be forgotten and DD had come to the rescue countless times in the driver's seat of the company Mercedes. When he was wearing his organisational hat, DD could be found doing any number of things, from scheduling meetings to arranging Jemme's haircuts. If the hat was firmly on, then something bigger would be afoot and DD would the unflinching helmsman, perfectly controlling and delivering a large function for the bank. From devising the guest-list to managing the caterers, he was unflappable and the event would be pulled off with élan, and exactly – to the letter – how Jemme had asked for it to be. Maybe there was something in the old adage about German efficiency, Jemme thought to himself as he finished the booklet. Whatever Germanic stock he drew on, and whatever hat he was wearing, DD was the very essence of a linchpin. He ensured the smooth running of things so deftly that often people did not realise he had even done anything.

Having finished his reading, Jemme slipped the documents into the Hermès briefcase he always carried, and made his way to the boardroom. The meeting was not a particularly challenging one, and everything went much as he had suspected, and exactly as DD had predicted. He'd had to do a lot of talking though, and now he was back behind his own desk, he could feel the toll it had taken on his throat. Reaching forward he flicked the intercom switch.

'Sir?' DD responded straight away.

'Hi DD, I'm feeling a little bit parched – would you mind bringing me some tea please?'

'Right away, Sir.'

Precisely three minutes later, DD rapped smartly on the door and entered, bearing a small silver tray. Jemme still preferred to drink his tea from glasses, in the Turkish fashion, rather than from porcelain cups, like the French. Sure enough, on top of the tray sat a tall glass filled exactly four-fifths of the way up with a light amber liquid. DD put the glass down in front of Jemme, who took a grateful sip. It had been sweetened with just the right amount of honey, and was the perfect temperature – not so hot that it couldn't be drunk and not so cold that it had lost its flavour.

'Fantastic, DD. Thank you.'

'Of course, Sir. Can I do anything else for you?'

'Not right now, I think I'll just prepare for this next meeting. Oh – actually, I'm going to be a bit pressed for time. Would you mind fixing up a lunch date with Hil?'

'Of course, Sir. Did you have anywhere in mind?'

'Not especially, I'll leave it up to you – somewhere special but not too fussy or pretentious.'

'Of course, Sir,' said DD one last time before leaving.

Four hours, one meeting and two further cups of tea later, Jemme was ready to leave the office. His throat was soothed, his meetings had been a success, and he felt he'd earned a nice lunch break. Following a brief, yet pleasant walk, he found the restaurant DD had chosen. He couldn't believe he hadn't been there before – he could have sworn that he'd eaten in every restaurant within a two mile radius of the bank. Hil was waiting for him outside, wearing a blue Chanel skirt suit and looking radiant. She beamed a smile at him, which caught him slightly between the ribs, in the way that she had the power to do.

'You look stunning, sweetheart,' he said genuinely as he embraced her.

Hil's creamy cheeks flushed slightly, 'Thank you. It's new – I thought you might like it.'

'I do, very much so. Come on, let's go inside. This morning has made me hungry.'

They were shown straight to their table, and as Jemme pulled the chair out for Hil he looked around admiringly. The restaurant was very Art Nouveau – a style of decoration he had been quite taken with recently.

'Special, but not too fussy,' he said approvingly.

'Who is?' asked Hil

Jemme laughed, 'Well, you, I suppose, but in this case I was admiring the restaurant. DD managed to pick exactly what I wanted.'

'Did you expect anything less?' said Hil.

'No, I suppose not!' Jemme chuckled, 'This menu looks good too; I think I'll start with the *pâté en croûte*. Are you ready?'

'I think so,' said Hil as Jemme caught the attention of a passing waiter.

Once their starters had arrived, Hil looked up from her salad,

'Is there any particular reason we're having lunch today? I mean, I always love to see you during the day, but I was just wondering if there was an occasion?'

'Well sort of. I mean, I hope there will be,' Jemme began. 'I have got some work coming up which will mean I have to spend a while abroad.'

Hil looked crestfallen and Jemme laughed, 'Don't look so sad, I think – I hope – it could be a good thing. I need to go to New York in a couple of weeks' time. I'll be out there for about ten days, and although there will definitely be business to attend to, I'll also be spending quite a bit of time kicking my heels. Well, I've thought about it and I can't think of anyone I'd rather be kicking my heels with...' he teased.

'You don't mean?!' Hil began excitedly.

'I do! I would love it if you would come with me, Hilyana.'

Hil did a poor job of concealing her excitement, and dropped her fork with a clatter. She reached over and took Jemme's hand, squeezing excitedly.

'I'd love to. Just think – our first holiday together!'

'The first of many I hope,' Jemme said, taking a sip of water and trying to pass the comment off as nonchalantly as possible.

Hil flushed slightly, but didn't say anything. She smiled at him and squeezed his hand again.

✻   ✻   ✻   ✻

Over the next few weeks, both Jemme and Hil's excitement about the upcoming trip grew. Hil hadn't been to New York before, and every time they saw each other she would regale Jemme with an even longer list of all the things she 'simply *had* to see' and shops she 'simply *couldn't* miss out on'. For his part, Jemme was trying to prepare as much as he could, so that the business part of the trip would encroach as little as possible on the pleasure side.

Finally, the day had arrived and Jemme made his way to Charles de Gaulle airport, light with a sense of excitement which never normally accompanied business trips. He had taken extra special care choosing his travelling outfit, and was wearing his most dapper suit over a handmade shirt with his monogrammed initials just visible under the jacket cuff. A pair of vintage Cartier cufflinks and some highly polished brogues finished the outfit with a dash of style. He was pleased to note that Hil had gone to similar efforts with her attire: the trip was obviously just as important to her. They cut quite the pair as they cruised their way through first class check in, and settled into the executive lounge.

'Is that another new outfit?' Jemme asked once they were sitting down.

'Oh goodness, don't say it like that, you'll make me feel guilty!' Hil said.

'That's the last thing I wanted to do! I just didn't think I'd seen it before and it looks absolutely lovely on you.'

'Thank you,' Hil said, managing to look self-conscious and pleased at the same time. 'It's rather exciting flying first class – I never have before.'

'It's only exciting if you're flying with someone else,' Jemme said rather dolefully, 'otherwise these business trips can turn into a rather lonely circuit of lounges and hotel rooms. Talking of which, here's the brochure for the hotel we'll be staying in,' he handed her a stiff piece of card, with florid writing at the top and glossy photos of luxurious looking rooms running the length of it.

'It's beautiful!' Hil exclaimed.

'I thought you'd like it. It's one of the nicest in Manhattan. I really wanted to show it to you, but I also chose it because of the location. It's not too far from where I'll be working, so we can maximise our time together, but it's also not too far from the Met.'

'The Met's pretty high up my list of "must-sees",' said Hil.

'Ahhh, you and your list! I knew you wanted to see it and I'd really like it if we could see it together. It's one of my favourite places, and whenever I'm there on business and feeling bored, lonely or just in need of some culture I head down there. It would be so much more special if I could go with you.'

'That sounds wonderful. I'd like that very much.' Hil said, slipping an arm through his as they got up to go to the gate.

The flight felt like the first part of the holiday. When there was someone special to share it with, the niceties of first class were all the more noticeable, Jemme realised. They both enjoyed the novelty of choosing from an in-flight menu, and the devoted attention of all the staff. Even though he had been through the motions hundreds of times, this felt like the first time he had ever travelled in such a way, and Jemme was thoroughly enjoying himself.

'My grandmother always used to enjoy the journey as much as the final destination,' he told Hil.

'If she travelled like this, I can see why!' she replied without removing the warm flannel she had been given for her face.

Jemme laughed, 'This couldn't have been further from how she did, in fact how she does all her travelling. Grandma likes things as simple as possible. She would not be impressed by any of this. In fact her favourite way to travel is her own two feet. She's known in Istanbul for her walking, and when I was a child we used to walk all over the city for hours. I learned so much in those walks; she would point out so many interesting things along the way, and tell me all about them – things I might not even have noticed, but also things I'd see every day but never stop to think about.'

'She sounds like a very interesting character,' said Hil, turning to face him, and removing the flannel.

'She is,' sighed Jemme slightly wistfully, 'I have to say, it was a wrench leaving her. I hope maybe you can meet her at some point,' he ventured.

'I'd like that very much,' Hil said, flashing him another beaming smile.

The journey flew past, and they moved effortlessly from airport to taxi to hotel. It was just as plush as the brochure had promised and, travel-weary, they sank gratefully into the soft coverings of the large bed.

The next day Hil heard a scrabbling at the door, and woke with a start. Jemme was already dressed, and was letting himself back in, holding a tray laden with food.

'I thought you should start your day with a proper New York breakfast,' he said, placing it on her lap. 'I'm afraid I have my first meeting, but I asked room service to bring this up for you, and by the time you've eaten it all and got up and dressed, I'll probably be finished and we can go exploring.' He handed Hil her silk dressing gown and kissed her on the forehead. She looked down and saw that there was a rose on the tray, next to the glass of orange juice.

She smiled up at him, 'You are too good to me,' she said happily.

'Nonsense!' said Jemme, 'You enjoy that – New York is famous for its breakfasts. I'll call through to the room as soon as I finish.'

'I hope it goes well,' called Hil after him, as she picked up a piece of bagel with one hand and a mug of coffee with the other.

As promised, some three hours later, Jemme phoned through to the hotel room and arranged to meet Hil outside the Met. He was at the Rockefeller Centre, and thought it would take them each about half an hour. He gave her careful directions and, sure enough, thirty minutes later Hil saw Jemme approaching the entranceway, exactly as she was.

He saw her and his face lit up, 'Hello! I hope you haven't been here long.'

'Not at all, I arrived just as you did,' she replied, hugging him.

'Oh good. Right, let's go in!' Jemme said, wrapping one arm around her waist.

'Is there anything in particular you would like to see?' he asked, as he paid their entrance fare.

'Not especially. There are so many things I would love to see that I won't be able to see them all. I'm more here for the actual museum, rather than any one specific thing in it. Why don't you show me one of your favourite things?'

'That's a great idea. Well…where to start? There's so much I love in here. I know!' he said suddenly, and steered Hil to the right of the entranceway. They climbed up a few steps and entered a long, narrow gallery. 'The Met has an incredible collection of Byzantine art, which is a subject close to my heart.'

'I didn't know that,' said Hil softly.

'It reminds me of home, of my childhood and of all the beautiful things I've seen over the years. It's been so influential on other art forms, that I've seen it crop up in many of my different travels.'

They walked slowly down the gallery. It was a veritable treasure trove of precious objects, from small figurines to large canvases, mosaic work and manuscripts. Every so often they would pause by a showcase and take a moment to study its contents properly. When they reached a wall-mounted mosaic fragment, Jemme inhaled sharply.

'What's the matter?' asked Hil.

'Nothing – nothing at all. It's just that piece of mosaic takes me back. It's just reminded me of about three different things, all at once!'

'Really? Do tell me about it.'

'Well, I suppose it's the gilding which is the most evocative. That's very typically Byzantine. You see it in many of the high churches and mosques of the Levant. It's difficult to get the same feeling from a small fragment like that, but when you're standing in a sacred building looking up at a ceiling completely blanketed in gold its absolutely breathtaking.'

'I can imagine.'

'It's more than just the aesthetic of it; it's as if the original builders are trying to convey to you how important the building was to them – how special it was. It's as if all the important and reverent thoughts about the building have been trapped in the gold somehow. You can't help but experience them yourself when you're there. It's quite humbling, knowing that you're standing in the same spot as men and women have been for more than a hundred years, reacting in exactly the same way to your surroundings as they would have done. In fact I think, if it's possible, the gold would have represented even more to them – it would have been so expensive and luxurious. It was probably the most impressive thing that any of them would ever see. I love the fact the religious direction of the building is almost irrelevant in terms of such decorative art. It doesn't matter whether it's a mosque or a church; the people react in the same way to the art, and it inspires the same feelings of awe and wonder in them.'

'I suppose you're right. It must be quite something – to look up and see nothing but gold.'

'It really is. But this piece is also directly reminding me of Hagia Sophia, back in Istanbul. It's the centre of a long-lasting love affair with my family. I think at some point I've heard every member of my family call it "the most beautiful building in the world." It's more than just its beauty though; I think it's the fact that it was such a huge part of the scenery of my childhood. It's so emblematic of the city, and whenever I was returning after some time away, its minarets would be the first thing I would see on the horizon and then I'd know that I was home.'

'It sounds like a really special place,' said Hil softly, touched that Jemme was sharing these memories with her.

'It is, without a shadow of a doubt. There's something else about this piece though, something which is bringing back powerful memories. Remember I was saying that Byzantine art was highly influential?'

Hil nodded.

'Well, when I was very young – the first time I'd properly left home in fact – I went on a Scouting trip to Venice. We visited San Marco's and I remember looking up once we were inside and seeing an entire ceiling of endless gold. I was mesmerised by it. It instantly took me back to home and Hagia Sophia. At the time I didn't understand how two buildings could be so similar, and yet so far apart from each other. I suppose it was the first time I truly understood the concept of the spread of art. It was during that trip that I realised culture and art could move away from their original homes, taken with merchants and diplomats to far off places. I realised that this could combine with other cultures and create something new. It made a profound impression on me and I suppose it's shaped the way I've thought about a lot of things in my adult life.' He paused and looked at the mosaic fragment again, 'It's funny, the feelings and memories one object can conjure up. I almost feel like I want to include this piece in my flat somehow.'

'I think you've got quite enough decorations, not to mention gold for the time being!' Hil chided, lightly.

Jemme laughed, 'You're probably right.'

They continued down the gallery, with Jemme pointing out various paintings which chronicled the Fall of Constantinople and statues which had arisen from various Ottoman fashions. Hil hung on his every word, and seemed genuinely interested. As they reached the end of the gallery they carried on walking, entering the mediaeval section. Something caught Hil's attention immediately, '*Belles Heures de Jean de France, Duc de Berry*,' she read aloud.

'Now, I can tell you something about that – I didn't go to Catholic school without being able to recognise a Book of Hours.'

'Go on, tell me all about it,' Jemme encouraged.

'Well, Books of Hours were prayer books from the Middle Ages. They were hugely popular in Europe and they were all unique to their owners, with favourite prayers, special illustrations and so on. Even the bindings could be customised. This is a really beautiful example. I don't know who Jean de France was, but he must have been a wealthy man to be able to afford such a lavish book as this one. You see these small illustrations?' Jemme nodded, 'Well, they're called miniatures,' Hil continued. 'It's a very specialised form of art, and the amount of skill shown in some of them is remarkable; you almost need a magnifying glass to be able to see all the detail involved.'

'Miniatures are a really big feature of Byzantine art too,' said Jemme.

'Really? I didn't know that.'

'Absolutely,' Jemme nodded, 'this is exactly what I was saying about art and ideas spreading and becoming wrapped up with new ideas. Manuscripts fascinate me – my family has always collected them and so I sort of grew up around them. I'd love to start my own collection, but I just haven't got round to it yet. I've got a couple here and there, but nothing major. I didn't realise it was something you were interested in, too.'

Hil nodded emphatically, 'Same with me. There were always beautiful manuscripts both at home and in school. For me they're almost part of the furniture. If you're serious about starting a proper collection, I'd love to help you.'

'Well that sounds very promising indeed!' Jemme said, slipping his arm back round Hil's waist, 'Now, what would you say to lunch?'

'I think *that* sounds very promising!' Hil laughed.

The rest of their time in New York passed in a similar way. Jemme's meetings seemed to take up minimal time, leaving them free for long walks, even longer dinners, and frequent trips to galleries and museums. Jemme was delighted that he was able to show Hil objects and artefacts from nearly all his favourite eras. He had never fully explained his passion for different civilisations to anyone outside his own family before, and to do it all in one go was exhilarating and only furthered his enthusiasm for it. As he showed Hil things, he was learning himself. Sometimes a piece would catch him off-guard, and challenge what he thought he knew. He wouldn't understand where it would fit into things, and wouldn't be happy until the curator or gallery attendant had explained it fully to him. Finally he would be satisfied at how it had integrated, and he was more confident of his knowledge than ever before. Hil watched all these discussions with a growing sense of warmth. She had never met anyone with such passion, and with such a thirst for knowledge too. Highly intelligent herself, she found that Jemme was the perfect foil for her; he challenged and stretched her in new ways, and she felt like she was growing as a person whilst she was with him.

When it finally became time for them to return to Paris, they found themselves sitting in another executive lounge, this time in JFK. It could have been anywhere as far as they were concerned, for they sat together in a blissful haze, feeling more in love than ever. Finally, just before it was time to head back to the gate, Jemme felt he had to ask,

'Hil, I've had an amazing time with you – it's been more than perfect. In fact, I can't wait to go away with you again. For our next trip, I was wondering if you might consider Turkey? There are some people I'd really like you to meet.'

Chapter Six

Since returning from New York, Jemme had become further immured in his den of treasures. Much as he had tried to hold back and reason with himself, that he simply didn't have the space, he and Hil had seen so many beautiful objects and trinkets that he hadn't been able to resist. They had visited several museums and galleries, and whilst the gift shops were mostly filled with worthless tat, occasionally they hid a rare treasure. Sometimes this could be a beautifully produced guide, full of thoughtful research and glossy pictures, which perfectly illustrated a particular exhibition they'd enjoyed. Sometimes it was a small tile, formed, fired and painted using ancient techniques, or a hand-blown glass vase with delicate millefiore trapped inside the glazing. Jemme had loved the fact that each object told several stories. Firstly, it was as it seemed at face value: a souvenir from a special trip. However, it also told the story of the museum it came from and, in turn, the civilisation whose story the museum was telling. It served as a symbolic conjunction, the point at which various stories met and collided, merging into a single object which had somehow become representative of all that was important to him, Yet he could hold it in the palm of his hand. He had bought just such a tile, and when he had unpacked it back at home, and felt its cool smooth face under his palm, it had reminded him of about three different things at once. He had thought of Hil, excitedly pulling it out from the middle of a stack of near-identical ones, yet proclaiming, 'This is the one!' But its classic *iznik* markings also reminded him of the blue and white colourings of his childhood. The swirling leaves and geometric designs could be found all over Turkey, and were even more concentrated in Anatolia, the area surrounding the eponymous tile producing town. Iznik had a fascinating history, as richly embellished as its famous tiles. It had been the capital of the Seljuks, battled the Crusaders and fallen to the Ottomans. The stories were familiar ones to Jemme, and he had heard them many times during his boyhood. However, recently he had also learned that the city was famous in the Christian world, for being the site of the First and Second Councils of Nicaea. These events had been formative in the early Christian church, and were crystallised within the liturgy of the church in the Nicean Creed. Jemme had only recently become interested in the birth of Christianity, and was determined to discover more. Different faiths had always interested him, and he had long been interested in Christianity from a historical point of view. The

Levant had cradled the nascent religion, and major early believers tied many other areas of history into the story. He turned the tile over, and noted the fineness of the workmanship. Quite apart from all it represented, it was a lovely object in itself. He liked the fact that traditional methods had been used to make it – it somehow made the tile's story more real and kept something important alive. 'This is exactly the type of thing museum gift shops should be selling,' he thought to himself. When people leave an exhibition, full of what they've just seen, they shouldn't be confronted with meaningless plastic tokens – they should have the chance to take something meaningful away. A piece like this allows them to keep a part of the exhibition in their homes, and reminds them of the sense of wonder they felt when they saw such beautiful and ancient homes. He was deep in his thoughts, and hadn't heard Hil approaching him from behind. He jumped slightly when she wrapped her arms around him and she laughed.

'Sorry, I didn't mean to startle you!'

'That's alright, my love, I was just looking for a new home for the tile you chose,' Jemme replied.

Hil followed his gaze as he turned to the bookshelves. There was absolutely no possibility there, as trinkets and ornaments looked set to spill off the shelves at any point. They looked around the flat in unison. As their gaze settled on various places, they silently dismissed them, before moving on to the next place. Jemme hadn't really stopped to take stock of just how much he had been buying recently. The odd painting here and there, maybe a small etching – they all seemed so small and manageable at the time; but now when he was actually confronted with the full scale of his collecting, he was quite taken aback. The whole place was teaming with treasures. He slipped an arm around Hil's waist, as they slowly turned around and took in the salon they were standing in. She giggled, 'I can't believe you can't even find enough space for that thing!' she said. Jemme looked down at the small, square tile he was still holding between his thumb and forefinger. Its small size made it look faintly absurd, especially when compared with the some of the other objects he was looking at in the room.

'Oh dear,' he said, slightly mournfully and put the tile back down on an occasional table.

Hil remained chipper, 'I think you either need to reign in your buying, or look for somewhere bigger!' she teased.

Jemme laughed with her, and kissed her forehead, 'I just can't help myself when I'm with you!' he said. However, what Hil had said stuck with him – maybe he did need to start thinking about somewhere bigger.

Clutter aside, Jemme was deliriously happy. In fact, the clutter only really bothered him from a practical point of view. He quite liked the fact that his flat was starting to tell its own story. It was as if its old walls were pages in a scrapbook, already begun by someone else. Now he was pasting in his own memories, and making the space his. He remembered seeing a picture of a fat little bird, lining its comfortable nest with feathers and sitting, satisfied, in the middle. He understood how the bird felt, and couldn't help but share its warm sense of contentment. Things were looking up in all areas of his life. Hil was almost too good to be true. Everything about her seemed to fit perfectly; her views chimed with his own, her interests interested him too and she had melded so seamlessly into his life he now found it impossible to consider a time when she was not there. He had already taken her to several important bank functions, and been proud to have her on his arm. She had an instinctive understanding of the form and protocol involved in events which muddled the social and the professional, and was the model of polished refinement. She was so well acquainted with what to do and what was required of her that it was almost as if she was following a set pattern of behaviour somehow, as if she had divined the prescriptive qualities of womanhood from the old manuscripts she professed to love. The code for womanly behaviour within much heroic verse was set out just as clearly as the rules governing social conduct for chivalric knights, and Jemme could just imagine Hil soaking up such information. Sometimes he liked to think that the strict social guidelines of *fin amour* in mediaeval times were also governing their courtship in modern Paris.

Life within the bank was also fruitful. Jemme's hard-earned success had established him with an enviable reputation, and he rarely had to seek out business anymore. Things were starting to level out a little too now, and he found his hours were, mercifully, more manageable and predictable, and phone calls rarely intruded into his home life anymore. He still kept an office at home though, a small sanctuary for himself, just as his father's had been during his childhood. He sat in it now, and absentmindedly shuffled some papers. As he did so, something caught his eye. The corner of one page bore a note in DD's unmistakable writing. Much like its scribe, the writing was formal, accomplished and elegant. Jemme knew that the slender loops and tilted letters had all flowed from DD's antique fountain pen – his prized possession. It was a lovely item, with its golden barrel and onyx lid, and he was never without it. Jemme glanced at the page the note had been written on. It was the record of a deposit which had been made earlier that week. It all seemed fairly regular and the amount involved wasn't anything to get excited about, but DD had clearly written '*Most interesting. Shall discuss with you further,*' above it. Jemme resolved to bring it up with him during their morning meeting. As he slipped the papers into his Hermès briefcase, his eyes fell onto a wrapped brown package leaning against the wall near the office door. He looked at it for a fleeting moment, before remembering it was yet another painting he had brought back from New York. He groaned inwardly, 'Where on earth am I going to hang it?!' he said out loud.

✣ ✣ ✣ ✣

Picking a different route to work, Jemme set off at a brisk pace. He was running over the pleasures of the New York trip, and willing himself to pick a favourite moment. It was impossible; every time he thought he'd pinpointed the moment of superlative happiness, another memory would drift across, trumping the last. It was a most pleasant way to pass the walk, and in no to time at all the bank's familiar façade hove into view, and Jemme was running his hands up the brass banister as he climbed the stairs. He exchanged his usual morning greetings with the staff at reception, and made his way straight to the fourth floor. DD was waiting for him in a well-cut dark charcoal suit. 'Good morning, Sir,' he greeted Jemme as he opened the door to the office for him.

'Hello, DD. How are you this morning?'

'Well, thank you, Sir. I have some figures to review with you, some proposals to be discussed and something I think might be of interest.'

'Ah, yes – I was going to ask you about that,' said Jemme as DD ushered him into the room and then closed the door behind both of them. He ran over all of the business with his usual efficiency, and Jemme concentrated, nodding occasionally and once interrupting him to clarify something. Everything was wrapped up relatively quickly and as DD paused to rearrange his papers, Jemme's curiosity got the better of him,

'Come on, DD, do tell – I'm dying to know!'

'Sir?' said DD as he raised his head from the papers.

'The thing you thought might be of interest – you, know – the one you wrote me a note about too. I'm intrigued.'

'Ah, of course. Professor Johnston.'

'Professor Johnston? Do I know him?' asked Jemme.

'No, Sir, at least not yet. He came in this week to make a deposit, and whilst we were in the cashiers' plaza we had quite a conversation. I must say he's a very personable individual and highly informed too. He's a visiting professor at Leiden University, and a fellow at Oxford University too. He was just here to deliver a paper on Ottoman art to a conference, which is what made me think he might be of some interest to you. He's an absolute expert on the Levant and completely passionate about it too. It's rare that one meets someone so knowledgeable and enthusiastic, and it was very contagious indeed. He specialises in Turkish history and I felt quite educated after our short meeting. As soon as he started talking about the Hagia Sophia I thought of you. I think you'll find him very interesting, especially in light of your upcoming trip. I've taken down his details – he'll be here for another week or so, before heading back to Oxford.'

'He sounds fascinating, DD, I look forward to meeting him, thank you.' Jemme beamed at his right hand man as he took the note. Although DD tried hard not to show it, Jemme could tell that he was pleased.

The day passed in a rather routine fashion. By now the bank was large and well-oiled enough to run itself, if needs be. The machinery rolled relentlessly on, and allowed Jemme to concentrate on more troublesome and intricate problems; complicated deals and ambitious acquisitions would have been frustrated if he had had to focus his energies on the mundane daily goings-on. DD played no small role in ensuring that operations ran as smoothly as one of his silk ties, and Jemme was eternally grateful to him for this. Today he had even telephoned Professor Johnston to organise a rendezvous with Jemme after work. Jemme was looking forward to meeting this professor, and whizzed through his afternoon tasks with zeal, finishing them much earlier than expected.

'I'm off, DD,' he called, poking his head around DD's office door, as he put on his jacket.

'Very well, Sir, I hope the meeting proves to be satisfactory,' DD replied.

'I'm sure it will, thanks again.'

DD replied with a slight inclination of the head and Jemme set off. Paris was full of Turkish cafés and restaurants, if one knew where to look, and DD apparently did. Jemme had been impressed when DD had passed him a slip of paper with the details of the location. To start with, meeting in a Turkish café was a great idea – it hadn't even occurred to Jemme, who would have naturally picked one of the upmarket yet slightly sterile bars which he usually used for client and business meetings. They would both be more relaxed in this setting, and it might even inspire the Professor. Secondly, Jemme was surprised that DD had even heard of this place. There was a definite divide in the city's 'ethnic' food offerings. On the one hand, there were expensive restaurants, with equally expensive menus; they were decorated to the rafters and felt like some kind of lurid theme park. The menus bore the French translation for each dish, and the food had been toned down a great deal, and made 'safe' for the Gallic palate. The clientele were unlikely to find anything too *outré* or intimidating there, but they were equally unlikely to find anything authentic, or with real flavour. However, these were the places which were widely known about, and could be found in indexes and listings. The other type of restaurant did not advertise at all, would not dream of translating its menu, and rarely even had a menu. Usually tucked away in slightly insalubrious surroundings, these places were absolute gems, and patrons usually kept their existence a closely guarded secret. The decoration would be minimal and usually from the home of whoever was running the place. Likewise, the food would usually have been imported directly, perhaps brought over by someone's brother or cousin. It would be whipped up into an exquisite feast by the owner of the restaurant, and that would be what was served that evening, regardless of whether a customer had any pretensions of choosing his supper from a menu. These places were dotted around the capital, and included every cuisine, from every continent. From fragrant Thai curries to proper Hungarian goulash, if you knew where to look there would be something authentic, cheap and packed full of flavour. The place DD had chosen was actually one of Jemme's favourites, and he knew it well. The lady who owned it was from the Anatolian region and a fantastic cook. He had never seen it empty, and it was a wonderful retreat. Sometimes if he felt a twinge of homesickness, or a longing for a well-made piece of flaky *börek,* he would head down here. The place was usually packed full of Turkish people, and he could sit happily for hours wrapped in the warm, cozy fug of cooking smells and listening to old men telling their stories and the excited chatter of younger people growing up here. He was pleased to have an opportunity to head that way, but quite surprised DD knew of the place – he hadn't realised that anyone outside the Turkish community had ever even heard of it.

He nodded his greetings to the owner and settled into a comfortably worn seat. A couple of minutes later, a slightly dishevelled man appeared in the doorway. His jacket was buttoned up on the wrong buttons, and his hair looked like it hadn't seen a comb in several days. He carried an attaché case which was too stuffed with papers to be able to clip the flap down. With his library-paled skin and greying blond hair, he couldn't have looked more different to everyone else in the café. He didn't seem to feel out of place however, and his scatty appearance belied an alertness and focus which could be seen glinting in his eyes. Jemme knew who he was, instantly, and waved him over.

The man made his way over, 'Mr Mafeze,' he said, shifting his attaché case and extending a hand to Jemme.

'Professor Johnston,' Jemme replied, shaking his hand warmly, 'pleased to meet you, although you must call me Jemme.'

'Very well, in that case you must call me –'

Jemme held up a hand and interrupted him, 'Please, if it's all the same with you, I'd much rather stick with "Professor". I don't get to meet many very often, and I quite enjoy the way it sounds, if you wouldn't mind indulging me.'

The Professor paused for a brief moment before breaking into a wide smile. 'Of course, of course,' he chuckled, helping himself to a chair and stowing the case under the table, evidently with some relief.

'I understand you've just finished a conference?' Jemme said,

'Yes, yesterday in fact. It was on Ottoman art and it went quite well actually. There were some very interesting questions at the end, which have prompted heaps of ideas. I scribbled lots of notes down, but I've barely had the chance to put them in order,' he gestured at the case, 'my whole life seems to be dominated by notes at the moment. I'm either preparing them, reading from them or trying to sort them out – I barely keep on top of them as it is, and I can't imagine the chaos which would ensue if I let anything slip for a moment!'

He shuddered slightly, and Jemme shuddered sympathetically. He remembered, in the early days of the bank, the vast amount of paperwork he'd had to plough through. It sometimes felt like he was trying to swim through it, and had to focus all his energies just to keep his head above the water. It had been about that time he'd hired DD.

'I understand you met Dieter Dietz?' he asked the Professor.

'DD? Yes, I did – what a character! He seemed really interested in what I had to say too.'

'Yes, that's a particular talent of his,' Jemme reflected.

Professor Johnston looked momentarily crushed and Jemme leapt in, 'Oh, I'm sorry – he would definitely have been genuinely interested in what *you* were talking about!' he tried to assure him. Before he could add anything further, the waitress had appeared and Professor Johnston was ordering a coffee in perfect Turkish.

Jemme was impressed, 'I'll have the same,' he said to the waitress, who made a note and departed.

'When did you learn Turkish?' he asked the Professor.

'Do you know, I don't think I can remember,' Professor Johnston replied, seeming genuinely puzzled, 'I suppose it must have been whilst I was an undergraduate. I've been studying that region for so long you see, and a great deal of the scholarship has yet to be translated into English. I'd read various journal entries with a dictionary in one hand and a notebook in the other, and over the course of my studies it was just accretive. The same happened with Arabic.'

'I'm impressed,' said Jemme genuinely, 'especially regarding Arabic, it's notoriously difficult to learn.'

Professor Johnston laughed, 'Yes, it was, especially at the beginning – I found it all so frustrating. It only really started coming together when I began visiting the Arabian Peninsular on research trips, and I was forced to speak in the language every day. It made such a difference, not least because I suddenly understood the context of everything I'd been studying. It's all very well learning about something in the Bodleian, but ultimately your understanding is finite. It's not until you immerse yourself in the place and culture which created it that you can gain true *understanding*.'

'Do you believe you have... gained true understanding of things through your studies, I mean?' Jemme asked.

Professor Johnston looked thoughtful, 'I think it's in the nature of history that one can never achieve perfect understanding. Our outlook is always clouded by historiography, not matter how academic our approach. However, I believe that by spending time in and around your subject, one can come as close to a pure understanding as it is possible to do. I certainly forged a long-lasting love of the people of the Levant, and their cultures and customs.'

As if to prove his point, as he said this the waitress arrived bearing a small tray with two tiny cups and saucers.

'Oh good!' the Professor said emphatically.

Jemme laughed. He had never seen anyone who wasn't Turkish react with anything other than a grimace to what he thought of as 'proper' coffee.

The waitress set the cups in front of them and returned with two glasses of water.

'*Teşekkür ederim,*' they both said in union.

Jemme looked at the Professor, the thick sludge at the bottom of his coffee cup had caused the *petit-cuillère* to stand directly upwards. 'Tell me your favourite places in Istanbul,' he said.

The Professor took on a dreamy look, and thought for a while, before beginning an animated description of the beauties of Istanbul. His vivid descriptions were interwoven with historical accounts. Listening to him felt like being taken on a guided tour, and Jemme was fascinated to hear facts and historical snippets about his home city which he hadn't even known before. The image of a tour stuck with him, as he listened to the Professor speak. He chatted fluently and confidently, only breaking off to take short, staccato sips of bitter liquid from his tiny coffee cup.

After a while he paused.

'I'm sorry – you must be getting bored. I'm afraid when I get onto one of my pet interests I just talk until someone stops me.'

'Not bored at all,' Jemme replied earnestly, 'in fact quite the opposite. I'm something of an amateur historian myself, but I don't get the opportunity to read and research as much as I like. My grandmother is a complete buff though, and listening to you now is reminding me of many happy afternoons spent listening to her in my childhood. I'm discovering new things too, which I'm sure Grandma will be surprised to hear! It's fascinating listening to an outsider's perspective on the city I grew up in. In fact, that gives me an idea: I'm shortly going to be taking my girlfriend to Turkey. I've got a rough itinerary in mind, but the problem is Istanbul. I know it so well that I don't even know how to begin showing someone around. Would you mind devising a tour for us? You could consider it a freelance project, I could listen to you talk, like you have, all day, and I'd be happy to pay to have some of it written down.'

The Professor looked a little taken aback.

'Of course, I understand you must be very busy,' Jemme began.

'Busy? Oh yes, I'm always busy! It's not that though; it's just that I've never done anything like this before. It will be nice to be able to make a little extra from my favourite subject and a welcome break from all the conferences too! I'd be happy to do it, thank you.'

'Excellent news,' Jemme said enthusiastically. He had been trying to map out the tour with Hil for a while, without much success. Every time he could see it taking shape, it dissolved again into an amorphous mess. He felt like he couldn't see the wood for trees, which was confounded by his earnest desire for the trip to be memorable and for Hil to have the best time possible.

They chatted for a while, about which sights simply had to be included, and things which could not be seen without seeing other things. Suddenly the Professor thought of something,

'I'm sure you probably don't have much time for this sort of thing,' he began.

'Go on,' said Jemme.

'Well, do you remember me telling you that a great deal of scholarship regarding the Levant was never translated into English?'

Jemme nodded.

'Well some important sources have been translated into French and the Bibliothèque Nationale has some beautiful early manuscripts. I've got a temporary readers' card because of the conference, and so if you'd be interested in seeing them I could sign you in.'

'Thank you, I'd like that very much,' said Jemme. He grabbed the waitress's attention and ordered another round of coffees. He was looking forward to spending the evening in the Professor's company.

※　※　※　※

Several hours later, and slightly buzzing with all the coffee had he drunk, Jemme left the café. He was at the edge of the edge of the XIV arrondissement, and would have to pass through the VII to get back to Avenue Foch, so he decided to call on Hil.

A rather frantic voice greeted him over the intercom.

'Hello!' he said cheerfully, 'It's me.'

The tinny voice softened, 'Come on up!' said Hil.

Jemme arrived to find the front door unlocked, but the sitting room empty.

'I'm in here!' Hil's voice came from the bedroom.

He followed it in, to find a scene of complete disarray. Hil was usually neat and tidy to a fault. Everything had a certain place, and if things strayed from their homes she would put them back in their correct places without even realising she had done it. Jemme couldn't believe the scene in front of him. Shopping bags were piled on top of each other; wardrobes were open; sleeves poked out of a suitcase hastily slammed, and Hil seemed to be entangled in a mass of coat hangers.

'Darling, whatever's going on?' Jemme asked, as he went over to kiss her, gently lifting a hanger which had attached itself to her elbow.

'I'm just trying to work out what on earth to take with me!' Hil said, looking flustered as she folded and unfolded a shirt again.

'But it's ages before we go!'

'I know, I know, but I was thinking about it when I got home from work, and I suddenly had a moment of panic. I couldn't think of a single thing I owned that might be suitable. I mean, I've never even been to Turkey, so I don't know what I should wear there to start with, and then there's the prospect of meeting your whole family too – which is more than a little intimidating. I started pulling a few things out of the wardrobe and then some cases out from under the bed... and it sort of escalated out of control,' she gestured around, slightly wildly.

Jemme gently took the shirt from her and put it on the bed. He smoothed down her hair, which was usually perfectly styled but had become slightly flyaway.

'You're being silly,' he told her gently, 'you've got absolutely no reason to worry. They will absolutely love you. I know I do,' he added, feeling his face turn warm.

Hil looked up. Her face was flushed too. She dropped the shirt which she had unconsciously picked up again, and embraced Jemme tenderly.

'I love you too,' she murmured.

They stayed rooted to the spot for several minutes, before gently disentangling themselves. Jemme looked down at Hil, 'How about we leave this for now, and I make us both a cup of tea?'

Hil smiled and nodded.

'I think that's an excellent idea,' she said.

They made their way into the sitting room, which was Jemme's favourite room in the flat. It was a perfect expression of Hil: as if her character had somehow seeped into every piece of furniture and scrap of decoration. The flat was not vast, especially when compared with Jemme's own place on Avenue Foch, but the rooms were generously proportioned enough that it didn't feel cramped, yet small enough to retain a sense of cosiness. It had all been beautifully and carefully decorated. Using the same consideration she showed for most things, Hil had been sympathetic to the building's age and location, and the size of the rooms. Just as her influence had been creeping in to Jemme's flat, as he entered Hil's sitting room and looked around he could see his own influence spreading into her space. There were a couple of etchings they had bought together over the fireplace, and a small *Ghom* rug Jemme had given her sat just in front of the sofa.

There were also less perceptible differences: Hil's book collection was starting to display a more masculine bias, as she began to buy books recommended by Jemme. Nestling between her well-thumbed copies of favourite novels and Wordsworth classics were a growing number of history books which directly reflected Jemme's interests, and places they had visited together. Jemme flicked his eyes over them and was pleased that his interests were as important to Hil as hers were to him.

'You sit down, sweetheart, and I'll go and fix us some tea,' he said.

Hil sank down into the sofa. Jemme pulled the footstool up, lifted her legs gently and placed them on top of it.

'There!' he said, pleased.

Hil laughed, 'You spoil me!'

Jemme smiled and turned to the kitchen. He was quite familiar with it by now and found the kettle and tea jar with ease. He rarely drank black tea, preferring either proper coffee, or fresh mint tea; but endless cups of milky tea had been a fixture of Hil's childhood in Ireland, and she drank gallons of the stuff. It was probably just as well this evening, he thought, he didn't need any more coffee after his meeting with Professor Johnston.

He decided to do things properly and gently pulled two delicate cups and their saucers from one of the wooden cupboards. They were exquisite yet fragile, and he handled them with great care. They were the only two remaining from a set of six, and he remembered buying them at auction with Hil. She had told him that she had never been to an auction before, and as they were rapidly becoming one of his favourite activities, he had suggested they go straight away. Hil had been a little apprehensive that prices would spiral out of control, and wasn't expecting to come away with anything. Jemme was getting the hang of how things worked however, and spent some time trawling the catalogue in preparation. He had found the cups and knew that Hil would love them. He also knew that the price would plateau quite quickly, as serious collectors would not be interested in an incomplete set. Hil wouldn't need all six anyhow; a pair would be perfect for her flat, and perhaps for making tea for two. She was delighted to win them, and they left the auction house buzzing with the adrenaline he had begun to associate with the experience. Hil chattered excitedly on the way home, stopping suddenly when they reached the bottom of her street. 'But they're even more perfect than I thought! Look, rue Sèvres!' she exclaimed pointing up at the blue street sign, 'and they're antique Sèvres porcelain! It's like it was meant to be!'

'I know,' said Jemme smiling to himself: all his planning had paid off.

He smiled again as he thought of Hil's excitement and filled each cup with sweet-smelling Pluckley tea, with a tiny splash of milk in Hil's – just how she liked her speciality teas. He put them on a painted wooden tray she kept stowed under the sink, and at the last minute noticed a slim tin. He had a quick look inside. Hil quite often kept her treats in it, and he struck lucky, finding two golden madeleines inside. He slipped one of the small, pillowy cakes onto each saucer, and took the tray next door.

'Wonderful,' Hil said from the settee, already looking more relaxed than when he had left her. He carried the tray carefully over to her, and with one hand moved a paperback from the side table next to the settee, and then set the cup down.

'Thank you,' she said beaming up at him. There was something about the warmth of the room, the way she had arranged herself on the sofa and the happiness of her smile, in that captured moment, that made her look utterly radiant. Jemme felt a huge surge of love as he gazed at her.

'My absolute pleasure,' he replied, moving round to sit next to her, 'I was thinking of another reason you don't need to worry, whilst I was in the kitchen.'

'Oh?' said Hil as she nibbled on her madeleine.

'It's to do with the clothes. I suddenly realised that they'll probably give you some.'

'Who will?' she asked, looking confused.

'My family. It's a Turkish tradition. They'll give us both sets of clothes as a sort of welcome. It only happens on very special occasions – usually when someone has been away from the family home for a long time and then returns. Or when someone brings a very special guest home with him…both of which are exactly what's going to happen,' he said, and popped his madeleine in his mouth whole.

'Goodness, I hadn't expected anything like that,' said Hil, as she continued to eat her cake in an altogether more dainty fashion. 'It will be so lovely to be involved in something traditional whilst I'm there. I'm so lucky – I'm sure most visitors only ever get to see the tourist sites, and don't get a proper feel for the place.'

'Well you're not most visitors, my love!' said Jemme, 'In fact, I've been thinking quite carefully about what we'll see whilst we're there. I want to make sure that you don't miss out on anything, but I also don't want to exhaust you with sites, and I want to make sure you get to spend some time with my family.'

'Absolutely,' Hil nodded enthusiastically.

'Well, like I said, I'm thinking about it at the moment, and I've also enlisted the help of a professor, so we can put together quite an itinerary.'

'A professor! Wherever did you find him?!'

'DD.'

'Of course – why did I ask? Thank you for going to so much trouble, sweetheart, I really appreciate it. I hope you know that I'm looking forward to it lots, I think I just allowed my nerves to get the better of me for a moment.'

'Of course I do. I'm looking forward to it lots, too.'

'Here,' Hil extended her arm, 'you can have the rest of my madeleine.'

❖ ❖ ❖ ❖

Jemme met with Professor Johnston on a daily basis for the remainder of the Professor's stay. He seemed to be relishing the project, and each time they met would complain that Jemme wasn't going for long enough.

'Now you know how I was feeling when I hired you,' laughed Jemme, one particular morning. He had rescheduled his morning appointments, to take the Professor up on his Bibliothèque Nationale offer. They had met early for breakfast so that they could head straight to the library as soon as it opened. Over buttery croissants and two very short *café noirs* which they had unanimously agreed were 'not as good as the "real" thing', they discussed what they had planned for the morning.

'I've been quite a few times,' explained the Professor, 'and I've finished my research for the trip, so this is just for fun, as far as I'm concerned. There are a few books I've seen before which I think might interest you, and a couple I've seen on this trip too which I think you'll like. I dropped in my request forms last night, so the books should be ready for us in the reading room when we arrive.'

'Excellent, I'm looking forward to it,' Jemme replied, noting the time and emptying some francs onto the table to pay for breakfast. 'Shall we make a move?'

Professor Johnston flapped about, trying to shove all his papers back into his attaché case, and losing himself in his scarf for a while, but was soon trotting after Jemme.

They arrived at the library just as the great ornate doors were being unlocked, '*vous êtes très vifs, messieurs,*' chuckled the custodian as they passed him and made their way to the entrance of the long reading room. Even though the library was springing to life with whirrs of heating, clicks of light switches and the banging of doors as the day's visitors began to arrive, there was an impenetrable silence within the cavernous reading room.

Professor Johnston made his way over the enquiries desk, and murmured something at the bespectacled woman behind it. He handed her a small card, which she studied for a while before handing him a slip of paper in return, and pointing towards a desk. The Professor waved Jemme over and showed him the slip of paper: '*place 67,*' it said on it. They worked their way through the desks, each one of which was designed to seat four people, and bore a small, bronze, numbered disc in each corner. They found 67 and, sure enough, there was a small stack of books waiting for them. A note on the top gave Professor Johnston's name, the books' shelf numbers and the memo '*FRAGILES: veuillez utiliser des coussins de protection S.V.P.*'

The Professor pulled out a chair for Jemme, and motioned at him to sit down whilst he bustled off to get some of the triangular shaped pieces of padding, which were used to support fragile books and manuscripts. The silence of the room was all encompassing, and the high ceilings seemed to amplify any sound, even the Professor's soft footfall. It made it difficult to have any kind of conversation about the books. Occasionally the Professor would breathe a fact to Jemme, or try to whisper something, but for the most part they stared at the books together in silence.

Jemme soon realised that this was the best way to appreciate them. Each book told its own remarkable story. Scars in the bindings showed how previous owners had stored them on the shelves, whilst cracks and creases in the spine betrayed favourite pages and chapters. Traces of bookplates removed, and scrubbed out names on the flyleaf hinted at the soluble nature of book ownership – as if the object itself transcended personal claim. Jemme was fascinated by the stories that each of these old books had captured and stored; the smells which were released when turning various pages, the fading marginalia; they were all deeply personal and added to the story of the book, before he had even got started on the contents.

For the next three hours they carefully examined the Professor's selection. There was a nice amount of variety, both in terms of content and the books themselves. Jemme was fascinated by a handwritten *Abécédaire*, a primer for the study of the Turkish language. Its pages were handcut and uneven, unlike the regularity of the looped writing inside, which spread in brown ink across the pages. The pastedowns had been made from beautiful marbled paper, and the book bound with leather in such a way that the four edges were completely protected when the book was shut, and it looked like a small leather box.

As he looked at it, Jemme tried to imagine the original owner of the book, desperately trying to unlock secrets in the Turkish language as he sat with his trusty guide – much like the Professor would do years later. He wondered if this man would have been studying from the comforts of his homeland, like the Professor, or if he was trying to make his way in Turkey, unable to speak to people in their own tongue.

They leafed their way through early Turkish encyclopaedias, evidently made to be luxury objects, with their heavy gilding and opulent leather bindings in heraldic colours: Sanguine, Sable and Gules. They pored over illustrated travel accounts of voyages in the Levant, written by adventurous Frenchmen of centuries past. Some bore pen and ink drawings of famous landmarks, so deftly rendered that Jemme was able to identify them instantly. He read through the accounts carefully, sometimes turning to the Professor for help with certain words: Professor Johnston had been studying such material for years and had a practiced eye for the nuances of old handwriting. As he methodically worked his way through these particular books, the thing which stood out most for Jemme was the way in which other people, from a different country and a different time, had perceived his homeland. He was so accustomed to the landscape, so familiar with the cities that they represented completely different things to him, as opposed to someone seeing them for the first time. He wondered how Hil would react, and whether she could ever forge the relationship with the land that he enjoyed. For that matter, he wondered how he would react. It had been a long time since he had been in Turkey, and he had changed a great deal during his time in France. He would be interested to see the city of his childhood, after so many years of nostalgia and yearning for the homeland; he wondered if he would understand it in the same way, if it would mean as much to him now that he had built a new home for himself in a new life far away.

It dominated his thoughts, as he stared at the sketchy outlines of Hagia Sophia's familiar shape in the book; not a record of the building, so much a record of how it had appeared to a French traveller some two hundred years before. Time and pages flew past, and before he knew it the Professor had softly closed the last book, and written '*tea?*' on the back of the reservation slip. He nodded and smiled to himself; no matter how much the Professor loved Turkey and its rich coffee, there was no changing an Englishman.

Jemme found himself rather saddened when the Professor's stay came to an end. He had enjoyed discussing subjects which interested him with someone so knowledgeable. What's more, he had been impressed with the itinerary the Professor had put together for him. It was just about the right length, and included all the buildings Jemme was anxious to ensure they saw, as well as a couple of others he wouldn't have thought of. Looking at the Professor's notes which accompanied the list, he understood: the buildings were important to completing the story of the city and he was satisfied that the tour the Professor was sending them on would tell a good story. He hoped it would make Hil love the city as much as he did. He had thanked Professor Johnston profusely when he received the notes, and offered to drive him to the airport.

'Excellent plan, thank you!' the Professor had enthused.

Waiting for him now, Jemme was amused to see him emerge from his hotel, bearing a suitcase as overstuffed and haphazardly packed as his attaché case. He dropped him off at Charles de Gaulle and shook his hand warmly. They had exchanged business cards during the car journey, and Jemme looked at the Professor's now.

'I hope this isn't the last time we meet, I've very much enjoyed spending time with you,' he said.

'I hope it's not as well,' said the Professor, 'it's rare to find someone with such interests outside academic circles, and one can tire of talking to academics fairly rapidly, believe me.'

Jemme laughed, 'I do. I meant what I said about calling me up next time you find yourself in Paris, and as soon as I can think of any projects which might be of interest I'll be in touch.'

'I look forward to it,' replied the Professor. Jemme handed his suitcase over to him.

'Goodbye,' he said.

'*Hoşçakalın*!' said Professor Johnston, before turning and disappearing into the bustle of the airport.

Slightly subdued, Jemme paused for a moment before leaving for the car. He wondered when he would next see the Professor, or meet someone so likeminded again. He had felt so stimulated in his company, and it had re-fired the passion for studying historic civilisations and peoples which he had held since childhood. Although he had spent most of his life in pursuit of knowledge, hungry to understand his dream, he still considered his studying efforts somewhat hobbyist, and himself something of an amateur. Maybe it was because he held himself up to Grandma for comparison, but he would never have considered himself in the same league as an Oxford academic before. Being able to hold his own during animated discussions with the Professor, and even contribute information the Professor hadn't known, had filled him with confidence. Whilst he was setting up the bank, and now that Hil was such a big part of his life, he found that he was spending increasingly less time chasing books on different civilisations. He missed it, and was filled with renewed enthusiasm to apply himself to studying again. Most of all though, he felt a burning desire to return to Turkey. He had been looking forward to the trip before, but now he was positively impatient.

He wasn't punished for long; preparations for the trip and sorting out his affairs at the bank meant that the time had flown by. Whilst Hil fretted over sundresses and evening wear, he worried about gifts. He knew his extended family would come to the house to greet them, and he wanted to make sure that no one was left out. He knew his family would shower them with generosity when they were there, and he didn't want to turn up empty handed. He had searched high and low for the most suitable gifts. He had thought about each person individually, and tried to buy them a meaningful gift which showcased the best Paris had to offer. After some thinking he had bought his mother a pistachio coloured silk scarf from Hermès, and his father a leather cufflink tray from Longchamp. It was a beautifully made item and the leather was of a very high quality. He wasn't entirely sure what the French distribution channels were for his father's leather, but he thought there was a reasonable chance this piece had started its life in his father's tanneries, and he was sure this would amuse Baba. He had stalled over Grandma. Her love of Istanbul was a huge part of her character, and he felt slightly guilty choosing another city to live in. He hoped it hadn't wounded her too much. After a great deal of searching, he had found himself in a little antiques shop in the VII on his way back from Hil's one evening. He had pottered around until he came across two small antique prints of Paris. They reminded Jemme of two which had hung in Grandma's room throughout his childhood, in both composition and aspect. Whereas hers showed Istanbul behind the Bosphorous in the early morning light, these showed Paris and the Seine. He was sure Grandma would draw the comparison, and pleased he could show her that Paris could be as beautiful as Istanbul. The presents had been carefully packed into one of the many cases they were taking, and he found himself back at Charles de Gaulle again, standing next to Hil and surrounded by cases. Jemme looked up at the boards and found their check-in desk. He turned to tell Hil but stopped. She was looking up at the board herself, relaxed and unselfconscious. Jemme studied her for a moment. Her head was tilted slightly up and her long hair tumbled down her back. She had picked an outfit that was both elegant and stylish and, not for the first time, Jemme was struck by the comparison with Grace Kelly. Hil suddenly realised he was looking at her, and the moment was broken. She flushed slightly,

'What?' she asked, looking a little self-conscious.

'Nothing. You look lovely, that's all.'

'Thank you!' she smiled, but the flush did not recede.

'You need to learn to take a compliment, my love,' Jemme said teasingly, 'and we need to go to desk three. Wait there, I'll get a trolley,' he said, eyeing up the cases warily.

Finally airborne, Jemme leaned across and squeezed Hil's hand, pulling it up to sit with his on the armrest. He sat, deep in thought. He was excited about the trip, he knew that much. Certainly, he was excited about the Professor's city tour and keen to show Hil around, since he knew he would enjoy the opportunity to see Istanbul through new eyes, both by experiencing Hil's excitement on sighting things for the first time and also by reacquainting himself with familiar sights. Hil should meet Grandma and the rest of his family, and he wanted her to stay in the house that meant so much to him and walk through the streets of the city he could never leave for too long. He almost felt as if this trip was going to unite all the things that he loved, bringing them all together under Turkish skies and creating a collection of everything and everyone who had moulded and shaped him into the person he was in that moment. However, it was laced with a certain trepidation – a lagging sense of fear which was too intangible for him to understand. He concentrated, prodding his subconscious and forcing himself to confront whatever it was in there which was making him feel uncomfortable. Perhaps it was returning after so long, he reasoned. Perhaps there were nerves about being reunited with people he hadn't seen in years. Jemme wasn't satisfied with either reason, but at least it went some way to providing an explanation. He dug deeper, poking at thoughts which recoiled away from him like worms exposed under a rock. If he was being completely honest with himself, the trip was more significant than he was letting on. Even on his own it would be a big trip, something of a grand homecoming after all this time away. The fact he was bringing Hil to Turkey was meaningful in itself, but the fact he was bringing her on this particular trip was telling. He pondered this fact for a little while, not quite ready to admit to himself exactly what it was telling *of.* Jemme realised that he was also slightly nervous about introducing Hil to his family; he knew how hectic it would be once they arrived, with all sorts of relations, neighbours and friends wanting to come over. Then he was shaken from his thoughts by an air hostess offering him coffee. He nodded gratefully and she passed him cup. When he looked over at Hil, who had already finished hers, she smiled at him and he realised that he had absolutely no reason to be nervous about introducing her to anyone.

'What?!' she asked, fidgeting under his gaze.

'What do you mean "what"?'

'You're giving me that funny look again, just like you were in the airport.'

'Was I? Sorry, sweetheart, I didn't mean to. How was your coffee?' he asked, looking at the thing brown liquid in front of him, unconvinced.

'Not great, but it did the job,' said Hil brightly, 'and they gave us a piece of Turkish Delight to go with it too.'

Jemme looked at the small, rubbery cube on the saucer. It was a rather alarming shade of pink and looked as if it had welded itself to the airline plastic cup. 'You just wait until you've tasted the real thing,' he said.

'I can't wait,' Hil replied.

Jemme felt much more relaxed than he had when they had taken off, and settled into his seat. Before he knew it, they were preparing for landing and he realised that he had returned to the land of his childhood. Stepping off the plane, a wall of heat enveloped him like an embrace. He sniffed and took a deep breath of Turkish air, before breathing out slowly and smiling to himself.

'Welcome to Istanbul,' he said, turning to Hil behind him.

'I can't believe how warm it is!' she replied.

'You'd better get used to it,' he laughed.

They moved down the staircase, and with each step Jemme was flooded with memories. No matter how long he left Turkey for; in fact, even if he never returned, she had an inescapable hold over him: she had been his first love.

A young Turkish boy heaved their suitcases off the carousel and piled them onto a trolley for them, and then stood around looking expectant. Jemme tipped him a handful of lira and he scuttled off to do the same for a couple standing at the next luggage belt. Jemme took the handle of the trolley and turned to Hil,

'Ready?'

'Ready.'

'Right. Well, in that case, let's see who's waiting for us on the other side.'

He had only pushed the trolley a couple of yards into arrivals when he heard a familiar boom, 'Jemme!'

He looked around to see his father waiting for him, with outstretched arms and a huge smile on his face. He felt a huge wave of homesickness rush over him, and had to fight the urge to drop everything and run into his father's arms as he had done as a child. He moved over to him, pushed the trolley to one side and embraced him,

'Baba!' he couldn't help uttering. His father's embrace wasn't as tight as it used to be and his boom had softened a little, but other than that he was exactly the same. He was still dressed in a well-fitting suit and looked exactly as Jemme saw him in his mind's eye, every time he thought of home.

'It's so good to see you,' he told Wadeah emphatically.

'And you, son,' his father replied, emotion creeping into his voice.

'I have someone I'd like you to meet,' Jemme said, turning and offering a hand to Hil. She moved forward and held it, and he noticed the tightness of her grip.

'Wa –' he hesitated. Could he still call his father Baba? It was the name by which he knew him best after all. He decided so.

'Baba. There is someone I'm very keen for you to meet. This is my girlfriend, Hilyana. Hil, this is my father, Wadeah.'

Hil moved forward and offered her hand.

'I'm so pleased to finally meet you, Mr Mafeze. Jemme has told me so much about you.'

Wadeah ignored her outstretched hand, and gripped her in the bear hug Jemme recognised from childhood. Hil looked a little taken aback at first, but then Jemme saw a smile spread across her face. She visibly relaxed, although, that could have been because she'd had the air squeezed out of her, Jemme thought to himself wryly.

'You must call me Wadeah,' said his father, finally releasing Hil, 'and I am pleased to finally meet you too! We've all been waiting, and there has been so much excited chatter at the house these past couple of days that I'm quite glad of the excuse to leave for an hour or so, to be honest.'

At the mention of 'we' Jemme looked at his father questioningly.

'It's just me at the airport I'm afraid. Everyone wanted to get the house and the food prepared for you, and I thought that if I came to collect you it would give you a little bit of breathing space to recover from the flight, before the onslaught of relatives.'

'Oh dear,' Hil laughed, 'that sounds rather daunting.'

'I hope you haven't eaten for a week my dear,' said Wadeah with mock gravity. 'Half of Istanbul's women seem to be in my house, and I don't think you're going to be able to answer their thousands of questions for all the pastries they'll want you to try, and stews and kebabs they'll want you to eat.'

'He's teasing you,' Jemme whispered to Hil as they moved towards the car.

'I know,' said Hil.

Jemme smiled. Hil had already got the measure of his father, which was an auspicious beginning.

Wadeah might have been teasing, but he wasn't exaggerating. The house was alive with colour, smells and noise. Jemme could hear sound coming from it when they were parking the car, and was instantly transported to significant events of his childhood. Every milestone had been marked in a similar way, and the house had been packed to the rafters with friends, family, neighbours and well-wishers, all come to offer their greetings, respects or congratulations, and each bearing plates and bowls of food. He remembered how it had been when his eldest sister, Astarté, had been born and how he could barely move for all the gifts. It had been exactly the same at the birth of each one of his subsequent eight brothers and sisters. What a happy childhood, he thought, to have been marked by such celebration.

'Leave the bags,' said Wadeah, 'I'll sort them out. You take Hil in to meet everyone.'

'Thanks Baba,' said Jemme and turned to Hil.

'Ready?'

'Ready.'

Just as when he had left the plane, with every step he took across the courtyard Jemme felt like he was taking a step further into his own memories. Everything looked exactly as he had left it, and exactly as he had been keeping it alive in his memory. The smooth black and white tiles shone under the sunlight, and had obviously been scrubbed for the occasion. As they passed underfoot he thought about all the games he had played on them in his youth. They had hosted simple pebble games for which he had invented intricate and complex rules; he had run across them with friends, variously kicking and catching balls; and he had sat on them during late summer evenings listening to Grandma tell her stories. He reached the familiar wooden door, which had been left ajar for him, just as it had been whenever he was returning home as a boy. He took a deep breath and pushed it open.

'Jemme!' his aunt Varda greeted him, planting a huge kiss on his cheek. 'What a delight it is to see you, young man! And looking so handsome too!' she wiped the lipstick mark she had left from his cheek with a dishcloth she had been holding.

'Aunt Varda, it's lovely to see you too,' said Jemme. He had barely got the words out of his mouth before he felt a huge clap on his shoulder,

'Jemme!' he looked up to see Uncle Faisaloo grinning at him. Of all his father's brothers, Faisaloo was the one who looked most like Wadeah, and Jemme could see that, like his father, Faisaloo had barely aged. There were a few more wrinkles around his eyes and he looked a little more worn around the edges, but apart from that he was just as Jemme remembered. What he couldn't believe was how big he felt, compared with Faisaloo. He remembered his father and all his uncles towering over him in childhood. He thought of them as giant men, strong and powerful as they talked knowledgably about the leather business. Although he had been almost the same height and size as them when he had first left, he still couldn't shake the impression he held of them as tall and mighty. Now, confronted with these heroes of his childhood, he felt like he had grown into a man during his time away and he could look them in the eye as equals.

'It's so good to see you Uncle Faisaloo,' he said. Barely had the words left his mouth when another aunt passed through the hallway and uttered a squeal,

'He's here! He's here!' she shouted back down the corridor.

'Aunt Inaam!' Jemme greeted her.

She almost ran over to him, giving him a huge kiss and trying to wrap her arms around him. Her hands didn't quite meet at the back and she laughed,

'My, you're bigger than I remember! I'm glad you're eating alright in Paris at least.'

'The food in France is very good, Aunt Inaam,' Jemme said, 'in fact France is famous for its cuisine.'

Aunt Inaam looked less than convinced, 'Hmmm, well I don't know about that. We've prepared quite the feast for you though, so at least you'll be able to eat some good, honest Turkish cuisine,' she said meaningfully. 'Ah, here's my sister, at last.'

Jemme looked behind her to see his mother moving towards him. She wore a smile on her face, but her eyes brimmed with tears.

'Mama!' he hugged her tenderly. If he had lionised his uncles in childhood, he had known even then that his mother was small, and now she seemed even more so. He felt intensely protective of her, and pulled her away gently to study her face. She had aged, but rather than detract from it, it gave her beauty an added feeling of wisdom. She was still deft and graceful in her movements and held herself with a poise which reminded Jemme of Hil. He turned to her now. Hil had been standing slightly behind him, taking everything in.

'Mama, there's someone very special I'd like you to meet,' he said looking back to his mother, 'this is my girlfriend, Hilyana.'

Hil moved forward and held out her hand, 'Hil,' she said.

Jama squeezed Jemme's hand and turned to Hil. Much like her husband, she ignored the outstretched hand and hugged her.

'I'm so pleased to meet you,' she said, the tears finally spilling over and flowing down her cheeks.

'Mama, are you alright?' Jemme asked.

Jama dabbed at her face with a handkerchief, and laughed at herself a little, 'Oh I'm sorry, I'm being silly. I'm just so pleased to see you, Jemme. I've missed you so very much, and I've been looking forward to this for so long that when I finally saw you, it all got a bit much. I've been looking forward to meeting you too my dear,' she said to Hil. 'We've all been hearing about you for so long and I know how happy you've been making my son.'

'Thank you, Mrs Mafeze,' said Hil.

'Please, you must call me Jama. Have you met everyone here?' she asked, gesturing around the hallway.

'Not quite yet,' laughed Hil as Varda, Faisaloo and Inaam rushed forward to introduce themselves.

'Well, before it gets too crowded in here, why don't we move to the liwan,' said Jama.

'Your grandmother will be here any minute now,' Wadeah told Jemme, emerging from sorting out the cases. 'She's been at a Sufi gathering.'

Jemme felt himself being ushered towards the liwan, with Hil in tow. The room was filled with people and the sound of chatter. There was a heady scent of flowers, and Jemme could see that his mother had brought out all of her favourite vases and filled them with typically Turkish blooms. Deep blue irises and purple lisianthus stood tall in the beautifully cut Murano glass vases on the side tables, whilst small jars on the bookshelves were bursting with fat bunches of lily-of-the-valley, crocuses and freesias.

'It looks beautiful in here, Mama,' he said to his mother, who was talking to Hil and didn't hear him. Before he had time to repeat himself he found his hand being shaken, his cheek kissed and scores of people asking him scores of different questions. What was Paris like? What was the food like? How did it compare with Turkey? When was he moving back?

He found himself introducing Hil to his brothers and sisters, his cousins, the remainder of his aunts and uncles, not to mention neighbours and friends. Hil shook hands, made earnest attempts to remember names, and fielded her own questions – what was Ireland like? How long had she known Jemme for? What did she think of Turkey so far?

As they moved around the room, there was a brief moment of respite. Jemme put his arm around her,

'I'm sorry,' he said, 'I thought it would be like this.'

'Don't be sorry,' said Hil, 'it's lovely that you have so many people that care about you. I've been wanting to meet them all for ages and see this whole part of your life.'

Jemme smiled at her, 'Well you're certainly handling it incredibly well, I'm exhausted already!' He knew Hil thrived on meeting new people, and was immensely proud to show her off. They were standing by a table which bore a heavy crystal vase, filled with strongly scented lilies. He sighed slightly,

'There's one person I still really want you to meet, and I can't see her anywhere.'

'I'm sure she'll be here any minute,' soothed Hil. 'Look!' she said excitedly, 'isn't that her over there?'

As he followed her finger, Jemme realised that he had told Hil about Grandma so often that she was able to recognise her straight away. Sure enough, entering the liwan with a spring in her step was Grandma, still in her black and white Sufi clothes and heading a group of her friends who were similarly attired. Jemme grabbed Hil's hand and made his way through the room to the group.

'Jemme!' he felt his grandmother bundle him into her bony grip. He grinned to himself, pleased to see that her strength hadn't dimmed in the slightest. She held onto him for a long time, and eventually he had to prise himself free, with a little more difficulty than he was expecting.

'I'm so pleased to see you, Grandma!'

'And I you, Jemme,' said Grandma, wreathed in smiles. The contrast to his reunion with his mother could not have been more pronounced. Lily seemed in fine sorts, and before he had a chance to say anything she had beaten him to it, 'Well, don't keep me waiting young man. Aren't you going to introduce me to your *paramour?*'

Jemme laughed, 'Grandma, this is Hil.'

Hil offered her hand and Grandma shook it warmly, 'Lily,' she said.

Jemme smiled slightly at Hil's face. She had evidently been expecting the slightly feeble handshake of an elderly lady.

'Welcome to our home,' Grandma said, 'and for that matter, welcome to Istanbul too. I'm sure Jemme will do a splendid job of showing you around, but I would be happy to take you around too. In fact I would enjoy showing you some of my favourite places.'

'Thank you, Lily, I would like that very much,' said Hil, looking touched.

Jemme suddenly felt a little anxious, 'Grandma, there's probably something I should mention.'

'What is it my love?'

'Well,' Jemme cursed his stupidity. He had become so enthusiastic when talking to the professor, he hadn't stopped to think that Grandma might be put out by someone else devising a tour of her city. 'I'm sorry – I wasn't thinking,

I asked a Professor I met recently to put together a tour of the city for us. I should have just asked you, I just wanted to make sure I had something planned for Hil.'

Lily didn't bat an eyelid, 'Well, that's no problem at all! Don't worry yourself about such things. In fact, I'd very interested to see what this professor makes of Istanbul. It's always interesting to see someone else's take on something you know very well.'

'That's what I was thinking when I asked him to put something together,' Jemme agreed. 'Are you sure you don't mind?'

'Of course not! I can still show Hil some of my favourite places here, and I can show her a bigger picture of Turkey too.' She turned to Hil, 'This country has a beautiful and rich history, which cannot be understood from looking at Istanbul alone. If you have time for some smaller trips whilst you're here, I will make sure you see some things I don't think you can leave Turkey without having visited.'

'I'd like that very much,' said Hil, 'thank you.'

Grandma smiled at her, and Jemme could tell that she had already decided she liked Hil. Lily had just enough time to introduce her friends, many of whom Jemme knew from childhood, before it was time to eat. Gradually everyone in the liwan made their way into the large dining room where the remainder of Jemme's aunts and cousins were laying out platters of food onto low tables, surrounded by cushions which had been brought in especially for the occasion. The dining table had been pushed to one side slightly, to accommodate the extra tables, but was still just as Jemme remembered, with its patina developed with use over the years. Everyone took their places, with immediate family at the dining table, and extended family at the others.

'It all smells so delicious,' said Hil to Jama.

'Thank you,' Jama replied, looking pleased. 'You must help yourself. Take something from each platter – here, start with some *pide*,' she said as she offered a basked of warm bread. Before long they all had plates piled high with delicious mezze. Jemme was impressed by how much effort his family had gone too. Kebabs, crispy *kibbeh,* and bowls of smoky *baba ganoush* seemed to flow endlessly. The crowning glory however, was a lamb, roasted whole on a spit in the kitchen. It had been stuffed with apricots, bulgar, almonds and pine nuts, and cooked slowly so that the meat was tender and infused with flavour. Jemme knew how long it would have taken to prepare and cook, and he was grateful. Such a dish was usually reserved for a very special occasion, and he was pleased that this trip was as important to his parents as it was for him.

Sitting in a room surrounded by everyone he loved and eating wonderful food, Jemme felt a surge of happiness. He remembered one of Grandma's favourite sayings, that there was no greater pleasure than breaking bread with friends, and as he looked around he couldn't have agreed more. There was something else about this meal though. He remembered celebratory feasts from childhood: whenever they were to mark his father's return from a trip, Baba would sit in the central seat at the table. Everyone would be asking him questions and hanging on his answers. He was the sole focus of attention, was passed all the dishes first, and offered more of everything before anyone else. Jemme looked at where he was sitting now, and observed Hil being asked yet another question about France by his sister. He realised that they were the focus of attention for this meal. He had returned to Istanbul an adult, and his family were treating him thus.

The feasting and celebrations continued long into the night, with food, dancing and music. As he had expected, both he and Hil were presented with traditional outfits. Hil looked moved, and he was touched himself. They were made of high quality silk and he was fairly certain the rich embroidery on them had been done by hand. It was yet another sign of the new way in which his family saw him, and he was proud that they were according such an honour to both him and Hil. His father and uncles had also given him a beautiful Hereke carpet. It was just like the one in the liwan, which he knew his parents had received as a wedding present, and the significance was not lost on him. Finally the evening began to draw to a close as people stared to drift back to their respective homes, sated and happy. After all the excitement, Jemme suddenly felt exhausted. It had been a very long day. He looked over at Hil, and although she was listening to Grandma attentively, he could tell that she was tired too.

'Mama, where are we sleeping?' he asked.

'I've put you in your old room and made up one of the guest rooms for Hil,' Jama replied, 'I hope she likes it. I've tried to make it nice and feminine for her, with some flowers and cushions.'

'She'll love it. Do you mind if we head to bed? It's been such a wonderful evening, thank you so much.'

'It's been my pleasure, sweetheart, I hope it was a nice welcome back. Of course you should go to bed, I can imagine how tired you must be after your long journey.'

Jemme waited for Hil to finish her conversation, thanked his parents again and hugged his Grandmother. Hil did the same and they turned to leave.

'Get as much sleep as you can,' Lily told them, 'Tomorrow you must begin exploring Turkey.'

'We will. Thank you all so much again,' Hil said.

As soon as they had left the room, Jemme turned and hugged Hil. He held her for a very long time. 'You were wonderful,' he said eventually. 'They all loved you.'

Slowly separating, they made their way to their rooms, heavy with sleep. Jemme felt almost as if his feet were walking him along the familiar route to his childhood room of their own accord. He yawned as he opened the door and stumbled straight towards the bed, where he instantly fell into a deep and blissful sleep – the sort that can only be experienced by a profoundly happy man. Several hours later, the rest of the family drifted their way to bed. As Jama made her way past Jemme's room to her own, she noticed that the door was ajar and the light on. Softly opening it to bid Jemme a final goodnight, she found her son lying flat on his chest with his hands under the pillow. She smiled, turned out the light for him and shut the door behind herself. Back in the corridor she shook her head; *No matter how important and grown-up Jemme had become, regardless of girlfriends and banks and Paris, he still sleeps just like he did when he was a baby,* she thought.

Chapter Seven

Jemme had slept soundly. There was something wonderful about being back in his childhood room. It was a reliquary of memories, preserved in photos, books and toys. It was familiar and comforting. There was something more though; it was as if this room retained a sort of innocence, preserved outside time. Jemme almost felt as if all his adult worries and concerns had been suspended, as soon as he entered the room. They simply melted away as he took a step back into his childhood. After a deep and dreamless sleep, he woke refreshed and full of excitement. He could hear the house's familiar noises – the birds in the larch tree by his window, the echo of footsteps across the courtyard, and the tiny creaks and groans of wood warming up in the morning sunshine. He washed and dressed, and made his way to the kitchen to find Hil already there, deep in conversation with his mother.

'Good morning, darling,' he said in surprise.

'Morning!' said Hil, kissing him, 'Your mother was just teaching me how to make yoghurt.'

'Oh really?' Jemme asked, knowing his mother would be pleased by Hil's interest, 'Well, you are in for a treat. Turkish breakfasts are a wonderful start to the day, but the Turkish breakfasts in this house are really something special indeed.'

'It's all ready for you next door,' Jama said, 'I'll bring the tea through when it's made.' She shooed them into the liwan, where some of Jemme's aunts were clearing up from the night before. One of the smaller tables had been set for two, with a bright table cloth, covered in small glass dishes.

'I love the amount of choice in meals here,' said Hil.

Jemme laughed, 'I hadn't really thought of it that way, but I suppose you're right – Turkish cooking is very much "a little of what you fancy." Help yourself,' he said, gesturing around. The spread featured all of his favourite breakfast things and he was pleased to see Hil trying different things with enthusiasm, murmuring at little surprises, 'Olives for breakfast!' and '...so much flavour!' as she tried something from every dish. He finished on a chunk of freshly-baked bread, slathered with thick, amber-coloured honey.

'I think I'm full!'

'Me too,' Hil agreed, 'that was one of the most delicious breakfasts I think I've ever had. It was certainly the biggest,' she added.

'You'd better get used to it!' Jemme told her, 'At least it should see us through this morning. Are you ready to get started on the Professor's tour?'

'Absolutely,' said Hil. Jama appeared and took the dishes out of Hil's hands,

'You leave those my dear, I'll deal with them. Go out and explore Istanbul.'

Outside it was sunny with a refreshing breeze, and they walked along hand in hand.

'This is the way I used to walk to school,' Jemme told Hil. She squeezed his hand,

'You must point out all of your favourite places to me. I'm going to imagine you as a young boy here.'

They strolled along, taking in various old shops, coffee houses and restaurants which had featured in Jemme's childhood. Hil was completely taken with the souk and Jemme had some trouble dragging her away.

'I've never seen anything like it in my life,' she said, 'so many things for sale! So many colours! And all the smells too – it was all so….exciting.'

'That's Turkey,' said Jemme happily. He was pleased that Hil was starting to understand.

Everything they visited seemed to further her understanding, revealing a little bit more of the picture to her, just as Jemme had hoped. He had enjoyed her delight at the Topkapi Palace and was pleased to be able to talk her through everything they were seeing there. Over its six hundred years, its four courtyards had been expanded and adapted, and it illustrated the story of the sultans who had lived there perfectly. As they moved through the Gate of Salutation, *Bâb-üs Selâm*, into the second courtyard, Jemme explained the fall of the Ottoman Empire and the passing of the palace into the hands of the government, before becoming an imperial museum. Hil listened attentively whilst Jemme talked her through the different phases of the empire, which roughly matched the different phases of construction in the courtyards they were walking through. They spent several hours taking in the collections of porcelain, ceremonial robes, weapons, shields and murals which were scattered around the palace. Several rooms seemed to be positively filled with treasures, and Hil was fascinated by the beautiful Islamic calligraphic manuscripts, jewellery and Ottoman miniatures. For his part, Jemme was impressed by the way they had been displayed. The showcases were subtle and did not distract from the pieces. What's more they were sympathetic to them, and allowed them to be seen in their rich original contexts. It was a refreshing change to a trope he had been noticing in museums recently which he did not like at all. He had first noticed it in a small French museum and found it deeply irritating, but the more he thought about it, the more he began to notice it elsewhere, sometimes in world-famous institutions. It was all to do with presentation of objects and artefacts. To his mind, an object was a product of its environment. It was an expression of the individual and culture which created it, and often served more as a pointer to certain elements in that culture than as a piece in its own right. Ignoring that was to cut away a hugely important function of the object itself. Furthermore, it altered the way in which people reacted to the artefact. He was tired of seeing beautiful objects put on plain plinths in white rooms underneath harsh lighting. They were utterly devoid of context and anaesthetised from their own meaning. It radically altered the way people perceived them. A hunting spear in a glass case in a museum is looked at merely as an old spear. Jemme felt that the museum's job was to ask questions: What kind of person would have made the spear? Was it a specialist job within the society? Why did they choose this design? Had they experimented with others? Similarly, he had been dismayed once to find a beautifully illustrated mediaeval manuscript on a completely plain white slab, inside a glass box. It was so sterile, and presented the object merely as something to look at, a pretty piece of history rather than a tool which could be used to understand the past. Here in the Topkapi, objects were displayed in their original setting. It gave them so much more meaning; he could imagine them being used by the occupants of the palace in daily life and on special occasions. Helpful little plaques provided interesting information for each piece, and Professor Johnston's notes filled in anything extra.

As they finished at the palace, Jemme made a mental note about the things which had impressed him the most about the museum. Whilst Hil enthused about the history and the objects they had seen, it was the techniques involved in the museum which had interested him most. He didn't know why it seemed a good idea to remember it, but he somehow felt it could be useful in the future. He was visiting so many museums at the moment that he had the opportunity to compare different styles and approaches. He somehow felt that if he could take the best of each, he could put it to good use.

As they continued with the Professor's tour, Jemme was pleased with his decision to commission the project. Professor Johnston had put together an itinerary which gave a very balanced synoptic view. It provided a clear and focussed narrative, which also included a look at Western influence. Jemme was particularly pleased by this element: it would not have been something he would have thought to explore, but it was interesting being able to look at such familiar sights through a different prism. The more he studied the city, in fact, the more he began to see the influence of the West. He wondered if he would have noticed, had it not featured in the Professor's tour. He suspected he might not have done – as a child, he had taken the architecture of all the buildings at face value. It was only later he had started to analyse the traces of different cultures which could be found in a building's makeup. However, by then it was too late to begin analysing any of Istanbul's buildings. He knew them too well; they were as familiar as the faces of old friends. Now he had been away and lived in Western Europe, he could see its influences screaming out at him from every corner. There were classically Beaux-Arts pedimented doors and the distinctive Ionic scrolls and guillouche of the Goût grec period. They were some of the things he had admired most in Parisian architecture, and it seemed odd to see them here. They were familiar from Paris; completely out of context, yet known as part of buildings from his childhood.

The Professor had included a visit to the Dolmabahçe Palace, where the Western influence was so prevalent, Jemme couldn't believe he hadn't noticed it before. As he led Hil around, he explained the history of the place to her, half from his own memory and half from the Professor's notes.

'This was built on land reclaimed from the Bosphorous' he began, 'it was meant to be a replacement for the Topkapi.'

'A replacement?' asked Hil.

'Yes, the sultan, Abdül Mecit I, decided that he wanted a new, modern palace and ordered the construction of the Dolmabahçe.'

'But they're so different!'

'I know, that's what I've been thinking since we arrived. The Topkapi is so Ottoman it's almost a cliché, whilst this is altogether more…'

'European?' suggested Hil.

Jemme smiled at her, 'Exactly. This whole building represents a huge break with tradition. Think about the Topkapi: it was filled with Islamic calligraphy and patterned tiles. Here, it's not just the architecture which reflects European taste, it's the floorplan, the building materials used and the decoration too. It's quite remarkable really, when you think about how quickly the ruling classes changed their idea of what amounted to prestige.'

'It still feels very Turkish though,' remarked Hil.

'Yes, it does, doesn't it? It's quite a hybrid. I think both styles have come together to make something quite beautiful, don't you?'

'Absolutely!' Hil nodded, It's so grand as well – easily more so than many of the palaces I've visited in Europe.'

'Here, let me show you something really special,' said Jemme, taking her hand. He led her into the Ceremonial Hall. She breathed in sharply as they entered, and even though he had been there before, he was still momentarily stopped in his tracks.

'It's magnificent,' said Hil, 'It's unbelievably big too.'

Jemme glanced down at the Professor's notes, 'Apparently it's capable of holding two and a half thousand people,' he said. They both looked around, and then up at the domed ceiling. A vast chandelier shimmered with light, and Jemme was reminded of the one his father had brought back from Venice many years before. He looked at his notes again. Professor Johnston had diligently provided facts on everything, and he was able to tell Hil that the chandelier was four and a half tons and probably the heaviest in the world. They wandered through the hall and continued exploring. The palace was just as impressive as the Topkapi, but for completely different reasons, and it provided a nice counterbalance. Hil was deeply impressed by the Crystal Staircase, with its banisters of pure Baccarat crystal, whilst Jemme was mesmerised by the ceilings. Almost every one was a work of art. There was something special about ceiling decoration, and he found himself drawn to it instantly. It was one of the first things he noticed in museums and galleries, and it was easily his favourite feature amongst the riches of Versailles. He found it staggering that sometimes people simply did not look up. They could spend hours wandering around a palace completely oblivious to the fabulous decoration above their heads.

'What does "Dolmabahçe" mean?' asked Hil.

'I suppose it translates literally as "filled garden",' said Jemme, as they turned a corner and he realised they had come full circle 'Have you seen enough? I could do with a coffee break, and we can get you some of that proper Turkish Delight I promised you on the plane.

'That sounds wonderful,' said Hil.

They left the palace and wandered along the Bosphorous, which glittered and glinted under the sun.

'I had no idea it was all so beautiful,' said Hil, 'I know that's how you described it, but I don't think you can truly understand until you've seen it with your own eyes.'

'I know. It's odd though, I'm seeing it through slightly different eyes now. It's not any the less beautiful, but I'm certainly noticing things I didn't when I was living here. I suppose as I've grown up and learned more, I'm understanding things differently and certain things take on new meaning for me too.'

'I suppose that's inevitable when you've been away from somewhere for a while, especially if it's a place where you spent a very formative period,' said Hil, 'I sometimes feel a little like that when I go back to Ireland, and I visit fairly regularly. I can imagine how it must feel for you, coming back here.'

Jemme was pleased she understood. He took her hand, 'Let's see about that coffee,' he said.

By the time they returned home that evening they both felt they had learned something about Istanbul.

Lily was waiting for them in the courtyard, 'How was it?'

'Fantastic,' enthused Hil, 'I felt like we saw so much. I really got a feel for what it was like for Jemme to be here as a child, and I learned so much about the city too.'

'Good, good – I'm pleased,' said Lily, 'what about you, Jemme?' she asked, turning to her grandson, 'Was everything as you left it?' she teased.

'Sort of, Grandma.'

'"Sort of?' Has something been moved?' she said with a little cackle.

'No everything looked exactly as I remembered it; there's just lots that I hadn't noticed before.'

Lily looked interested, 'Really? Anything in particular?'

'I think it's mostly the amount of Western influences in the buildings. Throughout my childhood I never questioned it, but today it was all I seemed to notice.'

'It was a good observation, my love. There are traces of Western influences throughout this city. Sometimes I even feel as if there are two worlds here: the old Ottoman imperial world with all its splendours, and then the modern world of the nineteenth-century empire. The latter is heavily influenced by the West, but no less Turkish for it. One might think external influences would dilute the culture somehow, but it just enriches it, stretching the tradition and adding to it. I believe some people even call it "Ottoman Rococo" or something along those lines. I hope you got to see some proper examples of it. I know you'd be very interested in it, Jemme, and it sounds like you might be too, Hil.'

'Oh yes, definitely!' said Hil, 'In fact we visited somewhere exactly like that today. We spent a good couple of hours at the Dolmabahçe Palace this afternoon. So much of it looked like places I have visited back in France, but yet it was married with an incredibly Turkish style of decoration.'

'You're starting to sound like Jemme!' said Grandma. 'The decoration of a place is one of the first things he notices too. I'm pleased you went though, and pleased you enjoyed your day as well. I think supper is nearly ready, I can tell you all about the ideas I've had over whilst we eat. Come on!' She set off at a sprightly pace and led the way to the dining room.

Over another delicious Levantine meal, Hil and Jemme told Jemme's family all about their day. The evening was much more sedate than the night before, with just siblings, parents and Grandma. Even though that made some fifteen people, it still felt like an intimate gathering, especially compared with the previous evening, and Hil was glad of the chance to spend some time with the immediate family. As they discussed their day, Lily added little pieces of information – small bits of history, long-forgotten folk tales attached to particular places and poems written about certain palaces and buildings. It coloured the stories and wove them all together. Hil studied her as she spoke. She was clearly an old lady and yet her face was as smooth as the tiles in the courtyard. She spoke with authority, and moved with a suppleness and deftness which belied her years. She seemed to have perfect recall and her knowledge was staggeringly broad and yet incredibly detailed too. As Hil listened to her explaining the reasons Western influences had begun to creep in during the nineteenth century, she shook her head slightly in wonder. It was clear why Jemme was fiercely loyal to his grandmother and why he had such keen respect for her too.

After the meal, everyone moved to the liwan and Jama brought in a large tray full of cups. She set it down and returned a moment later with a large teapot, steaming at the spout.

Lily saw Hil looking at it, 'Green tea,' she said, 'it's wonderful for the digestion. Here, let me pour you a cup,' she said springing to her feet.

As Jemme and Hil sipped their teas Lily talked to them about Turkey. She was a natural storyteller and Hil realised where Jemme's love of stories had grown from. She sat spellbound, listening to Lily talking of imperial palaces, splendid caliphs and wise sufis. There was almost something magical about the tales and they left her hungry for more. Lily told them of places where they could find Arabic thoroughbreds, desert ruins and holy places of pilgrimage. Hil wanted to visit them all – she wanted to see and experience everything she had heard about, and to grab Turkey with both hands, as if it were a precious treasure. By the time she went to bed her head was swimming with excitement and vivid images of camel caravans into the desert, and great leaders in their ceremonial dress.

Jemme came to wake her the next morning, 'Good morning, sweetheart, did you sleep well?'

'Yes, I did,' she replied. 'I had such vivid dreams though – I think it's hearing all of your Grandma's stories right before bed time.'

'I can well understand that!' said Jemme, smiling privately to himself.

'You looked like you were enjoying listening to her last night.'

'I was, very much. She has a way of describing things that's almost.....magical. There was once a great tradition of storytelling in Ireland too you know. People who excelled at it were legendary, and people would come from miles around to hear them speak. It's almost completely died out now though.' Hil said a little sorrowfully, 'That's why I enjoyed hearing your Grandma talk so much. It's such a wonderful gift to have, and so pleasing to find that there are parts of the world where the tradition is thriving.'

'I wouldn't go that far; it's dying out in Turkey too I'm afraid,' said Jemme, 'Grandma's part of the old guard. It's like she's a repository of forgotten practices and crafts. She tries to teach them to younger people as much as she can: the continuity of tradition is one of her big passions.'

'Well, I'm pleased it is,' said Hil, 'I'm glad that certain things are being kept alive.'

'Absolutely. Are you still keen to visit the places she mentioned?'

Hil nodded, 'Definitely.'

'Me too. I was thinking about it this morning. They're all quite spread out and we don't want to have to spend days and days travelling, so I think it might be best if we fly. I just wanted to check with you first.'

'That's absolutely fine, I'm looking forward to it,' said Hil.

The next couple of days continued as the first two. Tours of Istanbul were interspersed with breaks in little cafés, feasts with Jemme's family, and stories with Grandma. They took in the Galata Tower with its distinctive cone cap, the Bankalar Caddesi at the heart of the Ottoman financial world and, of course, the beautiful Hagia Sophia. Piles of kebabs, huge bowls of *tabbouleh* and great platters of mezze later, they found themselves packing small cases for their next destination, and wishing everyone a temporary farewell. Wadeah drove them back to the airport, 'I told you about the feeding, didn't I?' he said light heartedly during the journey.

'Goodness yes!' exclaimed Hil, 'I don't think I've ever eaten so much in my life. It's all so delicious, though that I find it difficult to refuse anything.'

Wadeah caught her eye in the rear-view mirror and smiled, 'Well I'm pleased, and I know Jama will be delighted to hear that her cooking's been so well received. Here we are now,' he said, drawing up the car and opening the doors for them. He took their cases in with them, hugged them both and wished them a pleasant trip. Jemme lead Hil to a different section of the airport, which dealt with domestic flights, and found the check-in desk. Compared with the plane they had arrived in from France, the aircraft was tiny, with two furiously spinning propellers which caused strange jittering shafts of light to fall across the seats inside. The flight only lasted for an hour or so, and as the little plane touched down onto the tarmac again, Jemme squeezed Hil's hand, 'You're becoming quite the Turkish adventurer, my love – another city already!'

'I know, it's so exciting,' said Hil, as the plane drew to a halt.

'Well here we are,' said Jemme, 'welcome to Konya, sweetheart.'

After they found their way through arrivals and out onto the street, Jemme hailed them a taxi, 'It's no way near as big as Istanbul,' he told Hil, 'but it would still take us too long to walk.' He shut her safely inside and ran around to sit in the front passenger seat, showing the driver the address on a piece of paper. The driver nodded and took off at breakneck speed. Hil looked alarmed and grabbed the armrest. Jemme laughed, 'Not everyone in Turkey drives like my father, I'm afraid!'

The driver darted down back streets, undertook and cut across before finally screeching to a halt outside a small white house with cobalt shutters. Jemme thanked him and laughed again when he saw Hil's face,

'We're here now, sweetheart, don't worry.' He took their bags up the steps and knocked on the front door. A tiny woman opened it, saw Jemme and squealed,

'Jemme! I've been looking forward to seeing you!' she said, squeezing his arm.

'*Salamat*, Maimy Badriya,' Jemme said, leaning down to kiss her on the cheek. 'I'd like you to meet my girlfriend, Hil. Hil, this Badriya; she's a great friend of my grandmother's and we're going to be staying in her guesthouse here.'

'*Salamat,* Hil,' said Badriya smiling welcomingly at Hil.

'*Mahrabat*, Badriya,' Hil replied, a little nervously.

Badriya laughed, 'That was perfect, well done! Come in, I'll show you around.'

The guesthouse was clean and comfortable, and Badriya fussed around after them, making sure they had everything they needed. 'Have a mint tea with me before you head out,' she said, 'I haven't seen you since you were just a boy and I'd love to hear all about your adventures.' The three of them sat at a wobbly table in the cosy kitchen and drank their tea, whilst Jemme recounted his life in Paris to date. When Badriya looked satisfied, Hil took her turn, 'I understand you're one of Lily's Sufi friends?'

'I am, yes. My goodness, Lily and I have probably known each other since before you were born! We were dervishes together and we still practice *dhikr* together sometimes. Of course, we don't see each other nearly as much now as we did when we were younger. I suppose she's told you about the history of Sufism?'

Hil nodded, 'Both she and Jemme have given me a good background.'

'You do know that not all Sufis are Dervishes though, my dear? That's something very specific to the Mevlevi order.'

'Yes, Lily told me a great deal about the Mevlevis – that's why we're here. She wanted us to be able to see the birthplace of the order, and to visit Rumi's tomb.'

'I'm pleased you're so interested. Often people do not take the trouble to understand such things. I'm sure you'll find lots here that will interest you and perhaps even surprise you.'

'I'm sure we will,' said Hil.

'It was lovely to catch up with you, Maimy Badriya,' said Jemme, rising from the table, 'but if you don't mind, I think we should get started – we've got lots to see.'

'Of course, of course. Will you join me for supper when you've finished?'

'We'd like that very much,' said Hil warmly.

It took Jemme a little while to find his bearings once they were outside, but soon they were making their way into the centre. As they walked, Jemme told Hil a little more about the history of the place. Grandma had told him stories of Konya throughout his childhood, and he remembered them all with ease. He told her of its early history under the Hittites and then the Phrygians. He described its capture by Alexander the Great and then its rule under the kings of Pergamon.

'It all sounds so romantic,' said Hil, 'all these ancient rulers and civilisations, with their wonderful names.'

'Romantic maybe, but not exactly peaceable. The whole town was destroyed more than once by Arab invaders and the Seljuk Turks did quite a bit of damage before they eventually made it their capital. They're not the only ones who took the city either; even the Crusaders tried their luck.'

'The Crusaders?'

'Yes, Godefroi de Bouillon and then Frederick Barbarossa some hundred years later, but neither had much success.'

'It's so interesting seeing Crusader history from the other side.' said Hil, 'It's something that gets taught to us in a very simplistic fashion at school, but they never stop to explain what the impact in the Levant might have been, or what its consequences were.'

'That's another of Grandma's favourite points.' said Jemme, 'She believes that history cannot be properly understood before thoroughly examining both sides. She believes someone who's never thought about something from the other side is condemned to a life of half-knowledge.'

'She's a wise lady.'

'Yes she is,' said Jemme, slipping his hand around Hil's waist.

He took her around some of the notable sights in the centre and showed her the Alaeddin Mosque, which began life as a church. However, it was Rumi's mausoleum and the Mevlâna Museum attached to it which took up the majority of their day. The museum was excellent and gave a clear but interesting account of Sufi history. Again, Jemme found himself taking note of presentation, and the way that certain ideas were communicated. He was impressed by the diligent research which had evidently gone into each information plaque, and enjoyed seeing the collection of antique Sufi instruments; they reminded him exactly of the ones Grandma's friends used to carry when he would watch them gather for their Sufi meetings. They had both been impressed by the mausoleum itself. It was highly decorated with carved wood and brocade. Rumi's sarcophagus sat on a raised platform, and Hil looked quite moved as she stared at it.

When they finally left, Jemme asked her if she'd enjoyed being able to see such a historic figure's burial place.

'Yes, I did,' Hil replied. 'There was something about that room too. I could feel it as soon as we stepped in. There was a very solemn and dignified atmosphere – it made the hairs on the back of my neck stand up, and it reminded me of holy sites of pilgrimage they would sometimes take us to, when I was at school in Ireland.'

'I'm pleased it made an impression,' said Jemme. 'I'm sure Badriya will be interested to hear all about it too.'

✻   ✻   ✻   ✻

The trip to Konya was only a short one, and after dinner and then breakfast with Badriya, they had said their farewells, promised to visit again and got another taxi back to the airport.

'Where's our next stop?' asked Hil, more to distract herself from the driver's swerving and honking than anything else.

'Aleppo,' said Jemme, 'and then we'll stop at Palmyra on the way back.'

'I can't believe we're visiting another country already!' said Hil.

'I know. It's been quite the whistle-stop tour. Turkey and Syria have a lot in common though and often people study their shared history in the context of the history of the Levant.'

'Is that why Lily recommended we come here?'

'Probably, although I have to confess I may have influenced her decision a little. There's a piece of history here which interests me a great deal and I'd love to show you.'

'How intriguing,' said Hil.

Several hours and another small plane later they found themselves in Aleppo. As they made their way into the centre in yet another taxi, Hil stared out of the window,

'It's so big, especially after Konya.'

'I know, it's still the biggest city in Syria. It was the third largest in the Ottoman Empire for hundreds of years too.'

'Really? After which cities?'

'Ah, now you're testing me! Cairo and Constantinople I believe.'

As they found the hotel Jemme had reserved, he recounted a potted history of the city,

'But that's barely even scratching the surface,' he concluded, 'there have been people here since the Bronze Age – it's one of the oldest continuously inhabited cities in the world. I've given you the briefest outline of the Ottoman and French periods, I haven't even mentioned Alexander the Great, or got started on the Sassanids.'

Eventually they found the hotel and checked in. Although it was perfectly nice, it felt a little cold after the homely atmosphere of the guesthouse in Konya. They were only staying one night though, before heading off on the next leg of their tour. By now it was lunchtime and so they made their way towards the large Sabaa Bahrat square to find some food. As they wandered, Hil took in her surroundings.

'I can't believe the mix on styles here. Some of these buildings look baroque and some even look Norman. They're all so different in age too.'

'That's what comes from such a long period of continuous occupation – the Romans, Byzantines, Seljuks, Ottomans and French have all left their traces here – even the Mamluks, if you look closely enough. There are all sorts of architectural styles and ideas at work within the city, sometimes completely at odds with each other. I love it though. I would hate everything to look exactly the same, like some purpose-built town. Personally I think it all comes together here to give the city a unique identity.'

'I agree. I was thinking the same thing back in Istanbul – when two different styles come together, the new hybrid style is often better than the original two were individually. It's as if people have the opportunity to pick the best parts of each and make something more refined.'

'My thinking exactly. Goodness, you're starting to sound like me.'

'That's what your grandmother said.'

'Did she? Well, like you said, she's a wise lady.'

After a quick kebab lunch they made their way along the ancient town walls.

'There's so much you simply must see here,' said Jemme, 'and I promise we'll come back at some point and do a proper trip. For now though, I really wanted to show you this.' They stopped outside an inconspicuous door.

'I thought we were going to a museum,' said Hil.

'We are. This is a little privately run museum – it's not always open and you won't find it in any of the guidebooks.'

Hil looked curious, but stooped through the low doorway as Jemme held the door open for her.

She straightened up inside and looked around the room they were in. The walls were completely covered with paintings of horses, prints of horses and sketches of horses. Display cabinets contained old yellowing documents outlining what looked like family trees, and a small bronze figurine of a horse sat on a plinth in three of the room's four corners.

'I don't understand,' said Hil, 'what has Aleppo got to do with horses?'

'Absolutely everything,' said Jemme. Hil looked none the wiser, so he guided her over to one of the walls, 'Let's start here. I'll show you round – I have no idea where the curator is,' he added, looking around.

'I don't think I've ever told you, but riding is a passion of mine,' he began

'No, you haven't – I had absolutely no idea.'

'Well, it's something I haven't been able to do for a long time, because I've been busy with the bank, but I've ridden since childhood. If I find myself living outside Paris I would dearly love to have my own thoroughbred, but it's just not practical at the moment. Anyway, that brings me to why we're here. People use the word "thoroughbred" all the time, but not many people know what it truly means. The purity of the line is very important, which is why you can see all these pedigree charts here,' he gestured to the cabinets. 'Ultimately though, every thoroughbred must be able to trace its origins back to one of three founding stallions.'

'You mean to tell me that all thoroughbred horses are all descended from the same three original horses?'

'That's exactly what I mean.'

'I still don't understand why the museum is here though.'

'Well, although the three horses ended up in England, each one was imported from this area.'

'Really?'

'Yes – Arabian stallions have been famous for a long time, and these horses were legendary. Their names were Darley Arabian, Byerly Turk and Godolphin Arabian. The Darley Arabian was brought to England at the beginning of the eighteenth century, by one Darley Thomas. He had travelled all the way to Aleppo, to this exact spot, to buy the horse. This little museum has been built over the site of the stables.'

Hil looked around at the pictures on the walls and took in the documents in the cabinet. She took a moment to study her surroundings, 'This has all been so interesting. I don't just mean this part, I mean this whole trip. I've learned so much about Turkey and the Levant, and I've learned so much about you too. I feel like I know you so much better now that I've seen where you come from and met your family. I've loved finding out all these new things about you too.'

'I'm so pleased you're enjoying yourself, sweetheart.'

'Of course I am,' said Hil, reaching out to embrace him, 'I can't wait for our next adventure.

Chapter Eight

Only four days after leaving Istanbul, Jemme and Hil found themselves in yet another city. Palmyra was around two hundred kilometres north of Damascus, and hadn't taken them too long to reach from Aleppo. It provided a nice stopping point on the journey back, and as she sat in the courtyard of the small guesthouse they had checked into, Hil was grateful for the rest. Although the trip so far had been enjoyable, it had also been tiring and this small moment of respite was greatly needed. The sun shone fiercely down onto the tiled courtyard, but a small table and two rickety chairs sat underneath the shade of a slightly saggy palm tree. She took a sip of pomegranate juice and stretched lazily. Looking around the courtyard she realised that it could have been a scene from any era. She took in her white linen trousers and billowy kaftan top, and realised that she too could be a figure from a different era, an extension of the ancient adobe house whose walls surrounded the courtyard.

She knew little about the town, but already had begun to feel the romance of the desert. Perhaps it was the timelessness of the place, the endless sweeping desolation which had drawn so many to it and started a life-long love affair for the likes of T.E. Lawrence. It had occupied its own unique place in culture, literature and art: a vast, immutable landscape that modern man could no more leave his mark on than the Palmyrans had, two millennia ago. She couldn't believe how foreign the Levant had been to her until so recently. It had seemed so far away, so 'other', emerging only in fleeting references within Western literature and art. Now she was here, she found it intoxicating. She was already keen to explore Palmyra, which she knew was the jewel in the desert crown. Lily had spoken about it with an infectious passion, and Hil couldn't wait to see it for herself. A shadow was cast across the book she was reading, and she looked up to see Jemme approaching,

'Good afternoon, sweetheart.' he said leaning down to kiss her, 'You look just like Grace Kelly in that hat.'

'Really?'

'Absolutely, sort of like a glamorous desert traveller.'

'Well, I don't know about glamour – I think it's too hot for that, but I've been thinking about how romantic this place feels.'

'It's amazing isn't it?' said Jemme, 'There's something about the desert that feels so mysterious and yet alluring – once you've lived in a country like this it never leaves you. No matter how much I think of myself as a Parisian now, a part of me has never left places like this.'

Hil cocked her head and squinted up at him, 'I can see why. I can't imagine how grey, sprawling European cities would look after this endless freedom.'

'Not so much for me, because I grew up in a city too; but the nomadic peoples here, like the Bedouins sometimes find it extremely difficult to adapt to a sedentary lifestyle. It must be so strange; living within four solid walls in a fixed place after a lifetime of being able to pack up camp and head off whenever you liked.'

Hil nodded her head in agreement, it all seemed so far away from her own upbringing; back in Ireland.

The rest of the afternoon passed in a warm golden haze. Hil and Jemme relaxed in the courtyard; eating dates and discussing their journey whilst the sun came down. The darkness was total except for the little oil lamps set outside the guest house to guide people back to their rooms. It brought an intense chill with it and, shivering slightly, they returned to their rooms for an early night ahead of an early start.

The next morning Hil softly woke Jemme up,

'What time is it?' he asked gruffly turning over,

'Just before five,' Hil replied, turning on the lamp on the bedside table.

Jemme groaned and Hil prodded him, 'You said it would be worth it,'

'I know, I know… and it will be,' he said stirring to life, 'I just wish it wasn't so early!'

Hil chuckled and began pulling on her clothes. It was far too early to be contemplating breakfast, and so only about ten minutes after waking they found themselves standing in the inky blackness outside the guesthouse.

'What if he doesn't come?' whispered Hil, stamping her feet a little to wake herself up.

'He's the owner's cousin. I'm sure he's reliable. Look! Here he is now,' Jemme said pointing in front of him.

It was a slightly useless gesture – he couldn't see his own hand, and so it was unlikely Hil could either. What they both could see however were the two circles of light coming towards them from the distance. As they drew closer they became bigger and the gentle thrum of an engine became audible. Eventually the Jeep drew up next to them and a shortish man got out, looking just as sleepy as Hil and James.

Jemme greeted him in Turkish and thanked him for agreeing to drive them. Hil stepped forward and smiled at him, and he cracked a wide grin before talking animatedly to Jemme again and gesturing at Hil. She looked questioningly at Jemme, who laughed.

'I'm afraid he doesn't speak any English my love, but he said you are very beautiful and well worth driving through the desert for.'

Hil blushed slightly, '*Teşekkür ederim*,' she said as gracefully as she could.

The man smiled again and opened the door for her. Jemme climbed in after her and soon they were off.

Driving through the desert was a strange experience. Initially Hil found it terrifying; she was used to city driving down broad, brightly-lit roads. There was only one way to do everything and cars hurtled past each other at high speeds, safe within the confines of their narrow lanes. It was complete anathema to drive into the black and the unknown like this. She kept bracing herself for some sort of collision. Jemme squeezed her knee,

'Are you alright, sweetheart?'

'I'm fine, I'm just finding this a little strange, that's all – we can't see anything!'

Jemme laughed kindly, 'But there's nothing to see!'

Hil thought about it a little and began to relax. It was true: the two channels of light the headlights picked out showed up nothing but indistinguishable tracks of sand. There seemed little chance of bumping into anything in any direction, even if they drove for hours and hours. That was something else, Hil thought to herself: they could drive for hours and hours and not look like they'd left this exact spot. There was absolutely nothing to give any idea of distance or scale. The darkness only made it more disorientating.

She leaned in to Jemme, 'How does he know where he's going?!' she whispered.

'To be honest, I don't know. People like Faisal know the desert like the back of their hands though. Families who have been here for centuries pass the knowledge down through the generations, and the children grow up learning how to navigate their way through landscapes like this. I think now everyone has cars, it's sort of accelerated that learning: they get to see a lot more of the desert a lot faster and so they really understand how it all fits together. They still have a healthy respect for it, though. I would never drive out here with anyone who wasn't a local. You always hear of tourists who don't understand the desert and head out without any fear of it. They always find themselves in some sort of sticky situation – so many people don't understand how inhospitable it can be here.'

Hil nodded, 'I can imagine,' she said, now completely relaxed.

The driver too seemed relaxed, his earlier tiredness completely gone. He chattered away, frequently leaving the wheel completely to turn around to them and cackle at some joke he'd just made, or point out various features in the rickety Jeep.

Jemme joined in gamely and Hil tried to laugh in the right places, and look suitably impressed when shown a seatbelt buckle that still weakly functioned.

As they drove on, the sky began to lighten around them. The black peeled back from the desert floor and a cold blue began to rise on the horizon. Soon they were slowing to a stop and the driver was opening the door for Hil again. She stepped out and looked around. There was enough light to be able to make out four or five blurry shapes next to them, and she was amazed to see that they were other vehicles. She couldn't believe that after an hour and a half's drive into the nothingness they had ended up in exactly the same spot as at least five other people. The driver saw her gaze, nodded, and said something to Jemme who turned back to Hil,

'He says the sunrise draws many people. He expects more will arrive in the next twenty minutes or so.' Jemme drew Hil to him and hugged one arm around her. She was swaddled in scarves but still shivered slightly in the dawn air.

'Let's find a good spot,' he said.

She nodded and walked with him along the ridge of sand they'd parked next to. The driver yawned and looked at his watch. He rummaged in his pocket and pulled out a pack of cigarettes, then went off to find the other drivers.

Jemme and Hil wandered along the ridge for a little while before it turned into a small plateau.

'This will be perfect,' said Jemme, stopping. He unwound the thick kufiya he was wearing around his neck and smoothed it out onto the ground. It was as large as a picnic blanket and they both sat down, huddling in next to each other. Just visible about two hundred yards away, he saw another couple doing a similar thing,

'I thought this was a good spot!' he said.

'I'm sure it is,' said Hil, 'how long do you think it will be?'

'It's hard to tell – it's not really something you can pinpoint,' Jemme replied, 'strictly speaking, it's already started. You saw the blue sky emerging as we were driving here. I suppose it's all just an extension of that. You're in for a treat though sweetheart: seeing the sun rise over Palmyra is an incredible experience, and something I feel everyone should see before they die.'

'Well, let's hope it's worth getting up for,' she said teasing him slightly.

Sure enough, over the next twenty minutes the sand around them gradually became dotted with other couples and young families. Some had come prepared with flasks of tea, others had not, and looked wistfully at the kufiya Hil and Jemme sat on as they fidgeted on the sand.

Just as Jemme had said, the sunrise had been underway for some time. The sky had been turning slowly from indigo to a light blue as they had been speaking, when suddenly a bolt of brilliant pink pierced the horizon. As it shimmered, swathes of rich yolky yellow spilled out either side and painted their way across the blurry line where sand met sky. Hil was mesmerised; she had seen sunrises before, but the colours were so vivid that she couldn't quite believe they were real. As it gradually emerged and revealed its shape, the sun seemed so massive too. It was as if there was nothing between her and the great sphere of brilliant, colourful light in front of her. It felt like a rare and special encounter in an otherworldly landscape. She was completely spellbound.

As the sun pulled into the sky it illuminated the valley below, which was thick with early morning mist. The mist seemed to scatter the red light of the rising sun, making the stone structures glow orange. Hil gasped, 'I had no idea there was so much of it!'

Jemme put his arm around her and they watched the desert town slowly reveal itself.

Huge amounts of stone grew up out of the desert floor, arching over into porticos and tunnelling out into long, elegant colonnades. As the sky became lighter, they began to see temples and great columned buildings too. Finally, the last vestiges of darkness had been washed away, and there it was in front of them, sand-blown and dusty – the perfect remains of a city.

'I'm so pleased you got to see it like this,' Jemme said to Hil.

'I can't think of a more perfect way of seeing it,' she said. 'It's beautiful.'

'I know. I've seen it a few times, but always as a child. Watching the sun rise with a group of other thirteen year old boys is a very different experience to watching it as an adult with someone you love. In many ways I feel like I'm seeing it for the first time too. Are you ready to explore?'

He held out his hand and pulled Hil up. As she stretched out her stiff limbs, he shook the sand from the scarf and wound it around his neck again. They slowly edged their way down from the plateau and made their way towards the city below them. The ground soon flattened out and they found the stone path which lead the way to one of the major gates.

'This is an original path,' Jemme said, 'This is exactly how people would have approached the city in ancient times.' He squeezed Hil's hand.

As they neared the city, it loomed large over them, 'It's hard to get an idea of scale when you're seeing it from above,' Hil said.

'I know what you mean,' said Jemme, 'you can appreciate how big the site is, but not how impressive all of the features are in their own right.'

Hil nodded as she craned her neck backwards to take in the tops of the columns they were walking past. The steady sunshine turned the stone from pinkish gold to warm yellow, revealing the high quality of the masonry and the preservation of the ruins themselves, something which Hil commented on.

'I suppose it's the perfect conditions for them to survive,' said Jemme, 'people sometimes say that this place is "More Rome than Rome" and I'm only now beginning to see why.'

'How do you mean?'

'Well, firstly, it's the character and style of the place. It's so quintessentially Roman. Perversely, if it had been in Italy it might have shown more influences from different cultures. It's such a remote outpost that it's almost as if they've made more of an effort to recreate Rome. It's a bit like when you find ex-pat communities far from home today – their version of their home countries is always an exaggerated version. It's a little bit of a caricature, and almost a bit like a theme park.'

Hil nodded, 'That's definitely true. I suppose it's because they're so protectionist – they want to preserve a perfect little slice of home.'

'Exactly, whereas "home" will be a dynamic, constantly changing and evolving place, their recreation will be static and almost museum-esque. I feel that Palmyra is almost a bit like that. It sort of leads me to my second point too, which is also slightly counterintuitive. I think the fact that Palmyra is a ruined city is what has preserved it so well.'

'How can that have preserved it?'

'Well it makes it into a snapshot – a frozen image if you like. If it had been continuously inhabited then it would have been modified and adapted. It's not like there were heritage preservation societies in Roman times, so bits would have been lopped off, burnt down and materials reused. Who knows what might have been lost, if it hadn't been ruined.'

'I see what you mean. I suppose the location has helped in a different way too,' Hil said. 'It's not as if the ruins are competing with anything else for space. I mean, when it comes to it, Rome is still a modern, functioning capital city. Over time, ruins have been built over and incorporated into other things. Here, there's no pollution, no damp and heaps of space. It could sit here for a hundred years completely undisturbed and look exactly the same at the end of it as it does today.'

'Exactly,' said Jemme, pleased that Hil was thinking about things in the same way he was.

They found themselves walking along a broad colonnade, flanked by columns which still soared proudly into the air two thousand years after they had first been planted into the ground.

Hil looked upwards and took in the crumbled figures topping the better-preserved columns.

'Are those statues?'

Jemme followed her gaze.

'Sadly, they're not very well preserved, but yes. Each one is modelled on a real member of the patrician class who benefited the city in some way. It's quite a nice piece of civic innovation. Historians believe that town authorities ran a campaign to raise money for the construction of this colonnade; wealthy merchants were encouraged to sponsor a column, and anyone who paid for the full construction of a column could top it with a statue of himself. It demonstrates quite a bit of modern marketing savvy, I think: the town gained a prestigious entranceway, and the wealthy had the opportunity to become a visible part of that prestige, immortalising themselves in the process.'

The statues were in various states of repair; much like the gargoyles on a cathedral, some were no more than a shapeless lump but some were strikingly detailed, with folds on togas and curls in beards still clearly visible. As they walked past them, they imagined the grain and cloth merchants who would have sponsored their construction, and stood on the same stone path to look proudly up at their own marble likenesses.

'How was the rest of the city financed?' Hil asked, 'Do you know if whole buildings were sponsored by different individuals in the same way as these columns?'

'I don't know,' said Jemme, 'it's hard to tell when there's no obvious sign, like these statues. The city was very wealthy though – I think Grandma was telling you a little about its history, and how it was an important stop on the caravan route.'

'Yes, she was;' said Hil, 'she told me all about the trade routes criss-crossing through this area and how strategically placed this city was. She didn't go into too much detail though; she said she wanted me to experience it in its purest form, so that I could build a completely unprejudiced mental picture which I could start to colour later.'

Jemme laughed, 'She was exactly the same with me when I was a child. When I was excited about going somewhere she would become infuriatingly recalcitrant and go completely silent on some topics. I think she knew what she was doing though – I really feel that so many of the experiences I had were more meaningful because she left me just enough space for my own imagination. I'm glad you've heard a bit of Palmyra's history though; perhaps I can tell you what I know as we wander around. Where do you fancy heading next?'

Hil pointed to a square building with a large porticoed entrance, 'Over there,' she said.

As they made their way over, Jemme told her everything he could remember about Palmyra; how the wealthy caravan city stood at the cross-roads of several civilisations, and how it was at one time considered one of the most important cultural centres in the world. Hil ran her eyes over the column stumps and the temple ruins, trying to imagine how they would have looked in an oasis thriving with culture and industry.

'Here we go;' said Jemme as they reached the building Hil had pointed out, 'this is the Temple of Ba'al,' he added. 'It was one of the first things I can remember seeing here when I came with the Scouts.'

'Can you remember anything about it?' Hil asked.

'Let's see,' Jemme screwed up his face a little, 'I can remember that this isn't the whole temple by any means. It would have been much, much bigger than this. This is only the most central part – it would have been the shrine.'

Hil looked at the beautiful columns, which enclosed the shrine protectively. It seemed strange to think that the most sacred and holy part of the temple, the inner sanctum, had been bared to the desert like this, 'It's odd – it looks so Roman, but at the same time, it's almost a little bit Greek,' she said to Jemme, as they began to walk around the temple's shrine.

'Ah, now that's something I can remember learning about. It's because of these pilasters – they're very Corinthian. In fact the front is very Corinthian too with the double set of columns in the portico.'

Hil looked at him admiringly, 'Very impressive!'

Jemme smiled; sometimes he felt awkward talking about things which interested him, around other people, as if they might think he was showing off. It was so easy around Hil though; she was genuinely interested to hear and often contributed things of her own too.

'If you've seen enough here, I'll show you the Camp of Diocletian,' he said, 'It's at the exact opposite end of the city and the best way to approach it is from here.'

Hil looked intrigued, 'Lead the way,' she said.

They continued walking around the temple until they were behind it. Standing with their backs to the temple they could see a great path stretching out in front of them. It was broad and lined with evenly cut smooth flagstones, although this was far from being the most impressive feature: colonnades ran down either side of them, defining the edges of the path and turning it into a grand entranceway. Many of the columns were in a remarkable state of repair and it was obvious that they had all been richly decorated at one point. Although they had crumbled and broke the line in places, the colonnades ran in an almost uninterrupted continuous chain from the start of the path to the end.

'It's so long!' Hil said as she squinted towards the end.

'I know,' said Jemme, 'it's remarkable isn't it? From memory it's just over a kilometre, so that makes two kilometres of columns. You can see how detailed they were too – look,' he said pointing to embellishments around the base of one column.

'Would this have been the main route through the town?' Hil asked.

'It would have been more than that,' said Jemme, 'the whole town would have been planned around this pathway.'

'But that seems to be in completely the wrong order; a path is only defined by what it leads from and to. If there weren't any buildings in place then it's completely redundant,' Hil reasoned.

'It's a good point, but this is all part of a set system of town planning that the Romans took very seriously. This is actually called a *decamanus*. In fact, properly speaking it's a *decamanus maximus*, seeing as it's the grand colonnade. The Romans would have begun planning by building a *decamanus* like this which ran from East to West, directly facing the enemy.'

'What do you mean?'

'I mean that the town would have been orientated around this central axis, which pointed in the exact direction of the enemy. There would have been a gate at either end of this to provide access into the city. One would have been closest to the enemy and one farthest away. It means that the access points are easier to control, and the town is easier to defend.'

'I see,' said Hil, turning it over in her mind.

'There would have been another street running across this one,' Jemme added, 'and this cross axis formed the central structure around which the rest of the town could be organised.'

By now the site was starting to get busy and other people were making their way up and down the *decamanus* too.

'In a way, I almost like the fact we haven't got it just to ourselves,' said Hil. 'Seeing this street busy is a bit like seeing it as it would have been.'

'I completely agree.' said Jemme warmly, 'Actually, you've hit on one of my pet causes at the moment. I don't like this idea of sealing off history and purposefully distancing it. It happens everywhere, and I think it causes it to lose a great deal of its meaning. What is the use of a book inside a glass case? How can you understand a town if you have to look at it from behind a rope? I started talking about this when we were in New York, but I've been thinking about it lots since then. I think museums and archaeological sites need to be a great deal more dynamic in their approach to their exhibits. I think this is the best way of seeing something, and leads to the richest understanding. Are you hungry?' he asked, breaking off.

Hil nodded, and Jemme stopped next to a man who was selling food from a tiny cart. They bought some flat breads with hummus, and as Jemme handed one to Hil he began to warm to his theme again, 'See, this is exactly what I mean. Here we are in this wonderful city, buying food which is as ancient as these stones. This is exactly as it's meant to be – Roman towns would have been buzzing with people selling street food, and it's that continuity which provides the purest form of experience in a place.'

They continued wandering along the path, both thinking about what Jemme had said. The Camp of Diocletian had not survived very well compared with the rest of the town, and so after a quick tour of the ruins, Jemme asked if there was anything else Hil wanted to see.

'Your Grandmother mentioned a theatre;' Hil replied, 'she said it was really quite impressive and definitely worth a visit.'

'That's a great idea,' said Jemme, 'I'd completely forgotten about the theatre. Do you know, I haven't actually seen it myself? For one reason or another there never turned out to be enough time on any of my childhood visits. Grandma mentioned it to me too – I'd love to see it.'

They made their way back to the central colonnade. It was flanked with lateral passages and the theatre could be accessed through two arches, slightly further up from where they were standing. As they walked Jemme unravelled some more of Palmyra's story; of all the distinguished military commanders and prominent politicians, there was one proud queen who stuck in his mind. Her name was Zenobia, and she had been queen of Palmrya in the third century. Jemme had heard her story long before he had heard of Palmyra. Grandma had told him of her fearless conquering, pushing the boundaries of her empire out across Egypt, Anatolia and Syria. She had described the beheading of Zenobia's husband Odaenathus and Zenobia's pride in widowhood. He related all of these facts to Hil, adding in things he had learned since.

'I find her such a fascinating character,' he said, 'I remember reading once that she was the finest incarnation of both female and male virtues.'

'What happened to her?' asked Hil.

'I suppose you could say her fortunes mirrored those of Palmyra. The Emperor Aurelian, back in Rome, tried to reunite the Roman Empire – the Eastern Roman Empire had become too powerful and Zenobia controlled too many trade routes. She would not submit to him and so she had to face him in battle. It was a crushing defeat which gave way to a full-scale siege on the city. It was really the event which began a long period of decline for Palmyra.'

'Did she survive the battle?'

'Legend has it that she was captured on the banks of the Euphrates, but Aurelian was so taken with her beauty that he spared her life and took her back to Rome, and paraded her through the streets in golden chains. I don't know how true that story is, but it certainly creates a powerful image. I can just imagine Zenobia, standing proudly and refusing to be humbled.'

'What do you imagine she looked like?'

'I've got a really clear picture in my head, but it's based more on my imagination than anything else. There are only one or two pieces of evidence for what she actually looked like, and they don't give very clear pictures. Anyway, once she reached Rome there are all sorts of conflicting stories about what happened next. Most of them end with her death in captivity, but there is one theory which I greatly prefer: some people believe that Zenobia's dignity impressed Aurelian as much as her beauty and he spared her life. Allegedly he installed her in a villa in Tivoli, just outside Rome. She lived out the rest of her days as a prominent Roman matron and socialite. Who knows what happened, but I know this is the version I prefer!'

They reached the arches which marked the entrance way to the theatre, and passed through them. Each gasped as they were greeted with their respective first views of the theatre.

For her part, Hil was astonished by the complexity of the place. It had been extensively restored and it was not difficult to imagine how it would have looked in its heyday. In fact, it looked as if it was ready to be called into action at any moment. The stage façade still stood and appeared to have been designed as if it were the entranceway to a great palace, with tall, elegant columns and a beautifully carved pediment. Unlike Roman amphitheatres, the performance space here was at ground level; it made it feel like a theatre in the modern sense, with a stage enclosed on three-quarters by tiered seating. The more Hil looked around, the more she could picture people performing in the scooped out area in front of her.

Jemme, however, had gasped for an entirely different reason.

'I've seen this before,' he murmured.

'I thought you said you'd never had the time to,' said Hil.

'No, I don't mean I've seen it here,' he said, trailing off as he focussed his attention on the seats behind them.

'What do you mean you didn't see it here?' asked Hil. 'Where on earth could you have seen it?!'

Jemme appeared not to hear, and carried on looking at the seats, 'She was sitting right here,' he said to himself.

'Sweetheart, you're not making any sense. Who was sitting there? Where did you see this place if not here?'

Jemme appeared to snap out of his reverie, 'Sorry, I just…. this is all…I just mean that I've seen it before. I recognised it as soon as I came in – it was such a powerful image. I could see everything exactly as I saw it before, when she was sitting there.'

He saw Hil looking at him in confusion and laughed a little. 'Sorry, I'm not making myself any clearer. It's a bit of a long story to be honest, and it began a long time ago too. When I was a child I had a very powerful dream. It was more of a vision than anything else, and I think it's shaped my life more than anything else. The things I saw were so vivid that they have never, ever left me. I had intense visions of all sorts of historical figures in their original contexts; their whole landscapes were contained with the rooms of a palace, and I crawled through tiny doors to see famous figures, scenes and battles of the past. It was so vivid when I woke, that I was unsure of what was reality and whereabouts I existed. I was completely fascinated by it, as was my Grandma. I remember telling her all about it, and her just shaking her head as I described all the details. Neither of us had any idea how I could have created such accurate mental pictures, which were not rooted in my own knowledge at all. I have no idea, even today; the details were intriguing enough in themselves, but I saw some things in their entirety without ever having learned anything about them at all.' He paused, 'Sorry, I can imagine that it must sound a bit strange when hearing it all at once.'

Hil studied him carefully, 'Not strange at all, I'm just trying to make sense of it, that's all. Do you mean you dreamt of things which you didn't know you knew, and then found out that you had dreamed them accurately?'

'Exactly. Except, it wasn't just that they were accurate – they were so accurate and so detailed that we had to consult multiple history books to verify things. There was no way I could have possibly known such things at that young age. Grandma and I were utterly confounded by the whole thing.'

'And you were saying that you can remember everything as clearly as when you first dreamed it?'

'Absolutely. At least, that might be where my memory springs from. You see, I've had the dream many, many times since then. Sometimes it's as brilliant as the first time I saw it, and sometimes it's just a dull reflection. Sometimes I see the whole palace again, and sometimes I'll just see a little bit of one room. There's often something different as well – I've seen some figures so often they feel like old friends, but just when I think that I've seen everything before, suddenly I'll find a new room, or notice something has changed about one of the others.'

'It certainly would explain lots of things,' said Hil thoughtfully. 'I suppose that's where your love of history comes from?'

'Possibly, although Grandma is a big factor in that too. I suppose it's hard to remember whether the dream was the product of an obsession with history or was what inspired it in the first place.'

'Was this theatre in your dream?'

Jemme nodded, 'I can't remember when I first dreamt it, but as soon as we came in I recognised it. I've seen it before exactly as it is here – every step and every column. Except, actually not exactly as it is here, because I saw it as it would have been. Zenobia herself was sitting on that step, right over there. It was before the performance had started, but everyone else was already sitting down. They all stood up when she came in.'

Hil looked at the spot he had pointed to, as if willing Zenobia to appear. 'I wonder how you could have seen it all in such detail,' she said softly, looking genuinely curious.

Jemme felt a surge of relief. He had suddenly realised that he had revealed something deeply personal to Hil. He had shared everything else with her so far, but this, this strange and complex experience had been kept private. It wasn't that he didn't trust her with it, it was more that he didn't understand it enough himself to be able to describe it. He knew that he was meant to use this dream in some way, but he still hadn't worked out how. He felt immensely grateful that Hil had accepted his revelation unquestioningly. Instead of doubting him and prodding holes in its veracity or likeliness, she had joined him in wondering how and why it had happened. He contemplated her, as she continued to look at the spot, and the last vestiges of his vision melted away; Zenobia had vanished and he was back in modern day, ruined Palmyra, standing with the reality of his dream and his life now.

'I've always been interested in dreams and visions – in literature and reality. They're such a rich source of allegory, metaphor and imagery, but they're complex too. Sometimes it takes years to un-knot everything in them and begin to interpret them properly. Don't worry, we'll work yours out.'

'You're so wonderful,' Jemme said happily, pulling her into an embrace. 'Thank you.'

* * * *

By the time the sun had begun to set, and the stone had begun to change its colour again, Hil and Jemme had found their driver and made their way back to their guesthouse. Most of the journey passed in silence, whilst they contemplated the treasures they had seen, hidden in a desert oasis. After a while they began discussing the day, which turned into a conversation about the dream again. Jemme tried to describe what he had seen. It seemed so strange to vocalise; whilst so many of the images were as familiar as the back of his own hand, he rarely talked about them. He had only ever explained things to Grandma, and that was a long time ago with the vocabulary and self-expression of a child. Suddenly, his words felt hollow and inadequate. He felt he couldn't come close to explaining things to Hil; no matter how hard he tried he could not convey the splendour of the golds he had seen, the richness of the reds, the excitement of the chariots and the exhilaration of seeing history as it was being made.

Hil sat quietly and listened to everything. She asked intelligent questions, and deliberated his responses. She could obviously sense Jemme's growing frustration, in trying to paint her a picture which was as vivid as his own.

'It's so interesting listening to you describing things to me.'

'Really? I feel like I'm not doing a particularly good job of it at the moment.'

'I don't think that even matters – the interesting thing is what you're trying to describe; you're focussing on the bits which are obviously most important to you.'

'I suppose I would do,' said Jemme, trying to work out which parts of the dream he had been giving the most amount of attention to.

'Everything is starting to make so much more sense, and I'm starting to understand you in a completely different way now,' said Hil.

'What do you mean?

'Well, hearing you talk, it's so obvious – I can't believe I've never noticed it before.'

'Noticed what before?' asked Jemme.

'That you're completely obsessed with decoration!'

'Am I?' he said in slight surprise.

'Of course! Think about it: it's one of the first things you notice whenever we go somewhere new. It doesn't matter if it's an Art Nouveau restaurant or a Restoration-era library, you always notice and you always comment on it. More than that, you remember it too and compare it to similar things you've seen before. For other people it's the background, but for you it's the focus.'

Jemme thought over what she had said; it was something he had never thought to question before, 'I suppose you're right,' he said eventually.

'Of course I am!' said Hil, looking rather pleased with her realisation. 'Look at all the things we saw today. What did you zoom in on straight away?'

Jemme thought for a moment, 'Probably the carvings in the colonnade.'

'Exactly,' said Hil, 'and if it wasn't the carvings, then it was the pilasters or the pediments.'

Jemme looked a little self-conscious as he turned over all the things he had pointed out that day. Hil rushed to reassure him, 'It's no bad thing; in fact, completely the opposite. It's an incredibly intelligent way of viewing things, and one which most people are not nearly alive enough to share. It's obviously driven by passion too – look at all the things you're describing to me about the dream; the vast majority are to do with how the rooms were decorated and how they looked. It's much more meaningful than an obsession with the aesthetic though – I think it stems from a more considered and observant understanding of history.'

'Thank you,' said Jemme, flattered. Hil was completely right, he was just surprised he hadn't noticed it himself. He thought about his flat, back in Paris, and how measured he had been in his approach to its decoration. He had never thought of colours as being merely decorative, but signifiers of something, invoking history, evoking emotion and inspiring thought. He had once painted a room purple because it contained several books on Phoenicia, as well as a genuine Phoenician artefact. It had been a deliberate and calculated act. The Phoenicians had all but invented the colour, and he wanted to pay homage to this; through careful research he had discovered that the first dye had come from one specific mollusc which was found on the shores of the ancient city of Tyre. Only the wealthy could afford such a luxury item, and so it became a symbol of power and status. Throughout history it had been associated with imperial power, with great figures always robed in rich purple. He had thought carefully about what the colour symbolised and how it related to the purpose of the room. The idea of blithely slapping a dreary colour on a wall without giving it a second thought was complete anathema to him.

He realised that it wasn't just colours, but embellishments too. He noticed and studied every piece of enamel, every baroque scroll and every detail which existed purely for ornamentation. It mattered to him; at heart it was another medium through which a story could be told and also understood years later. He wondered if his attitude towards such things would change now he was aware of them. More importantly, he wondered if he would have the dream again, now he had told Hil. Now that it had been transposed from the visual to the vocal, had it lost any of its meaning? He couldn't make sense of any of it – he still didn't even understand what any of it actually meant.

He sighed, 'I don't know what to make of any of this Hil.'

'I don't think you have to make sense of it,' Hil replied. 'As far as I'm concerned, it's the expression of an intelligent and passionate mind. I'm pleased you've told me, I feel like it's brought me even closer to you. I'm also sure that there's lots more meaning within your dream, but it will unveil itself to you when you're ready; you won't be able to force an interpretation out of it. For now, I think you should accept it as a mark of your talent as a historian.'

Jemme smiled again, but didn't look completely satisfied, 'I don't know...' he began again, 'I don't know whether I'm a historian or just deluded. Sometimes it's hard not to think I'm uncomfortably close to Don Quixote, tilting at my mad visions.'

'You shouldn't be so hard on yourself,' Hil chided, 'Think about all the times in history the wise man has been taken for the fool because people didn't understand what he was saying. It's the same with prophets convincing people of their visions; think about how often in literature and the annals they're recorded as being mad.'

As the car drew up to the guest house, they both fell silent, thinking over their conversation. By now it was completely dark again, and the car's departure was picked out by two tunnels of light, much as its arrival had been. It had been a long, but deeply satisfying day and they were both asleep almost as soon as they had slipped below the cool cotton sheets.

❖   ❖   ❖   ❖

Several bumpy car journeys and one rickety flight later, they found themselves back in Istanbul. After several days' travelling, it was nice to feel settled somewhere for a while. Hil had noticed that parts of the city were starting to feel familiar, and elicited the same feeling of home in her as parts of Ireland and Paris did.

Wadeah met them at the airport again, and they soon found themselves the centre of attention back at the house, with everyone eager to hear stories. Aunts wanted to know what Hil thought of the Levant, cousins wanted to know whether she had liked Syria better than Turkey, and uncles had hopeful questions about whether or not they had seen much of the leather trade on their travels. The evening went much the same way as those Hil had already experienced in the Mafeze household; it was a joyous, noisy occasion with plenty of food and chatter. Grandma sat in silence for the most part, listening to their stories and taking in every detail. Occasionally she would ask a question and when she did so, she was afforded the requisite amount of hush. It amused Hil that in the midst of the hubbub, everyone would still notice that this small old lady wanted to talk, and would quiet down instantly, herself included. She marvelled at the amount of respect Grandma commanded without even saying anything. Likewise, Lily had been eyeing Hil shrewdly. She was pleased with the younger woman's observation, and impressed by her knowledge too. Listening to Hil describe the theatre at Palmyra, and the breeds of thoroughbred they had learned about, she felt convinced that the girl was Jemme's intellectual equal and was pleased he had found someone to challenge and evidently inspire him too.

That night, after everyone had gone to bed she found Jemme sitting on a bench in the courtyard.

'Hello Grandma,' he said, hearing her soft footfall.

'I was hoping to catch you alone,' Lily said.

'I'm just getting some fresh air – I couldn't sleep after all that travelling.'

'Where's Hil?'

'She didn't have the same problem, she's fast asleep!'

Lily chuckled, 'Good for her! How did she find your trip? It sounds like she might even have found it as interesting as I'm sure you did.'

'I really think she did, Grandma; it was amazing. I hadn't expected anything less of her, but it was certainly a trip focussed around my interests.'

'That's true enough, but you make it sound selfish when you describe it that way. It was as much for her as it was for you; it was another way of you showing her some of your story. No matter how well she thinks she understands you in Paris, I don't think she truly can, until she's seen your background and the landscape which shaped you.'

'You're absolutely right, Grandma. This trip has brought us together in so many ways. I feel closer to Hil because I'm sharing the places and people I love with her, and she feels closer to me because she is seeing first-hand what has made me who I am.'

'Well put, my love,' Lily said approvingly.

'There's something more though,' said Jemme.

'What's that?'

'I told her about my dream too.'

Lily was silent for a moment. Her heart soared. She had known that this girl was very special indeed, but this was all she had needed to hear to confirm it.

'Did you?' she said casually, just as she had done when Jemme was a child and she had not wanted to prejudice his thoughts, by drawing attention to the significance of the situation.

'I did,' said Jemme, 'and I'm pleased I did too. I think it's already changed things for the better. I feel like I've let her in to the last part of my life, and we're closer now than ever before.'

'I think it's going to continue to change things for the better,' Lily said slightly mysteriously. Before Jemme had time to pick up on her meaning, she changed the subject, satisfied she had discovered what she was looking for. 'Tell me about Palmyra;' she said, 'was it as you remembered?'

'Sort of. Well, it's been standing for nearly 1,700 years, so I suppose it's more a question of whether or not I've changed!'

Lily laughed, 'That's a good point. Our reaction to places and people change as we evolve and our experiences broaden, though. I'd be surprised if you felt the same way seeing it today as you did when you saw it for the first time as a boy.'

'It definitely felt different seeing it with Hil – it turned it into a shared experience, rather than something that was just for me. I felt like I was seeing it all through someone else's eyes.'

'I'm so pleased,' Lily said, standing up, 'It sounds like it was an extremely productive trip indeed. I hope sleep comes to you soon,' she said, bending to kiss Jemme.

'Good night, Grandma,' he said. Lily pulled her shawl around her shoulders, and headed back into the house.

Their trip soon drew to a close and Jemme found that packing to return to France was far more difficult than he had imagined. First of all, there were the logistical and practical difficulties. They had brought huge amounts of luggage with them, but he had mistakenly though that once all the presents had been distributed, they would be travelling light on the return journey. As he wrestled with a suitcase and looked at the growing pile on the floor, he regretted his optimism. It seemed that they were taking back even more than they had arrived with. For every gift they had given, they had received two in return. Family members, neighbours and friends had all wanted to give them something to take back with them. Then there were all the things which he and Hil had bought on their various trips, not to mention the presents they had bought to take back for colleagues and friends in Paris. Jemme gave up on his suitcase and let it spring back open. He sat down next to it on the bed. It wasn't just the packing which was hard; leaving was more of a wrench than he'd realised. There had been so much to occupy him in Paris since he'd arrived that he had barely had time to think He didn't realise how much he missed his family and his city. Seeing Hil slip so seamlessly into life here made him wonder why on earth he would want to live anywhere other than Turkey. The weather was beautiful, the food was fantastic and the people were a great deal friendlier than they were in Paris. He sighed. He had responsibilities back in Paris, he knew that. He couldn't abandon the bank just like that. It had been a much needed break, though. He felt sunned, relaxed and refreshed. He had enjoyed returning to his roots and being reminded of the most important things and people in his life. Turkey had made him and would always be a part of him. He stood up and tackled the suitcase again with renewed vigour.

Chapter Nine

Back in Paris, Jemme found himself in a familiar situation. As he opened various suitcases and boxes, he looked helplessly around the flat, willing some space to open up. His bed, the table and various armchairs had become repositories of various things which he had unpacked, then given up on. Boxes of candies and tins of stuffed vine leaves nestled in piles of shirts, and book corners poked out from underneath mounds of linen. He was resigned to the fact that most of it would have to be returned to various cases, whilst he decided what to do with it all. He couldn't believe how small the flat was beginning to feel; for an apartment in central Paris it was enormous, and he had rattled around in it when he had first moved in. It seemed that it had begun to reflect his life, both becoming fuller in tandem. He accepted that he might have to clear out some clutter, but there was a more pressing issue: he had brought back a great deal of art with him too. In retrospect he wondered if he had been mad. When he had left for Turkey, he had already amassed more pieces than he could ever hang, and now the problem had been exacerbated. There was no way he could display even half of his collection without the flat beginning to look like a gallery.

Baggage aside, his return had been a relatively smooth one. Goodbyes in Turkey had been variously tearful, reproachful and joyful. He had promised he would not leave it so long the next time, and he had promised that he would bring Hil back soon too. He was pleased to note that his family and Hil seemed sad to be parted too, and pleased that the big introduction had gone even better than expected. The first night back in Paris had been a strange one. Although the glow of Levantine sunshine still lingered on his skin, the city he returned to was cloaked in rain and cloud, which began to seep into his mood. He was dreading his first day back at work after such an extended period away. He had never left the bank for more than a day or two, and making preparations before he left had been somewhat stressful. Although he trusted his staff, he was convinced that a great pile of work had been developing in his absence. He had managed to put it to the back of his mind whilst he had been on holiday, but now he was back, with the reality of the bank less than a mile away, he shuddered at the thought of the backlog he would have to plough through.

The next morning he left his flat-full of jumbled possessions very early, and walked briskly to the bank, grimacing slightly at the puddles underfoot. It had been a while since he had been the first one in the bank, and he had had to rummage through the mess at home to find his keys. Head bowed against the drizzle, he marched up the steps, not noticing the warm glow of light emanating from the bank's glass doors. As he put his key out to the lock he looked up. *Well, at least someone's already here,* he thought to himself. He swung the door open and was cheered by the sight of two people already on the reception desk. He nodded his greetings and went straight for the lift, comforted by the thought that even though he would arrive before DD, he wouldn't arrive to a mess of paperwork. DD had known he was coming back today and Jemme knew that he would have left everything exactly as he would like it to be found. There would be a great deal to work through, but at least it would be in a logical order, and thoroughly annotated.

However, Jemme had underestimated his second-in-command. Rather than merely leaving the paperwork in order, DD himself was waiting when the lift reached the fourth floor.

Jemme started.

'Good morning, Sir,' said DD unflinchingly, 'I trust that your trip was an enjoyable one.'

'Yes…it was very… how did you – I mean, DD you could have been standing there for hours!' Jemme finally concluded.

DD smiled very slightly. 'I knew you would be arriving early this morning, Sir.'

'But, how?'

'I just knew, Sir,' said DD, holding out his hand for Jemme's jacket. He opened the door to the office and Jemme was heartened to see a cup of coffee waiting for him. Easing himself into his seat, he took a grateful sip.

'It's the perfect temperature, what excellent timing!'

DD nodded slightly, 'I'm afraid it must seem a little weak. I should imagine you've become accustomed to drinking Turkish coffees.'

Jemme laughed, 'Weak yes, but no less flavour for it.' He took another sip, 'Mmmm, wonderful. Now I feel ready to tackle it – can you bring all the paperwork through please DD?'

DD unzipped the black leather folder he was holding and placed it open in front of Jemme. It was the folder which contained everything for the day ahead, as well as a review of yesterday; their days always began with Jemme sorting his way through its contents, and he was pleased to see that it was relatively empty today – at least it would not take him too long.

'Thanks DD – I'll have a look at this. Could you bring in all the rest though? I'm quite keen to get started on it.'

'Rest, Sir?'

'Yes, all the outstanding paperwork. I want to get rid of the backlog as soon as possible.'

'Backlog, Sir?' said DD, as if the word was slightly distasteful to him.

'Yes, the backlog,' said Jemme, wondering why DD was being so uncharacteristically slow on the uptake.

'But there is no backlog, Sir,'

Jemme stared at him agog, 'You mean to tell me that in the whole time I've been away, no work has accumulated – no work at all? What about things I need to sign, and decisions I need to make? Correspondence?'

'With respect, Sir, you authorised me to both sign on your behalf and to make decisions. I recall you saying that you trusted my judgement in the bank's affairs.'

'I did… I mean, I do – I'm sorry, DD, I didn't mean to insult you; I should have known that you would have kept everything shipshape whilst I was gone. I just assumed that some things might have gone undone, and that work might have snowballed somewhat…' he trailed off a little. Although DD's face retained its usual inscrutability, Jemme could imagine some cartoonish indignation fighting its way through.

'However, clearly I was wrong,' he said, moving on quickly, 'It looks like you've done an excellent job. It even feels like there's less daily paperwork than usual!'

'Thank you, Sir. I've included a summary of business on the first page. It details all the decisions I made *in absentia*. I trust they'll meet with your approval.'

'I'm sure they will, DD, I look forward to reading through them,' said Jemme spreading the pages out in front of him and settling into his chair.

'Another coffee, Sir?' asked DD, as he picked up the empty cup.

'You read my mind,' replied Jemme. As DD shut the door quietly behind him, the corners of a smile were just perceptible around the corners of his mouth.

The first day back had flown by. Jemme even found that he had finished a little earlier than usual after having coming in so early. He walked back home with a spring in his step. He had been completely satisfied with everything that had occurred in his absence, and he felt that the bank had been kept running exactly as if he had been there. Although he hadn't needed to, DD had proved himself, and Jemme was even more confident about taking time off in the future. It had got him thinking though; maybe it was time to start taking more of a backseat role. The bank had consumed so much of his life at the beginning. It had been exhilarating, and he had been proud to see the results of his hard work. However, now it had reached the stage where he didn't need to be personally involved in every decision, or to be on call around the clock, perhaps it was time to step back a little. He thought about how happy he had been recently, now he was spending less time at work and more time exploring museums, meeting interesting professors and spending time with Hil. If he could do all of these things with no repercussions for the business, then why stop now?

He pondered the matter, as he walked back to the flat. If he gave DD more long-term executive authority then he would need to visit the bank less, and could relinquish responsibility without sacrificing control. It was certainly an attractive prospect. Back at the flat, he was confronted with the mess he had left. It felt even more trying after a successful day – perhaps his affairs were not as in order as he would have liked. He decided to abandon the clothes and personal effects – they didn't really interest him that much. He was much more excited about the art he had brought back with him. A neat stack of flat oblong parcels leant up against the wall, and he unwrapped them excitedly, revealing a selection of prints and etchings, with one small oil painting. He remembered buying each and every one, and the smell of their wooden frames evoked ghostly images of market places and antiques shops in another home, far away. He looked around at the walls surrounding him, studying them closely. He was loathe to remove any of the art which was already hanging; he had become so accustomed to seeing the pieces where they were. They were the first things he saw when he opened the front door after a hard day's work, and the things which made the apartment home for him. However, he didn't want the flat to turn into some sort of museum – he reasoned that it should reflect his changing tastes and experiences and so it was important to change things around. After much deliberation he took down a oil painting of Venice, which had been done in the style of Canaletto. Jemme adored it, and was one day hoping to own the real thing. He looked through the packages he had just unwrapped and selected a lithograph of the Bosphorus, as seen from the Galata Tower. It was a fine piece and in its original frame too. However, once hung, it sat between two, much larger, Impressionist pieces. The open composition and soft edges of the larger paintings made the rigid black lines of the lithograph seem slightly prim and unimaginative. By contrast, the larger paintings seemed fussy and unfocussed. Hanging them together detracted from all three. Jemme sadly took the lithograph down again. He realised this was going to be a bigger project than he had thought.

Over the next week he arranged and rearranged. He took things out of boxes and packed them away again; every time he looked at an artefact, he would become filled with enthusiasm for displaying it, then move it seemingly endlessly around his flat before realising that there was no appropriate home for it, and he would sorrowfully pack it back into its casing before moving on to the next piece. His rearranging gathered momentum and spread throughout the flat. As he placed objects on shelves and moved them about, he began to question what it was that made them jar when next to each other. He moved and reshuffled, initially arranging by colour and then size. However, this was not enough. The deep indigo of a glazed plate did not represent enough of a link with the powdery cornflower of the vase he had placed next to it. He found it unsatisfying somehow, and wondered what unifying factors, if any, would bring things together harmoniously. He thought about the values of each object – there was colour, texture, form, shape and size to consider. The art was even more complicated – should he arrange his paintings by subject? How about grouping them by school or by painter? The more he thought about it, the more the possibilities began to unfold in front of him. There seemed to be an endless array of categories to consider, and he wondered at his naivety in first displaying his collections. Back then, as he recalled, space seemed to be the only consideration.

As the weekend drew near, an obsessive taxonomy was already beginning to take over him. He was engrossed by the perfect positioning of every piece within the flat. A chance positioning of two objects together made him realise what had been missing. He had brought back a small, antique, walnut box with him from Turkey. It was a pretty piece, and very typically Levantine, with decorative inlays of ivory and mother-of-pearl. He had been keen to display it, and had put it down on the shelf temporarily and then forgotten about it when he became involved in something else. On Saturday morning, he rose early and began work on his new project. He pulled a large cardboard box out from the bottom of the wardrobe. It contained small antiques which he had put in storage whilst he conducted his grand reshuffle. He opened it again and the first piece he pulled out was a small box made of a light-coloured wood. Its lid bore geometric designs picked out in glimmering mother-of-pearl. *That's strange,'* he had thought to himself, *'I could have sworn that I'd already put that box out.* He turned it over. It was exactly the right size and shape for the small shelf above his desk, and he took it over there. He had to do a double-take when he realised that the box seemed to be there already, yet also sitting in his hand. Suddenly he remembered: the one he held had been in storage for a while. It was a piece he had bought some time ago, from an antiques dealer in Paris. It was a small Venetian artefact, probably from the house of a wealthy merchant or important civic figure. He put the boxes next to each other on the shelf. They were strikingly similar, and it was little wonder he had mistaken one for the other.

He looked at them for a while, happy with the placement. There was something unifying about the shapes, colours and materials, but there was something else too. He kicked himself when he realised: sat side by side, the two objects silently told a story. They were the perfect expression of the Silk Route, documenting the passage of wealth and ideas between Venice and the Levant.

The rich decorative influence of the East was clearly visible in the Venetian box; it brought both objects together and tied them into the same story. Suddenly he began to see every other object he had ever collected as a building piece for a larger story. He realised that each one needed to incorporated into some sort of over-arching narrative.

He couldn't believe he hadn't thought of this earlier; it made perfect sense. Since as long as he could remember, he had been fascinated by the influence of East on West and West on East. It had shaped his learning and guided his thought. It was one of the earliest themes he had spoken with Grandma about, and one which had been a constant undercurrent in so many of their conversations. It would mean he would have to completely reclassify everything again, but it would definitely be worth it.

* * * *

By Sunday, Jemme had made some progress. The project was starting to come together, and he had constructed the beginnings of a narrative. However, he was frustrated. There were huge holes in the story – gaps and lacunae which could not be bridged because of a missing piece. Any artefact would have done, as long as it was from the missing period or place, but the story he was creating stumbled, within the confines of his collection.

He was so absorbed in the project that he didn't hear the knocking on the door. It wasn't until he heard Hil's voice, calling through the letter box, he realised both that she was at the door and that he hadn't spoken to her all weekend.

He opened the door, 'I'm so sorry, sweetheart, I've been so preoccupied,' he said bashfully.

Hil came in and looked around at the mess, 'So I see!' she said, hugging him. 'What on earth have you been up to? You don't look as if you've slept in days!'

Jemme caught sight of himself in the mirror, which hung by the door. He looked a mess – his hair hadn't been brushed and he had been wearing the same old jumper for two days, whilst he dealt with the dust of unpacking. He had snagged it on something the day before and it had sprung a hole, which had been working its way across the front.

'Goodness, I look a little mad,' he said, attempting to find a comb. He found one and set about returning himself to his usual state of sartorial nicety. Before he did so, he took another look at himself, 'Actually, I think I look rather like Professor Johnston,' he said and chuckled to himself.

'Is that your Anatolian professor friend?' asked Hil.

'He's English, but yes. In fact he'd be really interested in what I'm doing here,' Jemme said gesturing around.

'What on earth *are* you doing here?' said Hil, attempting to hang her coat on the hat stand but finding it had been moved.

Jemme saw her looking quizzically at the space where it had been, 'Oh I moved that. It was a Victorian antique from England, and completely unsuitable next to that table.'

'Unsuitable? But it was right by the door! Where have you put it?'

'Oh, I just put it in the kitchen whilst I decided what to do with it,' said Jemme absent-mindedly.

'Now you really are starting to sound like an eccentric professor.' said Hil, 'Why don't you sit down over there; I'll make us some coffee and you can tell me all about it. If you haven't moved the settee that is,' she teased.

After she had picked her way over various obstacles, Hil was soon carefully making her way back with a small tray bearing two cups.

'I've made it French style. I'm afraid it's going to taste rather weak after all that Turkish coffee,' she said.

Jemme laughed, 'You're the second person to say that to me this week,' he said, his attention now fully focussed on Hil. He took a large swig of coffee and pretty much knocked it back in one go, 'That's better! I was up late last night, and I've been so absorbed in all this that I've forgotten to really eat or drink anything today.'

'So,' said Hil, 'why don't you tell me about "all this"?'

Jemme put his coffee cup down, and told her about the evolution of his ideas since he had returned from Turkey. He explained that clashes between objects and paintings were much, much deeper than the stylistic. He brought two contrasting pieces together to demonstrate, but Hil seemed unmoved, 'Don't you think that two very different things can complement each other?' she asked.

'Certainly, but there's more to it than that. They have to complement each other in the right way.'

'You've lost me again, my love.'

'Well,' Jemme began, unsure of how to explain himself, 'if they are different within the right categorisation, then they can complement each other wonderfully. If they bear no relation to each other then any semblance of complementariness is entirely false.'

Hil looked none the wiser, 'How can it be false? If I can see two pieces with my own eyes and think that they complement each other, then that's a manifestly true fact.'

'Ah, but there is no meaning to either piece,' said Jemme triumphantly.

Hil took a sip of her coffee, 'I think you're going to have to explain it to me some more,' she said patiently.

'Well, I've always thought that everything in this flat should tell a story, I must have mentioned that to you before?'

'Absolutely. In fact I know the story of a good half of the pieces here,' Hil replied.

'Well, this week, I began to realise that not only should the pieces tell their own, individual stories, they should also come together to tell a much larger, more important story. If something is isolated from its context, then it is divested of a great deal of its meaning.'

'How do you mean?'

'Well, take this tile;' said Jemme, pulling it off the shelf, 'it's meant to sit with dozens of others on the side of a fountain on a mosque's courtyard. It makes sense in that context, and that's specifically what its designer created it for. However, it's on its own, on a shelf, in my flat in cold Paris – a far cry from being in a sunny courtyard somewhere in the Levant.'

'Granted,' said Hil readily. 'But that's just the nature of ownership. Things are always going to be removed from their original context at some point.'

'It's a good point,' said Jemme, slightly grudgingly, 'but this piece is so far removed that it has lost some of its meaning, and thus its value.'

'But unless you recreate a mosque's courtyard in your salon, you can never hope to return its meaning to it. Or, rather, its meaning as you understand it,' reasoned Hil.

'Ah! That's what I've been thinking of. You're right – I can't recreate the courtyard in this room, although you probably will believe that the thought did briefly flick across my mind. However, I can use my knowledge of this tile to position it around other artefacts, and allow it to tell a story. It can show the transition of influence from Iznik ware to Majolica pottery and then even on to Delft ware. The tile can become part of a story, and therefore a different form of meaning and value can be returned to it.' He paused, 'Do you see?'

'I do. I think those are some very interesting points, but… well, why?'

'Why what?'

'Why try and reconstruct some sort of narrative? I think it's an excellent idea, philosophically and academically, but not practically. Look at your flat – it's completely topsy-turvy, you can't live like this.'

Jemme paused and looked around, but Hil continued, 'It's not a concept for a home. Listen to you with your talk about artefacts and narratives. You sound more like you're trying to create a museum than arrange your furniture.'

Jemme looked around the flat, trying to see things through Hil's eyes. It was certainly a mess; everything had been churned up and there seemed to be no rhyme or reason to where anything was. However, in his head, things had never been clearer. He knew exactly where everything needed to be, and exactly what needed to be done.

'I need to do some serious antiques hunting,' he said.

'More things?! That's the complete opposite of what you need! Did you hear anything I said?'

Jemme snapped back again and refocused his attention on Hil, 'Yes, I did. I'm sorry, sweetheart – I definitely did listen to you, I was just thinking aloud. I know this all looks a little chaotic, but it's all under control. I can't really explain *why* I'm doing it, just what it is that I'm doing. I don't think I even know myself. I've just got an overwhelming sense of purpose about it.'

Hil sighed a little, 'Whatever makes you happy, my love. I was going to suggest we stayed here, but why don't you come over to mine and I can cook you some supper.'

Jemme felt a pang of reluctance. He didn't really want to leave the flat until the project was completed, no matter how long that took. He saw Hil looking at him expectantly and suppressed his desire to stay. After all, he hadn't seen her all weekend and it might be nice to spend a little bit of time somewhere neat and tidy.

※ ※ ※ ※

Several weeks later, Jemme had still come no closer to completing his project. In fact, the more he worked at it, the more it seemed to expand. He felt he could not address one aspect of the story of influence without including another. However, being back in the routine of work and life in Paris had made him realise that he would have to put things on the back burner for a little while. Hil was right, he was in danger of turning his house into a museum. Besides, he realised that the project was not finite; as he continued to collect more pieces, so the story would continue to evolve and develop. Perhaps it would be a life-long project, he had mused to himself.

Stepping back from his work in the flat had reminded him that he had been abandoning Hil since they'd been back, something he'd been quick to redress. He thought about how happy he had been with her in Turkey, about how much his family had loved her, and about all the veiled hints his family had dropped around him, including his Grandma. Hil had become a cornerstone of his life, and he needed to do something to show her that. He couldn't imagine a future without her, and he couldn't wait to begin a future with her.

The decision to propose had been a relatively easy one. It had been staring him in the face for a while; he just hadn't realised it. The difficulty was in planning the actual event. He had thought of a hundred different scenarios, but none of them were right. He wanted it to take place somewhere which was meaningful for both of them, and he wanted to ask in a way which expressed just how much he loved her and how much she meant to him. He had even been jotting down some notes in preparation. However, nothing sounded as he wanted it to. He screwed up page after page: too long, too short, too bland, too sentimental. He had been in constant contact with his family since he had made the decision (which had been much to their excitement) and just when he was beginning to despair, he telephoned his mother for some advice.

'Just be yourself,' she said simply. 'If you try and over-think it and put too much effort into it, it won't be natural. You don't want anything to be forced or to be false – it's the simplest question you could ever ask someone, in many ways.'

He had also spoken to Lily, who had similar advice, 'The situation will make itself – you don't need to plan how it will look or feel.'

'I know, Grandma, and I appreciate that, I just don't know what to say,' he'd said.

'Well, why don't you look to the poets? They've always provided inspiration to me. Think how old *Layla and Majnun* is – it dates all the way back to the Umayyad period, but its message of love is completely timeless.'

'That's a good idea, Grandma.'

'Whatever you do, don't copy from it though. You must use your own voice – would you really want Hil to agree to marry you because you'd asked in someone else's words?' Lily cautioned.

'No, I suppose not, Grandma. Although, at the moment I don't mind whose words I ask her in, just as long as she agrees!'

'Of course she will – don't be silly. Let us know the news as soon as possible. Good luck.'

It felt strange to hear Grandma's disembodied voice down the telephone. She had such a presence when she spoke and was so expressive, that it almost felt like talking to a different person. The distance did not lessen her ability to impart wisdom though, and her advice was as thoughtful and useful as ever. After scanning through some old Arabic and Turkish poems, Jemme felt much more confident in what he was going to say.

In the event, it had turned out that both his mother and grandmother had been right. He had had only had a rough idea of what he was going to say, but once he began it came naturally. They had both become quite emotional, especially after Hil had accepted. 'How romantic, to be proposed to in Paris!' Hil had said and Jemme felt inclined to agree.

✲ ✲ ✲ ✲

The preparations for the wedding meant that any attempt to further the flat project had to be completely abandoned for the time being. Jemme was unendingly grateful for DD's capabilities, and found himself delegating increasing amounts of responsibility to him. It freed him up to tackle the never-ending amounts of decisions. Firstly, and most importantly, they had to decide where to get married. Neither Turkey nor Ireland had felt quite right. Their two respective home countries had little direct relevance to their relationship. Eventually they decided on Paris; it was their home, where they had met and where they had decided to get married after all. It did mean that both families would have to travel, but they reasoned that that was much fairer than expecting the Mafezes to go to Ireland or the Rattisons to go to Turkey.

They had also struggled with the guest list. With such large extended families on both sides, they already had a sizeable congregation, before they had even begun to factor in French friends, colleagues and neighbours. Jemme had deliberated over his invitations for a while. He had a number of high profile clients with whom he had become increasingly friendly. He would have liked to have invited them, and it would certainly have eased business along well too. However, in doing so he would have snubbed other clients, who could easily have taken umbrage. In the end he decided to stick to just friends and family. Although it was regrettable that he'd have to skip over some people, there were plenty of clients he wouldn't have wanted to pass the time of day with, let alone share the most special day of his life. The more he thought about it, the more he was pleased with his decision. He thought of the rowdy, cosy evenings with his family back in Turkey. That was exactly the atmosphere he wanted to recreate at his wedding, surrounded by loved ones.

As well as dealing with his affairs at the bank, DD had somehow, miraculously, managed to find time to help Jemme in the planning. Jemme had protested, but had been met with a simple, 'It's no trouble, Sir.' It might not have been any trouble to DD, but it certainly had been to Jemme. He was relieved when DD brought his organisational touch to the plans. He was a natural at it too, prompting Jemme to ask him if he'd planned many weddings before -- to which DD cryptically replied, 'Weddings? No, not weddings, Sir.'

As the day grew closer, preparations became more frantic. Jemme felt he barely saw his fiancée anymore. They passed like ships in the night and all conversation seemed to focus on buttonholes, place settings and other such fripperies. Crises seemed to crop up at every turn; delayed deliveries, dramas with the florist, but DD was on hand to deal with them at every turn. He did so discreetly and deftly, so that sometimes it would be days before Jemme and Hil had even realised that there had been a problem.

Slowly, it all started to come together. The relatives' flights had been booked, the menus finalised and the dresses fitted. There was just one thing left, which had completely escaped even DD's attention. Four days before the wedding, Jemme suddenly realised with a jolt that he had completely forgotten to organise a best man. It hadn't even been something he'd considered, but he realised people would be expecting it. He racked his brain trying to work out who he could ask at such short notice. Ideally, he'd like one of his brothers, but he wouldn't have been able to pick just one, and besides, they were only arriving the day before the wedding. He thought over the role of the best man; they were supposed to provide help with last minute emergencies and support in the run up to the big day. It would need to be someone who lived nearby too; it wouldn't be any good having someone from another city, let alone another country. He ran through all the people he could ask, but each seemed to be unsuitable in a different way. It felt like an imposition too, so close to the date. It seemed like a lot to ask, and as he had never worked with any of the friends he was considering he didn't know how they coped in a slightly stressful situation. He didn't want it to ruin their day. He ran through the guest list again and again without any success.

With only a few days left he was starting to panic. He went over to Hil's flat to run over last minute arrangements and alterations. She looked as tired as he did, but still greeted him with a large smile,

'Hello, sweetheart;' he said, 'how's everything been going at this end of things?'

'Not too badly,' she replied, 'I think – I hope – it's just about under control now. I have to say, the way I'm feeling at the moment, one of the best things about being married must be not having to organise a wedding.'

Jemme laughed, 'I know what you mean! Much as I'm looking forward to the day and seeing all our friends and family, a little bit of me will be relieved when it's all over and done with, and we can look forward to starting our lives together – that's the really exciting part.'

'Absolutely,' said Hil warmly.

'Have you got anything left to organise?'

'Actually, I think it's all sorted now. I'm sure there will be some last minute things, but apart from that everything is pretty much done. How about you?'

'I'm the same really. I've got everything sorted except for one big thing. Well, I say "I", really I mean DD has. He's been an absolute God-send, both in the bank and in planning the wedding. I don't know how I would have managed without him.'

'Yes, he's been fantastic, hasn't he. What's the one big thing you still need to do?'

'I haven't sorted a best man.'

'Oh goodness! You're right – what with everything else I'd completely forgotten. I suppose it's because DD's been doing all the things a best man traditionally does to help it wasn't particularly obvious we were missing one.'

'Exactly. I'm completely out of ideas, I thought you might be able to help.'

'Mmm, it's such short notice though.' Hil thought for a bit, 'Actually, I can think of one person who could help – it's so obvious! We've both mentioned him about four times already.'

Jemme thought for a moment, 'DD?'

'Exactly!'

'That's a great idea,' said Jemme, 'I'll ask DD what he thinks.'

'No!' cried Hil, 'Ask DD to be your best man!'

Jemme paused. It made perfect sense. Unwittingly, DD had been acting as his best man thus far anyway. Jemme already knew that he was up to the job, and knew he would be indispensable on the big day. He also thought it would be a nice way of thanking DD for all his hard work.

'Now that really is a good idea,' he said to Hil, giving her a kiss on the cheek.

In no time at all, the big day had arrived, and Jemme found himself standing in his flat with DD helping do up his cufflinks. The past twenty-four hours had flown past in a blur of excitement. Families had been picked up from airports and introduced to each other, and feasting had begun. Hil's Irish family were as close-knit as Jemme's Turkish family, and had exactly the same attitude to large family events. Once they had all convened in the same room for the pre-wedding supper, the levels of excited chatter and story-telling were quite unbelievable. Jemme had looked at Hil and smiled, 'And this is only the beginning!' he said, prompting Hil to roll her eyes and giggle.

He had been tired the next morning, but barely noticed it. He felt like one major milestone had already been passed: the families had met and liked each other. Family was so important to both him and Hil, even more so when they were both living so far from their respective relatives. Now that both sets had been introduced, he felt like his extended family had just doubled, and he hoped Hil felt the same. As the car pulled up outside he felt a surge of excitement. He was going to be marrying the woman he loved in under an hour and that was all that mattered.

Much like the previous twenty-four hours, the next twelve passed by in an haze of excitement and happiness. The ceremony and reception had itself been a marriage of Eastern and Western traditions. The costumes, music, food and dancing had synthesised the two, creating a unique day for the couple, which perfectly embodied their relationship. Hil had looked absolutely stunning in her dress. It had been a gift from Jemme's parents, and was woven from finest Turkish silk. A dressmaker friend of his grandmother's had designed the pattern, and everything had been made in her workshop, right down to the beautiful needlework on the bodice. Hand crafted lace appliqués of Turkish and Irish flowers had been individually applied to the ivory silk tulle, with tiny organza buttons fastened with rouleau loops running down the back. French Chantilly lace trimmed the skirting and referenced the city the wedding was taking place in. After the ceremony had finished, when the guests had departed, and the last of the reception was cleared away, Jemme looked at his new bride, she looked as radiantly happy as he was. The whole day had been a great success, marked by the fusion of Eastern and Western. It was just as he remembered Grandma always saying; together, two cultures could combine to form something new, which was richer than either of its constituent elements. He couldn't wait to see how this would apply to the rest of his life.

Chapter Ten

Several months had flown past since the wedding; families had returned to their respective homelands, the last of the cake had been finished and Hil's beautiful dress had been carefully packed away in tissue paper, wonderful memories stored in every fold. They had easily slipped into the comfortable pattern of married life, and enjoyed the warmth and security of the domesticity it brought. Although she had kept her small *appartement,* with vague intentions of subletting at some point, Hil had moved in with Jemme. In some ways, little had changed; they had been spending such a large amount of time in each other's flats beforehand, it merely felt like a convenient extension of their courtship, and removed the need to cross Paris every time one of them wanted to pick up a clean shirt or drop off some shopping. Their lives had slipped seamlessly together, and Jemme was already finding it difficult to conceptualise just how things had been before Hil. However, in other ways it felt like a great deal had changed.

Hil had brought with her all of her things – her clothes, her books, her art, her trinkets, an entire adult life's worth of possessions. She was naturally very tidy, in fact much more so than Jemme, but that did little to address the problem of the sheer volume of belongings and gadgets they now found themselves dealing with. No matter how neatly things were packed away or returned to boxes, it was undeniably a problem. Every time a cupboard door was opened, a drawer tentatively pulled open or a book cautiously eked from a bookcase, it seemed to precipitate some sort of explosion. Clothes would fly from wardrobes, an entire shelf would disgorge itself of books and a flutter of scarves, cufflinks and other bits and bobs would surround the hapless individual. Jemme had been conscious of the need to move to somewhere larger before Hil had moved in, but now it seemed to be even more pressing than ever. No matter how orderly and ship-shape they tried to keep things, it seemed as if they were being suffocated in an efflux of their own possessions.

There was another reason pressing on Jemme's mind, though. During the wedding preparations he had allowed his classification and rearranging to take a backseat. His burning obsession with taxonomy, and his overwhelming desire to thread all of his objects together to create some form of overarching narrative, had been dampened. Later, in the golden warmth of the days following the wedding, he had been too preoccupied with Hil moving in to think about his project. He had enjoyed the excitement of seeing her things arrive in a van, and relished the excitement he had felt when he saw all of her possessions interleaved with his own, cosy as two spoons in a drawer. He loved the feel of permanency it brought too: Hil was now woven into the tapestry of his life as tightly as the finest Flemish wool. Their lives were knotted together intransigently. However, as he looked around his flat, struggling to contain the life they were building together, something else came to him too. Now that Hil's life was interwoven with his, the pattern of his life had to change. There had been little enough room for him to create the story he was trying to tell when he just had his own narrative tools to deal with, but now the problem had been compounded. Hil's things sat on the shelves, hung on the walls and stood tall on the floor. He loved them, but they interrupted the flow of what he was trying to create. He still couldn't work out why it was so important to him, but he knew that he had to continue with his project; he felt as if it had some wider importance and this sense of purpose sat in the pit of his stomach like a large pebble.

His mind was made up enough already, but there was one further reason. As much as he felt Hil was interrupting the story he wanted to tell, he was also keen to live in a space in which they could both create a story together. He longed for their new home to be a blank canvas – somewhere they could decorate together and fill with memories. He was excited, but also vexed by the problem – he wanted the new place to be so many things, he didn't even know how to go about looking for it.

However, apart from this one, small element, life was treating him well. He felt blissfully happy – almost as if he had been numbed to any negativity of feeling at all. Married life had been everything he had been hoping for. It had consolidated and codified their bond and he felt proud to have upheld such an ancient institution. He felt as if together, there was nothing he and Hil could not take on. All of the stresses and strains of daily life seemed to have been magically smoothed out and he found it difficult to imagine being troubled by anything niggling or irksome again. Although he knew how stressful moving house could be, he was confident that with Hil by his side they would sail though the process, and probably be even closer as a result.

Life at the bank was also going from strength to strength. After returning as a married man, he had found everything just as he had left it. DD had easily kept things running, and continued operations just as he would have done himself. Jemme sometimes felt as if he could see pale reflections of the bond he shared with Hil reflected in his relationship with DD. He trusted DD absolutely and unhesitatingly. Furthermore, he felt that with DD by his side there were no obstacles the bank could not overcome. He felt confident and unassailable.

Bounding up the bank's stairs, with the late summer sunshine reflecting off the familiar burnished copper rail, he thought to himself how thoroughly satisfying it was when the pieces of one's life fell together in such a way. It was as if he had finally made sense of the puzzle, and now smooth edges sat neatly confluent with each other whilst jagged pieces tessellated in a most pleasing and gratifying manner. By the time he reached the fourth floor, DD was waiting to greet him and take his jacket.

This had had become such a habitual fixture of their mornings that Jemme scarcely noticed it any more. It was a pattern of behaviour so ingrained that, if DD had not been there for some unforeseeable reason, he would probably hand his jacket to thin air before realising. However, on occasions the sight of this solemn German waiting for him caught him off guard, and made him chuckle.

'Good morning, Sir,' said DD gravely. Noticing Jemme's smile he raised his eyebrow a fraction, questioningly.

'Sorry, DD, I wasn't laughing at you, I was just thinking about the fact that you're always here to greet me.'

'Yes, Sir,' DD agreed, equally gravely.

'No, I mean...... never mind,' Jemme eventually concluded. He knew DD took pride in his impeccable professionalism, and it would have wounded him to hear that sometimes he put Jemme in mind of a stuffed owl. He had no idea how long DD stood there in the mornings, solemnly and silently waiting for Jemme to hand over his coat, but Jemme wouldn't have been surprised if he had slept standing up, one hand dutifully and expectantly extended, just in case.

'Sir, I have prepared the notes for you, as usual,' DD said, opening the door to the office, where Jemme noticed a cup of coffee waiting for him on his desk. He knew that DD's timing would be faultless too and that the coffee would be at exactly the right temperature. He didn't know what dark arts DD employed to get this right, but he presumed it was the same method that meant he always knew when Jemme arrived, and when he should stand expectantly by the lift. 'Or maybe that's not it at all,' thought Jemme to himself. 'Maybe he really does sleep there and maintain a round-the-clock vigil, just in case. Maybe that's what he does with the coffee too – it's not perfect timing at all, but rather he just makes endless cups of coffee all morning so there's always a hot one waiting.'

Actually, it doesn't matter either way, Jemme thought to himself as he happily took a sip of the rich, earthy liquid before him.

'Thank you, DD, this is delicious.'

DD nodded, 'Thank you, Sir. Now, if we start with yesterday's figures.'

They proceeded to go over the paperwork with the same easy fluidity as had become their custom. However, it meant that Jemme allowed his mind to wander slightly and run over the housing issue. When they had finished, he snapped the folder shut and sighed.

'Is everything alright, Sir? You seem a little distracted.'

'No, everything's fine thanks, DD. In almost every way it's never been better. There's just something I need to sort out.'

'Is it anything I can help with, Sir?'

'No, thank you it's – actually, now I think about it, it's exactly the kind of thing which is your forte.'

'Sir?' DD said, with his eyebrow creeping perceptibly skywards again.

'Well, it's to do with the flat.'

'I was wondering how long it would be before you began to think of moving.'

Jemme looked startled, 'How on earth did you know that? I've only just come to the conclusion myself in the last couple of days.'

'It just seems like a natural progression, Sir,' said DD, 'Also, I'm sure the place must feel a great deal smaller, now that there are two of you properly living there.'

'You're exactly right, DD. Small is definitely the word. The problem is that I've got no idea where to go next, both geographically and domestically. I don't know what type of flat or house I want to live in, or whereabouts I'd like it to be.'

'Would it be presumptuous to assume you'd like me to start looking around?'

'Now you mention it, that would be a capital idea. I'm sure you'll hunt out the best places going, and it would be an excellent starting point, thank you, DD.'

'My pleasure, Sir. To be honest, I'll quite enjoy the task.'

Jemme stood up and put the folder under his arm, 'I knew I could count on you, DD,' he said warmly as they left the office. With that weight off his mind, the rest of the day passed with ease, and Jemme went home, comforted by the confirmation that there really was no obstacle insurmountable.

Over the next few weeks, DD rooted out a range of properties and handed their details over to Jemme, who saved them until he could pore over them with Hil. She had practically fallen on the idea of moving,

'It's not that I don't like this flat,' she had said, 'It's absolutely beautiful and I'm so happy to be living here with you; it's just that it would be nice not be tripping over ourselves at every turn.' Jemme had heartily agreed and they had studied the first batch of properties with excitement. However, Jemme's enthusiasm had quickly turned to disappointment. There was no denying that the properties were beautiful, or that DD had found an excellent range. There was no faulting the roomy townhouses or the luxury flats, and all in fantastic Parisian locations too. However, they all failed to excite Jemme. They were all lacking an ineffable something, a *je ne sais quoi* which, try as he might, he just could not identify.

'Maybe it's the location?' suggested Hil helpfully, 'Maybe you're tired of living in central Paris and that's why they don't appeal.'

Jemme thought that probably had a ring of truth. He was fed up with the increasing volumes of traffic and the pollution it brought. He was jaded by the dirtiness of everything, and the inescapable petty street crime. He knew that at some point they were going to want to start a family, and he couldn't imagine Paris providing the best environment for that. Furthermore, now everything was running smoothly back at the bank, he could afford to deal with a commute. He would no longer have to drop everything and run to the office in the middle of the night, so it did not make as much sense to live so close by.

He relayed his thoughts to DD, and the next batch of properties they looked at were scattered through the *banlieue*. They were larger, and on leafier streets, but whilst they appealed a little bit more, they still failed to elicit the right response.

Hil was similarly disappointed, 'Do you know, I think we could go even further out,' she said as they leafed through the details of a property in St Germain en Laye. 'Once we're going this far out, it doesn't make that much of a difference if we tack an extra twenty minutes onto the commute, and we'll get so much more space too.'

'You're right,' Jemme replied, 'I wouldn't object to being a little bit further out at all. We would have to cap it at some point though.'

'How do you mean?'

'I mean we'd have to put some kind of limit on things. I don't want to have to be driving for six hours of the day, and I'm sure you don't either. We should agree an upper limit and then discount properties which go beyond that.'

'That's a good idea. Why don't we say one hour from Paris as the absolute maximum distance we'd be prepared to travel.'

'Perfect,' Jemme said with conviction and kissed Hil on the forehead.

As they continued to look at property details DD sent through, they continued to add various criteria to their list. After looking at one photo which made a house look so dingy and depressing they didn't even bother reading the specifications, they decided that light was an essential criterion. The search grew wider and the properties they considered diversified. Hil realised that if they really were going to live an hour outside Paris, then good transport links were essential, and so that was added to the list. Jemme got carried away and added 'proximity to beach' too, but Hil cautiously put a question mark after it. 'We don't want to set ourselves up for disappointment.' she said, 'We're never going to find somewhere that's got everything.' Jemme nodded sagely, but secretly he didn't believe her. He felt so confident in himself, in life and in them at the moment, that he was convinced they would definitely find *exactly* what it was they were looking for.

Although he didn't doubt his confidence, he did accept that the search might be a long one; six months in and they still hadn't even looked at a property.

However, it had not been in vain, as they had an ever-firmer idea of what it was they were looking for. By now, they had completely discounted Paris as a location and were starting to refer to their 'move to the country' with increasing levels of sureness and excitement. They decided to pay a visit to some friends who had had similar ideas, and had recently left the City of Lights for what sounded like a bucolic idyll. The reality had been a little different however, and they spent a slightly tedious weekend listening to their friends, still city-slickers at heart, complaining about insulation problems, how far they had to drive to buy a half-litre of milk and how much it had cost them to fix the roof (almost as much as the house had been in the first place, apparently). Dejected and slightly deflated they drove home in thoughtful silence.

'I hope that hasn't put you off too much, sweetheart,' Jemme said eventually.

Hil broke into a wide smile, 'It's certainly put me off seeing them again, but it hasn't put me off moving to the countryside!' she said. 'We'll just have to do it much, much better than them,' she added, with vim.

As soon as they got home, they both added 'good insulation', 'excellent roof' and 'proximity to shops' to the list. After recalling one particularly unpleasant conversation over dinner, Hil shuddered and also added 'linked with the municipal sewerage system'.

Time continued, and they still hadn't found anywhere they liked enough on paper to arrange to see. Jemme felt that he was the source of most of the prevaricating, and raised the subject with Hil.

'I'm sorry sweetheart, I feel as if I'm the one stopping us from finding anywhere with all my fussiness.'

'Don't be silly,' said Hil, 'I don't want to live anywhere unless we're both happy with it from the very beginning. I just wish I could understand why nothing we've seen so far is appealing.'

'I don't know; I'm not sure either. I think when we find the right place we'll just know. In the meantime I think we're going about it in the right way, by working out what our exclusion criteria are.'

'I know, I know – it would just be easier if I knew what our inclusion criteria were!'

Jemme laughed and kissed her, 'I'm sorry, sweetheart, I'm not sure myself either. I just want this next place to be something special – somewhere that's more than just the place we live in.'

'What do you mean?'

'I mean that I don't want it just to be a house, I want it to have *meaning*.'

'Surely the meaning is what we create out of the house – we're the ones who invest meaning in the place, not the other way around.'

'Sort of, and it's a good point. I just want us to start off in a place which is already significant in some way and then go from there. I know I'm not explaining myself very well, and it's because I don't really know what I'm looking for myself. I just feel as if there's a wider purpose to our search. I really want to continue the project I started here and I feel it's all connected with my dream somehow.'

'Oh,' said Hil simply. She thought for a moment, 'In that case, my love, we shall continue looking for as long as it takes.'

Jemme smiled, gratified.

✳　✳　✳　✳

Several fruitless months later, Jemme received an unexpected note in the post. It was no more than a scrap of paper and had been stuffed inside a scruffy envelope. On it a scrawled note read, '*Have got to come to Paris for another lecture. Meet me in Turkish place Wed. 12ᵗʰ noon? Johnston*'. Jemme had to read it several times before he could make out what all the words said, or even who it was from. Once he had deciphered the 'Johnston' he broke out into a wide smile,

'Fantastic!' he said out loud.

'What is?' Hil asked, looking up from her breakfast.

'The Professor is coming to Paris,' said Jemme, tearing off a corner of fluffy croissant, 'I'm so pleased – I was beginning to wonder when I would see him again.'

'Professor Johnston? That's nice, he's such an interesting man,' said Hil.

Jemme smiled broadly, and popped the piece of croissant in his mouth; he had a lot of catching up to do with the Professor and he felt sure that Johnston was just the man to help him understand how his dream related to his search for a house.

Before he knew it, Wednesday 12ᵗʰ came around, and Jemme found himself looking forward to an early lunch break. He flew through his paperwork, and was soon navigating the warren of back streets to find the little Anatolian café where he had first met the Professor. Turkish writing on a board outside proclaimed that the special today was *tarhana* soup and Jemme smiled. He could just imagine the cousin of the owner turning up with a 50kg sack of tarhana – a mix of grain and fermented yoghurt -- and the owner flinging up her hands before declaring that for the next three weeks, all anyone would eat at her café would be soup.

He poked his head inside. It had been a while since he had last visited; what with the wedding and then settling into married life, he'd been busy. Besides, the trips back to Turkey, not to mention all the food his extended family had brought over with them, meant that he'd been well stocked up on Anatolian specialities. He hadn't suffered from the pangs of homesickness or sudden cravings for good mezze and fresh pide he had in the past. Nevertheless, he was pleased to see that the place was just as he remembered. As he opened the door a cloud of smoke and smells greeted him. He stepped inside, the air thronged with Turkish voices and he stopped to listen for a moment. It reminded him of his wedding day, and the peculiarity of feeling almost as if one were in an Istanbul coffee house or an Ankara restaurant, right in the heart of Paris. He let the sonorous noise wash over him for a moment, as he looked around for the Professor. He luxuriated in the different sounds, picking out various regional accents and smiling at long-forgotten expressions. Suddenly he noticed the Professor. Johnston too was just as he remembered. He looked utterly out of place, yet seemed completely blind to this fact. He had the air of a man supremely at ease within familiar surroundings. It was hot and noisy in the café, but Johnston was blissfully impervious to this. Despite the warmth and apparently deaf to the shouting from the kitchen, he sat there in a shabby tweed jacket, sipping on Turkish coffee and reading through his notes – every inch the cliché. His attaché case was full to bursting, just as Jemme remembered, and he would have wagered that there were holes in the Professor's socks, yet it was hard not to be envious of his apparent contentment.

Jemme strode over to him, 'Professor!' he said, with a hand extended.

'Jemme, *merhaba*,' Professor Johnston greeted him. A waitress was passing by and the Professor flapped his hand slightly manically at her. She approached cautiously, 'Another coffee for my friend please,' the Professor asked in flawless Turkish, and beamed at her. She smiled to herself as she turned to fetch it for them.

'Thank you,' said Jemme, taking a seat, 'How are you? What brings you to Paris? I'm sure it's not for the mezze!'

The Professor laughed, 'No, you're right, although it is uncommonly good here. I've been delivering a guest lecture at the Sorbonne. They're revitalising their Oriental Studies programme and so have had a series of guest lectures to get people interested. I was quite flattered to be asked, to be honest.'

'I'm sure they were honoured to have you,' said Jemme generously, 'what was the lecture about?'

The Professor flushed, 'Well, I don't know about honoured!' He laughed a little nervously, 'But I hope they liked the lecture; it was on "Ottoman Diplomacy and the European State System".'

'Really? That sounds fascinating!' said Jemme, genuinely meaning it. The waitress arrived with his coffee, '*Teşekkür ederim*,' he said, enjoying the shape of the Turkish words in his mouth. *How strange that throughout my childhood I spoke nothing else, and yet it feels like a novelty or even a treat to use Turkish now*, he thought to himself. He turned his attention back to the Professor, who was fishing around in his attaché case.

'I thought you might be interested, so I photocopied the notes for you,' said Johnston as he rummaged, 'I know they're in here somewhere, I just can't for the life of me....'

Jemme smiled, 'Don't worry, Professor, I'm sure they'll resurface at some point. It was kind of you to copy them for me.'

'Not at all, not at all,' Johnston muttered. 'I know they're around here somewhere, if only I could...' he carried on diving his hand into the case. Jemme had images of the whole thing exploding and eyed it with slight wariness. He thought it prudent to change the subject.

'Is that the only reason you're over?' he asked.

'It's the main reason, but I'm also hoping to have sorted something else out by the time I've left,' said the Professor, resigning himself to leaving the papers, and sipping his coffee.

Jemme looked curious, 'Go on,'

'Do you remember me telling you that there is a large amount of Eastern scholarship that has never been translated out of its original language? Huge tracts in fact. It's criminal, it really is. Vast numbers of primary sources have never even been translated into English. Can you imagine such a thing? Primary sources?!'

Jemme shook his head, 'I'm sure the lack of scholarship hasn't really helped foster Western learning about the East.'

'That's exactly the problem! I was at a symposium recently which examined the idea of modern-day Orientalism, and how little academia has really changed its approach to the East in a post-modern... anyway, I'm running away with myself. The point is that large amounts of work still needs to be translated. I think it's a matter of the utmost urgency, and that our culture and learning is poorer for lack of it. Rather happily, the Bibliothèque Nationale is wont to agree, and is beginning a huge translation project. I'm hoping to play a large role in things – if not leading then at least translating myself.'

'Professor, that's wonderful news! I can't think of anyone more suited to such a project; I'm sure they'll want you on board from the off.'

The Professor flushed a little again.

'It's interesting you mention this though,' said Jemme, 'because the dialogue between East and West is something that's been preoccupying me recently. Not literally, of course, I mean more in terms of the marriage of the two historical narratives.'

'That's a rather weighty thing for a banker-historian to be preoccupied with,' the Professor teased.

Jemme smiled, but was secretly pleased that the Professor had referred to him as an historian.

'Well, Hil and I are thinking of moving soon, which has raised all sorts of issues, but also opportunities. I've been taking stock recently, and I've actually managed to amass a healthy collection of art, and bits and bobs.'

The Professor nodded vigorously, 'I'll say – a most respectable one at that.'

'Thank you. Well, I've been reappraising my approach to it all recently. When it was just a few pieces here and there, it was fine to hang them on the wall and admire them as individual things of beauty. Now that it's taking shape as a collection, I feel that I need to do something more meaningful than that. I can't simply dump everything on shelves and on hooks on the walls without thinking about it.'

'Certainly not,' agreed the Professor.

'But then again, I've got such a diverse assemblage that sometimes there appears to be little cohesion, and I can't think of the most logical or the best way to arrange everything.'

'Hmm,' said the Professor as he finished the last of his coffee and winced slightly at its bitterness. 'I have a couple of curator friends, and so I understand just how much thought and research goes into organising a museum collection.'

'I think "museum collection" might be overstating it a little!' said Jemme, 'Although it does sometimes feel that way,' he added pensively.

'How did you begin to arrange things? I think your first reaction was probably quite telling.'

'Well, I started off looking at things individually – Impressionist art together, examples of Levantine carpentry together, all of that kind of thing.'

'I see. That sounds like a reasonable first approach.'

'But then I ended up with the same problem, but on a much larger scale. Instead of having lots of isolated pieces, I had lots of isolated groups, some with only two or three pieces within them, but nevertheless they bore as little relation to each other as the individual pieces had. So, I started to think about how the groups could be part of a larger whole. I realised that there could be a much larger, overarching narrative, which could link everything together. But then my problem became the fact that I didn't have *enough* works, which seemed a little paradoxical. It was true though – as I looked around I could see nothing but lacunae and gaps – great striking holes in the narrative I was trying to create. I felt as if I was in the situation where I could go one of two ways. I either needed to get rid of a great deal, or acquire a large amount for my collections to make any sense.'

'A conundrum indeed. And then what happened?'

'Well, then Hil moved in and brought even more objects with her, and the project kind of lost momentum a little. The thing is, if we're thinking about moving into somewhere bigger, then it seems like the perfect opportunity to pick up where I left off. I just want to go about things in the right way.'

Professor Johnston toyed thoughtfully with his spoon. 'I think you're right on two levels. Firstly to be so critical in your approach to your collection. I agree with you: once a person acquires enough objects, it becomes a collection and takes on a greater significance. I think it brings with it a large amount of responsibility, and also changes the nature of the collection – look at Sloane or Bodley: their collections are remembered because of the nature of the assemblages, not the individual items within them. Anyway, I also think you're right on a second count – that this move presents a great opportunity. There's so much potential for you to house and nurture a great collection of your own; you've already got off to such an auspicious start. It's quite an exciting prospect… think about it, you could be a latter day Hans Sloane!'

Jemme certainly did think about it as they chattered away over a lunch of tarhana soup. The thought continued to occupy him over the next few days, as he variously looked at and rejected property details DD gave him. The Professor was in town for another week and it wasn't long before Jemme was meeting him for another coffee. They chatted about the translation project and Jemme's ideas too. Johnston had given it some thought, and Jemme was grateful for the effort, especially when the Professor obviously had so much else on.

'I think that your problem was that you were starting off so big,' said Johnston as he finished yet another tiny cupful of punchy coffee. 'It sounds as if you were trying to weave a narrative around everything you own.'

'I was, I am,' said Jemme as he looked wistfully at a tray of glistening baklava and honeyed lokma. 'Shall we?' he said to the Professor.

'Absolutely,' said Johnston, smacking his lips, 'and some more coffees whilst we're about it, I should say!'

Jemme signalled to the waitress and asked to see the tray. She brought it over, and it looked even more appealing up close. They chose a couple of pastries each, and ordered another round of coffees.

'Think about it,' said Johnston, returning to the matter in hand. 'From what I know, you've got some pieces which don't even qualify as antiques, they're bone fide antiquities.'

Jemme nodded, 'I suppose you could put it that way, yes.'

'But you've also got some pieces that are from this very century?'

'Yes, I have a fair amount of Art Nouveau art and artefacts – it's fast becoming my favourite epoch.'

'Well, there you go then!'

'What?'

'You're trying to create a narrative around pieces from the Antique period all the way up until the turn of the century!'

'I suppose, but….'

'It's lunacy!' cried the Professor, apparently feeling the effects of all the sugar and coffee.

Jemme chuckled.

'Think about it – what are you trying to do? It sounds like you're trying to create a testament to all human endeavour, Eastern and Western, over the course of several millennia, all in a handful of medium-sized rooms in a flat in central Paris. Do you know how insane that sounds?!'

Jemme laughed again, 'Alright, alright, when you put it like that I will admit that it certainly sounds a little Quixotic. I've been constricted by my surroundings though, so go easy on me.'

Johnston took a swig of water and calmed down a little.

'It's a gallant first attempt, there's no two ways about it, but, as I said. I think you've started off too big. You need to be more selective: if you pick several key periods to illustrate certain points, then you can elaborate with larger collections around those points. That way, you can be concise, but detailed at the same time.'

'I see what you mean,' said Jemme, 'That all sounds sensible.'

'Your points can be anything too!' said Johnston, 'It could be an era, a movement in art, or even a civilisation. You could focus on one area geographically or perhaps look at the interplay between two civilisations or areas,' he said, warming to his theme. 'There's so much potential here, I think it's a really exciting opportunity.'

Jemme started to see things as the Professor did, with clear, concise narratives illuminating his favourite subjects and elucidating subjects close to his heart. He couldn't help but share his excitement, 'And you think there's the potential to do all of this?' he asked keenly.

'Absolutely! History is your oyster. The only thing that will limit you is your choice of your next property.'

Jemme mulled the thought over in his head on the journey home. Once he got back he dug out the slightly dog-eared list and added 'rooms – at least ten' to the bottom. He sat in his study and flicked through some of his favourite books in an absent minded way whilst he contemplated the potential the project had. He thought about his favourite civilisations, and the periods of history that had most excited him as a child. He thought about the sources of continued interest into adulthood, the trips he had shared with Hil and the treasures they had discovered in all manner of different places. His head was swimming with possibilities, and his mind felt alive with the excitement of it all. Before he went to bed that evening he found the list for the second time and crossed out 'ten' and wrote in 'twenty' instead.

※　※　※　※

The Professor's visit was shortly drawing to a close and Jemme and Hil had still not come any closer to organising viewings on any property. The number of rooms had now become Jemme's primary concern, and he had since scribbled out 'twenty' and written in 'thirty' and then 'thirty-five' in its place. Hil had initially looked a little sceptical, but seeing his enthusiasm had left him to it. Two days before Johnston was due to leave, he asked Jemme if he would like to accompany him on a trip 'to the country.' Even in the late summer, Paris was feeling hot and sticky, and Jemme readily agreed. Johnston had to go and cast his professorial eye over the book collection of some aristocrat in his crumbling chateau, apparently.

'It won't take very long,' he told Jemme, 'but I thought you might enjoy the opportunity to have a bit of a nose around.'

They left early on Saturday and drove south of Paris for about an hour and a half. Jemme greatly enjoyed watching the scenery change, from urbane and upright to rambling and ramshackle. They drove past sprawling farms, and through tiny villages. The air was fresh out here, and the warm early morning light made everything look like a Gainsborough painting. Jemme drank it all in greedily, and thought about how excited he was to be leaving the city. They eventually found the chateau, which was in a poor state of repair. The roof seemed to have sprung holes and some of the windows were boarded over. The owner looked in an equally poor state of repair. They had been ushered into a *salon* by a rather doleful housekeeper, who had offered them *café* but then turned up with something that was anything but. Jemme drank the lukewarm watery concoction as gamely as he could, and exchanged pleasantries with the owner. The man looked as though he were pushing a hundred, and shuffled slowly around the dim room in laboured fashion, which was quite painful to watch.

'Shall I open some of these shutters?' asked Jemme, 'It might help the Professor if there was some more light in here.'

The old man looked at him and cupped his ear, '*Comment?*'

Jemme repeated his question a few more times before the old man shrank away from him, '*Les volets? Non, non, non, Monsieur!* My tapestries and my carpets, *Monsieur!*' he croaked, and shuffled off, muttering to himself.

Jemme gave up trying to be helpful, and waited for Johnston to finish. The Professor soon joined him, 'Would you like to have a look around? I've cleared it with the housekeeper – her son is going to show us about.'

Jemme agreed, although he wasn't keen to spend any more time in the house than was strictly necessary. The son turned out to be just as doleful as his mother, and led them on a rather subdued route around the house, before depositing them at the front door and bidding them a baleful '*au revoir*'.

'Sorry about that,' said Johnston on the drive back, 'I wasn't expecting it to be quite as…'

'Depressing?' Jemme finished for him.

Johnston laughed, 'It was rather, wasn't it? I'm afraid so many of those chateaux are like that. You find these old aristocrats clinging on to their hereditary homes, which are crumbling at the same rate they are. They're so proud, and they still act as if France is the class-driven society of Louis XVI's time. They haven't got a penny to support themselves of course, and you'll find them selling off the family portraits to fix the roof. It's sad, but sometimes it's hard to feel sorry for people who are just so….'

'Snobbish?' Jemme ventured again.

Johnston laughed, 'I suppose so.'

'What was that business with the shutters all about?'

'Oh that. That will have been because he'll have some priceless rug, or something or other which he won't allow light anywhere near. They're all the same – it's like they're living in museums or even mausoleums. It's like they've enshrined the past and will protect it at every cost. It's no way to live – shuffling around in the dark to protect a rug which you won't allow anyone to ever see.'

'No,' Jemme agreed. The whole thing had got him thinking though. Whilst the chateau had been dark and somewhat dank, he couldn't help but notice the potential it held. Granted, his host had shut up all his paintings, and Jemme imagined that he couldn't even remember where most of them were, but that didn't prevent Jemme from noticing how much space there had been in which to hang them all. The peculiarities of the space and shapes the old building created afforded a number and size of walls that Jemme could only dream of. What's more, old chateaux such as that one were full of myriad defunct rooms. There was no longer any need for a scullery maid's chambers or a game pantry, and so now they sat empty in buildings just such as this one. Jemme knew exactly what he would do if he got his hands on them, and he knew that the countryside was dotted with empty chateaux.

He mulled the idea over for a couple of days, turning it over to see it from every angle and prodding at it. He knew it was folly to imagine himself as king of a castle, but it definitely retained an appeal. A few days later, DD brought up the subject anyway.

'I notice that I still haven't been able to find anything which appeals to you, Sir,' he said, almost remorsefully.

'It's not you DD, I'm afraid it's me, I'm being rather picky.'

'Perhaps I could be a little bit more specific in my search; have you thought of any further criteria, Sir?'

'Well, it's funny you should mention that; as a matter of fact I have. I was thinking that perhaps you could start to look for houses which were more… chateau-like.'

DD managed to suppress whatever he was feeling and merely asked, '"Chateau-like" Sir?'

'Well, I say chateau-*like*… what I actually mean is just plain chateau. I'd really like it if you could find me a chateau for sale.'

Although his face registered no difference, DD sounded as if every last breath was being squeezed out of him, 'Sir?' he rasped.

'It would still have to meet the other criteria, of course. I mean, I don't want to have to start looking at places which are more than one hour out of Paris!'

'No, sir, of course not. I shall see what I can find,' DD intoned, although it sounded more like a death rattle.

To his credit, only a few days later, at the end of the morning meeting, he presented Jemme with the printed details of a chateau for sale. It wasn't too far from Paris and had apparently been re-roofed recently. Tall, elegant windows made it look as if it would be beautifully light inside and the façade made it look like a castle straight from a fairy tale. Jemme presented the papers to Hil, who looked at him slightly goggle-eyed,

'Are you serious?'

'I know it seems a little whacky, but...'

'Whacky? It's completely crazy! Are you actually, *actually* suggesting that we start looking at chateaux now? We've had enough trouble finding a house which we liked – how on earth is looking at chateaux going to make things any easier?!'

'I know it seems fanciful, and I'll admit that it is, but it's just for fun. Please, just indulge me on this one – we can go and have a look around a beautiful chateau and then get back to the search proper. I was just struck by something when I went on that visit with the Professor; I'm sure once I've seen one and got it out of my system, then I'll be completely over the idea.'

'Fine,' Hil sighed.

Jemme grinned at her and her irritated face melted away, 'You're just like an excitable child at times!' she said, giving him a playful kiss on the cheek.

That weekend they drove eastwards out of Paris. It was not an auspicious start; Jemme hated east Paris at the best of times and avoided it at all costs. If he ever did find himself there, then he inevitably got lost in the complicated one-way system, and always emerged in a temper with a resolve not to come back for as long as was possible. Eventually they reached the outskirts of Paris, and carried on driving east. They found the chateau without too much difficulty, and turned off the road where the gate signposted the beginning of the driveway. As they caught their first glimpse of the chateau, they both gasped slightly. Sitting at the crest of the long entry drive, it really was like something straight out of a fairy tale, with spires tapering up from its roof and turrets stacked on top of each other. They parked up the car and crunched their way across the gravel. Yellow roses grew up against the grey stone walls and the grounds they had driven past on the way down appeared to stretch all the way behind the chateau too. A small set of steps led up to the main entrance, and as they went up them, Hil slipped her hand into Jemme's and squeezed it. He smiled at her – it was difficult not to get caught up in the romance of the situation. He knocked on the door and then noticed a long, fine chain hanging to one side. He pulled on it and heard a far off bell ring inside the building somewhere. Several moments later the door creaked open on its massive hinges, and a small man with greasy hair and yellowed eyes stood before them.

'*Oui?*' he drew out questioningly.

'We're the Mafezes,' said Jemme, we're here for the viewing.'

The small man broke into smiles, 'Of course, of course; I am the *procurateur*, I am managing the sale. I will show you round!' he said rather dramatically.

Jemme and Hil exchanged amused glances and followed him inside. He led them along the corridor which was flanked by large windows, affording beautiful views over the grounds. Hil stopped to admire them.

'We noticed how lovely the grounds were on the way in. Do you know how big they are?' she asked.

'Yes, the grounds are as lovely as Madame,' said the *procurateur*, looking Hil up and down lasciviously. 'I believe there are one hundred and ten hectares here.' He flashed a toothsome smile at her, which revealed that his teeth were as yellow as his eyes. Hil looked a little uncomfortable, and smiled at him stiffly.

As he took them around the various rooms, he gave the majority of the explanation to Jemme, before turning and leering at Hil. If he hadn't been so enamoured with the chateau itself, Jemme would have upped and left there and then. However, there was no denying that it had its merits. It was extremely large – two thousand square metres apparently, with beautifully high ceilings and generously proportioned rooms. It was full of original features with lintels, cornices and balusters. He could genuinely see himself living there with his young family. He saw his future children playing safely on the grass outside, he saw huge paintings hanging on the walls, he saw statues standing in the long corridors and he saw enough rooms to be able to create whatever it was he was hankering for. It was all a little bit too good to be true. The strange, greasy little chap was making it difficult to enjoy, though. He kept making meaningful references, and shooting long sideways looks at Jemme. Jemme didn't have a clue what he was talking about, but he wasn't particularly comfortable around him. When they finally got to the master bedroom, the little man was positively ringing his hands with glee.

'Oh, hoooo, here we are!' he said excitedly.

'Is this the largest bedroom in the house?' asked Hil innocently.

'Oh, oh, it is a large bedroom Madame wants?!' he said, barely believing his luck, 'I am not surprised – oh! This house!' he licked his lips and then winked sleazily at Jemme. It was the final straw,

'Look, what on earth are you talking about?' said Jemme, resenting his assumed chumminess, his lack of professionalism and his creepy behaviour.

'But Monsieur does not know?'

'Does not know what?' Jemme asked tetchily.

'Why, the story of this house of course!'

'What story? What are you talking about?'

The man made a low guttural noise of pleasure. Evidently he enjoyed the opportunity to tell the story.

'This chateau,' he said dramatically, 'is the former residence of Alphonse François, Marquis de Sade!'

A slow smile crept across his swarthy face again, 'So, you can see why I am wondering why it is that Madame would like a large bedroom...'

'Are there any other rooms to see?' asked Jemme curtly, cutting him short, as Hil tried to suppress a shudder.

It turned out there were indeed a good many more rooms to see, all of which Jemme looked at wistfully as he tried to block out the noise of the odious *procurateur*. He was positively revelling in his role. He seemed to have decided that since the young couple he was with knew nothing of the chateau's history, it was now his duty to impart as much candid knowledge as he could muster. They couldn't pass a single room, or even alcove, without him describing in lurid detail what he 'thought might have happened there'. By the end of the tour, all Jemme and Hil wanted to do was jump in the car and drive westwards towards a hot shower, as quickly as possible.

Once they were safely back in the suburbs of Paris, they both looked at each other and burst out laughing.

'That was about the creepiest experience of my life,' said Hil.

'Me too,' Jemme agreed.

'I'm guessing it's a no then?' she asked.

'Definitely a no to that place, but not to chateaux in general.'

Hil looked at him questioningly.

'Imagine that place without any of its history, and without that horrible man showing us round. Wasn't it beautiful? Couldn't you see us raising a family there? The children would have their own forest to play in and own lake to swim in. We could fill it with lovely art and antiques and there would be enough space for everyone and everything – we could have guest rooms for our parents when they came to stay.'

Hil thought about it for a moment, 'I suppose you do have a point. We were both so impressed by it from the outside as well,'

'Exactly,'

'In fact, I was impressed by it from the inside too, right up until I started to think something was amiss with our ghoulish tour guide.'

'Mmmmadame,' said Jemme, mimicking the *procurateur*'s lecherous tones.

'Stop!' squealed Hil, shuddering.

A few days later, Jemme received a phone call from the very same ghoulish guide.

'I hope Monsieur enjoyed seeing the chateau,' he said.

'Enjoyed? Ah, yes...very much. Thank you, we'll be in touch,' said Jemme, keen to get off the phone.

'Well, if Monsieur is not completely convinced already, there is one thing which might make up your mind.'

'Really,' said Jemme doubtfully.

'Yes, it is most exciting news, most exciting indeed. We have just heard that the Disney Corporation are planning on building a theme park right opposite the chateau!'

'I see. Thank you for letting me know. Like I said, we'll be in touch,' Jemme said in completely neutral tones. He hung up and stared at the receiver for a few seconds. He didn't know whether to laugh or grimace. After repeating the news to himself, he shook his head and chuckled. If his mind hadn't been solidly made up before, it certainly was now. He couldn't think of anything more surreal, or anywhere less desirable. He definitely had no plans to start a family in a place where saccharine cartoons danced in view of the lair of the original arch-libertine.

✻ ✻ ✻ ✻

Bizarre as the incident had been, it had not altered Jemme's desire to continue to look at chateaux. Once he had seen the space it could afford him, it felt like a huge step down to consider ordinary or modern houses. He still wasn't sure what it was he was trying to create there, but his idea was taking shape, and he liked the extra tissue of history which an ancient chateau or manor house would bring. Hil too had been quite taken with the idea. In her naturally understanding way, she had soon realised why Jemme was so set on the idea and supported him in it.

'After all, it's been nearly a year already – we might as well wait until we've found exactly what we're looking for,' she had told him.

Jemme had thought about it carefully, and after their initial experience added 'must have a story to tell' to the list. He ran over all the things he had liked about the chateau they had seen, and then added 'must be built of stone' and 'must have French character or beauty from the outside'. He thought about it for a while, and weighed up whether or not they were reasonable criteria, then added '..or brick, or a combination of both,' to 'made of stone'. A couple of days later he noticed the list was sitting on his desk, and an extra item had been added onto the bottom in Hil's handwriting: 'Parquet floors' it said.

'I didn't like the stone floors of the last place,' she said when he raised it with her. Too draughty. Parquet is much warmer and nicer.'

'Absolutely,' he agreed, pleased at this sign that she was now fully on board.

By this point he had realised that the search was going to be a much bigger project than anyone had first imagined. It was no longer fair to rely on DD as their only source for finding property, especially now they were being so specific. Jemme put the word about with his colleagues and contacts, established links with several agents and signed up to a number of monthly publications. Soon enough, it paid off and several months later, an elderly French gentleman Jemme had done business with wrote to him, saying that an acquaintance of his was selling up his chateau in Burgundy, and, if Jemme was amenable to the suggestion, could he organise a meeting? Jemme wrote a polite letter back, and they set up a date for the following month.

Jemme and Hil decided to make a weekend of it, and packed a couple of small bags before heading south-east to Burgundy. It was a lovely drive through rolling hills and beautiful countryside, but by the time they had arrived it had already been two hours since they had left Paris. However, the small town nearest the chateau was incredibly pretty, with lots of good food on offer in the shops and appetising looking regional specialities, not to mention an abundance of excellent red wine. The gardens were boxed in by a smartly cut hedge, and the chateau itself was a soft grey French stone. The first thing that either of them noticed was how small it was, especially compared with the first one they had seen. The second thing they noticed was the fact that it appeared to be an island in a sea of vineyards. A young man of about twenty came out to meet them, and introduced himself as the owner's son. He was perfectly pleasant and the chateau was very nice, but they both knew from the beginning it really wasn't what they were looking for. It was very obviously a gentleman's retreat, with huge antlers mounted above large open fireplaces. Oil paintings on the walls showed various illustrious ancestors with rifles cocked over their arms and trusty spaniels by their feet. Books about game lined the shelves, and polished antique spears shone in glass display cases.

'My father enjoys *la chasse*,' the young man said, somewhat unnecessarily.

He showed them to the cellar, which was musty with a faint hint of pipe smoke. It was probably the biggest wine cellar Jemme had ever seen, with rows and rows of dusty bottles, carefully placed in special racks which stretched from end to end. The young man walked them slowly up the middle, pointing out the various Viré-Clessé and Petit-Chablis and enthusing about the number of Mâcon-Villages. The tour of the cellar took almost as long as the tour of the house, which Jemme found slightly puzzling until he heard that the sale of the wines was included in the sale of the house.

It was a tempting offer, and had he been a committed oenophile it would have been a fantastic bargain. Furthermore, if he had been that way inclined, the vineyards surrounding the chateau represented a hefty source of income, and he could have set up a respectable wine business without too much trouble. However, it was not at all what he wanted to do. He thanked the young man warmly, and when he said that he hoped they found the right buyer soon he genuinely meant it. He could imagine the chateau making someone very happy exactly as it was – it just wouldn't be him. After he and Hil had checked into a charming guesthouse in the nearby town, they talked it over. She completely agreed with him, but was very emphatic about the space too.

'You surprise me,' said Jemme, 'at the beginning you were the one shunning the idea of a chateau, because it was unnecessarily large, and now look at you!

'I know,' said Hil as she sipped a glass of excellent Côte de Chouchois, 'but once you've seen what's on offer…' she trailed off.

'Agreed,' Jemme said. 'Let's add "space" to the list. We can start off with two thousand square metres and see how that goes.'

'Excellent,' said Hil, 'cheers!' she raised her glass.

'Cheers,' said Jemme and clinked his with hers.

Chapter Eleven

One rainy September morning Jemme found himself thinking back to that Summer morning when he had tried to convince Hil to see the first chateau with him. He remembered it exactly as if it were yesterday,

'I'm sure once I've seen one, and got it out of my system, then I'll be completely over the idea,' he had said.

He also remembered the surging optimism and supreme confidence he had had as a newlywed, believing that nothing was insurmountable, and that he and Hil could achieve anything they put their minds to. Some four years had passed now, and they had still not found the home of their dreams. At times Jemme had worried that they were only looking for the home of his dreams, and that he was the driving force behind things. He worried that if things had been left to Hil, they would have long since found somewhere, and be completely settled in by now. She was always quick to reassure him that this wasn't the case, though. She variously soothed, indulged and reasoned that it wouldn't be the perfect place unless both of them were happy with it. There was something of the grail quest about the search, and Jemme sometimes wondered if he would ever really find what he was looking for, or if it was merely the act of searching he craved. The length of the search to date definitely put pressure on the final result – having waited for so long, the final property couldn't be anything less than perfect, and would have to satisfy pretty much every criterion on the list.

The list had changed and evolved over the years too, variously growing and then shrinking, reflecting the shining examples and houses of horror they'd seen. There had been the manor house with wiring so dangerous it looked as if Tesla had left, mid-experiment. Hil swore she saw sparks jumping along the electric cables, and they had tried to look at one room in the dark after deciding they would rather not risk touching the light switch. They had decided against it pretty quickly, and Jemme had not wasted any time in adding 'recently rewired' to the list. Six months later he had extended that to 'electricity in every room', after visiting one place which seemed to be trapped in the last century.

One particular place had sat next to a beautiful lake. Clear as crystal, it provided a perfect, inverted image of the grand chateau above it. It was an arresting sight, and had prompted Hil to suggest 'lake or river' for the list. They were both rather enjoying the specific nature of their search. Now that they had accepted that they were going to have to wait, they could afford to be as picky as they liked. Seeing so many chateaux had been an education too. They felt like experts on French neo-classical architecture, cess-pit storage, subsidence and dry rot. They now knew exactly what to look out for, and had become attuned to the various fibs and exaggerations of the agents and *procurateurs* who showed them around. They could tell when something was a white elephant within about the first ten minutes of arriving. Hil had even developed a theory that the difficulty the agent had experienced in shifting the property thus far was directly proportionate to the broadness of his smile and his enthusiasm when he was showing them around, and Jemme was inclined to agree. It had been an education on the crumbling remnants of the French aristocracy too. Many of the imperious, cash-strapped people they had encountered had been similar to the owner of the first chateau Jemme had visited with the Professor. Haughty and proud to the last, they were a fragmented class, surrounding themselves with the very heritage that was proving to be a millstone around their necks. They shuffled around in their darkened castles in summer, and in winter lived out their lives in the only two rooms they could afford to heat. It was a fairly dismal existence, but Jemme found it difficult to empathise with many of them. They were still tightly bound by the stratifications of a defunct class system, and often outright hostile during visitations. It was a life and an ideology which was ultimately unsustainable, and Jemme had been surprised they had managed to eke a living out of their property and inheritance thus far. He very much viewed them as the last hurrah of the French Empire; although sometimes uncomfortable, meeting such people had been a very interesting experience, and allowed him a greater depth of understanding of the French psyche and attitude towards their own history.

Despite the fact they had still not found anywhere, they both agreed that the viewings they had been to had been invaluable. In addition to the experience they had gained and the insight they had been exposed to, it had also helped shape their search. Certain things had remained on the list, but it was a fairly fluid set of criteria and things were just as likely to be removed. For about a year and a half, Jemme was fixed on the idea of having a *pigeonnier*. At first it had been a complete flight of fancy, but having seen several manor houses with their own pigeon lofts, he had become set on the idea of having one himself. It had a long history in both the East and West, and noble associations with aristocracy and kings. Their agents' ears had perked up at the news of this interest and seemed to use it as a focal point in their respective searches. They had bombarded Hil and Jemme with news of 'the perfect chateau,' and 'the manor house of their dreams.' Hil and Jemme would duly drive for hours and hours to the middle of nowhere, to find an awful property in a dire state of repair. They would look questioningly at the agent who would point skywards and say happily, 'But look, Monsieur, the *pigeonnier*!' They decided to cross it off the list for the time being.

'Why don't we say that if it's there, it's an added bonus, and if it's not then it's not a deal breaker?' Hil suggested.

'That sounds reasonable enough,' Jemme had replied, although secretly still held out hope that they would find somewhere with its own pigeon house.

They had also come up with several other loose categories: whilst they weren't worthy of proper list mention, they were certainly things to bear in mind whilst looking at a place. It had to be private, for example. Jemme had thought it wasn't worth mentioning, but after looking at a place which had been dwarfed by a modern development right on its doorstep, he resolved that if there was any chance they might be overlooked, then he would want, at the very least, a high, thick hedge.

As Jemme thought back over the search so far and idly wondered how much longer it would continue for, he flicked through the details of the latest property. This one had been found by DD, who still hadn't tired of looking around on their behalf. Jemme admired his indefatigability, which seemed to match his own. Whilst he and Hil had initially been disappointed, they had not been discouraged. There seemed to be no question about the fact that they would eventually find a place; it was just a question of how long it took them. Jemme had put his various projects on hold and they had put most of their art and antiques into storage. He still caved and occasionally bought the odd piece, but if it cluttered up the house too much, Hil soon whipped it into storage with the rest of them. It felt like everything was ready, and they were living in a state of anticipation whilst they waited for the next stage of their lives to begin.

Jemme thumbed through the details DD had given him. The chateau looked promising, although he had learned not to get excited until he had seen the place. The photo was a little too blurry to make out, and so he read over the details; just south of Fontainebleau, it was certainly within the right distance of Paris and the surveyor had given it a favourable report too. A small map showed its proximity to the *autoroute,* and a paragraph of rather florid prose outlined its colourful history. Variously home to knights, cardinals and priests, it had stood tall through battles won and fortunes lost. Its story appealed to Jemme as soon as he read it, and the details of the grounds did too. It was set in one hundred hectares of beautifully landscaped gardens. They didn't need a thing doing to them; all he would have to do would be employ a gardener. Best of all, the family were willing to leave all their statuary behind. Jemme couldn't discern much about the marbles from the photo, but they were well placed in their surroundings, and would be a pleasant extra if he took the property. Hil seemed equally keen on the place and so he made arrangements to go the following weekend. Apart from anything else, he was dying to give the new Mercedes a run-out and the long straight road down to the chateau provided the perfect opportunity.

The car had a colourful history of its own, and Jemme was already quite attached to it. He had bought it from a dealership on the Champs-Élysées, where it had been marked as *d'occasion,* but it had looked brand new. There wasn't a single mark on its glossy champagne-coloured finish, its interior still smelled of brand new leather, and the meaty engine under the bonnet positively gleamed. He had liked the car when he tried it: it was luxurious and yet comfortable, with a feeling of stability and solidity. He had liked the price even more, and asked the dealer why it wasn't being sold as new. The dealer assured him that it was 'as good as new' but hadn't been able to answer his question. Eventually Jemme had wangled the truth out of the manager. The car had been bought by the despotic leader of an African state. He had paid for it to be fully reinforced and shipped over, but had been deposed before he had even had the chance to drive the thing. Jemme remembered seeing footage of the coup on the news, and couldn't believe that the object he was thinking of buying provided such a tangible link to the story. The dealer had told him that the car was completely bullet proof, and had had a huge steel plate let into the chassis, which was thick enough to withstand antipersonnel landmines. 'Not that you'll need to worry about anything like that in the eighth Arrondissement,' he had joked, before confessing that all of these things made the car quite petrol hungry. Jemme didn't need to think about it for too long. The reduction on the car was incredible, and vastly made up for any extra fuel costs. He had bought it on the spot, and it had been delivered later that day. So far he had only made short inner-city trips in it. He'd been stuck in traffic for most of them as well, and so he jumped at this opportunity to actually hear the roar of the car's V8 engine.

The weather had cleared up a little by the next weekend, and so they drove out of Paris with the windows rolled down and high hopes. Once they had finally freed themselves from the bumper-to-bumper traffic, Jemme tickled the accelerator with his foot. He felt a satisfying *VROOOM* from underneath him, and the car shot forward. He stepped down slightly harder on the pedal. *VROOOOOOOOOM* growled the car as he took himself into the fast lane. He drove at the speed limit all the way to the chateau, thoroughly enjoying himself. Despite the speed at which he was travelling, the car still felt as if it was cruising along at a stately fifteen kilometres per hour. It felt just like he was sitting on the comfortable leather sofa in his office's foyer.

Just as the map had promised, the chateau was not far from the *autoroute* and they found it very easily. He parked the car and got out of it slightly reluctantly. As Hil headed to walk to the chateau, he turned back for another look at the gleaming Mercedes, its hot engine still clicking slightly under the bonnet. He joined Hil with a big grin on his face, prompting her to mutter something about boys and their toys.

As they walked up the flagstone path to the chateau they took in the impressive façade. The grainy photo really hadn't done it justice – Jemme hadn't even known that it had a beautiful Italianate bell-tower, and the picture had made the whole building look a great deal smaller, too.

He suddenly realised something, 'The camera!' he exclaimed and fished in his pocket for the car keys. 'Stay there, I'll only be ten seconds,' he said to Hil as he dashed back to the car. The camera was the newest tool in their search. Huge recent developments in photography meant that pocket cameras were growing ever smaller, yet still producing impressive results. They had invested in one which was small enough to slip into Hil's handbag, and it had proved to be a valuable resource during the search. They were now in the habit of taking several photos during each viewing, which they could pore over later. Sometimes it was because they simply forgot what certain features looked like – after a while they all seemed to blur into one. Sometimes, it was for comparative purposes, and they could flick through photos from several different chateaux trying to determine which room was the most sizeable, or which elements they liked the most. Jemme had even found somewhere selling films with forty-two shots on them, which had proved useful on several occasions when he had become slightly carried away whilst photographing various properties. He locked the car up for the second time, 'Smile!' he called over at Hil, and leant back to get the entire façade into the viewfinder.

They were met at the entrance by the concierge, a rather dishevelled fellow with two missing front teeth. Jemme privately thought that he looked a little as if one of the gargoyles had fallen from the eaves of the house and then sprung to life.

'*Bienvenu, Monsieur,*' he said, looking anything but welcoming. He introduced the stout little grey-haired woman by his side as 'Mère Marie'. 'She is an Abbess,' he said, 'She insisted on coming with us.' Mère Marie nodded primly but neither of them offered any further explanation. They both led Jemme and Hil around, with the concierge offering as little information as possible, and the Abbess occasionally shaking her head and tutting.

'May I ask,' said Hil in French, 'did this used to be a religious building? I was led to believe that priests lived here at one point.'

Mère Marie looked incensed.

'I only ask out of interest, because I'm from a Catholic background myself,' said Hil, attempting to soften the stern looking Abbess. It achieved the desired result, and she consented to talk.

'Not just priests, Madame, but nuns too! This was a convent and I was a nun here.'

'Really? Were you Abbess here too?'

Mère Marie's face darkened, '*Non*. I was Abbess at another convent – a more moral convent nearby. I was very young when I left here and I left as soon as I discovered that *le péché* was so rife amongst the sisters here. I would have nothing to do with it I tell you – *rien*!'

'Sin, mother?' Hil ventured.

The abbess nodded her tiny head, '*Oui, oui, Madame*, but I would have nothing to do with it – *rien*! I come back now to warn people. God frowns on this place and all who live here must know this.'

Hil didn't look, but she was pretty certain Jemme would be rolling his eyes. So far, Marie was fitting his profile of a religious eccentric. He had no doubt already written her off as a slightly senile, superstitious old lady. Hil, however, had grown up around people just like this, and was much more sympathetic. They continued to follow Marie and the concierge – a very strange pair indeed. In fact, the four of them together made a very odd sight. As Marie continued to mutter about the *pécheurs*, Hil continued to listen and try to coax details out of her. The gap-toothed concierge silently showed Jemme the different rooms, and Jemme cheerfully photographed them. Eventually they arrived in a large central hallway. A sheet of tarpaulin had been spread out on the floor and was covered with plaster dust. Jemme peered up and could see daylight through the high ceiling above.

'What happened here?' he asked.

'The ceiling fell in, Monsieur,' the concierge answered in a matter-of-fact way.

Mère Marie's muttering increased and Hil frowned. Jemme remained the only one unconcerned by the situation.

'Oh dear!' he said jovially, 'do you think it will be a difficult job to fix it?'

The concierge executed a perfect Gallic shrug, '*Je ne sais pas, Monsieur*, it is always the same. A new owner buys the property, and the day they move in a piece of the ceiling falls in. It is always in this same spot too.'

'Vengeance!' Mère Marie suddenly piped up. 'It is God's vengeance!'

'Shhhhttt!' the concierge said, 'Nonsense!'

Hil eyed Marie, who continued to mutter something about sinners and 'seeing things with her own eyes.'

'Well, it doesn't look like anything too serious,' said Jemme, completely ignoring her as he took a photo. 'I'm sure a good architect would get a builder to sort it out in a matter of days. Shall we go on?'

The strange little foursome continued touring the chateau. Marie's mutterings intensified, Hil looked increasingly uneasy, and the concierge did a poor job of hiding his irritation at Marie's fevered head-shaking and sighing. Jemme on the other hand was becoming increasingly cheerful, snapping away with his camera and declaring things 'magnificent' and 'wonderful.' Once they had seen everything in the chateau he turned to the concierge. 'I know it sounds like an odd request, but I was wondering if we could look in the cellar? I'd quite like to have a look over the plumbing, and the electrics and that sort of thing, just to check they're in order.'

The concierge shrugged and turned to lead the way. Jemme turned to Hil,

'Are you going to come with us?'

'No, thanks. It's so sunny it seems a shame to go into a dark basement. I'll stay up here and have a look at the grounds,' she said.

'Whatever you like, my love,' Jemme said. As he turned to follow the concierge he could hear Marie saying something to Hil about showing her 'where it all began.' He chuckled slightly, glad he wasn't going to have to deal with the strange woman.

A recce downstairs produced positive results, and he was pleased by the overall condition of everything. He found Hil waiting upstairs for him.

'Hello darling, I-'

'Let's go,' Hil hissed, interrupting him.

'Go? But I wanted to have a look at the grounds too!'

'I'm serious!' she said, 'Let's go now.'

Jemme took in her ashen face, and decided it would probably be best to do as she said. Besides, he didn't really have much choice in the matter; Hil had already linked her arm through his, and was steering him towards the exit.

They passed the concierge and the Abbess. Jemme started to say goodbye, but was interrupted by Marie's cries of, 'I told you! I saw it with my own eyes!' Hil picked up the pace and Jemme trotted after her. Neither of the two figures they left behind looked surprised to see them leave.

Hil slammed the car door shut and told him that she wanted to leave as soon as possible.

'What was all that about?' Jemme asked when they were safely back on the main road. 'You look positively spooked. Is everything ok?'

'No, not really. I hated that place and I don't ever want to go back.'

'You hated it? What do you mean? I thought it was lovely, I'm feeling really excited about it.'

'It was anything but lovely. Mother Marie told me some horrible stories about the sinning that went on there. I think the sisters were anything but chaste, and they didn't deal very well with the consequences. The whole place is cursed, and she doesn't think it will ever be absolved.'

'Cursed? You're being silly,'

'I'm not – Marie said all the bad things that have happened there are just showing God's wrath.'

'God's wrath?! What nonsense. I'm sure there's a perfectly rational explanation for everything she was droning on about.'

'Well how do you explain the ceiling falling in at the exact same spot, every time a new person bought the house? Marie says it's because something bad happened exactly where the roof falls through.'

'That's ridiculous! I'm sure if the roof keeps falling down in the same place it's because of a structural weakness – like I said, a good architect will sort that out in no time.'

'But it's every time someone new comes in!' Hil said obstinately.

'Well I expect that's because they send a surveyor up to have a look at the roof, and he loosens it. I'm sure there's something logical behind it. Really Hil, I'm surprised at you taking that funny little nun seriously. She was positively falling over herself to have an audience.' No sooner had he uttered the words than there was an almighty BANG! The steering wheel jerked sideways and Jemme completely lost control of the car. The back swung out suddenly from behind them, sending the car into a skid. He grabbed the steering wheel, and tried to straighten the car, but this only sent the front careering into the opposite direction and made the car start to snake. They had been driving in the outer lane, and Hil screamed as the car started to veer towards the middle lane. Jemme tried to grapple with the wheel and regain control of the car, but everything was happening too fast. He knew that braking would only exacerbate the situation, and so he had no choice but to lean on the horn and try to get them safely to the hard shoulder. As he tried to guide them across the middle lane, he didn't notice a lorry coming up behind him on the inner lane. Hil screamed again, but it was too late. The huge vehicle smashed into the back of them, sending the car into a spin, which took them clean off the road. The driver drove off, sounding his horn, and it was only as he was watching him disappear that Jemme realised he had safely managed to stop the car. The force of the lorry's impact had been enough to stop the car snaking, and also to send it off the road. He counted slowly to five and then exhaled fully until there was no breath left in his lungs at all. He had to do the same again before he felt ready to turn to Hil. She was as white as a sheet, and visibly shaking. As calmly as he could he undid his seatbelt and went round to her side of the car. She was in shock and looked a little faint, but she was made of stern stuff and, by the time the breakdown service had arrived, a little colour had returned to her cheeks.

Wrapped in a blanket and sipping a cup of very sugary tea back at the garage, Hil soon looked a little less peaky and listened attentively as a gaggle of French mechanics tinkered with the car. Eventually one of them came over.

'We'll be able to fix it for you, but it's going to take several weeks to sort it out – that's a very nasty dent you've got in the back.'

'What happened?' asked Jemme, who was sipping some much-needed sugary tea of his own.

'Tyre blow-out, Monsieur. Extremely unlucky on such a new vehicle. Extremely unlucky indeed – to have one would be unfortunate, but to have four…well, that's completely unheard of!'

'*Four* of my tyres blew?'

'Yes, Monsieur. In all my years as a mechanic I've never seen such a thing – and at exactly the same time too. I could maybe understand it a little if it was an old car with bald tyres, but these look practically new – I've never seen treads so thick!'

'It is nearly new,' Jemme said.

'Most unfortunate,' the mechanic murmured. 'You are fortunate in other ways though, Monsieur. I see that the car has been reinforced?'

Jemme nodded.

'Well, I am pretty sure that that has saved your lives. The weight of all that extra metal is what kept all four tyres on the road. If it had been an average car it would have probably rolled, as soon as the second tyre blew. If it hadn't then, then it definitely would have done when that lorry hit you.' He whistled, 'That lorry would have made mincemeat of you in a normal car!'

Hil shuddered, and Jemme turned a slight shade of green. He reached across with his free hand and squeezed her knee. He didn't want to talk about it again, but he knew that she was thinking of the spooky nun, and all her portentous damnations.

True to his word, within a couple of weeks the mechanic had the car straightened out for them and as good as new. During this time, Jemme hadn't raised the subject of the chateau. As little as he allowed himself to become unsettled by what he thought of as 'superstitious clap-trap', he could understand the unease Hil felt. About a week after the accident, he had developed the photographs he had taken whilst they were at the chateau. Once they had been returned he had flicked through them with a slightly confused look on his face. There were his pictures, exactly as he had taken them, and yet, something was different. The colours were odd and there appeared to be a red mist over everything, as if a strange veil had been pulled over the scene to distance the viewer from it. He looked at the first photo he had taken, with Hil smiling in the foreground. The chateau loomed up behind her, and was much darker and more intimidating than he remembered. Towards the edges, the sky looked almost crimson and the lake in the background was an unsettling shade of red too. He reasoned that it was a fault at the processing laboratory and that there had been a developing error, or that there was a problem with the camera's lens, yet all the other photos on the reel were completely fine. It wasn't just the colours either, it was the general mood of the pictures. They were creepy and odd. He resolved not to show them to Hil and not to think anymore about the strangest chateau he had seen yet.

* * * *

The search continued apace, and the seasons continued to change. One day Jemme was flicking through the photos he had taken during various visitations. It was odd to think that he could have picked any one of those buildings, and they would now have been living in it for several years. He was still glad they had not though, and still felt confident in their choices. He shook his head as he remembered the various broken staircases, sprawling patches of damp, and eccentric proprietors. He thought sadly about the condition of some of the properties and people he had seen. Although the chateau might have looked palatial from the outside, sometimes the occupants were living in little more than squalor. Miles from anywhere and cut off even from the community around them, theirs was a strange existence. It was one they clung to ferociously however, and seemed to want to do anything to protect.

He glanced at some photos of a manor house they had seen in Limoges. He remembered it well. Although he had been encouraged by the grand reception rooms, he had been astounded to see the living quarters. In the smaller bedrooms he had been able to stand in the middle of the room and touch all four walls, and the larger bedrooms weren't much better. The concierge who had shown them round had been as glum as most of his type Jemme had encountered thus far,

'It is always this way, Monsieur;' he said morosely, 'a building such as this is not for sleeping and living in, it is for entertaining in.'

Jemme remembered smiling to himself as he tried to imagine this man doing anything remotely entertaining. However, as soon as he got home, he had also added 'grand reception rooms' and 'well divided' to the list.

Hil interrupted his thoughts with a cup of tea and a slice of the buttery *tarte aux abricots* she had just finished making. She placed them down gently on the table, and saw the box of photos open in front of him.

'Ah, journeying through the past?'

'So to speak yes; I've just been having a look through some of these places, and wondering if I could have imagined us living there.'

Hil leant over and looked at some of the places.

'Gosh, do you remember this one?!' she said, picking up one photo.

Jemme smiled, 'Goodness yes!'

'Just as the agent had finished telling you what excellent repair it was in, he put his foot right through the floor!'

Jemme laughed, 'I remember – the place was rotten, all the way through.'

'Can I have a look?'

'Of course,' Jemme shifted over to let Hil sit next to him. She looked at the photos that were out, and then tipped some more out of the box. They both looked through them, variously sighing and giggling as they remembered the chateaux they had seen and the characters they had met. Hil leaned the box over and saw that less than half of the photos had been taken out.

'My goodness, there are still so many photos left! We didn't even start taking pictures until we'd already seen a good eight though. How many have we seen?'

'I've lost count,' said Jemme, 'do you know, it's been about seven years since we started this search?'

'Seven! I suppose it would have been. It's just become such an established thing that I've almost stopped thinking about the fact we're doing it.'

They both screwed their faces up, as they thought back over the places they'd looked.

'Fifty,' said Jemme eventually, 'I make it fifty altogether.'

'I'd just made it forty-eight,' said Hil.

'Remember those two we looked at, at the same time, in Rouen?'

'Ugh, I'd tried to forget!' said Hil, thinking back to the first one they'd seen, where the agent was potentially as sleazy as the man they had met at the Marquis de Sade's chateau. The second one had seemed promising, until a stiff southern breeze had revealed the fact that a fertiliser plant had been built just behind the chateau. 'I suppose you're right though, that would make fifty. Gosh – did you ever think that it would take this long or that we would see this many when we first began.'

'Not for a second. Any regrets?'

'None at all,' Hil replied, pinching a little of Jemme's tarte as she looked at the papers in front of him. 'Is this the next place?'

'Yes, I've just been having a look. It's in Orléans which is quite convenient.'

'Mmmm. I like Orléans too. Ooh – the garden looks nice.'

'Yes, it's good to have a colour photo isn't it? These are all Greco-Roman marbles from the eighteenth century, according to the literature. The plinths they're on are antiques too, and they all come within the sale of the place, which is a nice touch.'

'How big is the plot?'

'It's a hundred and twenty hectares.'

'Oh wow; is there a story to the house?'

'It seems so, although I don't know much about it. Apparently it was the home of a famous artist who died about ten years ago or so. Only his widow lives there now.'

'Poor lady, that must be rather lonely.'

'I should imagine it would be – especially in somewhere so large. It's two thousand square metres all together.'

'Well, I'm looking forward to seeing it. I expect the old lady wouldn't mind a visit either,' said Hil, swiping the last of Jemme's tarte.

'Hey!' he said and gave her a playful nudge.

✳   ✳   ✳   ✳

The chateau was an easy drive from Paris, and Jemme was satisfied to note that it was sixty minutes on the dot from door to door. As first impressions went, this was amongst the best so far. The chateau was quintessentially French, with its interlocking stone and brick and *porte-cochère*. Opened, white shutters revealed tall windows still with their original eighteenth century 'shaky' glass. The grounds spread out around the chateau, carpeted with a thick, velvety grass. A large copse was visible in the distance, and a small stream appeared to be running through it. There seemed to be some sort of terrace on the western side of the chateau, which had been smartly landscaped, and Jemme could imagine it catching a good deal of evening sunshine. He was pleased by what he had seen so far, and that was before he had even looked at the part of the gardens detailed in the advertisement.

'I wonder what she'll be like,' said Hil as they approached the front door.

'I haven't a clue,' replied Jemme, 'I arranged the viewing through our own agent. He's been dealing with her though, and says she's a delight – really vivacious and sparkly for someone her age. I don't know who'll be showing us around though; the agent had other appointments today.'

His question was soon answered when a rakishly good-looking man answered the door.

'*Bonjour!*' he said warmly, '*Monsieur et Madame Mafeze*, I presume?' He didn't wait for an answer before pumping their hands energetically. 'I'm Roget; come in, come in – we've been expecting you.' He didn't elaborate on who he was and swept them inside.

'How was journey? I heard you were coming from Paris – *magnifique!* I adore Paris; it's such a wonderful city. Here let me take your coats,' he whipped the coats away from Jemme and hung them on a peg, 'Well, let's begin, my friends. There's no point hanging around. What shall I show you first? This is such a marvellous place it's hard to know where to start – *la plus belle chateau dans la monde*, we always say,' he laughed. 'Come, follow me!' he said and began leading the way.

Hil and Jemme trotted meekly behind him, slightly bamboozled. He was the most enthusiastic concierge they'd had so far, but he was a little too bombastic.

Hil was wondering where the charming old lady she'd been expecting was, and Jemme was wondering if the young man striding in front of them even was an agent. As they slowed down to enter the first room, he caught up with them,

'I'm sorry, in the rush back there I didn't actually catch who you were?'

'I'm Roget,' the man repeated. Before Jemme had a chance to ask any more questions, Roget had flung the door open, and was gesturing inside the door, 'The cuisine, *Monsieur et Madame*! *C'est formidable, non?* We think it is the best chateau kitchen we have ever seen, but of course we would say that!' he chuckled.

'We?' Hil mouthed at Jemme. Jemme shrugged, and was about to whisper something, but Roget was already beckoning them in,

'Come, come! You must see it all!'

They went inside and looked around. He hadn't been exaggerating, it really was *formidable*. In fact, it was probably the best chateau kitchen Hil and Jemme had seen, too. The vast majority they had seen so far had been in basements, where aristocratic French families had no doubt been keen to secrete the 'below stairs' staff. This one however was on the ground floor, and light poured in from the floor-to-ceiling windows. Copper pots and pans hung on the wall, catching the sunlight, and a large vase of meadow flowers sat on the broad wooden counter. Hil could imagine it filled with the warmth of a family and bustling with activity around the large cooker.

As Hil looked around the kitchen, Jemme looked Roget up and down. He put him at twenty-one, perhaps twenty-two at a pinch. He exuded a confidence bordering on arrogance, of the sort that only one who is young and aware of his good looks can experience. He was tall and slim with clear, tanned skin and long floppy hair, artfully swept back. He wore a pair of berry-coloured trousers, an open white shirt and dark linen jacket. He almost seemed a caricature of himself, a turn-of-the-century bounder and cad, who had somehow found himself in charge of a chateau. Jemme wasn't even sure if he *was* in charge, or on what kind of authority he was acting, but he thought for now he would follow him around and then ask questions at the end.

After seeing several rooms, he had all but forgotten his reservations about his guide. The chateau was simply beautiful. Although he had trained himself to be sceptical, he couldn't prevent a surging sense of hope. They looked at several further rooms, and he began to feel butterflies of excitement stirring up in his stomach. It was everything they had been looking for. None of the things they had hated about the previous chateaux were present. Everything here was working and in excellent condition. It was bright and airy, and a pleasure to walk around. What's more, it had been exquisitely decorated by someone with apparently impeccable taste.

'Wouldn't it be amazing if some of the furniture came with the sale?' said Hil to Jemme, apparently sharing his thoughts.

Roget heard and spun round, 'That could easily be arranged,' he said, a little too readily. Jemme was a little too preoccupied with his thoughts to pick up on it however. He had abandoned his caution and given in to excitement. As they explored various rooms, he began to visualise himself and Hil living there. He could see them sharing cosy dinners in the little *salle à manger*, and entertaining friends with more lavish fare in the grand *salon*. He could see his grandmother staying with them in a room he would decorate just like a Turkish *majlis*, and he could see his art hanging in the long corridors, as sequential and collated as his heart desired. The whole place was ripe for his project. He could take as many rooms as he wanted, and there would still be enough space for an entire, completely independent family section. In fact, he could take whole rooms to explore just one small section of his art or collection. He imagined what fun it would be to walk along a French corridor, and open an innocuous looking door to find an entire room filled with Phoenician artefacts. Seeing as he has the space, he could even decorate the whole room and recreate a tiny slice of Phoenicia deep within an historic French castle. How delightfully incongruous, he thought to himself, to open a door and suddenly find yourself within ancient Phoenicia, or perhaps a door further down the corridor would open to reveal a scene directly from the palace of Ashurbanipal. He couldn't believe he had finally found somewhere that would allow him to realise all of these visions. It was the chateau of his dreams. As soon as he had thought that, he suddenly stopped in his tracks: it really *was* the chateau of his dreams. Finally he understood. He couldn't believe that it had taken him seven years to realise what he was trying to do. In fact, it had taken longer than that – it had taken his entire life. Suddenly it all made complete sense: he was recreating his dream. Everything had fallen into place – the strange fixation with arranging his collection and his obsession over the project without really understanding why; the dissatisfaction with all the chateaux he had seen so far – the very fact that he was looking at chateaux even! He realised his dream had been the driving force all along. It had been the reason he had collected art, rare books and antiques. They were all things he had seen before; he had in fact spent his adult life seeking out the real, tangible versions of the objects he had imagined in childhood. He experienced a deep and profound sense of happiness and completion, feeling like he had finally achieved an enlightened level of understanding and purpose. This chateau was the perfect setting too; there was very little structural work to be done in terms of internal divisions. Based on the rooms they had seen so far, there was a natural division between family quarters and…. he struggled to think what the second half would be – dream quarters? Gallery quarters? It was too much to call them 'museum' quarters, although that would be a reasonable next step. The corridor they were standing in right now could form the heart of the 'dream quarters.' It was almost exactly as he had imagined it: long and narrow with many rooms of equal proportions leading off it. He could picture recreating a different civilisation in every room, and became quite giddy with the prospect. Suddenly he felt an elbow in his ribs.

'Ow!' he said, and looked up. Hil was glaring at him, and Roget was beaming expectantly.

'Well, what do you think, Monsieur?'

'Oh, I…um,' Jemme mumbled.

Hil stepped in to rescue him, 'I think we're getting a little ahead of ourselves,' she said firmly, 'why don't we see the rest of the place first?'

'As Madame wishes,' said Roget graciously with a winning smile, 'Come, come let us continue.' He turned and led the way down the corridor.

'Thank you,' Jemme muttered to Hil. Her words had rung true more than she could have realised – he was definitely getting ahead of himself.

'Sorry,' he said, slightly guiltily, 'what was all that about anyway?'

Hil pointed down at the carpet, 'It was a bit odd. I was just admiring the carpet and no sooner had I got the words out of my mouth than he said we could have it. I don't know if any of these things are his to give away.'

'Hmm,' said Jemme, not really listening. He was trying to put all images of his dream and ownership of the chateau out of his mind, and focus, but it was difficult. Every time they saw something new, he imagined how well it would fit into things, and started planning how he could incorporate it.

By the time Roget finally led them back to the hall in which they had started, Jemme was almost completely in his dream world. He already knew that the chateau was perfect, and was wondering how long it would take them to move in.

'Do Madame and Monsieur have any questions?' Roget asked them.

'Yes actually, I do. Where is the lady who owns the chateau?' Hil asked bluntly.

Jemme had completely forgotten that there was meant to be a widow living there, and tried to refocus, 'Yes, I was wondering that too,' he said.

Roget's smile faltered for a moment, but when it came back it was even broader than before.

'What a good question,' he said, then assumed a sorrowful look. 'Ahh, poor Madame Aguillon,' he sighed. 'She is not in a very good way.'

'Oh?' said Hil.

'No, Madame, she did not take the death of her poor husband very well at all. Between you and I – and I hate to speak ill of such a dear lady *châtelaine* – I think it's what started her decline.'

'Decline?' asked Hil.

'Oh yes, Madame. As I said, she is not very well at all. She suffers from a terrible grief which makes her struggle to think properly. Unkind people say it has driven her mad, but I know it is only because she is so distressed.'

'How awful,' said Hil sympathetically.

'Quite, Madame. I only do these tours so as to bother her as little as possible; anything I can do to make her life easier.'

Hil softened a little, 'How long ago did her husband die?'

Roget shrugged, 'About ten years ago, Madame. She has been completely housebound ever since.'

Hil looked a little surprised. She had been expecting to hear that the lady was freshly widowed. 'I'd very much like to meet her in that case.'

Roget looked a little reluctant, 'Oh no, Madame…' he began.

'If we're seriously considering buying this place, then I think it's out of the question that we wouldn't meet the owner. Besides, if she's housebound, then we'll know exactly where to find her, won't we?'

Roget squirmed a little and looked very put out. 'As Madame wishes,' he said in a slightly sulky way, before turning on the charm again, 'Madame strikes me as a sensitive lady who knows how to deal with an elderly widow. I'm sure you'll understand that most of what she says isn't true.'

It was a slightly clumsy remark, which Hil met with an assumed charm of her own, 'Why don't you lead the way, Roget?'

Roget led them to a small corridor they hadn't yet seen. A single door at the end opened into a suite of rooms. He knocked on it and opened, 'Madame Aguillon,' he called in, 'the buyers have insisted on meeting you.' He ushered Jemme and Hil in, his early effusiveness severely diminished.

As Hil entered a petite lady jumped up from the chair she was sitting on, 'Come in, my dear. How delightful!' she said. Although she was small, she seemed full of energy. Her glossy grey hair was piled up on top of her head, and her eyes were a startlingly bright blue. They sparkled a little as she shook Hil's hand, 'It's so nice to have visitors; my room is so tucked away in this corner that usually Roget's shown the viewers out before I've even realised they were here! Oh this, must be your husband,' she said as Jemme came in. He introduced himself, and she shook his hand with a warm smile, 'I was just saying to your wife that it's nice to finally put some faces to some of our visitors. It's strange to think that how many people have been round and looked at my home without me meeting them, or even realising they've been here. Still, one can't be too sentimental about these things, I suppose!'

Hil looked at the room. It was decidedly feminine, with soft drapes and walls papered in a cornflower blue. It seemed to be an extension of the lady herself, who wore a cream cashmere shawl wrapped loosely around her shoulders. It revealed a beautiful twist of pearls fastened around an elegant neck. It was clear that she had been a great beauty in her day.

'I'm sorry, I hope we didn't disturb you,' she said to the lady.

'Not at all dear, I wasn't doing anything important,' she said, gesturing to the desk she had been sitting at. It was in front of a window that offered sweeping views over the grounds. Right next to the window was a peony bush, and full, fat, pink flowers pressed up against the glass. A sketchbook lay open on the desk and some oil pastels were scattered next to it.

'You're a very talented draughtsman,' said Hil, admiring the half-finished picture of a peony.

'Oh, not really -- it's just my little hobby,' said the lady, 'My dear late husband was the truly talented one. Look, that's him,' she said, pointing fondly to a framed black and white photo on the wall. 'That was taken on his sixtieth birthday – wasn't he handsome? Still, probably a bit too old for you, dear,' she said mischievously to Hil. 'Come, I'll show you some of his pieces I've got in my sitting room.' Hil frowned slightly at Jemme and followed the lady through. Jemme fell into line behind her. He knew what Hil was thinking; even though he had been wrapped up in his reverie he could still notice that this sprightly and bubbly lady was far from the picture of a confused, half-mad old woman Roget had painted. Roget for his part had been completely silent since they had arrived, and skulked around in the background.

The sitting room was decorated in much the same way as the bedroom, and Jemme joined Hil in admiring the art on the walls. The lady chattered about her husband and his great talent, which both Jemme and Hil agreed was evident in the masterful work displayed.

'These aren't even his best pieces;' Madame Aguillon explained, 'these are just little things he thought weren't good enough to send to galleries. I love them though; they remind me so much of him and all our memories together. I was blessed with a very happy marriage and it's such a wonderful thing. I hope you two are as happy as we were,' she said, and smiled at them. Although she clearly missed her husband, she wasn't exactly a grief-ravaged widow and Jemme looked thoughtfully at Roget, wondering why he had led them to believe such a thing.

'I know you must be eager to get off, but I really would love it if you could stay for a little tea,' Madame Aguillon said. 'We have a wonderful cook here and she makes excellent pastries, you simply must try them.'

Hil smiled, 'Well in that case we'll definitely stay!'

'Oh good! Roget, would you be an absolute dear, and run and ask cook to send up tea for four, please?'

Roget grunted something and left.

Madame Aguillon watched him go, 'Such a star, you know. I'd be completely lost without him.'

'Oh really?' said Hil, not looking particularly convinced.

'Absolutely,' nodded Madame Aguillon shaking loose a curl from her tall chignon. 'I didn't realise what a dreadful muddle my affairs were in before he started to sort things out for me,' she said tucking the curl behind her ear. 'You see, I suppose I'm a little old fashioned and my husband always dealt with all of our financial and legal affairs. During his final years he was very careful to set everything up for me, and I thought things would just carry on as they had been and run themselves. I don't know what happened – I think it was a combination of my naivety and my poor, dear husband not expecting all the tax changes. Anyway, it seems it all got in a terrible mess, and I'm so grateful to Roget for helping out.'

'Tax changes?' Jemme asked.

'Yes, it's very complicated and I'm afraid I still don't understand it properly. I'm so cut off from everything here. I didn't even know there had been any changes. Roget told me all about it. He said the government had introduced some new laws and changed lots of their policies. I'm not quite sure why, but they all seem to have been targeted at people just like me. Anyway, to cut a rather dull story short, it seems that I'm going to have to sell this place. It's not really viable for me to keep it anymore.'

'*That's* why you're selling?' asked Jemme. The dreamy look had left his eyes and he now looked completely on the ball and alert. 'Because of these "tax changes?"'

Madame Aguillon nodded, 'Precisely. It's a shame to be losing my home after so many years here, but Roget explained it all to me – it's the only real option. At least this way I get to keep hold of all my lovely furniture and art.'

Jemme looked concerned. As a banker he was well-versed in government fiscal policy, and he knew for a fact that there had not been any such 'tax changes', or, at least, not of the sort which would require an elderly lady to sell off her investments. He thought back to his initial misgivings on meeting Roget, and about how totally the young man's behaviour had changed once they had asked to meet the owner. He was clearly used to talking people into his way of doing things, but Jemme couldn't quite work out what was going on. He didn't know who the man was, how he fitted into things or what he stood to gain. If he was related to the lady, he could be making a grab for his inheritance, but that didn't make sense. The chateau was being offered at a very reasonable price and if he stood to inherit it anyway, then he was short-changing himself by pushing for an early sale when he would have to wait to receive the bequest in any case. He didn't appear to be with any agency, and his familiarity with the property and his reference to 'we' undermined that theory anyway. Jemme started to feel uneasy, as niggling doubts poked their way through his contentment at having found somewhere so perfect.

Sitting face to face with such a charming and warm elderly lady was not making things any easier, and when he heard her innocently say, 'Anyway, it's like Roget keeps saying: it doesn't pay to be sentimental,' he groaned inwardly. It punctured his bubble of elation and he realised that something was sorely amiss.

After tea and what turned out to be really rather remarkable pastries, they started to make their goodbyes. Madame Aguillon looked sorry to see them go and made them promise to drop in if ever they were in the area again, regardless of whether they ended up buying the place or not. Roget leapt up, his former charm returning, 'I will show to your car,' he said, opening the door and hurrying them out. Once they had reached the entrance hall, he turned and flashed a winning smile at Hil, 'Perhaps Madame would care to wait in the car whilst I talk business with Monsieur?' he said.

Both Jemme and Hil's hackles immediately went up.

'Whatever you've got to say to me, you can say in front of my wife,' said Jemme coldly, 'This will be a joint decision.'

Roget fidgeted, 'Fine,' said Hil, 'I wanted to get some fresh air anyway. Jemme, I'm sure you'll fill me in on the way home,'

'Of course,' Jemme said as she left. He turned back to the young man and stared at him expectantly.

'Yes?'

'As I'm sure Monsieur couldn't fail to notice, the venerable Madame Aguillon is not quite "all there". This house is a weight around her poor neck – the very last thing she needs in her state is to be burdened by all the stress that goes with owning such a large lump as this. You'd be doing her a great kindness in taking it off her hands as quickly as possible. All I want is to help her shift it.'

Jemme looked at him sceptically. He had winced a little at the mention of such a spirited lady being 'not all there'. It seemed so disrespectful. He still hadn't worked out what Roget's game was though.

'With that in mind,' said Roget, running his hand through his tousled hair and smiling conspiratorially, 'I wondered if I might propose something? I'm sure you're keen to secure such a wonderful property for you and your lovely wife, and we're keen to sell very quickly. As you've seen, Madame Aguillon is very open to suggestions, and so I'll suggest something beneficial to all parties: why don't I persuade her to let you take the property for half its market value?'

'Go on,' said Jemme flatly.

'In exchange for my efforts, perhaps you could slip me a little cash tip – somewhere between one and two million francs? We could have this whole thing wrapped up in no time at all. Of course, we'd keep the matter between the two of us. Businessman to businessman.'

'I really must go. I will get back to you,' said Jemme, and left before Roget could say anything more. His walk back to the car was heavy with disappointment. The man had just confirmed what he had feared, and shattered the singing sense of hope he had felt since they'd arrived. Roget's words about Madame Aguillon being 'open to suggestion' rang nastily in his ears. The thought of such a lovely lady being so horribly manipulated and deceived made him feel sick.

Hil was waiting for him in the car, not looking especially pleased at having been excluded from 'men's talk.'

'Well?' she said

Jemme sighed heavily. 'I'm afraid we have a moral dilemma on our hands.'

* * * *

Jemme drove in the vague direction of Paris, but he felt slightly aimless. His mind was full of conflicting emotions, and he didn't know what to think. On the one hand he still felt a vestigial happiness at having realised what he wanted. He also couldn't quite suppress the excitement he felt about the chateau, and how perfect it was. He desperately wanted to live there and to own it, but to do so would displace its rightful owner. He had a heavy feeling of moral responsibility about the whole affair, and even thinking about living there made him feel huge stabbing pangs of guilt. Hil had already made her feelings on Roget quite clear. He hadn't yet told her the deal he had been offered, but before he'd even got into the car she had surmised what was going on. He sighed heavily,

'I can't think straight. I don't want to go home.'

'I know what you mean,' said Hil 'although I don't know where else we're going to go.'

'Why don't I take you out for dinner, and we can talk the whole thing over?'

'That sounds nice,' said Hil, with a rather wan smile. 'Did you have anywhere particular in mind?

Jemme thought for a moment, and as he pondered their favourite restaurants he drove past a sign. 'Deauville,' he said decisively.

'Deauville?! Are you crazy? We can't drive two hundred kilometres for dinner!'

'Why not? It's still early, we'll make it in plenty of time.'

'Because, it's ridiculous, that's why.'

'Come on,' said Jemme, a smile spreading across his face for the first time since they'd left, 'It's not ridiculous, it's romantic! We've had such happy times there. We'll get there in time for dinner and then if we don't fancy driving back later this evening, we can rent a room somewhere. Breakfast on the coast – it will be lovely!'

'But I don't have anything with me,' Hil protested feebly.

'You don't need anything; it will be lovely, I promise,' said Jemme. Hil looked at his broad smile and caved in.

'All right then, why not – I suppose it is quite romantic,' she said, as she smiled back at him.

Jemme turned off at the next junction, and they headed northwest for a couple of hours until they reached the outskirts of the seaside town. Deauville had always been one of their favourite destinations. Within easy reach of Paris, it was full of upmarket boutiques and old-world glamour.

They made their way to their favourite restaurant, which looked out onto the harbour, and were extremely gratified when the proprietor recognised them. He ushered them straight to one of the best tables on the terrace outside. The sun was just beginning to set, and one of the waiters had lit the candles set out on each table. It was still comfortably warm and as they raised a glass of crisp, cold white wine they both felt a great deal more relaxed.

'Santé,' said Hil and took a sip. 'My, that's better. It's all been feeling a little tense since we left, hasn't it?'

'Absolutely,' Jemme agreed. 'I just can't stop thinking about the place and that lady.'

'No, me too,' said Hil, 'You still haven't told me what happened with the abominable Roget. I'm guessing he wasn't the great friend-in-need he was making out?'

'No,' said Jemme grimly and outlined what had happened. Even though he played it down a little for Hil, she still shook her head and frowned.

'Disgusting,' she said when he had finished. 'I can't believe how deceitful he's being. I feel we should tell her.'

'It's such a difficult situation though – I don't want her to know she's been lied to and manipulated; it would break her heart.'

'I know, but we can't let him cheat her out of her home like that,' said Hil.

They continued in that vein for a while, discussing the various moral implications of their actions and inactions.

'One thing's for certain;' said Hil eventually, 'there's absolutely no way we can buy the place.'

'I was afraid you might say that,' said Jemme. 'Although I've been turning it over, I couldn't come to any other decision myself. It's such a pity, because to my mind it was absolutely perfect. I could see us living there, and having as happy a life as she evidently has there. There's another thing too, though. I could see something significant happening there and I finally understood what's been driving this search from my point of view.'

As they sat, he explained everything. They had worked their way through three courses, dessert, the cheese board and coffee before he had finished discussing his dream and his vision of realising it. Hil listened attentively, and asked questions; although she protested at some elements, on the whole she was enthusiastic about the idea.

'You're right,' she said, 'it is something significant. What a wonderful opportunity – to have enough space to create something really meaningful. I can't believe neither of us has thought of this before. It's as if everything has been leading you to this point – the recurring dream, all the trips we've been on, the museums and libraries you've visited, even your friendship with the Professor.'

Jemme thought about it, 'That's true enough, and I feel like I understand what it all means now, but I still don't know what its purpose is. I mean, once I've built all of this, what do we do with it? I don't want to create some sort of peculiar private museum you and I rattle around in. It's no better than these strange shrines the old aristocrats we've met have turned their chateaux into.'

'So why make it just for you and me?'

'What do you mean?' asked Jemme.

'Well, why make it a museum only you and I visit? Why not think big? What you've been describing is essentially a museum anyway, albeit a slightly novel one. Even when you were rearranging everything back at the flat, you were acting like a curator. Why not change a few little things and make it into a proper museum? It would certainly pay for the work, and you almost have a duty to share a collection as large as yours is becoming. It seems a shame to deprive others of the chance to see it.'

'That's a very, very interesting idea,' said Jemme slowly.

By now it was fully night-time, the other diners had paid up and left, and the waiter was collecting cloths from the tables around them. Heading back to Paris was the last thing either of them felt like, and so they found a charming little hotel and checked in for the night. After such a large meal, Hil fell asleep pretty much straight away. Even though he was tired too, Jemme couldn't sleep. He lay awake on the bed, staring up at the ceiling and thinking about what Hil had said. It made perfect sense, and he was excited by the idea, but it seemed a cruel disappointment that as soon as such a monumental decision had been made, he should lose the very place which inspired the decision. What if he had to search for another seven years before he found somewhere as good again? he thought to himself despondently. It could be decades before he had found anywhere and got it up and running. Eventually he drifted into a light sleep, punctuated by dreams of concierges and broken roofs.

The next morning they took a leisurely stroll along the seafront, and stopped for breakfast at a café with a bright red awning. They sipped big cupfuls of milky coffee, and ate excellently flaky pain-au-chocolats. Hil took in a deep breath of salty sea air and sighed.

'It's hard to feel down at times like these, isn't it?' she said.

Despite his lack of sleep, and the disappointment he felt, Jemme was inclined to agree. Once they had finished, they sat for a while longer before walking a little further down the promenade. There was a stiff breeze, and the sea was speckled with white sails as weekend enthusiasts took to the water.

'Look how big that boat is!' said Hil pointing to one not too far off. It had a distinctive blue bow and its sails flapped in the wind.

'That's my neighbour's,' said a voice behind them, 'and I'm glad he's too far out to hear you. He's got a big enough head as it is.'

Hil and Jemme laughed and turned round. The man behind them introduced himself.

'I own this *estate agent*,' he said, 'although I was just shutting up shop to take a guilty sunshine break.'

They laughed again, 'I don't think there's any need to feel guilty on a day like this,' said Hil, 'If anything, you should feel guilty about staying indoors.'

The man chuckled, 'Forgive me, Madame, I'm having trouble placing your accent. You sound almost Parisian, but not quite.'

'I think that pretty much sums both of us up! My husband and I have lived in Paris for some time, but neither of us is French. I'm originally from Ireland and he's Turkish, but it's been a while since we lived there.'

'Ah, I see – that explains it. What brings you to Deauville?'

'We fancied treating ourselves to a relaxing dinner at the seaside, and it sort of went from there,' said Jemme, 'We had some slightly disappointing news and wanted to make up for it.'

'I'm sorry to hear that, Monsieur,'

'Well, we're house-hunting at the moment, so I suppose it's kind of inevitable.'

'House-hunting, Monsieur? Well you are standing in front of the best estate agent in all of Deauville!'

Jemme laughed, 'I'm afraid we're being quite picky though,'

'I'm sure you're no more picky than some of the rich Deauvilloise I deal with. What is it you're looking for?' he asked.

'Well, actually, now you come to mention it – a chateau,' said Jemme, expecting the man to look surprised.

'What sort of chateau?' he asked, without even blinking.

'Umm…well,' Jemme stammered, slightly taken aback. He proceeded to describe the place they'd just seen in Orléans and how it was completely perfect, except for one thing.

The agent tutted, 'You did well not to have anything to do with it, Monsieur; I don't like the sound of this "Roget" at all.' He thought for a while, 'However, perhaps he has been a blessing in disguise if he has brought you here. As it happens

I have the details for a place which sounds very similar to the chateau you've just described.'

'Really?'

'Yes, it popped into my mind as soon as you started talking about this Orléans place – I'd be happy to show you the details.'

'Oh, well, you've only just locked up...' began Hil.

'Nonsense! It's no trouble,' said the man, who was already twiddling at locks and fiddling with keys.

They were soon sitting in front of his desk whilst he rummaged in a drawer.

'How irritating, I'm afraid I can't find the details. You see it's not properly back on the market yet, otherwise you would have seen it in the window.'

'Back on the market?' asked Jemme.

'Yes – it was sold, and we thought the whole thing was all wrapped up, but it unravelled pretty quickly. We should have looked into the buyer a little more, I suppose. It was originally the property of the French government, and, as I'm sure you know they've been divesting themselves of assets at the moment.'

Jemme nodded.

'Well anyway, we thought we had a buyer lined up – an American. He seemed enthusiastic enough, and pretty much bought on the spot. After only about three weeks, he walked away; he hasn't even reclaimed his deposit.'

'What happened?'

'Oh, it was nothing to do with the place,' the estate agent was quick to reassure, 'well, I suppose it was a bit, but not because it wasn't up to scratch. He had this preposterous idea that he was going to turn it into a golf course.'

'A golf course!' said Hil.

'Yes. If only he'd mentioned this to someone at the beginning, we would have naturally dissuaded him. It didn't come out until the sale had been finalised, and his advisers started looking over the place and telling him how hopelessly unsuitable it was. He left in a bit of a hurry after that, and I don't think he's going to bother getting his deposit back. It's now back in the possession of the French government, who aren't particularly pleased about it. I think they're keen to bounce it on as quickly as possible.'

'It certainly sounds like an interesting place.'

'It is. I'm just sorry I can't find the details. Why don't you tell me exactly what it is you're looking for, and I can tell you how it matches up? You'll have to trust me a little bit on it, but I can make a compromise: if I think it's right for you, I'll take you there myself tomorrow. I'm not even open, and it would mean giving up my Sunday, so I wouldn't do it unless I thought it was right.'

He smiled at them.

'Deal,' said Jemme.

'*Super.* I haven't heard much from you, Madame. Why don't you start off by telling me what you're looking for?'

Hil looked pleasantly taken aback.

'I can do a little better than that;' she said, fishing in her bag, 'we've actually got a list we've been using. It's a little battered I'm afraid, but it's the result of many, many viewings, so it's pretty accurate.' She handed it over.

'Excellent!' said the agent. 'Ahhh, if only all clients knew what they wanted as clearly as you two,' he sighed as he began to scrutinise it.

Jemme and Hil sat there for a few moments whilst he read the list, occasionally asking them what a particularly scrawled note said. When he had finished he looked up with a wide smile.

'Well, I can see I'll be giving up my Sunday!'

'It's a good fit?'

'Monsieur, it is the best fit I've seen in all my years working as an estate agent. You have here what, twenty criteria?'

'Twenty-one, I think,' said Hil.

'Ah, yes, I see. Well I can safely say that the place I'm taking you to see satisfies twenty out of those twenty-one requirements.'

'Really?'

'Truly, Madame. In fact, the only one which is missing is your request for the place to be no more than an hour outside Paris. I wouldn't try and trick you on that front – it's a good two hours' drive. However, there is some good news. I know that there are plans to build a TGV connection at some point, which will link up the nearby town to the capital in about fifty minutes.'

Jemme looked impressed.

'Like I said, Monsieur, I don't want to mislead you. I don't have a clue when the railway will be finished – or even when it will be started, but I know it will definitely go ahead. It's been in the local news a lot recently.'

'In that case, I look forward to seeing this place tomorrow,' said Jemme who had already decided that he liked this man.

* * * *

Having stayed another impromptu night in the hotel, Jemme and Hil were feeling in a holiday kind of mood. They were optimistic about the meeting, and reasoned that as it had come about so spontaneously when their hopes weren't particularly high, so they were unlikely to be disappointed. They rendezvoused with the estate agent, who was looking very 'off-duty' in a straw hat and short-sleeved shirt. He greeted them warmly and showed them to his car.

The drive there was an extremely pleasant one, and the estate agent chattered away about the property. He seemed to have a genuine interest in matching it with the right buyer, and was as keen as they were for the viewing to go well.

'I must tell you both that I was thinking about it last night. I'm not sure that this place is actually a chateau. I was looking through the ancient property details, and it describes itself as a "manor house." It has chateau in its name though.'

Jemme laughed, 'Now we're really splitting hairs – don't worry we won't hold it against you if it's been incorrectly classified. What is its name by the way.'

'Chateau Coeur-de-Neige.'

'Chateau Coeur-de-Neige,' Jemme repeated. 'I like it.'

'Well I hope you do!'

The agent needn't have worried. As soon as they turned in from the driveway, they were sold. Without even needing to look at each other, both Jemme and Hil knew what the other one was thinking. The place was beautiful; it was a mix of warm red brick and grey granite, with a pretty bell tower on top of a sloping slate roof. The grounds surrounding it were among some of the most lush they had seen so far, and perhaps the biggest too. As they neared the building, various details came into view. There was pretty scrollwork and embellishment on all the cast iron, and a thriving rose bed on either side of the steps leading up to the main entrance. They parked up. 'Ready?' asked the agent.

'Definitely,' said Hil, holding hands with Jemme.

The agent led them on a thorough tour of the property and its grounds. He was completely honest with them about any problems (of which there were few) and didn't exaggerate any of claims (there was simply no need). As they walked around, Jemme felt the same surging sense of hope he had experienced in Orléans. He felt the same flutter of excitement when he saw the handsomely proportioned rooms, and imagined with the same vividness his museum growing and developing within them. Although it wasn't as big as the Orléans kitchen, the kitchen here still bought a lump to his throat as he visualised his family chattering and eating around the large wooden table, kept all warm and cosy in winter by the large cooker.

A beautiful orangerie housed trees that still bore fruit, and gave the air a delicate citrus perfume. Hil took a small sniff and sighed.

'I know,' Jemme whispered.

From there they went out for a look around the grounds. A large stone *dos-à-dos* bench wrapped its way around the trunk of a tall oak in a thicket of rustling trees.

'Sit down,' urged the agent, 'the views from here are lovely.'

They sat down and saw that he was right. From there they could see the whole of the building in all its glory, and the verdant blanket of green around it which extended all the way down to the clear, calm lake. Hil sighed again,

'It's all so peaceful,' she murmured.

The agent was looking the other way, and so she whispered to Jemme,

'Shall we?'

Jemme didn't need to be asked twice. There was just one thing holding him back, 'Tell me,' he said to the agent, 'if we were to buy this place then would we be able to do so through you? I don't want to have to deal with any more crooks or cheats!'

The agent laughed, 'Unfortunately you wouldn't be able to complete the whole sale with me, but you would be dealing directly with the French government, so you can rest assured you won't encounter any cheats – the reputation of the country depends on it!'

Jemme smiled and offered his hand, 'In that case, consider your Sunday well sacrificed – we'll take it.'

Chapter Twelve

Hil and Jemme sat on the same bench Jemme had sat on with the estate agent only a few hours beforehand. They looked out over the chateau's grounds, taking in the velvety swathes of lawn, the glassy smoothness of the lake and the knot of trees beyond.

'I can't really believe what's just happened,' said Hil.

'I know, it's all a little much to take in,' sighed Jemme, 'To think, this is the kind of place we would visit for a weekend away or even pay to see as a museum or country park. Now it's ours!'

'Ours,' sighed Hil. 'It sounds so wonderful. I'm sure it will all sink in soon enough; it's just that it's all been so spontaneous and unexpected. I mean, I'm still wearing the same clothes I was when we were Orléans – we never planned to get as far as Deauville, let alone come all the way out here and then, well, buy a chateau!'

'I know, it's remarkable, isn't it?' said Jemme.

'Remarkable?' Hil giggled as the scale of everything that had happened started to sink in. 'It's completely mad! Who drives two hundred kilometres to go for dinner? Who pitches up in a holiday seaside town and ends up buying an entire chateau on the spot?'

'A romantic…?' Jemme ventured hopefully.

Hil relented, 'I suppose that's one word for it. It just seems that it's happened all at once, I really can't take it in.'

Jemme put his arm around her shoulders and pulled her in close, kissing the top of her head, 'Neither can I my love. It's so exciting though – everything you can see will belong to us. I can teach our children to fish in that lake; we can have picnics in these woods, it will be our own little empire.'

They looked out over the grounds together again, taking in the sweeping views all the way up to the house. It all seemed a little too good to be true, like something straight out of a fairy story. As Hil looked at the tiny attic windows, the grand front doors and the spiralling turrets, she imagined it coming to life. She saw the cobwebs swept out, the floors scrubbed and the shutters flung open. She imagined their possessions carefully installed, with colourful rugs on the floor, beautiful paintings on the wall and cosy furnishings in the smaller rooms. Her heart fluttered slightly as she imagined the family rooms ringing with laughter, and the sounds of happy family life. She felt almost a bit giddy when she pictured the grand reception rooms, and the lavish formal dinners they could host in them. She had been to just such dinners with Jemme, and always wondered at the people who lived in such houses and chateaux. It seemed like a completely different life, and she was struggling to believe that it would soon be her life, and that she would be one of those people.

Jemme was struggling to believe it too, but for slightly different reasons. He had been focussed on this idea for much longer than Hil, and realising the first stage of his plan had felt like an inevitability. What he couldn't believe was the manner in which it had happened. It had been an improbable string of coincidences: causal contingencies, each of which had played perfectly into the next. If he hadn't been paying attention when they drove past the sign for Deauville, he might not have taken the spontaneous decision to drive there; if they hadn't been walking along the promenade and stopped at the exact spot they had; if they hadn't been admiring exactly the right boat at exactly the second the estate agent came out of his office…. he turned it over and over in his mind.

'What are you thinking, sweetheart?' Hil asked, leaning over and squeezing his other hand.

'Just about the enormity of the whole thing I suppose. Not just this place either,' he said, nodding towards the chateau, 'I mean, I'm just taking in how significant the act of buying it actually was. I can't stop thinking about the journey that's led us here too.'

'I know,' sighed Hil, 'seven years and over fifty properties. It seems strange to think that this will be the final one.'

'Hmmm,' said Jemme, 'but it's not just that journey I'm talking about. It's the short-term journey. The one that led us right to this point and in this moment. It all just seems so…unlikely.'

'I know what you mean; there were so many things that could easily not have happened.'

'Absolutely. And, after all this time, all these endless disappointments, for everything to just fall into place like that makes me feel like there was some sort of external power influencing things.'

'What sort of power? Something like divine intervention?'

'Something like that, I can't quite put my finger on it. It's frustrating me. I like to think of myself as a man of science and I don't like not being able to explain things. It's as if there's a causality here that I don't understand.'

'What do you mean "causality"?'

'I mean the relationship between cause and effect. Think about two separate events – the fact we were in Deauville, and the fact that we bumped into the estate agent, for example.'

'Right,'

'Well, the second event can be understood to be a consequence of the first in this case. It's causal.'

'I understand what you're talking about, I just don't understand how it's relevant.'

'Neither do I really. It's just that causality is something that's always interested Grandma, and I was just wondering whether it could help me understand what's happened here. I understand the effect – I'm very happy with the effect indeed, in fact. I can understand the string of causal events that led to it too, it's just that I don't understand the relationship between the two. I don't see how everything could fall into place so perfectly, and nothing could interrupt the flow of causal events.'

'You're thinking about this too deeply,' said Hil, 'why not just enjoy this moment and take in what's happened. It's probably just one of those things that's just meant to be.'

Jemme gave her a half-smile but she could see he wasn't satisfied. It was always the same – he liked to be able to understand how and why things had happened. He liked to work backwards until he had found the initial spark which had ignited something much larger. It was one of the things that had made him such a success at banking. Hil knew him well enough to know that, although he was pretending to look at the lake again, his brain would be thrashing away, criticising and analysing until he reached some form of understanding.

'If you think that there was some sort of external force at work, then I think you're going to have to accept that you'll never be able to fully understand what happened, or why. Who knows? Maybe it was all coincidence, maybe it wasn't. Maybe it was even your Grandmother sending us positive wishes from Turkey!'

Jemme chuckled and kissed the top of Hil's head again, 'Sorry, you're right. I have been over-thinking this. Let's explore the rest of the grounds.'

Although he was notably more relaxed whilst they wandered around, hand in hand, thoughts of Eastern mysticism still swirled around his mind. Maybe Grandma had acted like the spark. Maybe she had done something tiny, which had set a series of events into motion, each larger and more significant than the last. 'What an auspicious way to begin a relationship with a place,' he thought to himself.

✳   ✳   ✳   ✳

Later that afternoon, Jemme and Hil returned to Paris. It was exactly two hours from door to door, just as the estate agent had said. They chattered excitedly all the way back. Things had finally begun to sink in, and they were both dizzy with anticipation. There were so many things to work out about the place. How were they going to decorate it? Where would all of their things go? How would Jemme's dream unfurl within its walls? They knew they wouldn't be able to move straight away; if there were going to be building and decorating works, it made much more sense to stick it out in the Paris flat, until the plasterers' dust had settled. How long they had to wait until they moved in really depended on how ambitious the development would be.

By the time they reached the outskirts of Paris, they had already talked the whole thing into reality. The chateau no longer seemed like an abstract dream in a far-off place; it was their home and their future. There was some paperwork to sort out first, and Jemme was to drive back out to meet the representatives of the French government in a couple of days, and sign on various ministerial dotted lines.

In the meantime, they settled back in to life as usual. Hil had wasted no time in disseminating the news amongst what seemed to be half of Paris. No matter what time of day, there always seemed to be a clutch of women in the flat, listening attentively and cooing in excitement. Jemme had enjoyed breaking the news too. By the time he was ready to drive back out into the country again, he thought about his first day back at work with a smile. As usual, DD had been waiting to greet him,

'Good morning, Sir. I trust you had a productive weekend,' he had said with his usual solemnity.

'Very productive indeed, DD, thank you. More productive than I think anyone had imagined,'

'Oh, Sir?' said DD with his imperceptible eyebrow-raise. 'I trust the chateau interested you,' he added as he took Jemme's jacket and ushered him in to the office.

Settling into his chair and taking a large gulp of the coffee waiting for him, Jemme smacked his lips 'Oh, very much, very much indeed.'

'Excellent news, Sir. It's been a while since a property has piqued your interest.'

'It has indeed DD, you're right. This one certainly piqued it though,' he said with a twinkle in his eye.

'Well that is good news. I hope that you'll consider a second viewing.'

'Oh I'm already long past that stage…'

'You've already been back to see it?' DD did a masterful job of containing his surprise, but didn't quite succeed. 'Forgive my tone, Sir, it's just that you've only been away for two days. I'm impressed that you liked somewhere enough to arrange a second viewing for the same weekend. This is a very promising start indeed.'

'Oh I definitely liked it enough to arrange a second viewing,' said Jemme teasingly, 'in fact…I liked it enough to buy the place, which is exactly what I did!'

'Sir?!' DD positively spluttered. Jemme looked pleased – the news had had exactly the dramatic effect he'd been hoping for.

'I bought it on the spot,' he continued to DD's increasing incredulity. DD collected himself, took a deep breath, rearranged his facial features back to their usual neutrality, and looked vaguely irritated with himself for allowing them to stray.

'I beg your pardon, Sir; it's just that that is the last news I was expecting to hear. I'm extremely pleased for you, naturally... it's just that after all this time and all these different properties, your search has seemed to come to a rather abrupt end.'

'It has rather, hasn't it,' Jemme said happily. 'It's been in the best possible way though. Both Hil and I are absolutely delighted with the place in every way possible. It's everything we've been looking for all this time. The only drawback is the distance from Paris, but that's a very minor point. Besides, they're thinking of building a high-speed connection very soon, so I won't be a long-term problem.'

'I see. Well, I suppose Orléans is about 120km from Paris, so you wouldn't be able to reach it in under an hour.'

Jemme looked momentarily puzzled, 'Orléans?' he laughed when he understood, 'Oh, I see. It's not actually in Orléans, DD, it's in the countryside.'

'Oh, my mistake, Sir, I thought you were going to Orléans, this weekend.'

'We were. That is to say, we did. We had a good look around the chateau there, too, and really liked it. We came very close to buying it in fact, but there was a deeply unpleasant and sleazy individual involved, who seemed to be exploiting the dear old lady Châtelaine, and we were too uncomfortable with the whole thing. So, we went to Deauville and by chance bumped into an estate agent, who took us to see Château Vigne-Verte, which we both loved and put in an offer for. Then we drove back to Paris and that pretty much brings us up to right now.'

If Jemme had enjoyed DD's surprise earlier, he was positively revelling in it now. He knew how linear DD was in his thinking and planning, and what anathema spontaneity and last-minuteness was to him.

'I don't understand, Sir. In one weekend you went to two different towns, saw two different chateaux and...bought one?'

'Well, three different towns if you count Deauville in the middle, but yes, that's the gist of it.'

DD shook his head and marvelled, 'I'm quite taken aback by the news,' he began.

'I can see,' said Jemme, playfully.

'But, I congratulate you on finally achieving your objectives, and hope very much that I might be of some assistance in realising the last stages of your plan,' DD finished, sounding much more like his old self.

Jemme smiled, 'Thank you, DD, I couldn't imagine doing it without you.'

DD looked gratified and they returned to the normal daily business of the bank.

Jemme thought back on it now, as he drove out of Paris, and chuckled again. He could probably count on one hand the number of times he'd seen DD lose his composure, and this incident had definitely featured highly amongst his favourites.

He was looking forward to visiting the chateau again, and had taken the day off work especially. He didn't expect the paperwork to take up much more than a couple of hours, and he had planned on spending the rest of the day exploring the chateau and then the nearby town and surrounding villages. He had told Hil not to worry about taking the time off work. It was bound to be quite an admin-heavy trip and not particularly fun, and they had both thought it would be quicker and easier if he dealt with the matter on his own. Besides, he had privately thought it might be quite nice to have a little time there on his own, taking in the canvas for his dream, before they started having to deal with all the fuss of moving. As he pulled up the gravel driveway again, and the magnificent chateau came into sight, he felt a blissful surge of validation – it was all as perfect and as real as he remembered. Butterflies whizzed around his stomach as he contemplated the fact that he would soon own it. It was dizzyingly exciting.

He parked up the car, and was pleased to note that there were several other cars outside the front entrance too. The ministers must be there already, which would speed things up nicely.

He crunched his way across the gravel, and knocked sharply on the front door. Nothing happened. He waited for a while and then knocked again, looking around for some kind of bell or buzzer. The door was so large it had all but absorbed the sound of his knocking. He waited a while longer, and was about to knock for a third time when he heard the muffled sound of shouting coming from within. It was too distorted to hear what was being said, but judging by the tone it was someone highly excitable. He heard something being slammed down, and then the door in front of him abruptly swung inwards. A small bespectacled man jumped when he saw him, and quickly looked indignant.

'*Oui?*' he said imperiously.

'*Bonjour, Monsieur.* I am here to complete the paperwork – my name is Jemme Mafeze.'

Jemme extended a hand, which the little man ignored. He pushed his glasses firmly up to the bridge of his nose and glowered at Jemme for a few minutes before bellowing, 'Claaaaaude! *Claude!*' behind him into the house. Someone who was evidently Claude appeared, clucking away to himself at the indignity of having been summoned thus. He completely ignored Jemme, and began a lengthy and dramatic discussion with the Frenchman, which became louder and accompanied by increasingly elaborate hand gestures. It soon became clear where the noises Jemme had heard had come from. Eventually the subject matter appeared to turn towards the stranger on the doorstep, and they both turned to inspect Jemme, whose presence was apparently distasteful to them. Finally Claude shrugged. The little man paused for a while, then shrugged too and opened the door to let Jemme in. 'Wait here,' he said abruptly, before disappearing off, arguing with Claude along the way

It was not exactly the reception Jemme had been expecting from the French government, and as he sat in the hallway feeling like an unwelcome guest, he struggled to hold on to the knowledge that this hallway was in fact his. Whilst he sat, various sour-faced officials crossed through, carrying bits of paperwork and an assortment of odds and ends. None of them paid him any attention whatsoever, and he began to wonder where the two men he had seen earlier had disappeared to. The minutes ticked on, and he grew impatient. His time could have been spent in a far more profitable way in the bank, with Hil, or exploring the surrounding area, as he had planned to do. Wasting time had always made him angry, and the idea of someone else wasting his time rankled deeply. The next time someone walked past him, he stopped him.

'*Excusez-moi, Monsieur,*' he began, firmly.

The man stopped dead in his tracks. He looked positively incensed, '*Oui?*' he snapped.

Jemme was not deterred, 'I am sorry to interrupt, but I have been waiting here for some time.'

'Waiting?' the man turned the word over as if it was new to him, 'Why are you waiting – who are you waiting for?'

'Well, to be honest, I'm not quite sure.'

'Hmph,' sniffed the man. 'I am very busy, Monsieur, I do not have time to waste with men who do not know what they are waiting around for.'

Jemme took a deep breath to prevent himself from losing his temper, 'I am a busy man too, Monsieur; that is why I would like you to help me find whoever it is I need to talk to. I am here to sign some paperwork. I am the new owner of the house,' he finished, thinking that revealing this fact would jolt some kind of urgency, or maybe even respect into the man. It didn't seem to make a blind bit of difference, and Jemme got the feeling that even if he had said he was Napoleon himself, he would still have been treated with the same imperious aloofness. The man narrowed his eyes and took a long, slow look at Jemme.

'Well, in that case, *Monsieur,*' he said with sarcastic deference, 'you will need to speak to the notary. I do not have any idea when he will be free. He is a very busy man – he is a minister in the French government! I suggest you continue to wait here, and when he is ready to see you someone will come and find you.'

This was just about the final straw for Jemme who jumped to his feet, 'Look here, I have driven all the way from Paris-' he stopped himself, took a deep breath and told the man in icy tones that he would be walking in the grounds and when the minister deigned to see him, he should come and find him himself.

He swept out of the hall to the sound of the man's protests about how unseemly it would be for a minister *of the French government* to go looking in the gardens for someone.

'Unbelievable,' Jemme muttered to himself as he tramped back down the same driveway he had walked up with so much excitement earlier that day. To think, he had been actually looking forward to this opportunity to meet government officials – he had thought it a rather grand way to take ownership of the place and an amusing story to look back on in later years. He was irritated that so much of the morning had been wasted – at this rate he was only going to have time to finish the paperwork before he had to head back to Paris. He sighed to himself; at least Hil hadn't come along on this trip. He looked up, and felt the early autumn sun on his face. It made him smile slightly. It was impossible to feel angry in such beautiful surroundings, and doubly so when he knew that he was tantalisingly close to owning them. He carried on walking up the driveway towards the wrought iron gates, which led in from the main road. When he had been here with Hil they had only explored the apron-shaped lawn, which spread out behind the chateau. However, the long driveway cut through a large amount of land, and he was keen to look around. With every step he took away from the houseful of irritating officials, he felt a little better. After about a hundred yards he stopped and took in his surroundings. He couldn't believe how much more extensive the grounds were than he had initially thought. Looking around him now he could see a thicket of pine on one side, and a rockery on the other, with beeches gently waving in the breeze behind it. He left the drive and went to explore the rockery first. It was full of interesting plants, and obviously well-maintained. 'Well, that's one thing the government has been doing right!' he thought to himself approvingly. Next to the rockery was what looked like a stone pedestal of some sort. It was a curious piece, with some ironwork arching over the top of it, and some sort of wooden plank lying flat on the surface. He went over to investigate and soon saw that it wasn't a pedestal at all, but rather a well. The pretty ironwork at the top was the bucket hoist. *I wonder if it still works*, he thought. It was all a little too perfect, and he could imagine Hil falling in love with the idea of having a working well in the garden. 'Charming', she would call it. He smiled to himself and lifted the wooden lid. It was too dark to see to the bottom, but he picked up a small pebble from the rockery and dropped it down the shaft, to hear the reassuring noise of a splash. He carefully replaced the lid, pleased with his discovery.

By the time he wandered across the driveway to look at the pine thicket, he had all but forgotten his earlier irritation. He judged that he had left it long enough, and whatever the notary was up to would probably have come to a finish by now. After all, he too was there to sign the paperwork, so he couldn't be that busy. He looked up at the waxy needles of the trees surrounding him. One of the trunks was oozing a syrupy, amber-coloured sap, which reminded him of the beautiful chunks of amber seen in Baltic jewellery. As he looked at it, and wondered if it too would one day dangle from a silver chain, he heard a twig snap behind him. He turned around to see find a weather-beaten man following his gaze.

'*Des pins, Monsieur,*' the man said. 'Although I will be surprised if these *idiots* do not try and box that up and take it with them. He took a final drag on the cigarette he was puffing, then, slowly and deliberately stubbed it out on the sole of his work-boot before carefully stowing the butt in his pocket. Despite his calloused hands, there was something sure and deft about his movements.

'*Des mégots,*' he explained. 'I do not like to see them littering the ground.'

'Absolutely,' Jemme nodded. The man looked at him curiously, 'You do not act like the others. Are you with the government?'

Jemme shook his head, 'Most definitely not,' he laughed. 'Jemme Mafeze,' he said, offering his hand and adding, 'I'm the new owner.'

This provoked the results he had been hoping for with the officials earlier. The man raised his eyebrows and looked impressed. He shook his hand, 'Well, I hope you make a better job of it than these men have; although that won't be difficult,' he shook his head lugubriously. Jemme took him in; of medium height and relatively stout, he had the kind of ruddy skin that only comes of a lifetime spent outdoors. He could have stepped straight from a D.H. Lawrence novel, with his green velveteens, grizzled beard and shabby oilskin gilet.

'If you don't mind me saying, you don't seem like the others either – I take it you're also not with the government?'

'Pah, I am not, Sir,' he said emphatically. Jemme laughed and the man softened a little, 'Well, I am not one of them, but I must confess I am with them.'

Jemme looked a little puzzled, 'I'm sorry, I never actually caught your name.'

The man sized Jemme up for a moment longer with curiously distant hazel eyes. 'I am Philby,' he said. 'I am the gardener here.'

'Well you've done a fantastic job, based on what I've seen so far,' said Jemme warmly, 'I was just thinking to myself how well the rockery looked.'

A slow smile spread across the man's face. 'Thank you, Monsieur. The lavender there was planted by my father. He was the gardener here before me, and he kept these grounds for all of his life. The roses by the front of the chateau were his pride and joy.'

'Roses?' asked Jemme, 'I must look out for them, my wife is particularly fond of roses and she'll be delighted to know that there are some here.'

'You won't see them, Monsieur; there are only a few left now. These government fools picked the flowers before they were ready and flattened the plants with their trucks.' He sighed bitterly.

'What a pity, I'm so sorry to hear that,' said Jemme. The man looked at him again and Jemme felt like he was still being sized up.

'Tell me,' said Jemme, 'what happens to you now? I hope you'll consider staying and maybe help my wife re-grow those roses.'

'Well, that all depends on you, Monsieur. I have spent my whole life gardening here, and when the government took over, they took me on as an employee. Now that they are moving from this property I will be deployed to another, apparently. They cannot tell me where, though and so it seems that I might be uprooted at a moment's notice, and have to leave my home. My family has lived in this village for generations!' He shook his head again.

'What nonsense!' said Jemme, 'I have been thinking about how we'll have to staff a property like this since I arrived. I'm lucky to have found you – I wouldn't consider having anyone else in the gardens here. Who better than a man who's spent his whole life here, and already knows the grounds inside out? I'd be honoured if you'd consider staying.'

A warm and genuine smile spread out across the man's weathered face. '*Merci*, Monsieur, of course I will stay.'

'Excellent news, glad to have you as the first one on the team, Philby!'

Philby put out his hand to shake Jemme's, '*Bienvenu, Monsieur, bienvenu.*'

'Thank you, Philby. I'll have my lawyers draw up a new contract for you. Don't worry, I'll make sure it compares favourably with the one the government has you on at the moment.'

At the mention of the government, Philby's face clouded over, 'I just remembered, Monsieur – the government.'

'Yes?'

'Well, seeing as you are the new owner, and you are a *gentilhomme*, there is really something you should know.'

'What's that?'

'Well, there have been two large urns sitting either side of the main entrance for as long as I can remember. Even was I a child coming here to help my father at work, they were there. They are part of the house and now they should belong to you.'

'I don't remember seeing any urns,' said Jemme.

'Precisely, Monsieur; they have gone the same way as the roses,' said Philby. 'I think they must be valuable – they are certainly old. Two of the ministers moved them this morning. I heard them talking about it – quite a fuss they made about it too. They're heavy, and the men weren't much up to the job,' he said with an edge of scorn, 'Anyway, they've hidden them in the *cave*, though I'm not sure what they're planning on doing with them. I wouldn't put anything past them.'

'Thank you Philby, I really appreciate you bringing this to my attention. I was heading back to the house anyway and I'll make sure I bring this up. I'll come and find you to say goodbye before I head back to Paris.' He shook Philby's hand again, 'I'm pleased to have you on board.'

Philby nodded, and fumbled in his pocket for another cigarette.

As Jemme strode back to the house, all the anger and irritation he had felt earlier in the morning bubbled up inside him again – how dare they try and deceive him? Who were they to try and make a profit from what was his? What on earth was this country coming to if the government itself could not be relied on to be an arbiter of morality?! The only thing tempering his bad mood was the early display of loyalty from Philby. He was pleased to have secured his first chateau employee, and already knew that he was in good hands. There was something earthy and honest about the man, and Jemme liked the way that Philby had been slow to warm to him too. It was the sign of a good judge of character.

As he reached the front door, and noticed the space where the urns should have been, his ire increased. Finding the front door was once again shut against him didn't improve matters, and he pounded on it with his fist. The little man opened the door again and looked just as displeased to see him. 'Oh. It's you again, Monsieur.'

'Yes, it is, and I would like to see the notary immediately. I don't have any more time to waste. If you want me to take this chateau off your hands, I suggest you take me to see him this instant.'

The man shrugged, 'Very well, Monsieur. There is no need to be so impatient,' he said, only infuriating Jemme even further. He led him down the corridor to a small room, which was being used as a makeshift office.

'Wait here, I shall go and fetch him.' The rudeness of the man set Jemme's teeth on edge, and by the time the notary finally arrived, Jemme was spoiling for a fight.

About five minutes later the notary finally swept into the room. Despite his rising anger, Jemme couldn't but be amused by the man in front of him. He was a parody of a cliché, all wrapped up in cloak of pastiche. He had bouffant hair and a spivvy little pencil moustache. A colourful square of chiffon tucked into the breast pocket of his jacket matched the cravat around his neck.

'Monsieur!' he said commandingly, as soon as he entered the room. He strode towards Jemme with his hand outstretched and gave him a powerful handshake.

'I'm-' Jemme began.

'Jemme Mafeze,' the notary interrupted him. 'We have been expecting you, Monsieur Mafeze.' He was a strange mix of virulent masculinity and yet at the same oddly effeminate in his actions. The paradox of the Frenchman, Jemme thought to himself, and smiled.

'Well,' the notary said with a slight flourish, 'I suppose we should get these proceedings underway as soon as possible, *non*?'

He slipped a pair of spectacles on and pushed them up his pendulous nose, 'Now, I have already prepared the deeds. Here you will see the seal of the French government,' he gestured, 'it is impressive, *non*? Here, you will see my signatures and those of my colleagues. All that remains for you to do, Monsieur, is to sign here – on this small line and that will conclude our business.' He smiled a lizard-like grin at Jemme and extended a hand to him, in which he was loosely holding an expensive-looking fountain pen.

Jemme did not return his smile, and the notary withdrew his hand with a wounded look.

'Is there a problem, Monsieur?'

'Well, actually, yes, there is,' said Jemme.

The man blinked behind his glasses, before slowly removing them and methodically polishing them on the silk pocket square. 'I can't imagine what that could be, Monsieur,' he said. 'As you'll see, this document has been signed by six of my colleagues as well as by myself. Seven, Monsieur, seven employees of the French government all together. Now, what could the problem be with that?'

He smiled a slightly twisted little smile at Jemme, and proffered the fountain pen again. 'What was it you said you did again, Monsieur Mafeze?' he asked in syrupy tones.

Jemme could see straight through him, and respected him none the better for it. He seemed to embody everything about the French attitude to authority and entitlement that had made Jemme's business and personal life difficult since he had moved to France. Although he loved his adopted homeland, and had no desire to leave at any point soon, there were still some aspects of life he found exasperating. The cronyism, the bureaucracy, the sense of entitlement which some members of society seemed to exude – they were all frequently occurring obstacles and he tired of having to deal with them. He had no doubt that this man in front of him had received this grace-and-favour job because he was someone's son or school-friend. Once he was safely ensconced within the cosy folds of the government's hierarchy, it would be nigh on impossible to rout him out. He was all but guaranteed a job for life, and the worst part was that he seemed to know it.

As he slicked his moustache down with his little finger, he stared, unblinking at Jemme. 'We both know you can't touch me,' he seemed to be saying.

'I'm a banker,' said Jemme curtly, 'but that's not important. What is important is that this sale is conducted correctly and legally.'

'Oh, but I agree, Monsieur. The French government never behaves in any other way. Why do you raise this point?'

'I don't know how the French government behaves in other affairs,' said Jemme, 'but in this matter I believe that they are not acting either correctly or legally.'

The notary sat up in his chair. He gasped dramatically and let the square of chiffon flutter down to his lap.

'Mon-sieur,' he inhaled, 'are you accusing *la gouvernement Française* of wrongdoing? Are you sullying the good name of *la Republique?* Never, in all my time as a humble servant of *la France...*' he shook his head.

Jemme was entirely unimpressed, 'As I said, I'm sure in all other matters you act with nothing but transparency and probity, but I'm afraid in this one you have not.'

'Have not? Have not! Look!' he waved the document in Jemme's face. 'Seven signatures, Monsieur, *seven* signatories of the French government. All good men – all men of excellent repute. Who are you, a, a banker to cast aspersions on their-'

Jemme had had enough of this posturing, 'Where are the urns?' he interrupted.

'The urns? I don't know anything about urns! I am a notary of the French government, not a housemaid!' spluttered the man, his eyes bulging with indignation.

'There were two urns,' said Jemme very calmly. 'They were either side of the front door and they have been there for generations. As I am now the new owner, they are now my property. However, they have been removed.'

'*Removed?*' cried the notary.

'Yes, removed. I'm afraid I consider that tantamount to theft, and I would like to resolve this matter as soon as possible.'

If the notary had been apoplectic before, the idea that the French government was being accused of theft looked like it was enough to make him faint. He slid down in his chair, looking withered and shaking his head,

'*Incroyable*,' he muttered to himself, '*incroyable*.' He picked up the phone on the desk, '*Marcel*,' he muttered into it weakly, '*venez ici*.'

Another man soon trotted into the room and looked around, '*Oui?*' he asked

'This man – this man,' said the notary, gesturing with a fey hand, 'has accused us of stealing some urns. Do you know anything about this matter?'

'Urns, Monsieur? I, um, well....' The new character ground his foot into the carpet and looked nervous.

The notary was sitting in his seat with his head in has hand, acting every inch the slandered gentleman. At the sound of Marcel's hesitancy he opened one eye and looked over.

'Speak up, man,' he said sharply.

'Well, I – we didn't mean any harm, we just thought that maybe, what with the banker from Paris not knowing what came with the house....'

Both Jemme and the notary glared at him.

'I am the "banker from Paris",' said Jemme, 'and I would quite like to know why you have put my urns in the cellar.'

Marcel jumped guiltily, 'I... how did you – '

'And I would quite like to know what on earth is going on!' said the notary.

Eventually the story came out. Marcel and another magistrate, Jean-Maurice, had stashed the urns in the cellar for 'safe-keeping.' He was sorry (even though he hadn't done anything wrong) and would move them back immediately for the new owner. It would be his pleasure, and Jean-Maurice's too.

The explanation was paper-thin and threw up more questions than it answered, but Jemme just wanted to get everything sorted.

He nodded his thanks to Marcel, who was dispatched with a cold stare from the notary. As soon as the door had closed behind him, the notary turned to Jemme, 'Monsieur, you must accept my most sincere apologies. I had no idea – ' he was a completely different person, now that his pride had been completely punctured, and Jemme even warmed to him a little.

'These magistrates – they are all so greedy. Anything they can make for themselves they will. I sometimes wonder if they would sell their own mothers!'

Jemme smiled, 'Keep your enemies close, Monsieur.'

The notary cracked a smile, a much more genuine one this time. Stripped of his hubris he actually seemed to be quite a nice guy.

'I think it's safe to say he won't be trying anything like that for a while!' said Jemme.

The notary had the grace to chuckle, '*Mon Dieu*, his face, Monsieur! I've never seen anyone look so guilty in all my life!'

Jemme smiled, 'He was slightly caught red-handed wasn't he? I think he was confused by the fact I knew they were in the cellar too.'

The notary chuckled again, and extended his hand for Jemme to shake.

'My unreserved apologies, again, Mr Mafeze. All we need is your signature, and I will do everything in my powers to ensure that this sale is sorted out as quickly as possible.' He passed the pen over and this time Jemme took it and signed.

He paused for a moment. 'I can't believe it's all real,' he said, trying to take in the significance of the occasion.

The notary smiled, 'Congratulations, Monsieur. Welcome to your new home! I will make it my personal responsibility to ensure those urns are put back before you move in. I tell you what, as a moving-in present, I will even make sure they're filled with flowers!'

As he drove up his own driveway to head back to Paris, Jemme thought about what a successful day it had turned out to be. Although it hadn't been the one he had been planning, it had still worked out rather well. He was now the official, legal owner, he had employed his first member of staff, and he had even drawn a smile out of a notary of the government of France!

✻   ✻   ✻   ✻

Back in Paris he presented Hil with a small packet of fudge, a local speciality.

'I picked these up for you on the way back,' he said, 'I thought you should probably get a taste for them now, considering we'll be eating a lot more of them in the future.' Hil squealed with excitement and hugged him.

'I can't believe it's all ours!' she said. 'All that time we've spent searching, all those trips to the countryside to see horrible draughty, creaking chateaux, not to mention the downright creepy ones. Just think – we won't have to do any of it any more! We won't have to meet any more of the strange people that seem to live out there, or have our hopes raised and dashed on a regular basis.'

'I know,' smiled Jemme, 'after all we've been through that's almost the best bit.'

They sat together on the sofa, wrapped one of Hil's broad cashmere scarves around them and ate chunks of crumbly fudge whilst they thought about the new house.

'There's so much to do, still,' said Hil, 'I suppose this is only just the beginning. I think that signing only feels like such a big deal because we've been looking for so long. Think how much we've got to do! It would be arduous enough moving into a new, larger house, let alone a chateau, and that's before we've even begun to think about the fact we'll be running your project alongside everything.'

'I know,' said Jemme, finishing his piece, 'I still think we've got the best plan though. Let's stay here until all the building and wiring is complete, and then we can move over – we've put up with things here up until now, I'm sure we can deal with it for a little longer.'

'If all the shops sell things as tasty as this, then I'm not sure I want to stay away for much longer,' said Hil, finishing off the last square.

The next weekend, they drove back out of Paris with a small overnight bag in the boot of the car, looking forward to spending their first night in the chateau. As they pulled up the driveway, Hil sighed, 'It's just as beautiful as I remembered it.

I was worried that I might have exaggerated it in my mind, or misremembered it as how I wanted it to be, rather than how it was, but it's just wonderful.'

'I know, I went though exactly the same thought process, but it was just as I remembered too. It's strange, finding precisely what you've been looking for. After becoming so acclimatised to the search and this endless quest for perfection, to be confronted with it is very disorientating.'

'Sometimes understanding that you're finally getting what you want can be absolutely terrifying,' said Hil thoughtfully, 'especially if you've enjoyed the search for it. I don't know how much we've necessarily enjoyed it, but we've certainly become used to looking – it's been such a large part of our lives, and it's a big change, a large shift in focus. I suppose we've got to adapt to the idea of moving and creating a new home for ourselves now.'

'You're right, I think it's the change that I'm most nervous about at the moment. It feels so strange, knowing that I could be on the brink of realising my dream after all these years.'

'I'm looking forward to it,' said Hil, 'After all this time hearing about it, I can't wait to be able to see its physical realisation. How many people are given the opportunity to see the tangible manifestation of their husband's childhood visions? Especially one which has guided you and shaped your outlook for your entire adult life.'

'I suppose not many people do. That's something else I'm finding strange as well – now I've finally found the chateau, I'm starting to focus on the dream. But, what do I do if, when, I realise that? What have I got left? I will have completed a lifetime's ambitions, and ended the thing which has been driving me for years. I don't know if I'm ready to cut it away quite yet.'

'But you won't be cutting it away; you'll be nurturing it and developing it. Do you think that a vision can be finite? When something is based within such shifting parameters, I don't think you'll ever be able to able to look at it and say, "That's it, I've finished, that's everything I ever expected it to be."'

'No I expect not,' said Jemme, looking affectionately at Hil. He was lucky to have a wife who was so perspicacious and thoughtful. She was right too – in many ways this project would continue to develop throughout the rest of his life. The dream had changed slightly every time he had had it, so the project was unlikely to be a simple and clear task.

They walked to the front door, holding hands. The government had sent a courier to the bank with a bunch of keys which Jemme now held in his free hand. It was a strange set, with innocuous looking every-day keys looped onto the same ring as large, weighty iron ones. Holding them all together felt good – the keys to his empire. Excitedly, he slipped the longest one into the lock on the front door and turned it. A heavy, reassuring clunk on the other side was audible, and he pushed at the door. It swung open with surprising ease – the government had obviously kept the hinges well oiled. He stepped to one side and gestured for Hil to go in, in front of him.

'Welcome to your castle, Mrs Mafeze.'

Hil smiled, 'How exciting! Thank you, Mr Mafeze,' she said with mock solemnity and went in through the door.

Light spilled into the entrance hall from the tall windows. A residual smell of beeswax lingered – a ghostly reminder of the generations who had lovingly cared for the place. They wandered slowly through the building, drinking it all in. They passed interesting little architectural details, remarking at pretty embellishments.

'These are all the little things that really make a house a home,' said Hil, as she ran her fingers over a large knot in the wooden panel in a window seat. 'Once you get to know these little quirks, then you really feel a sense of attachment to a place.'

'I know exactly what you mean,' said Jemme, taking in the old, shaky glass in the window above the seat. 'I'm looking forward to getting to know this place with you. I think it will be a while before we start to become acquainted with the details though – it's so large, it's going to take us forever just to remember where all the rooms are!'

'That's true,' Hil laughed.

'We bought it in such a hurry too; did you know that there are rooms we haven't even seen?'

'Actually? That's completely ridiculous!'

'I know, I couldn't believe it either. I've been trawling through the paperwork the government sent me, and the blueprints of the chateau. There are a couple of small rooms I didn't recognise, but there was an even bigger surprise than that.'

'More than finding whole new rooms?!'

'Much more. There's a whole library!'

'A library!'

'Apparently. I was just as surprised as you. I looked over the details again and again, but it's there on the list of rooms and there on the plans too – *bibliothèque*. It's really quite large, judging by the scale on the plans at least. It takes up the whole of the front corner, in fact. I have no idea how we missed it – I suppose we must have just walked straight past the door, because we've seen the rooms either side of it.'

'How bizarre. How exciting though -- our own library.'

'I know, I'm really looking forward to seeing it. There are some scribbled notes on the paperwork about original features and bookcases. If it's all still there, it would be the perfect place to display some of our books and manuscripts.'

'Wouldn't it just. It would be wonderful to be able to have them out; it's such a shame to keep them on a couple of ordinary shelves like we do at the moment. I feel like they're a little neglected.'

'Well, it's all been on hold, waiting for an opportunity like this I suppose,' said Jemme.

'What are we waiting for? Why haven't we gone and looked at it yet?' asked Hil.

Jemme laughed, 'Good question! Let's go. It's at the end of this corridor and to the right.'

They reached the end of the corridor and turned the corner. Just to the right of the corner was a wooden door. It was slightly awkwardly placed, and if they hadn't been looking out for it they probably would have missed it all together. With all their excitement in exploring the other rooms on the same corridor it was obvious they must have sailed straight past it when they were there before. Jemme turned the brass handle, which was in need of a good polish, and pushed the door open.

Hil followed him in and looked around, 'Oh,' she said flatly, trying not to sound disappointed.

Jemme looked around puzzled, 'I don't understand,' he said.

'Well, it's certainly big,' said Hil, hopefully. 'I was just expecting a little more. I thought you said that there were some original features?' Jemme continued to furrow his brow as he looked around.

'Unbelieveable!'

'What is?'

'Those government weasels! After everything we went through with the wretched urns too – and this is something I actually care about!'

'What is darling? What are you talking about?'

'They've obviously ripped it all out to take with them!'

'Who has? What have they ripped out?'

'Everything! Look!'

Hil looked around her. Jemme was right – the room had been completely gutted, and very recently too. Someone had obviously pulled the fixtures and fittings out with very little care. The beautiful wood blocked wallpaper had been torn and chunks of plaster wrenched out from the walls, littering the antique carpet with masonry dust. It was a sad sight; the room had handsome proportions, and even in its burgled state it was still quite grand, and Hil could only imagine how impressive it would have looked.

She slipped an arm around Jemme, 'Never mind, sweetheart, it's a bit like a blank canvas now – we can do anything we like with it.'

Jemme was not to be placated though, and muttered angrily about having been taken for a fool. The rest of the tour was somewhat subdued, and it wasn't until they were back outside that he started to perk up again.

'Ah, I'd forgotten – there's another addition to the house you haven't seen yet, or should I say, met yet.'

Hil looked intrigued as they made their way across the grounds away from the house. The ground dipped down around a knot of cedar trees, behind which sat a small brick bothy. In this slight depression it was well-screened from the house, and made for a quite a private little bolt-hole.

A slightly wonky chimney rose out of the roof, and it was easy to imagine smoke puffing out on a cold, frosty day.

'This looks like a cosy little spot,' said Hil.

Jemme knocked on the little wooden door and pushed it open, 'Ah Philby! I was hoping to find you here, excuse us for barging in.'

'Barging, Monsieur? *Non, non*, come in.'

Jemme stepped inside to the single room. An old table with a couple of rickety chairs sat on one side, and a small single-ring stove on the other. Hil followed him in, and once Philby saw that Jemme was not alone he leapt to his feet,

'*Madame, bonjour*, I am sorry – I didn't realise, please – have a seat,' he said, hurriedly sweeping the table down with one hand and pulling out a chair with the other.

'Philby, this is my wife, Hil. Hil, this is Philby. He's been the gardener here for years, and his father was before him. Luckily for us, he's agreed to stay on,' said Jemme, slightly amused by how flustered Philby looked.

'That's good news,' said Hil graciously.

'Thank you, Madame,' said Philby, 'Monsieur has told me that you might be interested in the rose beds, *non*? There were some beautiful roses, planted by my own father, but the government destroyed them through carelessness.'

'What a pity!'

'*Oui, Madame*. My father tended to them for years – they were his pride and joy. I hope to restore them to how they were.'

'That would be fantastic, I simply adore roses. I'm sure you can get them looking as magnificent as your father must have had them.'

'Thank you, Madame. It would please me to put right a wrong. I know this house so well, it saddens me to see it damaged by foolish owners.'

Jemme frowned, 'That reminds me, Philby, there was something I wanted to ask you about. I was very disappointed to see the state the library has been left in. All of the original fixtures and fittings have been ripped out and I was wondering if you knew what the government had done with them? I'm guessing they've all been sold off by now, but I was hoping there might be a chance of recovering just some of them.'

'Ah, no, Monsieur.'

'No?'

'It was not the government. They destroyed my roses and painted over many things inside the house, but they did not destroy the library.'

'Oh, I see. Well in that case, who on earth did?'

'It was the American who bought the chateau from them. He was crazy, *fou*, I tell you! He wanted to make a golf course out of the gardens and turn the chateau into some sort of clubhouse. I remember other Americans coming in and them destroying the library. It was a complete crime – that library is original to the house. It's like chopping down all the trees in an ancient wood.'

Jemme shook his head and grimaced slightly at the thought of the heavy-handed Americans splintering though beautifully carved wood and hacking out pieces of the wall in the process.

'Thankfully, he did not stay around for very long,' Philby continued, 'I dread to think what the place would have looked like if he'd been allowed to continue – he was *comme un chien dans un jeu de quills*!'

Jemme looked amused but then remembered the subject in hand.

'Regardless of who was responsible, I suppose it doesn't change the fact that a beautiful room has been ruined. Do you remember Philby, did they destroy the furniture or do you think there's any chance of repatriating any of it?'

'Ahh, there I think I might be able to help you, Monsieur,' Philby replied intriguingly.

Chapter Thirteen

Jemme and Hil woke the next morning not sure if they had enjoyed the first night in their new house or not. On the one hand it had been exciting going to sleep in a house that they now owned. They had chosen the largest bedroom on the first floor. It was from the Louis XIV period, with high ceilings and large windows looking out over the grounds. It was in desperate need of some attention, but still retained an air of faded grandeur. The paper was peeling and the carpet looked a little threadbare, whilst patches of damp bloomed out across the ceiling. However, despite all these things it was impossible to escape how impressive it was when first opening the door. Although it had seen better days, it was clear that the wallpaper had once been opulent; likewise, the paint was flaking on the coving and the ceiling embellishments were slightly discoloured, but nothing that a lick of new paint couldn't sort out. Even in their yellowed state, they still seemed to be markers of how important the room was, and indicated the status of its former occupants.

However, the bed was a completely different story. Hil remarked that it felt like sleeping on a sack of potatoes, and Jemme couldn't have agreed more. They had resolved that their first purchase for the chateau would be a king-sized bed, with no expenses spared on the mattress front. However, it hadn't just been their discomfort which had made for a rough night's sleep. It had been all the creaking and sighing of a house settling in to accommodating two new people. Any home has its own idiosyncrasies, a symphony of highly individual noises it makes when it winds down at the end of the day and warms up again in the morning. However, a very large, very old house produces an even stranger selection of sounds. One in the countryside is even stranger still. With wind whistling down the chimneys and rattling the ancient shutters, and the screeching sound of foxes in the garden, it had not been a particularly restful night. Once they had woken and, bleary-eyed, adjusted to being in an unexpected environment, they attempted to coax some life out of the ancient plumbing system in the bathroom. To their great surprise and delight, it spluttered to life and even managed to produce some hot water. Showered and dressed they were poking their way around the kitchen, trying to make sense of an odd variety of implements the government had left behind, and making tea with an industrial-sized pot, when Philby knocked on the door.

'*Excusez-moi,*' he said,

'Come in Philby!' called Hil warmly, 'We're just making some tea.' Philby entered and a small woman followed him.

'This is Madame Pilote,' he said. 'She keeps the archives in the village, and I thought she might be able to help with the library.'

'*Bonjour, Madame Pilote,*' said Jemme, 'thank you so much for coming.'

'It is my pleasure, Monsieur, especially if it will help restore some local history. I had heard that there had been some damage up here after the government sold it, but I didn't understand the extent.'

'To be honest, it's just the library,' said Jemme, 'everything else is in a rather poor state of repair, but can be spruced up relatively easily. The library, though… well, it's all been ripped out and I'm worried that we won't be able to replace it. Even if we can't track down the original pieces, then without knowing what it looked like we can't do a very good job of restoring it. We could be wildly out of alignment with how it was meant to look.'

Madame Pilote had been shaking her head sadly whilst she listened to Jemme.

'It is a shame, Monsieur, a great shame. I was lucky enough to visit the library here – it was very beautiful indeed. The jewel in the crown, in fact.'

Jemme looked disheartened.

'However, all is not lost, Monsieur. As I said, I was lucky enough to visit and I have a fairly strong memory of how it looked. Also, I have many archived documents and photos pertaining to the chateau. I'm sure I will be able to find something for you – maybe even photos of the library itself.'

'That would be fantastic, thank you very much indeed,' said Jemme.

Madame Pilote looked gratified.

'Will you stay and have some tea with us, Madame?' asked Hil.

'But of course!' she replied as Hil grappled with the large pot and rummaged around in the cupboard for four mugs.

✻   ✻   ✻   ✻

Hil and Jemme left for Paris late on Sunday, pleased to have spent their first weekend in their new home, but slightly daunted by how much work there was to do still. Even before they had left the chateau, they had resolved to come back the next weekend. There was so much to do, so many projects to get their teeth into, that staying away didn't really feel like an option. They had excitedly relayed all the details to their various friends and colleagues, describing the beautiful period bedroom they had chosen, and their pleasure at finding someone so local and connected with the chateau to tend to the garden. One of Jemme's friends had empathised with their delight and agreed that good gardeners were hard to come by, but expressed surprise that they were not going to continue looking. 'But I just told you, we already have a gardener. Why would we want another?' he had said. 'For a garden that size you'll need nothing less than a small team of gardeners,' his friend replied, 'By all means, keep the one you've got – make him head gardener in fact, but take on more staff. You don't want him so overworked he leaves!'

Jemme had thought it over. He certainly wanted to keep hold of Philby at all costs. What's more, it sounded like he'd been cut a rough deal under the government, and so he was keen to ensure that he treated him much better than the previous occupants had. He pondered on it some more, and realised that the chateau was much like the bank. So he had to start thinking of it that way. He was in charge of it, and it would require a full-scale team to run efficiently. It was his responsibility to hire and manage that team and he would need to start doing so as soon as possible. He resolved to find a second gardener for Philby the very next weekend.

The next journey to the chateau seemed to go much more quickly. They were becoming accustomed to the route, and started to recognise various landmarks along the way. As they completed the last section of the journey, and turned off the main road to the smaller road which led to the chateau, Hil experienced a prickling of the sense of familiarity which comes with feeling like a place is home. She smiled at Jemme, 'It's all starting to feel a little more real now,' she said.

'I know what you mean,' he replied as they turned down the driveway and the chateau, their chateau, hove into view.

Jemme had telephoned ahead and Philby was waiting to meet them. Hil could make him out from the top of the driveway, standing by the ruined rose beds.

'It's nice to know there's someone here – it feels quite welcoming, doesn't it?'

'Yes, definitely,' said Jemme, 'and it's more than that, it's the thought that there's someone here when we're not, almost as if there's life being breathed into the place. I'd hate to think of it all cold and empty whilst we're not here.'

Hil smiled again, 'I quite like the thought of Philby keeping it nice and warm for us whilst we're not here.'

'Me too.'

They parked up and Jemme got out of the door to open the door for Hil.

'Welcome back, Monsieur,' said Philby, 'how was the journey from Paris?'

'Incredibly easy actually, thank you Philby,' said Jemme as he opened the boot of the car to take their bags out. Philby watched him for a moment before an idea came to him.

'I can help you with those, Monsieur!'

'Oh, that's very kind of you, but there's no need.'

'No, Monsieur, it is no bother,' said Philby, grabbing the cases with his slightly gnarled hand. He headed into the house ahead of them. Once inside the hall, he turned around to Jemme, 'Shall I put these in the bedroom for you, Sir?'

'Oh I shouldn't worry about that, we can take them up,' Jemme replied.

'No, I will do it for you,' said Philby firmly. 'Also, your bed has arrived, Monsieur,' he said as they climbed.

'Already? That's great news!'

'Bed?' asked Hil.

'Yes, our new bed. I didn't think there was any point in wasting any time, so I ordered one as soon as we got back last week. I wanted them to deliver it this weekend so that there would be someone here to receive it, but it seems they sent it a little ahead of schedule.'

'I was here to sign for it, Monsieur, I hope you don't mind. I got them to take it upstairs and then wouldn't let one of them leave until he had unpacked it properly.'

'Well, thank you very much, Philby,' said Jemme, 'that's really quite a relief to hear – you're fast making yourself indispensable!'

Philby looked a little bashful, but covered it up by nodded gruffly.

'Also, Monsieur, it is good you told me when you were arriving. I was able to bring some fresh things to the kitchen for you. There is some bread there and some milk too, from one of the local dairies.'

'How thoughtful of you Philby, thank you,' said Hil, sounding touched.

Philby nodded even more gruffly, and Jemme and Hil exchanged smiles with each other. Jemme was resolved to find Philby some help as soon as possible hardened.

Later that Saturday, as arranged, they went to visit Madame Pilote in the village. They found her little office above a bakery on one of the small roads leading away from the square. The stairs were at the back of the shop, and a wonderful aroma of fresh bread greeted them as they passed through. Madame Pilote was waiting for them with a smile on her face.

'*Bonjour*! I hope you are both well. I am so pleased at what I have been able to find for you.'

'*Bonjour*, what excellent news, Madame,' said Jemme.

She offered them two seats, and they sat opposite her at the large, leather-topped desk which was far too big for the small office. A selection of files and loose papers were out in front of her and she scooped them up.

'Here, this is everything I found,' she said, laying them down on the other side of the table. She sorted through them, pulling various bits out and explaining them. Jemme was delighted. It was more than he could possibly have hoped for. There were old receipts, written on yellow dockets in loopy, elegant handwriting; there were typed documents, newspaper clippings, and best of all, photos. Some sepia, some black and white, they offered tantalising windows onto the library as it was. Some of them even showed close-up shots of particularly interesting features of the desk, the ceilings and the bookcases. Jemme felt a stabbing pang of regret. Much as he appreciated this insight, it only served to highlight what had been lost. The bookcases ran from floor to ceiling, with glass-fronted doors finishing the upper halves. Intricate marquetry and fleur-de-lys carvings decorated them, evidently the work of the same skilled craftsman who had fitted the cupboards perfectly flush with the walls. A thin, wheeled ladder spanned the shelves and looked like it could be slid along to the right section, so that a small librarian, or even the master of the house, could reach interesting tomes on the upper shelves.

For some reason, when he saw a close-up of a large tassel hanging from the end of the key for the case fronts, Jemme felt especially sad. He sighed,

'What a pity. I suppose at least we can commission some new cabinets and cases using these photographs.'

'But Monsieur, I think you might not have to do that! I have been asking around, as has Monsieur Philby and we have several leads for you. In a village like this, everyone knows everyone else's business. Some of these families have been here for hundreds of years – they know all the local business owners for miles around. My neighbour works in antiques and he has told me about a dealer in the next village who might know something about the bookcases. I think some of them might still be intact and I also think they might not even have left the *département* yet.'

'Really?' said Jemme, looking excited.

'*Vraiment, Monsieur.* I do not want to get your hopes up, but I think there is good reason to be positive. At the very least you have these documents, but we will both carry on looking around and hopefully find you something even more exciting.'

'Madame, this is the best possible news you could have given me. Thank you so much for your hard work. I really appreciate it.'

'Do not, mention it, Monsieur. Like I said, it's a pleasure to be able to restore a piece of local history.'

As they left the archives, stopping to buy a *pain rustique* on the way back through the bakery, their spirits were high.

'I know that it's going to be a long journey to get it all finished,' said Jemme, 'but it certainly feels like the first piece of the puzzle has fallen into place.'

'The first two pieces,' said Hil, 'don't forget we've already got Philby.'

Later that day, they wandered back into the village to find the little café Madame Pilote had recommended. Apparently it was a popular local spot for lunch, but it tended to get very busy. Knowing the French penchant for long, late lunches, they arrived early, hoping to beat the rush. Their promptness was rewarded with a small table, right next to the window. A waitress greeted them and asked them what they would like to drink.

'I think we'll see the menu first, if that's alright,' said Jemme.

'*Menu, Monsieur*? There is no menu. We just serve whatever *la Madame* has cooked.'

'Whatever she's cooked?'

'*Bien oui, Monsieur*,' said the girl as if it was the most natural thing in the world, 'in the morning she will see what is good at the market and then that is what we will eat for lunch.'

'Oh I see… well, what has she cooked today.'

'*Du lapin, Monsieur*. With fresh *estragon*.'

'Well that sounds good to me! We'll have two please.'

The waitress nodded and departed.

'It feels so local,' said Hil, somewhat unnecessarily. The low ceiling in the café also made it feel extremely cosy. It was a small building, and the kitchen must have been quite close to the eating area as delicious smells wafted through, making it feel even more homely. Behind the bar, postcards had been tacked to the wall, apparently sent from all over France by the regulars.

Although quite simple, especially compared with some of the restaurants they had been to in Paris, the food was utterly delicious.

'Good, honest fare,' declared Jemme satisfied. He was even more satisfied when he saw the modest bill, and made sure he left a generous tip.

As they wandered back through the square, they noticed a man standing on the central patch of green. He was bending down, and appeared to be looking for something in the decorative petunia border. They neared him and saw that actually he was carefully pulling off the browned, dead flowers, allowing the new buds space to push through.

They nodded their greetings as they passed him, 'You look like you're doing a good job, Monsieur,' said Jemme.

'*Merci*,' he replied. 'I don't think they look after this square enough. There is a paid gardener, but I don't think he is particularly good. I come down here quite regularly and tidy things up, and make sure that the beds are properly watered and the plants doing well.'

'That's very community-spirited of you,' said Hil.

The man shrugged, 'Not really, Madame. I love the outdoors. I have been a gardener all my life and I hate to be indoors during the day.'

'Oh, I see. Is that what you do now – are you still a gardener?'

He sighed heavily, '*Malheuresment pas*. For thirty years I was the only gardener at one of the big houses on the outskirts of the village. Then the owner sold the place and the new people brought their own man with them. I was out of a job and at my age it is not too easy to find another. Everyone around here seems to have someone already, and I can't travel too far to find work, as I don't have a car.'

'I'm so sorry to hear that, Monsieur,' said Hil sympathetically.

The man sighed again, 'A man is nothing without his work, Madame. My father used to tell me that there was no toil more honest than working the land. He was a farmer, and it's from him I gained my great love of the outdoors. Ah, well, I suppose every horse must eventually be put out to pasture.'

Hil looked at Jemme questioningly. He knew exactly what she was thinking and turned to the man.

'Monsieur, my name is Jemme Mafeze. I've recently bought Chateau Vigne-Verte, just outside this village. I've been looking for a gardener and hoping to find someone local. Would you be interested?'

'Really, Monsieur?'

'Absolutely,' said Jemme and Hil nodded too. 'Why don't you come along later today? I can show you around and we can discuss it a little bit further.'

'I will, *merci*! You have made my day, *merci*!'

They left a distinctly jolly-looking man still poking around in the petunias.

'I'm so glad we did that,' said Hil, 'It feels like we're starting to become involved in the village.'

'It does, doesn't it?'

They wandered slowly back to the chateau, drinking in the view,

'It's so timeless,' said Hil happily, 'there's nothing here to date things – this could easily be a hundred years ago.'

'I know,' said Jemme, 'just think, this is the exact path that previous owners will have been walking from the village back to the chateau for hundreds of years.'

'It feels a bit like we're becoming part of the story of this place. Maybe one day photos of the changes we've made to the inside will find their way into the archives, long after we've gone.'

Jemme squeezed her hand. It was exactly the kind of thought which would have occurred to him. He was could see the layers of stories forming before his eyes, and he was becoming increasingly excited. It was just as he had imagined – he was writing himself into the story of a place, inexorably weaving himself into its very fabric, whilst at the same time realising his dreams.

Once back at the chateau he went and sought out Philby in his bothy.

'Philby, I cannot thank you enough for your help. I went to visit Madame Pilote today.'

'I trust you were pleased, Monsieur?'

'Pleased? I was absolutely delighted, again, thank you.'

'It was no bother, Monsieur. I would much rather see everything that belongs to this chateau returned to it.'

'That's exactly what Madame Pilote said.'

'I am not surprised, Monsieur. This chateau is part of our history too – it's means a great deal to the villagers.'

Jemme was rapidly adjusting to the way Philby explained things. Although he was often curt, he always cut straight to the point and was incredibly observant. It was a point Jemme hadn't really considered until Hil had raised it on the way back. No matter how much he projected *his* dreams and ideas onto the chateau, there was only a certain extent to which he could make it his. It would always be part of other people's lives. It would crop up in other people's stories and futures. It defined the local landscape and so necessarily featured in the lives of local people too.

'You're right, of course, Philby. I hadn't considered that; how thoughtless of me.'

Philby shrugged, 'It's the same with any old building,' he said simply.

'I suppose it is. On a different subject, I think you'll be pleased to know, I've got you an assistant.'

'*Assistant*, Monsieur?' Philby repeated as if Jemme had just started speaking in a foreign language.

'Yes, a man from the village.'

'A man from the village, Monsieur?'

'Yes,' said Jemme, starting to wonder what was wrong with his gardener.

'But why, Monsieur? Do you not think that I will do a good job?'

'No, no, not at all,' Jemme rushed to reassure him. I'm sure you'll do an incredible job. I just thought that seeing as the grounds are so large, you would appreciate an assistant. I'd make you head gardener and you could deploy the assistant however you saw fit.'

'*Head* gardener?' Philby repeated, looking distinctly put out.

'Yes, you'd be in charge,' said Jemme, beginning to wonder if he had made a big mistake. 'He's going to come around later, I'll bring him over to meet you in the afternoon and you can see what you make of him.'

'I see,' said Philby quietly.

❖ ❖ ❖ ❖

Just as they had planned, later that day the man from the village knocked on the back door.

Hil let him in and shook his hand, 'It's nice to see you again, Monsieur, I hope you found the place without too much difficulty.'

'Found it! I grew up here Madame, I have known where this place is for my whole life.'

'Of course,' said Hil feeling slightly foolish.

Jemme appeared shortly afterwards and shook the man's hand too. He took him on a tour of the grounds. The man pointed out various plants, explaining that they were local to the area, or describing what Jemme could expect from them over the coming months. He made several useful suggestions about the rockery, and by the time Jemme took him to the bothy he had already made up his mind.

Arriving back at the small hut, he knocked on the door. Philby answered, looking slightly surly,

'*Bonjour, Monsieur*, this must be your "man from the village" *non?*'

'Ah yes, why as a matter of fact it is. I'm so sorry though, I've just remembered I have to make a rather urgent telephone call to the bank in Paris. If you'll excuse me I'm just going to run back to the house. I'll leave you two to get acquainted.'

He dashed back to the house, emerging about an hour later. Making his way down to the bothy, he hoped that the two men were getting along. It seemed he needn't have worried, as he opened the door again he could hear the distinct sound of conversation, so at least they weren't sitting around in awkward silence.

'Thank you so much for waiting,' he said, 'would you be able to start tomorrow, Monsieur?' he asked.

'*Bien sûr!*' the man from the village answered with a cheery grin, standing up to shake Jemme's hand.

It wasn't until after he'd left that Jemme realised he'd never even asked for the man's name.

'Well, what did you think?' he asked Philby.

'Of *Monsieur Oiseau*?' Philby asked sarcastically.

'Oiseau? Is that his name? How strange.'

'It is not his name, Monsieur, but it might as well be. The man did nothing but talk to me about birds for a solid hour.'

'Birds?'

'Birds, Monsieur. It is his hobby.'

'Oh. Well, each to his own I suppose. I guess it comes from a lifetime of being outside.'

'Hmph,' snorted Philby.

It was the first time Jemme had seen him so prickly, and he thought it was probably best to leave him to his own devices.

He headed back to the house where Hil had been preparing dinner, with ingredients they had bought in the little village square market earlier that day.

'That smells wonderful, sweetheart,' he said, kissing her on the cheek.

'Thank you, I hope it's as good as the lunch we had earlier!'

'I'm sure it will be delicious.'

After a large supper they were more than ready for bed. Slipping into their wonderfully comfortable new bed, they couldn't help but feel what a great improvement this weekend had been on the last. They had cooked themselves a meal in their own kitchen, begun to integrate themselves in village life, met some locals and were even starting to become accustomed to the house's strange creaks and sounds. It was feeling more like home by the day.

The next afternoon, once they had finished repacking for Paris, Jemme went to go and find Philby to say goodbye and see how 'Monsieur Oiseau' was settling in.

Not particularly well apparently. Philby scowled at the mere mention of his name. 'For two days, Monsieur, *two days*, he has done nothing but talk to me about birds. He has pointed at them in his little book and made me look at them through his *jumelles*. It is very tedious, Monsieur.'

'I'm sorry to hear that, Philby, I'm sure it is. Give him a while to settle in though, I'm sure it's just teething problems.'

'Hmph,' Philby grunted again.

It appeared to be more than teething problems, and by the time they next visited, the head gardener was barely on speaking terms with his deputy. Apparently the man's bird obsession extended far beyond dull conversation. According to Philby he was more a full-time twitcher than a gardener. He spent most of the day skulking around the grounds, looking for herons and sandpipers. When he wasn't staring optimistically though his binoculars, he was constructing make-shift hides.

'But I don't understand,' said Jemme, 'I thought he had been a gardener for all his life.'

'It is not his fault,' said Philby, slightly dolefully, 'I have seen this before. He worked in the same gardens for thirty years on his own. He is set in his ways. After that long, a man forms habits and they cannot be broken. Maybe his previous employer never checked on him. I don't think he is trying to cheat you, I think he no longer notices he isn't working.'

'That's very magnanimous of you, Philby. Would you like me to talk to him?'

Philby shrugged, 'You can, Monsieur, but I don't think it will do any good. Like I say, a man like that is set in his ways. Even if he understood what you were saying, I don't think he would change anything.'

'Oh dear,' sighed Jemme, 'what a pity. I thought we were doing such a good turn as well.'

'You don't owe him a living, Monsieur,' said Philby.

Although it sounded a little harsh, Jemme realised that it was completely true and he thought back to his realisation that he needed to run the chateau like he did the bank. If one of his employees back in Paris had behaved in this way he would not think twice about sacking them. He realised that that was exactly what he was going to have to do, but it didn't make him feel any better about the task.

Later on, as he was mulling it over with Hil, he understood where he had gone wrong.

'I shouldn't have hired someone to work with Philby, without consulting him. They're going to be working so closely together and spend so much time together, that it was unfair of me to try and foist someone on him without even talking to him. I still think he needs someone, but I don't want a repeat of this incident.'

'Well, it's simple,' said Hil, 'why don't you just ask him first? I'm sure he probably even knows someone he can recommend, especially if he comes from a gardening family.'

'Of course,' said Jemme, 'it's so obvious, I can't believe I didn't do that in the first place. We both already know that we can trust him and that he's got great connections too – look how helpful he was with the whole library thing.'

'Mmmm,' said Hil, already drifting off to sleep.

✳   ✳   ✳   ✳

They woke up the next morning after a very good night's sleep.

'I can't believe what a difference this bed has made!' said Hil, stretching lazily.

'It's great, isn't it?' said Jemme. 'I bought the best one in the shop – there are some things I'm just not prepared to scrimp on!'

'Well, I'm very glad,' said Hil, rolling over to kiss him good morning.

Feeling buoyant and refreshed, Jemme went out to find Philby after breakfast.

'Good morning Philby, I've been thinking things over and I'm sorry that I didn't even talk to you before I hired a colleague for you.'

Philby shrugged, 'I'm just as set in my ways as he is. I've worked outside on my own for most of my adult life too.'

'Well, that may be the case, but I know that I definitely want to keep hold of you for as long as possible, so we'll just have to find someone that can fit around you rather than the other way around.'

Philby grunted a laugh, 'I don't know how easy you would find that, Monsieur.'

'Well, I was thinking about it, and I was wondering – do you know anyone? I thought perhaps you might have someone in mind.'

Philby leaned back on his chair, 'I could choose?'

'Of course. In fact, I'm counting on it.'

'Well, it's funny you should mention that. As it happens, I think I might just know the person.'

'Excellent! Where can I find him?'

'In the village, Monsieur. His name is Xelifon and he is the son of my neighbour. I think this would be the best thing for him, as long as you didn't mind being a bit patient.'

'Patient?'

'*Oui, Monsieur.* Xelifon is a good man, but in many ways he is still a boy. He had very severe learning difficulties, but he is truly gifted when it comes to the garden.'

'Well, he sounds perfect.'

'I think so, Monsieur. I hope you will be impressed by him. Although I don't think he can read or write, he will be able to tell you the name of every single flower, plant and leaf in the garden.'

'I'm looking forward to meeting him, do you think you can arrange for him to come up here at some point?'

'*Oui, Monsieur*, of course. I can bring him up tomorrow. In fact only last Wednesday I was talking to his father. He was worried about him.'

'Really? Why's that?'

'Nothing he has done, Monsieur, it is more for his future. Like I told you, he has difficulties learning and so he is very limited in the sort of job he can take. They are worried that he won't be able to find anything. But they are also worried that he won't be able to make the most of his talent. This would sort out both problems. Also, you would get a very good gardener.'

'Well, in that case, everything seems to have fallen into place! Bring him up as soon as you can, I'm looking forward to meeting him.'

Back at the house, Hil was turning her hand to preparing another meal, using locally-bought fresh ingredients.

'You're turning into quite the bucolic housewife!' said Jemme teasingly.

'I know, it's all been rather fun. I don't think that I could do it the whole time, but I feel like I'm playing the part quite well at the moment.'

'You are indeed! I spoke to Philby, by the way.'

'How did it go?'

'Really well, you were completely right, I should have just asked him in the first place. I think he was quite pleased that I did too. He's recommended someone to me. It's the son of a neighbour of his – apparently he's got some learning problems, but is an absolute whiz in the garden.'

'He sounds perfect. When's are we going to meet him?'

'As soon as possible hopefully.'

'Great. Hopefully lunch will be ready as soon as possible too.'

'Well, everything seems to be turning out quite well this morning!' said Jemme pulling up a chair and looking hungrily at the pot on the stove.

✻ ✻ ✻ ✻

The next day, Jemme heard a knock on the kitchen door, and saw Philby waiting outside with a younger man.

'Hello. Come in, both of you – you must be Xelifon,' he said offering his hand.

The young man looked shy and took his hand slightly limply. Philby ushered him in to the kitchen,

'I have told Xelifon about the gardens here, and what we're hoping to do with them.'

'Oh really? What did you think?' Jemme said to Xelifon.

Xelifon looked away shyly. He seemed not to enjoy eye contact.

'Good,' he said softly and nodded his head.

'Do you think you would be interested in working for us here with Monsieur Philby?'

Xelifon studied his shoes intently. Philby elbowed him and he looked up,

'Well?'

'*Oui, Monsieur,*' said Xelifon and blushed slightly.

'Excellent,' said Jemme, 'well, why don't we do a three-week trial period and see how we all get along, and then we can go from here?'

'*Merci,*' murmured Xelifon.

'Let's go and I will show you where we keep all the tools,' said Philby

Xelifon followed him out and very carefully shut the door behind him.

Moments later Hil arrived in the kitchen.

'Hello sweetheart, you just missed our second member of staff.'

'The chap Philby recommended? What was he like?'

'Painfully shy, but he seemed like a good guy – very gentle. I can imagine him being a dab hand with the plants. Philby's just showing him around now.'

'Oh, good. I hope it works out – I suppose at least Philby's on side from the beginning this time.'

'I think that's the most important thing, to be honest. They're going to be spending so much time together, that them getting along with each other is the first thing to get right. I think everything will come from there. If it works out, I'm thinking of asking

Philby to find us some other staff. I reckon we're going to need lots more people, and I can't think of anyone better to find us really good staff from the local area.'

'Do you think we're going to need lots more staff?'

'Definitely – well, I mean there are going to be all the building works to start with, so we're going to need builders and architects and all manner of specialists to help get things ready. I'm sure we'll need restorers and experts – I have no idea how things are going to pan out, but if we need things gilded, or plastered or mosaicked, then we'll need people who know what they're doing. That's before we've even considered domestic staff. I'm sure we'll want some cleaners once we've settled in a bit better, and started using more of the rooms.'

'I suppose you're right. Goodness, it sounds like it's going to be a quite a large-scale operation. If we're going to be taking on lots of new people, I'd really like them to be from around here though. I think it's important we become involved as much as possible.'

'I couldn't agree more, I've been thinking about this a lot recently, and I suppose I've been realising that owning this property comes with a great deal of responsibility. Not just in terms of the building – I realised that a while ago. I feel we're duty bound to care for the house – the older a building is, the more you become a custodian for it, rather than an owner. But it's more than that though – I think we've got an obligation to the surrounding area too. The chateau is obviously an important feature of this area, and we can't live our lives here as if we're completely cut off from it.'

'I completely agree. Whilst we're here I think we should explore some more of the area too. Let's go a little further afield – there's a cathedral town not far from here I've heard some really good things about.'

✻ ✻ ✻ ✻

The following weekend, Jemme was pleased to note how well Xelifon was settling in. He was completely at home in the garden, and contrary to what Jemme had been expecting, he also seemed to be an incredibly quick learner. Philby was right – this really was the environment in which he flourished, and Jemme was pleased that the situation was so mutually beneficial. He also seemed to be a little less shy around Jemme the second time around, and proudly showed him some herbs that he was growing near the kitchen, giving him the English and French names for each. Jemme translated a couple into Turkish, and Xelifon looked delighted, repeating them quietly to himself. There was something in his general mien that made Jemme think he wouldn't forget them.

He and Hil had left some of their possessions each time they had visited, and so their weekends in the countryside were generally becoming easier. With a few home comforts around them, they turned their attention to exploring the rest of the chateau and making plans for its various rooms. People around the village were starting to recognise their faces too, and they were getting to know their way around quite well.

On the Saturday of their third trip, they made a morning visit to the cathedral city Hil had wanted to see. It was a rather quaint place, more town than city. It was fairly typical of the towns in the surrounding area, with its biggest claim to fame seeming to be a passing connection with St. Thérèse of Lisieux, who had visited the nearby Carmelite convent and ended up staying there for six months during the 1890s. The cathedral was dedicated to her, and had several devotional statues at the end of the south transept. A large copy of a very early black and white photograph hung on the wall behind, showing St. Thérèse in her habit, seated with her hands folded in her lap, as if in quiet contemplation.

They wandered through the cathedral, attempting to keep their footsteps from echoing up and down the nave. Hil spotted the devotional area, and motioned to Jemme; they both went over for a closer look. Once they had got there, and allowed their eyes to adjust to the murky darkness, Jemme stared, transfixed, at the photograph.

'It's amazing, isn't it,' murmured Hil, 'it's so rare you know what the face of a saint looked like and actually get to see them like this.'

'It's not just that,' whispered Jemme back, 'I think she looks exactly like my grandma.'

Hil tilted her head to one side, 'I suppose you're right,' she smiled before turning to study one of the statues.

Jemme however couldn't tear himself away from the photograph. The resemblance was striking. It wasn't just the high cheekbones and the almond-shaped eyes, it was something about the way she sat, serene and assured, as if she had somehow gained a greater understanding of the world around her.

Staring at the photo, Jemme began to feel comforted. He had always held onto the thought that Lily had some how played a role in helping him find the chateau, no matter how irrational it may have seemed. Now, seeing her likeness, in the most unlikely of circumstances, felt like an assurance that he was doing the right thing. He knew he had made the right decisions about the future of the chateau and its staffing and he felt like he had begun to understand the role he would play in recreating the dream.

Chapter Fourteen

Turning into the driveway after driving straight from work, on yet another Friday, Jemme reflected on how much their lives had changed in the few short months since they had bought the chateau. He thought carefully – no, he was right: they hadn't spent a single weekend in the Paris flat, nominally 'home', since they had bought this place. It had taken over their lives, shifting their focus, altering their goals and nudging its way into their subconscious. As well as dreaming of the palace from childhood, Jemme now dreamt of his own chateau too. He saw walls being torn down and built up as it was carefully apportioned, gilding being delicately applied and plasterwork sculpted. On a particularly lucid night, he would see the rooms being filled with treasures and painted with frescoes, until they began to look like windows onto various civilisations. Sometimes the rooms were so vivid and lifelike that he couldn't tell if he was having a recurrence of his childhood dream instead. Despite the intensity of these dreams, he always woke from them refreshed and full of enthusiasm and drive. He knew that the harder he worked, the more one dream would slip into the other.

On this particular occasion he entered the main entrance hall, which he had since learned used to be called the Halle d'Honneur, and looked around. He was pleased with how everything was progressing. Although he was a long way from getting stuck into the meaty part of the project, whilst he acquainted himself with the house and developed his ideas, he was making sure that everything was prepared. It was always good to start with a blank canvas, and although he had never undertaken any kind of construction project before, he was savvy enough to know that he wouldn't want to be dealing with faulty wiring or discovering dry rot halfway through something. He had been pleasantly surprised so far. Whilst the interior décor left a lot to be desired, it appeared that the government had kept the chateau running like a well-oiled machine. There were good, modern drains, fed by sturdy guttering, which looked like it had been cleaned and cleared on a fairly regular basis. There didn't appear to be anything untoward with the wiring either, and there had been no unpleasant surprises when they had flicked various switches and twiddled various knobs, unlike in other, rather memorable chateaux they had visited. Philby and Xelifon had been working diligently in the garden, keeping everything weeded, mown and generally neat and tidy, as well as starting work on a few new projects, such as re-growing the roses at the front of the property. For the most part he had let them get on with it. He trusted Philby to work autonomously, and Philby had done nothing to show him that that trust had been misplaced. On the contrary, every time he visited the chateau again, he silently thanked his lucky stars that Philby had stayed on. To start with, he hadn't appreciated how much consideration the grounds of the chateau would need. He had thought the focus of his work would be exclusively on the interior, and had mentally prepared for the architects, builders and craftsmen he would need. However, the grounds needed just as much work. They were larger than the chateau, and continuously evolving too. They required constant attention, otherwise the lake would mulch over, the beds overgrow and the statuary become mossy. Philby seemed to be in complete control of all of these things, and went about them without needing instruction or guidance. Furthermore, he was turning his hand to lots of little projects Jemme was creating for him in the garden, without so much as a whisper about his increased workload. He was also excellent with Xelifon. He gave him just the right amount of work, and seemed to know intuitively how much he needed to monitor and then praise him at the end. Jemme had picked up on this flair for management at an early stage and knew that it would be useful at some point.

As well as all his work in the garden, however, Philby had also proved his worth in the day to day running of the chateau. Whilst Jemme was in Paris during the week, Philby was sometimes the only person at the chateau. On several occasions, Jemme had realised a little too late that he wouldn't arrive at the chateau in time to sign for a particular delivery or to meet someone, and he was stuck, several hundred miles away, not able to do anything about it. To have someone at the end of the phone who was already on-site had been hugely helpful. Jemme looked around him as he stood in the hallway. He was pleased to note that the tall windows were squeaky clean. Philby had found a window-cleaner from the village and he had done an excellent job. Likewise, the local French-polisher had done a fine job and the floors gleamed with an almost mirror-like sheen. He took everything in; satisfied he went straight to the kitchen to get a glass of water and something to snack on. As he drew a glass from the tap, he saw Philby's flustered face at the window.

Jemme opened the door for him and the gardener entered the kitchen, with his red face looking even more flushed than usual.

'Monsieur, I was on the other side of the grounds, I did not hear the car – I wasn't expecting you for another hour.'

'I wasn't expecting to be here for another hour or so either, but I made good time on the autoroute. How are you?'

'*Bien, Monsieur*, thank you,' mumbled Philby, still looking perturbed, 'but I am sorry that I was not there to greet you.'

'I shouldn't worry about that!' said Jemme, good-naturedly. He saw Philby's face and realised how methodical he was, and what pride he took in the property. They had already established their own little routines together, and he was sure that Philby felt slighted when the patterns were altered.

'Although, it does make such a difference when you are – makes it feel like I'm really coming home,' he said tactfully. Philby looked appeased.

'Why don't you show me what's new?' he asked. This in itself had become something of a routine. As he only saw the chateau once a week, the changes were always more dramatic than they seemed to Philby, who had overseen their gradual development.

Philby looked around expectantly, 'Where is Madame Mafeze?'

'Oh, she didn't come with me this time. She's got a big party this weekend that she didn't want to miss, so I thought I'd pop down for a little solo visit.'

'Ah, *bon*. I will show just you then. Did you see the windows and the floor in the Halle, Monsieur?'

'I did – very impressive. Thank you again for sorting that all out. It took quite a bit of hassle out of it for me, I can tell you.'

Philby merely shrugged and opened the door to the garden again.

'The herb garden of Xelifon, Monsieur,' he said, indicating the kitchen garden Xelifon had been working on since his arrival. It was coming along nicely, with fat bunches of fragrant herbs growing out into the space around them. As Jemme looked over them approvingly, Xelifon appeared and nodded to him. Although he was significantly less shy around him, he was still far from chatty, and generally uncomfortable with prolonged eye-contact.

'This is all looking excellent, Xelifon,' said Jemme.

Xelifon smiled and mumbled, '*Merci.*'

Jemme squatted down beside a wild mustard plant, rubbing its broad, dark green leaves to release its scent.

'*Hardalotu*,' said Xelifon. Jemme was impressed. It was the Turkish name for the plant he had given Xelifon, several weeks ago.

'I can't believe how well you've got it to grow here, I remember the difficulties my mother always used to have trying to coax it to grow, and that was in much more hospitable climes than these! The smell reminds me so much of childhood though,' said Jemme, smelling his thumb again. 'Do you think you could grow some *Iğnelik*? I don't know what it's called in French, but it grew all around my home in Istanbul, and I would love to be surrounded by it again.'

Xelifon tilted his head and slowly sounded out the word, perfectly mimicking Jemme's Turkish accent.

'It's got a long, pointed head which is filled with seeds and flowers in spring,' said Jemme. He racked his brains trying to remember anything else distinctive. 'It usually grows by the roadside,' he added.

Xelifon slowly scratched his neck whilst he thought, 'Flowers,' he repeated softly, with a look of intense concentration.

'Yes, bright pink ones – the leaves smell quite strongly too.'

Xelifon's face suddenly cleared, 'Cranesbill,' he said with a decisiveness and confidence Jemme hadn't heard before. Jemme looked impressed and then doubly so when Xelifon added, '*Erodium.*'

'Is that the Latin name?'

He nodded.

'Well, I have struck lucky in that case. Do you think you might be able to grow some here?'

Xelifon nodded again.

Jemme smiled broadly as nostalgia surged through him. For a moment he was standing in the middle of the sun-baked Turkish road outside his house, looking at the bright pink flowers of the plant with Grandma. He could almost smell their pungent leaves as he remembered Grandma telling him that they needed to be used in moderation, because their flavour was strong.

'Excellent,' he said to Xelifon. 'It will be a pleasure to be able to use them in the kitchen and even more so if they've been grown right here in the garden.' He momentarily drifted off again, whilst he remembered the distinctive taste of İğnelik, added to börek fillings and cooked in a hearty burgul. The sight of his two gardeners looking expectantly at him soon snapped him out of his reverie.

'Thank you so much for your hard work, Xelifon. Philby, why don't we continue to look over what you've been up to?'

Philby nodded, and led the way to some trees he had coppicing. Usually Jemme enjoyed these tours, but he was finding it hard to focus. Wistful memories of childhood kept drifting back across his mind, edged in sepia and whimsy. After they had finished looking around the grounds, Jemme went back in and unpacked his little weekend bag. He had now built up such a large bank of his possessions in the bedroom of the chateau, that the bags he brought with him were growing increasingly small. He pottered around the room for a while, mulling over his plans. It felt strange being in the chateau without Hil, and by the evening he was at a bit of a loose end. He was longing for the heavy duty work to start on the chateau, but he knew he had quite a bit of preparation to do first. As he ate his supper on his own, he idly began to map out the different processes which would be necessary to implement his plans. He tried to think things through in an analytical and objective way. Applying his banker's mind, he mentally created flow charts, analysed procedures and modelled strategies.

The next morning he was up early, and drank a large cup of milky tea in front of the open kitchen doors. The early morning sunshine streamed in, and he suddenly missed Hil. So many of her habits had rubbed off onto him over the years, drinking tea with milk for breakfast to start with. Basking in the crisp, golden light like this was just the sort of simple thing she would draw pleasure from, and Jemme felt himself enjoying it now, both in itself and because it made him think of her.

At around eight-thirty Madame Agnes Poirier knocked on the frame of the open door and leaned in,

'*Bonjour*?' she called out.

'Ah Madame, come in, I'm just putting the kettle on,' Jemme called out from around the corner.

He came over and shook her hand, 'Thank you for calling me in Paris, and for all your hard work on this, I really do appreciate it. I'm also dying to hear what you've come across – it all sounded very mysterious on the phone!'

Madame Poirier looked mischievous, 'All in good time, Monsieur,' she teased.

Jemme groaned, 'Please, don't keep me in suspense any longer!'

'*D'accord,*' she said, the curls in her tightly coiffed hair shaking in amusement. 'I have very good news for you, Monsieur. The best, in fact.'

'Really?'

'*Vraiment,*' she nodded vigorously, setting her curls bouncing again. 'Since we first met, I have spoken to many people on this matter. As I told you, my neighbour works in antiques and he put me in touch with a dealer in the next village. Anyway, he told me that he might-' Jemme was doing a poor job of containing his impatience and Madame Poirier decided to cut a long story short. 'Alors, I shall get straight to the end. The library has been found, Monsieur!'

'What?!' said Jemme startled, 'what do you mean 'found' – all of it?!'

'Yes, absolutely, Monsieur. Every piece of it! I can tell you the full story if you like, but I asked around a great deal, and with my neighbour we chased the paper trail until we finally tracked it all down. It has not gone far – it's not more than five kilometres from here in fact. It's with a local dealer who is a passing acquaintance of mine. He's looked over everything and by his estimation he has the panelling, vitrines and shelving for a room of the exact proportions of the library, which is what makes me think it is all there. It is unlikely it would have been split up, too – these things always go for more money when they're intact.'

'Oh Madame, that is the most wonderful news! I don't know how I can begin to thank you, I... I...' Jemme trailed off, 'honestly, I'm speechless with gratitude!'

'Then that is thanks enough for me, Monsieur. It was fun too, getting to play detective. Sometimes life can be a bit repetitive in a small village such as ours, so helping the newcomer track down something precious has been rather exciting!'

Jemme smiled, picturing Madame Poirier sleuthing away in her little office above the bakery, every inch the French Miss Marple. He thanked her warmly again and she left him with the details for her contact. Before she went, she also invited him to the local church to look at the full file of the chateau, which had so many tidbits and anecdotes.

Jemme couldn't see any point in delaying, so as soon as he had cleared up the breakfast things he set off for the place on the slip of paper. Madame Poirier had been right. The furniture hadn't got far. Less than half an hour after he had left his kitchen, somewhat strangely, Jemme found himself staring at his library. Although it had been disassembled, and the panels stacked against each other, he recognised it instantly. The fleur-de-lys carvings and the delicate marquetry were exactly as they had been in the photos. However, more than that, there was something familiar about the assemblage. Its grand form, its lines, even the knots in its wood were echoed throughout the chateau and Jemme had the curious sense of looking at a piece of extra-mural home. He struck a very favourable deal with the antiques dealer, who was as delighted to have played a part in the adventure as Madame Poirier had been. The man even offered to arrange for a specialist removal team to bring the pieces over to Chateau Vigne-Verte for him. Jemme departed with a slightly lighter wallet, but full of excitement.

He spent the rest of the day preparing the library for the team's arrival on Sunday morning. He picked the largest chunks of plaster off the floor by hand, and then rummaged around in the various maintenance cupboards until he found a rather creaky vacuum cleaner, which eventually whirred into life. Once the majority of the masonry dust had gone, the library already looked miles better. He looked around sadly at the holes in the wall where the panels had originally been torn out and realised there was still quite a bit to do. He would have to employ a specialist to refit the library anyway though, so they might as well treat the plasterwork underneath whilst they were at it. Satisfied, he went and prepared some supper for himself, thinking again how much he wished Hil was there to share in his excitement about the arrival of the library.

As promised, the next morning, the team arrived and very carefully moved the wooden panels, glass-fronted cabinets and other fixtures and fittings back into the empty library-shell. After sizing up various walls and shuffling the pieces around a little, they left each part in front of the place they thought it probably would originally have come from. Once they had left, Jemme wandered around having a look. The team seemed to have guessed fairly accurately, and he could imagine how all the pieces would look once mounted on the walls. For now though, it remained his very own, Louis XIV, flat-pack library kit.

✳   ✳   ✳   ✳

The following weekend, Jemme once again found himself driving straight to the chateau from work on Friday evening. This time, however, Hil sat next to him in the passenger seat. They chattered about their days, and about the weekend ahead, with Hil asking all sorts of questions about the library.

'Honestly, it was as simple as that,' said Jemme, 'Everyone sought me out with information – I barely had to leave the house. Sorry to disappoint, I get the impression you're hoping for a little more drama and intrigue.'

'It's got so much potential to have all sorts of Sherlock Holmes twists and turns,' sighed Hil, 'although it is still pretty incredible as a story, so I'm satisfied.'

They neared the chateau, and Jemme was pleased to note that Philby was waiting outside to greet them this time. He wasn't too bothered about this formality, one way or the other, but he knew how cross Philby would be if he had missed their arrival twice in a row.

He greeted them and helped take their bags inside.

'Philby's got lots to show you in the garden, Hil,' said Jemme.

'Really?' asked Hil, looking at Philby, who nodded in his slightly gruff way, 'Well, I suppose it's been a whole two weeks since I last saw it, and at the rate you seem to be progressing, anything could have happened.'

'Is the library finished, Philby?' asked Jemme eagerly.

Philby shook his head. '*Non, Monsieur.* The men were hoping to have finished yesterday, but they had to repair the plaster damage twice and allow it to dry out both times. They will work here until the late evening, so that it will be finished by the time you wake up.'

'That's an impressive level of commitment,' said Jemme approvingly, 'Thank you again for all your help – I'm sure you've done a fantastic job in managing them.'

Philby shrugged.

'I think we should just leave them to it,' said Jemme to Hil. 'I'm sure that it's all rather hectic in the final stages, and the last thing they want is to be disturbed. Also, it will be quite a nice surprise to go and see it tomorrow when it's all finished.'

'It's rather strange to think that, whilst we're going about our normal business, there's a whole team of hidden craftsmen working away on our home,' said Hil.

'You'd better get used to it sweetheart. I predict that there's going to be a lot more of that in the future,' said Jemme.

Bar the odd muffled thump and strange thud, by and large the craftsmen were completely inaudible, and it would have been easy to forget that they were there at all, had it not been for Jemme's excitement and impatience to see the finished room. The next morning, he had barely brushed the sleep from his eyes before he had jumped into a pair of trousers, and pulled a jumper over his head.

'Morning,' he said brightly, rolling Hil over. She mumbled something and didn't open her eyes. He decided that he wouldn't wait for her and scuttled off downstairs, every inch the child at Christmas. He found the strangely missable door and turned its tarnished handle. Stepping into the room was like stepping into a different world. Where last weekend he had been standing in a derelict space, full of rubble and bare walls, now he felt as if he had walked straight into a room from the time of the Sun King. He slowly turned around, taking in every detail. The men had done a wonderful job, and he felt he would have a hard job convincing a visitor that this room had not merely sat, undisturbed since the time of Louis XIV. Every last fixture and fitting had been returned to its proper place, and the library had seamlessly slotted together like some grand jigsaw. Amazingly, it did all seem to be there. There was no chink, or missing piece, but rather an integral, decorative whole, just as the ébénistes of Louis XIV would have designed. In parting, the craftsmen had polished the wood and buffed the gilded handles, and so the room smelled pleasantly of beeswax, just as Jemme imagined it would have done four hundred years ago. He sighed contentedly. He was incredibly pleased with the finished result, on more than one level: it had turned into an exemplar, and he hoped it would set a precedent for the rest of the future project he was imagining. In addition to the process of tracking down and reuniting original fittings, he was pleased with the effect they had created. The moment he had stepped into the room it had felt as if he was crossing a threshold. The door had been an entry to a liminal world. He suddenly felt as if he had stepped into the time of Louis XIV, a perfectly rendered microcosm of the era. It was exactly the effect he was hoping to achieve with all his rooms, and exactly the feeling he had had when wandering through the corridors of his dream palace. He was heartened by this early auspicious example, and wondered again if Grandma was somehow playing some sort of role in sending good wishes his way.

He heard a noise behind him, and turned around. Hil was coming into the room, bearing two mugs of tea. She was wrapped up in her dressing gown, and still looked a little sleepy.

'Goodness, this all looks impressive,' she said, handing over a mug to Jemme.

'Doesn't it? I've just been taking it all in – I can't believe it, but I'm pretty sure it's all whole too.'

'It certainly looks it,' said Hil looking around, 'What's that?' she asked, pointing to what looked like a strange railing on the end cabinet.

'Hmm, I'm not sure – I hadn't actually noticed that,' said Jemme as they both went over to investigate. Up close the 'railing' had five horizontal bars that ran from floor to waist height. It sat flush with the lower cabinet and ended just where the bookshelves started. It was highly polished and obviously made with the same expertise as the rest of library, although it was made from a darker type of wood.

'How strange,' said Hil, looking closely at it. 'I wonder how you're meant to open this cabinet with this thing in front.' She prodded it slightly and it slowly slid away from her. She looked slightly alarmed. 'Goodness, I hope I haven't broken anything,' she said, trying to move everything back to exactly how she had found it. The railing slid back into position with the same ease it had moved away from her.

Jemme looked at it for a moment, then, frowning, reached out and very gently pushed it in the opposite direction. It glided along, to a different position along the bookcase, still fixed in its slot from floor to waist height.

His face suddenly cleared, 'It's a ladder!' he said. 'Look!' he got close to the top rung and peered behind it, 'You can barely see because it's been so well made, but it's on runners – it runs the whole length of this wall so that you can get to books on the higher shelves. I can't believe it works so smoothly; the craftsmen must have oiled everything up for us before they left. It looks like it's an original piece too. In fact, I bet…' he looked around the room, 'yes! Look Hil, there's one on each wall!'

He moved over to another bookcase and, sure enough, tucked away neatly at one end was another sliding ladder. The case by the door had one too, as did the one running along the opposite wall. All of them were in perfect working order, as if they had been made yesterday. Jemme couldn't stop himself from smiling. It had been a completely unexpected surprise, and a marvellous bonus too.

'How wonderful to have everything back exactly as it was intended,' said Hil. 'I can't believe these things have survived being moved around either. I would have expected something like that to snap off, or at the very least be damaged in transit.'

'I know, it's almost as if they were all meant to get back to us together,' said Jemme.

Hil smiled. 'I suppose it all just shows that this furniture was built to last. Old carpenters had such an eye for detail too – they're always hiding things away and adding things on. I wonder if these pieces hold any more secrets.'

She ran her fingers over the bevelled edges, which jutted out to form boxed corners at the end of the shelves. They seemed the perfect location for something hidden, but yielded nothing. She moved round the edge to the end of the bookcase and looked closely at the wall of highly polished wood in front of her. Pensively she pushed at the bevelled strip of wood again. This time her curiosity was rewarded. The piece of dado clicked inwards and then slid out to reveal a hidden desk. It wasn't very large, but would certainly have been big enough to accommodate a librarian's record book, whilst someone jotted down the volumes which had just been removed from the shelves. Hil clapped her hands delightedly, 'See! What did I tell you?!'

'Well done,' said Jemme, impressed, 'fancy that – two extra little details we weren't expecting at all. I wonder if we'll find any more?'

Hil laughed, 'I think that might be pushing our luck for today a little.'

'I think you're right. To be honest, I would have been pleased enough just to have the library back together, and then to find the ladders was a treat enough.'

'I'm sure this house has got its fair share of secrets too,' said Hil, 'I expect there are all sorts of hidey-holes around and about. I imagine there are more than just physical secrets too. I wonder what's gone on here over the years – who's lived here, who's visited, I bet it could fill a book.'

✻ ✻ ✻ ✻

Several weeks later, faced with something very similar, Jemme thought back to that morning in his own library. Banking business had taken him to London, but a cancelled appointment had afforded him a rare afternoon off. He had decided to travel just outside London to Windsor. He had never visited the castle there, and was keen to make the most of this opportunity. He had always been fascinated by old buildings and museums, but castles and chateaux held an even greater pull for him now, and he tried to visit as many as he could. Since he had bought Chateau Vigne-Vert, he was surprised at how much his attitude and priorities had changed during visits. No longer was his attention drawn by fine Flemish tapestries and burnished escutcheons. Instead, he looked to see how the owners had concealed their light switches, where the radiators were, how seamlessly the electrics had been wired in. He was constantly looking for tips and inspiration. On this particular occasion, he felt as if he was conducting a meta-visit. Not only was he standing within Windsor Castle, having investigated its inner workings, but a guide was now showing him the inside of Queen Mary's dollhouse. A grand home within a grand home, he thought to himself. The guide had just pulled out a secret drawer underneath the house, to reveal a vast garden, rendered in tiny form, and complete with gardening tools, formal hedges and ornamental borders. It was very impressive, and Jemme didn't know whether he enjoyed its actual form more, or the fact that it was so cleverly hidden. It had made him think of the hidden drawers within his own library which revealed what he had since found out were called tirettes.

The dollhouse was a perfect miniature. Although it was famous for its detail and accuracy, it had to be seen to be believed. Leading architects had worked on it, and treated it with all the gravity and reverence due to a royal commission. Jemme listened, enraptured, to details of the tiny pipes which ran with water and flushed a miniature loo, and observed the working light switches. The furnishings in the house were all faithful replicas of leading designers' carpets, curtains and upholstery patterns. The guide even showed him the specially commissioned miniature works by leading authors of the day, such as Conan Doyle and Somerset Maugham, which had been perfectly bound by the Queen's own bookbinders, Sangorski and Sutcliffe. Even the bottles in the wine cellar were corked, sealed and labelled exactly as their larger counterparts. Jemme felt like a giant looking in on a tiny, perfectly formed world. He suddenly had a sense of being outside his dream, looking in. The dollhouse was a microcosm of what he hoped to achieve in the chateau, and the experience of looking into tiny, separate worlds was exactly what he wanted to reproduce. Seeing this miniaturised cross-section was exactly what he had needed, to visualise what he wanted to do. Cut straight through the middle, with the rooms neatly stacked on top of each other, he recognised how he needed to divide the chateau internally. It would take a while, and he would need a good architect too, but at last he understood. He knew the first thing he would have to do when he got back to France.

Chapter Fifteen

Since he had returned to France, Jemme had lost no time in seeking out an architect. However, things had not been as easy as he had hoped. Although he had little experience in hiring craftsmen, he had recruited countless, highly skilled professionals for the bank over the years, and saw no reason why this should be any different. As with most of these matters, he turned to DD for help; sure enough, within the week, DD presented him with a sheaf of smartly produced resumés, some of which accompanied impressive portfolios. Leafing through them, Jemme felt a small frisson of excitement. It was the first step towards modelling, and building, something permanent and meaningful.

Seeing the work these architects had already created just made things feel even more real. Faced with the photographs, sketches and blueprints of rooms, and even buildings, they had created, he felt ready to propagate a tradition. The physical manifestations of other people's dreams, spread out in front of him, offered him a tantalising flavour of what it would feel like to realise his own. Choosing an architect was an important first step. He knew he would need a highly skilled and experienced professional, on whom he could rely. The architect would act as the cornerstone on which the chateau project was built, and play an important managerial role too. Jemme imagined the other craftsmen consulting the master architect in his absence, and the architect overseeing work, checking for quality and artistic continuity. He thought back to the time when Grandma had pointed out a special stone to him and explained its significance. At the crown of the arch they had been looking at, it was the smallest piece in the whole feature. However, this thin, wedge-shaped piece of stone, which was called a 'keystone', was the most important part. It marked the apex, and locked all the other stones into position. Without it, the structural integrity was broken and the arch would crumble. However, when it was slotted into its position, the arch could stand tall for hundreds of years and would be strong enough to support the weight of a person if necessary. He had always remembered Grandma pointing this special stone out to him, and thinking back on it now, he couldn't help but draw parallels with the function of the architect. Without him, the project would crumble – it wouldn't matter how good the other stones were.

He slowly turned his way through the pages of one portfolio. Whereas most of the others had been produced on glossed paper, the matt pages of this one made it stand out. It was in keeping with the washed out browns and dull greys of the architect's Brutalist aesthetic. He was a fine draftsman, and his drawings magnificently captured the sharp angles and sheer concrete faces of the modernist buildings he had designed. However, he was all wrong for the project. His designs expressed an ethos that was totally at odds with Jemme's. Whilst Jemme wanted to create an elaborate paean to the past, variously enshrining and exalting, this applicant used stark structures to communicate egalitarian and socialist principles. His entire body of work was future-facing and deconstructed, whilst Jemme's ideas were retrospective, in both form and function. Based on what he had seen so far, he respected this man as an architect, but couldn't see any way in which he could use him. He moved the portfolio to one side, and drew another across the desk towards him.

This one included a short personal statement on the flyleaf, which described the architect's fascination with the Egyptian Revival style. Jemme's interest was immediately piqued, as it married what he expected would be two important themes within the museum. Firstly, he was fascinated by Egyptian history, and as the project was destined to explore civilisations of major significance he thought it inescapable that the Egyptians would be included somehow. Even if they were not directly, their influence would certainly be felt. However, it was the revival element that really appealed to him. In the eighteenth and nineteenth century, the use of ancient Egyptian imagery and decorative motifs had been incredibly popular in Western Europe, following Napoleon's incursions into Egypt and his battle with Nelson on the Nile. The publication of the *Description de l'Égypte*, the work of the scholars who had accompanied Napoleon, had proved enormously popular and influential on both art and architecture in France, Italy and England. Jemme felt that some of the chateau's exposition must include its own context. It would be antithetical to his aims to create a space which did not reference the country in which it was located, or the history of that country. He was keen to explore French history, as well as the chateau's own history. He wasn't sure yet how synoptic his treatment would be, but he knew he would have to reference Napoleon somewhere, and to focus on the emperor within Egypt killed two birds with one stone. He flicked through this architect's portfolio keenly, wanting to see how he had interpreted the sense of excitement and exoticism with which the subject matter had been treated by nineteenth-century society. With every page he turned, he felt a rising disappointment. Treatment of any revival style always had to be done deftly, with a sure hand. The key was not to emulate the original style, but rather to recreate the way in which it had been interpreted, by the revivalists. It was a two-tiered challenge, in which the architect must simultaneously reference the style's roots, but also the prism through which they were seen by later society. This architect had failed miserably. There was nothing subtle, intelligent or nuanced about his designs whatsoever. They were brash, crass and overblown. Instead of showcasing the arrogance and pride of Imperial French architecture, he had created something that would not have looked out of place in a theme park. His gaudy statues and oversized motifs were more akin to pastiche than anything else and looked like they were in response to a brief from a Vegas casino. The highly saturated colours applied during the photography development process and the glossy paper didn't really help matters, and only exacerbated the tastelessness and cheapness of his designs.

Jemme pushed his portfolio back across the desk, making a mental note to be wary of any evidence of kitsch or garishness. The point was rammed home a little harder when he flicked through the next book. This architect had seemingly taken the idea of 'Rococo' and run away with it. Every florid inch of his designs was dripping in ornate curlicues and ostentatious flourishes. It was all too much, and Jemme felt a little nauseous just looking at the pictures. Like the architect before, this man seemed to have used modern materials and techniques, meaning that the hideous designs throbbed in brilliant Technicolor. His portfolio rapidly went the same way as the Egyptian Revivalist's.

His enthusiasm somewhat dampened, Jemme idly looked at the work of the next contender. He was very much a product of the Bauhaus school and his designs centred on the idea that ultimately there could be synergy between all art. Again, Jemme admired his work and thought his artistic ideals held a certain amount of truck, but he was completely wrong for the chateau. Sighing he let the cover of the portfolio flip shut and leant back in his chair. Perhaps everything would seem better after lunch.

There is a great deal to be said for the powers of a fine luncheon and by the time he returned, Jemme was filled with renewed optimism. He flicked through several further portfolios, finally arriving at one which held promise. The architect didn't seem to be governed by a particular style or a specific school. Rather, his portfolio showcased his response to a variety of different briefs, each of which seemed to have been executed with skill and a dash of élan. Each plan had been carefully thought through, right down to the tiniest detail. Several innovative touches were particularly impressive, and demonstrated both the man's intelligence and deep understanding of how his buildings would function and be integrated into their landscapes. Jemme snapped the front cover down decisively. He would see this man as soon as possible.

Later that week Jemme sat opposite Emile Dahan, in a small café around the corner from the bank. So far, he had proved himself to be quite a raconteur, and with a quick wit to match. Jemme had instantly warmed to him. He had an interesting story to tell too: the son of an Armenian immigrant, he had studied architecture in Lyon before setting up his own practice in Paris.

'I'm originally from Turkey myself,' Jemme told him as his coffee arrived and the waiter set a mint tea in front of Emile.

'Ah, so we are practically neighbours!' Emile replied.

'I suppose so,' Jemme smiled, 'although for all my travelling in the Levant and trips back home, I don't think I've ever been to Armenia. I'd be interested to hear if you thought your roots influenced your work though. Do you think of yourself as more Western or Eastern?'

'That's an interesting question and one I've thought about quite a bit too. I suppose every second-generation immigrant has to consider it at some point – does he have more in common with his kin or the country he grew up in? I guess I've reached the same conclusion everyone else does eventually: that it's a mix of both. I think it's doubly so for people from my area – from our area. Armenia is at a cultural crossroads, it's on the eastern-most edge of Europe and the western-most edge of Asia. I don't know if Armenians think of themselves as particularly Western or particularly Eastern when they're at home, so it's even stranger to consider the question when I've been in France for my whole life.'

'Does it influence your work though?'

'Oh that I can answer easily: undoubtedly, yes. Even if I had grown up in Armenia, I think I would still have the same fascination about the interplay between East and West, culturally and artistically. It's such a huge part of the Armenian cultural landscape, as I'm sure you've noticed in Turkey too – you can see both Western and Eastern influences everywhere you look. However, growing up here in France has meant that I'm even more fascinated by the relation between the two.'

Jemme listened thoughtfully, 'The project I'm recruiting for is a bit of an unusual one, but at its heart will be an expression of Eastern art, culture and history expressed in a Western context. I want to find some way of marrying the two so that both are represented properly, but one does not detract from the other.'

Emile looked interested, and they discussed the matter animatedly until Jemme looked at his watch and realised that nearly an hour had slipped by. He made his apologies and dashed back to the bank, pleased at having found someone so well suited to the project. His afternoon was rather frantic, and so Jemme didn't have another opportunity to think about Emile. As he was finishing up for day, he shuffled his papers together and put them neatly to one side of his desk, ready to go through the next morning. In doing so, he uncovered Emile's portfolio once again. He flicked through it again; he liked his work, he had liked the man in person and he liked his outlook. Furthermore, he seemed to have a perfect understanding of the Eastern/Western ends that Jemme was trying to express. 'No time like the present,' Jemme thought to himself, and picked up the phone to call Emile. He invited him to spend a week in the chateau and present his ideas at the end. Emile had agreed instantly, and Jemme directed him to DD to arrange the dates. He went home satisfied at the progress he had made.

✽ ✽ ✽ ✽

Several weeks later, Jemme stood at the front door to the chateau, ready to welcome Emile. He had been hoping to take the week off work, and stay there during the architect's mini-residency. However, he had been extremely busy recently and was reluctant to take a day away from the bank, and the idea of being away for a whole week made him feel a little green around the gills. Anyway, as Hil had pointed out – his presence wouldn't really make any difference. If anything it would be a hindrance and slow Emile down. Instead he had arranged for Emile's visit to span two weekends, during both of which he and Hil would stay at the chateau.

Emile arrived full of bonhomie, and had them both laughing within moments. He was charming and interesting, and Jemme couldn't wait to see what he would produce; he was only sorry that he wasn't going to get to spend the whole week there. Over the weekend, Jemme showed Emile around the chateau, pointing out original features he wanted to accent, bits he wanted to restore and empty spaces he was trying to convert. Emile was observant and engaging; he explained about the articulation of joints, describing how parts could be joined in such a way that each separate piece looked as if it was a separate and distinct whole. Jemme had never examined buildings on such a granular level, and he listened carefully, absorbing everything. By the end of the day he had started to notice ashlar, large blocks cut by an expert mason so that the faces were even and the edges square, and he could tell the difference between a Corinthian and Doric column. The following day he sat down with Emile at the large antique desk in the library. Although it wasn't original to the room, it was roughly contemporaneous, and Jemme had been thrilled when he had found it in an antique shop, not far from the chateau. It had a very old, if slight shabby emerald green leather topper, with gracefully turned mahogany legs. He felt quite commanding when he was sitting behind it, almost as if he was king of his castle.

'This is a lovely piece,' said Emile as he sat down on the other side.

'Thank you,' said Jemme, 'One day I hope that this place will be full of thoughtfully sourced antiques. It's going to take a while to build up the collection, if I do it one piece at a time, but this is as good a starting point as any.'

'These handles are lovely,' said Emile, looking at the delicate hinged draw-pulls on their punched gilded backing plates. 'You can tell that they haven't been changed since this thing was made – look at these screws,' he pointed out the tiny screws which affixed each plate to the drawer. They had been there for so long that layers of lacquer had built up around them, where the desk had been polished and cleaned, and been allowed to become dirty, over the years. They almost looked as if they had melded into one unit.

'I would never have noticed that,' Jemme murmured as he scrutinised the tiny fittings.

'It's a really easy way to tell,' replied Emile. 'Sometimes features like this are stripped off and sold separately and then replaced with facsimiles or later fittings. The screws and nails are always a dead give away. I won't, but if I unscrewed one of these now you'd see that they were all handmade and slightly uneven. They've got very thin little threads, which would have been hand-whittled by the *ébéniste* who made this piece.'

'Fascinating,' Jemme said, running his finger over the small screw caps, trying to imagine the hands that would have originally fitted them.

Emile shrugged, '*C'est dans les vieilles marmites qu'on fait les meilleures soups,*' he said.

Jemme frowned.

'It's a silly expression,' said Emile, 'I guess it just means that the best broths are made in the oldest pots. I think the best poems are written at desks such as these too. A symphony composed on an antique Stradivarius, which has been handled and played by many great violinists, is bound to be of a higher quality than one composed on a mass-produced, shop-bought new instrument. The history of a piece is important.'

'A man after my own heart!' said Jemme enthusiastically. 'It's strange though, in all the time I've been living in France, I don't think I've ever come across that expression.'

Emile shrugged nonchalantly, looking every inch the Frenchman. Jemme smiled again: he was an excellent choice. Not only was he a perfect hybrid of Eastern and Western, he seemed well informed and sensitive, both to the building and its furniture. He seemed to share Jemme's attitude towards antique pieces and Jemme was sure he would share his vision too. It was a highly auspicious start, and Jemme couldn't wait to see what he was going to come up with.

The following weekend, Jemme left for the chateau with a spring in his step. He was looking forward to hearing what Emile thought, seeing his plans and generally getting the project started. As he drove up the long gravel approach to the building, he tried to imagine what the insides would look like once they had realised Emile's plans. He tried to squeeze the rooms of his dream within the walls of the chateau, and picture everything slotting together. He couldn't believe that he was about to see the black and white plans which would enable him to realise something he had been driven towards for so long. He thought back to something Hil had said – she was excited to be able to see something that only he had experienced. He felt a bit like that now; although he could visualise what he wanted with a remarkable degree of clarity, until now it had only been inside his head. He was on the verge of seeing it laid out in front of him, as if it had been extracted from his mind's eye and made real. He was pleased he had the whole weekend in front of him; he would go over the plans with Emile this evening and then spend the next couple of days wandering around the chateau with the architect, letting him point out where various things would go, and painting him a picture of how things would look; exactly like last weekend, but with inverted roles.

Emile was waiting to meet him in the Halle d'Honneur, with a long roll of paper under his arm.

'How was your journey?' he asked.

'Good,' replied Jemme cheerfully. 'How have you enjoyed being here for the past week? I hope it hasn't been too strange, rattling around on your own!'

Emile laughed, 'Not at all, I've had Philby and Xelifon for company and it's given me the chance to really get to know the place. I've put together some ambitious designs for you – I really hope you like them.'

'I'm sure I will, I've been dying to see them,' said Jemme, feelings his fingers almost twitch as he said it, as if to prove his point.

'Shall we look at them now, or would you like some time to settle in?'

'No, no, not at all! Let's look at them now!' said Jemme, trying not to sound too impatient.

Emile led the way to the library, evidently having settled in quite well. They went back to the desk, and he unrolled the plans, smoothing them across the table. Jemme looked at them, puzzled. Instead of a climactic moment of excitement, he just felt mild confusion. He didn't understand any of what he saw before him – where was everything? Where were the sumptuous original decorations which restored the grand rooms to their original functions? Where were the rooms which embodied Eastern civilisations? Where was the carefully observed fusion between the two? He looked at them again. He couldn't even tell if they were the right way up or not.

Emile looked expectantly at Jemme's expression, 'I'll talk you through everything,' he said when he realised that his plans were not going to be met with the elation he was hoping for.

'Do,' said Jemme, looking at him with an expression that bordered on the plaintive.

'Well, first of all, let me explain the concept. I thought over all of our discussions, and tried to work out what you were trying to achieve with the project.'

'But I don't think there is a goal – I think the project's an end in itself. That's why it's such a unique job,' Jemme said.

'I know, but think about how you explained it to me, and try and think about how that sounds,' said Emile.

Jemme looked none the wiser.

'Well, you wanted individual rooms which showcased a particular civilisation or people didn't you?'

'Broadly speaking, yes.'

'Well, think what that sounds like – multiple small rooms, filled with antiques, not necessarily bearing a correlation to each other, and yet housed within the same building?'

Emile looked expectantly at Jemme.

'I know what you're driving at, but that's just not really what I was…I mean, I want there to be a narrative between the rooms, that's the whole-'

'A museum!' interrupted Emile. 'It's so obvious!'

'Well, I mean, yes, on the surface of it, but really, it's all so much more than-' Jemme mumbled, struggling not to give in to dismay at the fact that Emile perhaps didn't share his vision after all.

Emile ploughed on, apparently oblivious to Jemme's disappointment.

'Once I understood what it is that you wanted, the rest became easy.'

'But again, it's not exactly what I-' before Jemme had chance to finish, Emile interrupted him again, waving his hands dismissively.

'Clients often don't know what they want at the beginning of a project. It's my job to help them work that out. Then, it becomes a process of distillation. I refine and I refine until we are left with a product at the end which is the completely pure realisation of their vision.'

He looked expectantly at Jemme, who didn't return his enthusiasm.

'It's a bit like taking the crudest form of oil and refining it until it becomes as pure as aviation fuel,' he said helpfully.

'Yes, I understand that,' said Jemme, growing a little tetchy, 'What I don't understand is how things seem to have got so distorted; you didn't need to refine anything. I understood what I wanted from the beginning, and I never said I wanted a museum.'

'But that is what you want! You just don't realise it yet, perhaps. Once *I* realised it though, the whole project became much easier. I started to deconstruct the concept of the museum, and came up with something for you which will be original, new and ground breaking.'

'But the concept itself was original,' argued Jemme.

Emile barely registered the fact he'd heard anything, and continued in full flow, 'I started thinking about museology and how I could use current thinking to create something forward-facing, rather than being mired in tradition,'

'But tradition is exactly what I want!'

'Are you familiar with the concept of museology?'

Jemme shook his head.

'It's the study of what gives the objects meaning. I mean, obviously it's their context, but it evaluates what it is about that context that provides meaning, and seeks to exploit it. It's a theory that is constantly evolving and changing.'

Jemme's ears pricked up for the first time. This was the kind of thing he was interested in, and what he'd been hoping to explore in the plans. Perhaps Emile was just getting off to a bad start. He backed off a little and let him continue his explanation.

'Well, traditional museums would have you believe that the only way to display an artefact is in some fancy, elaborate milieu, dripping in decoration and completely overblown. Current thinking challenges that, and completely reinvents the whole approach to display and interpretation.'

Jemme listened intently, but failed to see what point Emile was making. Displaying things in 'a fancy milieu' was exactly what he'd been wanting to do.

'Go on,' he said slowly.

'Well, in line with current thinking, and vogues all across Europe, I've developed a modern, sleek design for you,' said Emile, 'It's more than just a design, it's an expression of a philosophy. It recognises the artefact as the primary source, and strips away everything which might detract from that. Clean lines, white walls and plenty of light are the only things which are needed in a museum. The rest is all down to the display objects themselves. Anything further is just background noise. These designs allow pure dialogue between visitor and artefact.'

'Hold on,' said Jemme, firmly, pulling himself together. 'We're getting completely carried away. First of all, you've told me that what I really want is a museum. I'll admit there are certain similarities between my concept and a small-scale museum, but that's where it ends. I feel like you've taken that idea and run away with it – now we're talking about visitors?! It's all too much. I appreciate what you're saying, and I agree with some of your philosophy, but it's all wrong for this place. I thought we understood each other, but these plans are the total opposite of what I was hoping for. I wanted to draw out the character of the chateau, not mute it as much as possible with bright lights and whitewashed walls. I thought you understood that? These cases are all wrong too – I want to create a totally immersive experience in each of the rooms, not single out one piece for study. I want it to feel as if you've *actually* entered an ancient palace or stepped straight into Phoenician times when you open each door, not into another identical, bland room as if you're going to the high fashion district in Paris. I really thought you'd understood that. You recognise that I don't want any plastics, any phony varnishes, brushed aluminium, or any pressed wood or veneers.'

Emile looked crestfallen. He paused for a moment. 'What I had understood,' he said, slowly, 'was that you had commissioned me on the basis of my expertise and experience. What I *understood* was that I was trusted to develop plans for you.'

He was obviously angry, but Jemme didn't feel in the mood to placate him. He was feeling angry and disappointed himself. 'You were trusted to come up with the designs,' he told Emile, 'but what you've come up with is so far removed from what I want, it's as if we didn't discuss it at all. This all represents your vision and your ideas.'

'But that's because I'm the architect! Of course it represents my vision, that's why people hire me.'

'No! People hire you so that you can use your skills as an architect to help them realise their vision,' said Jemme, starting to lose his cool. He checked his temper. 'Perhaps I didn't communicate my ideas to you clearly enough,' he offered.

Emile softened slightly, 'I'm not prepared to redesign these,' he said, 'I can't take on a commission which compromises my design philosophy. I just can't.'

Jemme sighed heavily, 'In that case, it pains me to say it, but I'm afraid we can't work on this project together. I wouldn't just need you to compromise, I would need you to completely redo all of this. It's a shame, because I was really hoping to work with you.'

Emile looked pained, 'I just can't compromise,' he repeated again.

'I know, I understand,' said Jemme. 'I'll still pay you for the designs of course, but that's where it has to end.'

Emile executed another perfect Gallic shrug and rolled up his designs, 'I am sorry too. It would have been a wonderful project, and a good collaboration too, I think,' he sighed, 'However, I think you're right. It will not work. I also don't think there's too much point in me sticking around. If I leave now I should be back in Paris before midnight.'

He offered a hand which Jemme shook, 'Thank you for all your hard work.'

'Thank you for the opportunity. I wish you every success with the project.'

Jemme showed him to the door and shut it slowly behind him. He had been so excited about this weekend being the weekend that began everything. He was so sure about Emile too; he couldn't believe that things had turned out the way they had. He took a deep breath; if he was being honest with himself he knew that he would encounter multiple problems over the course of the project. He shouldn't have expected to get such an important part right first time. At the very least, it had been interesting to have his first proper encounter with an architect. It hadn't been at all like he was expecting. A few friends had told him to expect extreme arrogance, yet Emile had seemed pleasantly accessible and down to earth. Jemme thought about it some more, and ran through what had just happened. Upon reflection, he realised that Emile had frequently referred to his vision and his plans, with very little acknowledgement of Jemme's role. He had also completely steam-rollered Jemme in conversation, and barely acknowledged anything he had said. In fact, the way in which his plans didn't acknowledge Jemme's concept was pretty arrogant in itself. *Maybe he was quite arrogant*, thought Jemme to himself at last. *Perhaps it was just that he was such a pleasant person I didn't really notice it at first. At least I know what to look for next time*, he mused as he went to phone Hil with the latest news.

With nothing else to do over the next day, Jemme wandered around the chateau trying to see things as Emile had seen them. He visualised stark white walls and huge-paned glass windows; he imagined bleached wooden surfaces and clean simple lines, and shook his head. It might work in a modernist setting, but it was completely inappropriate in an ancient building such as this one. It forsook the context for the sake of the artefacts, whereas Jemme wanted to create as much cohesion between the two as possible. Having the extra day to himself, and alone with his thoughts, he had time to consider his approach to the project and his own interpretation of museology. He still was not sure that he wanted to create what others would term a museum, but it would have to share certain attributes with a museum, such as the emphasis on, and understanding of, conservation. There was a duty of care and a duty of scholarship too. He thought about it some more; it wasn't just the 'museum' part he needed to develop though, he needed to work out how it was going to integrate into the rest of the house. Emile's plans had involved the whole chateau, but that was far too ambitious. First and foremost, it was to be a family home. He and Hil had talked excitedly about raising children in its grounds, and that was still an important priority. He had absolutely no intention of allowing this project to squeeze out his current or future family. However, he wasn't sure how much he wanted family rooms intermingling with the special gallery-style rooms. It would be too strange, and create too much fragmentation. Would it be possible to have two completely separate areas within the chateau? Could he divide it so that one half was purely for family and guests, and one half exclusively dedicated to housing antiques and exploring history? It was strange to think of the place divided, but it was certainly an option. He realised he needed someone with whom he could discuss all of this and, with a sinking heart, knew he would have to turn back to the stack of CVs and portfolios once he returned to Paris.

A busy week at work followed and Jemme barely had time to look through the fresh slew of CVs that DD had rustled up for him. He decided to spend the first weekend for a long time in Paris, and enjoy some much needed quality time with Hil. She had been sympathetic when she had heard that the thing had not gone as planned with Emile, but after a Saturday morning spent with a very morose Jemme she had ticked him off for sulking.

'You said yourself, you're not going to get it right first time,' she said, 'so there's no need to be so glum about it. This is the first person you interviewed for the first position at the chateau in the first part of the project. It's really not so bad.'

'Actually, he's not the first person I interviewed,' said Jemme glumly.

'Really?' Hil asked as she tried to think back over the past few months.

'No – I mean it wasn't exactly a proper interview, but I've hired Philby and Xelifon already.'

'Well there you go! Unless things have changed dramatically, that's all working out very well, isn't it?'

Jemme was forced to concede that it was.

'Well then!' Hil said, brightly.

Jemme raised an unconvincing smile.

'Look, why don't you go and fetch the CVs you've got so far, and we'll go through them together over a nice cup of tea. By the time you've got back, I'll have bought us some of those *financiers* you like from the boulangerie.'

Jemme looked at her for a moment,

'Go on! Go,' she said in mock sternness, ushering him out of the door.

He smiled again, earnestly this time, and kissed Hil as she tried to shut the door on him.

About an hour later, Jemme was chasing financier crumbs around a saucer with his finger, and they had whittled the shortlist down to about three. Only one had really made any impression, but even he wasn't particularly impressive – his ideas seemed completely at odds with Jemme's, even though they had been executed well. His name was Michael, he was Anglo-Irish and had some experience of working on museums. Although Jemme still wasn't sure if that's how he wanted to describe his project, at least Michael was au fait with the way in which antiques and artefacts needed to be treated. Hil read his personal statement aloud again. Although he had lived in England for most of his life, there was a fiery passion in the way he wrote about architecture, which was decidedly Mediterranean.

'Well, he's certainly enthusiastic,' she said.

'Mmm, it's just a pity I don't feel the same way about him,' said Jemme, nosing around the crumpled paper bag to see if there were any biscuits left.

'Well, he's keen. He's worked on some interesting pieces before and we don't really have many other options at the moment. Why don't we at least meet him?'

Jemme shrugged, 'I don't see why not, I suppose. You should be there though,' he added.

'Do you think so?'

'Absolutely. I've been treating this process as if it's just another recruitment for the bank. It's going to affect your home too, and you should have an equal say in who we pick to work on it. Plus, you're an excellent judge of character.'

'Thank you,' said Hil, breaking the rest of her biscuit in half and giving half to Jemme. 'I think we should chat to him as soon as possible. Once you've started these things rolling it's a shame to lose momentum.'

'I agree. I'll ask DD to get in touch with him and see when he can come and meet us.'

It turned out Jemme was in luck. Although Michael was a highly sought after architect, a commission had been abruptly pulled, meaning that he was available immediately. Just a few days later, he sat opposite Jemme and Hil in Hil's favourite café, telling them the story of the man who had pulled the plug on the project. His dislike of this backer seemed to be as passionate as his adoration of another patron, and he seemed rather stereotypically Italianate in mien. He was extremely likable and talked very eloquently and Jemme had been impressed straight away. However, he wanted to err on the side of caution after his experience with Emile, and so got straight to the heart of the matter.

'How much do you think the client's vision is important?'

Michael blinked slightly at his bluntness, but only paused for a moment, 'The client's vision is everything,' he replied, looking serious. 'Without it the project is just a vehicle for the architect. Of course, I would love a building to be built purely to my designs, but I also enjoy the collaborative process. I make designs which are completely my own, but these are just for my portfolio. Besides, I learn something new every time I work with a client. I have to force myself to see something from someone else's point of view.'

Jemme and Hil exchanged quick glances. Jemme was impressed and he could tell Hil was too. Michael seemed to pick up on this, and quickly brought out a large scrapbook.

'This is my file of press clippings, which I thought you might like to see,' he said and handed it over to Hil.

It was an impressive collection, featuring highly favourable reviews and interviews from all over the world, and in a whole host of different languages.

'How long have you been collecting these?' she asked Michael.

'Pretty much since the first one appeared,' he replied. 'I thought I should probably keep it, and then when I had about five or six I started putting them all together in a book.'

Hil turned the pages slowly and Jemme looked over her shoulder.

'It probably hasn't done much for my ego!' Michael joked, and Hil smiled at him. She had been pleased to note that he didn't seem to be particularly egotistical. She too, had heard from the same friend as Jemme that this was something to be particularly wary of. She chatted with him for a while longer, and Jemme noticed that despite being friendly, she remained formal at all times. He realised that that was probably the mistake he made with Emile. He had been too eager to get the project started, and had allowed this keenness and the fact he liked the man to cloud his judgement. He followed Hil's lead, and remained appropriately detached. They chatted some more and then said goodbye. On the way home, Jemme was keen to hear,

'So, what did you think?'

'I thought he seemed to have racked up some good experience,'

'Yes?'

'..and I thought that his references were impressive,'

'Yes?'

'but, I'm not convinced he's the right person for the project.'

There was a slight silence whilst Jemme formed his thoughts.

'You see, what I realised during that conversation is that that doesn't really matter.'

'Doesn't matter! I'm surprised to hear you say that – surely it's the most important thing?'

'Well, it is and it isn't. In almost every way Emile was the perfect man for the project. He was everything I'd been looking for and it should have all worked effortlessly. However, what he produced was the complete opposite of what I was looking for.'

'But at least you started off with one thing right! If you start off with an architect who's not right for the job, then where on earth will you finish up? I'm pretty certain he's guaranteed to produce something wildly unsuitable.'

'But that's what I realised – I don't think it really matters. It was something Michael said that made me realise it actually. He talked about learning from his clients, even when he didn't like the work they wanted him to produce. When Emile showed me his plans, I was disappointed, of course, but in hindsight they were still incredibly useful. Even though they're not going further than drawing board stage, they'll still shape the overall project. His plans gave me so many ideas and made me think about what I really wanted from this whole thing. It forced me to criticise my own understanding, and see what needed to be changed and reworked. I think it could be the same with Michael. I've already got enough material to know the rough shape of the plan I want, but I'm not sure on a couple of points. I want Michael to give me ideas and guide my own plans, rather than give me the finished product.'

Hil thought it over, 'I suppose I can see what you mean, but isn't that terribly unfair on him?'

'I've already thought about that and, honestly, I don't think it is. I'm still going to pay him for the design consultation, just like I did with Emile. Think about it – he's really quite a successful architect and is used to working on much larger projects than this. The only reason I suspect he even came and met with us was because his last commission fell through. This would work perfectly for him – it would be something to keep him ticking over until the next big thing comes along.'

Hil frowned, 'I suppose you've got a point. It would definitely make things a lot easier.' She didn't look too convinced by the idea of Jemme coming up with all the plans on his own, but for now she didn't say anything, and they walked back home together feeling that they had, at least, taken a step in the right direction.

Several weeks later, Michael had produced a set of plans. Although his use of space was interesting, they were heavily modernist and far too incongruous with the setting – in other words, completely wrong for the chateau. However, just as Jemme had hoped, they sparked off several ideas of his own, and helped him resolve several problems which had been occupying him. Just as he had predicted, Michael did not react badly to the news that he was not to be hired.

'It's probably for the best. I've just been approached about a major commission in New York; it's something I've been working towards for years, and I would hate to have had to turn it down because I was already committed to something else,' he said.

Jemme shook his hand and wished him all the best. He thanked him again for his hard work, although he wasn't convinced Michael understood exactly what he was thanking him for.

Once Michael had left, Jemme and Hil pored over his plans. He hadn't latched on to the idea of a museum in the same way Emile had, but he had drawn a clear distinction between 'display space' and 'family space'. He had also sectioned off what he called 'working space'. It had all been done very neatly, and was obviously the work of someone who thought about the functionality of a space as well as its aesthetic. In a way it was a shame they weren't employing him. However, when he looked at the 'display space' Jemme remembered why not. In this respect Michael had very similar ideas to Emile, and was obviously influenced by current fashions and academic theories on the use of space and light around ancient objects. Jemme looked at the way he had divided the building again. It was sensitive to the shape and its varying age. Parts of the chateau were original and stood exactly as they had been built, several hundred years ago; parts were later additions or adaptations, and parts were reconstructions after some fire damage at the turn of the last century. There were also parts which were decidedly modern additions, and had evidently been built by some ham-fisted architect who didn't give two hoots about how much it clashed with the original building – someone, Jemme suspected, who was in the employ of the French ministry. All of these different elements made for a building which was complex and multi-layered and Jemme was keen to treat it thus. He felt that the age and location of the rooms should play a fundamental role in their functions, and Michael's suggestions offered a natural way of determining just what those functions should be.

The slightly unattractive modern additions could be the 'work' areas. Jemme had already thought about the fact that there would be a great number of craftsmen coming and going over the course of the project. The builders, plasterers and woodworkers would all need somewhere to store their tools when they working, and perhaps even a place to stay. It would depend on where they came from of course, but he doubted he would be able to find sufficient specialists in the surrounding villages. If they had to come from Paris, or even further afield, then they wouldn't be able to go home at the end of every day. He would be able to convert some of the space in the later additions into comfortable living quarters, with quite a good deal of ease. There was an old stable block which would do nicely if needed, too.

He realised that Hil was looking at him, and he had been silent for a while.

'Sorry sweetheart, I've just been thinking about the way Michael's divided things up.'

'Yes, I was just looking at that too. I'm not sure about this "work space" bit – do we really need that?'

'Absolutely. In fact, that's what I was just thinking about. We're going to need so many builders and decorators over the course of this project, it makes sense to have them in a separate area. There'll be room for them to stay here if need's be and all their equipment can be stored here too. It's fine now, when the place is relatively empty, but as we finish various rooms it doesn't really make sense to have people carrying paint pots and ladders through them, when they could bash into things or damage various bits.'

'I suppose so. I hadn't really imagined that we would need quite so many people coming and going, though. I had rather hoped that we might start to settle in soon enough – I didn't realise it was going to be a building site for so long.'

Jemme rubbed Hil's arm, 'I'm afraid it is, my love, I want to be absolutely clear with you on that from the beginning. However, that's the beauty of dividing things up like this. If we have the family section completely separate, then we can get that area sorted and be all snug and homely there without even realising that there are building works going on elsewhere.'

Hil looked sceptical, but smiled at him, 'Well, I suppose it's worth giving it a go. I like the idea of having the living area separate from these display areas too. It means we've got two completely different properties here.'

'I like it too, and I like the way he's sectioned things off. It solves something that has been worrying me for a while. I've been wondering how I could retain the character of the chateau, whilst also creating something which was completely immersive.'

'What do you mean "immersive"?'

'I mean that in what Michael's called "the display rooms", I want to recreate an entire tiny world – a bit like a room in a dollhouse. You open the door and are completely subsumed into that world.'

'I see…'

'But, if that world is an Assyrian throne room or a Phoenician harbour, then it's not really in keeping with its context.'

'Not really.'

'So, this solves both problems. These sections here, which are not part of the original chateau, can be used as museum rooms, gallery rooms or display rooms – whatever you want to call it. They're not particularly old, and they're certainly not being used for their original function right now. I would have no qualms about dividing them up internally so that we can get the right number of rooms, and of the right proportions. They wouldn't detract from the character of the chateau because they were never intended to be here in the first place.'

'I suppose not. It would make sense, and I guess it wouldn't affect the general flow of things.'

'Precisely. Now, these rooms on the other hand,' he pointed to several on the plans in front of him. 'These are original to the chateau. They're what I think I'm going to call "the Noble Rooms".'

'Noble?'

'They just have a certain air of nobility about them. There's the size of them to start with, and the proportions. Then there's the fact they were almost certainly designed with some sort of aristocratic pastime in mind. These are the ones I want to protect at all cost. They're all in a reasonably shabby state at the moment, and are going to require quite a bit of care; several of them need immediate, specialist attention, but I want to conserve them, preserve them and restore them to their original glory. We'll fit them with carpets, tapestries – everything. We can have these all to ourselves; they'll be family rooms. Look how large this salon is! Can you imagine entertaining our friends when it's been put back to how it would have been when the chateau was first built.'

A smile spread across Hil's face, 'That would be rather wonderful,' she said, 'that's the sort of idea that's been exciting me since we first bought this place.'

Jemme was smiling too, 'In that case, I shall make that my priority. This is going to be a chateau of three parts, and there'll be something for everyone by the time I've finished, I'm sure. We've finished, I mean,' he said, quickly correcting himself.

'So, now we just need to find a good architect without any of his own ideas. I guess we need someone who is willing just to take on the plans whole, as they are, and fine-tune them for us.'

'Mmmmm.' Jemme didn't sound convinced.

'Well what do you think we need, then?'

'Actually, I don't think we need anyone at all.'

'What?' Hil seemed cross rather than confused. 'That's madness. You surely can't be thinking about taking on the project yourself?'

'Well, I'm already half-way there. It would just be a matter of-'

'Please, sweetheart, this is already going to drain our savings accounts, and rumble on for way longer than I expected. Don't let it sap up the precious little free time you have.'

Jemme paused for a while. He could see that Hil wasn't happy, and he really didn't want to start the things off on the wrong foot. The project could potentially create something unique and amazing, but it could also drive a wedge between them, and he knew he would have to be sensitive in his handling of it from the beginning.

'I'm sorry, I know the past few days have really driven home what a large-scale operation this is going to be. I want you to be involved at every stage, and I want to do everything in my power to ensure that not one single piece of this whole plan becomes a bone of contention between us.'

'I just think it's such a big responsibility to be taking on at such an early stage. You're going to need to focus on so many other things, later down the line, that I'm worried you're going to have no time left at all. This is the time in our lives when I was hoping we'd be thinking about starting a family, and I don't want to have to compete for your time or attention.'

'And neither should you,' said Jemme, squeezing her upper arm. 'I want those things too, I just also want to build a future for our family. I promise that I'll always have time for you and I'll always prioritise us. I do understand your concerns, but I really don't think it's too great a burden at this stage. I've already got a plan, formed after consulting two professional architects – the hard part's already finished. I'll talk it through with a design consultant who'll be able to draw up some proper blueprints for me, and then I'll run it past a couple of engineers who can test the structural viability of everything. I've already started thinking about it, but I need to talk to some chartered professionals to check my calculations are right.'

Hil sighed, 'When you put it like that, I suppose it won't be too bad. As long as you've got a couple of people to help guide you, and if the majority of the work is already done…'

'It is, and I genuinely think things are better this way. Can you imagine how much more work there would be for me to do if I entrusted it all to one architect, and he ran amok with things? Managing such a high-ranking professional, not to mention an arty type, would take up so much time. Then, what if I found out that five, six weeks down the line, he'd gone in completely the wrong direction? Can you imagine how long it would take to put that all right?'

'Maybe you're right, although it does seem odd to think that someone you've hired to save you time could end up causing extra work for you.'

Jemme laughed, 'Believe me, after some of the employees I've had at the bank it wouldn't be the first time!'

Chapter Sixteen

With the first stage of the project set in motion, Jemme's excitement was palpable. Even Hil's earlier misgivings seemed to have been subsumed by the magnitude of his enthusiasm.

'You're like a child!' she told him teasingly, after he had just finished showing her the blueprints for the third time. They had been produced, precisely to specification, by a leading Parisian design consultant.

'It's just so exciting though! This is exactly – exactly! – what I would have done if I had the skills. I can't believe he's done it so perfectly!'

'They have been nicely done,' Hil agreed.

'Nicely done? They're perfect!'

'Yes, you mentioned,' she said, smiling at him.

'It feels a bit like receiving the instruction manual ahead of a really exciting new present,' said Jemme happily. 'Now I've seen how it's all going to work, I just want to get on with the real thing.'

'Like I said, just like a child,' said Hil, pinching his shoulder playfully. She looked over the plans again. 'It's hard to imagine it all in the flesh,' she said. 'I'll have to learn my way around all over again!'

'I know what you mean,' said Jemme, looking over it all again himself. Just as he had wanted, the disused stable block and some of the modern wing had been given over to staff quarters, storage and workshop space. The central core of the chateau comprised the 'Noble Rooms' with their full, original proportions. The access points and entranceways had also not been altered, to ensure a continuous flow of grandeur within this section, and eschew any peculiar bathos. Finally, the display rooms sat in the reconstructed area. The plans showed the area neatly divided into rooms of equal portions, perfectly tessellating little blank canvases, ready for Jemme to decorate in any way he liked. He knew Hil would compare them to little toy boxes for him to fill with his treasures, so he decided to keep quiet. This was the part of the house he was most excited about, and the part he couldn't wait to get started on. However, he intended to be true to his word to Hil and he was anxious to get the family part of the chateau sorted as soon as possible, so that their living space would be ready: this was a family home first and foremost.

'Now that this is all sorted, what's the next stage?' asked Hil.

'That's a good question. I've been so focussed on this part that I'd almost forgotten that this was just the beginning!'

'And I suppose asking if you're going to hire a project manager to worry about this kind of thing for us is fairly redundant?'

'Pretty much – if I've got this far without an architect already, I'm reluctant to hand my project over to somebody else.'

Hil sighed, 'I should have guessed as much. So, with your manager's hat on, what do we need to sort next?'

Jemme didn't think about it for very long, 'Now that we've got the plans sorted, we need to hire in builders to make these alterations. I'll ask Philby for his help and see if we can get some local people. I'm going to budget three weeks for it. It's not particularly complicated; the technical stuff will come later. Right now we're literally still at the bricks and mortar stage.'

Hil smiled, 'Well it's comforting to see that you seem to know what you're doing at least.'

'I really feel like I do. There's something so exhilarating about being in charge of something so big, and knowing I'm responsible for getting everything exactly as I want it. Maybe it's the adrenaline,' he paused and suddenly realised what he'd said, 'sorry sweetheart, I meant getting everything the way *we* want it.'

'I know,' said Hil, giving him a small kiss on the cheek, 'you just get so carried away, that's all.'

'Talking of getting carried away; something I can be doing whilst the builders are working on the place is deciding what I want to showcase in each display room. I know myself, and I know that if I don't plan it before hand I'll try and cram everything in and we'll need to buy a second chateau!'

'Heaven forefend!' said Hil, affecting being aghast. At least, Jemme thought she was affecting.

'Don't worry, I'll keep control of myself. When would you next like to visit?'

'Well, I don't much fancy going down there whilst it's still a building site, but I think we really should at some point to check on progress. When do you think the builders can start?'

'Well, it's hard to say exactly. I haven't even spoken to Philby yet, but in a rural area like that there always seem to be tradesmen available for work. I'm sure there won't be much of a delay in getting people to start and these plans are fairly straightforward. We can hand a copy straight over to the foreman. So, if I can get them to start at some point this week, how would next weekend sound? We can do some fun things whilst we're there too – maybe go on a couple of little day trips.'

Hil perked up, 'That sounds fun – next weekend would be perfect.'

Philby was more than happy to source some local builders, and shared Jemme's opinion that it would not be difficult to find people to start straight away. With one of his best men on the job, Jemme was free to turn his mind to the all important gallery list. He didn't even know where to begin. He was faced with the rather terrifying prospect of realising his dreams, and getting everything he wanted. It was a little daunting. Perhaps thinking back to the first time he had the dream would be a good starting point. He didn't even need to close his eyes to recall the images, first seen in childhood, which had become so familiar to him. The pink arches of the Doge's Palace sprang out from the shifting walls in front of him, as he imagined the outside of his dream palace. They blended into and emerged from its shifting facades which, over the years, had accumulated more and features as he had visited more and more stately homes and chateaux throughout the world. They served as a repository for visual memories, stored for posterity in this mental scrapbook, which was ever mutable and forever changing. He remembered walking along the corridors of this palace as a young boy, and the first ever room he had opened. He had seen Hammurabi devising his law code with an assistant. They had been committing the code into writing, with the assistant inscribing on a tall stone stele with slow, methodical chisel work. *The first written law code*, Jemme thought. *That merits a place in the display rooms*. It was a significant act by an important figure, but did it merit a whole room to itself? He thought about it some more; he'd already promised Hil that he wouldn't get carried away and he didn't want to at the first turn. How about the looking at Hammurabi more generically, in terms of the Babylonians? They were an important civilisation, who made huge advances in astronomy, medicine, literature and philosophy. He thought about the legendary Hanging Gardens and the fabled Tower of Babel, conceived to reach the gods, great symbols of success and prowess which exposed the vanity of some leaders.

Grandma was highly knowledgeable about the Babylonians; she would certainly tell him that one room alone was barely big enough to catalogue all their achievements, but it would be a start. Yes, he would dedicate the first room on the list to the Babylonian Empire and its successes, perhaps picking out several specific pieces or people. He cast his mind back to boyhood and Grandma showing him a drawing of mysterious cuts and scratches into the face of stone tablets. Jemme remembered being fascinated by the idea that these intriguing cuts into clay and stone represented a huge advance in the spreading of stories. Now the story teller didn't need to even meet with his audience – indeed he might not even have intended it to be for the audience it ended up with; if the tablet was lost and found hundreds of years later, the story, or perhaps poem would be rediscovered. He remembered looking at the little symbols, half-way between pictures and letters. Their minims were straight and neat, with bowed serifs and triangular-shaped terminals, like tiny pennant flags. He had researched it in great detail since this first encounter. Grandma had taken some time to explain how it wasn't a language, but a system for expressing a language. It was like thinking about the Latin alphabet – it could be used in Turkey, and people would read and understand it as if it was the most natural thing in the world. However, in France, people would be using exactly the same alphabet amongst themselves. Neither would be able to understand a text in the other's language; even thought the letters would be so familiar, they would be configured in a totally incomprehensible way. Grandma had made it so easy to understand that, instead of confusing Jemme, it had fascinated him. This scrawling script had been in ancient lands, whose very names felt mysterious – Phoenicia, Sumer... How could he omit such places if he was to include Babylon? Ancient Mesopotamia was full of cultures, civilisations and people worthy of exaltation and recognition – had the Assyrians not left a lasting trace in the annals of history? The library of Ashurbanipal, the epic of Gilgamesh – they could not be ignored where there was space to chronicle Eastern achievements.

He stopped himself: was that even what he wanted to do? He wanted to showcase certain flourishings in Eastern history, certainly, but that was not an end in itself, merely a by-product of something else: the physicalisation of his childhood dream. He realised he would have to refocus, and try to think about what he had actually seen in the dream over the years. Trying to banish thoughts of the great collection of Ashurbanipal's clay tablets in Nineveh, he put himself back into the corridors of the dream palace. Mentally opening one door, he remembered a crowd of richly cloaked Venetian ambassadors. Another set of ambassadors surrounded him, but now he recognised himself as being in the midst of a Bellini painting. Venetian ambassadors, clad in black, were being received by the reclining Mamluk governor of Damascus. Eastern dignitaries in colourful raiment thronged the courtyard, and an opening in the perimeter wall led to a vaulted *liwan*. Jemme felt as if he was visiting a familiar haunt. The faces were always the same and their positions unchanged when he entered the room. In some of the other rooms, things were always different when he walked in; people came and left, furniture moved and conversation altered. Sometimes it was as if he was coming in at the height of the action, and sometimes he felt as if he'd got there too late and had just missed a great battle or speech. However, he felt as if these characters were frozen somewhere within this space, collected by Bellini and trapped within a canvas prison. They became animated only when he entered the room, and he imagined them becoming two-dimensional and flattened when he left again. However, this was one of his favourite rooms. Since moving to Paris, he had been to visit the original Bellini painting in the Louvre many times. It seemed strange to see it hanging, flat and lifeless, on a wall; to look directly into the painted eyes of the Mamluk governor, and know that he had dreamt him into life and recognised the sound of his voice. He desperately wanted to include this painting somewhere in the galleries, even in the house, but he didn't know where it would fit in. He could perhaps put it in an area dedicated to Venice, or in a room for Venetian ambassadors, but then he wanted to reference Damascus somewhere too. He also wanted to show the interaction between the two, rather than having two, completely separate, rooms.

He thought of all the other things he wanted to include, and tried to work out how they could all fit together. The more he thought about it, the more his plans expanded. His dream had expanded and evolved, keeping pace with his learning, and was too vast and nebulous to squeeze into the confines of fixed rooms. He also couldn't escape the nagging feeling that he wanted to do more than merely exposite his dream. He had the opportunity to explore so many other features of history which had fascinated him over the years. If he was going to create a room dedicated to the Babylonians, and visualise his dream, then what was stopping him from doing the same for the Assyrians, who had been just as important, but hadn't featured in his imagined palace? He considered it for a moment. It would turn it from a private project into a more museum-like enterprise, but perhaps that was what he had been destined to do anyway. It was an interesting new direction, and he pondered civilisations he could include. However, if he'd had problems making a list, when he was solely focussed on his dream, now it was all but impossible. As he ran over different cultures, his list grew exponentially. He couldn't include one civilisation without including two more to demonstrate their enduring legacy. Similarly, he couldn't focus on great and remarkable caliphs of history, without fitting them into their wider contexts and exploring their cultures.

It was all too much, and it seemed that, the more he tried to solve the problem, the harder it became. He realised he had gone off-course again, and tried to refocus for the second time. He would have to stick with his original plan and have a single room for each civilisation, with special focus on any particular person, place or event of interest. The problem was now how to arrange the rooms. They were never in the same place in the palace, and it would make sense to have some form of order to them, but how? Should he do it by timescale? The gap between some civilisations was only a couple of hundred years, but almost an entire millennium between others. It might make things seem patchy. He could arrange everything according to geographical location, perhaps starting with the westernmost cultures and drifting further east. This didn't work either – some civilisations had occupied the same lands, but centuries apart. He sighed. There must some way of making his ideas work ideologically. He wanted a narrative thread that would weave together people and places, from East to West, over an extended period of time.

Suddenly it came to him – it was so obvious! One thing had been a recurring theme in Grandma's stories and a trope of his own learning. Its silken threads had tied together East and West from ancient times, bringing the two spheres into contact with each other and slowly diffusing culture, ideas and learning in the process. The Silk Route had beaten a path through history, connecting mercantile Venice with the opulent produce of China. It wasn't just silk either: jewels, silver, spices, glassware and carpets travelled in both directions; crafts, materials and learning spread along its winding route, melding with indigenous practice and moulding new ideas. It was the ultimate paradigm of cultural hybridism and enrichment and one which provided Grandma with an endless source of faith in reconciliation and the ability of foreign cultures not just to co-exist, but to co-operate too.

If this provided his central theme, he could link so many different things in to it. He would no longer have to choose between two separate rooms for the Bellini painting, but rather it could be used to show the influence between the two. He could chart the progress of art, ideas and scholarship from the Far East, through the Levant and into Western Europe. He could follow how they had become fused with other ideas along the way, and the rich, multi-layered, unique objects and philosophies which had emerged as a result. He could examine the parity between Eastern and Western belief systems, and the disparity in their expression. It all started to come together, and his enthusiasm rose again. It was a bold new direction, but one which made perfect sense. It allowed him to create something greater than just his dream. It was an extension of it, but it had far greater meaning: opening a dialogue between East and West was a significant act. Even if it only remained within the confines of the chateau and even if he and Hil were the only ones ever to see it, it was still an important scholastic endeavour. If he found that there was something new to say as a result, then all the better. On reflection, this had been what he had been trying to do all that time ago in the Paris flat. When he had first started to rearrange his objects, he had been trying to create some sort of narrative with them. With careful positioning he had attempted to coerce a story out of them, merely from their configuration. This was essentially the same, but on a much, much larger scale. His antiques and artefacts would take on far greater meaning, be more significant and in a way *be better* once they had become integral parts of this new plan. Their history would be enriched and explained by the context in which he would place them. It was the complete opposite of the museological beliefs Emile had espoused. Emile had wanted to quieten the room with plain walls and bright lights, to allow the artefact to do the talking; Jemme wanted to use the room to explain the artefact.

It all seemed to make sense, and with enthusiasm coursing through his veins again he wrote two words at the bottom of his list: 'Silk Road'. Suddenly he paused. Would this really be enough? It couldn't, for example, be used to connect the Babylonians with the Tudors. He didn't have to think for very long; with his mind alive with new thoughts, inspiration came to him fairly quickly: he would subdivide. Whilst the Silk Route would provide the thematic core of the museum, it would just be one level. The chateau had many floors – as many as six in its highest parts, and so he would tier his ideas. The image of the dolls house flashed across his mind again, as he imagined everything stacked up on top of itself. He picked up his pencil again and wrote 'First floor – ancient civilisations.' This would be for Phoenicia, Assyria, Babylonia and suchlike. The second floor would cover the peoples of the first one and half thousand years BC. This left the next floor to explore the mediaeval to early modern period. Here he could examine significant stops along the route, as well as examining the mounting influence these stops had upon each other. He hoped by the end he would show that cultural assimilation had brought the two terminals together, shortening the route and bridging the divide between East and West.

He wasn't completely sure how to deal with the next floor yet, but he didn't let it slow him down; he merely put a question mark next to it. If he dealt with the Silk Route through to the height of Venetian power, and perhaps the collapse of the Republic too, then it would leave him with a nice narrative space for the third floor to fill as he pleased. It would give him around three hundred years to play with, and he was sure that the subject matter would become obvious as the project progressed. The fourth floor, where the majority of the family rooms were, would continue to be in keeping with the chateau's history, with perhaps some exhibition space given to local history; maybe he could hang a few paintings of French kings, or prints of the area as it was. There was plenty to be thinking about, but for now he was thrilled with his new direction. It allowed for a larger scale project with much more ambitious intentions, but all within the dream framework. He still wanted to retain the immersive experience. He wanted to open the door and feel as if he had stepped into a particular time or place, except now a full tour of the chateau would allow the visitor to feel as if they had just undertaken a truncated trip throughout the whole of history.

✻   ✻   ✻   ✻

Jemme was so engrossed in his idea he barely noticed Hil over dinner. The more he focused on the subject, and the deeper in concentration he became, the more the links between different civilisation shimmered in to view, as if they were fine silvery strands being coaxed from the depths of a quagmire. He felt almost irritated when Hil spoke, and he could feel the threads slipping from his grasp and disappearing back into the murkiness. At one point he sighed audibly. Hil looked injured,

'It's been like this every time I've tried to speak to you over the last few days. You're beginning to make me feel like I've done something wrong.'

'Mmmmm,' said Jemme absentmindedly.

'You're not even listening now! I have to say I think you're being rather unfair.'

'Unfair?'

'Yes, I haven't done anything, and all I'm doing at the moment is trying to make conversation, but you're making me feel like a bit of a nuisance.'

Jemme shook himself free of the last vestiges of his imagination, 'A nuisance?' he looked pained. 'Darling, I'm so sorry – you could never be a nuisance.'

He gathered himself, 'I've been neglecting you, haven't I?'

Hil winced, 'Don't put it like that. It makes it sound like I'm hungry for attention. I just feel like we've been strangers to each other recently.'

'I know, I can understand that. I'm just so engrossed in the project at the moment that it seems to be absorbing every thought I've got. I've been completely wrapped up in it, and I seem to have forgotten about the things which are much more important. I'm sorry, it was very selfish of me.'

Hil softened, 'Don't be too hard on yourself. I just felt like you'd disappeared inside your own mind for a bit that's all.'

'I think I did, to be honest. Let's shelve all talk of the project for the rest of the week, until we actually go there. We can do whatever you like tomorrow evening, and I haven't forgotten that day trip once we're back in the countryside either.'

'I'm looking forward to it,' said Hil with an affectionate smile, looking slightly appeased.

Jemme was true to his word and the rest of the week passed with barely a mention of the chateau. He did his level best not to think about it too, although as Friday neared it became increasingly difficult to quash his rising excitement about seeing the building works which were going on in his home, right now.

As had become their routine, on Friday morning Jemme put their overnight bags in the boot of the car, and drove the short distance to work. Within about half an hour of finishing, he was heading north out of the city, with Hil in the driver's seat.

'I can't believe there's been a team of strangers there all week whilst we've been in Paris,' said Hil, 'I'd got used to the idea of Philby and Xelifon being there, and it's actually quite nice to know they're keeping things ticking over whilst we're away, but the idea of a group of people we've never met chopping and sawing away at our house is definitely strange.'

'I know what you mean. I don't really mind the idea of them being there too much, it's the thought of what they might have done that's been troubling me. I'm sure Philby's done a masterful job of keeping them in line, but I'm finding it hard not to get nervous – what if there was a mix up with the plans and they've knocked the wrong wall down? What if they're just not that skilled?'

'Well, even if that is the case, there's not much we can do about it now. Let's just get there. Anyway, like you said, I'm sure Philby's done a great job.'

'I expect you're right,' said Jemme as they pulled into the driveway after what seemed like an exceptionally long journey.

It didn't take Jemme more than about five minutes to see that Hil had been completely right. Everything was going exactly as he had wanted, and exactly to the timings Philby had given him. He shook his hand vigorously when he saw him,

'Thank you, Philby, it looks like you've got matters well and truly under control.'

Philby shrugged, as if slightly perplexed by the idea that things might be otherwise. 'Monsieur said I should find local builders,' he stated matter-of-factly.

'Yes, yes I did, and I'm glad I left it to you. Where does everyone come from?'

'Some from this village, some from the next. They are all known to me in one way or another. They are good men.'

'I'm sure they are. I'd like to meet them if possible – do you think it would interrupt their work?'

Philby shrugged again, and led the way to the source of the hammering noise.

Despite the dustsheets everywhere and the clouds of fine plaster, Jemme could see straight away that the work had come on leaps and bounds.

'This is all coming along very nicely, Philby,' he said excitedly. A couple of paces behind him, Hil looked much less convinced.

Philby merely nodded, and moved over to a man who was on his hands and knees, sanding away the last piece of the false wall which he had just removed. Philby laid a gnarled hand on his shoulder and muttered a couple of words to him. The man frowned, stood up, dusted off one filthy hand and extended it to Jemme,

'*Monsieur,*' he said gruffly.

Jemme shook his hand warmly, 'It looks like you've been doing an excellent job so far, thank you,' he said. The man merely nodded, in exactly the same way as Philby, yet it communicated a great deal. Jemme thought it wisest to leave them to their own devices. Turning to leave, he saw Hil standing behind him,

'Oh, hello darling, I didn't realise you'd come in too.'

Hil looked irritated.

'It's impossible to hear anything above all this noise,' Jemme explained hurriedly, 'come on – let's go and unpack.' He put an arm around her waist and steered her out of the room, 'What did you think?' he asked eagerly. Hil raised an eyebrow and didn't say anything.

* * * *

Back in the kitchen, they scrabbled around in the cupboards looking for food. They had got into the habit of keeping the pantry relatively well-stocked with dried and tinned goods, and Philby usually ensured there were some fresh things in the fridge waiting for them on their arrival. However, Jemme had told Philby that the builders could help themselves to food whilst they were working, and it appeared that they had done just that. Hil unearthed half a packet of crispbread biscuits and Jemme found a tin of peaches. It made for rather a dismal supper and Hil didn't look too impressed.

'I'm afraid everything's going to be shut in the village at this time,' said Jemme, offering her a crispbread, 'I guess for tonight we'll just have to make do with this I'm afraid, sweetheart. Still, I suppose that's all part of the fun of it!'

Hil gave a rather wan smile and bit into the cracker, which very quickly revealed itself to be stale.

As he looked for a tin opener and two forks, Jemme wondered why he hadn't pre-empted this situation. The builders were only half-way through, and would need a great deal more feeding before the end of the project. They could always go to the village, but it was a bit of a walk, and if they left every time they wanted lunch or even supper, by the time they had walked there, found a café and then walked back again it would take a good chunk out of the working day. They were always free to bring their own food, of course, but it would be nice to be able to offer them something here. He thought some more. Of course, the builders were only really the start of it. In the near future, he envisioned the house being filled with decorators and craftsmen. Regardless of whether or not there was enough food for them in the kitchen, they would still need somewhere to wash their sheets and their clothes. Presumably they would generate a lot of mess too – it would be better to clear it up as is it happened, so that things didn't build up or get ground into the carpet. He didn't want to task the decorators and artists with such a job, as it would slow overall progress. He found what he was looking for, and opened the tin,

'Dinner is served!' he announced with a flourish, handing Hil a fork.

She couldn't help smiling, '*Bon appetit*!' she laughed. 'Goodness, look at us, in this great, historic building, eating straight from a can.'

'I know, it's not really ideal. You're being a good sport about it though, thank you. I've just been thinking about the whole thing. This is just the beginning of everything, and we're already encountering little problems like this. I want to make sure we're fully prepared for when work starts in earnest.'

'What do you mean?'

'I mean that embarking on this project is going to involve more than just hiring the specialists to work on the interiors.'

'Who else do you want to hire?!'

'Don't look so aghast,' Jemme laughed, 'I've just been realising that we're not going to get away without having domestic staff as well.'

'Domestic staff? But we already have Philby and Xelifon.'

'I know, and they're fantastic, but I suppose what I'm looking for is an indoor version of both of them. I need somebody to keep the same watchful eye over the house as they do over the garden.'

'A sort of housekeeper figure?'

'Precisely. I think I want exactly what the French would call a *regisseuse*: someone who could keep watch over the house and check that everything's in good working order. Once we start installing proper carpets in some of the rooms, and our antique furniture too, we're going to need everything to be kept clean and dust-free too. Also, it will mean we've got someone to manage the kitchen – they can make sure it's always stocked whilst there are people working here and when we're about to visit, too. If we're really lucky we'll find someone who's able to cook. Can you imagine how nice that would be? After the long drive from Paris, we'll arrive all tired and hungry after a full day's work, to find that there's a delicious, hot, home-cooked meal waiting for us.'

'That would be rather wonderful,' said Hil, looking at the domed piece of tinned fruit she had speared on the end of her fork. It was preternaturally bright, and she eyed it suspiciously, 'Rather wonderful indeed,' she muttered.

'That's what I thought,' Jemme said brightly, 'I thought we might as well start looking straight away. We can ask Philby if he could recommend anyone, and then maybe even interview them this weekend.'

'Sounds like a good idea,' said Hil, having another look at the peach and deciding against it. She forked it back into the tin and left it bobbing around in the syrupy liquid.

Hil woke a little before Jemme the next morning,

'Morning,' he said sleepily as he tried to focus his eyes on her.

'Morning – it's a lovely sunny day today.'

'Good, good,' he mumbled. 'I wonder why I'm so hungry,' he said, sitting up and rubbing his eyes, 'I'm not normally like this first thing in the morning.'

'You're hungry because we barely had any supper last night – I'm absolutely starving. The bad news is that there's nothing for breakfast either.'

'Ugh,' said Jemme sliding back down into bed again.

'Are we still going to go on a day trip?'

'Of course!'

'Well, why don't we get going as soon as possible – we can get breakfast somewhere along the way.'

Jemme looked heartened and sat back up again, 'That, my love, is the kind of thinking that makes me glad I married you.'

He got out of bed, pulled on some trousers and, whilst tucking a shirt into them, went off to find Philby. He found him near the rose beds at the front of the house, and explained that he was hoping to take on some more domestic staff.

Philby looked puzzled, and so he clarified, 'Someone who can manage the house in the same way you manage its grounds. I really want someone who's a sort of housekeeper, cook and domestic manager all rolled into one.'

'Ahhh, a *regisseuse,* Monsieur?'

'Precisely! Do you think you'll be able to find anyone?'

Philby leaned on the top of his spade and thought for a moment, 'Might do, Monsieur. I will think.'

'Thank you, I should add that I don't want anyone to replace you – both Hil and I are tremendously grateful for everything you've done so far. The *regisseur* – or *regisseuse* – would be complementing you, rather than taking over from you.'

The edges of Philby's weather-beaten face softened slightly, and Jemme knew him well enough by now to know that that signalled he was gratified. He left him tending to the roses whilst he went back in to find Hil. She was already dressed and waiting for him in the hall.

'Excellent – you were quick. Shall we head off?'

'Absolutely. The sooner we find somewhere to eat the better!'

'I couldn't agree more!'

They headed over to the car, with Hil stopping to admire Philby's work along the way.

'So, where are we off to?' asked Hil, once they had turned off at the top of the driveway.

'I know we never got round to actually discussing it, but I thought of a place yesterday which would be nice to explore, and might be of interest.'

Hil looked at him questioningly.

'Lisieux,' said Jemme, 'it's not actually that far from here and I thought it would be interesting to visit the birthplace of a local saint, having recently seen a shrine to her.'

'That's a nice idea. Do you know much about the place?'

'Not really to be honest, just that it's very old, was the birthplace of St Thérèse and was bombed quite heavily during the war. Parts of it are really lovely though.'

'Well, I'm looking forward to exploring it.'

'Me too – do say when you see somewhere you'd like to stop for breakfast by the way.'

Only a few moments later, Hil saw a café on the left,

'Oooh, here! Stop!'

Jemme pulled up outside a typical little Norman café. Clad in grey stone with window boxes of brightly coloured geraniums, it had cheerful yellow awnings which had been pulled out, with a couple of tables set up underneath each one.

'I think it might be warm enough to sit out. What do you reckon?' Jemme asked Hil.

'I think so,' she replied. Moments later they were greedily tearing chunks out of the basket of fluffy pastries Madame had set in front of them. They washed them down with large *bols* of café-au-lait whilst the car sat in front of them, its engine ticking and clicking as it cooled. Refreshed and replenished, they settled their very modest bill and continued on the road to the cathedral city. It was just after ten-thirty when they arrived, and a little market was already well underway in front of the town hall. It was all classically French, and they wandered between the stalls where old men stood behind boxes of vegetables, shouting their wares, and pretty young girls sold brightly coloured sugared almonds from stalls decorated with dainty lace table cloths. Hil bought a couple of glossy red apples for them to snack on later, and they strolled along to the basilica. The old town was cobbled and charming, with old fashioned little shops in half-timbered buildings. However, every so often a stark reminder of the town's suffering poked its way through this fairy-tale fabric, like a jagged tooth. Halfway along an ancient street, a starkly modern building, utilitarian and functional, served as a reminder of the hurried reconstruction in the post-war aftermath. Bleak concrete walls sat side by side with delicately carved stone arches and elaborately carved window frames.

'What a pity they couldn't have made things blend in a little more,' said Hil as they walked past one particularly charmless edifice.

'You see this all over France, especially in areas of strategic importance, such as this,' said Jemme. 'You're right, it is a pity, and half of me wishes that things had been restored to exactly as they were before. However, half of me also thinks it's important that we have these reminders. It's all part of the town's story, and we can't choose to visually erase such an important episode.'

'I suppose you're right, and it is a rather forceful reminder. It's just easy to become rather sentimental and yearn for something a bit more picture-postcard. It's a rather strange pattern though – look how a whole row of houses has survived except one. I wouldn't have expected it to be as precise as that.'

'I know, sometimes it almost seems as if its predetermined – you'll find whole towns have been flattened, but the oldest or most beautiful buildings have been left completely intact, standing unscratched in the middle of the rubble. The cathedral here is a good example of that.'

'Did it survive?'

'Perfectly. I suppose once something has stood strong for eight hundred years, a bit of bombing isn't going to phase it.'

'I suppose not!'

Labour *of* Love

'Here we are now, it should be just around this corner,' said Jemme as they turned off the narrow street they were on.

A small square spread out in front of them and sitting on the opposite side was the Cathédral Saint Pierre de Lisieux. They both stood for a moment and looked at it.

'It's beautiful,' said Hil, 'I think even more so, knowing what it's survived.'

'I know, it feels like it has even more significance in some way.'

They crossed the small square, craning their heads backwards as they approached, trying to take in the façade. It was very gothic, with flying buttresses, ribbed vaulting and fearsome gargoyles. It was difficult not to be filled with a vague sense of awe whilst looking at it, something which was only magnified when considering how many people would have experienced a similar sensation looking up, standing on the exact spot over the centuries. Inside, the cathedral was a little more austere. A long nave led them up to a high altar, sumptuously decorated with an embroidered cover. The side chapels commemorated various sons of the town, and a particularly moving dedication in one of them acknowledged the sacrifices of the young men in the region during both World Wars. Finally they reached the Lady Chapel, which was dedicated to Saint Thérèse. A large painting of her hung from the wall, and was surrounded by small bronze dedicational plaques, which gave the name of the benefactor, the date and often a heartfelt message. In front of the painting, the floor was covered with posies of flowers and small candles, flickering in jars. She was obviously a much cherished saint and, judging by some of the messages left with the flowers, people had come from far and wide to visit her chapel. Another wall was hung with black and white photos, featuring the same rounded face with piercing eyes which had so reminded Jemme of Grandma before. Boards either side of the photos gave further information about her life and her connection with the town. Jemme and Hil stood in the silent stillness of the chapel, hand-in-hand, reading about the young woman's life and beatification. Suddenly, something fired off inside Jemme's mind. He experienced the same sense of tingling consciousness he had before when he had realised that St Thérèse bore a remarkable resemblance to Lily. He studied the information at the top of the second plaque again, but he had been right. Thérèse's life had crossed over with Lily's by quite a significant margin. His grandmother would have been about fifteen when St Thérèse had died; an intriguing thought. He liked the idea of them both existing within the same age and time, with the potential, however remote, that they might even have met. Regardless of whether they had or not, there were still so many things which would have connected them, and which keyed St Thérèse into Grandma's sphere and own story. They both would have looked at the same moon every night, and experienced the world change in the same way. On any given night, whilst Thérèse was lying in her bed in a Carmelite cell, gazing through the window at the stars, Lily might have been looking up at the same stars, lying in the cushioned liwan on a hot Turkish night. As they lay, they might have shared the same thoughts, questioned the same pieces of wisdom and divined new understanding and wisdom of their very own. There were so many personality traits they shared as well – intellectual curiosity and rigour, sagacity, gentleness. Jemme felt the warmth of comfort spread out across his body, reaching the very tips of his fingers. It felt as if he understood yet another connection, and he had taken one step further in arriving at where he was meant to be. He knew that he had made the right decision about the house, and that his grandmother would approve. The chateau was meant to be looked at as part of an integrated whole, just as these two women's lives had been. Satisfied, he squeezed Hil's hand and looked at her questioningly. She nodded, and they both left the cathedral as silently as they had entered it.

Once back outside they wandered from crêperie to café. Just like many of Normandy's market towns, this one was a cradle of produce; shops groaned with stacks of cheeses and bottles of Calvados, whilst menus positively dripped with butter and cream, great choices of Camembert and other famous cheeses. By the time they finally got back to the car, they were both carrying very full bags, and there was no danger of being without food in the chateau for a while. The drive back was a happy and relaxed one, with both of them chattering eagerly about the town and the area in general. Having looked at the cathedral, they had discovered an even bigger monument to St Thérèse – a basilica which was the second greatest pilgrimage site in France, after Lourdes. Hil was looking forward to telling her mother – a staunch Catholic – that they had been to such an important place. For his part, Jemme shared his realisation that Thérèse and Lily had both been alive at the same time. Although Hil thought it was interesting, she clearly didn't feel the same way about what Jemme felt was its great significance. By the time they reached the chateau, it was dark again. They went straight to the kitchen to unpack all their goods. Seeing them all laid out on the kitchen counter, they both started to feel slightly hungry and, within moments, Jemme was emptying a glass jar of lobster bisque into a saucepan, and Hil was gently sliding a tarte tatin onto a serving plate. They had just settled down to enjoy their feast when there was a knock on the kitchen door.

'*Excusez-moi, Monsieur, Madame*, I did not mean to interrupt.'

'Not at all, Philby, please – come in, we're just having an early supper.'

'How did you find Lisieux?' he asked politely.

'Very nice indeed, thank you,' replied Hil, 'there were very pretty bits indeed.'

'Did you like the Cathèdral, Madame?'

'Yes, I did – we did in fact. It's remarkable it's survived this long when there was so much damage to the area. You can see it all over the town – great modern buildings right next to very old ones.'

A momentary sadness flickered in Philby's eyes, 'Much of this area suffered, Madame. There are many towns in northern France like that.'

'Yes, that's just what Jemme said.' Hil said. 'Still, it was a lovely place, and I expect I'll go back at some point.'

'What have you been up to today, Philby?' asked Jemme jovially as he spooned delicate bisque into his mouth.

'Today I have worked on the roses, Monsieur, but in the afternoon I went into the village to see if I could find a *regisseuse*.'

'Ah, excellent. Do you know, I'd almost forgotten about that! How did you get along?'

'Well, Monsieur. The aunt of my neighbour's friend is available for work. She has spent twenty years in Lyon, managing a small hotel there, so she is used to running households. I have asked her to come and meet you tomorrow.'

'Well that's very good news -- and what quick work too. Thank you, Philby. By the way, do you know if she can cook?'

'*Oui, Monsieur*, she is a cook *par excellence*. My neighbour talked to me for a full ten minutes about her coq-au-vin.'

Jemme's mouth twitched at the sides slightly as he struggled to suppress a smile, 'Well, in that case I shall make sure to ask her about it tomorrow. What's her name, by way Philby?'

'Marguerite.'

'That's a nice name,' said Hil, 'We're looking forward to meeting her already. Thank you for arranging it all.'

As was his wont, Philby furrowed his brow and nodded gruffly to acknowledge their thanks.

The following day Jemme and Hil woke with the knowledge that an excellent breakfast was waiting for them in the kitchen. They spent a pleasant morning, during which the noise of the builders was barely audible. Hil seemed to have relaxed a great deal about the fact that the work was going on, and even seemed amenable to the idea that it would be on a prolonged basis. In the afternoon, she curled up and read, on the pretty velvet chaise longue in the bedroom, and Jemme thought some more about the previous day. He realised that there was another reason he had been so fascinated by Thérèse and Grandma's co-existence. He thought back to childhood, and how he would wonder at Grandma's great age. He remembered thinking about how, if Grandma was together with her own grandmother, just how much time their combined life spanned. He remembered the wonder with which he had thought of Grandma's grandma, at her very oldest, providing a tangible, living link with history and the past. Memories of that realisation had flooded back to him in the cathedral in Lisieux. If only he could meet someone who had actually met Thérèse, he would once again experience the thrill which came with engaging directly with history. He recalled the date she had died – it would be highly unlikely that that was possible. Even if, by some remote chance there was someone who was still alive, they would have been no more than an infant at the time Thérèse died. It was a shame, but he had enjoyed the hypothetical link with Grandma all the same. As he waited for Marguerite to arrive, he thought that it might be nice to include the saint somewhere in the chateau – perhaps reference her in one of the French rooms.

Jemme had just gone down to make Hil and himself a cup of tea when there was a knock at the kitchen door. Philby stood next to a middle-aged woman with a thick crop of curly brown hair and flushed cheeks.

'Come in!' said Jemme opening the door for them both, 'you must be Marguerite – here, take a seat. You can have one of these teas too – I'll just make my wife another.'

'Oooh, *magnifique!*' said the woman, squeezing herself into the seat Jemme had pulled out for her. She was plump and jolly and seemed like the sturdy type of country woman, raised on a diet of eggs and beef, who was so loved by novelists of the last century. Her face was smooth, and her hair richly coloured, which made her difficult to age, but Jemme put her in her mid-forties. When he handed her her tea, he noticed that in contrast to the smooth skin of her cheeks, her hands were rough with short nails – evidently those of someone who had spent a lifetime working. As she fussed around, unwinding her long scarf and settling into the chair, Jemme couldn't help warming to her – she had the air of a mother goose and he could just picture her telling off various burly builders for traipsing mud into the house.

She took a sip of tea and smacked her lips, 'Ahh, this is excellent, Monsieur! I do like tea the way the English take it!'

Jemme smiled, 'Well, actually I'm Turkish, and my wife's Irish, but I'm pleased you like the tea!'

'Oh, I see – it's just that Monsieur Philby told me that English is always spoken in this household.'

'Yes, my wife and I speak English to each other – I've been fluent for all of my adult life, and we just find it easier that way. Do you speak any at all?'

Marguerite shook her head, and her curls bobbed around, '*Non, monsieur,*' she said emphatically. 'Sometimes I have tried, but it does not come out right.' She paused and with great concentration pursed her lips and enunciated the word '*Taaay.*' Jemme looked confused.

'It is how the English pronounce *thé,* Monsieur,' she said brightly.

Jemme looked amused, 'Of course, my apologies. There's no need for you to worry though. Both my wife and I are fluent in French. We've lived in Paris for many years.'

'Is that where you live now, Monsieur? Would you not rather live here where the air is fresh and the cream is thick?'

'To be honest, at the moment that's all I want. It's a bit more complicated than that though. We both work over in Paris, and this place needs a lot more to be done on it before we could move in. We spend pretty much every weekend here though, and it's rapidly becoming my favourite part of the week.'

'*Ah bon*,' said Marguerite, stretching back in her chair, 'I can see why – I love this place. I've wanted to see what it looks like on the inside since I was a little girl.'

'Well, I hope you're not too disappointed.'

'Disappointed, Monsieur? No, no not at all. Tell me though, if you and Madame are not here during the week, why do you need a *regisseuse*?'

'Ah, well, although we won't be here during the week, we're expecting lots of people will be.'

Marguerite cocked her head to one side like a small bird, 'Monsieur?'

'Well, like I said – we're doing a lot of work on the house. Some rooms need restoring back to how they were originally, and we're converting some of them too. It means we'll have lots of builders around and then, towards the end, lots of painters and decorators too.'

Marguerite nodded slowly, 'Do the rooms need restoring, Monsieur?'

'I'm afraid so. Whilst some of them are all right, it's just the bare bones – we'll need to buy the right kind of curtains, carpets and antiques for them, to bring them back to how they would have looked. Others are in a rather sorry state though. I don't know if it was due to one specific owner or generations of neglect, but they've not been treated with the respect they were due.'

Marguerite tutted, 'I'm sure that it will have been the *gouvernement*, Monsieur. They were not popular around here, and I would not be surprised if they had done awful things to this place. There were all sorts of rumours going around the village when they left – some people said that an American had bought it and he was going to knock it down.' She shook her head, 'I am glad I have finally met the new owner though, and that you are going to be doing such good things for the chateau. It's an important part of our history here.'

'I'm pleased to hear it; I'm really looking forward to bringing everything back to life again too. As I mentioned though, there will be lots of people coming and going and we'll need someone on hand to coordinate things and make sure the house is kept in shape.'

Marguerite sat up in her chair. She had so far been chirpy, bordering on the scatty. Once Jemme mentioned household management however, she instantly focussed, and was as sharp as a pin. She talked him through her experience so far, and asked him some pertinent questions about the project. She rattled off a list of things he would need to think about – regular suppliers, surveyors, gas safety inspectors and the suchlike. 'If I am to cook for everyone,' she said, 'the kitchen will need to be up to commercial standards. It will need a deep clean straight away, a new cooker, which will mean new grease traps, and you'll need a larger fridge too.' She ticked off a few more points on her fingers and Jemme listened carefully. They were things he hadn't really thought of, but she was right – if the project was going to be big enough to warrant a household manager, he would need to start thinking about certain things in a new light. Marguerite seemed to know exactly what those things were, and what's more, she seemed to know how to deal with them too. Jemme was impressed.

'Thank you, that's all excellent advice. I'd like you to meet my wife, if that's all right. She's just upstairs – if you wait here a moment I'll go and fetch her.'

Jemme dashed off and returned a few minutes later, 'She'll be down shortly. Whilst we're waiting for her, why don't you tell me a little about what sort of food you like to cook?'

'Oooh, Monsieur,' said Marguerite, squeezing her hands in glee, 'I make the most *formidable* coq-au-vin....'

Jemme smiled as she descended into an adjective-heavy description, which lasted for a good five minutes.

✻ ✻ ✻ ✻

Driving to the chateau the following weekend, Jemme turned to Hil,

'Isn't it strange to think what a difference a week can make? By the time we get there, the builders will have finished their work and our new housekeeper will have prepared a delicious meal for us.'

'I know. I have to say I'm pleased about both of those things. I really liked Marguerite too, although she was chatty and bubbly, I got the impression she wouldn't suffer fools gladly, which is exactly what we need.'

'I thought so too – I can imagine her whipping everyone into shape. I bet she's settled in already.'

'I really like the way we're employing so many people from the area, too. It makes us seem less like the out-of-towners.'

'Definitely. Marguerite was saying that there was some hostility between the locals and the ministry when they owned the place, and I don't want that to be the case with us. Also, the advantage of being on good terms with local people is that we get to hear stories from the chateau's past. I bet Marguerite's full of them; she reeled off about three during our interview alone.'

Marguerite was waiting to greet them with Philby. She had an apron tied round her waist and a small smudge of flour on her forehead.

'*Bienvenu, Bienvenu!*' she said, bustling around them, '*Monsieur Philby, les valises!*' she trilled.

Jemme looked on in slight concern. He didn't think Philby would respond to such direct orders particularly well. To his surprise, however, Philby was actually smiling in amusement. Jemme thought it was probably the first time he had seen an outright grin on his gardener's face. Although he didn't rush to it, he at least lumbered over and picked up the suitcases for them.

'Thank you, Philby,' said Jemme.

Philby shrugged, 'I always carry the suitcases for Monsieur.'

Jemme and Hil followed them both in. Even from the hall they could smell something delicious emanating from the kitchen.

'Marguerite, something is making me hungry already!' said Jemme.

'*Ah bon, Monsieur*?' Marguerite chuckled as she wiped her hands on her apron. 'That is the dessert you smell'

'Mmmm, what is it?' asked Hil.

'It is *teurgoule*, Madame – a typical dish from this area.'

'How exciting! What's in it?'

'*Du riz, Madame*. It is like a pudding made from rice. We add the special, thick milk from our cows, then cinnamon, and bake it all afternoon in the oven as it cools down from making bread in the morning.'

'We have a similar thing back in Ireland, but it doesn't smell half as good as yours – I'm looking forward to trying it.'

'Does that mean you were making bread this morning as well, Marguerite?' Jemme interjected.

Marguerite shrugged, '*Bien sur, Monsieur*.' She led them upstairs, and Philby fell into line behind them, bringing up their cases. Jemme and Hil exchanged glances behind her back – things were working out well already.

Up in the bedroom, she had made the bed up with clean sheets for them and put out fresh towels.

'The wardrobe was a bit dusty, so I have cleaned it out for you. Also, I have put in some more hangers – I don't know *what* you put your clothes on before!' Marguerite chuckled. '*Dîner* is ready whenever you like. I'll talk to you about breakfast after you've finished eating.'

Hil yawned contentedly, 'Marguerite, I can't tell you how wonderful this all is – this is the reception I've always dreamed of!'

'Tsk, Madame, it is nothing,' Marguerite scolded, 'When will you eat? I will keep your food warm for you.'

'Actually, we'll probably follow you down now,' said Jemme, 'I'll look at the builders' work with Philby tomorrow morning.'

'*Bon*,' said Marguerite decisively and spun round to lead the way back downstairs again.

Getting back to the kitchen involved descending down the grand main staircase and crossing the reception Halle d'Honneur. However, the landing the bedroom opened onto was a large platform which jutted out over the hallway below, enclosed by stone balustrade. It was like a large, internal balcony and made a rather striking, but intriguing feature. As they crossed over it, a thought struck Jemme,

'Marguerite, I've always wondered about this–'

'The *balcon*, Monsieur?'

'Yes, the *balcon*. I've never really understood its purpose. It seems to be original to this part of the house, but I don't really know much about it. I was wondering if you had any idea?'

'*Ben oui*, of course, Monsieur! This is for the master of the house to receive guests. You see – it is attached to the master bedroom, where you and Madame sleep. In olden times, the servant would allow the guests into the hall here and welcome them, then fetch the master via the back stairs. He can walk out onto this balcony and greet his guest before going down to meet them. It is a common feature in French chateaux like this one, especially ones which were popular with society.'

'Was this chateau popular with society?' asked Hil.

'Oh, Madame, yes! My grandmother lived in the village her whole life, and when I was younger I remember she would tell me of the fancy balls they would have here. She worked as a kitchen maid when she was young, and she used to go home and entertain her whole family with stories of the ladies' dresses and the parties they would have.'

'How wonderful!' said Hil, 'I don't suppose you remember any of them?'

'Ah, Madame, it was a long time ago now. I think she said that there were very popular parties here for debutantes. All the young ladies from the polite society in Rouen and Bayeux would come here.'

Hil smiled, evidently imagining the old world glamour of the occasion, and the excitement of carriages making their way down the long driveway and their beautiful occupants making their way into the grand hall, lit by candles.

'Do you remember anything else?' she urged.

'Not too much, Madame, I know that the young ladies would have gathered up here before being presented below. Some fancy liveried man would have called their name and they would have walked down these stairs. I think people might have applauded as they came down, but I'm not sure. *La classe, non*?' she asked, noticing Hil's enraptured expression.

'It's all quite fairy-tale like,' Hil said happily, 'I'm just trying to imagine it now. It's so fascinating to think about the furniture of this chateau cropping up in other people's lives in the past, and having completely different meanings.'

Marguerite clasped her hands to her chest, 'Oh, but that is just the beginning! I can tell you so many more stories just about these *escaliers*!'

'Really?' asked Jemme.

Marguerite nodded vigorously, '*Oui, oui*, although it may take me a while to remember all of them... Ha! I can think of one though which might amuse you. Did you know that this chateau was occupied during the war?'

'I think so, although that's something I've been wanting to research a little more,' said Jemme.

Marguerite shook her head, '*Nazies, Monsieur, pleine de Nazies.* When *la France* was occupied, they took many chateaux in the north as their military bases. Some were used as headquarters in Normandy, some were used as a second defence line, and other were used only for fun. They did dreadful things, Monsieur – they ripped down paintings, used noble families' china for shooting practice and all sorts. I am sure this place would have lost many of its treasures during that time. It is a long story, and if you ever look at the local history of this area you will see why it is all so strange, but the Germans here should have left ages beforehand.'

Jemme and Hil looked confused.

'I mean that most of their side had already retreated,' explained Marguerite. 'There was a large Canadian siege on Falaise and it turned the tide for the Germans. But! There was still a chance for them to escape!' she said dramatically, 'the Falaise-Argentan pocket was unprotected by the Allies, so the Germans could escape. So many of them did, as fast as they could. I don't know why the Germans here didn't, maybe they were exhausted from fighting; maybe it is because our village has some of the best produce in the whole of the *Département;* maybe it was even because the chateau was so comfortable for them and the grounds so pleasant, but they did not even try to escape. There is a story in the village that a young private ran into this very hall early in the morning, before the sun was even up. He was in a flurry and began shouting at the top of his voice as soon as he got in. He stood below this very balcony and shouted up "General, General!" – the general would have been in this master bedroom you see – "General, Falaise has fallen and the Allies are coming." The general appeared from this very bedroom – as he was doing up his dressing gown no less! He looked down at the young soldier, and the soldier shouted up at him, "General, General, we are outnumbered – we have lost many men! What are your orders?"'

Jemme and Hil looked at Marguerite in anticipation, 'What happened next?!'

'Well, like I said, Monsieur, I think they must have been weary of the battle. The general looked down at the young soldier with his panicked face and he swore in German – "*Sheiße*!" Then he said, "I'm going back to bed. Those are my orders – go to bed." Can you imagine such a thing?' she chuckled, 'I prefer to think of it as a compliment to our village. They would rather be captured than run away from such a place. Now – no more stories or my *teurgoule* will burn to the bottom of the pan.' She shooed them downstairs like they were naughty children, and then wouldn't take no for an answer when doling out seconds in the kitchen. By the time they went to bed, with very full bellies, it was with the comforting sense that comes from knowing that one is being looked after, a sort of nursery-like sense of security.

'I'm so pleased we've got her here,' said Hil sleepily, 'It feels like a weight's been taken off my shoulders and we can really relax whilst we're down here. Plus, I can't wait to hear more of her stories.'

'I know!' said Jemme, shaking his head and laughing, 'What a character she is. It's so nice knowing that someone else will deal with all the day to day running of things, too – you're right, it feels like a lot of pressure has been removed and we can focus on other things whilst we're here.'

'Like relaxing?' said Hil hopefully.

'Sort of,' said Jemme, 'more a mix of relaxing and ploughing onwards with the project.'

'I don't really see how one lends itself to the other,' said Hil plainly, before rolling over and going to sleep.

The next morning her spirits were lifted again by coming downstairs to a wonderful breakfast, laid out for them by Marguerite.

'No more foraging in the cupboards for us!' said Jemme as he tucked a napkin to his neck and sat down. 'Marguerite, this is delicious!' he called through to the pantry, and tore off a hunk of the homemade bread she had baked yesterday.

Marguerite emerged into the kitchen, '*Ah, bonjour! Merci, Monsieur* – I am glad you are enjoying it, I enjoy making bread, it is a very satisfying thing. Although, I don't know if I shall bother when it is just the builders,' she said with a slight note of conspiracy in her voice.

'I shouldn't think they'll complain too much!' said Jemme.

'*Ah bon*,' Marguerite shrugged, 'Tell me, Monsieur, I've been wondering – what do people eat for breakfast in Turkey?'

Whilst Jemme described the bowls of creamy yoghurt, dishes of exotic spices and jars of honey, Hil made the most of the opportunity to help herself to the lion's share of the pot of jam Marguerite had put out. It was a rich, purplish-red colour, and whole, pristine cherries had survived the jam-making process.

'Did you make this, Marguerite?' asked Hil, 'it's wonderful.'

'Of course!' said Marguerite, 'I enjoy making jam – it is so satisfying. I don't like buying these jam and pickles they sell in shops – you never know what they've put in them. There were so many cherries left in my garden last summer – far too many to eat, so I made jam out of them. Monsieur Philby tells me he is to discuss the orchard with you. There used to be a wonderful orchard here, but it needs some attention. If you restore it I would like to make things from any produce you don't eat – jams and pies and so on. I'm already enjoying using the herbs Xelifon has grown.'

'I'd like that too – there's something about eating things grown in your own garden. It's so...'

'Satisfying?' ventured Marguerite.

Jemme smiled, 'Something like that! I'm looking forward to discussing this orchard plan with Philby, once we've inspected the building works.'

After finishing breakfast, which Hil described as 'very satisfying', Jemme went off to find Philby. He didn't have to look far and soon came across him in the rose beds at the front. Although he had only been working on them for a few short weeks, they had already come along in leaps and bounds.

'Philby, these look fantastic, Hil will be delighted when she sees them!'

'*Merci, Monsieur*. They seem to be taking to the soil very well. It is nice that so much of the house is being put back to how it should be.'

'I'm pleased you think so; from my point of view, it all feels like it's finally getting started. Talking of which, how did everything go with the builders?'

'*Très bien, Monsieur*. They finished on time, and cleared away properly after themselves. Madame Marguerite went around after them and cleaned everything afterwards – you'd never know they were there.'

'Well that's all excellent news. I wasn't expecting it all to be that easy to be honest. Let's hope the rest of the project goes as smoothly! Can we go and look when you've finished?'

'We can go now, Monsieur,' said Philby, removing his gloves and stepping out of the rose beds.

'Oh, no I don't want to interrupt,' said Jemme.

'It's no trouble, Monsieur,' said Philby, phlegmatic as ever.

He led the way into the section of the chateau which had had been covered in dustsheets and filled with burly builders the last time Jemme had seen it. Now, it was completely transformed. Philby was right – if it hadn't been for the slight smell of new paint, no-one would ever have guessed that only a few days ago it was still a *chantier*.

'This is fantastic,' Jemme murmured, 'precisely what I was hoping for.'

He walked down the newly formed corridor. Either side of him, doors opened onto small, perfectly proportioned individual rooms. Each was fresh and white, and brand-new, factory-fresh blank canvas. He could do whatever he liked with them. He felt a thrill of excitement and was reminded again of seeing the dollhouse. Each room was like a little secret cubbyhole for him to fill. It was impossible to ignore the sense of play he felt. Things could be put into these rooms and taken out, rearranged and removed at his whim until he had created something perfect. The project was stirring to life in front of his eyes. Just like the rooms of his dream, which shifted their shape and grew and shrank, in front of his very eyes, these rooms had sprung up from nowhere, morphing and adapting the topography of his home until it matched the vision in his head. He felt strangely powerful and alive with excitement at what the future could hold. This was just the very beginning.

Chapter Seventeen

Jemme couldn't wait to get started on his new rooms. Even though they were smaller than the other rooms in the house, they felt cavernously empty and he yearned to stock them with treasures and fill them with meaning. However, he recognised that these rooms were very much for him. Although Hil had taken a great interest in them, they were still his pet project, and would transform a part of the house that he would enjoy the most. She had been so understanding and flexible around the project recently, and had barely even mentioned the fact that they were spending so much time out of Paris. It seemed only fair that the first room he should dedicate his time and efforts into finishing should be one that they could share equally. He wandered through the new rooms and down to the central core of the chateau, where the grand noble rooms spread out in front of him. He was excited about these being finished too, although in a completely different kind of way. The gallery display rooms marked the realisation of a childhood dream, a narrative impulse which had driven him forward throughout his life. However, the grand noble rooms would mark a different aspect of his realisation. With all their finery and lovingly restored history, they would endorse his success as a self-made man. No longer was he merely living in a rented Parisian flat; he would now become the guardian of a little piece of French history. He knew Hil had been longing for the completion of these rooms too. When they had first started looking at chateaux together, she had talked excitedly about hosting wonderful dinner receptions, and having friends and family over to stay.

She had persevered with him for so long, and been constantly by his side during all the terrible real estate viewings they had attended, that now it was time to do something for her. He wandered around the noble rooms, trying to imagine how he would like them to look when finished. It was hard to know where to start – with the most important, or the easiest? In a way it made sense to start with the most complicated room. It would lay bare all the problems it was possible to encounter, and help him understand what would be needed when taking on future rooms. If he could prepare properly, then he could ensure that the project would run as smoothly as possible. He wandered through the rooms, occasionally stopping to trace his path on the blueprints and check the proportions the architect had detailed. Although he was wandering without much direction or purpose, he kept finding himself back in one particular room. It was in a rather sorry state, with great patches of damp spreading out across the ceiling like clouds. He unfurled the plans and peered at them. The design consultants he had hired had simply labelled the room 'salon'. Rolling the plans up, he wandered thoughtfully around the room. It certainly needed a great deal of work, but what sort of work? How could he go about choosing a decorative theme and furniture when it wasn't governed by the same aims as the newly designed rooms?

He thought about the library and his desire to restore it to how it would have looked in its original state. This room could be transformed back into a magnificent salon, without any shadow of a doubt. Its high ceilings, large windows and grand proportions made for an impressive empty shell, and Jemme tried to imagine how it would look bedecked with rich tapestries, hung with sumptuous curtains and filled with ornate gilded furniture. A salon would also provide an excellent entertaining space, and give Hil a reassuring taste of what was to come. What's more, there was so much work to be done on this room that it posed the suitably tough challenge Jemme had been hoping for. The idea of starting with this room grew on him, the longer he stood in it. His feet had repeatedly led him back here for a reason and he had never had recourse to doubt his instinct before. As he looked around at the bare walls and scuffed floor, he tried to imagine the clinking of glasses and the sound of laughter of the room filled with friends and family. Yes, this was definitely the starting off point he had been looking for. He looked at the plans again and felt as if he was metaphorically putting in a pin within the square blue outlines of the room: this would be where it all began.

A brief, satisfied smile flickered across his face, only to disappear quickly when he remembered that he had no idea how to go about designing the room. He wanted there to be no element of fantasy, no vignettes of past civilisations, mythical leaders or splendid palaces. This was to be a proper, straight-forward room, of the sort one might expect to encounter in a grand property. However, it still had to have meaning of some sort. The whole chateau project revolved around the conceit that decoration was a pointer towards something more significant. He was planning on using the décor in the new rooms to tell a story, and could not let it exist here merely in an aesthetic state. He furrowed his brow; there had to be some way of incorporating the philosophy he was developing in the room, somehow. He wanted these noble rooms to reflect the chateau's French history and context, so perhaps he could reference a particular period or event with this room. Perhaps even a person? He had previously toyed with the idea of focusing on notable French kings in the *corps* of the chateau; perhaps that was where the answer lay. He could select antiques from a particular monarch's reign, and choose furnishings that reflected trends and fashions of the time. He warmed to the idea – what an excellent way of showcasing broader influences and various era-defining events it was. Sitting down on the sill of one of the windows, he mulled over various French kings in his mind. There were a few gaps, but on the whole he was quite well-versed in the royal houses, from Valois through to Bourbon. The trouble was that there were so many kings; he didn't know how to begin selecting just one. They were also well-known for different reasons too -and not always positive ones.

Charlemagne made an interesting choice: crowned Holy Roman Emperor, he had been instrumental in the development of Western Europe and defined the character of mediaeval European culture. However, he did not want to ape the decorative stylings of a ruler who lived in the eighth century, in one of the noble rooms. He thought again; Louis X was another interesting choice. He had freed the serfs and allowed the Jews to live freely in France, overturning the exile imposed by Philip IV before him. Jemme liked the idea of referencing a king who promoted harmonious co-existence between different peoples, and thought how neatly this symbolised some of his expositional aims within the chateau. However, Louis had also been known as *le Hutin*, the quarreller, and his reign had been characterised by tension arising from his headstrong personality, which also strained international relationships. That didn't sit very well with the philosophy of the chateau at all. He shifted round in his seat until he was looking out of the window across the grounds. 'What would make this room truly special?' he asked himself. The sun was beginning to set just behind the copse he had first sat in with Hil on the day they had bought the chateau. He stared at it for a few moments, allowing himself to wallow in nostalgia. He thought back to how fresh everything felt back then, and pondered the exciting nature of beginnings for a while. Suddenly it came to him – it seemed so obvious. Someone who represented not only the end of a chapter of French history, but the beginning of a new one: Louis XVI, the last king of France.

He looked at the setting sun again and smiled. It was perfect. Louis' reign saw the death of the *ancien regime* and also the birth of the First Republic. It was an important and transitional period in history, rich in decorative ideas and furnishings. He thought back to all the Louis XVI era artefacts he had seen in auction showrooms and museums over the years; the gilded furniture, the sumptuous late-baroque plasterwork and the playful curlicues of early rococo. They would all lend themselves perfectly to a formal reception room, and would set high standards for the rest of the chateau. It would be fun too, tracking down all the pieces of furniture he would need, and piecing the whole room together. Pleased and excited about this early first stage, he set the plans down on the windowsill and decided to catch the last of the evening's light outside.

Although the light was fading rapidly, there was still enough for a quick lap of the lake and Jemme enjoyed the chance of some fresh air before supper. It had been another weekend of Hil staying in Paris. He didn't blame her, and was pleased that ownership of the chateau wasn't forcing her to give up her old life. It was different for him; he didn't feel that he had fully relinquished one life, but he didn't feel like he had properly started another yet either. He couldn't completely think of the chateau as being home, but he no longer thought of the Paris flat as being home either. It was the eternal paradox of the immigrant and he remembered his discussion with Emil Dahan. The architect had told him that someone who leaves their homeland is destined never to feel at home in any one place, and he couldn't help but agree.

It didn't change how much he missed Hil when he was here on his own, though. Sometimes it was hard not to feel lonely and like he was rattling around in an empty old house. He knew it would be different when work was properly underway, and with all the staff he was never truly alone; but still, it just wasn't the same without Hil. He wished she was there to wander by the lake with. Everything was always so much more fun when she was there and time seemed to simply fly by. Although there never seemed to be enough hours in the day when he was working on plans for the chateau, the evenings seemed to positively drag. After so many years of marriage, he wasn't used to being on his own, and he was rapidly coming to realise that he didn't much like it.

Walking back through the copse to the house, he felt grateful that Marguerite would be busy at work in the kitchen. He had been working in a different section of the house and so hadn't seen another soul all day. As he approached the house from the western side he could see the kitchen window was a warm rectangle of light. His heart lifted and he tried to put his rather melancholy thoughts from his mind; he knew Marguerite would be making something tasty, cooking up some wonderful local speciality, and the kitchen would be a cosy enclave of spices and smells. It hit him as soon as he opened the door and a warm fug enveloped him.

'*Bonsoir, Marguerite!*' he said, slightly forcing the cheeriness.

Marguerite span round, wooden spoon in hand, 'Monsieur! Come in, come in – my! Were you walking around in the *jardin* in the dark?!' she scolded.

'It wasn't dark when I went out, I just wanted to get some fresh air and sharpen my appetite,' said Jemme, smiling much more genuinely this time.

Marguerite looked briefly approving and then cross again. She turned around and stirred her pot again, clucking about men who lurk around in the *jardin* like ghosts.

'What are you cooking?' asked Jemme, keen to get back in her good books, 'It smells wonderful!'

'Ah, Monsieur, you know how to charm an old *governant*,' Marguerite replied, wiping her hands down on her apron. She put the lid back on the large pot where it sat rattling as whatever was inside continued to bubble away. 'This,' she continued, evidently pleased by his curiosity, 'is *poule au pot*. It is quite simple, but very tasty. My grandmother told me that Henri IV said every family in France should be able to eat this dish at least once a week.'

'What's in it?' asked Jemme.

'A large hen, leeks, carrots, turnips *et bien sur*, the crème fraîche,' said Marguerite.

'Ah, of course,' said Jemme, who was rapidly acclimatising to the Northern style of heavy cooking. It was good, hearty fare and exactly what was needed when outside was rainy and windswept, even if it could be a little heavy on mild evenings like this one.

Marguerite shrugged, 'It is not a very complicated dish, but it is cooked very slowly for hours and hours, and the pot is filled with herbs. This one has only used herbs from the small garden of Xelifon, and the leeks are from him too.'

Jemme looked at her questioningly.

'Ah, Monsieur did not know? Xelifon has begun to grow *légumes* too. He is doing very well with them and I often use them in the cooking here.'

'Excellent!' said Jemme sitting down at the single place she had laid for him, 'What a self-sufficient little enclave we're becoming.'

Marguerite smiled as she took his plate over to the stove, 'You should tell Xelifon you are pleased, Monsieur. It will mean a lot to him. He has thrived as much as his plants have here. I did not know him before, but Monsieur Philby says it is the best thing that's ever happened to him. His parents are very happy too, I understand.'

'Well, I'm pleased that everyone else is pleased in that case,' said Jemme. 'All I want is to fit into the local area well, and the last thing I'd want would be to put anyone's back up.'

'Well, you're in no danger of doing that,' said Marguerite, '*voila*' she added as she put a plate full of steaming hot food down in front of Jemme.

'Marguerite, once again you've outdone yourself. This looks delicious.'

'Tssk, Monsieur – I told you, it is only a simple dish. Ai, careful! You will burn your mouth!' she rebuked him as Jemme tried to shovel a whole forkful in.

He smiled. 'It *is* delicious and I can't believe that so much of it came from within yards of where I'm sitting now.'

'It is good to eat food you have grown yourself, *non*?' said Marguerite, 'Ah, here are the *jardinières*! I hope you don't mind, Monsieur, it is such a big hen, I said that Philby and Xelifon could have some too – I shall set the table in the other room.'

'Nonsense, they can eat in here with me.'

'Monsieur? Are you sure?'

'Absolutely, I've been on my own all day and I don't want to eat supper alone too. Besides, it will give me a chance to catch up with them.'

Marguerite shrugged again and ushered the gardeners in, fussing around them and tutting at their muddied boots. She made them wash their hands whilst she set two more places at the table. Philby didn't respond to this change in routine and his face remained as dour and impenetrable as ever. Xelifon's eyes twinkled and he smiled softly, he definitely seemed pleased, Jemme noted. Marguerite was right – this job seemed to have done so much for him. There was a time when he wouldn't even meet Jemme's eye, and here he was approaching the table first and choosing the seat nearest to Jemme.

'Good evening, gentlemen. I trust you've had a good day. Even if you haven't, Marguerite's *poule* will soon put a smile on your face,' he said brightly as Marguerite put down two further plates.

Xelifon's smile broadened as soon as he saw what was on it, '*Mes poireaus*,' he said quietly.

'Ah, yes – I've been hearing all about these vegetables of yours, and very impressed I was too,' said Jemme. 'Whereabouts are you growing them? I went out for a walk this afternoon and I didn't come across any vegetable patches at all.'

'By the old orchard, Monsieur,' Xelifon said quietly, as he slowly and with laboured deliberation, began to cut up his food.

'I see. Excellent stuff, I'm pleased to hear it. What are you growing at the moment?'

'*Poireaus*, carrots, some beans and some marrows too.'

'Even better!' said Jemme. 'I hope you keep up the good work – are you planning on sowing any more?'

'*Oui, Monsieur*, but it is the wrong time of year for many vegetables.'

Jemme nodded his understanding. Although Xelifon had opened up a great deal since he had arrived, conversation could still feel quite laboured at times and was never anything other than questions and answers.

Jemme turned to Philby, 'How are you getting on? I know how hard you've been working recently, I hope it's not spoiling your enjoyment of the grounds.'

'*Non, non, Monsieur*, I will always love these grounds. It is good to be able to breathe new life into them. So many things were neglected under the ministry. Now we have the chance to make everything new.'

'I am going to restore the orchard,' Xelifon suddenly interjected to everyone's surprise.

'The orchard? Really? That's wonderful news.'

'Yes, Monsieur. That is why I have planted the vegetables there – the whole area will be a kitchen garden.'

'That's just how it's supposed to be;' said Marguerite, frowning at Philby who was picking chicken bones up with his fingers, 'it would have been the same when my grandmother was working here and in the *gentilhommières* throughout France.

'It's the best way of living, exactly the kind of thing my own grandmother would approve of,' said Jemme.

They ate in silence for a little while and Jemme savoured the sweet flavour of the leeks grown in his own little patch of France, and the earthy depth of taste the herbs gave the pot. Before long he was laying his fork down, satisfied. Marguerite appeared with a carafe of water and filled his glass. 'Finished, Monsieur?'

'I think so – it was utterly delicious, thank you.'

'I'm pleased – would you like a *tranche* of bread for the jus? Look how much you have left!'

'A slice of bread?'

'Yes Monsieur, you use it to mop up all the jus at the end of a meal. It is not a very sophisticated habit, I know, but it is very tasty!'

'I don't think I will, but thank you all the same,' said Jemme.

'I'll have some bread, Marguerite,' said Philby.

'Me too,' added Xelifon.

Jemme sat back and sipped his water whilst his two gardeners pushed hunks of crusty bread around their plates with gnarled hands. Whilst they were busy eating, he thought about the grounds and their future. Philby had been right – it was as if new life had been breathed into them. Not only were they restoring long-abandoned features, but they were introducing new ideas too. He remembered how he had realised that he was just as responsible for curating and maintaining the grounds as he was the interior of the house. It was a beautiful extension of his ambition, and extended the scope he was able to cultivate and develop. So far he had mostly left Xelifon and Philby to come up with their own ideas, which they periodically checked with him. Now, he was keen to include some of his own ideas. He didn't know much about horticulture though, and hadn't even considered the fact that seasonality would be important when planting in the vegetable garden. He thought about the gardens of his childhood, the waxy palms in the courtyards of the ancient mosques and the graceful formal gardens of the stately homes he had visited in Europe. Perhaps he could draw inspiration from them, or reference some of his most favourite in the grounds here somehow. Maybe he needed to keep the grounds congruous with the house though – maybe it would jar with the age and location of the house if he started putting in foreign ideas and plants. Worse still, he risked offending Philby and Xelifon. Could he approach it in the same way as the house? Maybe he could mix different elements together; the grounds were certainly large enough to be able to accommodate different elements and designs very comfortably. If he wanted, they wouldn't even be visible from the house.

Xelifon and Philby finished their suppers and Marguerite cleared away their plates, '*Magnifique!*' barked Philby with more gusto than usual, causing both Marguerite and Xelifon to giggle.

'I've just been thinking about the grounds,' Jemme said, turning to his gardeners. 'I really appreciate all the new work you're doing with them and I hope that's going to continue.'

Philby and Xelifon both nodded.

'Would you both be amenable to some ideas I might suggest?' he asked.

The two looked confused, 'But Monsieur, it is your garden,' said Philby plainly which was all Jemme needed to hear.

'I've been thinking, I'd like to include some of the same ideas I'm developing in the house.'

They both looked at him slightly blankly so he continued, 'I've talked to you about what I hope to do with the new rooms and you already know that I want to restore the grand rooms, and so I suppose that's what I want to extend into the garden.'

'Like restoring the orchard,' Xelifon said slowly.

'Exactly! Many more things like that. Except, I also want to include other influences – nods to famous gardens, features from Eastern gardens, all of that sort of thing. The grounds are big enough to spread them all out so that they won't clash or detract from each other.'

Both gardeners turned the information over thoughtfully.

'It will be a French country house and its gardens first and foremost,' Jemme added,' but I want to shape the character so that it's a little more than that. I'm hoping to show the influence of different cultures on each other's horticultures, if you see what I mean.'

Philby still looked a little blank but Xelifon seemed to be warming to the idea,

'An international garden,' he said softly – more of a statement than a question.

'Yes, yes, exactly!' said Jemme enthusiastically, 'although not the whole garden, just certain parts of it.'

Xelifon paused and furrowed his brow slightly, 'An international forest,' he said.

Jemme stared at him, 'A forest of trees, each from a different country,' he elaborated. Jemme thought a little more. It was perfect, something which represented the passage of influence he was trying to demonstrate, but would not be obtrusive or destroy harmony in the garden. He could include the tree which was most emblematic of each country: the tall, conical Syrian Junipers of his youth, the noble English oaks, and the clipped horse-chestnut trees which lined the boulevards of Paris.

'That's a great idea Xelifon,' he said, 'exactly the kind of thing I was hoping for. Did you have anything particular in mind?'

Xelifon nodded vigorously, 'Maple, Chinese willow –' he began before Philby interrupted him.

'Where exactly will this *forêt* go, eh? It is not easy planting trees, Xelifon – it is not as quick as herbs. You must work at them for years.'

Xelifon looked chastened, and Jemme interjected, 'We both know that – that's the beauty of the whole project, it's something that will take years to nurture and will then outlive all of us. In a way it will be much more of a legacy than this chateau will be.'

Xelifon smiled and nodded slowly.

'I love the idea and I'd like you to be in charge of it, Xelifon,' Jemme said. 'I'm going to give you suggestions and the names of a few specific trees I'd like included, but otherwise I'll leave it in your capable hands. If there are any particularly rare or exotic trees, I have a man back in Paris who will be able to track them down for you – he's an absolute marvel and he'll be able to help you out with pretty much anything you ask him to. Now, if you'll excuse me, I'm suddenly tired after all that wonderful food, so I think I'll get an early night. I'm going to head back to Paris earlier than usual tomorrow and spend the afternoon with Madame Mafeze.'

He drained the last of his water, thanked Marguerite again and left the room to a buzz of excited French chatter behind him.

❖   ❖   ❖   ❖

Back in the sixteenth Arrondissement, he was pleased with the time he'd made on the main autoroute. It was still early in the afternoon, and he'd already parked the car and had time to pick Hil up a large bunch of hand-tied flowers from her favourite florist. He crept the last few steps up to his appartement, wanting to keep everything as much of a surprise as possible. Arriving at the front door, he knocked three times and waited. There was a pause for a while and then he heard the clip-clop of high heels nearing the door from the other side. Feeling suddenly playful he moved the bunch of flowers up, hiding his face.

'Hello?' he heard Hil's voice through the gerberas.

He pulled them down quickly, revealing himself, 'Surprise!' She looked momentarily confused, and then a big smile broke out over her face, 'Jemme, darling! How lovely! Are these for me?'

'Of course they are – who else would they be for?' he teased, handing them over to her.

'I wasn't expecting you back until long after I'd gone to bed; why are you back so early? Is everything all right?' she asked quickly, sounding concerned.

'Of course everything's fine, does something have to be wrong for me to want to see you?'

'No, not at all, sorry – I just wasn't expecting you. It's absolutely lovely to see you though. What a treat.'

'Well, I was wandering in the grounds yesterday and I just really missed you. I wanted to be with you so badly, and so I thought instead of spending another Sunday on my own in a huge, empty house, I would spend it with my beautiful wife instead,' he stepped inside and pulled Hil in to kiss him.

'You charmer,' she teased him pulling away. 'It really is lovely to see you though – are you hungry?'

'Starving.'

'What luck – I haven't had lunch yet. We don't have any food in the house either, so why don't we treat ourselves and go out for a proper lunch in one of our favourite restaurants?'

'Now that sounds like an excellent plan – well worth driving back from the countryside for!'

'Just give me a second to put these in water and I'll be ready,' said Hil, disappearing into the kitchen. She reappeared a few moments later, stopping to apply some lipstick in the mirror in the hall. 'Right, ready! Where shall we go?'

'I thought that little place about fifteen minute's walk from here. We've been there a few times before and it's very Art Nouveau inside. I'm in a decorating frame of mind and I'd like to go somewhere inspirational.'

'You're always in a decorating frame of mind!' Hil chided, 'But luckily for you, their profiteroles are amazing and I'm in the mood for something sweet.'

Around twenty minutes later they sat at a table for two, poring over the menus. More accurately, Hil pored over the menu and Jemme looked around the restaurant. It was just as he remembered it, a glorious panegyric to a glamorous past. He adored the style and remembered the first time he had joyfully discovered it. Of all places, his first encounter with the form had been in Russia. Wandering through St Petersburg on the last afternoon of a business trip, he had come across the Eliseyev Emporium. Startled by its size and unusual form, he had found himself drawn to it. He was fascinated by the architect's use of stained glass, the incorporation of statues and the use of arches. As soon as he had arrived home, he had found out as much as he could about the building. His research had led him to the architect, who had in turn led him to the art movement. Once he had learned a little more about it, he had begun to see how wide Art Nouveau's reach was. He saw it in the paintings of Klimt and Mackintosh and in the glasswork of Tiffany; once he had moved to Paris it was hard to avoid it and he realised that despite his initial Eastern encounter with it, Western Europe had cradled its birth and nurtured its development. Its presence in Russia was merely evidence of how far-flung its influence had been.

He yearned to include it somehow in the chateau, but it had never featured in the dream, despite his late-found love of it. Furthermore, the style was completely wrong in both form and context for the noble rooms. However, it was such an iconic part of French decorative history and so redolent of Paris at the turn of the century. He felt it needed to be included somehow, just as many other eras of French history deserved to be referenced. He knew that he would think of many others which would probably jar with his overall scheme too. However, they were all pertinent to the narrative of the chateau. and demonstrated the spread of influence between different cultures. He thought about it some more as he stared at the furled ferns carved into a bronze pillar on the opposite wall. Suddenly he became aware of people staring at him.

'Well?' Hil asked.

Jemme looked confused, 'Well what?' he asked, noticing that a waiter standing behind Hil was also looking at him expectantly.

'Well, this poor waiter has been waiting to take your order for an eternity,' said Hil.

'Oh, sorry, the *agneau* please,' mumbled Jemme.

'*Bon, Monsieur,*' said the waiter and disappeared.

'Poor man,' said Hil looking after him, 'He was too polite to shake you, which is what I felt like doing!'

'Eh? Shake me?' asked Jemme, still distracted.

'Yes! You're doing it again!'

'Doing what?'

'You're disappearing off into your own little world and it's impossible to reach you.'

'Sorry,' said Jemme, forcing himself to focus.

'It's all right,' Hil smiled, 'I'm used to it by now. You used to only do it when you were thinking about something historical or dream-related, but now it seems to have expanded to include anything to do with architecture or decoration.'

Jemme sighed, 'You're right, I'm sorry again – I was miles away.'

'What was it this time?'

'You're right, it was decoration. I'm absolutely fascinated by this Art Nouveau style, and I'm trying to figure out a way of incorporating it in the chateau somehow, but I'm not quite sure where it will fit. Anyway, that's not the decorating I wanted to talk to you about.'

'Ah, I knew there would be some talking though – I thought it was silly to expect a straight-forward lunch.'

Jemme looked wounded.

'Sorry, I was only teasing. I'm still really glad to have you back early, regardless. I'd love to hear what you have to say about the place too.'

'Well, I had a very productive weekend down there. The project's starting to take shape and I'm getting many more ideas, not just about the display rooms, but about the rest of the house too. This weekend I really felt like I put a pin in things and now I have a proper starting point.'

'Really? That's exciting.'

'I think so too. I thought carefully about which area we should tackle first, and I realised that it wouldn't be in the new display rooms.'

'But I thought you couldn't wait to get started on them now that they were ready.'

'I couldn't – I still can't. But I realised that it wasn't fair on you. You've come so far with me already and you haven't received anything in return. The galleries and display rooms are my pet project, and you've been so patient putting up with me whilst I develop them. However, the entire house is our project and I think it's only fair to start on a room we can both enjoy. So, I've decided that I'm going to dedicate all my time and energy to completing the grand salon. I'm going to ensure that it's fitted with the best curtains and carpets money can buy, and filled with the finest furnishings it's possible to lay hands on. What's more, I'm going to do it all in the style of Louis XVI,' he paused and waited for Hil to reply. She was just looking at him. 'Well, what do you think?'

'I don't know what to think – how exciting! It's so thoughtful of you to do one of the rooms for both of us first.'

Jemme brushed her comment away, 'Don't be silly – it couldn't be any other way.'

'Well, thank you anyway. I can't wait to have our very own salon completed; we can finally invite friends and family around. All my Paris friends have given up asking me for invitations and almost started accusing me of making the whole place up.'

'I know, it must seem like ages since we bought the place. I realise it's been a slow beginning, but I think that it was a good idea to get everything sorted first. I just hope that you haven't lost enthusiasm with the whole thing.'

'Well, if I had, it's certainly been revived!' she paused, 'Why Louis XVI by the way?'

'I just thought he reigned during such an important part of French history. I wanted to include it in the chateau somehow. Also, I thought that the period lent itself well to an impressive formal room.'

'Absolutely!' Hil agreed, 'I can just picture it now – our very own beautiful reception room, just like a proper grand dominion, I'm getting excited already.'

Just as she had said it, their food arrived, 'This has been the best Sunday for as long as I can remember!' she said happily.

Chapter Eighteen

The following weekend, Hil joined Jemme on the trip into the countryside. Even though her support had never failed and she had stood by him at every step of this ambitious project so far, Jemme couldn't help but feel her enthusiasm for it had waned somewhat in recent weeks. It hadn't been anything she'd done or said – indeed, he'd only realised it in the week since he'd told her about his plans for the salon. She seemed re-energised and her interest in the whole thing had been revitalised. It wasn't until she started again that he realised she had stopped asking questions about the chateau, and no longer saved clippings from antiques magazines and auction catalogues for him. They chattered excitedly throughout the journey, and Jemme felt hugely gratified to hear Hil enthusing about going to auctions and tracking down genuine artefacts.

'I've been reading about Louis all week,' she said as they neared the little restaurant that marked the halfway spot.

'Really? Do you fancy stopping – the usual place is just coming up.'

'No, I'm keen to get there!'

Jemme grinned, 'You're starting to sound like me! Tell me what you've been reading about.'

'Well, I was thinking over what I actually knew about the whole period and I realised that it wasn't much. I knew the major facts, but the rest of it was pretty much just the clichés – Marie Antoinette with her towering hair and her "let them eat cake" and Louis giving her the little palace where she could play milkmaid in all her finery and jewels. Once I bothered to look into it even a little bit, I saw how narrow that whole popular view was. I suppose it makes a good story, but the situation was so much more complicated.'

Jemme listened attentively. Usually he was the driving force in any discussion about history, and so it made a pleasant change to hear Hil enthuse on a subject close to his heart.

'To start with,' she continued, 'the whole "cake" myth is probably just that – a myth. I suppose that history is littered with people who are remembered principally by their misquotes, but it does seem rather unfair. I read an article which said that it was a mistranslation of "brioche", and another which said that the whole thing was probably made up by Rousseau anyway. It made me think about how much of my knowledge was received wisdom I'd never challenged.'

'That's how I've felt for pretty much my entire adult life,' said Jemme. 'The more research I've done, the more I've realised how vital it is to question everything you think you know. It's so easy for inaccuracies to slip into historical scholarship, and the longer they're left unchallenged, the more they become seen as fact.'

'Just doing this small bit of research has really opened my eyes to that,' said Hil, 'it's made me realise how much there is still to learn. Even if you just dedicated yourself to one small era of one country's history, it still seems like it would be a life's work.'

Jemme smiled, 'Perhaps you can see why I've been obsessed with this sort of thing for so long now.'

'Perhaps I can. It's certainly highly addictive. Once I had found out about one thing, I wanted to find out about three other things so that I understood how they all fitted together.'

'I can definitely understand that!'

'I really enjoyed it and now I feel like I've something more to contribute when we're creating the room. Even if none of it's new to you, I'll feel like the room has more meaning to me, now I understand its context a little more.'

'I'm so pleased you feel the same way as me. I've been fixated with the idea of context for quite a while and I'm really concerned that everything in the chateau has meaning in some way. This whole project goes a great deal deeper than just the aesthetic. I think this room is going to be even more meaningful to me, now that I know it's piqued your interest too.'

'It definitely has. I've been living in this country long enough to take an interest in its history. I always thought I knew my way around the various kings and battles, but it turns out I was quite wrong. For example, I didn't even know that Marie Antoinette was Austrian! I suppose I'd always assumed that because she had a French sounding name that she must have been French. It turns out that Marie Antoinette isn't even her real name, it's just what the French called her. Her real name was Maria Antonia, and she was a Hapsburg. She was only fourteen when she married Louis; although I suppose that wasn't particularly unusual for the age, it just seems so shocking now.'

'I can see we're definitely going to have to have some sort of Marie Antoinette room if you're this interested!' said Jemme.

'I'm interested in Louis too,' said Hil, 'it's just that she was such a colourful character and I feel like history might have remembered her unfairly. It might have been the same for Louis too, come to think of it.'

'What might have been?'

'The case that Louis was remembered unfairly. People seem to think that he was universally hated at the time of his execution, but actually some people were sympathetic towards him. In fact, I read a piece that said that sympathy remained strong enough to be a factor in the Bourbon Restoration.'

'That's interesting. You're right though, sometimes events and people are remembered in a completely different way to how they actually were. I think in this case, it's all part of the great French Republic creation narrative. The French are keen to show that the republic was born out of the grand vanquishing of a hated and unfair aristocracy. It gives the present-day set up legitimacy and credibility. I suppose by portraying Louis and Marie in such a way, they side-step any awkward thoughts of the new, fair and equal republic being born out of regicide.'

'I suppose so. I hadn't really thought about *why* these things might be remembered differently. It's an interesting extra step.'

'It's one I can't help taking. I think it comes from a lifetime's fascination with this sort of thing. The more research I did as I was growing up, the longer my thought processes became, and I discovered all these extra levels and stages I could push my thoughts through. The study of history itself – not the events that happened in the past, I mean the way they have been remembered and transmitted, is something that fascinates me. It's called historiography and I suppose it's the greatest story of all.'

He flicked the car's indicator and pulled off to the top of the driveway, 'Here we are already, that last half of the journey seemed to fly past.'

'Didn't it?'

'I'm so pleased you're here with me this weekend,' said Jemme sincerely, as they parked up outside the house. He'd felt a sudden pang of guilt as soon as they'd turned off the driveway: Hil was expressing a genuine interest in something for the first time, but instead of listening intently he'd spoken at length about something that interested him instead. It was only because he was so excited to be able to speak with her about such things, but he hoped it didn't sound as if he was trying to trump her.

He looked over; Hil was peering up at the rounded buttress that encased the great spiral staircase running to every floor in the chateau. It was topped with a conical roof and tall, slim window ran down its length. A warm light emanated from each window, 'Well it appears someone's in at least,' she said, 'I wonder which floor they're on.'

'I should imagine it's Philby checking over the painter's work. He arranged for the painters and plasterers to prime the room so that it's ready to be decorated. It should be a nice, blank canvas now whereas before it was...'

'A rather dirty canvas?' Hil suggested.

Jemme laughed, 'Something like that!'

'Well, in any case, it's nice not to come back to somewhere that's in complete darkness.'

Jemme opened the door for her and went round to the boot to collect their bags. Philby still made the effort to come and greet them and Marguerite usually joined them too. Jemme could only assume he was a little earlier than they had expected, although he knew that they would feel a little affronted that they hadn't met him. He loved the way that they were all falling into their little routines already.

He opened the front door for Hil and followed her in.

'Mmmm, I can smell what Marguerite's cooking already,' she said, 'I didn't realise I was hungry, but perhaps I am!'

Jemme dropped their bags off at the foot of the stairs, 'What first my love – some supper, or looking at the room?'

'Looking at the room, definitely!'

'Ah, a girl after my own heart.'

They made their way from the hall through to the nexus of rooms which, for him symbolised the heart of the chateau as a family home. Just as he had predicted, they found Philby in the Louis XVI salon. He heard them come in and turned around. Also as Jemme had predicted, a noticeable flicker of chagrin passed across the gardener's ruddy face. He decided to jump in first.

'Sorry, Philby, I didn't mean to sneak in – I think we must have just arrived a bit early.'

Philby shrugged, 'It is your house, Monsieur,' although he looked slightly placated.

'How did the work go?'

'*Bien, Monsieur.* The men left this afternoon, so I have been checking their work.'

'Thank you Philby, again, for organising everything. It all seems to go seamlessly whilst you're at the helm.'

Philby nodded and Jemme could tell he was pleased. He looked around the room.

'It's been a while since I've been in here, but I can tell what an improvement they've made,' said Hil, looking around. 'Goodness – look at the floor! It's so glossy, I could see my face in it! I can't remember what it was like before, but it definitely wasn't like this.'

'There was a large carpet in here, Madame, but the Ministry took it with them,' said Philby.

'Oh, really? So, was it just bare floorboards in here then?'

'*Oui, Madame*, just the parquet. It was very dirty, so you probably didn't notice it.' Turning to Jemme, he said, 'The men have sanded it and oiled it and then polished it.'

'They must have worked so hard – it looks fantastic,' said Jemme, 'I can't believe what a difference it's made to the whole room; it almost makes it seem lighter in here.'

Hil nodded, 'It's a bit echoey in here, though.'

'I know what you mean. I think that will all change when we have some curtains and soft furnishings in here though. The floor looks so good we could almost leave it as it is. However, I think I'd still like to install some sort of carpet; maybe not a fitted one, but it definitely needs something. I think it's going to take a while finding something big enough, though!'

Hil looked around the room. The newly buffed floorboards drew attention to just how large the room was, 'I think you might well be right!' she said.

'What else has been done, Philby?' asked Jemme. 'I recall there was a big problem with damp, but it looks like it's been sorted.'

'*Oui, Monsieur*, but it was a big job – more than just painting over things. They have fixed a patch of the roof outside which we think was letting it in.'

'Excellent work, thank you.'

'The men have also sanded down the wood and reconditioned it and restored the plasterwork too. They painted over everything on Thursday morning so that it would be dry when you arrived. The gilding was only finished this afternoon.'

'It's all been done very well Philby, I'm extremely pleased. Hil, what do you think?'

'Very well,' echoed Hil '– thank you Philby. I love this gilding, it really brings out the plaster features, and I remember it looking very shabby before.'

Jemme looked at it with her for a moment and started to feel a twinge of excitement as he realised that things really were underway. The project had truly started. He slipped his hand around Hil's and squeezed it.

'Now comes the fun part,' he said, 'we take pleasure in making a huge shopping list of everything we want for the room.'

'I know,' said Hil smiling broadly, 'although, can I suggest we do it over a plate of whatever it is Marguerite is cooking?'

'I can't think of anywhere better,' said Jemme and they walked hand in hand to the kitchen.

Marguerite was thrilled to see them, especially Hil, whom she particularly enjoyed mothering.

'But I did not hear you arrive!' she said, looking slightly dejected.

'Not to worry, Marguerite, neither did Philby by the sound of things. We're pleased to see you nonetheless and were very pleased to smell whatever it is you are cooking as soon as we arrived.'

'*Ah, bon, bon,*' said Marguerite, '*asseyez-vous!*'

They sat at the great granite table, with Jemme remembering the sadness he had felt a week before when he had seen only one place set at the table.

'What are you making, Marguerite?' Hil called over to her.

Marguerite turned round, spoon, as ever, clasped in one hand.

'Ah, Madame, tonight I am making for you my famous coq-au-vin. Then, for the *dessert* a great *tarte aux pommes Normandes*.'

'Sounds wonderful,' said Hil.

'Will there be crème-fraîche to go with the tarte?' Jemme teased.

'*Bien-sur*,' Marguerite replied, looking confused.

Over a wonderfully tasty supper, which justified its own reputation, Jemme and Hil discussed the room. It was difficult knowing where to start, although Hil seemed to be full of sensible ideas.

'I think we should start with the lights she said.'

Jemme nodded. The present nineteenth-century situation was not ideal. Although the floor had been rewired, there was still no fitted lighting in the room. Instead there were free-standing spotlights, the decorators had used to work by. They trailed thick black electrical cables across the floor like tentacles and lit the room as brightly as a sports stadium.

'It's hard to see it properly when it's that bright in there,' Hil continued, 'if you see what I mean,' she added, 'I know that doesn't really make sense, but I just feel that when it's lit up like a modern petrol station, it's hard to imagine it filled with antiques and the sort of refined ambience we're hoping for.'

'It makes perfect sense,' said Jemme, 'and I think lighting is a great place to start.'

'I'm assuming that we'll have a chandelier?'

'No question about it. I don't think it will be too difficult to source some eighteenth century pieces at auction back in Paris. They come up all the time.'

'Great. Is there anything we can do whilst we're down here, apart from coming up with ideas?'

'I don't know. I'm sure we can use the time constructively somehow; being in the room is certainly quite inspirational. I would find it difficult to come up with ideas back behind my desk in the bank.'

'True, true, but I'm sure we can do something else whilst we're here. Oh – I know! We can go down to the archives. Madame Poirier told us to visit whenever we liked, and we might find out a bit of useful information. Even if it's not directly relevant, it might spark off an idea.'

'That's a brilliant idea,' said Jemme. Both pleased with their progress so far, the conversation dulled as they savoured the last of their delicious suppers.

❋   ❋   ❋   ❋

Just before breakfast the next morning, they walked into the village. Jemme had suggested a drive, but the weather was still mild and Hil thought that some fresh air was a pleasant way to start the day. They had purposefully skipped breakfast so that they would be able to have some of the wonderful croissants from the bakery underneath the archives.

About half an hour later, brushing golden crumbs from their fronts, they made their way up the little wooden staircase at the back of the shop.

'*Bonjour!*' said Hil cheerily as she knocked and opened the door. 'Oh, I'm sorry – I didn't expect –' instead of Madame Poirier's familiar face, a new, slightly-confused one looked back at her. There was a moment's silence.

'Oh, I see – you were expecting Madame Poirier,' said the young boy behind the desk. 'I'm her nephew; she's helping a friend who owns an antique shop today, so I'm running the archives for her.'

'I'm Madame Mafeze,' said Hil, approaching the desk and offering a hand, which the boy shook enthusiastically,

'*Ah, Monsieur et Madame Mafeze*, from the Chateau Vigne-Verte! My aunt has told me all about you. It's so nice to have new owners who take an interest in the building and are regulars in the village too.'

'Thank you,' said Hil, 'it's very nice to be regulars in the village – we're very taken with this part of the country and we very much look forward to our weekends here.'

'*Ah, bon*,' said the young man, and Hil recognised the same friendly twinkle in his eye as was familiar in his aunt's.

'I was wondering if you could help us,' said Hil as she and Jemme sat in the two chairs on the opposite side of the desk.

'Of course, Madame.'

'There's a file here on the chateau, which we've looked into a few times. It's always being added to and it's quite large, so we haven't seen the whole thing. We were hoping to browse through it and see if we can find something.'

'*Bien sur!*' said the young man, 'But perhaps it will help if you also tell me what it is you are looking for. I might have seen it in the file.'

'We're just about to start redecorating the grand salon,' said Jemme. 'We already know roughly what we want to do, but we were looking for inspiration. Anything would do from your old archives – ideally a photo, but even a reference in a newspaper or an old receipt, just something to give us an indication of how it looked in the past.'

'I see,' said the young man thoughtfully, '*excusez-moi*. I will return shortly.'

He disappeared, and after about five minutes reappeared with a foolscap file. It was open about half-way through and he carried it carefully, lest any of the scraps of paper stacked up on either side dislodged.

He set it down on the desk, 'I thought I remembered seeing something on the salon. A long time ago I helped my aunt catalogue some of these files during the school holidays. We had many clippings from a magazine called *Country Life* and

I had to put them in all the correct files. Here, look,' he plucked out several pieces of thin, glossy paper and turned them round to lay them on the table. It was more than Jemme and Hil could have hoped for. Before them lay clippings of an editorial feature on the chateau, complete with photos of its most impressive rooms.

'This is brilliant, thank you,' said Hil.

'Does it help you with what you were looking for?'

'Definitely!' said Jemme. 'Look at this,' he said, turning to his wife and pointing at a photo. Although the picture itself was grainy, and the magazine's reproduction not particularly good, the room it showed was instantly recognisable as the salon. They both strained their eyes to pick out the details. The carpet had obviously been very thick – the bottoms of the chair legs seemed to disappear into it completely. There were also several large tapestries hanging from the walls, which, together with the huge curtains pulled back at the windows, went a long way to soften the room.

'Look at this,' said Hil, staring intensely at the picture. 'Do you see?'

Jemme frowned, 'See what?'

Madame Poirier's nephew came round and joined them on their side of the table. 'I don't see anything either, Madame.'

'I'm sure there's something here, but I can't quite make it out.'

'Ah! My aunt keeps a *loupe* in the drawer!' the boy suddenly proclaimed and rummaged around for a short while before producing an old-fashioned magnifying glass on a bone handle. He passed it to Hil who peered through it at the picture.

'I thought so,' she said, sounding satisfied. 'Here,' she passed the magnifying glass to Jemme, 'do you see? There are cherubs in each corner of the room.'

'Oh yes,' said Jemme as he moved the magnifying glass towards the paper. 'They look as if they're holding up the ceiling.'

'That's quite common for chateaux in this area,' said the boy. 'I expect they were original features.'

'I wonder when they went missing. Based on experience, I'd hazard a guess that the Ministry took them with them,' said Jemme bitterly.

'What a pity;' said Hil, 'they survived so long, only to be ripped out by some bureaucrat.'

They looked over the magazines for a little while longer, but didn't glean anything especially useful. They thanked the young man, who, like his aunt, urged them to come back whenever they liked, and left.

On the walk home Jemme cursed the ministry once again, 'They're such crooks!' he said. 'And after the amount I pay in taxes too!'

Hil laughed at his irritation, 'It's certainly galling,' she said, 'although at least we know what it used to look like. Maybe we can try and recreate them. What do you think?'

'I don't know,' said Jemme. 'In some ways I'd like to, but I also don't really want any modern reproductions in the room, no matter how faithful. I'd rather it was all antiques. Besides, I'd like to keep it to the Louis XVI theme.'

'I know what you mean about the modern reproductions, but maybe we could put something in the corners, as a sort of homage to how the room was.'

'Maybe,' said Jemme, 'I'm just trying to work out where on earth we're going to find a carpet. As soon as we get back to Paris, I'm going to get DD on the case. Something tells me I'm going to need my best man on the job.'

'Well I can't think of anyone better,' said Hil.

'Tell you what,' Jemme said suddenly, 'how do you fancy a day trip tomorrow?'

'But I thought you would want to spend the whole day working on the chateau?'

'I'd rather spend the time with you and I don't really mind where we are – I feel like we've already completed a large amount of the work.'

'Well, I'd love to go somewhere in that case – where did you have in mind?'

'Nowhere new I'm afraid. I was thinking of going back to Lisieux. There's a huge basilica we missed there, last time we visited – I don't know how. Anyway, apparently it's completely finished in the Art Nouveau style, which is something I haven't been able to stop thinking about since that restaurant last Sunday. I thought that regardless of what it looked like, it would be an interesting place to visit.'

'Sounds good to me,' said Hil. 'I really enjoyed our last trip there and definitely wouldn't mind visiting again. I never told you how impressed my mother was when I told her I'd been. She knew the place straight away when I told her about it. I'm surprised I'd never heard of it, growing up to be honest. It's such an important place to Catholics – the second most visited pilgrimage site in the whole of France.'

'Even more reason to visit then,' said Jemme as they neared the chateau.

As they approached the front door, Hil stopped by the rose bed. 'These have really come along so much; it's nice to having such beautiful flowers right by the front door. I've really missed having a garden in Paris.'

They made their way into the salon and stood looking up at the ceiling.

'I can just imagine them here,' said Hil, 'what a pity.' She sighed, 'Ah well, I'm sure we'll sort something out.'

'I'm sure we will,' said Jemme, an idea starting to form in his head.

* * * *

The next day they set off for Lisieux again. Hil was keen to visit a few craft shops she had liked on the previous trip and was also looking forward to seeing the basilica.

'Did you know that St Thérèse was known as "the little flower of Jesus"?' Hil asked as they were pulling into a parking space.

'Really? Why "little"?'

'Well she was very sickly as a child – she nearly died of enteritis just after she was born, and in fact four of her siblings did. So, I think it was partly because she was physically small. But she was also so young when she became a nun. I guess it meant that she was always the littlest one in the abbey.'

'I remember reading that she was young,' said Jemme as they walked up a street past a café he recognised from their previous trip. 'I can't remember how old she was though.'

'She went to a school run by nuns when she was only about eight, but she had quite a few religious experiences as a young child; she used to suffer terrible tremors and the doctors could do nothing to help her. Then one day she looked at a statue of the Virgin Mary and became completely calm – the tremors stopped, just like that. When she was fourteen she was desperate to enter a Carmelite order, but was too young. She went all the way to Rome on a pilgrimage and begged the Pope, Leo XVII, to let her join.'

'Really? I didn't know that!' Jemme thought again about how Thérèse reminded him of Grandma. Driven, focussed and prone to refusing to take no for an answer. She was also meditative and equally as prone to spiritual tremors. Lily would probably have tracked the Pope down too if she had wanted the same thing.

'Yes, she was there as a novice from then on, although she travelled a great deal. One of the reasons she's so popular is her great humility. She never ceased to be aware of her own limitations, and repeatedly wrote about how insignificant she was and how small her own power to love was compared with God's. She even signed her letters with "*toute petite*" in front of her name. My mother told me a particular verse from Proverbs which Thérèse was famously attached to. It's "*If anyone is a very little one, let him come to me*". I suppose it's that attitude which has endeared her to people, and created this lasting reputation of littleness.'

By now they had reached the basilica, and they stopped to admire it from the outside. Jemme felt a rush of admiration for his wife. It was the second time this weekend she'd impressed him, not only with her knowledge, but with her clear enjoyment of it. He couldn't believe how much closer he felt to her, knowing that she was beginning to share his passion.

'It's so large,' said Hil taking in the basilica, 'I can't believe we didn't see it before.'

'I know, it's enormous, isn't it?'

The arched narthex in front of them was topped on either side by a spire; through the middle it was possible to see the large dome soaring up, and the subsidiary spires which flanked it. They walked down the narthex and entered through the heavy church doors.

Inside was even more impressive. It was almost completely covered with mosaics, with the warm, dull gold throwing the bright colours into sharp relief. It was fascinating to see such a beautiful building which was so modern. It incorporated all the classical features of a basilica and recalled elements of the canonical tradition. However, everything had been interpreted by twentieth-century architects. Despite looking old, it felt undeniably modern. It was an interesting contrast and Jemme remembered how he felt when he was looking at the work of the revivalist architects when he had first bought the chateau. Even though each of them was recalling an established, historical style, they brought something new to the form. No matter what the innovation, they added to it in some way and enriched the tradition.

Here, the interior was one, entire whole. There were no columns slicing through the space, nor ambulatory aisles running up and down the pews. Instead, there was a pureness of space, a single, uninterrupted expanse. There was something quite simple and quite beautiful about it. They wandered silently up the aisle, taking in the mosaics on the walls and craning their necks backwards to see those on the ceiling. They had been beautifully put together and, although not as overtly Art Nouveau as Jemme had expected, clearly demonstrated the style's influence in the depiction of robed angels and cloaked saints.

After a slow tour up and down the aisle, they left the basilica, blinking in the bright light outside.

'Well, I really enjoyed that,' said Jemme, 'It wasn't at all what I was expecting, but I'm definitely glad we saw it.'

'Me too,' Hil said. 'I think it might be one of the most modern places of worship I've ever been in. Well, most modern of the important ones, certainly. It was very interesting seeing how it was different – did you notice how there were no pillars?'

'I did, but only right at the end. I knew there was something missing, but I couldn't quite put my finger on it.'

'That's so all the congregation has an uninterrupted view of the service. In the older buildings, only the upper classes who sat nearer the front or in the family pews could see the important parts, and in some cases, the most sacred parts of the mass were actually hidden from the congregation. This is a much more egalitarian, modern approach.'

'That's interesting,' said Jemme, genuinely meaning it.

'Oh, this is the bell tower I wanted to see too,' said Hil as they turned back to face the square. 'I'd heard it was completely separate from the main building. How unusual.'

'It's quite often like that in Italy.'

'Yes, but the campanile is almost always next to the church in Italy. Here, it's completely detached.'

'You're right, I suppose that is a bit strange. The whole thing's a bit odd actually – it doesn't even look like it's finished.'

'It's not. They decided that charity was a bigger priority than finishing the belfry. I suppose it's quite symbolic that they've left it like that. Anyway, the bell was a devotional gift from Belgium and Holland, which I thought was quite an interesting fact.'

'I do too. Is there anything else you'd like to see, or shall we move on to some of those shops you were talking about?'

'No, I think I've finished here,' Hil said, flashing him a smile.

'Excellent,' said Jemme, 'because there are two seats at a café somewhere around here with our name on.' He slipped an arm around Hil's waist and guided her towards a café he'd seen on the way in.

* * * *

After a pleasant lunch and early afternoon's pottering, they made their way back to the chateau so that they could leave for Paris at a reasonable time. About half an hour out of Lisieux, they passed a small antique shop with some rather pretty urns outside. 'Actually, do you mind if we stop here for a little bit? I remember going past here before and thinking that I'd like to go in,' Jemme asked Hil.

'Absolutely, we have loads of time.'

Jemme pulled off the main road and they parked up outside. The antiques shop itself seemed to be as old as some of its wares, with low ceilings, slightly wobbly floors and dark wooden beams. As they opened the front door, a small bell attached to the frame jangled and a '*Bonjour*!' was shouted from a back room.

'I will be right with you,' said the disembodied voice, 'I'm just finishing winding a few watches.'

Jemme and Hil browsed the front section of the shop for a while. It was quite enjoyable knowing that they weren't looking for anything specific. Jemme admired a Davenport desk, but had no intention of buying it. He realised that he was in the happy position when he could now declare that an item of antique furniture was not big enough for his house. In the Paris flat, size had always been a consideration whenever he was considering new acquisitions. It seemed to be just as much of an issue in the chateau, only the situation was inverted. Small antiques were a waste of time as they would be utterly lost in the large rooms. The only rooms small enough to accommodate a piece such as this one were the new gallery rooms, and it simply wouldn't fit with any of the ambitious decorative schemes Jemme had for these rooms. He admired the turned, bow legs and moss-green leather inlay nevertheless, before moving on to look at a padded box filled with tiny sugar spoons.

Hil had been looking at a collection of amber, but had tired of it quickly. She wandered around the shop, and passed through the short corridor that connected the front and back show rooms. Very shortly afterwards, she reappeared, considerably more animated than before and gripped Jemme's arm.

'Come and see what I've just found,' she said.

Jemme followed her through and looked around. The pieces in here were much bigger and mostly comprised chairs, tables and the ilk.

'Which one?' he asked.

'Which one?! That one obviously!' He followed her finger and saw that she was pointing at a piano.

'The piano?'

'Of course the piano! Look at it!'

He tried to share her enthusiasm, but it seemed fairly ordinary to him.

'Come on,' said Hil, still holding onto his arm, 'have a proper look.'

She led him up to it, and Jemme started to see why she had been so taken with it. It was a decidedly feminine piece and had been painted a delicate shade of pistachio. The lid had been propped half-open and hand painted vignettes of elegant society ladies were clearly visible on the underneath. It was easy to imagine how pretty it would look when it was fully propped. The keys had the pearlised shimmer of ivory and had been worn rounded at the edges where it had been well-played.

'Isn't it beautiful?' Hil asked

'It's certainly a nice piece,' Jemme said thoughtfully, wondering how old it was. With its hand-painted detailing and delicate carvings it was a completely unique piece, and he couldn't recall seeing anything even similar before.

'I wonder if it still plays properly,' murmured Hil.

'Ah Madame, it produces a sound the Italians would call *dolce*,' said the voice they'd heard when they first came in. They turned and found a jovial, stocky man with a mop of straw-coloured hair beaming back at them.

'*Bonjour, Monsieur, Madame,*' he said, 'I'm sorry I have left you until now. I've been finishing a most delicate task.'

'Not at all,' said Jemme, 'I'm absolutely fascinated by clocks and watches, and I know how precise their handling has to be.'

'Fascinated, Monsieur? Then maybe I should show you some of my collection here.'

'I would love that, but at the moment my wife is quite taken with this piano you have here. Could you tell us a little more about it?'

'Ah the fortepiano, Madame – it is quite lovely, *non*?'

'Yes, I think it's beautiful, I didn't realise it was a fortepiano though. What's the difference?'

'Ah, you do not play?'

'No, but I've always wanted to,' Hil said slightly sadly.

The man smiled at her indulgently, 'Well, a fortepiano is the instrument of Beethoven and Haydn; it's what they would have played and what they would have written for, too. It's really just an earlier version of the piano: can you see how it looks smaller than a modern piano?' Hil nodded, 'Well this is how all pianos looked in the eighteenth century. Since then they have been in a near-constant state of evolution, becoming larger and including new technologies. The sound has changed of course, and if I was to play this for you you'd notice that the music was different to anything you'd hear a mass-produced shop one make.'

'Oh, I see.' said Hil, 'This one still plays?'

'Absolutely, Madame! It plays as well now as it did when it was first made. It will sound different to a modern piano as I say, but for many that is the best thing about instruments of this age. In fact, some musical societies will only play the music of Mozart and his contemporaries on instruments which are the same age as the music, so that it can be heard as it was intended.'

Hil looked fascinated by the story, 'I wish I could play,' she sighed, 'I love the idea of an instrument being contemporary with a cherished piece of music.

'But Madame it is never too late to learn!' the shop owner said good-naturedly. 'Besides,' he added, 'this is such a beautiful piece that it does not function merely as an instrument of music, it is also a wonderful antique, and would look good in any musical salon.'

At the mention of the word salon, Hil's interest was visibly piqued. She cast a meaningful look at Jemme, who scrutinised the piano again with renewed interest.

'You said it was from the eighteenth century?' he asked the man.

'*Oui, Monsieur*, this is very typical of the style and design of pieces that were being produced here in France during that period.'

The fact it was French had caught Jemme's attention. He could already tell that Hil was longing to have it in the salon and, as an eighteenth century French antique, it would certainly fit with the room. It would be a nice way to finish the weekend, buying their first proper piece for their first proper room, and he liked the fact that it was also something Hil had chosen.

He made a decision. Turning to the man he asked, 'And how much would you be looking for, for a piece like this?' As he did so, he caught sight of Hil suppressing a squeal of excitement.

✳ ✳ ✳ ✳

Back in Paris the next morning, Jemme flicked through the file DD had given him. Despite the fact that he no longer needed to take such a hands-on approach, business was no less busy. In fact, the deals passing across his desk seemed to grow in complexity by the day, and required as much of his attention and concentration as ever. The world of banking was always a reflection of the wider world, so he had to keep apace with current affairs as well as the machinations of the business world. It required so much focus, both during and outside work hours. He tried to force himself to put the chateau from his mind as he concentrated on the methodical lines of figures DD had placed in front of him, and worked his way slowly through the proofs. By lunchtime he had finished with everything and was looking forward to a break before he had to start thinking about everything again. With impeccable timing, DD knocked and put his head around the door.

'If you don't mind, I'm just leaving briefly. I'm going to buy a sandwich from the new Italian shop around the corner.'

Jemme waved him away, 'No of course I don't mind. Go, go have a proper lunch break.'

'Thank you, Sir, but I'm keen to press on with the afternoon's work, so I'll only be about fifteen minutes. Would you like me to get you anything?'

Jemme leant back in his chair and clasped his hands behind his head. He suddenly felt very tired, 'Actually, DD, that would be fantastic. I'll have whatever you're getting yourself,' he said, knowing DD would already know the best thing on the menu.

Precisely fifteen minutes later, he and DD sat at his desk, unwrapping waxed paper from what turned out to be the best sandwich Jemme had tasted in a long time.

'Sir, I couldn't help noticing that you haven't talked about the project all morning,' DD said.

'Goodness, don't say that, it makes me feel as if I do nothing but talk about it!' DD nodded his head, which Jemme interpreted as a smile. 'Well, I've been trying not to think about it today to be honest, but now I've stopped, there's still something niggling at me.'

DD looked at him questioningly.

'Well, I've been worrying about the carpet in the salon.'

'What's wrong with it, Sir?'

'Nothing – there isn't one, that's the problem. I want to try and find one at auction somewhere, but I've been thinking back over all the catalogues I've ever looked at, and I don't think I ever recall seeing one that big before. I have no idea where I'll go about finding one that's both in the style I want and the exact size I need.'

'What is it you're looking for, Sir?'

'I need something to either be from the Louis XVI era, or be in that sort of style and, crucially, it needs to be a hundred and one square metres.'

DD didn't so much as flinch; he merely noted down the dimensions and said in very even tones, 'That is a large carpet.'

Jemme smiled, 'Indeed. Do you remember ever seeing anything like that before? I need to find out if that's the sort of thing that even exists first, otherwise I'll have to rethink my plans.'

'Leave it with me, Sir. I'll look into it for you.'

'Thank you, DD. I knew I could count on you.'

DD merely nodded again as he collected up the sandwich wrappers and brushed the crumbs off the desk, 'Now, I have the figures for this afternoon's meeting,' he said, seamlessly moving back into business mode.

Jemme followed suit and was able to focus on banking business without interruption for the rest of the afternoon, knowing that at least one chateau matter was well on its way to being restored.

Later that week, he turned his attention to another matter: the ceiling decoration. Hil had been keen to replace the cherubs with another feature, and something she had said had caught his attention. She had loved the roses Philby had planted, and was enthusiastic about Xelifon's international forest idea. Her love of the garden had reminded Jemme of a series of photos he'd once seen on the interiors of grand French chateaux. He couldn't remember where they'd been, perhaps in the south of France. What he did remember though was the fact that several of the formal reception rooms had feature ceilings. His favourite had great bunches of flowers painted in each corner, tied with magnificent bows which trailed ribbons along the edges of the ceiling. He knew that Hil would love them, especially if they incorporated roses, and he set about making enquiries about reputable artists. He wanted to get someone started on the job straight away, so that it would be a pleasant surprise for Hil when they went back the next weekend. With her piano installed and the ceiling painted, he hoped she would feel like they were really starting to make progress.

Chapter Nineteen

Jemme had had a very good week as far as work was concerned, but a slightly frustrating week when it came to the chateau. Perhaps he had been spoiled by good luck, but everything about the project had seemed so easy until now. Once the hard part of actually finding the building had been dealt with, things seemed to have run a great deal more smoothly. With Philby finding reliable, trust-worthy staff for him at one end, and DD hunting for specific antiques at the other, everything had gone very well so far. He'd been pleased with the way that all work had been completed to time, and to very high standards too. However, he hadn't enlisted DD or Philby's help in finding an artist for the ceiling and he'd found the whole search rather frustrating. He wanted the artist to have started by the time they got down there, so he didn't have long to look and the artists he'd liked weren't always immediately available.

Knowing that they'd recently had some work done, he'd enquired at the Palais de l'Élysées about their decorators, but was told that as soon as they'd finished, the entire team had moved on to the Ritz Hotel in London. Chasing the trail, he phoned the Ritz, but was told by the receptionist there that half of the team were still working. However, she believed that some of them had gone on to the Hôtel Crillon in Paris. Back to where he started, he popped into the Crillon in person to ask, but didn't glean any more information. The concierge he spoke to evidently sensed his frustration, and offered to speak to the manager and see if he could find out any more information.

The next afternoon, he received a phone call from the manager himself.

'*Monsieur Mafeze, bonjour.* I thought I'd take the opportunity to call you in person.'

'That's very good of you,' said Jemme, 'I can imagine how busy you are.'

'Well, I recognised your name straight away; you are a valued customer and so I was pleased to be able to help out.'

Jemme felt a twinge of satisfaction. Although he'd never actually stayed at the Crillon, he regularly hired out one of their function rooms when he was meeting with especially prestigious clients, and it was nice to be recognised. He smiled to himself when he realised that a routine business arrangement had led to the manager of one of Paris's most exclusive hotels chasing painters and decorators for him.

'I appreciate the effort, thank you,' he said.

'I've spoken to the man who led the project here, and he knows of a team of highly skilled and experienced artists who are just finishing a project.'

'Oh, really?' said Jemme, interested.

'Yes, he knows the leader there personally; they finished this morning.'

'What have they been working on?'

'They've been restoring the Petit Trianon at Versailles, Monsieur,' Jemme's interest increased

'Of course, the overall project is a long way from being over,' the manager continued, 'but the section they've been working on is complete, and our artist says that his friend is one of the best in all of Paris.'

'Well this is fantastic news, thank you;' said Jemme, 'the only question is one of availability.'

'He could be available this afternoon if you needed,' said the manager. 'The only problem is that he'll only be available for a week.'

'That's no problem at all, I don't think the project will take more than three days at the most.'

'Ah, very good,' the manager said, and gave Jemme the man's contact details. 'His name is Dupré,' he said.

Jemme thanked him profusely.

'My pleasure, Monsieur. Next time you are in our hotel please ask for me and we can have a coffee together.'

'I should like that,' said Jemme and rang off.

By now it was Thursday, and if he wanted the painting to be started by the weekend, he wouldn't have time to actually meet the artist in person. He rang the number the manager had given him and spoke with Dupré. Although he wasn't especially friendly, he certainly seemed to know what he was talking about. He recognised the style of decoration Jemme described immediately, and even named the chateau. It might not have been the right one, seeing as Jemme himself couldn't even remember it, but it seemed like they were talking about the same thing. Dupré agreed to the work readily enough, and Jemme gave him his address.

'I'm afraid you're going to have to go straight there,' he said, 'My gardener will be able to meet you though and show you around. I'll also ask him to organise scaffolding for you and help you get any other equipment you might need.'

Dupré sniffed something about not needing a *gardener* to help him find artistic materials and muttered a rather curt *au revoir.*

Although a little taken aback, Jemme was still quite pleased. He'd managed to get something sorted without bothering DD or Philby, and his plans for the weekend were all falling into place. He wasn't employing the man to be personable, so his brusqueness didn't really matter. Besides, he'd only be there for three days.

＊　＊　＊　＊

That weekend, the drive down to the chateau slid past as quickly as it had the last weekend. Hil was even more enthusiastic about the room than before, telling Jemme about Louis's attempts to expel the British from India and his alliance with Vietnam.

'I had no idea that France had such interests in the East during that period,' she said, before going on to talk happily about the piano.

'Do you think it will have arrived yet? I really hope it has, I can't believe it's ours and it's going to be in our home, it's so exciting!'

'I know, although I wouldn't get your hopes up sweetheart, it takes a long time to arrange the specialist shipment of something like that, even if it is only travelling a short way. I wouldn't expect it until next weekend at the earliest,' Jemme told her, knowing full well that it had already arrived and been installed in the salon; he just wanted the surprise to be as big as possible for her.

'Oh,' said Hil, a little disappointed, 'never mind, I'm sure there's plenty we can be getting on with whilst we're there.'

They were soon pulling into the driveway again. This time Jemme had been sure to telephone ahead, so as to avoid hurting anyone's feelings. Sure enough, Marguerite, Philby and Xelifon waited outside, forming a rather home-spun, but no less welcoming, guard of honour.

'*Bonjour, bonjour,* welcome back!' said Marguerite, as soon as they had got out of the car. She had even more of a twinkle in her eye than usual, and shot Jemme a conspiratorial glance when Hil wasn't looking. Philby helped them in with their bags and yet another wonderful smell greeted them in hallway.

'Marguerite, I think one day I'm going to steal you and take you back to Paris with us,' said Hil, 'I wish I came home to cooking like this every day!'

Marguerite laughed, 'Tsk, tsk, Madame, what would I do in a big city like Paris? Now, supper is ready for both of you, but it won't spoil if you want to eat it later. I'll go back to the kitchen and leave you to decide.' She scuttled off and, after grunting his goodbyes, Philby slouched off to the garden with Xelifon in tow.

'Shall we follow her through?' said Hil.

'Are you particularly hungry?' Jemme asked.

'Not hugely, I can definitely wait if you wanted to do something else first.'

'I wouldn't mind having another look at the room first, just to get some ideas.'

Hil shrugged, 'Sure,' and followed him through the corridors to the salon. The door was shut and Jemme paused for a while before opening it, 'I'm hoping that there will be someone inside that I'd like you to meet. In fact, I'm hoping to meet him myself too.'

Hil looked intrigued, 'Inside the salon? But we've already seen Xelifon and Philby.'

'Aha,' said Jemme mysteriously and opened the door with a slight flourish.

Hil stepped in and suddenly the look of confusion on her face vanished, to be replaced with one of joy.

'Jemme! Did you do all of this?!'

'Of course! I wanted to show you what it could all be like.'

'I can't believe what a difference it's made already!'

He stood next to her as she looked around. It all seemed to have come together rather nicely. The piano had been installed and set up with the lid propped fully open. The antique shop owner had been as good as his word and managed to find a stool which was a very good match. Best of all, in Jemme's opinion, was the chandelier, which shimmered with warm light, in complete contrast to the blue-tinged strip lighting they'd had there a week before.

Hil followed his gaze up. 'I can't believe that you've managed to get that sorted in only a week,' she said.

'Neither can I, to be honest,' said Jemme, 'although I can't really claim the credit for the light. It was all DD's work.'

'In a week?'

'Yes, I told him what I wanted and he agreed that it wouldn't be that hard to come by. I trusted him to find one at auction, and he arranged for it to be shipped here, where Philby sorted the wiring out.'

'So efficient!' said Hil and smiled again.

'This is actually the first time I've seen it. I'm really pleased – it's done exactly what you talked about and completely changed the tone of the room.'

'It's wonderful, I'm really starting to imagine how it will look finished now. I love the flowers,' she said, looking to the corner of the room.

'Ah, I asked Marguerite to sort that out for me,' said Jemme, 'she's done a nice job.' Following Jemme's instructions, Marguerite had dutifully arranged a beautiful bunch of flowers in each of the four vases she had placed in the corners of the room. 'They're not just there to be pretty though, they're to show you something.'

'To show me something?' repeated Hil questioningly.

'Yes and I was rather hoping to introduce you to someone too. After last weekend I thought again about what you said – about having something in the corners. I think I was a little dismissive at the time and I'm sorry, because I think it's a great idea.'

Hil smiled, 'Thank you.'

'Well, I got thinking about what we could put there instead of having the cherubs. Then, I remembered you admiring Philby's rose beds and I realised, what better way to finish the ceiling than with a bunch of your favourite flowers in each corner. That's what the vases of flowers in the corner are all about – a sort of clue if you like.'

Hil looked stunned, 'Really?'

Jemme nodded, 'I've got an artist to come over straight from Versailles; I've spoken with him on the phone and described the flowers you like most to him, and he'll be completing the work this weekend. I don't know where he is though, I was hoping he'd be in here.'

Hil was still staring at him and Jemme looked momentarily confused, 'Are you pleased?'

'Of *course* I'm pleased, it's one of the nicest things anyone's ever done for me, I'm just taken aback, that's all,' she said, before adding a heartfelt 'thank you,' and wrapping Jemme in a tender embrace. Just as they were enjoying being locked together, the doors at the other end of the room opened and a man neither of them recognised entered.

He looked at them in a slightly surly fashion and made no acknowledgement of the fact he had just interrupted a private moment.

'Ah, hello, I'm hoping you are Dupré,' said Jemme in a friendly manner, freeing himself from Hil and walking towards the man with an outstretched hand. The man took it limply.

'You are Mafeze, *non*?' he said.

'Erm, yes. This is my wife, Madame Mafeze,' said Jemme gesturing to Hil, who reached out to shake the man's hand as well. 'She's the inspiration for this whole project, so it's her you'll have to please, not me,' he joked with the man.

Dupré looked even less impressed with Hil than he had with Jemme. He took her hand for as long as it took him to utter a deeply insincere '*enchanté*', before dropping it again.

Jemme was irritated, but tried not to let it show, 'Have you finished the plans yet?' he asked brightly.

'*Oui*,' replied Dupré.

'May we see them?'

'See them?' he repeated.

'Yes, have a look at them before you paint them on the ceiling.'

Dupré started, 'Monsieur, I will not be changing them,' he said.

'But I'm not asking you to change them yet, I just wanted to have a look before they were committed to the ceiling, I want to make sure that my wife and I are happy with them.'

'But *I'm* happy with them,' said Dupré, with two spots of anger growing in his cheeks.

'I'm pleased,' said Jemme, 'but really, I would be more comfortable if I could—'

'Mon-sieur,' Dupré said, his voice rising, 'I have come straight here from one of the most of prestigious assignments in this entire country. I have just finished working for the *government* on one France's most treasured assets. I am satisfied with these plans, I do not see why there is a problem.'

'But,' began Jemme again, before feeling Hil's soft touch on his elbow. He took in Dupré's expression. The artist stood rooted to the spot and was beginning to turn puce. His eyes bulged slightly and he looked as if he was teetering on the brink of completely losing his temper. Jemme wasn't sure what he had done to anger him so much, but he agreed with Hil; it was better to back down.

'Well, I'm sure you know best,' he said magnanimously, 'I look forward to seeing the finished results.'

Dupré nodded curtly and they left for the kitchen. Even before he had shut the doors to the salon Jemme could feel his ire rising. He realised that he had effectively been dismissed from one of the biggest rooms in his own house by a complete stranger. He had never let an employee talk to him like that before either – Dupré hadn't just been disrespectful, he'd been outright rude. He was annoyed at his manner with Hil too, especially after all the planning he'd done to make sure she had a special weekend. He seethed all the way to the kitchen, and not even Marguerite's excellent stew could put a smile on his face.

Hil put a hand on his arm, 'I can tell you're cross. Don't let him upset you – I think we're just not used to dealing with arty types like that.'

'But he was plain rude.'

'I know,' she soothed, 'but I think he was just affronted that you'd questioned his designs. I have a feeling that there's going to be a lot more where that came from over the course of this whole project, so we'd better get used to it early on.'

Jemme felt marginally placated, but he had a sinking feeling that Hil was right. This was unlikely to be the last temperamental artist he encountered. Fighting down his irritation he managed his best smile, and complimented Marguerite on the dinner. Before long, Hil's rhapsodising about the piano had put a smile on his face and he went to bed in much better humour.

✻ ✻ ✻ ✻

Tired after a busy week, Jemme allowed himself a lie-in the next morning. He awoke to find Hil sitting up in bed reading the papers.

'Morning,' she greeted him and kissed him on the forehead.

'Morning,' he mumbled sleepily, 'what's going on in the world?' he asked.

'Well I'm not sure about the world, but in this little corner of France there are lost cats, school plays and all sorts of other dramatic events.'

'Ah, local news,' said Jemme laughing and sitting up.

'Well the big news is that they're starting work on the high-speed connection to Paris.'

'That's good,' said Jemme, stretching.

'Hungry?'

'I am actually.'

'That's good, because I brought a tray of breakfast up with me,' said Hil, getting up to retrieve it from the dressing table.

'Fantastic, what a star you are,' said Jemme, rubbing the last of the sleep from his eyes.

'It's the least I can do after all your hard work planning this weekend,' Hil said. 'I'm looking forward to today; by the end of it we're going to be one step closer to finishing that room.'

'Mmm,' Jemme agreed as he took a sip of the coffee she'd made for him. 'For a life-long devotee of tea, this is a fine coffee my love,' he said, before adding, 'I'm looking forward to today too.'

They finished up their breakfast and pored over the local paper together, relishing the small-town nature of its stories compared with the faceless and crime-heavy features in the Parisian press. Eventually they made a leisurely move downstairs.

'What a lovely lazy morning,' Hil said.

'Goodness, it's nearly lunchtime!' Jemme laughed as he looked at his watch and noticed the time.

'I wonder how much things have come along whilst we've been sleeping said Hil, 'I can't wait to have a look – let's just drop this tray off with Marguerite first.'

'*Bonjour*,' Marguerite greeted them cheerfully as they entered the kitchen, 'ah, leave that on the side, Madame. I will deal with it.'

'Thanks Marguerite,' said Hil, 'we're just on our way to the salon to see how work's coming along.'

Marguerite's face clouded, 'Oh no, Madame, I would not advise that. He is crazy that man – Dupré? He is *fou*! I went in there to offer him a *petit café* and I thought he would bite my head off! He said no one is to disturb him until he is finished.' She shook her head, 'I don't know who he thinks he is to order us around like this; he has only been here two days!'

Hil frowned and looked at Jemme, 'Perhaps we had better leave him to it. I'm in too much of a nice mood to have my head bitten off.'

'I think you're right. Besides, I don't get the impression we'd be able to change much anyway. Let's go for a walk around the grounds instead. I can show you where Xelifon is planning to plant the international forest, and the vegetable patch is coming along nicely too. Where are the gardeners, Marguerite?'

Marguerite shrugged, 'Xelifon I know is in the village. There is a market today and his father has taken him to buy seeds. He will be back here just after lunch. Monsieur Philby though – I am not so sure. He went down into the *cave* very early this morning and he hasn't been back since.'

'What was he doing in the *cave*?' asked Hil

'He has gone down there to check for leaks, Madame; he has been concerned with trying to remove all the damp in the house.'

Jemme nodded, 'He got off to a good start with the salon, I'm pleased that he's taken matters into his own hands with the rest of the house.'

'Is there likely to be much in the *cave*?' Hil asked Jemme.

'Almost certainly, but it's more a question of whether it's coming up through to here from down there. It's quite complicated though – have you ever been down there?'

'I don't think so actually.'

'Well, it's not just one large cellar, it's a complete labyrinth of tunnels.'

'Tunnels?'

'Yes, they're original to the chateau and they're designed to ensure air moves properly underneath – it's meant to circulate hot air and help prevent damp from occurring. It's needed checking for ages though and I'm pleased Philby's doing it – I wouldn't have wanted to go down there!'

'It doesn't sound like much fun,' admitted Hil, 'Still, it's interesting knowing what's going on down there – I had no idea it was so much like a Roman villa!'

'I hadn't thought about it like that, but I suppose it is,' said Jemme, 'Marguerite, we'll see you later. We're off to wander around the garden if you need us.'

'*Très bien, Monsieur.* Enjoy your walk.'

As they wandered around, Hil kept expressing surprise at how much progress had been made, 'I had no idea there had been as much work outside as in!' she said.

'It's coming along nicely, isn't it?' said Jemme, 'It's strange to think though, Philby is somewhere underground as we speak – he could be close to our feet right now!'

Hil giggled, imagining the gruff gardener burrowing around like a little mole.

They wandered around, admiring the garden a little longer until they realised they had walked up quite a hunger. They turned back to the house, passing Xelifon on the way back. He nodded shyly to them, and Jemme noticed that he was not yet as comfortable around Hil as he was with him. Back in the kitchen, Marguerite shared their surprise that Philby had not yet returned, something which Jemme and Hil discussed over lunch.

'Maybe it's a lot more complicated down there than we thought,' said Hil.

'I hope he hasn't got lost,' Jemme said with a note of concern in his voice.

'I doubt it. Can you imagine Philby getting lost?' asked Hil.

'No, I suppose not!'

After pottering around the house for a few hours, Hil finally cracked,

'Right, I can't stand the suspense any longer. We've been killing time for the whole day, Dupré must be finished by now, and if he's not then he will just have to deal with us going in and having a look.'

'Fair enough,' said Jemme, smiling at his wife's impatience. They made their way over to the salon and exchanged glances with each other outside, giggling nervously.

They opened the door as quietly as they could and slipped into the room. The first thing Hil noticed was a filthy dustsheet tossed over the piano. She knew it had to be protected somehow, but the sheet was so dirty it was probably doing more harm than good. She furrowed her brow and looked up. At the top of the scaffolding with his back to them, Dupré was finishing off the last bouquet and hadn't heard them enter.

Hil looked up at the flowers he had already painted, and a look of dismay crept across her face. She tried to fight it down for Jemme's sake, but a quick glance at him showed that he was feeling the same as her. She looked again. The flowers were not at all as she had imagined and they certainly didn't include any of her favourites. They were stiff and staid, and painted in drab, washed-out colours. Instead of adding a beautiful accent to the room, they detracted from all its features and if anything, were a complete eyesore. The more she looked at them, the more she hated them. She looked over to Jemme, whose expression matched her own. Forgetting to whisper she asked him if he was disappointed.

Dupré heard them and span around on his platform. He threw his paintbrush down in anger,

'I told that woman that I was not to be disturbed!' he said vehemently.

'No, Dupré, there's no need to be angry,' Jemme said firmly, determined not to be browbeaten by the artist again.

'Angry?! You've interrupted my work!' he said, kicking at the paint pot on the platform and causing red paint to slop over the sides and splatter onto the parquet floor below.'

'Will you please be careful,' said Jemme, 'we've devoted a great deal of time to these floors.'

'But not enough time to allow an artist to complete his work!' Dupré shouted down. He kicked at the paint pot again, 'Gah! This kind of thing makes me so angry!' The temper they had seen a brief flash of yesterday seemed to have risen to the surface even faster than before.

'I do not like to show my work until it is finished,' he reiterated, clenching his hands into fists.

'Well, I'm glad we saw it before it was finished,' said Jemme, 'because to be honest, it's not at all what we wanted. I thought you'd understood during our discussions on the phone, but this is completely wrong.'

'Wrong?! WRONG! What do you mean WRONG!' Dupré was not holding anything back now and screamed down at them from the scaffolding tower.

'After all of my efforts, am I to understand that *you* are criticising my work? What do you know of art anyway?! Who are you to criticise me?'

He picked up another paint brush and this time hurled it towards them.

'That is enough!' said Jemme. 'Come down right now and we will discuss this. I may not know as much about art as you, but I know what I wanted for this room and this is not it.'

'Come down, Monsieur, come down? Well if my art is so bad, why don't I just jump down eh?'

He made to put one foot over the side to show he meant it, 'The man's completely mad,' muttered Hil to Jemme in alarm.

'You think I'm not serious, Monsieur eh? You think you know all about artists as well as art? Eh?'

Hil looked pleadingly at Jemme. Dupré had completely and utterly lost his temper and she couldn't tell whether his threats were empty or not.

'Listen, Monsieur Dupré,' she began in a soft voice.

'Ah, now *Madame* is going to try to talk to me is she?' Dupré screeched.

Jemme leaned over to Hil, 'Are you OK staying here for a moment on your own?' he asked. 'I'm going to go and get Philby, he'll know what to do. She nodded and Jemme ran off. He arrived in the kitchen out of breath, 'Marguerite, where's Philby? I need his help quickly, you were right – Dupré is completely *fou*!' He stopped, 'Marguerite, whatever's the matter?' he asked. The usually buoyant governant was pale and wringing her hands in distress.

'It's Monsieur Philby,' she said, 'he still hasn't come up from the *cave* and now it's dark. I am so worried!'

Jemme looked at her in disbelief; the weekend had started so auspiciously, and now it was completely unravelling.

Chapter Twenty

Marguerite sighed and continued her hand-wringing. Jemme was surprised to see his usually phlegmatic housekeeper taking a turn for the melodramatic as soon as there was a whiff of drama. Years of high-pressure situations at the bank had taught him to remain level-headed, even in the most trying of circumstances. He took a deep breath; one crisis at a time.

'Marguerite,' he said evenly, 'there's no need to worry. I'm sure Philby will be perfectly fine. If he's not back within the hour, then we will all go looking for him together. Think how cross he'd be if we all went charging after him when he was just going about his business.'

Marguerite stifled a sob and nodded.

'Now,' said Jemme, 'I'm afraid there is a situation brewing next door, which is much more urgent. Dupré' – despite her distress, Marguerite still managed to tut at the mention of the name – 'Dupré,' Jemme continued, 'has got rather carried away and is threatening to jump off his scaffolding. I don't seem to be making any difference, and I really need someone's help. I thought maybe a native French speaker would be able to cajole him in a way that I can't.'

'Tsk,' repeated Marguerite, 'I would be glad, Monsieur – glad! – if he jumped off. He is a ridiculous man,' she harrumphed.

'Well, no one's especially fond of him,' said Jemme, 'but this is quite an urgent situation. Marguerite, I really need you to come with me right now.'

Marguerite had resumed her kitchen duties, apparently much calmed by the news of Dupré's impending doom. She spun round and waggled a dishcloth at Jemme.

'And why would he listen to me, heh? He would say that I am only the cook – he would talk down his long nose to me, Monsieur. These artists, they are all the same. They need to feel that they are in control the whole time,' she threw up her hands and turned back to attending her work, 'they are so *hysterical*, these artists, they give French people a bad name.'

Sensing when to cut his losses, Jemme decided to head straight back to the salon. Something Marguerite had said had stuck with him – the artist likes to feel he is in control.

Entering the salon again, he saw that the situation had deteriorated since he was last there. Hil was looking even more distressed, and Dupré was even more excitable. He was dangling one foot over the edge of scaffolding again. Hil winced.

'Ah Madame doesn't like that? Doesn't like it as much as she doesn't like my flowers eh?' he said shrilly.

Feeling a great deal calmer, Jemme assessed the situation quickly. He highly doubted Dupré had any intention of jumping. For one thing, he seemed to be enjoying taunting Hil too much. It was as if it was his way of regaining the upper hand after his art had been slighted. Hil spun round and saw Jemme. She looked momentarily relieved, but then after looking around desperately and realising he hadn't brought anyone with him, seemed panicked again.

'Monsieur Dupré,' Jemme began in a calm, measured voice, 'I am sorry that we have got to this point. I am even sorrier when I remember how excited we were to hear that such a respected artist was coming to work with us,' he paused long enough to note that Dupré was no longer dangling his foot.

'You were lucky, Monsieur,' he muttered, glowering at Jemme.

'Indeed we were,' said Jemme indulgently, 'and the flowers you have created for us here are wonderful. I love them and in a perfect world I would love them to be here always. The only problem is that we have very, very specific plans for this room. Many of the fittings and furnishings have already been ordered, and so it is too late to change anything. I am extremely concerned that everything else in the room will clash with your flowers. The style is all wrong in the context of the room and, as I'm very keen for you to sign your work, I'm anxious that people would think unfairly of you. If they did not realise that the flowers came first, they might think – completely incorrectly – that the artist whose signature they saw had been insensitive to the room and the style here,' he paused tentatively again. Dupré had stopped pacing around and, although scowling furiously, he was looking somewhat placated.

'It's my fault entirely,' said Jemme, 'I should have discussed the rest of the room with you in great detail. I should have known you would understand the style in great detail, *as an artist*,' he said, emphasising the words, just slightly.

'*Oui, Monsieur*, it was foolish,' Dupré said haughtily.

Jemme was quick to jump on the opportunity, 'Oh yes, absolutely,' he said, nodding furiously, 'which is why I'm asking for your help and your advice – *as an artist*,' he said with the same subtle emphasis. 'I want to keep your flowers very much,' he began, talking in his normal voice.

'Monsieur – I cannot hear you if you are going to mumble like that,' Dupré interrupted, tetchily.

'My apologies,' Jemme said, continuing at exactly the same volume, 'as I was saying…'

Dupré flung up his hands, 'That is no better either! Wait, wait – I will come down,' he said, starting to climb the ladder. He turned his back just long enough for Hil and Jemme to exchange relieved glances and for Hil to mouth, 'Well done!' at Jemme.

Once on the same level, Jemme proposed covering his roses with a very thin layer of paint so that they would be preserved and could be uncovered, completely fresh when the room 'inevitably' changed at some point in the future. He emphasised the clashing décor again, and then swooped in with a peace offering,

'Seeing how beautifully you finished the roses, there's something I was wondering if you would consider undertaking. It's a much bigger job but it's also a much more prestigious commission. I don't know how you would feel about it...'

'Go on,' said Dupré, sounding more rational.

'Well, as you may know, there is another reception room, about the same size as this one,' said Jemme.

Dupré nodded, and wiped some paint from his hands onto his overall.

'Well, I have a very ambitious plan for the ceiling there, but I have been waiting until I could find someone I trusted enough with it,' said Jemme, laying it on as thickly as he could.

Dupré nodded again, clearly giving it his full attention.

'I want it to be painted as the sky, and for it to be done with the highest possible skill; I want it to be based on the most beautiful of all the ceilings at Versailles, and I want the artist who completes it for me to be able to equal the artist Louis XIV employed. It's a very big commission Dupré and it will be such a large feature that people are sure to ask about it. I want to be able to tell them who completed it with a sense of pride. Do you think you could be up to the challenge?'

Dupré stroked his chin slowly, 'I have been to Versailles many times, Monsieur,' he said thoughtfully, 'the ceilings there are *magnifique*.'

'Yes, yes, they are,' said Jemme encouraged.

'I can paint you one which is just as good as the finest that Versailles has to offer,' he said eventually, as a look of determination entered his eyes, and something akin to a smile flickered across his face. Realising that that was as good as he was going to get, Jemme rushed to express his 'huge gratitude' to him for 'taking on this difficult commission' and dashed off to the kitchen. One crisis averted, he thought to himself on the way, time to deal with the next one.

He arrived at the kitchen wondering if Marguerite had continued to calm down. He was pretty sure that news of Dupré's safe scaffolding dismount would actually worsen her mood, rather than improve it. Entering the room, he saw that Marguerite was once again in a high state of agitation. She rushed towards him when she saw him at the door,

'Ah Monsieur, I am so glad you're back – it is *'orrible, 'orrible!*'

'What is Marguerite?'

'Ai,' she sighed heavily, shaking her head. She moved aside and unblocked Jemme's view... revealing, for the first time, a very bedraggled Philby.

Even though Jemme hadn't ever considered Philby to be in serious danger, he was nonetheless concerned for one of his most trusted employee's welfare, and had started to feel a little anxious about his extended absence. He looked at him now. Philby was struggling to retain an air of his usual competence, but he couldn't help looking forlorn and a little helpless.

'Philby, whatever happened to you?!' Jemme said, 'You're soaked through!'

Philby sniffed and looked down at himself. It was true, he was dripping wet, and he turned to Jemme with wide, sorrowful eyes, as if to acknowledge the fact.

Marguerite was fussing around him, and wrapping towels about him and entreating him to take off his wet over-wear. A kettle was starting to sing on the hob, and she turned round to tend to it. Just at that moment Xelifon appeared at the door.

'Did you find it?' Philby rasped, speaking for the first time.

Xelifon nodded and smiled his usual slow smile, slipping Philby a small silver flask. Philby sneezed and with slightly shaky hands unscrewed the lid. He took a long draught from it, coughed profusely and then exhaled sharply, satisfied. A flicker of fire returned to his eyes and he smacked at his chest with his fist.

'*Bon*!' he said triumphantly.

Jemme looked at him questioningly.

'*Eau-de-vie, Monsieur*,' he explained in a rather hoarse voice. 'Made in the village.' Just as he was lifting the bottle to his mouth for a second swig, Marguerite finished with the kettle and turned around,

'HEH! Oh no you don't!' she said, swiping the bottle away from him. Philby looked crestfallen, but it appeared the first gulp had done its work as he smiled furtively whilst Marguerite lectured him,

'Here I am, making you a cup of tea and soup and warming you with towels so that you do not catch the *grippe,* and all you are doing is guzzling moonshine – it will poison you I tell you, poison you!'

Jemme couldn't help smiling himself. He was pleased to see his gardener's spirits were raised too, but it still didn't explain what had been going on.

'So, what on earth happened to you Philby?' he asked, 'You've been gone since the early morning – we were just about ready to mount a search party.'

Philby shuddered a little, and shook his head. Jemme was amused to see Xelifon make the most of Marguerite's turned back by snatching the bottle back from the counter and stuffing it into Philby's lap. He drained a large amount of it, coughed again and smiled,

'I was lost, Monsieur,' he said simply.

'Lost? But where? I thought you'd been in the *cave* looking for damp.'

'*Oui*, I was lost underground, Monsieur.'

'How horrible,' said Hil, coming into the kitchen and overhearing. 'You poor thing, we'd all been getting rather worried about you. We had no idea where you'd got to.'

'I was underground the whole time, Madame,' said Philby.

'But – how? I don't understand,' said Hil.

Marguerite had been looking at the spot where she had left the confiscated hip flask with some confusion, but on hearing Hil, returned to the conversation,

'Ah, Madame, the tunnels under these old chateaux – they stretch for miles!'

'Miles? Surely not, where would they go?'

'Well, they are like a maze, they turn and turn – if you unfolded them all and made them straight, then they would be miles long.'

'Oh, I see,' said Hil, 'I had no idea that the cellar was like that – I've never once been down there.'

'It is not a nice place for you, Madame,' said Philby. 'It is very cold and very damp.'

'Isn't there a stream right through there which feeds the lake?' asked Jemme 'I remember seeing it in the deeds. Someone told me that the water was pure enough to drink.'

'*Oui, Monsieur*, there is a stream. The water in it is very clear. I have drunk it myself.'

'What, when you were down there today?'

'*Oui, Monsieur*, I was very thirsty after walking for hours. It is very pure.'

'Well, that's interesting – I wonder if we could –'

Hil gave Jemme a stern look and interrupted him, 'I can't help feeling that we're getting a little sidetracked. The important thing is not the quality of the water, it's the fact that Philby has had a horrible experience today, and we need to make sure he is alright.'

'*Merci, Madame*. Although, I should say again that the water is very clear. Not clear enough though,' he added and his face darkened slightly again.

'Oh so you don't think we could pipe it up here?' Jemme asked, 'That's what I was going to say before I was interrupted – it would be amazing to be able to drink-' he trailed off as Hil gave him another stern look.

'Go on, Philby,' she said pointedly.

'Well, I mean it wasn't clear enough for me to see my torch – that's the problem. The tunnels are not always level and the stream in some places is very fast and quite deep – maybe as much as a foot, especially nearer the lake. I stopped by it to tie my shoelace, and dropped my torch. It rolled in and I tried to chase it, but the water carried it away. I ended up standing up to my knees in the water in the pitch black.'

Philby had apparently given up caring about Marguerite's disapproval and brazenly took another swig from the bottle. He was becoming quite garrulous, but everyone was too distracted by his tale to notice this change in character.

'Go on,' prompted Hil again.

'Well, I could feel the direction of the current, so I walked against it, to get upstream. Then I tried to feel my way along the tunnels using my hands. They turn around so much though, that I was disorientated after about five minutes and completely lost after about ten. I have no idea where I wandered – maybe I covered the whole *cave*, maybe I only stayed in the same small spot, but I have been walking and feeling my way for hours and hours. Sometimes I would find myself in the stream again, sometimes I couldn't even hear it.'

'Oh, Philby,' said Hil softly.

'Ah Madame, it was a misadventure,' said Philby with uncharacteristic joviality. 'It must have been around lunchtime, because suddenly I was very hungry and I sat down in a dry bit of tunnel and realised that it could be a very serious situation I'd got myself into – I thought I might have to spend the night down there!'

Hil shook her head sorrowfully. Jemme was amused to note that Philby was obviously enjoying her sympathy, and seemed to be enjoying the attention too. It was so unlike him.

'So,' Philby continued, 'I decided to get help. I couldn't find my way back to the entrance, so I started to shout. I shouted at the top of my voice and I banged against the wall tunnels with my fists, but no one heard me.'

Marguerite shook her head, 'But of course we didn't hear you! The walls in these chateaux – they are so thick! And you were *underground,* Monsieur Philby! How did you expect us to hear you heh?'

Philby looked a little chastened but continued, 'I realise that, Madame Marguerite, and so after I had shouted myself hoarse, I realised I would have to carry on walking.'

'So how did you manage to get out in the end?' asked Jemme, intrigued, 'Did you manage to find the entranceway again?'

Philby polished off the brandy and shook his head dramatically, '*Non, Monsieur.* That is when I had the idea.'

'The idea?' Jemme repeated, wryly.

'*Oui, Monsieur.* I remembered that the stream flows towards the lake. So, once I found the stream again, I followed it. Only, this time I went in the direction of the current. The stream got deeper and deeper and I knew I was meeting the place where it joined the lake.'

'But I don't understand how you would have been able to climb out,' said Jemme, 'I know the lake really well and I don't recall ever having seen any tunnels feeding into it.'

'You cannot see it, Monsieur, it does not come above the water.'

'So how did you manage to climb out?' asked Hil, just as intrigued.

Philby looked cunning, 'I did not climb, Madame,' he said, knowing that everyone was hanging on his every word. Pausing for maximum effect, he concluded, 'I swam!'

'You swam?!' shrieked Marguerite, 'Are you completely mad? No wonder you are so wet! I have never heard anything so ridiculous – you should never have gone down into those terrible tunnels in the first place.'

'Goodness, Philby, it does sound like quite the adventure. I'm glad you're back safe and sound, I hate the thought of you having to spend a moment longer down in those tunnels,' said Hil.

His story over, Philby regained some of his usual composure and shrugged off Hil's concern.

'It was not really swimming, Madame. I was only underwater for a very short period before I popped up, and then it wasn't far to the banks of the lake.'

'Well, even so, I hope it's your last adventure for a while,' said Hil.

They both expressed their relief that Philby was OK, and withdrew from the kitchen. As they walked back up the stairs, Jemme slipped an arm over Hil's shoulders.

'Goodness, what a weekend it's been!' he said squeezing her shoulder.

'I know,' said Hil, 'I'm utterly exhausted. What time is it?'

Jemme looked at his watch and started slightly, 'It's seven o'clock! We'd better head back for Paris soon or it will be very late by the time we get back. Do you want to have supper here, or shall we grab something on the way?'

'I think I'd rather get something on the way back actually,' said Hil wearily. 'It looks like Marguerite's got her hands full downstairs, and I don't want to get back too late.'

'Of course. Let's get our things together and we can leave pretty much now,' said Jemme. He looked at Hil and could tell that she wanted to put as much distance between herself and the chateau as possible, something which concerned him slightly. Back in the car, having said their farewells, he thought he'd check.

'You did still enjoy this weekend, didn't you?' he asked, pulling out of the driveway and turning left for Paris.

Hil exhaled slowly, 'I think *enjoy* might be rather a strong word,' she said.

Jemme looked concerned, 'But I thought you'd be pleased – the beautiful piano is installed and the room is coming along nicely. We've got somebody working on yet another room and everything is really coming together. We had such a nice time together on Saturday as well.'

Hil sighed, 'That's the problem with you, Jemme. You're so close to this project you can't see anything else. Think objectively, for one moment, about what actually happened this weekend. Someone we employ and are responsible for was trapped in the cold and dark underground. He could have drowned, and we wouldn't have known about it for hours. What if he had slipped and banged his head? He could have been lying in one of those tunnels all day and no one would have gone to help him.'

'But he was fine,' said Jemme, trying to soothe her.

'I know he was fine, but he could easily not have been. It's a horrible thought. As is the fact that a man I have never met before threatened to commit suicide in our home.'

'But that was fine as well. In fact I don't think he ever had any intention of seriously doing it.'

'It doesn't matter – the fact is that it still happened and it was very unpleasant. In fact, I think it was disturbing. But it's all water off a duck's back to you. You don't really seem to care at all, as long as the house is progressing. It's like when poor Philby was telling you that he'd lost his torch in the stream. I could tell what you were thinking – you were thinking about the stream and how we could use it, not listening to his story at all.' She finished and a silence fell over them. Jemme felt deeply hurt. Hil had essentially accused him of caring about the house more than anything. He tried to think back over the weekend and see if she had a point or not. He could admit that there had been set-backs, definitely. However, when he considered the net output, it had been a profitable one. There had been a couple of mishaps, granted, but at the end of the weekend they were definitely better off than they had been at the beginning. He looked over at Hil again. Her face was clouded by what looked dangerously close to a scowl. It was so wholly out of character for her that he realised there must be something he wasn't considering. He thought some more. Had he been too obsessed by the changes to notice how upsetting the events had been for her? He knew that when he applied himself to something he was focussed and driven, but that was just part of his character. It was what had made him a success professionally and he had thought it was something Hil loved and admired. Realising that perhaps he had misunderstood something over the weekend, he resolved to pay closer attention in future; the very last thing he wanted was for this project to drive them apart.

'I'm sorry things turned out the way they did sweetheart,' he said, still not really sure what the problem was. 'I promise to…pay more attention from now on,' he added tentatively, shooting Hil a sideways glance. She raised one eyebrow and uncrossed her arms. Jemme sensed he was on the right track, 'and I promise I'll think of you and us before anything else in this project,' he added quickly. Hil's shoulders went down and she looked a little more relaxed.

'If you like, we don't even have to go to the chateau next weekend,' he ventured, 'we can stay in Paris and do whatever you like.'

This time Hil actually smiled, 'Really?'

'Of course!' said Jemme, returning her smile. 'Then, as soon as this room is finished, we can have some of our oldest and closest friends over. We can have a wonderful dinner with them and show them what we've been up to all this time.'

Hil was fully smiling now, 'That sounds wonderful. I've missed seeing everyone with all these frequent trips out of Paris. I should like to have them all over very much.'

'Then that's exactly what we'll do,' said Jemme, pleased his wife was happy again. However, deep down he could feel the first twinges of anxiety at the prospect of having committed to a whole weekend away from the chateau.

* * * *

Back in Paris, Jemme was starting to feel as if he hadn't had a moment to catch his breath. The week had been in full swing since first thing on Monday morning, and showed no signs of slowing down. Back to back meetings and presentations meant that Jemme felt he had had very little time to get any actual work done, and so he had found himself staying much later than usual most evenings, often eating his supper at his desk whilst he went over reports and figures. Thursday morning saw the arrival of a long-anticipated meeting with a small team from the aerospace company, Airbus. The company had recently been expanding, and the question of who would handle the new accounts was the talk of the banking world. It would be a coup for Jemme on a professional and personal level. To bring in such a prestigious name would add to the bank's profile considerably, and raise them up a league too. DD had managed to set up a face-to-face meeting, which was a good first step, and three of the company's board, including the chairman, were coming up from Toulouse for the meeting. Jemme had been preparing for it for a while and was surprised to feel a twinge of nerves when he heard that the men had arrived.

He made his way to the boardroom, just as DD was ushering the trio in.

'Ah, gentlemen, good morning. I trust your trip up was a pleasant one,' he said brightly, shaking them all by the hand. Two of them returned his shake limply, and looked rather morose. The only one who actually looked pleased to be there introduced himself as Charles, the Finance Director. He then introduced Thierry, the Chief Executive and De Valéry, the Chairman. Whilst Jemme instantly warmed to Charles, he knew that he was the least powerful of the three, and the man he really needed to impress was the one who looked the most sullen, De Valéry, because he had political connections and much decision-making power. He smiled as warmly as he could, and ushered them into the boardroom where

DD had neatly laid out all the materials they would need: a bottle of mineral water and crystal glass for each person, a thick notepad and high quality pen, as well as a bound copy of the printed documents Jemme was going to talk them through. Once they were seated, DD asked them with all his usual politeness whether they would like a tea or a coffee. '*Café*', muttered De Valéry and Thierry whilst Charles looked genuinely grateful at the prospect.

'Ah, *un café* would be *magnifique!*' he said with relish. '*Merci, Monsieur..?*'

'Dietz,' DD informed him with a slight inclination of his head.

'*Ah, Monsieur Dietz, merci.*'

Jemme smiled inwardly. So far, everything was going to plan. He had anticipated that the men would want coffee after their long journeys, and so had arranged for a special packet of coffee to be brought from Paris' oldest café, Café Procope. As well as being the oldest, it was also one of the most interesting, and telling its story would be a nice ice-breaker, getting the men to engage with him early on about a subject which had nothing to do with business. It was a tactic that had worked for him many times before. It was a good way of getting people out of 'business mode' and relaxing a little.

DD emerged with a small tray, just as everyone had settled into their seats. He moved silently around the table, laying a gold-rimmed cup and saucer in front of everyone, before disappearing, equally silently. The men fell on their coffees and, after only a few sips, Jemme thought he could notice De Valéry and Thierry perk up.

'I hope the *café* is to your taste, gentlemen,' he said.

Charles nodded, 'Very much so,' he said approvingly.

De Valéry made a noise which sounded a little like a grunt and Jemme realised that he was going to have to work harder than he had initially thought.

'I'm glad,' he continued with a slightly forced jollity, 'because we actually bought it especially for you. It's from Café Procope in the sixth Arrondissement – on rue de l'Ancienne Comédie. It's the oldest café in France, and one of the first that served coffee.' He paused. Charles was looking at him with interest, but the other two were tipping their cups back to get the last few drops, and paid him little heed. 'It often entertained even Benjamin Franklin, one of the founders of the US and later ambassador to Paris. Even Jefferson was there, one of the most avid collectors of French wines and president of the US.

'In fact, it's been serving coffee since the late seventeenth century when it was completely unknown to Parisians – something I'm sure you'll agree seems a strange thought these days. Back then it was a very exotic import from Turkey, and caused quite a stir – the waiters serving it used to dress up in Turkish clothes for the occasion.'

'How interesting,' Charles smiled.

De Valéry finished his coffee and banged the cup down, 'To business,' he said so abruptly that Jemme had trouble disguising his surprise.

'Yes of course,' he said, trying to smooth things over. 'Now, if you'd like to look at the first page of the documents in front of you, I'll begin to explain them to you.'

De Valéry completely ignored him and skipped straight to page five. He saw a table of data and stubbed it with his finger, 'Explain this to me,' he said brusquely.

'Well, the first five pages actually build up to that particular table, so I think it might be easier if we start at –' Jemme began before De Valéry interrupted him by shaking his hand dismissively.

'Monsieur Mafeze, I have no interest in the first five pages, especially if they only lead to this point. Now, you created this document *n'est-ce pas?*'

'I –' Jemme began

'*Monsieur, oui ou non?*' asked De Valéry

'Yes.'

'Well then you'll be able to explain these figures to me clearly and succinctly, won't you?'

Jemme was a little taken aback. Far from disarming these men with a thoughtful gesture and talking to them as peers, they seemed completely hostile to him. He pulled himself together and talked them through the data in the table as clearly as he could. Every time he tried to issue a caveat, and reference the necessary preceding pages, De Valéry made the same imperious hand gesture. The rest of the meeting continued in the same vein, with Jemme unable to make any of the points he'd been hoping to. He felt like the chairman had wrested all control of the meeting from him, and instead of impressing them with carefully thought out strategies, he spent all his time fielding awkward questions and trying to redirect their attention towards certain graphs and tables in the document. He looked at his watch and realised that he didn't have long left, but felt like he was going to need a miracle to get them on his side at this point. De Valéry seemed to sense that the meeting was drawing to a close, too. Tossing the paper he was holding onto the table, he leant back in his chair and folded his arms.

'So, Monsieur Mafeze, from what I have seen today, you have nothing more to offer us than any of the other banks we have seen so far. Why is it I should pick you, a new, small bank over one of your bigger and more established competitors?'

He looked at Jemme as if he didn't expect him to have an answer to the question.

Jemme paused a moment, 'Actually, I think that our smallness is our strength.'

'Oh?'

'With us you would receive a personal service from the very beginning. You've seen our building – this is it. It's not some huge skyscraper where people on the first floor have never even met people on the seventeenth. In a large bank, you might have your meeting with one associate and then be managed by a team of around ten. There's no continuity, with people forgetting your name from one day to the next as your folder gets passed around. I built this business up from scratch, and so I take a great personal interest in every single one of my clients and employees. No one is hired until I have interviewed them, and no important decisions are made on client accounts without my approval.'

'That may be so, Monsieur Mafeze, but that means that you are asking us to trust you personally – we would be exposing ourselves to greater risk.'

'I would be happy for you to talk to any one of my clients,' said Jemme, feeling the deal slipping through his fingers. 'In fact, they would all be happy to talk to you – I have developed good relationships with them all, and many of them have even become friends. They would all tell you that when I have committed to something I will see it through, even if it means managing it on every level myself. I will not accept things if they are less than perfect. It's a character trait as much as a business one, and something that pervades every aspect of my life.'

No one said anything, and so he started speaking just to fill the silence.

'Take for example, my current personal project. At the moment I'm renovating a chateau, which is a second home at present, but which is destined to be my full time home very soon–' he paused, surprised to see that De Valéry had uncrossed his arms and was leaning forward in his seat. He looked interested for the first time since he had arrived.

'It's a huge project,' Jemme continued, encouraged, 'but I have ensured that I have complete control over the whole operation. I'm just as happy to roll my sleeves up and get involved with the manual labour as I am finding specialist gilders.

'And you *own* this chateau, Monsieur?' asked De Valéry.

'Yes, my wife and I bought it some time ago,' said Jemme.

'*Incroyable*,' breathed the chairman, 'and you have had to do much work on it?'

'Yes, I'm afraid so. I've had to start from the bottom up, right from hiring an architect.'

'It must have been in very bad condition in that case,' said De Valéry.

'Oh it was – dreadful. In fact, I didn't end up hiring the architect in the end. I created the plans myself and ran them past a design consultant.'

'Yourself, Monsieur – a banker?' asked De Valéry in disbelief.

'Yes, me, a banker,' returned Jemme with a smile. 'Like I said, I'll take on any task to make sure that the project is perfect.'

'*Incroyable*,' repeated De Valéry.

'How did it come to be in such poor condition?' asked Thierry, speaking for the first time.

'Well, before I bought it, it was actually the property of the government, who used it as a sort of office and holiday home combined.'

The three men hooted, 'No wonder it was in such a poor state!' laughed De Valéry, 'I'm surprised it was even standing at all.'

Jemme sensed an opening and jumped on the opportunity. He joined in the men's laughter about *le gouvernment stupide* and talked some more about his chateau and the developments in the time since he had bought it. The story of the American golfer who ripped out the library prompted more laughter, and he played to his audience well. Within about quarter of an hour, everyone had completely relaxed and the conversation was flowing easily and fluently. DD brought in another round of coffees and the story of the Café Procope was retold with great interest. Before he knew it, the atmosphere had turned from frosty to convivial. It turned out that the chateaux of Northern France were of particular interest to De Valéry, and he spent a great deal of his free time on the boards of various trusts concerned with their preservation. He wanted Jemme to tell him about every step he had taken to renovate and repair and listened keenly, completely ignoring the time.

'Well, Monsieur, I am impressed,' he said for the fourth or fifth time. 'Not just with your project, but with your dedication to it and your own personal involvement.'

Far from slipping through his fingers, Jemme could feel the deal bouncing back into his hands. He knew he needed to make some kind of gesture to cinch it.

'Actually, I'm soon to complete my first room,' he said. 'My wife and I would consider it a great honour if you would come as our first guests for an inaugural dinner party. It will be the first of many, I hope.'

'*Monsieur, bien sûr* we will come!' said De Valéry with a gleam in his eye. The conversation descended into what they could expect from the room, and Jemme breathed a sigh of relief internally, knowing that he had saved the deal just in the nick of time. It wasn't until the men had finally left, some three hours later and in much higher spirits, that he wondered if Hil would be as pleased as he was. He had promised to put her first and be sensitive to what she wanted, and he was trying to remember what she had said about the first dinner. He had a niggling feeling that she wanted it to be an intimate affair, with old friends she felt they had neglected. He brushed it aside – she would understand how important the deal had been, and besides, he was sure that the more people there, the merrier the whole evening would be.

Chapter Twenty-One

Following the success of his meeting with Airbus, Jemme had stayed in the office going through paperwork with DD, and making sure that everything was completely flawless. He had arrived home even later that evening than he had during the rest of the week. Nevertheless, he was in high spirits and keen to share the success of his day with Hil. He was also hugely hungry and was just wondering whether he could hold off telling her until after he'd finished eating, when Hil opened the door. He could tell instantly that she wasn't pleased, but could see she was doing her best to disguise it.

'I arrived home hours ago!' she said, greeting him with a small kiss on the cheek, 'I feel like I've barely seen you this week,' she added slightly sadly as she closed the door behind him.

'I know, sweetheart, I'm sorry. I've just had so much on recently, I feel like I've barely caught up with myself. It's all been good though – lots of exciting stuff and hopefully one very big deal indeed.'

'I thought that you were meant to be taking more of a back seat though. I thought that once everything was running on its own you were meant to be relinquishing control to DD, and freeing up your time for other things.'

'Yes, that is the overall plan,' said Jemme slowly, 'but there are still lots of things I need to attend to personally. Like today's deal. Besides, you know how hard it is for me to allow others to take over my projects,' he tried to sound jovial, but his patience was growing thin. He had left work on a real high after the Airbus success, and now it felt like they were inching dangerously close to a row.

'I know it's hard for you,' said Hil, 'but it's hard for me too. There's always got to be some big project on the go. First of all it was the bank. Then you said that you would take a step back from that, which was fine, but then the house swept in to occupy that space. If you haven't even taken a step back from the bank, then you've got two huge things on the go and – like you said – you find it impossible to allow anyone else to help. You have to be involved on every level, and it leaves very little room for anyone else.'

'It leaves plenty of room for other people – look how many people I employ at the bank! Look how many people we've taken on already at the house!'

'I don't mean within the projects. I mean that it leaves very little room for other people in your life.'

'Hil, that's completely unfair. I have always prioritised you; I know that I've not been around much this week, but it's one week!'

'It's not just one week, Jemme. If you don't – or can't – find enough time to have an evening meal with your wife once in a whole week, then how on earth are you going to find enough time to start a family.'

Jemme let out a small groan, 'Please, Hil, not this again. I don't have the time or energy for this discussion at the moment.'

Hil said nothing, but just stared at him, as if he had completely proved her point. Taking advantage of the silence to pull himself together, Jemme mustered all his remaining strength to fight down his anger and aggravation. He took a deep breath and exhaled slowly.

'Look, sweetheart, I'm really sorry that I'm home late this evening. Believe me, I am. I would obviously much rather be at home with my wonderful wife than stuck in my office with my assistant. However, I had an incredibly important meeting today, almost a career-defining one and I really couldn't get away any earlier. I understand why you're upset and I'd like to talk to you about it all, but I think the first thing I need to do is have something to eat, otherwise I'm not going to be able to think straight.'

Hil relented slightly, then glanced at her watch. She looked up at him in concern, 'It's a quarter to eleven – you must be absolutely starving!'

Jemme grinned at her, 'I am a little.'

'There's some supper left in the oven. I've already eaten.'

'I'm glad – I wouldn't have expected you to wait,' said Jemme kissing the top of her head as he passed by her to the kitchen.

Hil sat with him whilst he ate his supper. When he had nearly finished, she sighed, 'I'm sorry too, I suppose. I know how hard you've worked to set the bank up and I realise I can't expect you to just give so much up of it up, just like that. I know how important the chateau is to you, too. Maybe I should have understood how difficult it was for you to give up going this weekend. I really appreciate it though; it's a big gesture and it means a lot.'

Jemme swallowed the last mouthfuls of his food guiltily. He wondered if he could get away with telling Hil that he was planning on heading off on Saturday morning for a quick trip, as well as the fact he had invited a board of directors to their first evening there.

* * * *

That Saturday morning, Jemme drove out of Paris very early in the morning. He hadn't woken Hil to say goodbye and he wasn't even sure she would have responded if he had. He wasn't planning on staying in the chateau long; he just wanted to check that the work was all coming along as it was supposed to, and get back to Paris as soon as possible. He had reasoned that the earlier he was up then the earlier he could get back. As he drove along the near-empty autoroute, the silvery fingers of dawn poked their way up from the horizon. He watched the sun begin to rise and remembered the trip into the desert he and Hil had taken. He remembered sitting down on a blanket with her pressed against him and watching the vast orb of shimmering pink light slowly sail upwards. It saddened him that they didn't feel as close at the moment as they had then. They rarely fought, not least because Hil's capacity for tolerance and forgiveness was seemingly never-ending. He idly wondered whether he had asked her to put up with more than was fair. Perhaps coming to the chateau again was selfish. He tried to justify it to himself: it wasn't for his own sake he was coming, it was for both of them. He wasn't even doing it for pleasure, it was so that he could ensure that everything was as it was meant to be. After the fuss with Dupré, he was more aware than ever that errors needed to be caught as early as possible. If Dupré had been charged with decorating a much larger area and they had left him to his own devices until the whole thing was finished, it would have been a complete disaster. His reasons for checking up on everything were manifold. Firstly, from a quality point of view: it was better to identify a lacklustre artist or unskilled craftsman as early as possible. Secondly from a financial point of view: if work wasn't up to scratch then the more that was completed, the more it would cost to correct it. Also, the longer he would be paying someone to complete sub-par work. Thirdly, from a timings point of view: the longer someone worked on something unacceptable, the longer it longer it would take to correct, and further the deadlines would have to be extended. Hil was the one who was anxious to have things completed as soon as possible and so she stood most to benefit from this trip. Besides, in the absence of a project manager, it was just good practice. If everyone had been left to work unchecked and something had gone disastrously wrong, people would rightly point the finger at him and ask why he hadn't monitored things more closely, and had better control over proceedings. Yes, it was just good practice.

Feeling that he had fully justified the visit, he drove the rest of the journey to Chateau Vigne-Verte with a lighter heart.

It was only just light by the time he arrived, although, as ever, Philby was waiting to greet him.

'Good morning, Philby,' said Jemme cheerfully.

'*Bonjour, Monsieur*,' said Philby, just as he had every time Jemme had arrived. Only the puffiness surrounding his eyes betrayed the early hour.

'How has everything been over the past week?'

'*Bien, Monsieur*. Monsieur Dupré is keeping out of our way. He is very enthusiastic about the Versailles ceiling, and has already been there twice to make sketches.'

'Good, I'm pleased to hear it, and pleased to hear that he's keeping out of your way too!'

Philby grunted.

'How are you, anyway, Philby? I hope you're back to your normal self after last weekend's mishap.'

Philby shrugged, 'I am as usual, Monsieur,' he said simply.

'Excellent, glad to hear it. Now, is Marguerite up? I think some breakfast is in order. You can talk me through all the developments over coffee.'

'She is up, Monsieur,' said Philby as he looked around for Jemme's bag.

Jemme realised what he was doing, 'Ah, no Philby, no luggage, although thanks all the same. I'm only here for the day this time, remember?'

'*Ah, oui, Monsieur,*' he looked momentarily uncomfortable as he tried to find something to do with his gnarled hands instead. He settled for jamming them into his oilskin and marched ahead of Jemme, leading the way into the kitchen.

The kitchen was full of wonderful smells; within an instant Jemme could tell that coffee had just been made and buttery pastry of some sort was in the oven.

He inhaled deeply, 'Ah Marguerite, what a welcome! This is my home away from home.'

'Monsieur!' said Marguerite, head bobbing up from behind the counter where she had been looking for jam in a cupboard. '*Bonjour*! Have you had a pleasant journey? Please – sit, sit!'

'I have, thank you Marguerite, although I'm sorry you've all had to get up so early.'

Marguerite waved away his apology, 'Nonsense! We must have the house looking at its best! Now, you sit and I will get you breakfast. You are staying for lunch too, *non*?'

'Actually Marguerite, I'm not sure that I am.'

Marguerite's eyebrows flicked up.

'I know it's only a flying visit, but I must return to Paris as quickly as I can,' Jemme explained, 'In fact, I promised Hil that I wouldn't come up here at all this weekend, so I'm on borrowed time as it is.'

'Ah, Monsieur, I understand. Family is more important than anything, even when you don't have your own family yet.'

Jemme took a huge bite of the pastry Marguerite had just served him, to disguise his guilt. He wondered if his housekeeper knew how prescient she had just been.

Over breakfast, Philby outlined the progress which had been made so far in both the house and garden. Xelifon's herb garden was now a properly established feature and his plans for the international forest were going equally well. Some paintings Jemme had bought for the salon had arrived and were being professionally hung later that day, and a piece of sculpture was being delivered in the middle of next week. It was all starting to come together nicely. Draining the last of his coffee, Jemme stood up,

'Shall we go and have a look, Philby?' he asked cheerfully.

Philby nodded and lead the way to the salon.

Although by no means finished, it was looking more like a proper room with every visit. The paintings had been carefully placed on rolled-up blankets to protect their frames, and then leaned against the walls.

Jemme walked over to them, 'Who positioned them, Philby?' he asked, stopping and turning his head to one side.

'I did, Monsieur. I asked the men to put them where I thought you would like them most. If you want them moved, you say and I will tell them to move them.

'Actually, I think they look great where they are. I was only asking because that is exactly where I would have put them myself – good work Philby.'

Philby nodded, in the way that Jemme understood as a smile.

The paintings had been auction finds. Jemme had been too busy to go to the actual sales, which he had deeply regretted – he had always loved auctions and had been excited about the first few he'd need to attend for this house. DD had gone in his place and performed brilliantly. Whereas Jemme came out of a closely-fought sale pumping with adrenaline and full of energy, DD merely returned to the office, sat neatly down at his desk and picked up his pen again, almost as if he had never left. Sometimes Jemme had to come and stand over him, demanding with an impatient, 'Well?!' before he even heard any news. The news was always delivered in a collected and brief fashion. Instead of an ecstatic 'We won!' or other exciting news of snatching victory from the jaws of defeat, DD would merely say something along the lines of, 'The piece will be shipped to the chateau as soon as the paperwork is complete,' or, 'I remained within the budget bracket you set for me.'

Jemme smiled slightly as he looked at the paintings now. He couldn't imagine ever remaining so dispassionate in such a highly-charged atmosphere, but then maybe that was why he valued DD so highly. He had thought carefully about the style and type of art he wanted to include in this room. He wanted the pieces to be congruous with each other and to sit well together, and he also wanted them to fit within the context of the room. They would have to be sensitive to the age, style and function of the room. He had started off looking purely at eighteenth century art, deciding that he would only install paintings which had been completed during Louis XVI's reign. However, when he had considered it a little further, he realised that he wouldn't do more than merely recreate. If he only chose fittings and furnishings from Louis' period, he would be creating a museum room, which was not his intention at all. He wanted to reference the period and emulate it, but not repeat it. He wanted to rework it, fitting it around the space as it was today. He had thought about stately homes and manorial houses which had stayed in the same families for centuries. The rooms did not remain in a state of complete decorative stasis, but rather evolved to reflect the advancing generations and the times. Thus, a notable nineteenth or even twentieth century piece might be found in an early eighteenth century room, and it would make perfect sense.

He decided that Louis' reign would merely provide the stylistic start date for the room. If pieces were not contemporaneous with the original room then they had to have another reason for being there. He would look for pieces which were a great match in terms of style, colour and size, but he would also look for pieces which had a story to tell. The paintings DD had procured were a great starting point, and he was pleased with the sculpture too. He couldn't wait to see it as he was sure that the photos in the auction catalogue didn't properly do it justice.

Philby walked over to a light switch and flicked it on. As the chandelier shimmered to life, Jemme looked up and noticed the ceiling for the first time.

'You've painted over the flowers!' he said.

'*Oui, Monsieur*,' said Philby, the corners of his mouth turning up slightly.

'Who did it in the end?' asked Jemme.

'I did,' said Philby and Jemme understood why he was looking pleased with himself. Some decorative plaster cornicing had been added to the coving and whilst it wasn't nearly so much of a feature as the flowers would have been, it finished the ceiling off nicely.

Jemme was pleased to note that, despite all the work that had been going on, including further painting, the floor still retained its highly buffed sheen. It was so glossy in fact, that he was tempted to leave it as it was. However, he knew that it needed a carpet of some sort. He couldn't leave a formal reception room with bare floorboards – it might be in keeping with a sleek modern, minimalist aesthetic, but it would be completely wrong in a room of this age. The problem was, they'd had difficulty finding a carpet that would fit. Both he and DD had been trawling auction houses and tapping contacts, but to no avail, they hadn't found anything which was anywhere near as big yet.

'Philby, you don't know of anywhere in the area where I might be able to find a rug or carpet for this room do you?' he suddenly asked, turning to his gardener.

Philby thought for a moment, 'It is a very big room, Monsieur. There are many antique shops in the area that sell things from the local chateaux, but I haven't heard of any big carpets in a while. I will ask.'

'Thank you, Philby, it will be much appreciated.'

Philby shrugged. 'Where is it you are advertising, Monsieur?'

'Advertising?

'*Oui.*'

'Well, to tell you the truth we haven't been advertising actually; it's been the other way round – we've been chasing sellers and looking through catalogues.'

'*On peut pas faire le poireau, Monsieur,*' said Philby shaking his head.

Jemme looked at him in confusion, but Philby yielded nothing. He still hadn't fully got to grips with all the strange expressions everyone seemed to use in this part of the country, and so he thought it best merely to agree with him and work it out later. Besides, he thought he had a point. There was no point speculatively seeking out adverts and notices, he might as well place his own.

Pleased with the way the room was progressing, he looked down at his watch,

'Ah, good – we still have plenty of time. I'd like to have a look around the gardens and maybe a quick chat with Xelifon too. Then I think I'll just about have enough time to look at Dupré's plans before I have to head off.'

Philby nodded and lead the way out across the grounds to the small gardener's bothy. The creaky door swung open, and Xelifon looked up. He was sitting at the rickety table, perched on the edge of the little chair. He smiled softly when he saw who was at the door.

'Monsieur,' he said quietly, nodding his head slightly.

'Good morning, Xelifon. What are you up to there?'

'*C'est des pousses, Monsieur,*' said Xelifon as he carefully continued to poke lines of holes in the long planter on the table, before gently placing a seedling in each one.

'What are you growing?' asked Jemme

'These will be for the kitchen *salade*, Monsieur. There is *roquette*, *des laitues* and finally, *la frisée.*'

'Good work,' said Jemme approvingly, 'We'll be completely self-sufficient at this rate!'

Xelifon smiled again, 'It is good to grow something from nothing, Monsieur. It is very cheap to buy seeds, and we will know that they have been raised only in our own soil.'

'Well, I can't argue with that,' said Jemme, admiring his turn of phrase. 'I know you've been busy, but have you managed to make any advances on the international tree garden yet? I was hoping to have a quick look whilst I was here.'

Xelifon nodded, planted the last of his seedlings, carefully patted the earth down on top of it and got up. He opened a drawer in the battered side table leaning against the back wall of the bothy and carefully drew out a folder. He slowly wiped his fingers on a cloth so that he wouldn't get earth on the folder's contents, and Jemme noticed for the first time that, whilst Philby's hands were as gnarled and worn as tree roots, Xelifon's were soft – almost feminine. He slid out a piece of paper and laid it flat on the table.

'Here, Monsieur,' he said gesturing to it.

Jemme moved around to his side of the table and leant over to look at the plan with him. He stared at it for a while,

'Xelifon, this is very impressive,' he said eventually, 'I hadn't been expecting a plan at all, let alone one as detailed as this.

Xelifon looked pleased, 'Here, Monsieur,' he said again, and began to trace the outlines on the page with his finger, 'I will show you.'

Jemme hadn't even absorbed the contents of the plans yet; he had been so distracted by the quality of Xelifon's draughtsmanship. He had drawn a plan of the forest from numerous different angles. One showed how it might look from above and one depicted a cross-section. The bottom of the page showed lines and lines of trees, as if the forest had been cut up and arranged in neat rows. The trees had been so expertly drawn that, even without the little labels Xelifon had added, Jemme would have been able to recognise them. It was just as well, as what talent Xelifon had revealed in drawing, he certainly lacked in handwriting. Whereas his depictions of the trees were delicately drawn and perfectly rendered, his writing was faltering and unsure. The letters were uneven in size and inconsistent in shape. From the depth of depressions they'd made, Jemme could tell he'd been pressing hard on his pen and guessed that he'd been concentrating just as hard.

'What does this say, Xelifon?' he asked, pointing at one note.

'That says "aggressive root", Monsieur. I have made some special notes for some trees.'

'I didn't know that willow had an aggressive root.'

Xelifon nodded, 'Very aggressive,' he said shyly. 'That it why it is on the outside of the forest, so it will not disturb the other trees.'

Jemme looked impressed, and Xelifon continued, 'Its root is quick to take, Monsieur, and so we will plant it on the edge of the forest, near the lake. That means its roots will provide extra protection for the bank.'

'Good thinking – I would never have considered that.'

Xelifon smiled.

'Why don't you talk me through the rest of the trees here?' Jemme asked, and Xelifon slowly began to describe his choices and explain their positioning. Jemme was as impressed as he was pleased. It was exactly what he had been hoping for, but hadn't been able to realise himself. It was a perfect extension of his philosophy indoors to the outside. Xelifon had chosen a selection of trees from both East and West, and ordered them in a thoughtful manner. Some were emblematic of the countries they came from, some were steeped in myth and folklore and some had featured in notable historical events.

In the pictures, they melded seamlessly together, creating a harmonious woodland which would have looked like a pleasant natural feature to an outsider, but was imbued with meaning to Jemme. As he described the plans to Jemme, Jemme realised how much Xelifon must have laboured over them. There was far more than mere aesthetics guiding his careful placing of the trees. Beech could grow up to fifty metres tall, yet had shallow roots, Xelifon explained. It was therefore at the centre of the forest, creating an apex from which the treeline could slope downwards as it reached the peripheries. A few, neat botanical drawings of leaves showed Xelifon's plan to include a mix of copper and fern-leaf beeches. Similarly, a careful study of a Japanese maple leaf showed it to be completely different to its European cousin. The crimson-edged leaves were much spikier and the elegant lobes much thinner.

'I never knew maple could look so different,' Jemme said.

'*Acer palmatum*,' said Xelifon.

'Is that its Latin name?' asked Jemme.

'It is the name of the species, Monsieur, but there are many cultivars. Some you would not even recognise as maple.'

'Ah, I recognise this though!' said Jemme pointing to one, very distinctive broad tree.

Xelifon smiled softly again, 'I thought Monsieur would enjoy this tree.'

'Well you thought right – whenever I see a cedar tree it reminds me of growing up.'

'*Cedrus libani*,' said Xelifon. 'It is the Lebanese Cedar, which grows in Lebanon, Jordan, Syria and Turkey,' he reeled the names off carefully, as though they were fragile objects he didn't want to handle. 'There is another cedar, *stenocoma* which is called the Turkish Cedar, but it only grows in southwest Turkey. This one is much more recognisable.'

'It certainly is. It looks like you've positioned it to be a bit of a focal point too.'

Xelifon nodded.

'Do you think you can get it to grow though?' Jemme asked suddenly, 'I mean, I expect the beech and the oaks will be used to cold, wet climates, but northern France has rather different weather to southern Turkey.'

'It will not be a problem if we buy it as a sapling, Monsieur,' Xelifon shrugged. 'There are many famous cedars in the parks of Northern Europe, and if we care for it well it will be fine. With attention, all of these trees will grow well here. The only difficulty will be finding the trees.'

'Ah, well you don't need to worry about that. Like I told you, I have a man back in Paris who could find anything anywhere. If you could make me a list – or, better still, if I could make a copy of this plan, then I'll get him on the case straight away.'

Xelifon paused a little, 'There is one more thing, Monsieur,' he said slightly awkwardly. Jemme stopped – Xelifon was often shy, but never awkward.

'What's the matter?' he asked kindly.

'Some of the trees will be very expensive, Monsieur. The Chinese Maple for example, is something which is greatly prized, and a beautiful example might be very expensive indeed.'

'Well, there's no need to worry about that;' said Jemme, 'with the amount I expect we're going to end up spending indoors, I think we can dedicate a little bit of funding to the grounds.'

Another thought suddenly occurred to him, 'Xelifon, how do you know the Latin names of all of these trees?'

Xelifon looked at him as if it was a question he had never considered before, 'Some I know, some I learned,' he said simply, before going on to describe how he had also placed some European maples towards the centre of the forest as their early-spring flowers were a good source of nectar for bees, which would encourage flowers to grow on the forest floor. Jemme looked at him curiously. He didn't think he'd ever met a man of more hidden depths, and was astounded that there had been a point when his own family had considered him unemployable.

After a very enjoyable few hours poring over plans in the bothy and then touring the orchard and burgeoning kitchen garden, Jemme sought out Dupré. The moody artist was bent over his plans, utterly focussed. He didn't hear Jemme come in, or the polite few coughs Jemme attempted. Steeling himself for a terse reaction, Jemme took a deep breath and tried a breezy, 'Good morning, Monsieur Dupré.'

Dupré's head snapped up, 'Ah, Mafeze,' he said.

'How are the plans coming along?' asked Jemme.

Despite his rudeness, Jemme could tell that Dupré was in a good mood of sorts. His eyes were a little glassy and he had evidently been deeply involved in his work. Jemme had been expecting him to be cagey when questioned, but was surprised when after the briefest of pauses, Dupré told him that the work had been going well, and even voluntarily showed it to him.

Jemme's personal dislike of the man immediately gave way to his respect for him as an artist. The study was exquisite, and instantly redolent of the masterful work at Versailles. With a beautifully observed palette and deft brushwork, Dupré had created silken, diaphanous clouds, within a canvas that seemed to open a window to the heavens above.

'I like it very much, Monsieur Dupré,' said Jemme.

Dupré shrugged as if to say that he expected no less.

'I hear you've been visiting Versailles?' Jemme asked.

'*Oui*, I was concerned that my ceiling should be in exactly the right style – especially after the style clash of the salon.'

Jemme looked confused for a moment, and then remembered his emphasis on the clash during the flower debacle, 'Oh yes,' he agreed readily, 'dreadful clash – terrible, can't risk it again. Excellent idea to go to Versailles, very forward thinking.'

Dupré gave the same self-assured shrug. 'This is entirely my own work though, Monsieur. It is merely based on a careful study. I have not stolen from any other artist, I have just referenced their work.'

'I wouldn't have thought so for a minute,' said Jemme. 'It's quite excellent, thank you.'

He returned to the kitchen, pleased that, for the moment at least, everything seemed to be going to plan. Back in the kitchen he chatted with Marguerite for a while and raised the prospect of the dinner party. She was excited that the chateau would once again be a social seat, and started chattering about all the society dinner parties her grandmother served at. 'It will be just like it was, Monsieur!' she said enthusiastically, 'But I have just noticed the time! You will be wanting to get back to Paris, *non*? Ah, we have kept you too long – I will pack you up a lunch now.'

'Actually, Marguerite, I'm rather hungry now. I think I might just stay and have lunch here.'

It was mid-afternoon by the time Jemme finally got back to Paris. If truth be told, he was spinning out his visit for as long as possible. The longer he stayed, the angrier he knew Hil would be and so the more reluctant he was to return home. When he eventually got back, it was almost worse than he had imagined. Instead of being angry, Hil just looked hurt and incredibly sad.

'I thought we were going to have the weekend,' she said with a look on her face which broke Jemme's heart a little. He instantly regretted dragging his feet, and wished he'd stuck with his original plan.

'We were. I'm so sorry darling, I just got carried away.'

Hil didn't say anything, but fixed him with an injured look, which made Jemme cringe a little. He silently admonished himself and thought desperately, trying to work out what he could do to make amends.

'Look I understand how disappointed you must be, and believe me, if there was anything I could do to change that I would. I've finished at the chateau for the weekend though and we've got all of the rest of today, and then the whole of tomorrow together. We can do whatever you like. Anything – I promise.'

Hil sighed, 'I don't even want to do anything in particular, I just wanted us to spend the weekend together, just like we used to. We don't even need to leave the flat, I just want to spend some time with my husband.'

Jemme felt even worse than he had a few moments ago, 'What would you like to do this afternoon, sweetheart?' he asked, hoping he could make amends.

'I don't know,' said Hil, 'before we do anything though I need to have some lunch. I was waiting for you, but I suppose you've eaten?'

'Just a little snack,' said Jemme diplomatically, 'come on, get your coat, I know where we should go.'

He walked Hil out to the car and jumped into the driver's seat.

'Where are we going?' she asked as they started driving south.

'Somewhere that's guaranteed to fill you up until supper and cheer you up at the same time,' said Jemme.

Hil appeared mildly intrigued, but still didn't look as if she had forgiven Jemme yet.

The traffic was forgiving, and after about twenty minutes they pulled up in front of a slightly grubby looking café. Hil peered out of the car window, and after a moment's confusion recognised her surroundings and laughed. They were outside the only Irish restaurant either of them had ever found in Paris. It was a tatty, run-down sort of place with hideous interior decoration and chipped plastic tables. However, the food was excellent and the welcome warm. It was also completely authentic; it was run by a couple from Galway who had only been in Paris a couple of years longer than Hil. When she had first moved to the city, Hil often used to visit, whenever she felt a pang of homesickness, and, although her visits had become increasingly less frequent over the years, Jemme knew it still occupied a special place in her heart. She was incredibly gratified when the proprietors recognised her immediately, and happily listened to all their news from Ireland whilst she sat down and greedily snacked on the basket of soda bread on the table.

After a hearty dish of comforting coddle with barley, just as Jemme had hoped, her spirits lifted.

Having managed to find some space for some colcannon, he ordered them a dessert to share. When the goody came it looked just as stodgy and unappetising as he remembered it. Made of white bread, boiled in milk with spices, he had never liked it, but knew the enthusiasm with which it was devoured by Hil's family. Dangerously full after Marguerite's decidedly more appealing lunch, he managed to force a couple of spoonfuls down, and hoped Hil wouldn't notice his lack of enthusiasm. Fortunately she was happy to eat the majority of the dessert herself, and happily explained to him the tradition behind eating it on St John's Eve.

By the time they had settled the bill and lingered for a while talking, she was almost back to her old self. Jemme knew the underlying problems hadn't been resolved, but at least it looked like the weekend was going to be saved.

'What do you fancy now, my love?' he asked, slipping his hand around hers.

Hil smiled, 'I'm just trying to imagine what I would tell someone who'd never been here before to do with a free afternoon in Paris.'

'Any ideas?'

'I think I would tell them to go to the Musée d'Orsay. I think that's what we should do too. No matter how many times I've been, I still don't think I've seen even half of the treasures there and we're so lucky to live so close to it, I feel we should make the most of it.'

'Well, I never say no to a museum outing,' Jemme smiled. 'If the traffic holds, I can have us there within fifteen minutes.'

Sure enough, in no time at all they found themselves wandering around one of the world's most prestigious museums.

Several hours slipped happily by as they gradually lost themselves in the corridors of history. They finished looking at a display of exquisite Queen Anne's Lace and Hil turned to smile at Jemme. Rather than the sad little half-smile he had seen during the past week, it was the wide, genuine smile he loved. He felt a small sense of relief wash through him.

'It looks like you enjoyed the lace!'

'It's not just that, it's more the feeling of being here. It's so easy to take what we have for granted, and I don't think I stop often enough to appreciate what a wonderful city we live in. People spend years dreaming of a visit to Paris, and yet it's where we wake up every morning. It's so nice to have some time with you to appreciate it.'

'I'm pleased, sweetheart. It feels like ages since we've been here as well.'

'Doesn't it. There's something wonderful about museums too – I love the atmosphere inside them, and the feeling one has of being surrounded by priceless treasures. It makes me so excited about the fact we're building one of our own, of sorts.'

Jemme felt an even bigger surge of relief pass over him this time, 'You have no idea how happy it makes me to hear you say that,' he said.

'Well of course I'm excited. I'm still really cross you went up this weekend, but I want to hear all about it later on.'

'Well, in that case, I look forward to telling you. I reckon we've got time for one more thing before they shut – is there anything in particular you'd like to see?'

Hil shrugged, 'Why don't we just turn left at the end of this corridor, and see what we come across?'

'Sounds good to me.'

Reaching the end of the corridor, they turned to find themselves in a small gallery of paintings by Degas. Hil noticed one straight away, 'Jemme look!' she said, going over towards the small plaque to the left of the picture and reading aloud, '*Semiramis Building Babylon.*' Jemme came and stood next to her; he put his arm round her waist and they both studied the painting.

'I don't know much about Degas,' he said after a while, 'do you?'

'Not much. It says here that it was started in 1860 and probably stayed in Degas' studio until his death. It's a mythological scene, which shows Semiramis on the banks of the Euphrates, considering the construction of Babylon. Apparently they think that Degas took certain elements from Assyrian reliefs, which are now in the Louvre.'

Jemme listened carefully as he looked at the painting. He knew that he had to finish the first room before he could start another, but he felt himself become excited about the prospect of a Babylonian room. The more he thought about it, the keener he was to get started on it as soon as possible. His enthusiasm spilled out and he talked to Hil at length about Semiramis, Babylonia and the Assyrians, touching on his plans for a room. They were mostly stories she had heard before, but she listened patiently. When he had finished, she kissed him softly on the cheek.

'I forget how enthusiastic you get about all of this,' she said, 'it's one of the things I love about you – I don't want it to let it come between us.'

Chapter Twenty-Two

Having spent the rest of the weekend strolling around Paris, rediscovering old haunts, by the beginning of the next week both Jemme and Hil were decidedly more relaxed. However, Jemme was anxious not to become complacent, and knew that he would still have to make a great deal of effort. Hil was the most forgiving person he knew and he didn't want to take that for granted. Much as it pained him, he resolved that he wouldn't visit the chateau at all the next weekend, not even on a quick morning trip. Hil seemed to appreciate the gesture, and they had invited some of the friends she had complained about neglecting over for dinner in the Paris flat, ahead of the grand dinner in the chateau's salon. It gave them both something to look forward to, and Jemme hoped it would distract him from worrying about what was going on over in Chateau Vigne-Verte. Just to be on the safe side, he had thrown himself into helping Hil organise everything, ordering in special foods from the *grands magasins* and helping move the furniture around in the flat.

He had even managed to break the news about the Airbus board to Hil, and, although she was a little irritated, she was gracious enough to congratulate him on the deal. It seemed that the Paris dinner party for close friends was the pay-off for mixing in business with the chateau dinner party, so Jemme put even more effort into helping make it a special evening. It was thus with a clear conscience that he invited several further clients to the chateau. He had been wanting to impress them for a while, but hadn't been able to come up with any particularly inspiring ideas. He felt that bringing them to the chateau would provide the elusive something he had been searching for. Furthermore, they were sure to be impressed that the chairman of Airbus was also a guest.

As the week wore on, he found other ways to feel he was helping the progress of the work at the chateau. He dedicated a great deal more time to procuring the rug for the salon, helping DD place adverts in industry publications and spread word amongst specialist shops. Although everyone agreed to run the advert, no one seemed particularly optimistic about the results he might expect.

Towards the end of the week, he popped out on his lunch break to pick up some special olives for the party, from a Middle Eastern delicatessen. Throughout his childhood, Grandma was always telling him that the olives of Palmyra were the best and the biggest in all of the world: 'like plums' she would always say.

He thought it would be nice to have a couple of bowlfuls in the sitting room for his friends whilst they had drinks and talked about the chateau. This was the only place he had found which sold the fat, juicy olives he wanted, and he had phoned ahead to make sure they had them in stock. On the way back to the office, clutching the precious bag carefully, he noticed a carpet shop.

The handwritten signs in the window were in poorly-translated French and advertised antique carpets and genuine rugs from Ghoum and Isfahan. It looked promising, and Jemme decided to go in. The bell rang as he opened the door and a short man emerged from the back room. He was clearly from the Middle East, and so Jemme greeted him with a friendly, '*Salaam*,' relishing the sound of a language he rarely used.

The owner greeted him back with a hearty '*Salaam*!', which revealed him to be Iranian.

'What luck I have, to find a Persian to talk with about rugs!' Jemme joked.

The man spread his arms wide and bowed his head, 'How can I help you, friend?'

Jemme outlined what he was trying to find, describing the room and his search so far. 'So, I was wondering if you had heard of anything like that, or perhaps if I could ask you to contact me if you have?' he said, rummaging in his pocket for a business card with his free hand.

The man had listened carefully and took the business card from Jemme without saying a word. He turned it over in his hands whilst he carried on thinking.

'My friend, I have sold carpets all my life. My father did before me, and his before him – in fact my entire family has always been in the industry. I have seen thousands of carpets in my life, but I don't think I've ever seen one like you describe. Don't be disheartened though – unusual pieces sometimes turn up from the strangest of places. If you like I can send word back to my family in Iran to keep an eye out, and who knows what will be unearthed in the next few years? *Patience is the key to joy*, as Rumi said.'

Jemme smiled at the proverb, 'Indeed it is. However, and at the risk of sounding impatient, I'm afraid I can't wait for a couple of years, I was hoping to have something sorted in about three weeks' time.'

The man blinked, 'Well then, I feel a different course of action must be taken. If time is a problem, you will have to make your own luck.'

'What do you mean?'

'You will have to make it.'

'Make what?'

'The rug!'

'Make it?' Jemme paused. It was something he hadn't considered before. It certainly would solve the problem, but he didn't know if a modern piece could sit with the decorative philosophy he was developing for the chateau.

'Is it really such a strange idea? About half the carpets here are made in our workshops back in Iran, and they're just as popular as the antiques. Persian rugs are the best in the world, and the best craftsmen still make them using traditional methods. In fact the only difference between a custom-made one and an antique is that you have control over how a new one looks. That, and the fact it is a little bit newer,' he said and gave a wheezy little laugh at his joke.

'Do you have workshops yourself?' Jemme asked.

'Oh yes, my immediate family own several, and amongst my extended family there are hundreds, before I even begin to count neighbours and friends. Our whole town are rug-makers and we all use the same materials and methods as we have for generations.'

Jemme tried to consider how he would feel about having a modern piece in the room. His first instinct was that it was cheating, and against everything he had been trying to do within the chateau. However, as he thought about it some more, he realised that far from being antithetical to the chateau's aims, it was actually completely in line with them. By using traditional craftwork from ancient cities, he was helping keep a historical thread alive. He had no idea when, or indeed, if he would find the carpet he was looking for, and if he did, there was a chance that it might have come from one of the same workshops anyway. He had warmed to this man straight away too and felt that he could trust him.

'It's an interesting suggestion,' he said, 'I'm not quite sure what I want to do yet, but if I did decide to have one made, would you be able to recommend a reputable workshop?'

'Oh yes! The difficulty will be choosing which one. Come, I'll show you the most recent shipment from my brother's workshop.' He led the way to the back of the shop and a pile of silk rugs.

'They've only just arrived,' he explained, hauling several from the top and laying them out on the shop floor to reveal their intricate designs.

'They're all hand-knotted, look,' he said, turning one over.

They had obviously been expertly made, and Jemme spent an enjoyable quarter of an hour admiring them with him, before heading back to the office. He left him a small box of *Za'atar* he had picked up at the deli as a thank you.

Jemme's afternoon suddenly became very busy, so he didn't have any time to think further on the rug. Back at home, Hil just wanted to talk about the party. She was excitedly unwrapping some of their special wedding china, which they hadn't used since they bought the chateau and started spending weekends out of Paris. He was looking forward to catching up with old friends too, although even if he hadn't been, Hil was excited enough for both of them. He loved seeing her so enthusiastic; it made the fractious few weeks they'd had seem like a distant memory.

Despite having a busy day on Friday, Jemme managed to get away at the time he'd promised Hil he would. He knew he was leaving a mountain of work for Monday morning, but it definitely wasn't important enough to keep him. Grabbing his coat, he fairly flew out of the door, shouting a hurried goodbye to DD behind him, who was attending to the stack of papers on the desk in front of him, as if he had every intention of staying for the weekend to work on them. In fact DD had referenced his life outside work so seldom that, as far as Jemme knew, that's exactly what he did every weekend. Jemme remembered how he used to wonder if DD slept standing up, so that he could greet him with his morning coffee, and smiled as he took the steps two at a time.

Jemme had got so used to jumping in the car and heading north straight after work on Friday that it felt strange to be heading back to the flat. Depending on how things went, he was going to try and sneak in a phone call to Philby on either Saturday or Sunday, but apart from that, he tried to put all thoughts of the chateau out of his mind. Back at the flat, Hil had been busy getting everything ready. Vases of freshly cut flowers filled every windowsill, and the best linen had been taken out of the chest and laid on the table. The furniture had been rearranged, the silver polished, and slim, elegant candles fitted into the silver candelabra. Somehow she had also managed to find time to prepare a special meal for them.

'This is an unexpected treat,' said Jemme, when he arrived. He looked down at the bunch of flowers in his hand and realised that they might be somewhat redundant. Hil looked pleased to see them nonetheless.

'Well, I thought that, as we have the weekend together, we might as well have a nice meal tonight as well. We'll have everyone else here tomorrow, so this one is just for us.'

'Darling, how thoughtful,' said Jemme appreciatively.

Hil smiled, 'Come on, it's almost ready – why don't you take your coat off and sit down,' she said and pulled out one of the dining chairs for him.

'I could get used to this!' Jemme said, and sat down.

It was a sentiment he repeated following one of the best meals he'd tasted in ages. They had been eating Marguerite's food at the weekend, and grabbing their own quick suppers during the week, and he had almost forgotten just how good Hil was at cooking.

If Friday night was good, then Saturday night was even better. The evening was flawless, and went completely to plan. Catching up with their Paris friends was hugely refreshing. Since he had bought the chateau, Jemme had found that he was increasingly outward-facing whilst in Paris. Weekdays had become the inconvenient time between weekends when he was obliged to return to the city. Spending the evening with old friends reminded him that Paris had been his home for a long time, and still meant a great deal to him. Their friends proved themselves a ready audience too, listening to their stories of highs, lows and dramatic interludes experienced at the chateau so far. Some hooted with laughter at the story of Dupré, some looked concerned. They murmured sympathetically when hearing of Philby trapped in the tunnels, and expressed admiration when Jemme explained Xelifon's hidden talents. They all agreed that they couldn't wait to see the chateau and meet the colourful characters who had been illustrating these stories too.

They sat and talked until the small hours, gradually trickling out until it was just Jemme and Hil. Jemme yawned and stretched,

'Well, I don't know about you, but I think that went fantastically well.'

Hil sighed contentedly and began to absent-mindedly fold up napkins, 'It was exactly as I'd hoped it would be.'

'I'm so pleased. I had a wonderful time and, judging by all of their faces, so did they.'

'It was so nice seeing everyone. I feel like we haven't entertained in ages and we used to so much.'

'I know, I suppose it's because we haven't really been around much.'

'I suppose. It's something I really enjoy though, and want to get back into doing regularly.'

'Then you should. Tonight was a big success; there's no reason why you shouldn't do it more often.'

'No, I suppose you're right. The only thing was, I felt like this flat was a little small. It was just about all right for this evening, but I don't think we could have had any more people over. It was a bit limiting as well, I mean we can't do much about the furniture we've already got here, we can only move it around a little bit.'

'Well my love, imagine what it will be like when you have whole rooms which exist only for the purpose of entertaining,' Jemme said.

'I know!' Hil squealed, 'It's so exciting! I can't wait for it all to be finished!'

'A girl after my own heart,' said Jemme fondly.

Unfortunately the finish date was not as close as Jemme had hoped. Several of the artists and craftsmen he had engaged suddenly got called away to other projects at the last minute. He had to replace one, and agreed to keep the commissions open for the other two, but had to wait until they were finished. A delivery of important materials got held up, and caused a stall in production, but Jemme took all the problems in his stride. If anything, he had wanted there to be as many complications as possible when completing this room so that he could work out how to deal with them as the project progressed. He had already realised that he would need to allow much more time than anticipated, and decided that it would be wise to set a good precedent with laid-back artists early on. He resolved to be a little bit firmer and clearly set out the procedures for time off at the beginning. However, the biggest reason the completion date had been delayed was the carpet. Jemme had continued to toy with the idea of finding an antique for a while, or at least until he talked it over with DD. DD had instantly agreed with the shop owner. He listed his reasons practically and perspicaciously, and Jemme could see that he was right; the only reason he hadn't committed so far was a romantic attachment to the idea of something being old.

Eventually the desire for the room to be finished took over, and he spent some time with the Iranian looking through samples in his shop and discussing different designs and colours. He had drawn up some rough sketches and sent them to his brother, who had formalised them and sent them back with a price; there had been some back and forth over details, and no small amount of haggling, but they had reached an agreement everyone was happy with. Although the shopkeeper's brother promised to set his entire staff to work and make the rug a priority above all others, it would still take some time to complete. It was exciting nonetheless, and Jemme enjoyed thinking about the fact that, in a town he had never visited, unseen hands were carefully creating a piece of heritage for him, slowly taking shape, knot by knot.

With work stalling at the chateau, there wasn't much point visiting, and so Jemme spent another weekend in Paris. The timing turned out to be felicitous; staying late at work on Friday, he was surprised when DD knocked at his office door and announced a visitor. DD stood back to reveal Professor Johnston behind him.

'Professor!' cried Jemme, 'This is an unexpected pleasure!'

'Jemme! I'm glad I caught you here. I've misplaced my address book and couldn't remember where you lived. I was hoping to find you at work, but then it took me so long to find this place that I thought you must have gone home.'

Jemme remembered the Professor's overstuffed attaché case, which was wont to spill its contents at the slightest opportunity, and laughed, 'I'm sorry to hear you lost your address book, Professor – although I have to confess I'm not at all surprised! You're lucky to have caught me, I speed off as soon as I've finished on a Friday these days.'

'So I hear!'

'This Friday's a bit of an exception, and I'm incredibly glad it is – how long are you in town for?'

'Only the weekend, then I have to go back to London, but that's only for a few days then I'll be back. I might work as a visiting Professor at the Sorbonne for this academic year, so I'll be around quite a bit.'

'Well, that's very exciting news. Still I suppose we should make the most of you whilst you're here. Have you had supper yet?'

'No, not yet, I was rather preoccupied with getting lost on the way here.'

Jemme laughed again, although he sensed that the Professor was being earnest. 'Neither have I. If you don't mind waiting about ten minutes, I need to finish off a few vital bits here and then we can head off to my flat together.'

'Wait? No I don't mind at all! I've got some papers I need to read anyway,' he produced a rolled-up folder from inside his coat pocket and brandished it like a club. Jemme's mouth twitched a little at the corners; he'd forgotten how eccentric some of the Professor's mannerisms could be.

'DD, would you mind finding the Professor a comfy seat and seeing if he wants any tea or coffee?'

'Of course, Sir,' DD said.

'Also, if you've got a moment I'd really appreciate it if you could telephone Hil and tell her that there's one more for supper. I'm quite keen to focus on this and get it finished as soon as possible.'

'Of course,' said DD, leading the Professor into the antechamber.

Despite his best efforts, Jemme's work dragged on for longer than he had hoped. Finally emerging from his office, he saw that the Professor had barely noticed and was happily absorbed in his papers.

'Shall we head off?' he asked.

'What? Oh, off – yes,' said Professor Johnston, as he struggled to stop reading.

Back at the flat, Hil was just as delighted to see the Professor as Jemme had been, and they ran through the reel of stories they had entertained everyone with the previous weekend. Professor Johnston found them all very amusing, especially the one about the 'cartoonish' Dupré. He asked Jemme lots of questions about the salon and the restoration in general. Jemme thought it an opportune moment to raise the possibility of a Babylonian room, and was gratified when Professor Johnston shared his enthusiasm for it. They began discussing the most important, or most representative elements of the Babylonian civilisation which could be selected for the room.

'It feels strange to be boiling an entire civilisation down to such a microcosm,' Professor Johnston said, after failing to come up with a shortlist.

'I know, and I definitely felt that way at first, but then I started thinking about it like this: if you were writing a book about the Babylonians, you wouldn't include every single name, reference and piece of information, would you? You would select the most interesting, or most relevant to your chosen theme or topic. This is a little like that I guess; it's just going to be a visual realisation of what most historians commit to writing.'

'That's a very interesting way of looking at it,' said the Professor. 'In that case, why don't you give me a few days to think about it and I'm sure I'll be able to come up with a slightly more detailed list.'

'That would be great,' said Jemme, just as he noticed the time. 'Professor, it's so late – you must stay tonight, you can sleep in the spare room.'

'Well, that's very kind of you, thank you – I think I'll take you up on it.'

Just as he was closing the door to the spare room, he opened it a little and spoke to the Professor inside, 'Of course, it goes without saying that we'd love you to come to our first event at the chateau – more than that in fact, we demand you come!'

'Splendid!' called out the Professor from inside the room, 'Good night!'

Jemme smiled and tiptoed off to his own bed, trying as best he could not to wake Hil.

Thinking it would be of interest, the next day Jemme took the Professor to the carpet shop. To the owner's complete surprise and Jemme's slight amusement, Professor Johnston addressed him in fluent Arabic and began to ask him very specific questions about the rugs, the town in which they were made and the methods they used. Once he had got over the surprise of such knowledge and language coming from such an unlikely source, the shopkeeper disappeared into the back room and emerged with three cups of sweet, clear tea served in small glass cups.

'Ah, *chai*, excellent! It's been a while since I had a proper cup,' said the Professor enthusiastically.

They stayed for an hour, chatting about the plans for the rug – 'the biggest my brother has ever made' – and the shopkeeper's homeland in general. Emerging, refreshed, the Professor told Jemme that he was confident he had made the right decision, 'Otherwise, goodness knows how long you would have sat around waiting for something to turn up.'

'I agree. I'm pleased that I decided to take charge of the situation. I just hope that it turns out all right. It's such a large commission to trust to a man I've never met. I don't know what I'll do if it's not quite right.'

'You're right, it is a risk, but have faith. I had a good feeling about that chap. Everything in his shop was of a very high quality indeed, and he was very knowledgeable about the antiques he was selling too.'

'That's true, I didn't see anything there that I wouldn't have bought on the spot.'

'Exactly. Also, I've never been to his particular town, but I've been to many others like it in the same region. Rug-making is completely ingrained in the culture – the children can knot carpets almost before they're born. I'd be surprised if they turned out anything that was less than excellent.'

'That's what I was hoping, but it's good to hear it from someone else too. Are you in a hurry to get off?'

'No, not really, I don't have to be anywhere until just before lunch.'

'Well, in that case, do you fancy popping into the Musée d'Orsay with me quickly? I'll show you the painting I was talking about – the one that got me thinking about the Babylonian room.'

'Splendid, let's head over.'

Even though being in a museum with the Professor was one of Jemme's favourite activities, he was very disciplined, and only stayed to look at the one painting. He could have spent hours – days even, wandering round the museum and discussing its exhibits with the Professor, but he was anxious not to let himself get carried away, and to return to Hil as soon as possible. Telling the Professor to get in touch when he was back from London, he bade him a warm farewell and headed home.

'How was the carpet man?' asked Hil when he got back.

'He was well – I don't think he quite knew what to make of the Professor though!'

Hil laughed, 'I don't expect he did!'

'The rug's coming on well though, apparently. By the time it's finished, everything else in the room will be too, so as soon as we receive the shipment, the room will be complete!'

'How exciting!'

'I know. Seeing that we want to make this dinner such a special occasion, there's no harm in starting to plan it now. It means that it won't be such a rush nearer the time.'

'I suppose you're right. It took so much time and effort to get everything ready here, and that was only for a handful of people.'

'Exactly – plus, we already had most of the things we needed here because we've been living in this home properly. Think about everything we don't have over there – table cloths, cutlery and so on – we don't even have enough plates to eat off!'

'Well that's something that definitely needs sorting!'

'I'll help as much as you like, but I just thought that you might like to be in charge of everything, so that it's exactly as you'd like it to be.'

'That's nice of you. I don't just want it to be my thing though – you've worked so hard to get the room ready. I'll do everything you don't have time for, and we can discuss certain elements together, like the menus and so on.'

'Deal.'

'Actually, whilst we're thinking about it, what are we going to do about food? I mean, I don't especially want to be cooking all evening, especially if it's going to be a formal event.'

'Of course not. We can ask Marguerite if she'll mind.'

'Mmmm,' Hil didn't sound convinced. 'Her cooking is excellent, but I don't really think it's fair to ask her to cook for so many people.'

'Well then we'll get help for her. Once this room is finished and we start the next, we're going to have even more people coming and going. I originally hired her as a housekeeper with occasional cooking duties, but she's rapidly becoming the full-time cook. I don't think it will be difficult to find some help for her, and if they're girls from the village then they can start off only working a few days of the week before we get very busy.'

'Well, I suppose that won't do any harm,' said Hil hesitantly.

'I know what you're worried about, but are too nice to say,' said Jemme, looking at his wife shrewdly. Hil squirmed a little. 'You're worried that Marguerite's cooking is too homely, and that it won't be fancy enough for a proper dinner party.'

'No,' said Hil looking uncomfortable, 'it's not that, I love her cooking, you know that, I just...'

Jemme laughed, 'It's fine, I won't tell her and you're right. I don't even know if she'd want to cook for a dinner party. Why don't we talk to her about it when we're next down there and see if she'd even be comfortable doing it at all? We can ask her to cook a few test dishes and see how it goes. If it doesn't look like it will work, then we can easily hire in a chef.'

Hil raised her eyebrows.

'She definitely won't mind,' said Jemme, 'and it's very easy to hire a chef for one-off events. There are lots of excellent chefs here in Paris who work freelance, specifically on events like this.'

'That's an excellent idea. Why don't we go down next weekend? That way we've got plenty of time to sort everything out and audition new chefs if need's be. It would be good to check up on how everything's looking as well.'

'Really?'

Hil shrugged, 'Of course.'

Delighted he wouldn't even have to ask, Jemme smiled.

✳ ✳ ✳ ✳

Another busy week passed, and Jemme found himself looking forward to Friday with a growing sense of excitement. It was the longest period he had ever spent away from the chateau and, despite enjoying his time in Paris, he had missed it a great deal. As he and Hil drove down after work, he wondered aloud how everything would look.

'So much has happened since we were last there!' he said excitedly to Hil.

'I know, I'm looking forward to seeing it too,' she replied.

Pulling off onto the driveway, Jemme felt a surge of affection as the chateau came into view.

Home sweet home, he thought to himself. He was going to say it aloud, but despite Hil's recent renewed enthusiasm, he still wasn't sure she was on quite the same level as him. She certainly looked pleased to have arrived, which was a good sign.

The visit quickly fell into comforting old patterns. Xelifon, Philby and Marguerite greeted them. Philby took their bags and Marguerite frog-marched them into the kitchen, presenting them with plates piled high with supper before they'd so much as caught their breath.

Once they had finished, Jemme raised the subject of the dinner party. They didn't get very far with it, as the mere mention prompted Marguerite to go off into a ramble of second-hand anecdotes about the parties her grandmother had seen at the chateau, and the wonderful dresses of the beautiful society ladies.

Eventually Jemme realised he was going to have to interrupt her, 'Marguerite, I would love to hear all about parties of the past, but for the moment I was hoping that we might talk about the party that's coming up in a few weeks.'

'Oooh Monsieur!' Marguerite exclaimed in delight, 'It will be just like the old days!'

'Yes Marguerite, just like the old days. Now, we wanted to talk to you about the cooking.'

'Oh Monsieur, the food they used to eat, you would not believe it, such luxury! Such elegance! The best chefs in all of Paris used to come to this very chateau!'

Jemme rolled his eyes jokingly, 'Marguerite!'

'Sorry, Monsieur, I'm listening.'

'Well it's actually the chef element we wanted to talk to you about.'

'*Oui, Monsieur*?'

'Well, as you are our first – and best – cook, we thought it was only fair to talk to you first.'

'About what, Monsieur?'

'About the cooking of course'

Marguerite threw up her hands in horror, 'But, Monsieur, you cannot expect me to do it! I am not a professional chef! I am just a cook! I cook as your mother would, not for fancy guests!'

'Well your cooking is a little less Turkish than my mother's,' said Jemme smiling, 'But we all love your cooking and wouldn't have dreamt of asking someone else without talking to you first.'

'Of course, if you want me to, I will try my best,' said Marguerite looking slightly terrified.

'Don't worry, Marguerite,' said Hil kindly. 'We wouldn't make you do anything like that if you didn't want to. We just wanted to check to see if you wanted to do it yourself first, and make sure that you weren't offended it we asked someone else.'

'Offended, Madame? *Non*! It is exactly how if should be. You must hire a proper chef – that is the correct way for these things, *hé*, can you imagine if I served them up a big dish of my *coq-au-vin?*' she chuckled heartily.

'I'm sure they'd enjoy it,' said Hil, 'even if it wasn't what they were expecting.'

'Do you have any particular recommendations regarding chefs, Marguerite?' asked Jemme.

'*Non, Monsieur.* I am sorry I don't know anyone who works like that. I don't know anyone who would either. My sister went to Paris last year; maybe she met a chef then,' she added hopefully. 'I could ask her.'

'It's alright Marguerite,' Jemme said, 'I'm sure we won't have any problems getting hold of someone, I just wanted to see if you had any contacts first.'

Having sorted the matter of who would cook for them at the meal, and discussed the idea of hiring more help around the house, they went to the salon to see where they would be eating.

Jemme felt like he hadn't seen the room in ages, and for Hil the transformation was even more dramatic.

'I can't believe it!' she said as Jemme flicked on the chandelier, which slowly threw light onto a stately room, filled with graceful furniture and luxurious fittings.

Jemme looked around him approvingly. The room was completely finished; it was only waiting for the carpet. He took Hil's hand and slowly walked her around the various new pieces, taking in the paintings, furniture, curtains and drapery. She kept shaking her head and repeating that she didn't believe it. For Jemme's part, he certainly did believe it. It was everything he had hoped for; a perfect exemplar which would set the tone for the rest of the chateau.

'Are you pleased with it?' he asked Hil

'I'm more than pleased…. I just can't-'

'Believe it?' Jemme finished for her.

'Exactly! This is just like the rooms I have been looking at in books all my life. I can't believe it's in our own house and all for us. It's quite something to take in.'

'I know,' said Jemme as they wandered around, 'Imagine the whole house coming to life, just like this room has. You remember what a state it was in before.'

'I do,' said Hil, 'and some of the other rooms surrounding it are in an even worse state. This is like the jewel in a rather tatty crown. I can't believe the transformation it has undergone, and I can't believe that it's only the beginning either.'

'I'm so glad you're as pleased as I am, and you're right. It is only the beginning.

The rest of the visit passed by happily. Jemme inspected the suite of new rooms and Hil helped him pick out one which could be turned into the Babylonian room. Having someone to discuss things with and share decision-making made the whole process more exciting, and Jemme couldn't wait to get started on the next room. Over the next week, Jemme and Hil met several of the chefs DD had found for them. Just as Jemme had predicted, finding a talented chef in Paris was child's play. By the end of the week they had found someone they liked who was available on the right day, tasted some of his sample dishes and discussed and agreed on a menu. During the following week, Hil packed up their largest service of Sèvres porcelain, and carefully polished the antique silver canteen. Both were sent over to the chateau, where they joined a new shipment of Waterford crystal glasses. Marguerite telephoned to say that she had found a girl from the village, Aude, who was willing to start work straight away as her assistant. Jemme approved everything and the new girl joined Marguerite in polishing, dusting and readying the house. The giant rug finally arrived and was installed in the salon. Jemme felt as if he was a child who had been given a new toy and then told he couldn't play with it for another week. He kept himself busy by helping Hil organise the delivery of ingredients for the chef, and ensuring the florist brought his arrangements on the morning of the party.

With the invitations long-since sent and the date looming, Jemme had a sudden brainwave, just as he was about to leave work. He picked up the telephone and called through to DD's office.

'DD, I've got a rather unusual request for you, but I was wondering if you would be able to get hold of some peacocks for me...'

Chapter Twenty-Three

Jemme and Hil both left Paris at lunchtime that Friday. Jemme hadn't even thought twice about taking a half-day off work. He wanted the party to be perfect. Originally, he had wanted it to be purely for Hil's sake; he wanted to thank her for her patience so far and show her how things would be if she continued to persevere. However, there was now a greater significance riding on it. A great deal of financial and commercial enterprise was linked to the party's success. Since initially inviting the Airbus board, Jemme had also issued invitations to several other important directors, chief executives and heads of finance. The list had swelled to just under twenty, before he had even begun to count their actual friends. He felt a bit guilty that he was hijacking the evening, but his hands had been tied: after he had issued about five invitations, word had started to spread in business circles that Monsieur Mafeze was hosting an exclusive event for hand-selected guests. It meant he was obliged to ask certain key clients, for fear of putting their backs up. Then, once they had been invited, word spread further and he was hamstrung, having to invite another round of people. He was going to have to be on top form all evening, and didn't foresee a great deal of relaxation.

As they crawled along the road out of Paris, Jemme couldn't help noticing how much more traffic there was.

'I suppose we're never driving up there at this time of day – we must be hitting the lunchtime traffic,' he observed to Hil, as he fidgeted impatiently in his seat.

'Must be. We've never driven up there on a weekday before either, now I come to think about it. It will be nice to see the place on a normal working day.'

'It would be, but I don't think this is going to be a normal working day! There's going to be flowers and food and chefs flooding in all day!'

Hil laughed, 'Alright, maybe not. It will be nice having a bit more time up there though.'

Eventually the traffic cleared, and Jemme stamped on the accelerator, only to be forced to a grinding halt about a hundred yards later.

'This is so tedious! We'll be there at the normal time at this rate!'

Still earlier than usual, but not quite as early as he had hoped, they finally wound their way down the driveway at about three in the afternoon. Both of them were absolutely famished and allowed themselves to be whisked into the kitchen by Marguerite.

'They are only sandwiches, Monsieur, as we have been so busy since everyone started arriving,' she said apologetically.

Jemme had to restrain himself from snatching the plate from her. They might have been 'only sandwiches' but they were made on fresh, homemade bread, and crammed full of ripe, tasty ingredients. Despite their great size, Jemme managed to wolf his down in no time at all. As soon as he had finished, he sat back in his chair and sighed,

'Ah, that's better! Now, sorry, Marguerite, you were saying?' Whilst he had been eating Marguerite had been chattering away, but he had been so hungry he had completely phased out any conversation.

'Ah, Monsieur, I was saying that it will be just like the old days!' said Marguerite happily.

'Ah, yes,' said Jemme, 'the old days.' He exchanged a wry look with Hil who was being altogether more delicate with her lunch.

Just then a young girl bustled into the room with an armful of candlesticks.

'Madame Marguerite, I am ready to do the polishing!' she trilled.

'Tsk, child – you do not carry the *candélabre* like that! They are very *précieux*!' Marguerite scolded, fussing around the girl and removing the candlesticks one by one, gently placing them on the table.

The girl blushed and mumbled 'Sorry.' Looking over to the table her blush deepened when she saw Jemme and Hil.

Marguerite followed her gaze, 'Ah you have not yet met! Monsieur Jemme, Madame Hil, this is Aude.'

'*Bonjour*,' said Aude a little shyly but with a broad smile nonetheless. She was a short, pleasant-looking girl, with a moon-like face, rounded by a diet of cream and eggs. Her glossy hair fell loose about her shoulders and there was a healthy glow to her plump cheeks. Jemme instantly warmed to her.

'Aude, it's a pleasure to meet you. I understand that you live in the village?'

'*Oui, Monsieur*, my family have always lived there,' she said happily, nodding her head at him.

'Then you must know all sorts of stories about this place, just like Marguerite.'

Aude paused for a moment and chewed the inside of her cheek as she thought.

'Not really, Monsieur. My family are farmers and always have been. They would never have been to a place like this. A farm is hard work, Monsieur. They spend all their time there.'

Jemme felt slightly embarrassed, 'Yes of course, my apologies.'

Aude shrugged her shoulders, 'It is nothing,' she said earnestly. A grin spread across her face again, 'I am here now.'

'Yes, you are and you should be polishing. Now go and get the cloth and the special silver polish I showed you,' said Marguerite, shooing her across the room.

Once Aude had left, Marguerite returned to the table and cleared their plates.

'She seems nice, Marguerite,' said Hil.

'A yes, Madame, a nice girl – her family are so poor though! It is a very difficult life, farming, and they do not have many sons. They are honest though, these farm girls, but sometimes – ahhh, sometimes they are so slow!' she shook her head to herself.

'Marguerite!' Hil laughed.

Marguerite blinked innocently, '*Oui, Madame*?'

'Never mind,' said Hil, seeing her blank look, 'I'm glad you have someone like Aude to help you with all the housework.'

After a quick coffee and update with Philby, they went over to see the chef. The stable block was rapidly emerging as the 'staff quarters', and a small but comfortable room had been made up there.

Jemme knocked and they both went in.

'*Bonjour, Monsieur Mafeze*!' Jean-Louis greeted them as they entered, '*Madame Mafeze*,' he added, bowing his head as Hil entered.

'Hello, Jean-Louis. We just thought we'd drop in to say hello. How are you settling in?'

'Well, Monsieur, I have everything I need here, thank you.'

'I'm pleased to hear it. How is the room? We're hoping that eventually these will be permanent staff quarters, but we're just getting them up and running at the moment. I'd be interested to hear what they're like to stay in.'

'Fine, Monsieur, fine. I will only be here for a week and they are perfect for that amount of time, I cannot say what they would be like on a longer-term basis.'

'Hmm, that's a point,' said Jemme. 'And how have you found your neighbour.'

'Monsieur Dupré?'

'Yes.'

'He is an odd fellow. He has kept himself to himself mostly, which has suited me very well. He seems to be obsessed with some painting of a sky, or a ceiling – I couldn't work out which. Your cook, though, is a different matter.'

'Marguerite?'

'Yes, she seems to think that she is my mother!'

Jemme laughed, 'She's like that with everyone. If you can bear it, I'd ask you to just let her mother you a little, she'll be terribly put-out if you don't. That's one of the reasons she dislikes Dupré so intensely.'

'Well, I'm not complaining, it's nice to have someone else cook my meals for me for a change. On the night itself, it will be a slightly different matter though. I know it's her kitchen most of the time, but I need to be in charge and I need to be left alone. If I need her help I will ask for it, but if she is fussing around me then it will make things very difficult.'

'I understand, I'll have a word with her and make sure she's completely aware that the kitchen will be your territory. Now, how have you been since we met in Paris?'

They passed a pleasant half hour chatting with the chef, who had an impressive roster of clients and an amusing collection of anecdotes about them, then went out to the bothy to find Philby.

'There's one thing I'm particularly keen to see outside,' said Jemme.

'Ah, is this the thing you've been mysteriously arranging with DD?' asked Hil.

'It might be….'

Arriving outside the small hut, Philby came out to greet them.

'Is everything ready?' asked Jemme excitedly.

'*Oui, Monsieur.* They are in the cage so that you can see them.'

'Cage?' said Hil in surprise. 'Who's in the cage? What's going on?'

'Come on,' said Jemme grabbing her hand, 'let's go and have a look.' He led her to the copse where they had first sat on the day they had bought the house. As they neared the edge, a strange sound was carried on the breeze.

'What's that?' asked Hil. It was almost like the braying of a donkey, but much more high pitched.

'You'll see,' said Jemme, leading her into the wood and up to a large cage with a pitched roof.

'Here we are!' He stopped and looked in, 'They're beautiful, just as I'd imagined them.'

Hil took a step forward and peered into the cage. She looked down at the birds. They were low to the ground with long elegant necks and huge tails which trailed out behind them. They were a bit larger than a hen, but much more exotic looking.

'What are they?' she said.

'They're peacocks!'

Hil laughed, 'They're not peacocks!' she looked down at the birds again. They were as white as snow, from the crest on their heads to their downy underbelly. As the other three birds pecked around on the ground, one of them looked up and saw Hil staring at it. It made a hissing noise and in a flash had lifted its tail up and opened out a huge fan. Like the bird itself, the fan was a pure white. Where one would expect iridescent blues and greens and threatening eyes, there was nothing. The shape was instantly recognisable, but it was utterly devoid of any colour whatsoever, almost as if it had been entirely washed away in the rain.

Hil looked at Jemme in confusion, 'There's something wrong with your peacocks.'

Jemme laughed, 'There's nothing wrong with them, they're meant to be like this – they've been selectively bred to be just like this in fact. They're leucistic.'

Hil studied the birds again, and then Jemme.

'Why would anyone try and breed out the best part of a peacock?' she asked.

'Don't you think they're beautiful like this?'

Hil looked at the birds again. There was something incredibly beautiful and regal about them, but she couldn't see them as anything other than a poor version of what they should be.

'They're incredibly rare – they were pretty expensive if I'm being honest.'

'You paid *more* for peacocks with no colour?' she asked incredulously, looking at Jemme as if he had just bought some magic beans from a travelling salesman.

'Well, yes – like I said, they're very rare,' said Jemme, beginning to feel a little foolish.

'How much?'

'Well, I can't quite –' he mumbled guiltily. The birds had been eye-wateringly pricey and judging by her face, he was certain Hil would be outraged.

'I thought they would be a nice surprise for our guests, when they're wandering in the grounds.'

'Well they'll have to be wandering in a very specific part of them.'

'Oh – they're not going to be kept in the cage. They're going to be free to roam the grounds. I've had this installed so they have somewhere safe to be at night. Philby's just rounded them up and put them here so that we can see them.'

Hil narrowed her eyes and looked at the birds again, 'I suppose the guests will be quite surprised to see them,' she concluded slightly ambiguously.

They turned and walked back to the house, with Jemme struggling to shake the feeling that his plan had backfired slightly.

Back at the chateau, Hil went off to talk to Marguerite, and Jemme took the opportunity to inspect the Babylon room. He stood looking at its white walls, and trying to imagine how he could mould it and develop it into something which was more than just a room. He closed his eyes and thought of Ancient Mesopotamia, flanked by the mighty Tigris on one side and the Euphrates on the other. He pictured the floor of the room as marshland and mud flats with reed banks shoring up the corners, and the horizon stretching all the way to the Persian Gulf. He thought of the emergence of the written word, and imagined Sumerian, Akkadian and Aramaic unfurling in strange characters and symbols across the walls, mystifying and intriguing until they began to make sense and become one of humanity's most useful tools. He imagined Hammurabi sitting proudly on his throne and making his great laws, setting into stone mankind's first legal code and establishing the precedent for justice and jurisprudence. He thought of the Selucids, the Achaemenids, the Parthians and the Sassanids. He remembered Nebuchadnezzar and the beautiful Ishtar Gate, and wondered how he could possibly fit everything into this one, small room in France. And yet, he knew he would. He opened his eyes and looked around the room. It would be his own tiny Babylonian Empire.

✻ ✻ ✻ ✻

The next morning Hil and Jemme were both up bright and early.

'I feel like a child on the morning of his birthday,' said Jemme excitedly. 'I can't believe our first room is finally finished and we're going to host our very first event.'

'Mmmm,' Hil agreed, not yet as perky and alert as her husband.

'Come on!' said Jemme prodding her, 'Let's get up – there's lots to do!'

'Alright, alright,' she mumbled, rolling over.

Half an hour later, a very upbeat Jemme and a slightly puffy-eyed Hil were breakfasting in the kitchen. Marguerite seemed to match Jemme's excitement, and was chirruping about fancy society ladies and beautiful dishes. She was bustling around the kitchen, making a big show of keeping out of Jean-Louis's way. He had already been up for hours, preparing vegetables, chopping herbs and measuring out spices.

'You look busy,' Jemme said, as he wandered over to Jean-Louis, coffee in hand. Jean-Louis froze mid-action, evidently realising he couldn't shoo Jemme away in the same way he had been fending off Marguerite all morning. He looked at Jemme nervously and then eyed his carefully arranged equipment, desperately hoping his new employer wasn't about to undo hours of preparation with some idle fiddling. Jemme was oblivious to his fretting and picked up a strange looking tool,

'What's this?' he asked, turning it over in his hands, 'I don't think I've ever seen anything like this before.

Jean-Louis leaped towards him, carefully removing it from his hand and laying it back in precisely the right place. He inserted himself between Jemme and the work counter.

'It is a mandolin, Monsieur. It is used for slicing things very finely. At the moment, I am doing the *mise en place* – it is a very important part of the preparation,' he paused, allowing emphasis to fall on the words 'very' and 'important'. 'In fact, it is almost as important as the cooking,' he said meaningfully.

'The *mise en* what?' asked Jemme cheerfully, still blind to Jean-Louis's caginess.

'The *mise en place*, Monsieur. It is when a chef prepares all his ingredients and equipment. Everything must be in the right place, everything must be measured out and prepared so that as soon as he starts cooking, the chef has everything he needs and will not have to interrupt the process. It is like a symphony Monsieur, or a highly-coordinated military operation. Can you imagine if halfway through making a soufflé, at the most critical stage, a chef had to stop to refill his pepper mill or look for the eggs?!'

He looked at Jemme, who finally realised that perhaps his presence in the kitchen wasn't altogether helpful.

'Right, well, yes. It looks like you're doing an excellent job. I suppose I'd better leave you to it.'

Jean-Louis smiled and gestured towards the kitchen's exit with a bow of his head. Jemme shuffled out, coffee mug in hand. Slightly chastened, he went and rejoined Hil who had just finished her own breakfast.

'How's it all looking?' she asked.

'Excellent, although to tell you the truth I don't think Jean-Louis wanted me there at all. I think I was getting in the way.' He paused for a moment, 'I think I'm going to go and see how Aude is getting on in the salon.'

Hil rolled her eyes and went back to reading her book, 'I'm sure she'll be pleased to see you, too,' she said as Jemme left the kitchen.

As it turned out, Aude was much better at disguising the fact that Jemme was in the way than Jean-Louis had been. She smiled at him and answered his questions shyly. Even though it was only a little after nine in the morning, the room was already looking fit for a feast. Everything had been polished to a glossy sheen, and the table was already groaning with cutlery. Large floral centrepieces were so fresh that dewdrops still clung to the petals.

'These are beautiful!' he said to Aude. 'Where are the flowers from?'

'Some are from your own *jardin,* Monsieur,' she said. 'The roses, mostly.'

'Fantastic! Philby has worked hard on those rose beds; it's nice to see the fruits of his labour. Who made the arrangements? They're absolutely lovely.'

'I did, Monsieur,' said Aude blushing.

'Really?'

Aude bit her lip and looked at her shoe. 'It was me and my mother, Monsieur. She used to sell flowers.'

'Did she? How interesting. Well in that case, do pass on my congratulations – and the same to you too, these are wonderful.'

Aude nodded and turned an even deeper shade of purple.

Jemme paused and realised that it was going to be difficult to engage her in any further conversation.

'Right, well – it looks like you're doing an excellent job, I'd better leave you to it I suppose,' he said.

He left the salon and went to find Hil again.

'I don't really know what to do with myself,' he said, sitting down heavily in the chair next to hers. 'There's so much excitement around, but I don't seem to be involved in any of it – I really want to help get everything ready.'

Hil closed her book and smiled at him, 'Oh sweetheart, I'm sorry. I think the best help would be staying out of everyone's way and letting them get on with everything. I'm sure that nearer the time there will be lots you can do. Why don't I make us both some coffee and then we can leave the kitchen properly, so that Jean-Louis can sort out all his things. We can drink it on the bench outside and discuss this evening.'

'Alright,' said Jemme, still looking a bit dejected.

A little bit later, as he sat on their favourite stone bench, coffee in hand, he still hadn't perked up too much.

'I don't understand what the matter is,' said Hil, 'everything's been leading us to this point and you've been so excited – what's changed?'

'I'm still excited, I just feel a bit left out this morning I suppose.'

'Well, that's crazy. I'm not surprised though – this is just what you're like!'

Jemme looked at her questioningly.

'You have to be involved at every single level,' Hil explained. 'You're not satisfied unless you've had a personal involvement, right down to the minutiae.'

'Really?'

'Absolutely – think about this place! Progress has been slow because you've wanted to do it all yourself. From designing the thing, all the way down to choosing the paint.'

'I never realised that about myself,' Jemme said, looking a little sad, as if Hil had just revealed something deeply unpleasant about himself.

'It's no bad thing,' Hil said, softening, 'I think most of it stems from perfectionism – you just want to get involved because you want to make sure that everything is as good as it possibly can be.'

Jemme looked thoughtful.

'I suppose the rest of it is just eagerness,' Hil added.

'Really?'

Hil laughed, 'Definitely! It's that boyish enthusiasm of yours – you want to be involved because you get so fired up about these things.'

'Well I can definitely concede that!' Jemme said, lightening. 'I never really thought about it in terms of progress though. I hope my getting involved doesn't slow the project down more than is necessary.'

Hil shrugged, 'It depends what you want to get out of it I suppose. If it was a simple construction project which was crucial to future plans, then running to schedule is important. This is different though – it's much bigger to start with, but you don't want to just construct something, you want to create something. I think the whole process is as important to you as the end product.'

Jemme finally smiled, 'You know me so well,' he said, leaning over and kissing his wife. 'You're right too, I should just let everyone do their jobs. I think I'll keep well out of the way until this afternoon at least! Why don't we just have a nice morning together?'

'Wonderful!' said Hil, finishing her coffee and collecting both their mugs, 'Do you fancy a walk around the grounds? It's much warmer out than I thought it would be.'

'That sounds nice. We can let the peacocks out of their cage too.'

'Who does it normally?'

'Philby – he's the only one with the key. Like I said, they're only going to be in their cage during the night, to keep them safe. The rest of the time they're free to roam the grounds.'

They approached the cage, which was unexpectedly quiet. They both peered in to realise that it was empty.

'Philby must have let them out already,' said Hil.

'He must have done. That's strange though – he's locked the padlock again. I'll talk to him about that. I wanted the cage to be left unlocked during the day so that the birds can come and go as they please.'

'Well why don't we go and find him.'

It didn't take them long, and they soon came across Philby, digging in a new flowerbed.

'*Bonjour, Monsieur,*' he said shading his eyes against the early morning light. He straightened up and brushed the earth from his hands. 'Have you seen the flowers from the garden? The girl Aude has made them into decorations.'

'I have seen them, and I'm looking forward to showing them to my wife. They look fantastic. I actually wanted to talk to you about something else though.'

'*Monsieur?*'

'Oh it's nothing serious – it's just about the peacock cage. Do you remember, we discussed the fact that the cage would be left open during the day?'

'*Oui, Monsieur.*'

'Well, I'd still like to keep that as the practice, just so that you remember when you're letting them out in the morning.'

Philby looked confused, 'But of course I remember, Monsieur.'

'I'm sure you will, but it hasn't been done this morning – it's not a big deal though, don't worry about it.'

'I don't understand, Monsieur, I haven't let them out this morning yet.'

'Well someone has, and then they've locked the cage door afterwards.'

'That's impossible, Monsieur,' said Philby fishing around in the coat of his oilskin. He produced a small silver key at the end of a long piece of string. 'Look – this is the only key.'

'Oh. Well that's rather puzzling. Who could have let them out?'

'No one, Monsieur. I look after this key very carefully. I know that they are very valuable birds. I locked them all away last night and then put this key in my pocket. It hasn't left it since.'

'Well they're certainly not in the cage anymore,' said Jemme, starting to look as confused as his gardener.

Philby frowned, and the three of them made their way back to the cage. They stood at the edge peering in. It was plain that the peacocks were not there, but where they were was anything but clear.

'I don't understand, Monsieur,' Philby said.

'Neither do I, I'm afraid.'

'Have you been walking around the grounds, Monsieur?'

'We've been outside, but we haven't wandered around much, why?'

'They make a great noise, Monsieur; if they have got out we should be able to round them up easily – they like to stick together too.'

'But they couldn't have escaped,' said Hil.

'The cage is very sturdy, Madame, yes, but it is the only explanation.'

'No, they couldn't have escaped, because the cage was still locked. If they'd managed to break through the door, they would hardly stop to lock it behind them, would they? I think we're all agreed that they wouldn't have been able to slip between the bars too.'

Philby and Jemme both looked at her, and then at the decidedly locked padlock. She was completely right. The three of them stared at the cage for a while longer, turning the puzzle over and trying to come up with any logical conclusions.

'Well, I suppose we better start looking,' said Jemme eventually.

'But Monsieur, how would they have escaped?'

'I have no idea, but they were extremely expensive birds and regardless of how they magicked themselves out of their cage, I'm not yet prepared to conclude that we've lost them for good.'

They spent two fruitless hours wandering around the grounds looking for the birds.

'I just don't understand,' said Jemme, for the fourth or fifth time.

'I don't think we're going to find them, sweetheart. We've looked all over and Philby's right, we would have heard them by now. I think we're going to have to resign ourselves to the fact they're gone.'

'I don't understand though,' said Jemme again.

'They must have escaped somehow,' said Hil, trying to be as comforting as possible.

'But they couldn't have done – you saw the padlock – it was locked tight. I asked Philby to buy the most heavy-duty one possible too, to prevent exactly this sort of thing. There's no way they could have broken through that, even if they somehow organised themselves to rush the door in unison. Besides, it doesn't explain how it was locked again afterwards.'

Hil winced, 'Maybe a fox took them? It used to happen all the time in the chicken coop when we were children. They're very cunning and can reach through the bars of the cage.'

Jemme shook his head slowly. 'I don't think so – think about the racket all of them would have made if a fox came anywhere near them. Besides, a fox would have made a terrible mess – there's not so much as a single feather on the ground. Cunning as he might be, I think it's unlikely that a fox could reach in, past all that metal netting, dispatch all of them and then carefully remove each one from the cage.'

'I know, it was just a suggestion,' said Hil gently, 'I'm just as puzzled as you.' She thought for a moment longer, 'Did they come from nearby?'

'No, actually DD took a very long time sourcing them; they came up from Nice, but originally had been imported all the way from Singapore. Why?'

'I'm just wondering if lots of people were aware that they were here.'

'I don't think it was big news, per se, but I should imagine that it wouldn't have been difficult to find out. Besides, I'm sure Marguerite would have discussed it down in the village.'

'Hmmmm.'

'What are you thinking?'

'Well, you did say they were very expensive?'

'Yes, very, which is why I'm so keen to find them now.'

'The only conclusion I can come to is that they've been stolen, I'm afraid.'

'Stolen?!'

'They must have been. Think about it – incredibly expensive birds arrive up here. It's not difficult to hear about it, and just as easy to find out how much they're worth. I don't think it would have been that difficult for a couple of people to come in and make off with the lot, to resell.'

Jemme screwed up his face and thought about it.

'I don't think it was an opportunist,' said Hil, 'I suspect it would have been very carefully planned out.'

'That's crazy,' laughed Jemme, 'the great peacock heist!'

'Is it really crazy though? Do you remember that old lady who used to live in the flat below us in Paris?'

'The one with the dogs?'

'Precisely. She had quite a few dogs, but she also had that rather noisy Chow-Chow – do you remember?'

'Goodness, yes – it was some kind of pedigree wasn't it? She'd paid something astronomical for it too.'

'Exactly, it was a completely ridiculous sum. But do you remember what happened to it?'

'Ahh, I do. I see your point – it was stolen.'

'Not only was it stolen, but it was stolen and all the other dogs were left behind. Someone knew exactly what they were doing, and exactly how much that dog was worth. Think about it – any status symbol becomes a commodity and there's always a market for stolen commodities.'

Jemme sighed, 'I think you must be right; that's the only way I suppose makes any sense.'

He thought about it a bit more, 'Actually no, it doesn't really make sense – Philby said the key hadn't left his pocket – how could they have got into the cage? I can understand if they'd used bolt cutters or something, but there's still the wretched mystery of the locked lock. Also, how would they have got here? Aside from how they got past the entrance gate, if they had come on foot, someone would have heard the noise the peacocks made, and if they came in a van, someone would have heard the noise the van made.' He paused and frowned, 'It just doesn't make any sense,' he said again.

'I'm sorry sweetheart. I hope they weren't too expensive,' said Hil.

Jemme grimaced, 'Why don't we head back in. I'm a bit fed up of the garden.' He took the coffee cups from Hil and they headed back into the kitchen. Jean-Louis stopped in his tracks when they entered the kitchen, and stared at them meaningfully.

'Alright, alright, I hadn't forgotten – I was just bringing these back,' Jemme grumbled, before rejoining Hil in the corridor.

'I guess the kitchen's still out of bounds,' he said.

'Stop looking so grumpy! There's plenty of stuff we can be getting on with.'

'Like what?'

'Well, why don't you tell me about your plans for the next room? I know it's been on your mind a lot recently, so why don't you talk me through it?'

Jemme perked up a little, 'OK. In fact, why don't I show you? I'll take you to the room.'

'Great.'

On the way, they passed the second reception room Dupré was painting. Hil paused, 'Do we know if he's finished yet?'

'I'm not sure to be honest. I should imagine he'd be very close to the end, if he hasn't actually finished.'

'Well why don't we go and see? It would cheer you up lots to see a new piece finished – it will be exciting!'

'I don't know Hil, I've already been booted out of my own kitchen, I don't want to be kicked out of my own salon too!'

'Well, we'll sneak in then. If he's up on the scaffolding like last time then he probably won't even hear us.'

Jemme relented, 'OK.'

Hil gently pushed the door open and Jemme crept in behind her, feeling a little mischievous. The room smelled of paint, and they could hear Dupré creaking around on top of the ladder. The scaffolding had been ratcheted up so that it almost touched the ceiling, so he could only have been lying flat on his back whilst he painted the finishing touches. They looked up and slowly took in the ceiling. After a few moments Hil caught Jemme's eye and raised her eyebrows. He exhaled slowly and shook his head, both of them dumbstruck. Unfortunately, they had made enough noise to alert Dupré to their presence and he slid out from between the narrow, gap and swung round to sit on the top rung of the ladder.

'No, no, no, Monsieur! Not again!'

'I'm sorry to disturb you, Monsieur Dupré, but we just wanted to have a quick peek – I had no idea you were so advanced in your progress!'

Dupré appeared to be in too much of a reverie to become too angry. He sighed and wiped his hands on his overalls, fishing a half-finished hand-rolled cigarette from a pocket.

'If only you had waited half a day more you would have seen everything finished,' he chided. 'But, now I suppose is fine. She is nearly finished,' he said, gesturing with one hand and lighting the cigarette with the other. 'You are pleased, *non*?'

'I, um,' Jemme faltered, looking sideways at Hil who shrugged her shoulders, non-plussed.

'It's certainly very accomplished,' Jemme said finally.

'You do not like it?' Dupré asked, a dangerous note of anger rising in his voice.

'Oh, we do, very much,' rushed Hil, anxious to avoid a repeat of the last incident. 'I think we were just expecting something else, so were a little…surprised.'

'Yes, I think it's just not quite what we were expecting,' echoed Jemme. He and Hil looked up at the ceiling, taking it all in. Jemme had certainly not been lying – it truly was an accomplished piece of work. The brush strokes, use of light and careful renderings of the clouds was second to none. However, they had been expecting the elegant ceilings of Versailles with their wistful clouds, redolent of days spent in summer meadows. Instead, Dupré had spread a tumultuous sky across the ceilings, filled with squalls, and rent asunder by tempestuous clouds. It was dark, brooding and threatening; the sort of sky in which portent runs wild, and which is always seen by sailors before a mighty storm and soldiers on the eve of a brutal battle. Instead of opening the room to the lofty heavens above, it made them feel as if they were cowering beneath them. Hil began to feel stifled by the atmosphere the ceiling created. She felt oppressed beneath its weight and unsettled by the torment that shot through it like the silvery clouds. She shuddered a little and squeezed Jemme's hand,

'Come on, let's go.'

Jemme thanked Dupré, who was happily packing up his brushes, and followed Hil out into the corridor. Once the door was shut behind them, she breathed a small sigh of relief,

'Goodness, I feel *physically* lighter than when I was in there. I know Dupré has a slightly depressive temperament, but it feels like it takes a particular type of tortured soul to come up with something like that. What on earth are we going to say to him this time? I mean, it was fine when it was just the flowers, but how are we going to tell him we want to paint over the whole thing?'

'Paint over it?'

'Well I assume we're going to have to – there's no way we can work with what he's done and try to change it.'

'But why would we want to change it?'

They had been walking back to the gardens, but Hil suddenly stopped, 'You don't want to change it?'

Jemme looked slightly confused, 'But why would I want to change it?'

'But you saw it! It was tormented and terrifying. I felt like Lear on the heath just standing underneath it.'

'It's definitely dramatic, and like we both said, we weren't expecting that, I'll agree.'

'It's not just that it's dramatic though – it's beyond that! It's, it's…. you're not seriously contemplating keeping it?' Hil finished helplessly.

'But I don't understand why I wouldn't. You saw it; it's beautiful! It's some of the finest craftsmanship I've ever seen. In fact, it's better than some of the art I've seen in various galleries, and it's painted directly onto my own ceiling. Why would I want to change that?'

'Because it's horrible! It's intimidating and depressing and creates an awful atmosphere. It's completely wrong for a reception room like that, which needs to be light and airy.'

'I know it's not exactly like Versailles, but I'm still really pleased with it. I think he's done a fantastic job. It's so different – it creates a really striking first impression.'

Hil looked at him sadly, as if she had suddenly realised that they were never going to understand each other on the matter.

'In any case, it certainly gives us a story to tell!' said Jemme cheerfully.

'I suppose,' Hil sighed, sounding exceptionally glum.

Jemme didn't appear to hear it. 'Come on, we were planning on looking at the Babylonian Room!' he said, grabbing her hand and continuing down the corridor.'

✻ ✻ ✻ ✻

After an afternoon spent looking at the white walls of a room she couldn't visualise, Hil was feeling rather flat. The prospect of the long-awaited party failed to arouse much excitement in her, and she sat on the bed, wondering what had changed. She had been looking forward to showing off the chateau to her Paris friends for a long time, and indeed, looking forward to seeing her much-missed friends for a proper evening. However, something just didn't feel right. It couldn't be attributed to the ceiling though, it seemed too trivial. She lay back heavily. The more she thought about it though, the more she realised it was bothering her. It wasn't merely how it looked, it was the fact that she and Jemme were so out of tune with each other on the matter. No matter how this project had tested them, they had always understood one another; she knew instinctively what would delight Jemme and what would upset him too, and he her. They had wordlessly communicated with each other the entire time, and been seamlessly in-step with each other the whole way through. However, for whatever reason, Hil had had a strong reaction to something and Jemme had been completely deaf to it. It felt like a gap had been torn in the perfect harmony which had existed before, and it had become a jumble of discordant notes. She sighed as she realised that this clashing noise had been amplified when they had gone on to look at the next room. Usually she allowed herself to be enveloped by Jemme's dreams; she listened eagerly and followed the rich ideas he painted for her, soaking up every detail and trying to see things as he saw them. Occasionally when her imagination faltered and the colours dulled, she merely allowed his enthusiasm to wash over her, and enjoyed the feeling of seeing someone she loved so animated and enthralled. However, this room left her cold. She could not see beyond its stark white walls, even when Jemme attempted to conjure biblical rivers, mud-brick buildings and the fertile Mesopotamian plains.

Sighing again, she decided that perhaps she was just being obstinate because things hadn't been the way she had liked them. Just then Jemme came in with a suit bag draped over one arm,

'Sweetheart, you're not dressed? Have you seen the time?'

'Oh, I hadn't actually. Is it late?'

'A little, but don't worry – what have you been up to?'

'Just lying here thinking.'

'About anything in particular?'

'I... no, not really,' said Hil, sitting up and stretching, 'I suppose I'd better get ready.'

She wandered into the bathroom, still lost in her own thoughts. Turning the shower up to maximum heat, she stood underneath it completely still, letting the water wash over her as she tried to close off her thoughts, and let herself focus on the evening. Through the steam, she was alarmed to see that the hands on the clock weren't at all where she was expecting them to be; the realisation that she didn't have that much time left seemed to snap her into action and banished the last lingering thoughts.

Seeing Jemme in his best dinner jacket returned some of the tingling excitement about the evening, and by the time she felt the coolness of her silk dress on her body, the feeling of anticipation had properly returned.

'Is that the new dress you were talking about?' asked Jemme smiling at her.

'Yes, I bought it from Ungaro a few months ago especially for this evening. Do you like it?'

Jemme came and stood behind Hil, looking at both of their reflections in the mirror.

'I love it,' he said, 'you look beautiful.'

'Thank you,' said Hil, smiling as she fiddled with one earlobe, trying to slip in a dangling earring. She eventually pulled it down and straightened it, looking into the mirror. She shook her head slightly so that the light caught the diamonds.

'Beautiful,' said Jemme again, taking in her jade green dress and pearl and diamond jewellery. 'You look so elegant,' he said proudly, kissing her on the cheek.

They left the room together and made their way back downstairs, where the first guests were soon to be arriving. At the top of the stairs, Jemme offered Hil his arm. She slipped hers through and they made their way down. Hil's new shoes meant she had to walk a little more slowly than usual, so their unhurried descent seemed almost stately.

'Just think,' Hil said, 'this is just how they would have begun big society evenings in days gone by.'

'I know,' said Jemme, squeezing her arm, 'and now it's our turn to be lord and lady of the manor.'

On reaching the Halle d'Honneur at the bottom, they noticed how clean everything looked. They had become so acclimatised to the house being in a perpetual state of work that they ceased to notice various piles of masonry blocks, stacks of paint tins or huge swathes of dust cloths. For the first time in a long time, everything had been cleared out of sight, and all traces of building works had been swept and polished away. The hall was lit softly and filled with yet more fresh flowers. Hil could imagine it filled instead with excited debutantes, wearing the first proper evening dress of their young lives, standing around and watching their nervous peers descend the staircase. She pictured the young girls blushing, and imagined the sound of music wafting out from perhaps a string quartet in the ballroom. She thought about how the leading families from the entire *département* would have sent their daughters, and what a big event it would have been in the area's social calendar. Imagining the carriages arriving and the excitement of the festivities, she could see why Marguerite's grandmother would have cherished her memories of such events, and told the stories to her young grandchildren.

Wandering around, Hil began to feel a little like a debutante herself. She felt as if she was on the brink of announcing herself within her new role and position, and her friends would understand her in a whole new way. It felt like her own rite of passage.

Jemme too was feeling quite excited. He and Hil made a tour of all the rooms which would be open, before checking that everything was alright in the kitchen and the servery.

He slowly opened the doors of the salon so that they could see everything that had been prepared for the feast. As the setting within revealed itself, Hil couldn't help but gasp slightly. Shimmering in candlelight, it was a scene straight from a storybook. Between them, Aude and Marguerite had prepared a table groaning with flowers, and laden with cutlery that glinted in every place setting, and crystal glasses which shattered the light from the chandelier overhead, sending it scattered across the table. The furniture, tapestry hangings and art all pulled together and made the room look like it had always existed as a whole. It looked opulent and grand, yet still warm and inviting.

'Look at the piano!' said Hil, pointing over to the pistachio-green pianoforte they had bought together. The folding candelabra, which extended out from either side of the music stand, had been polished and fitted with tall rose-coloured tapers, which flickered. 'It looks completely at home in this room,' she said happily.

'It does, doesn't it? I think all our furniture does actually – I'm so pleased with how it all looks. I can't believe how lucky we've been with the carpet too. It was so elusive!'

'Commissioning it was a great idea, I don't think you would ever have been able to find anything that worked as well in the room as this one does. How did you come up with this design in the end?'

'It was a bit of a collaborative effort actually. It was partly me partly the Professor and partly the shop owner. There are all sorts of references in it, and I'm sure the Professor would be more than happy to talk you through them at length at some point,' he said wryly.

'I'm sure he would!'

'There is one thing I want to show you though. There's a special message in the carpet just for us.'

'A message? That's so exciting! Where is it? What does it say?'

'I'll show you,' said Jemme, taking her over to the edge of the carpet. 'Look, here,' he said pointing at the corner.

Hil followed his finger and looked at the swirling patterns which filled the corner. She glanced around the room and saw that the pattern was echoed exactly in each corner.

'Do you see?'

She shook her head.

'You'll have to look quite closely, but they're hidden in this part here, and it's the same in each corner.'

'What are?'

Jemme smiled, 'That would be telling, wouldn't it! Look I'll get you started by showing you the first one.' He knelt down and traced a path through the pattern, following one swirling line in particular. Suddenly, the line sprang out and made sense to Hil; it was not merely a line, but a letter 'H'. She squinted at the twisting and interweaving lines in front of her, trying to uncover further letters. Once she knew what she was looking for it didn't take her long and she had found all of their initials.

'What a lovely idea! I can't believe you managed to keep it a secret until now too! I'll enjoy knowing that they're there, especially when no one else can see them.'

'I thought you'd enjoy them, my love.'

Just as they were thinking of heading off to the kitchen, the first guest arrived.

Hil went and opened the door to find Valerie and Nicola, two of their oldest friends from Paris. They were cherished friends too, as they were the first joint friends they had made as a couple, meeting them on only the second occasion she and Jemme had been to dinner together. She greeted them warmly, and was just wondering where to put their coats when Marguerite bustled in. She saw Hil with an armful of coats and scarves looking slightly confused, and swept them away from her.

'Madame, I shall take these,' she said rather grandly.

'Oh, Marguerite, thank you – I was just wondering…. in the flat at home it's so much easier…'

Marguerite saw that the guests were facing the opposite direction, as Jemme pointed something out to them, and she shooed Hil back towards them, 'Madame, you do not need to worry about that kind of thing – I shall answer the door and take everyone's things. All you need to do is entertain them.'

'Thank you, Marguerite,' Hil said, smiling.

'*Tiens*! Go!' whispered Marguerite, ushering her away.

Valerie and Nicola were looking around, wide-eyed,

'I had no idea it would look like this. I mean I know you said "chateau", but you also said that it was in a complete state!' said Nicola.

Hil laughed, 'You should see the rest of the place. This is a bit of a showpiece entrance; the rest of the rooms are filled with ladders and paint buckets and all sorts. In fact, the room we're eating in was finished so recently, you'd be advised not to touch the walls!'

Valerie laughed, 'Well I think it's incredible. I can see why you've both been away from Paris so much. What a fantastic project to have for the weekends! I'm impressed, I really am.'

'Thank you,' said Hil warmly. 'It's a little more than just at the weekends though, I'll have to admit. It has a habit of creeping into our consciousnesses.'

'Well from what I've seen so far, it's been worth it, I can't imagine any other couple taking on something like this.'

Jemme and Hil began to show them around, explaining their various trials and tribulations so far, to much hilarity. The story of Philby stuck underground prompted much gasping, whilst the story of Dupré on the scaffolding elicited a great deal of tutting about 'the artistic temperament'. They finally led them to the salon, where their reaction was even greater than Hil's had been. Nicola looked almost tearful as she rhapsodised about how regal it all seemed. Hil laughed affectionately at her pleasure, and was just thinking about how enjoyable it was to share a special evening with friends, when Marguerite ushered two more guests in. She introduced them as Messieurs Granier and Coer-des-Roi of Total.

Hil politely offered her hand, and enquired about business, but she could feel the atmosphere slipping between her fingers. Jemme snapped straight into action as well. Although his demeanour didn't appear to change, she knew him well enough to know that he was in full 'work' mode and rather than being relaxed, was focussed and alert.

The six of them made polite small talk, and Valerie and Nicola asked lots of questions about the oil industry, but Hil couldn't help longing for the atmosphere of a few moments ago, when they were giggling at the grandeur of the place and with the excitement of the whole event.

Gradually the rest of the guests started to arrive. The business set seemed to keep mostly to themselves, and Hil could feel her loyalties divided. It was the perfect set-up in many ways; she could surround herself with friends and spend all night in their company. However, she knew it wasn't fair and she would have to spend at least some time talking to the assembled oligarchs and technocrats. She made her way over and found Jemme. On this side of the room, the sound of conversation was completely different. Amongst her friends it had been warm and lively, with plenty of laughter. Here there was laughter, but it was rasping and thin. The air hung with platitudes, but Hil felt instinctively that there was no great friendship between any of these men. In fact, as she caught snatches of conversation, she distinctly got the impression that each was sizing the others up, working out respective importance and industrial clout. It was difficult not to feel excluded, a feeling which only grew when she found Jemme, who introduced her to the chairman of Airbus, a man she took an instant dislike to. He offered her a half-hearted '*enchanté*' and a thin smile, before turning back to his conversation with Jemme.

Hil decided to persevere, 'I hope my husband has told you some of the stories of this place so far,' she said.

'*Ah, oui, Madame*, I have heard much about it. I am very involved with this sort of thing.'

'Oh, I see – how so?'

The chairman merely shrugged, and began to talk to Jemme about the new joint venture they had just agreed on. Hil was slightly taken aback by his rudeness, but after a moment realised that he wasn't going to acknowledge her any further so went off to find someone else, as Jemme shot her an apologetic look.

She noticed that a couple of men who were slightly on the fringes of the group had empty glasses, and she made her way over.

'Good evening, gentlemen. Would you care for a top-up?'

Almost as one, they extended their empty glasses to her. She looked around the room to where Aude was circulating with a bottle of champagne, and caught her eye.

'How do you do, I'm Mrs Mafeze,' she said, offering them a hand.

The men seemed more interested in the fact that their glasses were being refilled, but once Aude had finished, they became much more talkative.

One introduced himself as Monsieur Giscard of Thompson, an electrical company, and the other as the managing director of Total France.

'I was just talking to Monsieur Giscard about the difficulties I'm having at the moment,' he said.

'Difficulties? I'm sorry to hear that.'

'Ah, Madame, it is a small matter and a ridiculous one at that. We have discovered new oil in a previously untapped location – I cannot say where. It would be a significant boon for us. It would drive up our operating income and profit, not to mention assets and equity. It would create new jobs and be good for our shareholders.'

'Well that sounds like a good thing.'

The man smiled bitterly, '*Exactement*! But, for now, we are stuck!'

'How are you stuck?'

'A band of trouble-makers, Madame, are making life very difficult for us. They are trying to block drilling, and keep us out of the area permanently.'

'Why would they do that?'

The man drank deeply from his glass until it was empty again. He looked at it and then at Hil, who took the rather unsubtle hint and looked around for Aude again.

With his glass refilled, the man sighed, 'There are many reasons, they claim, Madame, but mostly it is the same as always – people who wish to stand in the way of progress and people who fear big business. Sometimes they call themselves "environmentalists", sometimes they say they are protecting indigenous rights – there is always something. I've even been accused of being a colonialist in the past!'

Hil looked slightly taken aback, 'Which is it in this case?' she asked.

'Ah, it is all of them, and some I have never heard before. We are having some difficulties because the land is protected – it is of scientific interest apparently, although I don't think that actually means much. Besides, it's never usually such a big obstacle, but these people are being so persistent. There is a tribe who have been living on the land for a long time, granted, but we would pay to have them rehoused. I'm sure the housing we provide will be a damned sight better than what they have now, but no one sees it that way. Campaigners are getting worked up about the fact that the people's way of life is being threatened, but what does that even mean? They've been living the same way for hundreds and hundreds of years, with reliance on the same primitive crafts and technologies. We're helping them progress!'

Hil looked appalled and couldn't help but stare at the man for a while. He saw her look of disgust, but misinterpreted it,

'I know, Madame! It is shocking how ungrateful some people can be!' The electrical man shook his head in sympathy.

'Is it likely that the campaigners will succeed?' asked Hil hopefully.

Monsieur Markette, the oil man, shook his head, 'I can't see how they could – they're a rag-tag bunch of amateurs. Principled, of course, but ultimately clueless. It's not like we haven't fought this battle before. We've got a hundred-strong team of lawyers on our side who know every loop-hole in every piece of legislature, like the back of their hands. *I* wouldn't like to get on the wrong side of those guys!' He laughed in a way which reminded Hil of a sea-lion barking. 'Of course, it might not even get that far. The ideal scenario would be one in which we could find someone high up in politics, who was sympathetic to our cause. The problem is that these people have been so noisy that our usual… "friends"… are reluctant to associate themselves with the problem.' He paused and looked like he was assessing Hil for the first time, 'You don't know anyone do you?'

'I, well – I don't think….'

'Well, let's start here – who do you know at this party?' the man interrupted her.

'What do you mean, who do I know?'

'Who's your main connection here? Who's your reason for coming?'

'My reason for coming? This is my party! My "main connection" if you will, is my husband!'

'Mafeze? No,' the man shook his head, 'no, Mafeze won't be any good for this.'

'Who are all those people?' he asked, gesturing towards the Paris crowd.

'Those are my friends from Paris, Monsieur.'

The man's eyes lit up a little, 'Oh? And do they know anyone?'

'Monsieur,' said Hil firmly, 'I highly doubt, even if they did know anyone of influence, that they would be willing to ally themselves with this cause. What's more, I know that they would not be willing to discuss the matter this evening. They have come all the way here to enjoy the chateau with us, and celebrate the work we have completed so far. I hope that you are able to join us in that matter and no other.'

The man looked disappointed, and eyed Hil warily as he drained his glass again. He had clearly decided that she wasn't going to be of particular use to him.

※　※　※　※

By the time the last of the food had been eaten, and taxis were queuing up to whisk their guests away, Hil was starting to feel very tired indeed. She had enjoyed herself, but the evening had not been completely what she was expecting. To start with, it had felt rather strained. There had been a distinct lack of cohesion, and making constant efforts to bridge the gulf between the two groups had been tiring. Listening to Jemme's business friends had been even more exhausting. She hadn't met a single one whose opinions, tastes or policies she agreed with, and she couldn't help but feel pleased as they drifted out.

Eventually the last of the guests, Nicola and Valerie, left too. Hil and Jemme bid them a very fond farewell and thanked them for coming.

'It really was wonderful to see everything at last,' said Valerie

'Yes, it was, and thank you so much for inviting us. It was an honour to be included,' Nicola added.

Hil looked hurt. 'An honour? I hope we haven't neglected you to that extent?'

Nicola laughed. 'Not at all, I just mean that we were touched to be included on such an important guest list.'

They embraced Jemme and Hil warmly, and then left.

Hil sat down on one of the antique armchairs, and gratefully kicked her shoes off. Jemme came and joined her, stretching out on his chair.

'Well, I would say that was a resounding success!' he leant over and kissed her. 'Are you pleased?'

'Mmmm,' Hil replied, distractedly. 'Did you not think that was odd?'

'What?'

'What Valerie and Nicola said as they left?'

'Odd? No, I just thought they were being rather sweet, that was all.'

'It almost felt like they thought it was a business-focussed event, and they were invited as an afterthought, rather than the other way around – they were the first people I thought of asking!'

'I think you're over-thinking it, sweetheart,' said Jemme, yawning.

'Maybe. Did you enjoy yourself then?'

'Very much so – what a success! The food was incredible, didn't you think?'

'Absolutely – I was very impressed, although poor Marguerite and Aude had their hands full.'

'I know. That was the only thing we didn't think through properly I think. Next time we do this I'll definitely hire waiting staff; it's not fair to expect them to do the whole thing.'

'No, although I think they rather enjoyed this one though – I thought Marguerite was ready to swoon when she overheard all your chums introducing themselves to each other!'

Jemme laughed. 'It was a very successful evening on that front too, actually. I thought it would be a way of consolidating a couple of outstanding pieces of business and impressing clients, but it was much more productive than that. I think I managed to generate some more business and actually gain a few more contacts. I think they all really valued the chance to meet each other, and the setting helped a great deal too.'

'Well, I'm pleased you got something from all of them,' said Hil, wishing she could say the same herself.

Chapter Twenty-Four

Jemme and Hil made their way back up the stairs in a considerably less regal fashion than they had descended them. Hil was holding her shoes in one hand, and Jemme had opened the top buttons of his shirt and undone his bow tie, leaving it draped around his neck.

He ran one hand through his hair and yawned extravagantly, 'Well, I am tired!'

'Me too,' sighed Hil, 'I feel I could sleep for a hundred hours.'

Jemme laughed and slipped an arm over her shoulder, 'I'm still thinking about how well everything went. I'll definitely use Jean-Louis for the next one, or, if he's not available, then another freelance chef – maybe he can recommend someone. I liked the way Marguerite had set up the salon too – that configuration really worked. I think next time I'd do things exactly the same way, seat-wise. I think the serving needs sorting though. I'm annoyed I didn't think about that – I wonder if DD can recommend anywhere that would provide good contract staff.' He paused and looked at Hil who was staring at him slightly goggle-eyed. 'What?'

'I'm exhausted just listening to you! Have a moment off – just for a second! I'm struggling to make it up the stairs I'm so tired, and you're already planning the next event. The dust hasn't even settled from this one yet.'

Jemme laughed, 'I'm sorry – it's the enthusiasm you were talking about the other day. I just enjoyed this one so much I can't wait to get started on the next one.'

Hil tried to reply, but was yawning too much.

'Come on, let's get you upstairs,' said Jemme cheerfully, as his wife wondered where he got all his energy from.

They both slept deeply and awoke late the next morning to find the bedroom filled with light.

'It must be nearly lunchtime!' said Jemme, rubbing his eyes and reaching for his watch on the bedside table with one sleepy hand.

'Mmmm,' Hil mumbled.

Jemme found his watch, and squinted at its face, 'Goodness it is! Hil it's nearly one. Come on, let's get up!'

'What?' Hil asked, eyes still closed.

'I said it's nearly one o'clock in the afternoon, we should get up!!'

'Why?'

'Because there's lots to be getting on with, that's why – we can't waste all day lying around in bed!'

With a mutinous groan, Hil opened one eye and gradually hauled herself into a sitting position. She was just contemplating opening the other eye when she saw that Jemme had already managed to get dressed and was opening the curtains.

'What is *wrong* with you?' she complained.

Eventually they both made it downstairs to find that Aude and Marguerite had already done sterling work, and the house was nearly returned to normal. The heavy curtains in the salon had been drawn back, and the room was flooded with light. The tables had been cleared, and Aude was rubbing beeswax into one as Marguerite picked up a few stray flower petals from the carpet.

'*Ah, Monsieur, Madame, bonjour!*' she called when she saw them. 'You slept well?'

'Yes, like a log, thank you, Marguerite,' said Hil, who laughed when she saw Marguerite's puzzled expression. 'It's just an expression,' she explained. 'You look like you've been hard at work whilst we've been lazing away though, thank you.'

'Ah, Madame, it has been easy,' said Marguerite. 'This girl is not as slow as she pretends to be,' she said, gesturing teasingly at Aude who smiled shyly.

'Actually, Marguerite, we wanted to thank both of you for your hard work last night too,' said Jemme. 'We both really appreciated it, and we could never have had an evening like that without you.'

'Oh, Monsieur!' said Marguerite, clasping her hands to her chest. 'We were just pleased to be there, eh, Aude?' Aude nodded. 'Oh, it was wonderful. So *élégant!*' continued Marguerite.

'Well I'm pleased that you both enjoyed it too,' said Jemme. 'I've already been thinking about the next one though –' Marguerite interrupted him with a squeak of excitement, 'and I was thinking that we'd need to get more help in.'

'More help, Monsieur?'

'I just feel that it wasn't fair to expect the two of you to serve the entire party. I'd feel much happier if we could bring in some agency staff for the evening to help out, that's all,' he looked at Marguerite anxiously.

'Just for the evening?'

'Yes, only on a very temporary basis. It's more to relieve my guilt than anything else, really. I thought that we could perhaps get a few people from one of the grand *école hôtelière* – perhaps even one in Lausanne. They'd be directly answerable to you, of course,' he added judiciously.

Marguerite's eyebrows shot up, 'To me, Monsieur?'

'Of course.'

'Well, I suppose I can never complain about extra help,' she said with a shrug. Jemme exchanged a quick smile with Hil.

'Excellent, I'll make sure we get that sorted in time for the next event.'

'Ahhh, the next event. When will it be, Monsieur?' asked Marguerite excitedly.

'You share my husband's enthusiasm,' said Hil, 'We haven't even finished cleaning up after this one yet.'

Jemme laughed, 'I'm not sure yet, but when I am you'll be one of the first to know. I've got some more people back in Paris I really need to impress, so I can't imagine it will be that long!'

Marguerite smiled contentedly, but a dark look momentarily clouded Hil's face when she realised his motivation.

※　※　※　※

Back in Paris, Jemme got in touch with the Professor. It turned out that, as luck would have it, his plans had fallen through and he was heading back to the Sorbonne the next day. Jemme set up a lunch meeting with him straight away, and in no time at all, he found himself sitting with Professor Johnston in the scruffy Turkish café they often visited.

'I thought you were going to have to stay in London for a lot longer,' said Jemme, taking a tiny sip of the rich bitter coffee they had just been served.

'So did I. It's typical of academics though I'm afraid – keep you waiting for ages and then let you know at the last minute that everything's been cancelled.'

'What a pity you didn't know a few days earlier, you could have come to the party.'

'I know, I know, a great shame. How was it?' asked the Professor, knocking half a glass of water over. It spread outwards and dangerously close to the stack of handwritten papers he had plonked on the table next to him. Jemme leaped up with a napkin but, completely undisturbed, the Professor merely picked the stack up with one hand and dumped them into the top of his open attaché case. It was a practiced move that suggested he was in the habit of having to save precious research documents from his own clumsiness. Jemme sat back down,

'It was rather good actually – a bit of a mix of business and pleasure, but I enjoyed myself nonetheless. The salon looked incredible too – it all came together really well.'

'The carpet turned out alright?'

'Yes, more than alright actually, it was perfect.'

'Ah, excellent. I had a good feeling about that chap. I might go back and visit him at some point. I'm considering a paper on tracing the motifs on certain rugs back to their geographical origins. I was thinking of focussing on the *boteh* but I'm not sure if it's a good starting point and I have the feeling that that fellow might be able to help.'

'What's a *boteh*?' asked Jemme.

'Oh it's a shape that you find everywhere in Azerbaijani art. It was used throughout Iran during the Qajar Dynasty to decorate all manner of regal things – crowns, court garments, that sort of thing. It's interesting because of how widespread its use is. I think it can be used to show the passage of influence and trade. You see, it crops up everywhere – it's a traditional decoration for Uzbek headdresses for example.'

'That sounds fascinating; it's exactly the kind of thing I'm interested in, but I don't think I've ever heard of it. What did you say it was called again?'

'Well it's called something slightly different by everyone. The Persians call it *boteh jegheh*. I believe the Punjabi call it *ambi*, and I know that people who stitch it into quilts in the west often refer to it as a "Persian pickle", because of its shape.'

'I still don't think I've ever seen it before,'

'Oh you'd recognise it if you saw it, I've no doubt.'

'And you think it can be used to demonstrate trade links?'

'Oh I know it can. There's enough later evidence that can be corroborated with other proof. It suggests that we could look at the spread of earlier influence in a similar kind of way.'

Jemme looked at him questioningly.

'Well, the East India Company brought it to Europe in the seventeenth century, and it was hugely popular, leading one town to rename it. In fact, even today I think lots of people still think that Paisley was invented in Scotland.'

'Oh, you're talking about *Paisley*!' said Jemme, enjoying a sudden moment of clarity.

'Yes I am, and that, I think, rather proves my point.'

Jemme thought for a moment, 'I wonder if I can explore similar things at the chateau.'

'Of course you can. In fact I think it's an indispensable part of the narrative you're trying to create. Sometimes a trend leaves one country and is adopted wholesale by another. It can be anything – an idea, piece of scientific discovery or an artistic practice. Sometimes it continues to develop and evolve, completely isolated from its original source, and ends up being something very different. The interesting point is when the original country re-adopts the trend, sometimes with even more enthusiasm than they had for the original. You see it all over the world – look at the craze for Indian chintzes in England in the eighteenth century. Sometimes it's a good thing though, and represents the very best parts of cultural hybridity.'

Jemme turned the thought over in his mind for a while. It was exactly the philosophy Grandma had always espoused: one culture can synergise with another to create something greater than either of them would be capable of alone. Even if they were not working in direct co-operation, synthesis could still occur and produce something meaningful.

He sat and tried to work out how he could incorporate the concept into his project. Then he wondered whether he was already doing so without realising, whether the idea of cultural co-operation was so elemental to human progress that it was intrinsic to every artefact and piece of history he was hoping to display. Whilst he thought, the Professor ordered another round of coffees and flicked through some of his notes. Jemme enjoyed sitting together in amiable silence, and when he had to return to work, suddenly realised that he had not discussed even half the things he was hoping to with the Professor.

He wandered back to the bank, remembering all the questions he had wanted to ask about Babylon and the new exhibition room.

Halfway through a reasonably busy afternoon, DD's discreet knock disturbed his thoughts.

'Come in, come in, DD, you don't need to knock,' said Jemme.

'It's not particularly urgent, Sir, and I didn't want to disturb you.'

'Well you're certainly not disturbing me – what is it?'

'I have some details for you from the École Hôtelière de Lausanne.' Jemme looked blank. 'For future hospitality engagements,' prompted DD.

'Oh, of course, thank you. You're so efficient, DD!'

'The school were highly amenable to my suggestion,' said DD. 'In the long vacation of their final year, they like students to gain as much practical experience as possible. They try to persuade local restaurants and hotels to take pupils on as interns, or to give them summer placements.'

'That sounds sensible. There's only so much you can learn in a classroom, especially studying a subject like that.'

DD inclined his head, 'I expect that was their reasoning too, Sir.'

'Did you explain that it wouldn't be a long-term placement, and that in fact it wouldn't actually be that local?'

'I did, Sir. They were most receptive to the idea on the proviso that we fund the travel costs and provide accommodation.'

'Of course.'

'I also needed to register our details, which I have done, and the chateau might be subject to a one-off inspection by one of their placement co-ordinators, although, considering the distance he or she would have to travel, I consider it unlikely.'

'Well that all sounds fair enough. What do I have to do?'

'Nothing, Sir, it is all taken care of. I have printed out a small summary in case you would like to look at it.' He laid a piece of paper in front of Jemme which outlined everything he had said, and bore the school's contact details. 'When you have next decided to host an event, just let me know, and I shall ensure that we are sent the correct number of students.'

'Thank you very much for your work on this, DD.'

DD nodded, and shut the door behind him, leaving Jemme to wonder who he would invite to his next party. Should it be new clients he wanted to impress early on? Perhaps people he had worked with for a while, as a way of thanking them for their loyalty. He knew it had to be handled diplomatically, as he wanted to make sure no one was offended. He also knew that he shouldn't let his enthusiasm run away with him. If he established a precedent early on, then the events would become *de rigeur* and people would feel slighted if they were not invited – they might question whether he took a particular deal seriously if he was not holding a party to either broker or celebrate it. He idly wondered how many people the salon could comfortably hold, and realised it was probably about as many as some of Paris's top restaurants. As long as he had enough staff, space was certainly not a problem. He didn't know whether to focus on planning the next party, starting the next room, or finishing that afternoon's work. He paused for a moment; he was good at multitasking so there was no reason he couldn't do all three.

Back at home Hil greeted his news about the next party with slightly less enthusiasm.

'It just feels like we should give ourselves a bit of a break before we fling ourselves in to the next thing,' she said.

'But I am giving myself a break, I'm starting to plan the Babylonian room with the Professor.'

'That's not the same thing at all. If anything, that's the complete opposite! You need to rest at some point, Jemme, you're still working just as hard at the bank. Something needs to scale back; it's just not tenable to carry on at full throttle the whole time.'

'But I'm not, I just told you – working on the room will be my way of relaxing. I like being busy, you know that. Besides, it's not like I'm overworking, I've still got time to do things like go to parties.'

'That definitely doesn't count!'

'Why not?'

'Well, because it wasn't restful for a start, and secondly because you were still working whilst you were at the party.'

Jemme realised that the conversation was steering dangerously close to a row and decided that it would be prudent to pre-empt it. He took a deep breath, 'Fine.'

Hil looked at him in a pained way, 'I don't think you really understand what I'm trying to say.'

'And I don't think you understand what *I'm* trying to say, but I really don't want to argue with you about it, so let's just leave it at that shall we?'

'Fine,' Hil replied, tight-lipped.

The next week, Jemme got a phone call from the Professor,

'They're still messing me around!' he said down a rather crackly phone line.

'Who are? Where are you?'

'Those pesky academics! I'm at the airport.'

'What?'

'After all of that, they think the conference might be back on. I've got to go back to London straight away.'

'But you've only just got here!'

'I know, I know. It's a pain. But listen, there's something in the British Museum I think might interest you. I was wondering if you could head over soon – maybe even this weekend?'

'This weekend? I'm not sure...'

'It would be a great starting point for your Babylonian room,' said the Professor. 'I've got to go, they're calling my gate.'

At home that evening, Hil was even less impressed to hear this particular piece of news.

'You're going to London, just like that?'

'It's only for two days; it seemed like an opportune moment.'

Hil shook her head and sat down on the bed.

'What's the matter? I didn't think you'd mind – I've been away without you lots of times before.'

Hil looked up to him and Jemme was surprised to see that her eyes were brimming with tears. Jemme sat down next to her,

'Sweetheart, whatever's the matter? Would you like to come with me? It's not too late, I can easily buy you a ticket.'

'No, it's fine.'

'Then what's the matter?'

'I wish you knew.'

Jemme felt a little exasperated, 'But how can I know if you won't tell me.'

Hil sighed and wiped her eyes, 'It's the fact that you think it's an opportune time.'

'Well I didn't think there was anything particularly special going on this weekend – have I forgotten something?'

'No, there's nothing this weekend, it's just this time in general.'

'What about "this time"?'

'I'm just worried, that's all. You think nothing of jumping off to London for the weekend, and you're constantly thinking about the next thing you can organise or throw yourself into.'

'But I don't understand why that is a problem.'

'Because it takes up all your energy and time, and it worries me.'

'But I still don't understand why.'

Hil took a deep breath, 'Because it means that you'll have no time or energy left to start a family.'

Jemme felt his heart sink like a stone. He knew that this subject had been playing on Hil's mind for the last couple of years, but so far they had managed to avoid having a serious conversation about it. There was no escaping the number of their peers who were starting families though, and it was a subject which confronted them at every turn, crying out for their attention. Although he had barely admitted it to himself, and had certainly not to Hil, starting a family was very low on Jemme's list of priorities. He knew it was something he wanted eventually, but there was so much he wanted to accomplish first. He felt like he'd only just started on the chateau, and the rest of the project lay tantalisingly ahead of him. It was such a large commitment, there was no way he could balance it with caring for infant children and he felt saddened when he considered everything he would have to sacrifice to have children. At some point he would be ready, but that time felt like a long way off.

He put his arm around Hil. 'Darling, I'm sorry. I know this is something we need to think about together. I also realise that it must be frustrating to see me jump from one thing to the next like this.'

Hil sniffed, 'I just feel like we've let so much time pass already, and we don't have forever.'

'I know, I know. I promise that this will be the year we discuss it though.'

'Thank you,' Hil smiled resignedly. She looked momentarily placated, but the sadness in her eyes was unmistakable.

Jemme replayed the conversation in his head on the short flight from Paris to London. He was pricked by guilt, but he didn't feel like he could offer Hil anything else at the moment. The promise of an open and honest discussion was all he had.

It had been a while since he'd been in England and so the conversation was soon put from his mind as he watched the belt of countryside between the airport and London slip past him from a taxi window. DD had found him a very pleasant hotel in Bloomsbury and so, after dropping his bag off, he strolled over to Museum

Street, stopping on the way for a quick cup of tea at his favourite café. The tea arrived in a pot, filled with loose leaves. With all the straining and different bits of equipment that came with it, there was a sort of ritual to its preparation and equipment that he rather enjoyed; it was meditative and calming.

The Professor was waiting for him on the grand steps that led up to the museum's entrance.

'Hullo, hullo,' he said cheerily.

'How are you?' asked Jemme, taking in the creases around the Professor's eye and the deep lines across his forehead.

'Well, thank you, although slightly more tired than I would like!'

'Really? I hope everything's alright.'

The Professor waved his hand nonchalantly, 'Oh as well as can be expected – it's just these wretched academics I was telling you about. They call me back to London at a moment's notice and tell me that the conference is on again, so I work through the night then head up to Oxford and work through the night there too, only to be told this morning that funding has been pulled and the conference is off again. I haven't slept in three days, and I'm behind in my other work now too.'

'I'm sorry to hear that. Are you sure you wouldn't rather get some rest?'

The Professor waved his hand again, 'This is rest enough for me! It's a nice change to the rather dry subject I've been focussing on, and I always feel a great deal more relaxed when I'm around my favourite subjects.'

'That's exactly how I feel too – I was trying to explain it to Hil, but she just didn't understand. I think it's because I look very busy; it seems to contradict the idea I might be relaxing. I find it so restful though.'

'That's just the way our sort are,' said the Professor, as they made their way through the Great Court, 'cursed to be at work always.'

It seemed an apt way of putting it, thought Jemme. He would always be at work, because he found it impossible to turn his thoughts off. His mind was always alert, asking questions, assessing its landscape, attempting to draw parallels and forever turning. Perhaps this would always be the way he relaxed.

The Professor led them all the way across the Great Court and through the long Ancient Egypt gallery to a small room.

'Here we are,' he said, 'the Middle East department.'

'It doesn't seem very big,' said Jemme, thinking about the long Egyptian gallery they had just crossed through.

'It's actually made up of a couple of rooms – this is just the Nimrud room. The Nineveh room's up there,' he pointed to one end of the gallery, 'then the Assyrian sculpture and Balawat Gates are down there and behind is the Assyrian Lion Hunts, siege of Lachish and Khorsabad.'

Jemme looked impressed, 'I didn't realise they had such a large collection here.'

'Oh goodness, yes! In fact, this is only the very tip of the iceberg. I would guess that only about ten per cent of the department's collection is on display here. In the archives they've got a huge assemblage of cuneiform inscriptions on clay tablets. Over 130,000 according to the curator I spoke to the other day.'

'130,000?!'

The Professor nodded, 'It's the largest collection of any modern museum and they're not even close to completing the cataloguing. The chap I spoke to has been here for five years and is still reading and translating inscriptions. He's spending a great deal of time working on ancient archives to identify text which belongs together, and filling in missing fragments. I thought that some of his work would be invaluable for your Babylonian room, and he's agreed to show us a few tablets later on. I've brought us here first though so that you can have a bit of a look around, and perhaps even get some ideas for other rooms in the chateau.'

'Excellent, thank you,' said Jemme, already moving over to inspect the walls, which were panelled with large stone reliefs. Despite the fact that the plaque gave their estimated date range as being from 883-859 BC, the detailing was still crisp and clear enough to show the curls of a tall man's beard and the ferocious look on a lion's face. They had been executed so masterfully that the drama of a charging horse was apparent, even through its stone depiction.

'Where are these from?' Jemme asked the Professor.

'From Nimrud. It's in the north of modern day Iraq. These are all from the palace there; I think most of them came from the throne room, but some of them would have been in other royal apartments. They're quite remarkable aren't they?'

Jemme nodded. 'Is this Ashurbanipal?' he asked, pointing at a figure riding in a chariot.

The Professor squinted at the stone, 'Ah, close, but no. That's Ashurnasirpal II – he was around about two hundred years earlier. He was a great expansionist, and the arts grew hugely under him too, but I'm afraid he was a bit of a thug. Still, I don't suppose any empire of that era was enlarged because of its leader's kind heart.' He looked at the panels with Jemme for a while, 'Here, look – you can see him leading a military campaign against his enemies. Ah, look, he's hunting in this one;' he pointed at the depiction of the king amongst lions, 'it was a very popular royal sport,' he added, leading Jemme towards the end of the gallery.

They wandered into the next room, which was similarly lined with stone panels.

'Are these from the same palace?' asked Jemme.

'No, these are from Nineveh, which is a little bit further south. These are from the palace of King Sennacherib, who ruled pretty much exactly between the Ashurbanipal and Ashurnasirpal. Personally I find these panels fascinating. They give away so many details about Assyrian life, and being able to see two sets from two separate palaces next to each other like this gives us a wonderful amount of information. Look, in this set you can see them getting the stone to make these slabs. Just in that one picture we can find out more about ancient quarrying and transportation techniques than we could from any text source.'

Jemme stared closely at the picture, intrigued by its value as a historical records and the amount of crucial evidence which was hidden in its imagery.

'What are these?' he asked, pointing to huge monster-like figures. Even though they were carved into the same material as everything else, Jemme could tell that they were shown as being made of stone.

'Ah, they're called *lamassu*,' said the Professor, 'they're quite frightening aren't they?'

Jemme took in the monsters, which had human heads, but the winged bodies of bulls and nodded.

The Professor chuckled, 'Well imagine seeing the actual sculptures then – they weighed about thirty tons! They were commissioned for the main entrance to the palace and would have made quite the first impression I'll bet!'

They spent a very pleasant hour and a half walking around the rest of the galleries. The Professor had been right – it was the best way of relaxing. Perhaps it was the pace at which they walked, or perhaps being surrounded by such objects put him into a reverie. Whatever it was, Jemme felt completely at peace. There was a simplicity about the silent engagement one could have with relics from the past. Contemplating them opened a sincere and unprejudiced connection between object and viewer, in which the viewer opened up his mind and sought learning. It was a very basic pleasure, and one which Jemme relished. His enjoyment of the Assyrian reliefs refreshed him. He had particularly enjoyed one of the smallest galleries, which depicted lion hunting, the sport of kings. Ashurbanipal was shown triumphantly engaging in his favourite pastime in hunting scenes that were full of tension and realism. According to the Professor they were considered amongst the finest achievements of Assyrian art.

When they had finished, Professor Johnston led the way to what appeared to be a piece of wall painted with 'staff only'. He felt around for the handle and Jemme realised that it was actually a door, painted in exactly the same way as the rest of the gallery so as to be as discreet as possible. Once they were on the other side, Jemme followed the Professor upstairs, through corridors and downstairs again as they negotiated the labyrinthine, behind-the-scenes part of the museum.

'I know that everything in there was Assyrian and not strictly related to what we're going to see now,' he said as they walked along, 'but since you're thinking about a Babylonian room anyway, and there's so much overlap between the two civilisations, I thought it might be useful. At the very least it will give you some context for the Babylonian room, and perhaps it might even get you excited about an Assyrian room!'

Since they had first set foot in the gallery, Jemme had already been imagining a palace lined entirely with pictures on stone, and with every panel he had looked at he had felt a mounting rush of excitement about the achievability of such a thing. Unlike the Babylonian room, he already knew where he could start. He already understood how he could capture the Assyrian civilisation for a room in the chateau, and its execution wouldn't even be that complicated.

'I'm finding myself extremely tempted!' he said to the Professor.

'Well that's good news. There's so much source material here, you'd better not look around too much in case you get any further ideas! Better to finish one room before you start the next, and you've been thinking about Babylon for a while.'

As they climbed up another set of stairs, which seemed more like a temporary fire escape than a proper staircase, Jemme thought about what the Professor had said. In a way it did make sense to finish one room first, but then he had already worked on the salon as his test room and that had been finished to perfection. He had been thinking about the Babylonian room for a while, it was true, but if he didn't have firm plans for it, then maybe it made sense to work on another, easier room at the same time. He might be able to use the same artists and craftsmen for both, which would be much more efficient, not just financially, but in terms of disruption at the chateau.

Finally reaching the cataloguing room, the Professor tried to open the door, but it wouldn't budge. It took a good few attempts with his shoulder before it would yield, and when it eventually swung open it revealed a room unlike any Jemme had ever seen before. It looked just like a bank vault, but one filled with historic treasures. Floor to ceiling shelves housed boxes with handwritten labels, bags with tagged artefacts, books and notebooks. A desk in the middle was covered in papers, small artefacts and a very high stack of books.

'Oh, he's not here,' said the Professor looking around.

'This place is incredible!' said Jemme.

'Do you think? Most departments look like this in museums, although this is a little tidier than lots I've seen. This is just everything he's working on at the moment, and again it's only a tiny amount of the whole collection. There will be boxes and boxes in storage somewhere.' The Professor wandered over to the desk to have a look at what the curator was working on. On top of all the papers was a note messily scrawled in Indian ink:

> *Prof. Johnston, was good to meet you the other day. Sorry I can't be there with you this afternoon. Here are some pieces I thought would be of interest. Feel free to look around. Hope to see you again, Yours, Prof. Jones.*

'Ah, well that's good of him,' said Professor Johnston, showing Jemme the note. 'Let's have a look at what he's left for us, shall we?'

He picked up a list and browsed through it. It made no sense to Jemme, but to the Professor it seemed to read like a fluent list of instructions. '829E97TA,' he read out, before looking around quickly. He went straight over to one shelf and, after only a few moments search, pulled out one small box which looked identical to those around it.

'Very good system,' he said approvingly to himself.

He laid the box on the chair, and lifted the lid off to reveal a selection of objects inside, each one of which was in a protective polythene bag, and bore a tag describing the object's provenance and giving its catalogue number. The Professor began to show them to Jemme, explaining where each had been found and what it meant. He referred frequently to the curator's notes, which were detailed and insightful.

Jemme was fascinated; he had always been interested by cuneiform and the birth of writing. To see such a rich collection of objects and to be handed them inside their plastic bags felt like a privilege. He thought about the fact they were kept in these boxes, and how few members of the public got to see them, and realised how rare this opportunity was. Moreover, if they were kept in storage like this, then the number of people who would have seen them at all could be extremely limited. Jemme felt a smile creep across his face as he held a fragment of a stone tablet in his hands.

'Where's this one from?' he asked.

The Professor read the tag, 'That one's actually an inventory of a grain store,' he said. 'It was found by a farmer during ploughing in 1873 apparently. The curator thinks that it was part of larger collection of records for tax collectors.'

Jemme smiled, 'Some things never change, I suppose!'

'Indeed,' agreed the Professor. 'Here,' he took the piece from Jemme's hand and changed it for another, 'this seems rather modern too.'

'What is it?' Jemme looked at the second piece. It was on a slightly lighter-coloured stone, but the letters had been formed in the same regular and precise way. Jemme stared at them, taking in their alien configurations of lines and crosses, and wishing he could unlock their secrets.

'That,' said the Professor, 'is an incredibly old text indeed, and one I thought you'd be interested to see.'

Jemme looked at it again, wishing he could make sense of it, 'What does it say?' he asked.

The Professor flicked through some more of the curator's paperwork, 'Aha, he's translated it – excellent man! It says "if a woman wine seller gives one flask of *pīḫum* on credit, she shall receive fifty *qu* at harvest-time".'

Jemme looked confused, 'What does that mean? What's a *qu*?'

The professor looked back to the notes, 'He really has been very thorough – these notes are exceptionally well annotated. He estimates that a "qu" is equal to just over three-quarters of a quart in dry measurement. This is law 111 of Hammurabi's code,' he explained.

Jemme laughed with pleasure. 'Incredible!' He looked down at the piece in his hand. It had been one of the very first things he'd seen in his dream as a young child, and he had seen it countless times since then. He had seen pictures of the stelae into which it was carved, he had seen archaeologist's sketches and lithographer's engravings, but nothing had ever compared to the first stele he had seen in his dream. He couldn't believe that now he was actually holding a piece of it in his hand. He mentally repeated what the Professor had read to him as he looked at the lines of engravings, wishing he could match up the words to the letters.

'You're right,' he said eventually. 'It is a very modern sentiment. It makes complete sense – if someone gives goods on credit then they should receive a greater amount back in repayment. It's one of the most fundamental tenets in banking. It certainly accords with me professionally.' He thought a little more, 'I like the proviso "at harvest time" too – it's evidence of good social planning and responsible lending.'

'Quite,' said the Professor, nodding in approval. 'This piece was found by farmers too, and according to the curator's notes there should be a few more fragments from the same stele in this crate and then there are three from a different stele in another box.'

'How many were made?' asked Jemme.

'I'm afraid that's impossible to say. The evidence of the stele themselves points to a strong social infrastructure, so it's likely that there were quite a few. They would have been hugely labour intensive, so they're also evidence of a literate and organised work force, which is interesting.'

'I remember reading about how large they were, so I suppose they would have taken quite a great deal of time and man power.'

'Oh, a great deal indeed, yes. More than that though, they would have required a great deal of craft specialisation. Think about the journey each stele would have made throughout production. They would have needed workers to quarry a block as big as a man, and then skilled masons to plane it flat and prepare the work surface. Finally, when it was finished they would have needed men to lift it into place and ensure that it stood steady, and that's before you've even considered the scribes.'

'Yes, I suppose each piece would have been an incredible undertaking,' Jemme agreed. 'Can we have a look at some more fragments?' he asked.

The Professor looked through the box. 'Aha, here we are,' he gently pulled out another piece and handed it to Jemme who studied it carefully. It was clearly from the same source as the other piece, although judging by the curvature of one side, it had been closer to the edge of the stone slab.

'*If a life is lost, the city and governor shall pay one mina of silver to his people,*' the professor read.

Jemme shook his head again, 'I just can't believe how contemporary these ideas feel when they're actually thousands of years old.'

'It's remarkable isn't it. It really shows a state-level society in action too. Imagine the administrative organisation and understanding of civic duty that goes into the creation of a law like that.'

'Does the curator have any notes on the units used in the law?' asked Jemme.

'He does actually, let me see *mina = about 500 gr, divided into 60 shekels,*' the professor read, 'he's also written *cf Deuteronomy 21:1 ff.*'

'I wonder what it says?' said Jemme.

'I should imagine it's a corresponding or similar law,' said the Professor. 'He's done his research very thoroughly and I expect he's been looking for cross-references and parallels. I'll wager that this verse in Deuteronomy says almost exactly the same thing – it's interesting how many similar or even identical ideas and laws occur in ancient texts, both religious and secular.'

'I agree. It was something that fascinated my grandmother too. She was always saying that there were indisputable common threads running through the world's major religions, despite obvious superficial differences. I can see this text as an extension of that idea. Grandma was always pointing out that the major Abrahamic faiths had their genesis in the same area, so it made sense that the same environment would govern their structuring and formation. It's interesting that these law codes are from exactly the same area too – she always said the Middle East was the cradle of civilisation.'

'A wise woman,' said the Professor.

Jemme smiled. 'Let's see the final fragment in this box.'

The Professor found it and consulted the notes, 'Ah, this one will appeal to your banker sensibilities too – *if he does not have the money to pay back grain or sesame at their market value in accordance with the ratio fixed by the king, he shall give to the merchant his money, which he borrowed from the merchant together with its interest.* The curator has added that in ancient Mesopotamia the ratio between silver and various commodities was fixed by the state.'

'You're right – that does appeal to me with my banker hat on! In fact, it was only within living memory that currency's value ceased to be tied to the value of gold and silver. It's probably why some European economies have been in trouble over the past few decades.

The Professor nodded, clearly several centuries out of his comfort zone. 'Let's see if we can find the other box.' They located it on the shelf without much effort, and Jemme smiled to himself when the Professor expressed more wonder at the efficiency of the curator's filing. Jemme dreaded to think what the Professor's own offices looked like. Once they had safely stowed away the first box, and opened up the second, they examined the different fragments and consulted the curator's notes. There was no duplication between any of text on the pieces of stone, and Jemme enjoyed seeing yet more original laws first hand. He learned that there were provisions against inactivity:

'*If a man rented a fallow field for three years for development, but became so lazy that he has not developed the field, in the fourth year he shall break up the field with mattocks, plough and harrow it, and he shall return it to the owner of the field; furthermore he shall measure out ten* kur (a measure equal to a little more than seven bushels, divided into 300 qu.) *of grain per eighteen iku* (a land measure equal to about 7/8 acre),' read the Professor, following the curator's scrawled notes with his finger tip.

He was also fascinated by the form of civil insurance that had been delineated:

'*If a man deposited his grain in another man's house for storage and a loss has then occurred at the granary, or the owner of the house opened the storage-room and took grain, or he has denied completely the receipt of the grain which was stored in his house, the owner of the grain shall set forth the particulars regarding his grain in the presence of god, and the owner of the house shall give to the owner of the grain double the grain that he took.*'

Jemme found a sheet of unused paper, and took notes of the rules which interested him most – those which seemed most prescient, or touched on subjects close to his own interests. He also carefully wrote down the cross-references the curator had cited, meaning to look them up later, '*Murder: Hammurabi first law – cf Deuteronomy 5:20 19:16-21/Exodus 23:1-3,*' he scribbled.

By the time they had finished, Jemme was filled with renewed zeal and couldn't wait to get back to the chateau and get started on both rooms straight away. He already had a clear picture in his mind of exactly how he wanted the Assyrian room to look and every time he closed his eyes he could imagine himself standing in the middle of it, surrounded by stone panelling with detailed reliefs. He pictured his favourite of the friezes he had seen, and transposed them directly onto the walls of the chateau. Being in the British Museum had been hugely inspirational in more ways than he had anticipated. As well as giving him the ideas for how the room would look, it had also given him ideas of how he would achieve this. On leaving the museum, he had wandered through a temporary exhibition on Venice. It had reminded him of his trip there as a young Scout and seeing the star attraction – a Tintoretto on loan from the Accademia – brought back memories of the art he seen there as a boy. He considered the life-long impression it had made on him, and enjoyed looking at the other exhibits in the gallery in a reverie of nostalgia.

One plaque described the craze for trompe l'oeil during the Republic's heyday, and he remembered how entranced he had been by it and the magical illusion it created. Everything about it drew him in – the visual deception itself and the reverence for the master painter who had created it. He knew that it was a technique he would use in the chateau, but as he thought about it, he realised that it was a more than merely a decorative choice – the technique could actually be of use to him. He considered the stone panelled room he was planning on creating in the Assyrian room. Although the picture in his mind was as clear as crystal, the practicalities of the whole thing were proving a little more elusive. He suspected he might have to reinforce the walls if he was to hang stone from them and he had no idea how long it would take both to find a craftsman skilled enough and for him to finish the work. He realised that trompe l'oeil provided a neat and easy shortcut. If he could find someone proficient enough, then he could create the illusion of stone-clad walls with nothing more than paint. It would take a fraction of the time and was mutable too – if the artist made a mistake, he could merely paint over it, whereas if a mason accidentally chiselled too much off, then the whole piece was ruined.

He was delighted with the solution. In addition to being infinitely practical, it also fitted within the philosophy of the project; it would continue a decorative tradition and provide employment for skilled artists. If he could find someone suitable, then he was tantalisingly close to a realisation of the room. It was too exciting to imagine.

By the time he caught his return flight, he had also formed a clear idea of how he would go about bringing the Babylonian room together. Again, the British Museum had provided inspiration. A chance look at a book in the gift shop had reminded him that the thing that most represented the Babylonian civilisation to him was his very first experience of it and encounter with it. He remembered the vision of the Ishtar Gate he had had in his dream. It had been one of the first things he had seen, and he and Grandma had unravelled his description of it later, with Lily patiently explaining each detail to him. He remembered his childish unease around his new sister at the time, and how Grandma had explained to him that the Babylonian goddess Ishtar was the counterpart to the north-west Semitic goddess Astarté. It had made him view his sister in a whole new light and as a figure of interest. Lily had told him that Astarté had been the goddess of love, war and fertility, and he had always thought that had been reflected in his sister's passionate temperament. The vision of the gate held a great deal of meaning for him and it would be a fitting way to begin the project. He liked the symbolism too, and the idea of creating a liminal entrance into a different world as his starting point for the project.

On the aeroplane, he began to sketch out different ideas. He held the image of the gate in his head as he tried to replicate it onto the paper in front of him. However, all that happened was that he drew a picture of the gate. In front of him was nothing more than the image in his mind, transferred onto paper. He thought about it some more as he chewed the end of his pencil. How could he turn the gate into a room? He looked at the paper again. All that would end up happening would be that his artist would paint a picture of the gate onto the wall. It was the same problem – shifting the image from one medium onto another. The project was designed to be immersive. He wanted to create something experiential rather than visual. As he stared at the sketch of the gate in front of him, he imagined shrinking down so that he was no bigger than a fly and walking through it. Suddenly he realised – that was it! He would create the room which was behind the gate. In entering the room, the visitor would be walking through a threshold of sorts anyway, and so it made sense that they would enter into whatever was on the other side of that gate or doorway. The room would allow him to create the innermost part of the city, which had been protected by this ancient gate.

He started to make a list of things and people he would need, and resolved to get started on things as soon has he returned to Paris. Satisfied, he folded the piece of paper neatly into four and slid it into his pocket next to the one bearing notes from the curator's office.

✻   ✻   ✻   ✻

Back at home Hil greeted him,

'I'm pleased you're back,' she said.

'So am I! Has everything been alright here?' he asked, taking in her tired face.

'Yes, I just missed you, that's all,'

'I'm sorry, darling, I missed you too,' he said, lifting her chin up and planting a kiss on her face.

'How was the trip? I hope you managed to get some rest.'

'I couldn't feel more rested,' said Jemme happily, 'it was absolutely wonderful – I've got so many ideas! I feel so reinvigorated and re-energised. It's marvellous!'

'Well, I'm pleased for you,' said Hil, a little flatly.

'Thank you!' said Jemme sitting down on the sofa and stretching. 'It's only a short flight, but it's definitely left me a little stiff,' he laughed as he stretched his neck out, 'must be getting old I suppose!'

Hil almost flinched at the words. 'What on earth's wrong with you?!' asked Jemme, playfully reaching out and grabbing her by waist. He pulled her down onto the sofa next to him and she sat heavily. Her downbeat mood seemed to be directly correlated to Jemme's ebullience, but he was too enthusiastic about his plans to notice that she seemed to become more withdrawn as he became more buoyant.

'London was looking beautiful,' he said, looping an arm around her and squeezing her in for a hug. 'I can't believe how long it is since I was last there and I don't think we've been together for years. We should go soon and have a mini holiday!'

'Mmmm,' said Hil.

'It was so useful as well. The Professor seemed to know exactly what I wanted, and had set up lots of interesting things. He's recently befriended the curator of the BM's Middle East department, which was an absolute boon. The man couldn't be there for some reason, but he'd left an excellent assortment of stuff for us to look at. I could have stayed in that one room for weeks; it was brilliant – all the things that interest me most and all carefully annotated by an intelligent man. Just brilliant.'

'It must be nice to have someone know exactly what you want,' said Hil dolefully.

'It was! It was fantastic!' said Jemme, deaf to any other meaning. 'I've got so many ideas for the Babylonian room; I'm going to start organising it tomorrow morning. The best part about the trip – actually I don't know if it was the best part, there were so many good bits! Anyway *one* of the best bits was the fact that I got so many unexpected ideas. I mean, I wasn't even looking for them; they just popped out! And I've already completed a second room in my mind. I know exactly how it's going to look, I can't wait to get started on it straight away.'

Hil looked aghast, 'You can't mean that!'

'Of course I do, why not? What do you mean?' asked Jemme, looking confused.

'So you'll be working on three rooms at the same time?!'

Jemme paused for a moment and thought, then shrugged his shoulders, 'Yes, I suppose it will be three. Why?'

'Because that's crazy. Have you not been listening to anything I've been saying? That's the exact opposite of what you need to be doing! I keep saying that you need to cut back, that there's too much in your life at the moment, and yet you're just taking on more. You're edging me out.'

Although she looked quite upset, Jemme couldn't feel too sorry for Hil; instead, he felt angry with her. He felt she was being irrational and what's more she was trying to bring down his positive mood because she was feeling sulky.

'Look Hil, that's not true and you know it. There might be three rooms but one of them is going to be really straight-forward. I already know precisely what it will look like, as I just told you. I've nearly finished the plans for the second, so that isn't going to be that complicated, and the third one is a completely separate matter altogether. It's one of the reception rooms, so will be much easier. There might be three on the go at the same time, but it's not like they all have to be finished at the same time. Besides, think about it, working on multiple rooms simultaneously is the most efficient way of doing things.'

However, instead of backing down, Hil just looked even more upset and shook her head sadly. 'I'm going to bed,' she said quietly, leaving Jemme sitting on the sofa looking confused and wondering why she didn't share his enthusiasm.

Chapter Twenty-Five

By the time Jemme got into bed, Hil was already fast asleep. Although he was travel weary, his mind was alive with images of the things he had seen in the museum. He stared up at the ceiling, and imagined it slowly calcifying. He concentrated hard until he could tease out shadows and textures. As he stared, they formed themselves into reliefs, depicted high drama, frozen into stone. He relaxed his eyes and smiled, satisfied. The stone pictures shimmered in front of him for a few moments and then vanished. Jemme shut his eyes, finally ready to drift off to sleep.

Within a few moments he began to feel a familiar sensation of air rushing up past him as he fell through the blackness of space. Soon he had landed softly on a grassy patch of land and, unhurt, he picked himself up and brushed dirt from his jacket. He straightened up and looked ahead to see his palace, moving and shifting in front of him. Over the years it had gradually come to look more and more like Chateau Vigne-Verte, and with the work he was conducting on his own chateau, the gap between the two was becoming ever narrower. He walked towards the palace, enjoying its altering dimensions; as it bloomed before his eyes, he suddenly felt small and child-like again. Nearing the door, he noticed that on this particular visit it had adopted the pillars from the British Museum's grand entrance. He wandered through its corridors, visiting rooms that were as familiar as old friends, until he found himself opening a door he had never seen before. As soon as the door swung open, it shrunk immediately downwards, meaning he had to get onto his hands and knees and crawl through. Standing up on the other side he looked around and instantly recognised his environment. He was surrounded by the stone panelling he had seen in the museum; it was exactly as he had imagined he would recreate it when building his own Assyrian room. Tall, bearded kings and ferocious lions strode across the stone reliefs, oblivious to his presence. He saw two wooden thrones in front of him and what looked like a small table next to one, raised on high on five slender legs. He wandered over to them and tried to climb into one. It sprung upwards suddenly and he looked around to see whether or not there was a small step or footstool. When he turned back, the throne had shrunk down again, and he jumped in it. He sat and surveyed the room, with its panels of endlessly moving characters. As he relaxed in the chair, he stared up at the ceiling. Just like his own ceiling had, it began to shift and change under his gaze. It gradually peeled away from the edges, shrinking into a suspended middle that disappeared like a puff of smoke. It revealed an indigo blue sky, pricked by the light of tiny stars. Jemme stared at it some more, reminded of evenings spent in the liwan of his childhood.

He sat in the throne, feeling completely relaxed and at ease. After a while, it began to feel as if the seat was falling in underneath him and, once again, he found himself in a pitch-black freefall. Eventually, his pace slowed, as if he was falling through treacle, and the darkness became milkier and lighter. He blinked his eyes several times and his surroundings slowly came into focus. Instantly he recognised his bedroom. The falling motion stopped and he realised that the dream was over. A broad smile spread out over his face and he rolled over to see if Hil was awake. Her back was to him and, despite him shaking her gently, she seemed fast asleep. He gave up and rolled back to stare at the ceiling. He always woke up from the dream feeling refreshed and this was no exception – he was filled with renewed zeal for the room. He decided to leave Hil to her own devices and get up. It was still early and the morning was ripe with possibilities.

He slipped on his dressing gown and padded into the kitchen to put the kettle on. No matter how excited he was, no proper work could begin without proper coffee. As he watched the syrupy black in the bottom of the *ibrik* start to bubble, he was reminded again of childhood, and the distinctive smell which meant his father was in the kitchen. Although his mother and aunts had prepared all the food at home, his father always made his own coffee. He was fastidious about the method, and stood watching the tiny pot with its long handle, carefully spooning in an exact amount of sugar at a precise time. Jemme remembered running into the kitchen to greet him, and Wadeah heaving him up so that he could peer at the top of the hob, before patiently explaining to him the origins of coffee and the best way to make the thick, bitter beverage for which the Turks were famed. It was a story Jemme had heard countless times, and as a young boy he had absorbed its details. As he picked the pot up by its long, cool, wooden handle, he recalled the pride with which his father explained that the first coffee was brewed in Yemen in the fifteenth century, right down in the south of the peninsular. Like his mother, Wadeah believed that the Middle East was the cradle of many things, and food was definitely one of them. Jemme poured the dark liquid into a small gilded espresso cup, a wedding gift from DD. He went through the sitting room and sat in his favourite chair, next to the bookcase.

After he had drained the liquid and winced slightly at its bitter taste, he felt prepared to tackle the next task. He ran his fingers along the shelves next to him, scanning the titles until he found the volume he was looking for. He pulled it out and sat back down again. Unlike many others on the shelves, this book's cover was pristine and its spine unbroken. Professor Johnston had brought it for him on his last trip over to Paris. However, it had coincided with an exceptionally busy period at the bank and, sorrowfully, Jemme had had to confine it to the shelves and all but forgotten about it. On the flight back from Paris he had been considering the Assyrian room and the book had suddenly popped into his mind. He remembered the Professor giving it to him – Johnston had said that it had recently been published by a friend of his, an expert in Akkadian kingdoms.

Jemme carefully opened the book and sat back to read. It had been well written, expertly treading the fine line between scholarly and engaging. About fifty pages in, he realised that he was never going to remember the important pieces of information, so got up to get a pen and notepad. Whilst he searched for both, he decided he might as well make some more coffee. It was only when he stood over the bubbling little *ibrik* again that he thought to check on Hil. He poked his head around the door to see her fast asleep still. Although he tried not to, he couldn't help feeling pleased. With his coffee, notebook and pen, he was looking forward to settling down again and would have been loath to interrupt it. Ensconced in the comfortable chair once again, he flicked back a few pages to something that had caught his eye.

'*Three periods*', he wrote in his book, '*Old Assyrian Period, c. 20th -15th century BC; Middle Assyrian period, 15th-10th century BC and NeoAssyrian Empire, from 911-612 BC.*'

He stopped and looked at the date range. He would have to cover nearly nineteen centuries in the room, if he was going to do it properly. He chewed the end of his pen and thought for a while. Starting on a clean page in the notebook, he sketched out the room, just as he had seen it in his dream. He drew the throne he had sat in and the slightly smaller one next to it, and the tall, five-legged table. He tried to freeze the moving characters from the panels in his mind for long enough to draw them. Alongside them, he drew details from the panels he had seen in the British Museum which had not featured in his dream. He thought some more about what he had seen, and eventually drew an arrow to the ceiling of the room and wrote *stars – liwan?* He wasn't sure how he would finish it, but supposed that it would come to him as the room evolved.

Even in its very rough form, he was pleased to see it existing on the paper before him. He now had a plan, a guide to follow. Underneath the drawing he scribbled some notes – *thrones – carpenter? Walls – trompe l'oeil artist?* It was a short list and not at all intimidating. He thought some more and tried to picture himself actually standing in the room. *What can I see?* he thought to himself. He knew what the walls would look like, and he had a rough idea of what he might do with the ceiling too. He thought – the floor was a different matter and so he added *carpet?* to his list. He mentally looked around the room, trying to be as pragmatic as possible, ignoring the detailed panels and the intricate thrones and tried to imagine the nuts and bolts holding the room together. What needed to be tucked away and hidden? He added *lighting?* to his list and then *electrician* shortly afterwards. Thinking about the ceiling some more, he realised that he couldn't task a trompe l'oeil artist with its execution. No matter how he decided to finally decorate it, he was fairly sure that it would require a different specialist, and so added *artist* to the bottom.

He reviewed the list, which was becoming slightly more intimidating. It was still manageable though, and he had always known that he would have to engage multiple craftsmen and artisans. He resolved to start his search for artists first thing on Monday morning. Stretching out in his chair and yawning with a satisfied flourish he decided it was high time he woke up Hil.

He strode up to the bed and shook her playfully, 'Come on!' he said.

Eventually, Hil stirred slightly and half-opened her eyes.

'What?' she asked flatly.

'It's definitely time to get up – I'm just about to start on my third coffee of the morning!'

'Fine.'

Jemme smiled at her, but she merely shut her eyes again, 'I'll come and find you when I'm up,' she said in the same, oddly low voice.

'Alright,' said Jemme cheerfully, secretly a little pleased he would be able to continue working on his projects for a while longer. He returned to the sitting room and pulled out his notebook again. He was just sketching some detailing from the panel when Hil finally arrived.

'Good morning, sweetheart. Sorry, I didn't mean to disturb you – did you sleep well?'

Hil nodded but didn't say anything. She went into the kitchen and emerged a few minutes later with a large mug of milky tea. She sat in the seat next to Jemme's and sipped it slowly whilst she looked at what he was sketching. After a while she finally spoke, 'What are you doing?' she asked him.

'I'm sketching out some of my plans for the Assyrian room,' he said happily, 'look – this is a piece of panelling we saw in the British Museum.'

'Did we?'

'Not "we" you and me, I mean the Professor and me.'

'Oh.'

'I'm really excited about it actually, I remember it so perfectly and I'm going to recreate it pretty much straight away.' He paused and frowned, before realising what was missing and adding an extra detail into the composition in front of him.

Hil said nothing and resumed sipping her tea in silence, eyeing the drawing warily.

* * * *

Just as he had planned, Jemme set to work first thing on Monday morning. He outlined his plans to DD, who made some very helpful suggestions, and then telephoned Philby and passed on the list of craftsmen he needed, hoping it would be possible to find them locally. He was rather satisfied that the wheels had been set in motion, and was planning on calling the Professor too, but had to turn his attention back to banking matters. The party had achieved exactly what he had hoped, and had helped him secure a great deal of highly prestigious business. However, it also meant that he was much busier than he had been before, and today was no exception. Before he realised it, it had crept round to eight in the evening, and he could feel the emptiness of his belly. He wasn't quite ready to finish what he was working on, but didn't want to wait any longer to have supper. He decided that it would just be easier to take supper at his desk and then he would be free to work as late as he liked. DD brought them both a couple of boxes of take away, and some plates he kept for just such an occasion, and he continued to work smoothly. By the time he eventually got home, Hil was already asleep, but as he slipped into bed beside her, he felt satisfied with the amount of work he'd managed to complete, and sighed contentedly before dropping into a deep and dreamless sleep.

The next day followed a similar pattern, and it wasn't until Wednesday lunchtime he realised that it had been three days since he'd actually seen his wife awake or spoken to her. Despite the work he still had to do, and the tempting stack of auction catalogues DD had put on his desk, he decided that he would finish at a reasonable time and head home. As he made his way up the stairs to the apartment, he glanced at his watch and was pleased to note it was only just after seven – there would be plenty of time for dinner and a whole evening together. He arrived at the door and was puzzled to see that it had been left ajar. He paused for a moment and heard voices coming from inside. He pushed the door open and the three people inside stopped talking and looked up.

'*Bonjour!*' two of them greeted him cheerfully.

Jemme paused for a moment, desperately trying to place the couple. He had been expecting to see Hil on her own, and so was slightly wrong-footed. He also realised with a slightly guilty pang that it had been so long since he'd seen Hil with any of her friends that he'd lost any context. Suddenly a moment of clarity pierced his brain, just before things became awkward,

'Eva! Roland! How nice it is to see you!' he said as enthusiastically as he could, trying to smooth over his initial stumble.

Hil stood up to greet him, 'I thought it might be nice to have some company this evening, so I invited Eva and Roland over,' she said pointedly.

'Well, I'm glad you did, it's been a very long time since I've seen either of them!' said Jemme.

'Well, you are always building away at this crazy chateau of yours, and so you're never around any more,' said Eva playfully.

'It's not crazy!' Jemme protested good-humouredly.

He sat down with them and listened to all they had been up to since he had last seen them. As they talked, he grabbed a handful of the olives Hil had set out in a little silver dish, and thought how genuinely pleased he was to see them. They were definitely more Hil's friends than his, but he had always been fond of Eva and her librarian husband Roland. She was fascinated by manuscripts, and had a modest collection of antiquarian books which she was always keen to discuss with Jemme. Whilst she was effusive with a flair for the dramatic, he was slightly Germanic in mien and a great deal more reserved. However, they were both incredibly well read, and their general speech was peppered with literary references. Jemme listened to the anecdote Eva was finishing and laughed. He was struggling to remember how long it had actually been since he'd last had any contact with them – no wonder he didn't recognise them at first. He noticed that Hil seemed a great deal more relaxed than she had been in days, and her eyes were sparkling with laughter as she added something to the end of Eva's story. All four of them laughed again and Jemme decided to make the most of the opportunity.

'How would you two like to see this "crazy chateau" that's been taking up so much of our time?'

'See it? Well we'd love to!' said Eva. Roland smiled and nodded his agreement.

'It's not finished by any means, and there will definitely still be works going on whilst you're there, but there's a really nice reception room we can use and another on its way. We've got some staff there too who keep the place ticking over. One of them is a fantastic cook, and we could have some nice supper.'

'*Fantastique*!' said Eva.

This time Hil directed her smile at Jemme, and he felt a warm sense of happiness wash over him.

'We'd love to have you over,' she said to them. 'I'm sure Jemme will be pleased to talk to you about the rooms he's planning, and we can show you round the grounds – you can even stay over if you like, there's plenty of space!'

'We would enjoy that, thank you,' said Roland.

'Excellent – are you free next weekend?'

'I believe so.'

'Well then, come for dinner! In fact, like Hil said, there's plenty of space, so let's make a weekend of it – stay both nights!' he said, swept away with enthusiasm. He paused and saw Hil looking a little uncomfortable.

'Actually, sweetheart, if it's alright with you, let's not make a *whole* weekend of it. Eva and I have already talked about going to see an exhibition at the Louvre next weekend, and it would be nice to spend some time in Paris. Also,' and Hil paused, 'there's not very much for us to do for a whole weekend.'

Jemme was disconcerted, but hid it behind a broad smile, 'Absolutely. One night it is. I'll drive us all down on Saturday afternoon.'

'I'm looking forward to seeing everything,' said Roland. 'There is so much history in these old chateaux. I will have a look through the library this week and see if I can find anything on the area, or perhaps even the chateau itself.'

'That would be great,' said Jemme, 'there's a great archive in the village, but it's very limited, so I'd be interested to see what a much larger library in Paris has to offer.'

'Me too,' said Roland, with a twinkle in his eye – the closest he ever came to making a joke.

They passed a pleasant evening talking, chatting and eating supper, and Jemme felt the tension which had been oddly present between him and Hil relax. Keen to capitalise on this renewed cordiality, he continued to ensure that he came home early for the rest of the week, and by Saturday everything seemed to be back to normal. He had been itching to drive down on Friday night and meet some of the craftsmen Philby and DD had found for him. It felt like a peculiar kind of torture to know that everything was in place and waiting for him, but he was stuck in a different city. However, he knew that it would be highly un-diplomatic to raise the matter with Hil, so he choked it down and didn't even mention it.

By Saturday afternoon he was champing at the bit. Philby had found him a carpenter and a few general handymen, and DD had found him a trompe l'oeil artist. He had arranged to see the artist back in Paris on Monday morning, but he would be able to meet the others this weekend and get them started straight away. As they packed their small overnight bags, he and Hil talked easily and comfortably, and he relaxed a little, trying to push the project to the back of his mind.

However, he couldn't help raising one issue, 'What did you mean by "not having much to do"?' he asked.

Hil paused and tried to remember, 'Oh, that – I only meant that it's not like there's lots to do with guests for a whole weekend.'

'But we always seem to fill the time when we head down there – if anything, the weekend always feels too short!'

'I know, but that's because there's work to be done, meeting new staff, looking over progress and so on. It's not really stuff you can do with guests, and besides that, there's not much else.'

'I see,' said Jemme, zipping his case shut and picking up Hil's too. He didn't really see at all, and had had no idea that Hil had felt that way. For him, the chateau was an endless source of occupation. He could have spent weeks there happily and not even set foot outside the perimeter fence. It just felt like there was so much do. Even when work was excluded, he could still wander in the grounds, talk with the staff, learn about the building and enjoy the rooms which had already been finished. He deposited the bags in the hall next to the front door and returned to the bedroom.

'We'll just have to make sure we're entertaining enough to keep them occupied then!' he said, kissing Hil on the nose.

She giggled just as the doorbell sounded, announcing the arrival of Eva and Roland.

'*Bonjour!*' trilled Eva through the letterbox. Jemme smiled and went to let them in. His smile only widened when he saw what Eva was wearing. She was dressed in a full skirt, which fell down to mid-calf length and a dainty jacket, cinched in at the waist. The look was topped off by a large brimmed hat and an elegant clutch bag. She was every inch the 'New Look' Christian Dior had designed in the 1940s to introduce glamour and style into war-ravaged Europe. It seemed hugely anachronistic, yet somehow it suited her perfectly,

'Eva, you look so elegant,' said Jemme, kissing her on both cheeks.

'*Ah, merci*! I thought we should dress smartly – it is not every day one gets to go to a chateau!' she said.

Jemme extended his hand to Roland who was wearing a rather sober grey suit. Nonetheless, it hung beautifully on him, and a very thin black tie gave it a stylish edge.

'It's great to see you both;' said Jemme, impressed to notice Roland's highly polished, pointed brogues, 'we're both ready so we can get started straight away, or you can come in for a coffee first. It's up to you.'

'Oh, I think we'd like to get going,' said Eva, 'we're very excited!'

'Excellent!' said Jemme, picking up his and Hil's case and calling back to her.

Hil emerged from the bedroom with her coat on, fiddling with an earring, 'Yes, alright, I'm ready! Hello,' she said, greeting her friends. 'Gosh don't the two of you look nice!'

'Well, thank you!' said Eva as Jemme ushered them all out of the corridor.

The trip to the chateau was a slow one. Jemme had forgotten about the terrible traffic they'd encountered last time they drove up on a Saturday afternoon, and it wasn't long before they found themselves bumper-to-bumper with everyone else trying to leave the city. It was nice to have some extra company in the car though, and Eva kept them entertained with a couple of amusing stories. Soon they were on their way again, only to come to a grinding halt another mile later. They sat in silence for a while, coming to terms with the tedium of the situation.

Eventually Roland spoke, 'At the risk of sounding solipsistic – have I ever told you where my name came from? I was just thinking about chateaux and knights and courtly tales, and I suddenly thought it might be of interest.'

Jemme turned around in his seat, 'No I don't think you have, and it definitely would be of interest.'

Although he spoke in quiet, measured tones, Roland had them all spellbound as he told them of the Frankish Roland, Charlemagne's military leader, and his role in the epic battle of Roncesvalles. It had survived in a heroic poem, the *Chanson de Roland*. Jemme was fascinated; it was something he had never heard of before, but the concept of ideas and texts surviving for longer than their physical records had always been one that fascinated him.

'I've never heard of this poem – how old is it?' he asked.

'Oh, it wasn't written until a couple of hundred years after the battle,' replied Eva, 'but it's still from the late eleventh century, and it's the oldest surviving work of French literature; it's definitely worth reading at some point, not just as a poem but for all the history it contains.'

'Absolutely,' Jemme agreed enthusiastically, 'I've always been fascinated by old poetry – my grandmother used to read me old Persian poems when I was a small boy.'

'Well, you should come to the library next week,' said Roland, 'we have a very good mediaeval section and there are lots of modern translations of the *Chanson de Roland* as well as various other *Chansons de Geste*.' He saw Hil's look, 'A cycle of poems,' he explained, 'they all come from around the same point in the early mediaeval period and represent the very beginnings of French literature. They record the heroic deeds of knights and kings and would have been performed by troubadours and jesters in the various courts of the country. Like you, Jemme, I was read them in childhood and it began a life-long fascination. My mother was a great scholar and fascinated by the Crusades. She always told me that the *Chanson de Geste* were the greatest source of evidence for that period. Anyway, that's why she named me Roland, and so I suppose it's inevitable that I've never managed to escape her interests.'

'That's very interesting,' said Jemme, 'I'm really keen to study this further. I suppose growing up, the stories and poems I was exposed to record the Crusades from a very different angle, but one of my Grandmother's greatest lessons was that no story was ever complete unless told from both sides. Perhaps there's even scope for some sort of Crusader room in the chateau. It would certainly fit with the French history narrative I'm trying to create.'

'You should,' Roland nodded, 'there is so much French history you can charter in this project. There are so many events and kings whose stories somehow touch that of the chateau, it would be fitting to chronicle them.'

'Don't give him ideas!' said Hil with a slightly nervous laugh.

'Like who? Did you find anything in your research?' Jemme asked eagerly.

'I did find a few useful things, yes, but then there are some obvious points you don't need to spend any time in a library to make.'

'What do you mean? Like what?'

'Well, off the top of my head, like the chateau's proximity to Falaise, for example. If you were thinking of examining French kings, William I is as good a place to start as any. If you haven't been yet I'd highly recommend it; there's an old castle there and it's a nice piece of French and local history.'

'What's its connection with William the Conqueror?' Hil asked.

'Oh – it was his birthplace,' answered Roland. 'But aside from that it's a fascinating place. It's been occupied since Mesolithic times, and there's been a castle there for at least a thousand years. It was the seat of the Dukes of Normandy too.'

'I didn't know that,' said Jemme. 'In fact, if I'm being honest, I've never even heard of it. You said it's nearby?'

'I'm not sure how far exactly, but it would be an easy day trip. I think you'd be interested in it too – I'm sure its history will have overlapped with your chateau's at some point.'

'Really?' asked Hil.

Roland shrugged, 'I don't see why not. I think it would only be about half a day's ride. It's highly probable that any of the various Dukes situated in Falaise would have visited, whether in a friendly capacity or not. Going back even further, it's possible that *Guillaume le Conquérant* himself might have visited. I mean, it would have been an earlier incarnation of the chateau of course, but I think I remember you saying that the site had been continuously occupied?'

'Yes. I'm not sure of the exact dates, but there has always been some sort of fortified house here.'

Roland smiled and spread his hands out, 'Well there you are then. Perhaps William would have passed through, or come here to collect tax, or even come for hunting.'

'How exciting!' said Hil, 'I remember thinking how lucky we were to be tied to such a piece of history when we first bought the place, but I think I'd started to forget that. It is really incredible that we have such a tangible connection to so many historical characters and events.'

Just then the traffic started moving again, and soon they were on their way.

Hil continued to ask Roland questions about the chateau, other chateaux in the area and the *Chanson de Geste*. Roland seemed pleased by her interest, although as he smiled to himself with relief, Jemme thought that Roland probably had no idea Jemme was ten times more pleased that Hil was asking so many questions. He too was interested in what Roland had to say, and he had felt himself fizzing with ideas as Roland had mentioned the Crusades and various mediaeval kings. He had always entertained the idea of referencing French sovereignty and notable monarchs in the chateau, and now he returned to it with renewed enthusiasm. Some rooms would obviously fall into the reign of a certain monarch, such as the Louis XVI salon. However, the stylistic influence of more ancient monarchs was unlikely to occur naturally during the course of decoration. He wondered if he should create rooms dedicated to them within the core of new rooms, or whether he could merely allude to them with a couple of artefacts, or a painting.

He was delighted by the idea of including some sort of Crusaders' room too. It tied together so many of the threads he wanted to explore in the chateau. It could examine local French history and the role of knights from this very area; however, it could also explore an extremely important historical convergence between East and West, which shaped history and continued to affect attitudes and learning today. Lastly, it could fulfil one of his dictums about both parts of the story. It seemed so appropriate to explore the Western and local side of the story in situ, and from an Eastern point of view.

'I'm looking forward to visiting you next week and taking out a copy of that poem,' he told Roland.

'Good. I'm looking forward to loaning it to you.'

'I'll be willing to bet that I can read through it and find certain elements that crop up in Eastern poems and perhaps certain characters too.'

'I don't doubt it; if both poems are commemorating the same event, then it stands to reason that there will be some cross-over between them! I suppose the difference is the way they describe the events as happening – a great victory in one will be a tragic defeat in the other.'

'Mmmm,' Jemme nodded, 'I'm just trying to think if there's anything in particular I want to look out for. Can you remember any parts which relate directly to the Levant?'

Roland laughed, 'It's a very long poem! Also, it's in Middle French, so it's not exactly easy to remember.'

'Fair enough,' Jemme couldn't help but look a little disappointed. As with everything which interested him, he had quickly become impassioned by the subject and wanted to fling himself into it, head first.

Roland obviously detected the note of disappointment in his voice, 'I'm sure I can remember something though – as I said, my mother used to read it to me all the time as a child.'

He paused for a moment and Eva put an affectionate hand on his knee, 'I've never known anyone to absorb books as much as this man,' she said. 'He's like a modern-day Denis Diderot.'

'A modern day who?' asked Hil.

'He was a philosopher and writer,' Eva explained, 'he was very important during the Enlightenment, not least because he was the co-founder and chief editor of the very first Encylopédia. I often think that Roland is like my very own *encylopédia*,' she said fondly, looking at Roland.

As if to prove her point, he suddenly snapped his fingers, 'I've remembered!' he said. 'It's because it's all in verse, it protects the text.'

'What do you mean?' asked Jemme.

'If it all rhymes then it is easier to remember it. All of these poems began in the oral tradition; they wouldn't have been written down until later. The jesters performing them would have found it much easier to remember them in verse – just like I have now. You only need to remember one line and another one comes back to you.'

'But how does that protect it?'

'Well, it makes it much harder for it to change as it is handed on from one person to another. If it's in verse, it's fastened to its original form. If someone forgets a line, or deliberately changes it, then they must change several other lines too.'

'Oh I see. I'd never really thought about it that way before.'

'Which was the piece you remembered, Roland?' asked Hil.

Roland laughed, 'Well, having said all of that, it won't rhyme, but that's only because it's the modern French version. Let me think,' he paused and drew breath, '*So Corbaran escaped across the plains of Syria / He took only two kings in his company. / He carried away Brohadas, son of the Sultan of Persia, /Who had been killed in the battle by the clean sword /Of the brave-spirited good duke Godfrey /Right in front of Antioch, down in the meadow.*'

Jemme was silent for a moment, before smiling broadly, 'Fascinating,' he said, shaking his head slowly, 'I recognise so many of those people and places.'

Before he could explain any further, he realised that they had reached the turning, and he flicked his indicator before pulling off the main road.

By this point it was late afternoon, and the light was turning dusky. As they turned again and drove down the driveway he was pleased to see that someone, presumably Marguerite, had turned the lights on for them. The slit windows running down the central staircase were on as well as the large windows either side of the front door. The warm yellow looked inviting, and set against the blue gloaming it gave the chateau a magical feel, showcasing it at its very best.

There was silence in the car, whilst Eva and Roland drank in their first view of the chateau. Jemme turned around and in the fading light was able to make out Hil's smile. Evidently she was enjoying their reactions.

Jemme pulled up the car and saw that a welcome party comprising Marguerite, Aude, Philby and Xelifon awaited them. As he got out of the car, Philby moved forward and opened the door for Eva. She looked a little taken aback, but got out and smoothed down her crumpled skirt. Donning her hat again she looked around her.

'Welcome,' said Hil, getting out of her side and putting an arm around Eva.

'Yes, welcome,' said Jemme.

Eva and Roland exchanged glances. They looked around again, taking in the line of staff waiting for them, and looked up, trying to see to the top of the roof with its spires and campanile.

Philby picked up their cases and they followed him in. As they passed Marguerite, they received an especially extravagant '*Bienvenu!*'

'Thank you,' said Eva.

'Ah Madame, you are most welcome,' said Marguerite in slightly grandiose tones. 'It is always wonderful to have visitors from Paris, and we enjoy welcoming the friends of Monsieur and Madame Mafeze very much.'

'Well, we're delighted to be here,' said Eva, as behind her Jemme's mouth twitched at the corners slightly.

Once in the Halle d'Honneur, Eva and Roland stopped and looked around them. Although it wasn't completely clear of tools and decorating clutter, Marguerite had done a good job of clearing most things away, and it looked almost like it had done for the party. Jemme had all but forgotten how impressive the hall looked on first view, with its grand sweeping staircase and balustraded balcony. They paused for a moment, and allowed Eva and Roland to enjoy taking everything in. Their enjoyment seemed to be shared by Hil, who was watching them look at their surroundings.

'Of course, we knew that you had bought a chateau, and you had told us there were original features, but it still doesn't prepare you for actually seeing it,' said Eva eventually. 'I feel almost as if we aren't meant to be here after dark and there will be a velvet rope keeping us back from the exhibits.'

Hil laughed, 'I know what you mean. I remember feeling that way at the beginning too. If you're thinking that in the hall though, wait until you've seen the finished salon! Come on, we'll show you to your room first.' She started climbing the stairs and the others followed her. 'I'm afraid it's not much, we haven't really worked on any of the bedrooms yet, but it's large with a nice view, and I'm sure Marguerite will have made it comfortable for you.'

She left Eva and Roland to settle in to the room. Although it was largely empty, it had been painted when the new rooms were prepared. The old carpet had been ripped out and the floorboards underneath buffed and polished. The original plasterwork on the ceiling had been restored, and Marguerite had left them a huge vase of flowers from the garden on a pretty antique sideboard. They both seemed impressed, and Hil only wished it was still light enough to be able to show them the view of the garden.

She left them to freshen up, and went downstairs to go and find Jemme who was talking to Philby.

'*Bonjour, Madame,*' he said, nodding to her.

'Hello, Philby, how are you?'

Philby shrugged, '*Bien, Madame, merci.* We are waiting for the *ébéniste.*'

Hil looked puzzled.

'I asked Philby if he could find us a carpenter, and he's going to come along shortly,' Jemme explained, 'I'm looking forward to meeting him.'

'But aren't we just about to have dinner?' asked Hil. 'I thought we'd spend some time with Eva and Roland in the salon before we ate,' she said, looking a little disappointed.

'Did I hear our names?' asked Eva coming down the stairs, wearing a different and equally elegant outfit.

'You look lovely!' said Hil, 'I was just saying that we'll be eating soon. Eva, Roland, this is Philby, our gardener, by the way.'

Eva smiled winningly and Philby nodded dourly in a rather comical exchange. Just then a small man came trotting out of the corridor. He wore round, wire-rimmed spectacles and a collar-less shirt tucked in to grey trousers. A white, wiry moustache had been waxed to a sharp point on either side, in contrast to the rather fluffy hair on top of his head. As he trotted, the glasses slipped to the end of his nose, and, stopping when he reached the group at the bottom of the stairs, he poked them back up again with a rather stubby finger and blinked.

'Monsieur Ledantec,' said Philby.

The short man turned around and looked up at the portly gardener, '*Ah, Monsieur, bonjour*! Sorry I am late,' he began.

'This is Monsieur Mafeze,' said Philby, pointing, 'and this, Madame Mafeze,' he added, jerking his thumb backwards towards Hil.

Hil smiled as she thought about how refined the introductions taking place in this exact spot would have been in days gone by.

'It's a pleasure to meet you, Monsieur Ledantec,' she said.

'Ahhh, Madame, the pleasure is all mine!' he said cheerfully, going round and shaking hands with everyone in the group to their general bemusement.

'Thank you for coming over this evening,' said Jemme, 'I've been looking forward to meeting you.'

Just then two further men appeared from the corridor. Considerably burlier than the carpenter, they were dressed in paint-spattered clothes, and one of them had a white smear of emulsion across his forehead.

They looked around at the new people with slight suspicion before turning to Philby, 'It is finished,' they said.

'*Bon.* This is Monsieur Mafeze,' said Philby again, pointing accusingly. Both men nodded at Jemme. 'These men have been painting,' said Philby, perhaps a little unnecessary. 'They are doing general jobs,' he added.

'Ah, excellent, thank you, *messieurs*,' said Jemme.

They nodded. 'Can we leave?' they asked.

'Of course – I hope you don't have far to go?'

They shook their heads in unison. 'The village. We will be back tomorrow.'

Jemme turned to Ledantec, feeling a little awkward, 'Have you got far to go?' he asked, 'It's just that, well, we're shortly going to be having supper.'

'*Ah, Monsieur, bien sûr*! It was my fault anyway, I was meant to be here much earlier. Of course, this evening it is too late to talk, but I am pleased that we have been able to meet.'

Jemme smiled, 'Me too. Will you be able to come by tomorrow and discuss things a little more?'

With a wide, expressive sweep of his hands, Ledantec agreed, 'But of course!' and bade them all good night, trotting out in the wake of the hefty handymen.

As if they were all running round in a revolving door, as soon as Ledantec had disappeared, Marguerite materialised.

'Everything is ready for you,' she said brightly, and began ushering them in the direction of the salon.

Whilst Eva seemed bemused by the events that had just taken place, Roland seemed perplexed. 'How many people do you have here?' he asked Hil who was walking next to him. She laughed,

'I wish I knew! It changes on a daily basis, and the number of people we see at the weekend is by no means a reflection of how many people have been here during the week.'

Roland knotted his eyebrows slightly and lowered his voice so that Marguerite couldn't hear, 'But doesn't it bother you? Having all these people here in your house whilst you're away?'

Hil frowned, 'Not at all, to be honest. I think I'm completely used to it. This house has never been a private place – we've had people coming in and out from the very first day, and that's only going to increase as we have more and more artists working for us. If it was the Paris flat, I'd feel differently, but it all comes with the territory here. Plus, we've got our core staff here all the time, people like Marguerite and Philby whom you just met. We trust them completely and they wouldn't so much as let anyone onto the property if they didn't think they were suitable.'

Roland didn't look particularly convinced, 'I couldn't do it,' he said simply. Just then, as they reached the salon, Marguerite stopped them all abruptly. Hil smiled to herself, knowing that Marguerite was pausing for maximum dramatic effect. True to form, with a theatrical flourish, she waited until she had all their attention before flinging open the doors. It achieved the desired effect in Eva, who gasped slightly, and Roland's eyebrows shot up. Hil and Jemme looked impressed too, and basking in their expressions, Marguerite let out a tiny, satisfied sigh.

'It's beautiful,' said Eva, smiling and looking slowly at the tableau in front of them.

'I know,' said Hil softly, looking around, 'we're very lucky.' The room was like a scaled down version of how it had been for the party. The table was set with crisp linen and shining silver cutlery and, judging by the amount of flower arrangements and tall vases filling every nook and cranny, Hil was surprised that there were any left in the garden.

'We can go in, you know!' laughed Jemme, trying to encourage his guests, who seemed rooted to the spot.

Eva and Roland wandered in, slowly looking around them as they did so.

'And you say that it was completely empty when you moved in?' asked Roland.

'Yes, it was, and it was in a bit of a state too actually – there was damp coming through the ceiling, the carpet was horrible and the paint was peeling. We had to strip it back to the bare bones and begin again.'

'Remarkable,' said Roland.

'I can't believe it hasn't always looked like this,' said Eva, 'it all fits together so perfectly. All the furniture too, it all seems so...seamless.' She stopped and noticed the pistachio piano for the first time, 'Oh, now that really is beautiful,' she breathed. 'Is is a harpsichord?'

'Close – it's a fortepiano,' said Hil, 'in fact, I think it's the first piece of furniture we bought for this chateau. It came from a little antique shop just outside Lisieux.'

They sat at the places Marguerite had laid for them, and Marguerite and Aude appeared with fresh crusty bread and big bowlfuls of *soupe de poisson*.

'It's nothing fancy, it's just something that is typical of this region,' Marguerite said, slightly mournfully, as she laid a bowl in front of each guest. No sooner had they all dipped a spoon into the silky soup than they were all agreed that they wouldn't have wanted anything else. After a chicken, roasted in Normandy butter, with vegetables from the garden and a particularly rich dessert, everyone sat back in their chairs, feeling very full and very satisfied.

'It's so nice to eat home-cooked food,' said Eva. 'Sometimes one can be so busy in Paris that it becomes a matter of grabbing bites to eat wherever possible. This is what life is all about – this is the proper French way of life. Simple, but delicious, honest food and the time to enjoy it with friends.'

'Absolutely,' smiled Hil.

Jemme nodded, but thought guiltily how many times he had eaten supper at his desk with DD recently.

They passed the rest of the evening chatting pleasantly about plans for the chateau, with Eva and Roland in turn being surprised and impressed, both by the ambition and how many people they would involve.

'But it seems that you have so many people working for you already!' said Eva.

'That is what I said,' said Roland, still not looking too convinced by the answer Hil had given him.

✻ ✻ ✻ ✻

The next morning, Jemme woke before Hil. Slipping out of bed as quietly as possible, he dressed and headed downstairs. He found Marguerite in the kitchen, and thanked her warmly for supper.

'But, Monsieur, it was nothing! I hope that your Paris friends liked it. I am sure they are used to something very different.'

'They might be, but I think that's the reason they liked it so much!'

Marguerite smiled broadly and shrugged, 'Pff, I am pleased they liked it, whatever the reason. Monsieur Ledantec will be here soon and those big men are already working.'

Jemme smiled and Marguerite shook her head, 'So clumsy,' she said, retying her apron strings, 'I am surprised they haven't broken anything already! I will tell Monsieur Philby again – they shouldn't be allowed near the china!'

'I'm sure Philby will keep a close eye on them,' said Jemme, 'Ah, excellent. Here he is now.'

Philby nodded an abrupt good morning to them all, and Marguerite poured him a cup of coffee.

'Thank you for organising some extra help. It will be really useful to have people on hand over the next couple of days,' said Jemme.

Philby shrugged, 'They are casual labourers, Monsieur. They will be glad of any work you can give them.'

'Do you have any idea what time Monsieur Ledantec might be coming in this morning?' asked Jemme.

Philby scratched at his stubbly chin and looked up at the clock above the kitchen door, 'Around half an hour,' he said.

Jemme and Marguerite both brightened. 'Excellent!' said Jemme.

'Ah, Monsieur, enough time for you to have breakfast!' enthused Marguerite, already turning round to fiddle with the stove. Jemme's original plan had been to wait for Hil and the other guests to get up, but he suddenly thought that if he had breakfast now he could spend all morning with Ledantec, and meet the others when he had finished. Before he had had time to sit back down again, Marguerite was cracking eggs and whisking them into a pan. 'No one ever uses enough cream,' she muttered to herself.

She fussed around the kitchen, finally serving up a huge plateful of rich yellow scrambled eggs, and topping up Jemme's coffee at the same time.

'You spoil me, Marguerite!' said Jemme, happily digging in. He was just finishing off the last morsels when he saw Ledantec approaching the open kitchen door. Jemme smiled to himself. With his oddly short legs, Ledantec always seemed to be scurrying everywhere he walked, reminding Jemme of a small Chihuahua. He rose to greet him,

'Monsieur Ledantec, thank you so much for coming back this morning.'

'My pleasure, Monsieur Mafeze,' said Ledantec, offering Jemme a hand and smiling warmly. His glasses slid down to the end of his nose as he shook Jemme's hand vigorously, and he slid them back up to the top of his nose and blinked several times.

Jemme divided the last of the coffee between two cups and handed one to Ledantec, before leading him to the room he was considering using as the Assyrian room. He gave a brief background to the project, and outlined his intentions for the chateau. Although he tried to keep it as succinct as possible, it still required a great deal of explanation, and as he heard himself explain the whole story to Ledantec, he was struck by a fleeting realisation that this artist might think he was mad. He had never had to describe the whole project from beginning to end in one go before, and so he had never had to consider how Quixotic it might sound. He finished, and watched Ledantec absorb everything he had said. The short carpenter remained silent for a while and sucked on his moustache as he mulled it over.

'It is a very ambitious project, Monsieur.'

Jemme let out a rather hollow laugh, 'I know!'

'And you have no project manager? No architect overseeing work?'

'That's right. I've been doing everything myself, with help from Philby.'

'And you are here only on the weekend, no?'

'That's correct too. Although Philby is here every day.'

'And you are also restoring the grander rooms in this house *at the same time* as working on this project?'

'Yes, again,' said Jemme, wincing a little at how crazy he must seem in this man's eyes. He looked warily at Ledantec, waiting for him to speak. Ledantec puffed out his cheeks with air and then slowly exhaled.

'*Bon*. I wanted to understand the scale.'

'And…?' Jemme asked.

'It is very ambitious. Extremely ambitious. But, it is good to breathe life back into these old buildings. If you are committed to it and you have the energy then it is a positive thing in my opinion.'

Jemme broke out in a wide smile. 'I'm very glad to hear it,' he said.

They had been standing at the top of the corridor and, draining the last of his coffee, Jemme flicked on the lights and led the way onwards again.

'These are all the new rooms I was telling you about,' he said as they came to the first door. He opened it and Ledantec peered in.

'To be honest, they're all pretty much identical,' said Jemme, moving on to the next door to show him. 'They're all plain white at the moment, and they've got nice, even proportions, so they're as close to a blank canvas as it's possible to get. I've been planning on starting the Babylonian one for a while, but recently I've been thinking about an Assyrian room too and that's the one I'd like your help with.'

They reached another door and Jemme swung it open, 'This is the room I was thinking of.'

They both stepped in and looked around. Ledantec twitched his nose, 'Why this room in particular? You just said that they all had similar proportions – I thought the whole point was that there was nothing particularly distinctive about any of them.'

'It is, you're right. I'm actually thinking of the long term. I want there to be some kind of sense to the rooms. Wandering along this corridor should be like a journey, and I don't want to suddenly jump from the Sumerians to sixteenth-century Venice, for example.'

Ledantec nodded, 'Like in a museum.'

'I suppose so, yes.'

Jemme looked around the room, and pointed out the various features he was already thinking of installing. He described the trompe l'oeil panelling, which caused Ledantec to nod approvingly, and he explained his proto-plans for the ceiling.

'All of which brings me to the last feature,' he said, 'which is where you come in. I want to install a couple of thrones against this wall here. I know exactly what I want them to look like, but they're complete one-offs so they'd have to be entirely custom made.'

Ledantec nodded.

'They'd be quite complicated pieces, both technically and in terms of trying to make sure that they look exactly right. I've got a very specific idea of how I'd like them to look, and so the success of the piece will rest on our ability to communicate with each other.'

The carpenter nodded again, 'Of course. It is very important that we work closely with each other. Perhaps we could begin with an outline – maybe you could describe the pieces to me and we can discuss them so that I can see if I've understood properly. Before I begin work for anyone, I always draw up very detailed plans – I'll discuss it for a long time before even cutting in to the first piece of wood.'

Jemme felt reassured, and, as they discussed the proposed commission, his respect for the carpenter deepened. Ledantec didn't know anything about Assyrian history, but he picked up details incredibly quickly. He was also as sharp as a knife, and impressed Jemme with some of his suggestions. Although they didn't discuss anything other than the thrones, Jemme was already considering asking Ledantec to have a more permanent role within the project. By the time they drew to a close, it was nearing lunchtime, and Jemme realised that he had abandoned his guests. He bade Ledantec a warm goodbye and told him he was looking forward to seeing his drawings. Making his way back to the kitchen, he found Marguerite half-way through preparing lunch,

'Tsk, Monsieur, where have you been?! Everyone was looking for you!' she scolded.

'Were they? Did they seem cross?'

Marguerite shrugged, 'Monsieur Roland and Madame Eva seemed confused that you weren't here, but Madame Hil did not.'

Poor Hil, Jemme thought to himself, she knows me too well. 'Do you know where they are?' he asked Marguerite.

'I think they are walking in the garden,' she replied. 'Lunch will be about half an hour, and Madame said you would be driving back to Paris soon after you had finished eating.'

'Alright, thank you Marguerite, I'll go and find them,' said Jemme, heading off for the grounds. He found them without too much difficulty, and jogged over to catch up with them. 'I'm so sorry to leave you for so long!' he said, slightly breathlessly when he reached them.

Hil gave him a small, resigned smile and a peck on the cheek.

'*Bonjour,*' Eva greeted him cheerfully. She was dressed as elegantly as she had been the day before and Roland too had clearly gone to some trouble. Jemme felt a pang of guilt as he remembered how excitedly they had talked about staying in the chateau. 'I had to speak with the new carpenter,' he explained, somewhat feebly.

Eva smiled at him and shook her head, 'I was just saying to Hil – we are so impressed by how many people you have working for you here. I had no idea it was such a complicated operation! Last night there seemed to be builders and carpenters popping out of the woodwork at every turn!'

'There did, didn't there?' said Hil looking meaningfully at Jemme. He squirmed a little under her gaze and she relented, asking how the new carpenter had been.

Jemme brightened, 'Excellent! I was really very impressed indeed. He's highly accomplished technically, but he also seemed very alert and intelligent too. He really listened to what I was saying and took my ideas on board. I think we're going to work very well together. Also, he's going to sketch out some drawings which we'll discuss at length before we even begin making anything.'

'Good,' said Hil emphatically. 'Because the last thing we want is another Dupré.' Eva and Roland looked at her questioningly, so as she led them back to the house she related the story of the temperamental artist atop his scaffolding, and his threats of jumping.

She had just finished as they reached the salon and as they settled down at the table, Eva shook her head,

'But it is horrible! I cannot believe that this happened in your own home – you must have been so upset!'

Roland too shook his head, 'I could not do it personally. I would find it strange enough to have all these people in my house to begin with, but for them to then go about threatening me…' he shuddered slightly.

Hil looked rather gratified, especially when Jemme's assertion that 'it had all been rather an adventure' seemed to fall on deaf ears. Once they had begun the meal, Eva asked Jemme for a little more detail about the carpenter and his plans for the room. Jemme had been feeling guilty for having left them all for so long in the morning, something which had only been intensified by remembering Hil's distress at Dupré. He was grateful for the chance to exonerate himself, and so described the thrones he wanted to build and how they would fit in with the decoration of the whole room. Eva and Roland listened, with interest.

'How compelling,' said Eva. 'I have never heard of such a thing outside a museum. Is that what you're building?'

'To be honest, I'm not really sure. I'm aware that a lot of the processes I'm going through are similar and, in a way, the goals are too. I want to conduct this project by the same rigorous standards a museum would, in terms of research and the provenance of pieces used. However, there's more to it than that. I also want to focus on artisanship and traditional crafts. I think I want the whole thing to be more integrated than a museum.'

'But then what? What about when it's all finished?'

Jemme laughed, 'Well that really is a long way off! I feel like we're so close to the beginning at the moment that it's not something I need to worry about yet.'

'Do you not have any idea at all though? Any small inkling?' Eva probed, 'It just sounds a lot like it will look like a museum when it's finished with all its galleries, or display rooms or whatever you call them. After all your hard work, maybe it would be a good thing to allow people to visit.'

'I'm not quite sure how my wife would feel about that,' said Jemme jokingly, trying to evade the subject. He caught Hil's eye and saw that she was giving him a rather beseeching please-don't-get-ideas look. 'It's enough to ask that we have workmen and artists traipsing in and out; I think I should leave it for a while before I broach the idea of members of the public coming along as well!'

He paused just long enough to hear Hil exhale softly, evidently relieved.

Eva shrugged, 'That is fair enough. I know Roland would never be happy with something like that,' She looked at her husband, who managed to smile in accordance and look horrified by the idea at the same time.

'I am interested in the grand rooms you are restoring,' he said. 'Rooms just like this one. You have done a very nice job here, and I think it is important to retain some of the original character of the chateau, no matter how you adapt the rest of it.'

'Oh I agree absolutely,' said Jemme, 'in fact, one of the most important things that's been developing in this project so far is my philosophy regarding everything. I've had to consider my approach on so many different levels – where I source furnishings from, what sort of methods I use in restoration, how I preserve various rooms and features. That's what I mean about the whole thing being more integrated than a museum – in a way I feel that there's much more responsibility.'

Roland looked thoughtful, 'But how have you chosen which rooms to restore and which to change?'

'Again, that's something I've had to think very hard about. With some rooms, such as this one, it seemed obvious that they should be restored to their original function and design. However, it's not as if this chateau would have looked the same throughout its history. The rooms would have been constantly changing in their use and decoration.'

'That's true,' nodded Roland.

'Well, I felt that part of my duty was to continue that. Although some rooms seem to be slightly museum-like, I didn't want to turn the whole property into a museum. I thought about how, over the years, the people who lived here would probably have bought the latest fashions and inventions, so the house would always have been filled with innovation and new technologies. I want to continue that tradition, but I also want to reference the place's history and location – just as we were discussing yesterday. There's also something else to think about: when I'm actually decorating the display rooms I want to use the most authentic methods and materials possible, even if they are authentic to, say, ancient Phoenicia, rather than these eighteenth century materials already used in the chateau,' he finished and took a sip of water. Roland sat, silently digesting what he had said for a while.

'You have certainly thought about it a great deal,' he said eventually, 'I had not considered that one might need to develop a philosophy for a project such as this, but I can see now how necessary it is.'

'I would say it is indispensable,' said Jemme.

Roland thought again, 'I know you've already decided to preserve one of the libraries, but I was wondering if you were thinking of preserving any of the others – or even creating one. I'm sure a house of this age would have had more than one library.'

'It's something I've been thinking about quite a bit recently, actually,' Jemme replied.

'We've got a sizable collection of antiquarian books, and a few rare manuscripts back in Paris that I'd be keen to bring here. There isn't a particularly cohesive theme to them though; it's just a collection that Hil and I have built up individually and then together. It can all go into the *Bibliothèque Régence* for now, but I've been wondering how we could split it up later on – I'm sure the collection is only going to get larger.'

'Ah, well now you are appealing to my special area of interest!' smiled Roland. 'Are you thinking of creating other libraries based on subject or age?'

'I'm not quite sure. I suppose it depends how the collection grows, and in which direction.'

'That is true. However, it might be something to think about when you're seeking out new acquisitions. For example, you could have a library based on a certain subject, such as travel. You could source classic travel literature and travelogues as well as antiquarian guides and maps. It could be really quite interesting, especially as the books would all be of different ages. Alternatively, you could collect a library of books of the same age – seventeenth century French works for example; you could collect based on provenance, or bindings even.'

Jemme looked at Roland eagerly, 'Those are fantastic ideas!' he said, already trying to imagine how everything would look, installed and finished in the chateau. 'I would certainly like a library concerning old classic languages, and languages of the East…'

Roland gave a small shrug, 'You are fortunate not to be limited in your scope. In fact there is enough room here to be able to do all of those things and a great deal more besides. You could even dedicate one of your display rooms to examining the origins of writing!'

By now it was far too late and, despite the intensity of Hil's pleading look, Jemme was already excitedly planning how he would go about creating everything Roland had just described.

Chapter Twenty-Six

Hil was silent for most of the drive home, whilst Jemme talked animatedly about Roland's language-room idea. Although the slightly more sedate Roland attempted to contribute to the discussion, and Eva occasionally asked questions, on the whole no one could keep up with him. By the time they neared the outskirts of Paris, Jemme had formed and discounted about three different plans, and was mulling over the details of a fourth.

'They all sound interesting,' said Eva, when he had finally stopped to draw breath. 'I suppose you'll have plenty of time to think about it though.'

Jemme looked at her blankly.

'Well, you've only just started a room haven't you?' she asked. 'And then I thought you had the next one all lined up,' she added, faltering slightly at Jemme's continued blank stare.

'Oh, no,' Jemme said dismissively, 'that won't be a problem. It's not like I have to wait for one to be finished before I can start on another. I can pretty much begin this any time I like.'

'Oh, I see,' said Eva, stealing a glance at Hil, who was staring fixedly out of the window. 'Well, I hope you're not taking too much on,' she said kindly, but firmly.

Jemme laughed, 'Not at all!'

He found a parking space right outside Eva and Roland's front door, so they were able to get out of the car and properly say goodbye. Eva and Roland thanked them warmly for the weekend, and reiterated what a pleasure it had been to stay in the chateau. Roland reminded Jemme that he could come into the library any time he liked, to pick up a copy of the *Chanson de Geste* or any other text he might find interesting, and they both said that they hoped to see more of the couple in the future. They stood outside their front door waving to the car until it reached the bottom of the street. Having watched them disappear in the rear view mirror, Hil turned round in her seat and sighed.

'They are such a nice couple.'

'Aren't they? What a fun weekend! I hope that was just the sort of cheering up you needed,' said Jemme.

'I suppose,' said Hil flatly.

'Sweetheart, why do you sound so sad? I thought this was exactly what you wanted – we didn't go for the whole weekend, we spent a lot of time with friends we haven't seen very much, we took guests to the chateau and had a nice dinner, what on earth was wrong with that?'

'It wasn't exactly like that though, was it?' said Hil, looking slightly sulky.

'What do you mean?'

'Well, we hardly saw you this morning to start with, then when we did, all you talked about was the chateau and your building project. It was the same yesterday – we got there late, the place was full of workmen and then you talked all evening about your plans and what you want to do. We haven't seen Eva and Roland in such a long time, and you didn't even ask about what they are doing, or how they are.'

Jemme looked stunned, 'But that's so unfair! We got there late because we left Paris late – I know there was traffic, but that's hardly my fault. I don't understand – you say you want to spend more time in Paris this weekend, so we do – even though it was the last thing I wanted to do – and then you complain about not spending enough time at the chateau!'

'The "last thing you wanted?!"'

'Come on, you know I don't mean it like that! Besides, I don't think it's unreasonable to expect that they would have wanted to hear about the chateau and the project during a stay *in* the chateau!'

'But not for the whole weekend! If you weren't talking about rooms you were planning, you were talking about rooms you were working on –' she paused and bit her lip, trying to collect herself, 'I just think it's a bit much, that's all. It would have been nice if it could have been a weekend with the chateau as a backdrop, rather than the focal point.'

'Well I'm sorry – I had no idea you would feel like that, otherwise I would have done things differently.'

'I know you didn't,' Hil said, sighing heavily and ignoring Jemme's confused look. Suddenly she remembered something, 'You weren't serious about starting new rooms were you?!'

Jemme looked confused again, 'But of course I was – why wouldn't I be? What's wrong with that?'

'I just thought that maybe you were caught up with the enthusiasm of the whole thing, but when you'd a chance to reflect you might…' she trailed off, looking sadly at Jemme's face, 'but of course not,' she concluded, mostly to herself.

'Sweetheart, what's the matter? I'm sorry this weekend wasn't what you were hoping for.'

'It's not that.'

'Well, what is it then?'

Hil closed her eyes and leaned her head back against the headrest. 'Never mind. Let's just go home.'

Things continued in a similar way for the rest of the week, much to Jemme's surprise. He had thought that everything had improved with the weekend away: Hil had seemed light-hearted and relaxed, and he had thought she was genuinely happy. Now things had slipped into how they had been the week before. He was working late, and getting home when Hil was already asleep, and then leaving before she was awake. It felt like they were ships passing in the night. Whenever they did find the chance to speak, Hil was quiet and withdrawn, and wouldn't engage with him, no matter how many times he tried to ask what the matter was and what he could do to help. He had started not to look forward to going home, and was beginning to think that there wasn't much point anyway – it was unlikely he would even see his wife, and if he did, even less likely that they'd have a proper conversation. He compensated for it by working even harder at the bank and sinking his time into the chateau projects. Ledantec had posted him a tube filled with plans for the thrones. One particular piece had been rolled up with a note attached, explaining that he had 'taken the liberty of sketching out a plan for the room, as it might help to have a visualisation'.

Jemme was pleased. Ledantec was an excellent draftsman – as good as any architect he had seen, and he was right, it really had helped to have a properly drawn out plan, which was an improvement on Jemme's own early sketches. The plan was perfect too – Ledantec had listened carefully, but also understood what it was he wanted and he felt a small thrill to see it laid out before him on a large sheet of paper. He had raised his concerns over the ceiling with the carpenter, and also briefly mentioned his memory of being in a *liwan*, and Ledantec had chosen to focus on this. The ceiling had been coloured as a dusky sky, filled with bright stars. As soon as he saw it, Jemme knew that that was exactly how he wanted it to be in the finished room, and he smiled. 'What a find this man is proving to be,' he thought to himself. After a few telephone calls to ensure they were both happy, he authorised Ledantec to go ahead with the piece.

'How long do you think it will take?' he asked him.

'It depends. I have a couple of other pieces I'm working on, but if you'd like it urgently then I am happy to delay them, and work on this full-time.'

'It's not "urgent" exactly, but it would be really nice to be able to see it next time I am down,' Jemme said hopefully.

'When will that be?'

'This weekend.'

There was silence on the line and Jemme could hear Ledantec sucking on his moustache as he thought.

'That will not be a problem at all,' he said with conviction. 'However, I don't know if I will be able to make the table too.'

'Oh, that's not a problem. That's a very simple thing, and it's quite clear what it needs to look like from your drawing. I should imagine we could pretty much give that to anyone and ask them to make it. I'll ask Philby to find a local woodworker or something.'

'No, it's alright, Monsieur. I can sort it out. It will be much easier – I'm already here and this way I can see whether their work is any good.'

'Well if you don't mind, that would be very helpful.' He wished Ledantec goodbye, and put the phone down, satisfied. Another success, he thought to himself.

By Thursday he had managed to speak to Hil for long enough to ascertain that she didn't want to come to the chateau that weekend. She said she was keen to spend more time in Paris and carry on catching up with old friends. When Jemme asked if she minded him going alone, she merely shrugged, which he took to mean 'no'.

That Friday morning, he arrived at work with a small overnight case, planning to drive straight to the chateau. Even though he was as busy as he had been throughout the week, he felt highly motivated and somehow managed to get his work finished earlier than he had done on any other night. Before he knew it, he was whizzing his way out of Paris with his overnight bag on the passenger's seat next to him. Pulling off the road onto the top of the driveway, he caught his first sight of the chateau, and felt the comforting sense of familiarity that comes with arriving home. He pulled up the car and slipped into the hallway. Putting his bag down, he took a deep breath in and exhaled slowly as he looked around him. He smiled and tried to imagine anywhere he'd rather be. Making his way to the kitchen, he readied himself for the inevitable telling-off he'd receive from Marguerite.

True to form, once she'd scolded him for not letting them come out and greet him, she filled him in on progress. He was pleased to hear that the room was coming along nicely, and amused by Marguerite's distaste for the 'big men' who apparently were still doing handiwork around the house. It seemed one of them had got ideas above his station, and Marguerite was less than impressed. Promising her he'd be back in an hour and a half for supper, he went off to the new room to see everything for himself. The room was empty, but was obviously in the process of being worked on. Half a cup of coffee stood on the floor, various tools were lying around and a portable freestanding spotlight had been plugged in to shine on the work in progress. He looked around. Although things were slightly messy, he could really see the room coming together. The first thing he noticed were the two thrones, in situ, exactly where they had been in the plans. He moved over and examined them carefully. It was the first time he had seen the physical manifestation of anything from his dream and he ran his hand over one of the thrones, excited to feel its solidity beneath his touch. Both thrones had been made from walnut, and had been expertly carved. The back on one of them was still a little rough, but judging by the pieces of sandpaper and pots of varnish lying around, Ledantec had not yet finished working on it. There were a few other rough edges which needed to be smoothed out, but on the whole, they looked just as he had imagined them, and just how he and Ledantec had discussed them. They were complicated pieces and their form was intended to reference the three different periods of Assyrian history. From the Professor's book, Jemme had adjusted the detailing of the thrones, so that they showed Persian, Assyrian and Parthian influences. He recalled seeing photographs of different artefacts in the book, and being fascinated by obvious influence of one on the other.

Someone had also begun to prepare the walls of the room too. Although he had not yet found his trompe l'oeil artist, the walls were covered with rough sketches of the panels. Judging by the quality of the work, even in draft form, he suspected Ledantec was responsible. Just then the carpenter appeared behind him, holding a handful of wet brushes.

'*Ah, Monsieur, bonjour*! I was just washing the varnish from these brushes – I see you have seen everything,' he said, nodding towards the thrones. 'They're not finished yet, but they will be by the end of the weekend. What do you think?'

'They're excellent – exactly what I was hoping for, thank you.'

Ledantec smiled, 'I'm pleased. We're getting closer to the plan.'

'Indeed we are – did you draw on the walls?'

'Yes, I hope you don't mind – it will be painted over anyway, I just wanted to create the right setting for the chairs, and give the feel of what the room will look like when it's finished.'

'It's made a huge difference, thank you – I can visualise it in front of my eyes now, instead of just in my mind.'

'I'm looking forward to seeing it all finished!' said Ledantec, putting his clean brushes down and picking up a very fine piece of sandpaper.

'Well, I can promise that you're not the only one,' said Jemme. 'By the way, did you manage to find someone to make the table?'

'Oh, yes, I did actually – I didn't have to look very far at all.'

'Really, anyone I'd know?'

'It's one of the local handymen Monsieur Philby hired from the village.'

Jemme thought back to the previous weekend, 'The slightly... hefty fellows?'

Ledantec laughed, 'Yes, that's right. Anyway, one of them heard I was looking for someone and practically begged me to let him have a go. He said that he had lots of woodworking experience, and that was his true calling. He got rather passionate about it too, and kept telling about how many craftsmen there were in his family and how they could gild, glaze and tile the piece if needed.'

'Well, I would never have guessed it.'

'No, me neither. I told him that we would just stick with making the piece for now and he's been off working on it for days. He seems to be very anxious to prove himself.'

'I'm looking forward to seeing the finished thing in that case,' said Jemme.

'So am I, out of curiosity if nothing else,' said Ledantec. 'He'll have finished it by this afternoon or tomorrow morning apparently. I also thought of one more thing, I might do it myself, but if this man turns out to be any good we can ask him too.'

'What's that?'

'Well, one of these thrones is rather high – it's alright for someone like you, but someone like me would almost need to jump to get up there. It depends on whether you want to use them, or just have them as installation pieces, but either way, I thought a small footstool might be useful. You could stand on it to get into the larger throne, and then rest your feet on it when you're sitting in the smaller throne.'

'That's an excellent idea, thank you,' said Jemme. He smiled to himself as he recalled looking around in his dream and wondering how he would get up into the high seat. It was only its suddenly shrinking proportions that allowed him to sit down in the end, but otherwise a stool would have been very handy.

He left Ledantec to his sanding, and went to look at the room he was planning on turning into the Babylonian room. Its pristine white walls made it seem characterless and empty, but having just seen the progress in the Assyrian room, Jemme could see past them; he imagined himself standing in front of the Ishtar Gate, staring up at its colours and carvings, knowing the wonders of the city it protected. He turned around, and against the opposite wall imagined himself as the unseen observer, watching Hammurabi dictate his great law code to a scribe. It was all so tantalisingly close to being realised. He would ask some of the artists from the Assyrian room to work in here when they had finished, so it could be started within the week. He could picture most of the room in his mind, but he was unsatisfied with his vision of Hammurabi. He had admired the great Babylonian since childhood, and his dream vision of the lawmaking process had been so vivid that it was inconceivable Hammurabi would not be referenced in this room. However, the idea of painting a representation of him on the wall did not appeal. The more he thought about it, the more it seemed too flat a representation of a character he saw so vividly in his mind. He tried to recall other depictions of Hammurabi. There were the carvings of him in the stele of course, but that didn't seem right either. It was too stylised and not detailed enough. He thought some more and gradually a trip to the Louvre with Hil crept into his consciousness. It had been a long time ago – before they were married even. He recalled taking her to the Assyrian gallery, and explaining to her his fascination with the long and rich history of civilisations of the Levant.

He closed his eyes and tried to remember what he had seen. He remembered talking about Hammurabi, and he was sure that they would have looked at something as he did so. Suddenly it came flowing back to him – there had been a statue. He dredged it from his memory and focussed on it. About three feet high, he thought. He remembered it being carved from black granite, which sparkled slightly under the museum's lights. He remembered how skilfully it had been carved, and how soft the features had looked, despite being hewn from stone. It would be perfect for the room, and he resolved to look it up as soon as he got back to Paris. He would find a sculptor and commission a reproduction, or, even better, perhaps some later versions were already in existence. He had several friendly contacts at the Louvre, and he was sure they would be able to point him in the right direction. Realising he had better keep his promise to Marguerite, he made his way back to the kitchen, pleased with how the evening was turning out.

The next morning panned out in a similarly satisfying way. Finally accepting that he would be more useful if he left everyone in the Assyrian room to finish their work, he settled in the library. He had visited Roland during the week and, amongst other things, he had picked up a book on the origins of the written word. He was keen to get this next idea started as soon as possible, and saw his research as the first step. He sat and sipped his morning coffee as Ugarit, Akkadian and Sumerian swirled around his head. He looked at the charts of letters, and struggled to try and memorise them. They seemed completely foreign, with no familiar curvature of serif he could assimilate. He struggled to develop a clear picture of what had happened too, and he flicked through the book, looking for a point he could work from. It seemed that writing had developed independently in two different places, worlds apart. The first was Mesoamerica, and, although that region held some interest for him, it was nothing compared with Mesopotamia, the second area, where written evidence dated back to 3200 BC. It was an awe-inspiringly large number, and he turned it over in his mind, trying to conceptualise five thousand years of writing. He tried to draw a timeline in his notebook, but it kept becoming tangled with logograms and syllabaries. He realised that understanding the history of writing was about more than just tracing the history of letters. There was a philosophy to be understood too; he must consider how writing had evolved as a means of record, for important state matters, magical incantations and to honour ancestors. The reasons for capturing and recording thought and facts were manifold and only increased as the concept became further ingrained in early societies. He understood that the process of developing that concept had been complex and lengthy, and wasn't easy to trace. It was this very thing that had fascinated him most in childhood though, the idea that people had begun to realise they could store their stories in a permanent way.

He took a deep breath, and returned to the book. Although it was complicated, he wouldn't have to include every detail in the room. As long as he represented significant milestones, and referenced something from each era, he would be providing the essence of the story. Flicking back to the beginning again, he read the chapter on Cuneiform. It was the oldest known system of pictographs, and began with over a thousand different individual characters. He looked at a photograph of a clay tablet bearing cuneiform script; the characters were strange to look at – not exactly pictures, more geometrical shapes incised into the clay with a blunt reed. They were regularly formed, and he tried to imagine the skill of a scribe capable of creating over a thousand different iterations of these small shapes, and the regard in which he would be held. He skimmed over a few more pages and learned that, over time, the number of characters lessened and their forms became simpler. One chart showed the evolution of a single character from something which almost looked like a picture of what it represented to a series of ever-simpler lines, which almost resembled a letter by the end. It was fascinating to be able to see this truncated evolution right before his eyes, and he idly sketched out the different shapes as he continued reading.

By the time he'd finished the chapter, he'd written *cuneiform* at the top of his notepad, next to the doodle, and underlined it twice. It was inconceivable that he would not include such an important writing system, which spanned so many languages and so much history. He followed the journey from cuneiform into a fully fledged orthographic system in which the letters represented sound. He discovered Ugaritic, the ancient language of modern-day Ras Sharma, and its thirty-character alphabet. He was fascinated by the Phoenician script, which evolved and mutated, eventually becoming the basis for Greek and, in turn, Roman alphabets, the progenitor for Latin and all Western alphabets. By the time he stopped for lunch, he already had a long list in his notebook and felt if he had travelled on an epic journey.

He made his way back to the kitchen, thinking about everything he had read, and trying to visualise how he would go about creating some form of paean to them. He found Marguerite looking rather flustered in the kitchen.

'Is everything alright?' he asked, looking hungrily at the pots bubbling away on the stove.

'*Oui, oui*, everything is fine, Monsieur, everything is just becoming busier that is all.'

'What, today?'

'No, no just in general – it is not a problem though. There are more mouths to feed and more rooms and furniture to clean, so Aude is in the kitchen much less.'

'I'm sorry to hear that, Marguerite, if I'd thought about it I would have realised. You know that I'm more than happy for you to take on someone else though, don't you? I'll leave it entirely up to your discretion – maybe Aude has a friend.'

'Ah, Monsieur, it is kind, but I think I will wait first and see how we get on with just the two of us.'

'Alright, but don't forget, if you need any help just ask for it.'

'*Merci, Monsieur,*' said Marguerite, looking as if that was the last thing she would ever consider. Jemme remembered how long it had taken her to get used to Aude and accept her help, and he realised that she would just have to come round to asking for more help in her own time.

'Everything is ready, Monsieur,' said Marguerite, gesturing at the table for him to sit down.

'Thank you, Marguerite, this all smells wonderful. There's so much of it as well, I can see why you've been in the kitchen all morning!'

Marguerite shrugged, 'These workmen are hungry, Monsieur, there has to be a lot.'

'It seems a shame that they always eat together, and I eat separately away from them,' said Jemme.

Marguerite looked slightly horrified, 'But that is the proper way, Monsieur. It would not be right for you to all eat at the same meal time.'

'Alright, alright,' said Jemme, keen to interject and change the subject before she started talking about 'the good old days' again. He ate his lunch in silence, wishing he had someone to talk his new ideas through with.

Later that afternoon, Ledantec came to find him, 'Everything is finished, Monsieur,' he said.

'Excellent, can I come and see it now?'

'*Bien*, of course. The man who has been working on the table is just bringing it over now and installing it. I haven't even seen it myself yet.'

'Well then, I hope we're both pleased! Shall we head over there now?'

Ledantec nodded and led the way back to the new rooms, explaining the finish he had put on the thrones and how they would need to be treated and cared for. Jemme was impressed by his knowledge and how much he seemed to care about his work too. 'I really enjoyed working on these pieces,' said Ledantec as they neared the top of the corridor. 'They were so different to the usual commissions of tables and cabinets.'

'I'm pleased,' said Jemme, 'I liked them very much when I saw them, and can only imagine I'll like them even more now they're finished!'

His expectations were confirmed when they entered the room and Jemme saw the two thrones sitting in front of him, exactly as he'd seen them in his dream. The dustsheets and equipment had been moved away, and the portable spotlight repositioned to show off the thrones which sat, resplendently regal, in their unfinished surroundings. Next to the larger one was a small footstool, just as Ledantec had promised. It had been beautifully finished, subtly echoing the style of the two seats. Jemme bent down to admire it, and then felt a shadow fall across his face. He looked up and recognised one of the burly workmen Philby had employed the previous week. He stood up, and the man beamed a smile at him, revealing two missing teeth.

'Ah, you must be…' Jemme began, struggling to remember if he had ever actually been introduced to the man.

'Mattrani,' said the man.

'Of course. Monsieur Ledantec has told me that you have been working on a piece for us.'

The man nodded, '*Oui, Monsieur* – I can do much more than painting. Here, I have finished it,' he said, turning behind him to retrieve something from the corridor. He returned, clasping something gently in his rather fleshy hands, before carefully setting it on the floor.

'Here,' he said, indicating the piece and watching them anxiously. Jemme and Ledantec looked at it curiously. It looked a bit like a table, but its proportions were very odd. The top was incredibly thick, and the legs very thin and spindly. There was something strange about the legs too, but Jemme couldn't quite put his finger on it. Their silence seemed to make Mattrani nervous, 'I made it exactly as the drawing you gave me,' he said to Ledantec.

Jemme recalled Ledantec telling him that he thought Mattrani was keen to prove himself, so he rushed to reassure him, 'No, no it's excellent, thank you. Perhaps it's just that I haven't seen the drawing for a while. Maybe I've forgotten what I was expecting it to look like,' he said diplomatically. He looked at the piece again. There wasn't anything wrong with it and the work had been nicely done, but it was just a little…odd. Mattrani fumbled in his pocket,

'Here, Monsieur, look,' he said, producing the plan, on a piece of paper which had become dog-eared and soft. Jemme looked at it and then up at the table in front of him. To give Mattrani his dues, they were exactly the same, and the drawing on the paper itself was an exact replica of a carving from the British Museum. Jemme concluded that it must have just lost something in the transition between mediums. He thanked Mattrani for all his hard work, and turned to Ledantec, about to ask about the trompe l'oeil work. Mattrani, however, looked a little wounded.

'But Monsieur, you haven't seen the best part yet,' he said.

'The best part?'

'Yes – this is the part that took me the longest. It wasn't just me who worked on it either. I told Monsieur Ledantec: I am from a family of craftsmen, I can do more than just paint!'

'So I can see,' said Jemme patiently. He was hoping that Mattrani would reveal the so-called 'best part' soon. He hadn't noticed anything particularly remarkable, but felt a little awkward asking him to point out which bit was better than the others when it was clear he thought it was obvious. Luckily, Mattrani was keen to divulge his crowning achievement.

'I will show you the inside,' he announced proudly, causing Jemme and Ledantec to exchange glances.

He carefully ran his hand around the edge of the tabletop, until he found what he was looking for, and slid his fingers underneath the wood, before lifting the top like a lid. Intrigued, Jemme and Ledantec both leaned forward and peered in, curious as to what had been revealed. Both seemed as surprised as the other to see that the thick top piece of the table had been concealing what appeared to be a golden bowl.

Jemme looked up at Mattrani who was beaming at him again. 'My cousin is a gilder,' he said by way of explanation.

'I see,' said Jemme, warily. 'Just out of interest though, why is it that you've hidden a bowl *inside* the table?'

'A bowl, Monsieur? No, no – it is a basin!'

'Aha.' Jemme paused, 'Well, I'm afraid the same question applies.'

Mattrani's expression turned from one of pride to one of concern, 'Look, look,' he said, pointing at the picture again. 'Here,' he said pointing to the table's legs.

Jemme look of confusion only intensified, but Ledantec started to eye the man as if he was dangerously mad.

'The pipe,' he explained.

Jemme looked at the picture and then at the table. He suddenly realised why the table had looked so strange – a fifth spindly leg sat right underneath the middle. He looked at it again and saw that it too had been gilded. He took a deep breath,

'Look, I'm really not understanding any of this. You've recreated the table from the drawing, but in the process it has acquired a fifth leg and a secret hidden golden bowl – sorry, basin. Maybe you could explain it to me from the beginning?'

'Table? It is not really a table though, Monsieur…' he trailed off and took in the way in which the other two men were looking at him.

'*Bon*, I will talk you through everything. I asked Monsieur Ledantec many questions about this room. It is the hunting room of an Assyrian king, no?'

'Well, I suppose that's one way of looking at it.'

'And this is the throne the king will sit in after his hunt?'

'Again, it's not exactly how I was thinking of it, but I suppose it is, yes.'

'Well, what would be the first thing a king in a hot country would do after coming back from hunting?'

They stared at him blankly, 'Wash his hands?' Ledantec ventured.

'Exactly!' Mattrani said, looking as if he was starting to wonder if they were idiots. 'So, this is the high basin which is next to the king's throne – high enough for him to reach into it when he is sitting in his throne. I know we don't know if it was golden, but it might have been, and anyway I thought it was right that it should be gold for a king. The lid was my invention too – I thought it could protect the basin, and also means it could be used as a table when it's not in use.'

He stopped and looked at them to see if they had taken it all in. Jemme slowly looked at the piece of paper again. Suddenly it all fell into place, and he could see exactly what had happened. The plan had been taken from a completely flat carving, which had made no attempt to represent perspective or depth. It only showed the 'table' face-on and didn't allow a view of the surface. Both he and the carpenter had seen it and assumed it had been a table. However, Mattrani had taken in the strange fifth leg and, no doubt anxious to make a good impression, had thought slightly more creatively and decided the object was a basin. He laughed out loud,

'Well, I didn't realise that I would be getting some gold-leafed plumbing for my first room! Thank you Mattrani. You've done a really good job – my apologies I didn't recognise that straight away, I think there was a bit of a misunderstanding.'

Mattrani returned to beaming, and Ledantec shrugged the whole affair off. After being reassured by everyone that his family was indeed one of talented craftsmen and he was, in fact, capable of a great deal more than painting, Mattrani finally left. As soon as he was out of earshot, Ledantec turned to Jemme, 'I am so sorry about all of that,' he began, 'I should have made sure he understood properly, and checked up on what he was doing.'

'Don't think anything of it,' said Jemme light-heartedly.

'But it was my responsibility to find someone to do the job, and he must have incurred terrible expenses with all this gold leaf nonsense,' Ledantec protested.

'Honestly, don't worry,' said Jemme. 'I'd rather spend the money and have the story to tell. Besides, who else can boast of a golden basin – and a hidden one at that!' he chuckled again.

* * * *

After yet another frosty week with Hil, Jemme couldn't wait to get back to the chateau the following weekend. He was excited to see all the transformations which had occurred since his last visit, and keen to get out of Paris with all its pollution and noise. He always felt better after a weekend of fresh air, home-cooked food and being outdoors, even if it made the trials of living in a big city even more noticeable when he returned. In the week since he'd left, he'd persuaded Ledantec to have a more involved role in the chateau project, and co-opted him into finding a trompe l'oeil artist; he'd spoken extensively with the Professor about his ideas for a writing or alphabet room and he'd asked DD to find him artists for the Babylonian room, as well as making enquiries about the statue in the Louvre himself. He was grateful to have so many helpful and cooperative people around him. It made progress so much easier and more enjoyable too. He was pleased that Ledantec was amenable to having a higher level of involvement too. He foresaw Philby continuing to help him find workers for construction, painting and decorating, whilst Ledantec could help with the more skilled craftsmen. If he needed anyone highly specialised then he could still rely on DD. In this instance he had been lucky and it had transpired that Ledantec had known a trompe l'oeil painter, and had got him to work straight away. It was a perfect set up, as Ledantec would be on-site to explain his own sketches on the walls and how the room was meant to look when it was finished.

He had been a little less lucky with the statue. After revisiting it, he had discovered that it was exactly as he remembered it, and it would be absolutely perfect for the room. However, unfortunately his contact was doubtful that any replicas existed, even after researching the statues' provenance and trying to trace any other objects which had passed through similar channels. Although he had wanted a piece which had a story to tell in its own right, the most important thing was that the piece told the story of Hammurabi, and so he had decided to commission a reproduction. His contact had been able to help out on that front, and assured him that they would get one of their regular artists on the job straight away.

It was therefore with a sense of satisfaction and excitement that he made the journey north on Friday evening. Everything in this area of his life was going exactly as he wanted it to and, in this respect, he couldn't be happier.

His first stop, once he had reached the chateau, was the Assyrian room. As he approached the room he could hear Ledantec's voice, and that of an unknown man. He was pleased that Ledantec had stayed so late to supervise the work, and had a feeling that he was going to prove himself again and again. Feeling slightly silly, he stopped and took a deep breath before he pushed at the door. It opened as if directly within his dream, revealing a tiny, self-contained world inside. An odd sense of déjà vu passed through him as he found himself staring at a scene he had seen a hundred times before. Although the room was unfinished, and Ledantec and his painter friend certainly hadn't featured in his dream, apart from that it was exactly as he had imagined. He stepped forward with a broad smile to greet the two men.

'I can't believe how wonderful this all looks!' he said, shaking his head. He looked around and laughed when he saw the basin – this time in 'table' mode, with its golden fifth leg.

'Is it as you hoped?' asked Ledantec, 'I think it's quite close to the plans we discussed, but then again Mattrani thought what he'd produced was…'

'It's more than I could have hoped for!' said Jemme, shaking the painter's hand and introducing himself. 'It's brilliant!' he said looking around again.

The trompe l'oeil painter, who introduced himself as Faito, laughed, 'If only all clients were as pleased as you are, Monsieur, my job would be a joy!'

Jemme came forward and looked at the work he was completing. From far away it had been obvious that he was highly skilled, but when right up next to them, it became even more obvious just how talented he really was.

'These are fantastic,' said Jemme. 'I could genuinely be fooled into thinking they were really made from stone.'

'Thank you, Monsieur, for a trompe l'oeil artist, to be told he is a master deceiver is the highest compliment!'

'I should imagine it is. This reminds me of my first visit to Venice when I was a boy. I went with the Scouts, and I was fascinated by how things which appeared to be so lifelike could in reality be completely flat.'

'That's what trompe l'oeil is all about, Monsieur, pushing another dimension through the flat and the uninspiring,' agreed Faito.

Jemme smiled, but thought how the artist couldn't possibly know how his words rang true on a different level too. It was an apt description of what he was trying to do with this whole project.

'I was hoping the ceiling would be finished by the time you saw the room for the first time,' said Ledantec, 'but it won't take very long to complete, and you'll be able to see the finished room in its entirety by the time you go back to Paris.'

'Have we already found someone to do it?' asked Jemme.

'Oh, I said I would if that's alright,' said Faito, deftly flicking his brush to create just a hint of shadow. It made the painted stonework pop out, and look exactly as it had when Jemme had seen the real thing in the British Museum. He looked on admiringly.

'Well if *you* wouldn't mind, that would be great.'

They talked for a while longer, and Jemme raised the idea of working on the Babylonian room too. The artist was very receptive to the idea, and, like Ledantec, seemed anxious to work collaboratively with him, which was a sweet relief after some of the artistic temperament Jemme had already been exposed to.

✳ ✳ ✳ ✳

The following day Jemme sketched out further plans for his writing room over breakfast. He still wasn't quite sure what kind of form it should take, and was mindful that it could easily be dull; at the moment all he had come up with were multiple clay tablets and stone steles bearing the different scripts, and he didn't think they would be especially scintillating viewing. It also wouldn't give the immersive experience he was creating with the other rooms. He wanted to step into the room and feel he had entered a different world, rather than feel as if he had entered a room in a museum. It would require some careful thought and perhaps some revision of his philosophy too.

With a flicker of excitement he wondered if the Assyrian room was finished yet. Although it pained him, he realised that he should leave them for as long as possible. He reasoned that the pleasure he would get from seeing it completed would reward his patience. In the meantime there was work to be done on the Babylonian room. He decided to sketch out how he wanted it to look, and thought that he might ask Ledantec to do some sort of a mock up on the walls again. First though, he was going to go and check over the wiring. Last week, Philby had told him that there had been a fault somewhere in that room and the lights wouldn't work. He had offered to find someone to fix the problem, but somewhere along the line, Mattrani had caught wind of things and insisted on helping. Jemme had expressed his preference for a qualified, experienced electrician, but Mattrani had become rather animated about creating some sort of lamp. He had emphasised his craftsman credentials, and carefully described just how many fellow craftsmen there were in his family, as if it was the first time anyone was hearing the news. Mainly to keep him quiet, Jemme said he could work on something, and had all but forgotten about it until he had announced on Saturday that it was almost complete.

Finishing his coffee, Jemme went off to find Philby and discuss the wiring. He was anxious that everything should be in a perfect state of repair before decoration started, and concerned that something had gone wrong already in one of the new rooms. Philby talked him through what they thought had happened and walked him over to the room to show him what the electrician had done to fix it. When they got there Mattrani was looming over the doorway, waiting for them. He grinned broadly,

'I have been expecting you, Monsieur,' he said. With his missing teeth and broad frame, the effect was slightly more menacing than he perhaps realised, and Jemme smiled weakly,

'Oh, of course, your light.'

'Everything is ready for you to see,' he beamed.

'It's inside is it?'

Mattrani nodded vigorously, 'Yes, it is all completely ready – it is even wired in.'

Jemme felt Philby bristle next to him, 'Who wired it in?'

'I did. I couldn't find the electrician. It is fine though, there are many electricians in my family.'

Philby stared daggers at the man, and Jemme felt a slight sense of foreboding creep over him.

'Well, let's have a look shall we?' he said, pushing open the door. Mattrani's handiwork was immediately obvious. In fact, it was inescapable. In a pristine white room it drew all the attention in a rather aggressive way. Jemme stared at it, transfixed.

'What do you think?' asked Mattrani eagerly.

'It's.... it's remarkable,' said Jemme, truthfully. He stared at it some more. Of all the things he had been expecting, this did certainly not feature. He had thought that perhaps Mattrani might present him with some strange lampshade, with the same sort of pride as cat who had recently dragged in a bird, but this was completely different.

'It's the hanging gardens of Babylon,' Mattrani announced when no one had spoken for a while.

'Yes…yes, I can see that,' said Jemme looking up at the installation. He truly did not know what to make of it. It was huge to start with, a good three feet by four feet. It had been clad in imitation stone with what appeared to be artificial foliage stuck, or glued, to it. He had created tiny staircases running between the different tiers and a couple of small figurines, mounting the stairs, kept the scale of the piece. Jemme didn't know whether to burst out laughing or continue to stare in wonder at the piece. It was bizarre, but in a way, brilliant.

Eventually he asked where the lighting element came in.

'Ah, I will show you. They would have lit the hanging gardens with braziers – correct?'

'Yes, I suppose they would have done,' said Jemme cautiously.

'Well, look,' he said, pointing. There were small slits cut into the stone cladding which could barely be seen when the light was off, but which – presumably – gave the effect of burning torches when turned on.

'Oh, um, yes, I see,' he said. He stole a sideways glance at Philby who was staring stonily at what he clearly considered to be a monstrosity.

'Well, I suppose we'd better see it on then,' he said, realising that was clearly what Mattrani was waiting for. Mattrani was already hovering excitedly by the light switch waiting for his big moment.

After a dramatic pause, he flicked the switch and said 'Voila!' They all looked up, waiting for the garden to spring to life. Unfortunately it sprang into life a little too much. With a large bang and a flicker of blue, the lights went out in the room and in the corridor behind them, too. A moment later, the gardens started smoking and tiny flames crept out through the burning brazier slits. Mattrani and Jemme both looked up at it in alarm. Jemme turned to find Philby, but he had already disappeared, plodding back in moments later with a fire extinguisher in one hand. He calmly doused Mattrani's creation in foam until the flames had disappeared. When everything had died down, Mattrani looked up in horror at his smouldering, foamy work of art.

'We'll need to redo the wiring now,' said Philby bitterly, and disappeared to replace the fire extinguisher.

Jemme stood for a moment longer, offered his condolences to Mattrani, and then excused himself, worried that he might burst out into laughter. It wasn't until he was safely back in the library that he exhaled slowly, and allowed himself a chuckle. The whole incident had been slightly ridiculous, from the over the top, bizarre chandelier to its untimely ending. He didn't know who had looked more horrified – Philby when he had seen it, or Mattrani when he had seen it go up in flames. He smiled again to himself, and wondered if any of Mattrani's family had worked on this particular marvel. As he thought about the incident, and considered what he would like to replace the feature, he did realise one thing: the lighting feature would have to be integrative somehow. Maybe not in such an over-the-top way as this one had been, but it would have to be carefully designed to fit it with whichever room it was in. If the rooms were to be microcosms of ancient worlds, then it would be jarring to suddenly come across a modern feature, and it would shatter the whole illusion. Each would have to be different, according to whichever room it was in, but it would have to be considered as part of the design technique.

By the time he headed back to Paris, he felt he'd had a weekend full of drama and success. It had been eventful, but ultimately rewarding, and he couldn't wait to return in a week's time.

Chapter Twenty-Seven

Sitting at his desk one afternoon that week, Jemme couldn't help but smile as he remembered Mattrani's horrified look as his majestic hanging gardens smoked and smouldered. He felt like the development of the chateau was really becoming a story in itself. He had always hoped that this would be the case, and he would be able to add his own chapters to the building's long history. He hadn't imagined these stories being so vital and personal though, and he could already imagine himself retelling some of them years down the line as he sat in the beautifully finished chateau.

When he thought of the chateau, he felt like he could see his future stretching out in front of him, clearly defined and full of promise. Learning and excitement were written through it, and a sense of purpose defined it. It was as if the chateau was the central point around which everything revolved. All the dreaming and ephemeral knowledge he had been building suddenly had a use and focus. It made him feel alive, and as if he understood life perfectly. The only thing that troubled him was Hil. Whilst the chateau filled him with understanding, it seemed to confuse her. It made increasingly less sense to her life, and clouded her vision of the future. For all that it made him firm and confident in his choices, it seemed to shake her in hers and unravel her resolve. He could see how unhappy it was making her, and feel how far it was driving them apart. He had no idea how to resolve it though. Everything he tried either seemed to make it worse or seemed only to be a temporary solution. He had thought that the weekend there with their friends would be a nice gesture, but it only seemed to have made the most superficial of differences. He wondered whether he hadn't made enough effort, and was even beginning to feel a little guilty when DD interrupted his thoughts.

'I have the auction brochures you wanted to look at, Sir,' he said, laying three glossy magazines down in front of Jemme.

Jemme pushed everything to the back of his mind, half-promising himself that he would think about it all later. He pulled one of the magazines towards himself and opened it enthusiastically.

'Was there anything in particular, you were looking for, Sir?' asked DD.

'Not really, I had a tip off from a client that there were a couple of big sales coming up, so I wanted to see what was around,' said Jemme, flicking through the pages and drinking in the pictures.

'I've heard that there are a few estates for sale, Sir,' said DD.

'Yes, another batch of France's grand old families selling off the silverware no doubt,' said Jemme absent-mindedly.

'Sir?' said DD looking perturbed.

Jemme looked up, 'I don't mean to sound insensitive, DD, but you know what these people are like! It's hard to feel sorry for them. They isolate themselves from the rest of the country and act as if it's still the heyday of the monarchy. I met enough of them whilst I was looking for the chateau – fussing over arcane etiquette whilst the plaster peels around them.'

'It is difficult to uphold tradition and acclimatise to a new world,' said DD, pragmatically.

'Well, that's true enough I suppose and I expect, in fact I know, that your tolerance for people like that is much higher than mine. My problem is that they don't even try to acclimatise. They're far too haughty. They don't make life easy for themselves and so I have no qualms whatsoever in buying up their treasures when they eventually have to sell them. Like this one!' he said, pointing at a piece half-way down the page. 'Now, this looks interesting.'

'Sir?' said DD peering over stiffly.

He looked at the oil painting Jemme was pointing to. It showed a Parisian street, with Sacré Couer just visible behind the parade of shops with their painted shutters. There was a certain crudeness to the scene, and the brushwork and the colours were very muted.

'It's not your usual style, Sir,' observed DD.

'No, no it's not at all,' agreed Jemme. 'I don't know why, but there's something compelling about it. *La Rue Norvins à Montmartre*,' he read. 'Utrillo,' he added. 'I don't even know if I've heard of him.'

'When was it painted, Sir?' asked DD blandly, evidently not nearly as interested as Jemme.

'1910,' Jemme said, reading the small section of text next to the printed picture. 'I know that was an interesting period for art in Montmartre, but I don't know much about it.' He stared at the painting for a while longer.

'I wonder where I could put it...?' he murmured out loud.

'Sir?' DD said with a note of concern in his voice.

'Oh, it's alright, DD, I can tell you don't like it. I'm just very drawn to it, that's all. I'm going to have a think about it this evening.'

For the rest of the day, whenever he had a spare moment, Jemme found his mind wandering back to the Utrillo painting. He completely forgot his resolve to think about Hil, and instead idly imagined the painting hanging on various walls of both the Paris flat and the chateau. He couldn't picture it anywhere, yet he was reluctant to let go of it and the idea of owning it.

He ended up working much later than he had intended, and arrived home after Hil had already eaten.

'I made some supper for you, too,' she said a little sadly, as she greeted him.

'Did you? That was nice of you!' said Jemme cheerfully as he gave her a kiss on the cheek. 'Good job too – I'm starving!'

'So was I, I waited for you for quite a while, but…' she trailed off.

Jemme waved her comment aside, 'Don't be silly, I wasn't expecting you to wait for me!'

'I know, I just thought it would be nice if we could…' Hil began, but Jemme was already in the kitchen, plating himself up some food, from the oven dish Hil had covered with tin foil.

He came back into the dining room and joined her at the table, 'This smells delicious sweetheart, thank you – is it a new recipe?'

Hil nodded, 'I thought I'd make a bit of an effort.'

'Well it certainly tastes like you have. You know, I was thinking – I might not head up to the chateau straight away.'

'Oh?' Hil sat up and a smile quickly flicked across her face.

'Well, I mean I'll still go up on the Saturday of course, but there's a rather exciting auction happening in Paris on the Friday evening, so I thought I might stick around for that.'

'Oh,' said Hil again.

'Would you like to come?' asked Jemme.

'To the auction, or to the chateau?'

'Both of course!'

'I'll see,' said Hil flatly.

'Alright,' said Jemme, feeling slightly exasperated. *She's so moody the whole time*, he thought to himself.

The next morning found Jemme in a good mood. Before he had gone to bed he had resolved to buy the painting, and worry about where it would go later on. However, when he had woken up, he had begun to think about the role of more modern works in the chateau. It had always been his intention to include pieces which post-dated the chateau, but it felt such a long way off he hadn't begun to think about how they would fit. They were a necessary part of the chateau's story; he just needed to work out which part they were.

By the time he had arrived at work, he was wondering if the painting could be the starting point for this. It didn't mean he had to commit himself to anything; if he changed his mind or direction later on, he would only have to relocate one painting after all. Once DD had finished the morning's briefing with him, he asked him if he could investigate a good book about turn of the century paintings from Montmartre. He didn't even know if there was a proper term for the movement, or even if there was a movement at all, so he decided to call it the *école Monmartre*. He hoped that DD would be able to find a book by Thursday afternoon so that he could flick through it before the auction but, true to form, when he returned from lunch, a brown paper bag sat on his desk.

Feeling a familiar rush of excitement, Jemme tipped it up and slid out a slim paperback. Its cover bore a painting similar in colour and technique to the one which he had found so enticing earlier. He carefully began to leaf through the book. It was obviously meant for academics rather than casual art fans, and each page was a block of tiny black text. He tried to skim read it, and picked out a few familiar names – Chagall, Modigliani ... but that was about it. Sadly he realised that he was going to have to sit down and read the book properly. He returned it to its bag, and turned his attention back to the spreadsheets he had been working on that morning.

By Friday lunchtime he had made a small amount of progress on the book, but he felt like Thor drinking the ocean. Every time he thought he had established something, or understood, suddenly he would come across something he realised he knew nothing about. He felt mired in a sea of cross references and, although it had initially been frustrating, he soon became positive again. This was just another opportunity to learn about a new area. He didn't have to discover everything before the auction; the painting could be his starting point for this too.

Normally he didn't worry too much about what time he finished work, but today he felt particularly motivated to finish early. He focussed on his work, and the afternoon sailed past. By seven he had finished for the day and disappeared into his en-suite bathroom to freshen up. He had worn one of his favourite suits with a crisp white shirt underneath and a silk Hermès tie. He straightened his cufflinks and smoothed down his hair in the mirror. Satisfied, he left the office, picking up his overcoat and the auction catalogue on the way back through.

'Good luck, Sir,' said DD sombrely as he walked past his desk.

'Thank you,' Jemme replied, then laughed when he saw DD's grave face, 'It's alright – if I win it I won't bring it into the office.'

DD's nostrils flared a fraction, but he didn't say anything.

Going down the stairs and heading to the famous Drouot auction house in the 9th Arrondissement, he felt a frisson of excitement. It had been a while since he had been to an auction for the fun of it. There was a time when he and Hil would go together, and make an evening of it. Then he began to see them as a necessary means of procurement and was grateful when DD went with a list for him. It was nice to be going along as if it was an occasion. He wished Hil had been a bit more enthusiastic about it. He hadn't heard from her all day, and so had assumed that she had decided against coming. It was a shame, especially as it meant he probably wouldn't see her all weekend now – especially not if he wanted to make an early start for the chateau on Saturday morning. Trying to ignore the tiny prick of resentment, he determined not to let it ruin his evening.

He strolled along to rue Drouot, enjoying the walk. It had been so long since he had spent time in Paris at the weekend, he had forgotten what it felt like. There was an excitement in the air that couldn't quite be described. It was a sense of anticipation and expectation, as candles were lit on restaurant tables, opera-goers queued at box offices, and holiday-makers clutching maps looked, wide-eyed, at their surroundings. He cheerfully made his way amongst them, until the imposing façade of the Hôtel Drouot came into view. Although he wasn't a particular fan of the building's modern incarnation, seeing it lit up and other people also dressed for the occasion lifted his heart. He made his way inside, to find the foyer thronged with Paris's collecting elite. There were some antique dealers and art-loving clients he recognised, and some faces he knew but couldn't quite place. One of the dealers he knew spotted him, and walked over,

'Monsieur Mafeze!'

'Hello, Jacques, how are you?'

'Well thank you, Monsieur. Quite a good turn out this evening, *non*?'

Jemme looked around him, 'I'll say there is. Is there a particular item everyone's after?'

Jacques shrugged emphatically, 'All of them, Monsieur! It is rare to have more than one of the *grandes familles* selling off their estates at once, and tonight there will be a wealth of treasures – many of them probably haven't been seen in public for at least a hundred years.'

'I suppose not,' said Jemme, 'how many families are selling off their estates this evening?'

Jacques shrugged again, this time a little more lugubriously, 'Ah Monsieur, too many. *La république* has treated some of her oldest families unkindly.'

Jemme decided to keep his opinions to himself, and wished Jacques good luck before heading off to find the room in which his sale was taking place. Although it wasn't due to start for another half an hour, the room was just as bustling as the foyer had been, and he had to take a seat near the back. After exchanging pleasantries with the people sitting either side of him, he settled in and read through the catalogue. Before long a hush settled over the room, and he looked up to see the auctioneer enter. The thin wiry man took to the podium and welcomed everyone to the evening's sale. He spoke with the quiet assurance of one who was used to commanding respect. The first couple of pieces sold for much more than their reserves, yet the man remained completely composed and didn't show any sign of the ripples of excitement passing through the room. The next piece sold for five times its estimated price, yet the auctioneer merely slid his glasses back up his nose and neatly banged his gavel. By the time the Utrillo painting came up, the room was filled with excited chatter. The auctioneer looked disapprovingly at the crowd, who, chastened, fell back into respectful silence.

'Maurice Utrillo, an oil on board painting, c.1910,' said the auctioneer. Jemme felt his pulse quicken. He shifted in his seat and sat upright. Old memories of past auctions floated up into his mind, and he smiled to himself as he remembered some favourite victories. He sat, calmly biding his time, as the auctioneer worked his way up and various people withdrew from the bidding. Within a short space of time, it had become a bidding war between four people – three at the front he couldn't see and a rather ruddy-faced man some way to his left. Still Jemme kept his hand down.

He subtly looked over and took in the ruddy-faced man. He could instantly tell that he was nervous; the man was too quick to bid for a start. The auctioneer would name a price and the man's hand would shoot up. He would repeat the price several times, looking around the room and be on the point of banging his gavel when one of the three at the front would laconically raise a hand. The man would have shifted forward to the front of his seat in excitement and would then sink back in disappointment before instantly raising his hand, as soon as the auctioneer named his next price.

Jemme shook his head to himself – he wouldn't last long. Sure enough, the man was soon permanently sitting back in disappointment, unable to raise his hand any more. The three at the front slowed the pace down, each leaving their bid until the last possible moment. Once one of them withdrew, Jemme decided it was time to step in. He judged his moment and raised a hand. There was a murmur of excitement at the new bidder. Jemme concentrated hard, and did not allow himself to bid too soon. The price gradually rose, yet each remained resolute in their bids. Despite the adrenaline auctions provoked in him, Jemme found them oddly relaxing. He was able to focus entirely on the task at hand and his desire to succeed at it. It was this ability which had driven his most successful deals at the bank, and it had never let him down yet. He was enjoying not being able to see his opponents -- it added an extra level to the cHallenge.

The bidding continued to rise until it evidently became too much for one contender. This was Jemme's favourite part of the whole process: a war of nerves between two people. He calmed the butterflies fluttering in his stomach, and did not allow himself to bid until the last possible moment, a procedure he called cold shoulder. Usually this flustered his opponents and deterred them, although without being able to see, it was hard to tell if this was working. In fact, it didn't seem to be. Every time he paused, his opponent paused for a fraction of a second longer. Every time he quickened his pace, his opponent would be even faster on the draw. *Whoever he is, he really knows what he's doing,* Jemme thought. His opponent continued, relentlessly teasing out the pauses and driving bidding down to the wire. Jemme felt his composure falter for a moment, then he recovered himself, and realised that he was amused by the game more than anything. He had found a worthy adversary, and he was enjoying the competition. Eventually he realised that the mystery bidder was not going to back down, and, despite having the stamina to continue all evening, he just didn't want the painting that much. It had been a spur-of-the-moment choice and was not worth spending a small fortune on. He conceded defeat, and smilingly shook his head when the auctioneer offered him the next bid. The auctioneer offered again, extending the offer to the room before finally bringing down his hammer to a smattering of applause.

Jemme stretched out in his chair. *Well*, he thought to himself, *that's a pity, but whoever won that fully earned it.*

He watched the rest of the sale with interest, waiting until it ended and he would be able to shake the hand of the man who outbid him. Once the auctioneer had brought his gavel down for the final time, and the crowd began to filter out, Jemme made his way to the front rows. He recognised a few dealers he had bought from before, and wondered if any of them were the new owners of the painting. He sized them up – although they were all highly competent, they had never shown any signs of fire in their dealings with him. To the best of Jemme's knowledge, they didn't have the grit or determination that was needed to win an auction such as the one he had just lost.

He decided it would be easiest just to ask the auctioneer. Turning to speak to him, he couldn't help but be struck by the beauty of the woman who was talking animatedly to him. She stood on high heels, which made her already long legs seem even longer. She obviously took care of her appearance and was expensively dressed in clothes which perfectly accessorised her slim curves. Dark, glossy hair tumbled around her shoulders and accentuated the creaminess of her flawless skin. She evidently knew the auctioneer well, and touched him on the shoulder from time to time as they spoke. Jemme walked over and stood patiently next to the auctioneer, waiting for his chance to speak with him. The woman noticed him and flashed him a quick smile, looking him directly in the eyes. Jemme faltered slightly before smiling back. As he waited he tried to think about the sale, but he kept finding himself thinking about how uncommonly piercing the woman's blue eyes had been and how unusually pillowy her lips were. He wasn't necessarily attracted to her, but he felt compelled to look at her, in much the same way he had been drawn to the painting when he first saw it. *She is extraordinarily beautiful, and I appreciate things of great beauty*, he reasoned with himself – *there's no need to feel guilty.*

The woman finished talking to the auctioneer, and flashed Jemme another winning smile.

'I'm sorry,' she said in velvety tones, 'I mustn't keep Monsieur Clogerard all to myself.'

'My dear, I always have time for you,' said the auctioneer smiling at her in an avuncular fashion.

'Oh, I – I don't mean to interrupt,' said Jemme, 'I was just hoping to ask you a quick question about the Utrillo painting.'

Both of them looked at him with interest.

'Yes, Monsieur?' asked the auctioneer, peering at him over the top of his half-moon glasses. 'Ah, you were bidding, *non*?'

'Yes, I was actually, I-'

'And now you want to know who won?' continued the auctioneer as if Jemme hadn't spoken.

'Well, yes, I did, but –' Jemme looked around at the rapidly emptying room, 'I think I must have missed him.'

The auctioneer's serious face twitched with the hint of a smile.

'Ah Monsieur, you are in luck. I can introduce you right now.'

Jemme raised his eyebrows, 'Excellent!' he looked around himself again in slight confusion – there were now very few people left in the room and he was almost certain none of them was the winner.

He turned back to see the woman smiling at him,

'Burbona,' she said, gracefully extending a hand.

'I think, Monsieur, you have just met your match,' said the auctioneer.

Jemme continued to look confused for a fraction of a second before realisation dawned and he felt his face flush, 'I'm so sorry – I didn't mean, I didn't realise, I mean I just assumed….' Burbona laughed huskily.

'Don't look so flustered, Monsieur…?'

'Mafeze,' Jemme said, earnestly shaking her hand, 'Jemme,' he added.

'Well, Jemme, I am delighted to meet my bidding rival. I was impressed!'

'Likewise,' said Jemme, with what he hoped was a winning smile, but feared was a leer.

'I hope you're not too bitter about the painting,' Burbona said.

'Oh goodness no,' said Jemme, a little too quickly. 'Well, what I mean is that it was a rather spontaneous decision on my part. It's not the style or era I usually go for at all. There was just something I liked about it, that's all.'

'I can understand that,' said Burbona. She spoke with the confidence of someone utterly at ease, and filled with self-assurance.

'So you are a regular auction goer, then, Jemme?' she asked.

'Reasonably regular,' said Jemme, flushing slightly when she said his name. 'It's been a while since I've been to a sale actually. There's usually someone who goes on my behalf. Like I said, I was just intrigued by this piece, and thought

I'd come along.' Burbona listened to him intently, but Jemme felt as if her gaze went right through him. He had a stern word with himself and tried to regain his composure.

'Do you know much about this particular era? I tried to read up a little on it, but I have to confess, I found it difficult to know where to start.'

'I expect you'll find that Burbona knows much about many eras,' said the auctioneer, 'but if you'll excuse me, I will leave you two to become acquainted. I must go and tend to some paperwork.'

Jemme shook his hand and thanked him for an exciting sale, whilst Burbona kissed him on both cheeks, and told him to send her love to his wife.

Once he had left, Burbona tossed her hair and laughed, 'Monsieur was being far too generous,' she said. 'I spread myself thinly.'

'Are you a collector?' asked Jemme.

Burbona smiled enigmatically, 'Of sorts, I suppose. Now tell me about you, Jemme. If not Utrillo, what is it you usually buy?'

Jemme felt his confidence return as he described the chateau, its various noble rooms and the pieces he had been collecting for it so far. He left out anything to do with his dream, and focussed instead on the art, statuary and furnishings he had been slowly amassing. Burbona listened intently, occasionally nodding in recognition, or raising her eyebrows in interest.

'What a fascinating project,' she said when he had finished. 'I think I might be able to help you out.' She reached into her handbag and drew out a slender, crocodile-skin calling-card box, which opened with a snap. She handed over a card to Jemme who read it and laughed.

'You certainly have a lot of surnames!'

Burbona smiled, 'I suppose I've been collecting those as well.'

Jemme laughed again. He couldn't help but feel that she was being modest though. He had recognised several names on the card, and was sure that they belonged to the *grande familles* who were still held in such hushed regard by people such as Jacques.

'I know most of Paris's auctioneers,' said Burbona, 'and I tend to know when the big sales like this are happening some time before they are announced, and so I could let you know when pieces are coming up which I think would be of interest to you.'

'That would be amazing,' said Jemme, genuinely. 'How is it that you know about the approaching lots before they've been announced though? I thought I was quite well connected, but it seems I'm a bit of an amateur!'

Burbona smiled enigmatically again, 'I suppose I know people on both sides of the sale,' she said. 'Sometimes,' she added, 'it's possible to remove an item from a sale for a client, before it's even been announced.'

Jemme felt hungry for the titbit that was being dangled in front of him, 'Really?' he asked casually.

Burbona smiled, 'Of course. We shall have dinner one night next week. I can get a more thorough idea for what it is you want.'

Jemme admired her forthrightness; it wasn't so much a question as a command. He wondered if he should mention the fact that he was married. 'My wife has never much liked auctions,' he said clumsily, and then winced to himself.

Burbona didn't react at all. 'I shall call you to confirm,' she said and looked expectantly at Jemme, who paused for a moment before realising what was expected of him, and fished in his jacket pocket for his own card.

Burbona saw someone else she knew and bade Jemme farewell, kissing him on both cheeks. Jemme walked home with a spring in his step. All in all it had been a successful evening, despite the fact he had lost the painting. He arrived home pleased to see the lights were on.

'Hello darling, I was hoping you'd be in,' he said opening the door. Hil looked up from the sofa and offered him a wan smile.

'Are those new clothes?' Jemme asked, not recognising the shapeless garments his wife was draped in.

'No. They're very old pyjamas. They're comfortable,' said Hil.

'Oh. Good,' said Jemme cheerfully. He headed over to the sofa and planted a kiss on Hil's cheek.

'You look a little pale my love, are you feeling alright?'

'I'm fine,' said Hil narrowing her eyes slightly, 'I'm just not wearing any make up.'

'Have you had a nice evening?' asked Jemme, sensing danger and changing the subject quickly.

'I suppose,' Hil replied flatly.

'What are you reading?' Jemme asked, tipping his head to see the cover of Hil's book.

'A friend lent it to me. It's about women who leave it too late and end up childless,' said Hil. Her words hung in the air meaningfully, and Jemme realised another rapid subject change was in order if he wanted to avoid another heavy conversation, in which Hil would expect things he couldn't promise.

'The auction was great fun. You really missed out!' he said.

Hil stared stonily at him and didn't say anything.

'The bidding for the painting I wanted was particularly exciting,' he said. 'Quite thrilling, actually. But listen to this! I lost! I can't even remember the last time that happened!' Hil remained silent, and Jemme realised he was going to have to carry the conversation, 'Well, anyway, I didn't mind,' he said, 'because it meant that I met the most fascinating woman. She gave me her card and we're going for dinner next week,' he handed the card to Hil who glanced at it fleetingly before putting it down on the table next to her.

'Did you see how many surnames she had?!' Jemme continued, unabated. 'I think she's a proper aristocrat, and member of the old guard. She wasn't at all stuck up though – I mean, she had an air of class to her, without a doubt, but she wasn't so far removed from reality as some of them are. In fact, completely the opposite! She seems to be right in the middle of the art world – I get the impression she knows anyone who matters. She's going to keep an eye out for me, and if there are any lots she thinks I'll like, she'll let me know about them before they're even published in the auction catalogue! How brilliant is that?! I've always known that there was an upper echelon of buying that I couldn't get into – a properly closed circle, and this is finally my chance!'

He paused. In all of that time Hil had said nothing. 'Isn't that great?' he said, trying to elicit some kind of response.

'Great,' repeated Hil unconvincingly. 'Was there anything else?'

'Anything else? Well not really, I was just chatting.'

Hil rose, 'In that case I'm going to bed to finish my book,' she said.

Once she had left, Jemme sat down heavily in the spot she had just vacated. It was hard not to feel like she had brought down his evening. He had arrived home filled with enthusiasm and buoyed up with excitement. Hil hadn't even made an effort to share in any of that, and had done her best to dampen the mood. He sighed and looked over to the coffee table at the card she had discarded. He picked it up, put it back in his pocket and smiled. Something exciting was definitely on the horizon.

* * * *

'How did the auction go, Sir?' DD asked at work the next Monday.

'Well, thank you, DD, very well indeed,' Jemme replied energetically.

DD looked mildly aggrieved, 'I see.'

'I mean, I didn't actually win the painting,' Jemme said. DD maintained a straight face, but Jemme could sense his relief.

'It was very interesting, though,' Jemme added, 'and I met someone particularly amazing,' he handed the card over and DD read it carefully.

'Have you ever heard of her?' he asked.

'Certainly,' said DD. 'She is a guaranteed presence at the most prestigious auctions and I even know her by sight. I have never had the pleasure of making her acquaintance, though.'

'Well I met her last night,' said Jemme.

DD raised one eyebrow slightly, 'A most interesting woman, I don't doubt, Sir.'

'Interesting indeed. I'm meeting her for dinner this week. I think she could prove a real asset during our acquisitions. Not that anyone could replace you, of course,' Jemme added quickly.

DD inclined his head slightly in recognition. 'And how was the chateau this weekend, Sir?' he asked.

'Good, thank you,' said Jemme. 'Everything's really coming along nicely. They've taken on a new girl in the kitchen too – Florence. She's a friend of Aude's, and Marguerite was really enjoying being able to boss both of them around. The girl seemed perfectly capable, but I must have heard Marguerite complain about her a dozen times. I think she was secretly enjoying the role of hard-done-by housekeeper.'

'An astute observation,' said DD.

They settled down for their morning briefing and Jemme tried to pay attention and stop himself from wondering how that week's dinner would turn out. He forced himself to focus and worked steadily all day, until a phone call interrupted the afternoon.

'Hello Jemme,' said a familiarly sultry voice.

'Burbona?' asked Jemme.

'Are you free tomorrow evening?' Burbona asked without clarifying who she was.

'Yes, I think so – I'll have to check, but...'

'Good. Eight o'clock at La Tour d'Argent,' said Burbona. She paused for long enough to ensure that Jemme had heard, and then hung up.

Jemme slowly put down the receiver and stared at it for a moment. He smiled. He had never encountered anyone – even amongst his most bullish clients – who was so direct. The only ones who came close were brash and loud, salesmen by nature and graceless in their manner. Burbona was obviously used to getting what she wanted. Jemme wondered how she could possibly have obtained reservations at one of Paris's most exclusive restaurants, at such short notice. He had sometimes waited months to take clients there, despite his friendship with Claude Terraille, the owner; he wondered if perhaps it was a long-standing reservation, but someone had dropped out at the last minute. If that was the case, then he only admired her audacity in filling the gap so smoothly.

He wore his favourite suit again the next morning, and took a couple of ties with him so that he would have a choice if he changed his mind that afternoon. The day flew by; if nothing else he was excited by the prospect of eating at the Tour d'Argent. It felt like a truly indulgent mid-week treat. He didn't allow it to distract him though, and was as diligent as ever in his afternoon's work. By seven he had finished, and was preparing his notes for the next morning. He made his way to the en-suite bathroom again, checked his appearance, and, satisfied, headed out. He noticed the book DD had bought on one of his shelves, and so slipped it into his jacket pocket – it would provide a good talking point if conversation dried up.

He made his way to the 5th Arondissement, trying to remember what had been his favourite dish the last time he had eaten there. Arriving at the famous restaurant he made his way inside and stopped at the reservations desk.

'I'm meant to be meeting someone,' he said to the Maître d'.

'What is your name, Sir?' asked the man imperiously.

'Jemme Mafeze.'

Suddenly the man's countenance changed. He smiled, '*Ah, Monsieur Mafeze, bienvenu!*' He took Jemme's coat and ushered him towards a table in one swift movement. He pulled out a chair at one of the best tables in the room, and Jemme sat down. He looked around and realised that he was the first to arrive.'

'Is–' he began, looking at the empty chair opposite him.

'*Non, Monsieur*, she is not here yet. Would you like some wine whilst you wait?'

Jemme nodded, wondering how, if Burbona wasn't there yet, the man knew both who he was and with whom he was dining.

Some ten minutes later, Burbona arrived. She was wearing high heels and a fitted dress with a string of delicate pearls around her neck. She made her way over to him, smiling. 'She's obviously used to making an entrance,' Jemme thought to himself.

She sat down opposite him, in the chair which had just been pulled out for her.

'How nice to see you again, Jemme,' she said. 'I'm really looking forward to hearing your plans and helping work out how I fit into them.

Chapter Twenty-Eight

Jemme shifted nervously in his seat. He forced himself to try and relax a little, but everything was conspiring to unsettle him – Burbona's unbroken stare, his uncomfortable chair, even the refined nature of his surroundings. For the first time in a long time, he found himself struggling to think of something to say. Burbona looked at him expectantly, and he looked around the room for inspiration. Suddenly his eyes alighted on a curious contraption which sat, gleaming on a small table towards the edge of the restaurant. It had a small wheel on top of a large, screw-like shaft, which led down to a domed section. It had been polished to high sheen, but it didn't seem to be an object used for decoration. Seizing the opportunity to start a conversation Jemme nodded towards the object,

'What do you reckon that strange thing could be for?' he asked.

Burbona followed his gaze and saw the machine. A flicker of confusion passed over her face, 'The press?' she asked.

'It does look like a press, doesn't it,' said Jemme.

'Of course. That's the machine for *canard à la presse*,' said Burbona, looking slightly confused again.

Jemme's newly-gained confidence began to falter again, 'Oh, yes, *canard…*' he began and trailed off, feeling highly embarrassed. He had no idea what the thing was, but felt as if he should.

Burbona looked at him in mild puzzlement for a moment longer before understanding the situation. She tossed her silky hair around her shoulders and laughed girlishly,

'I can't believe you have never had *canard à la presse*!' she exclaimed, 'This restaurant is famous for it!'

'I suppose I probably don't come here as often as you,' Jemme muttered.

Burbona smiled teasingly at him, 'Well, in that case we must order you a *canard*!' She flicked her eyes away from the table, and instantly caught a waiter's attention. She looked at the machine, and the man nodded his understanding. Moments later he approached the table with various bits of odd-looking cutlery and started making a fuss, setting them out.

'Just one please,' said Burbona, 'I'll have a *Niçoise*.'

Jemme looked at her. He still had no idea what he was letting himself in for, and felt like he was being abandoned.

Burbona laughed at him again, 'Well, you can't expect me to eat the duck twice in the same week,' she said.

'No. Of course not,' said Jemme, hoping that things would start to explain themselves very soon.

After a while, the same waiter reappeared, carrying a small, cloth-covered side table. He set it down next to them and another waiter, wearing gloves, placed a small machine on top of it. Without any finger prints, the burnished bronze shone furiously and Jemme stared at it with a mild sense of apprehension. It looked similar to the machine he had first spotted, but this one was slightly more ornate, and stood on four little bronze duck feet. There was apparently no escaping the fact that duck would feature at some point in the evening.

Burbona looked questioningly at Jemme, who still refused to back down and admit that he didn't know what was going on. He returned her gaze and smiled, wondering if they were both playing the same game. The waiter returned with Burbona's meal; sitting in the middle of an exceptionally large plate only made it look even smaller. Still, Jemme found himself looking slightly enviously at the pitiful collection of leaves – at least he knew what they were.

The waiter returned again, bearing a domed dish and several jugs. He placed them down on the table and began turning the wheel on the device so that the top rose up the shaft. He deftly lifted the dome from the platter he had been carrying and used a pair of tongs to flip whatever had been in there into the press, turning the wheel in the opposite direction and bringing the lid down again. Jemme had been attempting to appear disinterested throughout the whole process, and, maddeningly, couldn't see what was now inside the press. The waiter continued to turn the wheel, becoming slower when whatever he was pressing offered greater resistance. Soon a trickle of liquid began to flow out of a small spout at the bottom and straight into a *saucier*. Eventually he could turn the handle no longer, and proceeded to pour from the various jugs he had brought with him, carefully stirring their contents into the saucier. As he did so, another waiter appeared with a plate bearing a sliced duck breast and some artfully arranged vegetables. He placed it down in front of Jemme, and the first waiter poured over the contents of the saucier. They both disappeared, leaving Jemme to contemplate his supper with a slight air of scepticism. He was somewhat disappointed that all that fuss and intrigue had just lead to a sauce.

'Well, *bon appetit*, I suppose,' he said, tackling the duck breast. As soon as he bit into his first forkful he understood completely, and couldn't help letting out an appreciative noise.

'Ok, Burbona, you win. What is this?! It's one of the best things I've ever eaten,'

Burbona smiled sweetly, 'Well I do love winning, but I do also like seeing someone enjoy one of Paris's best dishes, so I'll relent. This is one of the most famous dishes in the whole city. It has been served here for over a hundred years.'

'But it's just duck,'

Burbona laughed again, 'Come on, Jemme, you've tasted it. It's not "just duck." To start with, it's a specially chosen duck. They're mostly taken from Rouen where they're plump, then, they're roasted in the kitchens here.'

'So what's in the press?'

'Everything except the legs and the breast. Think how juicy a roasted duck is. They don't completely finish the roasting job – they take it out of the oven just before, so it's at its moistest and most tasty. After they've taken off the legs and breast, they put the whole of the rest of it in the press. Think about all those beautiful cooking juices, slowly being squeezed out. That's why the sauce tastes so good.'

'But what else is in it?'

Burbona shrugged slightly and dabbed at her mouth with a napkin. 'I can't tell you all their secrets. Butter and cognac are pretty obvious though. Sometimes they add Madeira, sometimes Port. If you're feeling especially indulgent, sometimes they even add foie gras. It's always poured over the sliced breast like that and served. They're preparing the rest of it in the kitchen right now.'

'The rest of it?'

'They broil the legs; you'll be having them as the next course.'

Jemme couldn't help feeling like a complete novice. Although he had dined in some of the world's best restaurants, whilst he was with Burbona here he felt like a small boy who had left his village and seen the city for the first time.

'Now, tell me more about the chateau,' she said. 'Which room is next in your plan?'

'It's a good question,' said Jemme. 'To be honest, there's not really any rhyme or reason to it – it's almost a little haphazard. I tend to start a new room when I've seen something particularly inspiring for it. Sometimes DD will find a really interesting piece at an auction, and then it will take me in a completely new direction.'

'DD?'

'Dieter Dietz. I don't think I ever call him by his full name though. He's my second-in-command, I guess. I would be completely lost without him. He runs a tight ship at the bank, and helps in almost every area of my life. He was invaluable when we were looking for the chateau and I could never have furnished it without him. He's one of those rare types who just seems to be able to make things happen. I couldn't even begin to count the number of times something has looked impossible, only for DD to fix it as if it was the most natural thing in the world.'

'You are certainly loyal to your employees,' said Burbona.

'Well I suppose so, but he's so much more than that. Like I said, I would be lost without him,' Jemme paused, 'But, returning to your original question, I just don't know. If I had won that painting the other day, then I might have created some kind of *École Montmartre* section to the chateau, but as the better woman won, then I guess the next room will depend on which piece I come across next. I've been thinking recently about the lack of sculpture in the chateau. For all the paintings on the walls and rugs on the floor, there isn't really any statuary around the place and I'd really like to change that.'

'Do you have anything in mind?'

'Not at the moment. I don't know a huge amount about it actually. I think any stately home is incomplete without statues though, and I suppose they would have to be in a classic style, but that's about it.'

'Well, it's a start. Do you have any favourite sculptors?'

Jemme felt like a novice again and desperately tried to think of any sculptors, 'Like I said, it's not really my forte,' he said, feeling slightly embarrassed.

'But I'm sure a man with an art collection like yours must have at least a passing acquaintance with the canon of sculpture.'

Jemme floundered. He tried to think back over various museum trips, willing something to come to mind. All he could recall were endless rooms of marble, capturing heroes and figures from mythology in various poses. He thought back to visiting the Louvre for the first time with Hil. He remembered that they had spent a while in the sculpture gallery, and she had been particularly taken by one piece. He struggled to remember what it had looked like, but he recalled that Hil had been taken by the name of the sculptor – she had thought it sounded poetic, and he remembered looking the man up afterwards and discovering that Rodin had once been his assistant.

He thought hard and finally it popped into his head,

'I've always enjoyed Carrier-Belleuse,' he said.

Burbona smiled, 'Me too. This is an excellent starting point. We shall go from here.'

They finished the rest of the meal by discussing sculpture in general terms and notable pieces privately owned in various stately homes in France. 'Of course, I'll need to see the space before I can plan the acquisitions,' said Burbona. Jemme readily agreed and, as they said their goodbyes, Burbona told him she would be in touch to arrange a visit. It wasn't until he began to make his way home

Jemme realised that she had effectively decided the chateau's next development and invited herself over. He couldn't help but feel a stab of admiration at her forthrightness.

✳   ✳   ✳   ✳

The next week, Burbona rang up and informed him of her visit in a fortnight's time.

'It won't take long to drive,' she said, 'so I'll just come for the day.' Jemme had agreed readily, and then set his mind to thinking about how he could persuade Hil to come with him. She seemed ambivalent at best and he couldn't believe that she wouldn't share his excitement about his new acquaintance.

'But it's such a coup to have someone like her working with me on the chateau!' he said.

'Is it really?' sniffed Hil, 'How exactly?'

'Oh come on Hil, I told you about all of her surnames!'

'Yes, you did – apparently she has lots of them.'

'Exactly! She's related to Louis XVIII and all the house of Capet and Bourbon. She's proper old stock, she's the connection we've been missing all this time.'

'With what exactly?'

'With the chateau of course! I mean, no matter how long we both live here and how much we understand French society and culture – no matter how French we might *feel,* we will never really be French. We don't have the same connection to the chateau's past that she does.'

'There are millions of French people. I don't see why she has to be the specific one to provide this connection.'

'Oh come on Hil,' said Jemme again, growing increasingly exasperated. 'You know why – her blood is bluer than anyone else's I've ever met. She comes from exactly the type of family who would once have owned chateaux across all of France.'

'I'm sure she does; it's just that they don't appear to any more to start with, and, secondly, I don't know why you're suddenly chasing after the people you've spent years criticising. Don't you remember how difficult it was for us when we were looking for Vigne-Verte, and how much we both said we hated them? I'm just surprised to hear you've changed your mind, that's all.'

'I haven't changed my mind, I just think that it adds a crucial layer of credibility to everything I'm trying to achieve. I – look, are you going to come or not?'

'I'll think about it. When are you going?'

'The weekend after next.'

'I promised a friend I'd go shopping for baby clothes with her. I'll have to talk with her.'

'Ok, well you have a think and let me know. There's plenty of time,' said Jemme, anxious to steer away from a dangerous conversation.

He knew, without having to ask, that Hil wouldn't be coming with him the first weekend, so with a slight sadness he packed his bag alone on Friday morning. He was beginning to feel that the days they used to pack together so excitedly were rapidly becoming a distant memory. Perhaps they needed a holiday together, he thought to himself. He was sure that Hil would appreciate it, and it would probably be a wonderful balm for their relationship, healing the rapidly expanding rift between them. The only snag was that he couldn't imagine spending any of his free time anywhere other than at the chateau. For him every weekend felt like a holiday; he came back relaxed and refreshed and looking forward to the next weekend. He resented any leisure time he spent away from the chateau, and couldn't help feeling it was wasted time. His conscience pricked him, and he realised he was being supremely selfish. He would have to sacrifice at least a weekend away from his other home for Hil's sake. He spent that morning at work wondering where both of them could go. He wondered whether they should head somewhere romantic that was new to both of them, or go somewhere familiar which held special significance to them. He resolved to give it some considered thought, and then spent the afternoon thinking ahead to his chateau visit. Some new artists had begun work since his last visit, and he was keen to meet them. Since he had begun this project, he already felt like he had learned a great deal about various artistic techniques and he was hungry to learn more. He wanted to know about gold leafing, tile glazing and metal beating, and learn all the ancient crafts which had barely changed in hundreds of years. He could imagine them all being used in the chateau to recover its history, and he loved the continuity of it.

Arriving later that evening, he greeted Marguerite and Philby.

'And Madame?' asked Marguerite, looking hopefully at the car.

'Sorry, Marguerite, she hasn't come with me this time. She sends her love though and will be over soon.'

Marguerite looked disappointed but quickly cheered, 'Ah, Monsieur, one is better than none at all. Come,' she ushered him into the house and manoeuvred him into the kitchen, where a buttery roasted chicken sat resting on top of the oven. Jemme didn't protest as she served him out a large plateful, with helpings of vegetables.

'Marguerite, this is delicious!' he said after his first forkful.

'It's only a very simple dish, Monsieur, but there are two secrets. One is the herbs – they are from the herb garden of Xelifon, look,' she opened the double doors which led into the kitchen and in the dying light of the day Jemme could see the fruits of Xelifon's labour.

'Come, have a proper look,' Marguerite waved him over, 'I use herbs from this garden in every single meal, Monsieur, and look at it still!'

Jemme looked out of the door. The garden looked as if it had barely been touched. The herbs had fully bedded in, and the garden was neatly clipped, looking as if it had sat there for generations.

'It is wonderful to have such a thing right on the kitchen doorstep.' said Marguerite happily, 'Good herbs will make any meal taste fit for a king.'

A light breeze shook the herbs, carrying a waft of fragrant scents towards the door. Jemme breathed deeply, 'I have to agree, Marguerite. We're very lucky to have Xelifon. Now, you mentioned that there were two secrets. What's the other one?'

'Ah, Monsieur, that is Xelifon's doing as well. The vegetables we eat are the freshest in all of Normandy – these were in the ground only an hour ago!' she said, gesturing to the pots on the hob. 'They are the sweetest carrots I have ever tasted, and the creamiest potatoes.'

Jemme looked over to the vegetable patch and saw the neat rows of carrot tops, and runner beans creeping up carefully constructed trellising. He felt a sudden surge of happiness. Everything here worked and everything made sense.

'Fit for a king indeed,' he said smiling at Marguerite and returning to the table to finish his supper.

The next morning he took a cup of coffee from the kitchen and went to find Xelifon. He knew he was shy when it came to taking praise, but he wanted to make sure he knew that his work was valued. He found him in the small potting shed Philby had built, carefully poking seedlings into tiny cardboard pots. He was completely absorbed in his work, and it took a while for him to register that Jemme had even entered the small shed. He looked up with a dreamy gaze which slowly cleared,

'Monsieur,' he said softly, carefully wiping dirt from his hands onto a rag tucked into the side of a drawer.

'I didn't want to interrupt, I just wanted to let you know that I really enjoyed Marguerite's supper last night, and I understand that was mostly down to your hard work, so I wanted to thank you.'

Xelifon smiled, 'It is the season for carrots,' he mumbled.

'Well they tasted excellent.'

'Soon it will be cabbages,' he added, looking up.

'Well, I'm definitely looking forward to that!'

Xelifon smiled again. He looked relaxed and ready to talk. Jemme decided to take advantage of this rare situation, 'Why don't you show me what you've been up to recently?' he asked, 'I never see you on your own these days, and it would be nice to hear things from your point of view.'

Xelifon put the seedlings down and carefully wiped his hands again. He followed Jemme out into the grounds, and they walked along in silence for a while until they reached the edge of the international forest. Jemme turned to Xelifon.

'Do you know, this is so much a part of the landscape that I almost forget you planted it yourself. It feels like it's always been here.' Xelifon smiled and looked at his feet.

'Is there anything new here?' prompted Jemme.

Xelifon nodded and led the way forward. They came to a tree with long, waxy leaves.

'*Acacia bakeri*,' Xelifon said softly.

'I don't recognise it,' said Jemme, looking up at the tree which would have seemed more at home in a rainforest.

'It's endangered,' said Xelifon.

'Endangered? I didn't know trees could be endangered!'

Xelifon looked Jemme directly in the eye, '*Oui, Monsieur* – trees, plants, they can be just as endangered as animals.'

He broke off his gaze and looked up. 'It will grow very tall. It's from Australia. It's known as Marblewood,' he continued to look up, and Jemme realised he wasn't going to get any more out of him.

'Shall we move on? I understand you've planted some Chinese willows by the lake.'

They headed down to the lake, Jemme noticing that the dreamlike look had returned to Xelifon's face. Suddenly the look vanished and Xelifon began to giggle. 'What is it?' asked Jemme, wondering if he would be able to feign interest in some sort of plant-based joke.

'*L'artiste, Monsieur*,' said Xelifon, pointing towards the lake. Jemme followed his finger and saw a figure on the bank appearing to try and stand on his head.

'Who on earth is that?'

'Monsieur *Nori*,' Xelifon said, carefully trying to enunciate the word. 'He is the artist,' he added, rather unhelpfully.

'I see,'

'He is from a country I have never heard of.'

'Right.'

They both looked at the figure again. He was having some trouble with his balance and had ended up flat on his back. Xelifon giggled again.

'Does he do this often?' Jemme asked at length.

Xelifon nodded, 'Every day, Monsieur.'

'I think we should go and say hello to this Nori,' said Jemme, eyeing him with slight suspicion. The last thing he was in the mood for was artistic histrionics. As he neared the lake, Xelifon trotting in his wake, Jemme got a much better look at the man in question. He had a heavy brow with large, bushy eyebrows which hung low over his deep-set eyes. His neck-length black hair was slicked down straight, and contrasted with the wiry mess of his dark beard. Jemme couldn't help but think how much he looked like Rasputin. The man noticed them and sat up, offering his hand without standing. Jemme bent down to shake it and was struck by how surreal the situation was. He certainly hadn't expected to come across an up-ended doppelganger of the Black Monk by his own lake in the middle of the French countryside.

'Monsieur,' growled the man, squeezing Jemme's hand tightly and shaking it slowly.

'I understand your name is Nori,' said Jemme.

'Noury,' corrected the man in gravelly tones.

'I see. Well, welcome, Noury. My name is Jemme Mafeze.'

'Yes.' The man remained seated and stared up at Jemme expectantly, which was slightly confusing – Jemme was pretty certain it was not his turn to speak. Eventually, he began to feel uncomfortable under the man's unbroken stare, and the silence started to feel awkward.

'And – forgive me for being rude – who are you, Noury?'

Noury furrowed his thick brows, 'N-o-u-r-y,' he repeated, slightly confused. 'That is my name,' he explained, looking at Jemme as if he suspected he might be slow-witted. 'I come from Turkmenistan.'

'I see,' said Jemme. Xelifon gave him a conspiratorial look as if to say that he had never heard of this suspicious-sounding country either.

'And…what are you doing by the lake, Noury?' Jemme finally ventured.

'Attempting headstand,' said Noury matter-of-factly.

Jemme realised that he wasn't going to get anywhere with the conversation so decided to leave him to it.

He thanked Xelifon for showing him around, and returned to the house. He felt slightly worn out after a rather odd morning, and was ready for another coffee.

Back in the kitchen he found Marguerite, polishing some silver and scolding Aude.

'Hello, Marguerite. I've just had to oddest encounter by the lake –'

Before he had had a chance to continue, she had nearly slammed the candlestick she was holding down onto the table. 'Heh, Monsieur, I know *exactly* who you will have met by the lake! That crazy man from a country none of us have ever heard of!'

'Turkmenistan?'

'*Oui*, it sounds something like that. He is a strange, strange man, Monsieur.'

'Yes, I rather got that impression. What is he doing here?'

'He is some kind of artist apparently,' Marguerite said the word with some kind of distaste, 'but I have not yet seen any proof of that,' she added, looking knowingly at Jemme.

'What has he been working on?'

Marguerite shrugged expressively, 'I would like to know the same! He seems to spend all his time meditating and eating honey.'

'Honey?'

'*Oui, Monsieur*. He brought it with him. He won't touch our food. I told you – crazy!' she shook her head and resumed work on the candlestick. Aude looked nervously up from her polishing and shot a look at Jemme as if to confirm everything Marguerite had said.

Jemme decided that everyone in the chateau was a little crazy this morning and that he'd be better off on his own. He spent the rest of the morning planning how he would present things to Burbona when she arrived. Would he show her the rooms in order of completion, order of grandeur or chronological order? Did it make more sense to follow the narrative he was creating within the chateau, or to follow the chateau's own patterns. He felt a little like a curator, getting ready to show the public a museum in development, and he rather enjoyed the sensation.

By the end of the day, he had given some further thought to Roland's Crusader suggestion, come up with some rough ideas for a couple of other rooms and even managed to extract a little more information from Noury, whom he was privately struggling not to address as Rasputin. He was here to paint something to do with the Silk Route apparently, although Jemme didn't manage to work out what that was exactly, or who had asked him to come along. He did, however, see him eat a couple of spoonfuls from a large glass jar of honey, and wondered if he really had brought it with him.

By the time he was heading back to Paris on the Sunday, Jemme was looking back over the weekend with mixed feelings. He didn't feel like he'd achieved as much as he usually did, and there were parts of the weekend which had been downright perplexing. On the whole, the weekend had felt like a precursor to the next one. He could feel himself getting excited about it already. It had been a while since he'd had a visitor to the chateau. There had been Hil's friends of course, but a while since there had been anyone that mattered. He checked the thought – it wasn't really what he meant, and he was glad he hadn't said it out loud. Still, there was no harm in thinking that he hadn't taken anyone so *relevant* to the chateau in a while.

He arrived home in good time on Sunday evening, and was pleased to see that Hil was still awake. He was even more pleased that she appeared to be in such a good mood.

'Hello darling, how was your weekend?' he asked, greeting her with a kiss. 'Oh it was wonderful,' said Hil happily. 'We went to some beautiful cafes and visited some gorgeous baby shops. We got a little carried away actually and spent far too much money. I bought Nathalie lots of gifts – adorable little crocheted dresses for the baby, and a couple of nice new-mother things for her.'

'Well, whatever makes you happy my love,' Jemme said.

Hil smiled sadly, 'I wish some of the things had been for me,' she said.

'I'll take you shopping, darling, I promise, we'll go to Boulevard Hausseman and Galeries Lafayette – I remember how you used to love the dresses in there.'

Hil sighed inaudibly. 'That sounds nice,' she said, unconvincingly.

The next day at work, Jemme thought over the Crusader rooms. It was something he was keen to start on right away, and he wondered if Burbona might have any ideas. 'She's probably even related to some of the original knights,' he thought to himself. On his way to meet a client for lunch, he passed a poster for an exhibition on the mediaeval French court and decided that it was a sign that he should start working on the room straight away – maybe it was even a sign from his grandmother. He resolved to drop in on Roland on the way back from lunch and take him up on his offer of reading material.

That afternoon he talked over the lunch with DD. It had been a successful meeting and he was keen to draft up the decoration proposal straight away. They worked hard, raking over the details and building various pricing models. Eventually they produced a comprehensive pitch which would only need a tiny amount of polishing before it was ready to be sent over. Jemme leant back in his chair and stretched,

'Good work, DD, I think that's one of our best pieces in recent times. He's sure to go for it too.'

'I hope so, Sir.'

'I think we've earned a break, don't you?'

DD inclined his head slightly, 'Shall I make some coffee, Sir?'

'I think that sounds like an excellent plan – almost as good as this one,' he said, indicating the scattered papers on his desk.

DD returned a few minutes later bearing a small silver tray, which he set down on the desk. Carefully avoiding the papers they had been working on, he unloaded two tiny cups and saucers and a small bowl of sugared almonds.

As soon as he spied the jewelled colours in the bowl, Jemme sat up.

'Where did you get those?' he asked.

'A new Turkish confectioners has just opened in the 12th Arrondissement, Sir. It is run by a Turkish family. I thought perhaps you would appreciate something authentic, and it would be worth starting out with a safe option.'

'You thought right, DD – what a treat! I haven't had sugared almonds in years, but I adore them. I'm glad you've only bought a small bowl, I've got very little self-control around any Turkish treats.'

'Oh, Sir?' said DD without betraying a hint of irony.

'Whereabouts are they from?' asked Jemme, grabbing a handful of almonds and washing them down with some thick, bitter coffee.

'It was difficult to ascertain, Sir; he barely spoke any French. I understand that that it is a small town outside Istanbul.'

'Well, I shall pop in and see them at some point,' said Jemme, perking up as the sugar and coffee kicked in.

'I haven't yet had the opportunity to ask you about the chateau,' said DD, taking a very small sip from his coffee and carefully placing it down so that the pattern on the cup and saucer was exactly aligned – something he seemed to have been able to do without looking.

'It was a bit of an odd weekend actually, to be honest,' said Jemme.

'Oh, Sir?' said DD.

'Yes, everyone seemed to be acting rather strangely, and I don't know what to make of that new chap you've hired.'

'New member of staff, Sir?'

'Yes, the Turkmen fellow – Noury. He came across as being rather odd and, to be honest, I'm not even sure what he's doing there. Painting of some sort, I gather.'

'Painting, Sir?'

'Well that was the impression I got from the rest of the staff – I couldn't get much out of him at all.'

'Ah, the gilder from Azerbaijan. He came highly recommended, Sir. He is highly gifted in water gilding I believe.'

'What's water gilding?'

'It's a method of applying gold leaf to mouldings, Sir.'

'Oh, I see. It sounds a bit funny. Actually, wait – that's not the point at all. This guy is neither from Azerbaijan, nor is he a gilder. He's definitely from Turkmenistan, as everyone there was talking about it. I don't think many of them had heard of it to be honest. I suppose it's not that surprising – I'd hazard a guess that Marguerite has never left France. Wait, I'm getting off the point again – who is this Azerbaijani? Why didn't I meet him?'

'His name is Mahmoud, Sir. I am not expecting him to be arriving until next weekend, so he must have been early.'

'No, we're definitely not talking about the same person, DD. This man's name is Noury.'

DD paused momentarily, 'Perhaps he pronounced his name strangely, Sir, I have only seen it written down.'

'No, this is definitely how it was pronounced – he even spelled it out for me.'

DD came dangerously close to looking confused.

'In that case, Sir, I will need to establish whether this man was hired by the chateau staff, as he is certainly no one I have encountered.'

'I shouldn't imagine that they would have hired him – they all seemed highly suspicious of him, and I don't know where they would even have come into contact with him – I don't think there are too many Turkmen in the village!'

'I shall establish his identity immediately, Sir,' said DD looking very serious. 'Don't worry about it, DD. I'm sure it's all completely fine, it's just a bit of a mystery, that's all!'

Jemme finished the last of the sugared almonds and looked rather cheerful about having uncovered a mystery, whilst DD seemed to be somewhat concerned.

✳ ✳ ✳ ✳

Jemme spent the rest of the week fine tuning the proposal, and barely had time to get excited about the upcoming chateau weekend. On Thursday afternoon he suddenly realised he was going to have to pack his bag for the next morning, and he had barely given any thought to how he was going to host Burbona. He wanted to impress her with the work he had done so far, but he didn't want the project to look too polished, as he was looking forward to her input and was hoping she would have some interesting ideas. It was a great deal of surprise that he heard Hil announce her intention to visit the chateau with him for the weekend.

'That's fantastic news, darling!'

'Well, I suppose it's been a while since I was last there. It would be nice to see what's new.'

'Absolutely! There have been so many developments since you last came along – I've been dying to show you. I've also got lots of new ideas I can't wait to discuss with you. Everyone will be so pleased to see you too – I think it's going to be a really fun weekend,' Jemme said enthusiastically, wrapping Hil up in a hug.

She smiled weakly. 'I'm looking forward to it. When is your new friend coming – Burbona is it?'

'Yes it is, and she's just coming for the day on Saturday. She's not staying overnight unfortunately, but I'm hoping she'll be able to next time.'

'Next time?' said Hil, arching one eyebrow slightly.

'Well I'm hoping she'll be able to come quite a few times. It would be great if she could be a part of the project somehow; she would bring so much to it.'

'I suppose we'll see what she's made of this Saturday.'

'I suppose so, but it's a social visit as much as anything else. If she does become a part of the project I would expect to ease her in gradually, although knowing Burbona that's not how she'll do things!' Jemme chuckled to himself.

'Oh?'

'Well if she sees something, she tends to go for it, that's all. She's a real firebrand!'

'I see. Perhaps I should come up with you on the Friday night. It might be nice for both of us to spend the night there before she arrives.'

'That would be very nice – I was looking forward to this weekend before, but now I'm really looking forward to it!' he planted a large kiss on the top of Hil's head.

Chapter Twenty-Nine

As five o'clock neared on Friday evening, Jemme raced to finish his work and prepare his papers for Monday morning. At half-past on the dot, DD knocked on the door and entered,

'Madame Mafeze has telephoned to say she will be here in fifteen minutes, Sir.'

'Excellent, excellent. I'm actually running a little bit behind and I'm not quite sure I'll be ready then. When she gets here, do you mind telling her that I'll be with her as soon as I can?'

DD nodded once, 'Of course, Sir.' Jemme turned back to his papers. After a few moments he became aware that DD was still standing there and looked up.

'Was there anything else?' he asked, noticing that DD looked distinctly uncomfortable.

'The Turkmen you met, Sir.'

'Ah yes, that Noury chap. What about him?'

'I have been unable to ascertain who was responsible for hiring him, Sir.'

'Oh, really?'

'Unfortunately yes, Sir. It is very troubling.'

'Well I shouldn't worry about it too much, I'm sure we'll work it out!'

'Personnel should be properly authorised, Sir,' said DD looking slightly put out at Jemme's laissez-faire attitude. 'They have unregulated access to the property whilst you are absent, and your art and antique collection there is expanding.'

'I suppose that's true. It's not really that formal over there though. There are always people coming and going and I quite like that – you've got to remember that it's in the middle of the countryside, not Paris!'

'Yes, Sir, but personnel must be authorised,' insisted DD. Jemme could imagine how uncomfortable this irregularity in protocol was making his second in command, so decided to be charitable,

'It's a good point, DD. Thanks for bringing my attention to it. I'll look into it whilst I'm at the chateau this weekend.'

DD looked somewhat appeased, and bowed his head in acknowledgement before leaving the room.

Jemme went back to his work, smiling to himself – DD's stiffness was so out of place where the chateau was concerned, and he wondered what everyone over at the chateau would think about being referred to as personnel. He imagined that Marguerite would actually rather like it, but Philby would be deeply unimpressed. Sighing, he turned back to his work – the faster he finished it, the faster he could head off for Vigne-Verte. Around twenty minutes later, he clicked the lid back onto his pen and breathed a sigh of relief. He had finished everything he needed to, and left everything in a good state for Monday morning. He threw a couple of papers into his attaché case and left his office. Walking into DD's office he was pleased to see that Hil had already arrived. She was chatting animatedly, and looked happier than he'd seen her in a while. DD still looked uncomfortable, but was responding politely to Hil's questions. For a brief moment Jemme wondered if DD was still worrying about the 'personnel issue' and if this was the sort of thing DD thought about at the weekend. He hoped not, but suspected it might be the case. Hil heard him come in and looked up,

'Hello sweetheart, have you had a nice day?'

'Yes thank you, not bad at all. What about you?'

'Very good,' said Hil with a smile, 'I've just been telling DD how much I'm looking forward to our weekend.'

'Me too! Shall we make a move?'

They both bade goodbye to DD, and Jemme did his best to assure him that he would investigate matters thoroughly.

'What was all that about?' asked Hil on the way to the car.

'Oh nothing really – there's someone at the chateau we can't account for, and DD's getting himself rather worked up about it. He's from Turkmenistan and he's an artist of some sort, but no one seems to have hired him. He appears to have just arrived one day.'

'A rogue agent, how exciting!' said Hil.

Jemme laughed, 'that's what I thought too – it's rather fun having our own little mystery!'

'Absolutely. In fact, I'd go as far to say that no chateau is complete without a mystery or two!'

Jemme smiled at his wife, feeling a surge of love. It had been so long since they had shared jokes and been silly together, and he had missed it. With someone in the car to talk to, the journey passed in no time and they were soon turning up the driveway.

Hil breathed a small sigh when the chateau came into view.

'I'd forgotten how wonderful it looks when it's like this,' she said. 'It really is beautiful – there's no finer view than coming up the driveway and seeing it all lit up.'

'I couldn't agree more,' said Jemme, reaching over and squeezing her hand.

They parked up, and Hil looked pleased to see the reception party. She opened the door almost before Jemme had turned the engine off and jumped out.

'Marguerite!' she said, embracing her. Marguerite looked absolutely delighted,

'Madame! It is so nice to see you! We have all missed you so much!'

'I've missed you all too,' said Hil, letting go of Marguerite and shaking hands warmly with Philby.

'We thought you had gone to Paris and forgotten all about us,' Marguerite scolded.

'Oh, don't make me feel guilty Marguerite – I'm sorry I've abandoned you all slightly.'

'Ah, Madame! All is forgiven, come with me straight to the kitchen. I have supper all ready.'

Hil looked behind her to find Jemme.

'You'd better do as you're told,' he said nodding after the housekeeper. 'You don't want to get into any more trouble!'

Hil smiled mischievously at him and followed Marguerite indoors. A gorgeous smell had spread out of the kitchen towards the hallway.

'I've missed your cooking, Marguerite,' said Hil smiling.

'Bof, it is nothing, Madame – only simple home cooking. I have made your favourite dishes though, and we have cooked you a few more with ingredients from the garden.'

'Yes, I've been hearing all about Xelifon's efforts. Jemme was saying that there is a vegetable patch which is just as successful as the herb garden.'

'Oh, he is so talented, Xelifon. The plants respond to him so well. Even if a frost kills off all my beans at home, they will still be sweet and crisp here.'

'Well I'm looking forward to tasting the fruits of his labours. It's so satisfying to be able to eat food which was grown within walking distance of your front door.'

'But Madame, that is how it should be,' said Marguerite seriously. Hil decided to keep her mouth shut so she didn't get another telling off. They arrived at the kitchen where lids were clattering on bubbling pots and steam hissed from a giant pan. The windows were steamed up, and a very red-faced Aude was running around the kitchen tending to various pots.

'Goodness, Marguerite, how many people are you expecting?!'

'Just you and Monsieur,' said Marguerite, blinking. 'Are there guests this evening too?'

'No,' smiled Hil, 'just Jemme and me. I meant that you've cooked a lot of food, that's all.'

'But I thought you would be hungry,' said Marguerite, 'and it has been a while since you ate any of our food here.'

'Marguerite, what a feast!' said Jemme arriving in behind them.

'But I thought you would be hungry,' repeated Marguerite.

'We are, but you didn't have to go to so much effort – you must have been labouring for hours!'

'Ah Monsieur, it is never a chore,' said Marguerite smiling. Hil caught Aude's eye as she staggered from the stove with a large double-handled saucepan.

'Here, let me help you with that,' she said rushing over.

'Tsk, tsk, Madame, you are doing nothing,' said Marguerite. She took control of the pan and chided Aude, who by this time was perspiring slightly.

'She has been getting in the way since this morning!' said Marguerite turning to Hil and Jemme. Aude scuttled off, evidently keen to keep out of the way.

'I hope you haven't been cooking for us since this morning,' said Hil.

Marguerite brushed her comment aside, 'It is always good to take time over these things,' she said, pulling out two chairs.

Jemme and Hil sat down and looked, wide-eyed, at the plates in front of them as Marguerite spooned, ladled and dished out the feast she had worked so hard on.

They ate in happy silence, occasionally pausing to exchange knowing looks. 'I know – it's amazing, isn't it?' said Jemme after Hil had just glanced at him.

'It's so, so good,' she replied, 'but I don't think I can eat another mouthful! You're spoiling us, Marguerite!'

Marguerite looked over from the stove in concern, 'But there is so much more still to come, Madame! And you must try the desserts too.'

'There's dessert as well?' said Hil.

'Yes Madame, I've made three – you will try them, won't you?'

'For you, of course! I mean, I don't think I'll need to eat again for a week, but how can I refuse when you've gone to so much effort?'

Marguerite beamed at her, opened the oven and turned back around bearing a tray of huge stuffed marrows.

'Grown by Xelifon, Madame,' she said.

Hil and Jemme exchanged another glance and realised they were going to have to do a lot more eating before they were going to be allowed to go to bed.

* * * *

They awoke the next day after an extremely deep sleep.

'Morning,' said Hil, stretching.

Jemme groaned, 'I'm still so full!' Hil laughed and poked him playfully.

'I couldn't believe it, when we'd made our way through that blackberry pie and she arrived with that huge cake!' she giggled at the memory.

Jemme put his hand over his face and groaned again, 'Don't remind me. I haven't had to put so much effort into eating for a really long time!'

'She will have appreciated it though. She loves looking after people and mothering them, so I think the best thing we could have done was just let her.'

'I know, I know,' said Jemme removing his hand from his face and joining in when Hil giggled again. He stopped,

'I really am so happy you're here,' he said seriously.

'Me too,' said Hil flashing him a beautiful smile.

They got up and dressed and made their way downstairs. Hil had put on pretty printed dress and her hair hung loose around her shoulders. She wore no make-up, and her skin glowed with healthiness. Jemme looked at her appreciatively. He knew she would be offended if he told her how homely she looked, but he meant it in a wholly complimentary way. It was more that she looked perfectly at home within the chateau, as if this was where they always lived. He allowed himself to indulge in a moment of fantasy where that was the case. He imagined himself working from home all day and then working *on* home during the evenings and at the weekends. He imagined how quickly work on the chateau would progress, and all the exciting new directions the project could take when he was free to work on it every day.

'Are you coming?' asked Hil turning round and looking back up the stairs. A shaft of light from one of the stair tower's windows caught her face, and turned her hair a golden colour.

'Jemme? Are you coming?' she asked again.

Jemme snapped out of his reverie and suddenly realised that he had completely stopped in his tracks at the top of the stairs.

'Sorry sweetheart, I was daydreaming slightly.'

Hil laughed, 'I could tell! Good daydreams I hope.'

'Definitely.'

'I'm pleased,' she smiled back at him and waited for him to catch her up.

'We'd better get to the kitchen, and you'd better loosen your belt buckle, I think Marguerite's been at it again!'

About an hour later they sat over a couple of empty plates and in front of some not very empty bowls.

'I think she thinks we haven't eaten in weeks,' whispered Hil to Jemme when Marguerite was out of earshot.

'I know!' Jemme hissed back, looking at the platter of sausages in front of him with a certain wariness.

Just then Xelifon knocked shyly on the door,

'Good morning, Xelifon,' said Jemme cheerfully, 'Come in, come in.'

Xelifon stepped into the kitchen and looked around him. He was blushing slightly and tugged at one sleeve,

'*Bonjour, Monsieur*,' he said, not making eye contact with anyone. 'Monsieur Philby sent me.'

'I see.'

Xelifon continued to look around the room, avoiding eye contact.

'Why did he send you, Xelifon?' prompted Jemme.

'A lady, Monsieur.'

'A lady?'

'A lady has arrived, Monsieur,' he paused and looked around the room a little longer before making eye contact with Jemme, 'a very pretty lady, Monsieur,' he said, his blush deepening.

'Burbona must be here!' said Jemme, excitedly leaping to his feet. He rushed to the door, looking behind him as he left to Hil, who was still finishing her cup of tea. 'Are you coming?' he asked without stopping.

Hil deliberately finished her tea, before leisurely standing and making her way to the entrance hall. She paused for a moment before entering to smooth her hair down and check her dress, and she momentarily wished she was wearing lipstick. As soon as she entered the hallway she instantly regretted her decision not to, and wished she was wearing anything other than her dowdy dress. Jemme was chatting animatedly to a woman who could only have been Burbona. She was tall and slim and dressed expensively in a chic black outfit. A designer bag swung from her shoulder, and her glossy hair had been swept up into a salon-perfect chignon. Hil wriggled in her dress, and tried to do something with her hair, but to no avail. She realised she was just going to have to seize the initiative and make the first move. Mustering her confidence she strode towards Burbona, ready to introduce herself with an outstretched hand. Before she had had the chance, Burbona noticed her and turned around.

'Ah, you must be Madame Mafeze,' she said, landing a kiss on each of Hil's cheeks. Hil caught a waft of her perfume and recognised her earrings as Cartier. She took a breath to answer, but Burbona got there first again,

'It's a pleasure to meet you, I've been curious to see which lucky lady ended up with a husband like this!' she smiled coquettishly at Jemme, who laughed. Hil pursed her lips into a small smile,

'Welcome to our home,' she said, and was about to add 'I've heard so much about you,' but checked herself. 'My husband mentioned you were coming,' she said instead.

Burbona smiled winningly, but behind her back Jemme shot Hil a cross look. She wasn't extending the warm welcome he had hoped for.

'We're both so pleased you could make it,' he said, 'I know you're very busy in Paris and I'm flattered you were able to spare a day to come all the way out here.'

'We are all busy in Paris,' said Burbona, 'but I am never too busy for friends. Besides I have always had a soft spot for chateaux, and I adore seeing a new place.'

She looked around the Halle d'Honneur, 'Well I like what I see already,' her eyes followed the grand sweeping staircase to the top.

'Tell me, is the ballroom nearby?'

'Yes, as a matter of fact it's just through those doors,' said Jemme. 'How did you know that?'

'I just recognise the layout. This place would have been used for large social events, and I expect young ladies would have come out here. It's a very classic debutante entrance, coming down these stairs to be presented, and then moving on into the ballroom.'

Jemme looked at her delightedly, then shook his head and chuckled. 'I should have guessed that you would understand this place straight away. It took Hil and I years to discover that, and it was only through a chance glimpse into the local archives. Burbona knew how this place used to work within about five minutes!' he added, rather unnecessarily, to Hil.

Hil smiled even more tightly than before, 'Well, we both think that lifestyle is very outdated,' she said to Burbona. 'It's an obsolete, bygone era and it's rather irrelevant now.'

Jemme's smile dropped and he frowned fiercely at Hil, who refused to acknowledge his displeasure.

'But how can you say that when places like this still stand?' said Burbona. 'I agree with you that we are in a different age, but I do not agree that the old age is irrelevant, especially when there are places like this to remind us of it.'

'And people,' added Jemme.

Burbona flashed another winning smile, and Hil came dangerously close to a scowl.

'Are you ready to look around?' Jemme asked.

'Yes, but I'm afraid I must make some calls first. Do you have a telephone here?'

'Of course, let me show you where it is, then we can meet in the kitchen afterwards.' He ushered Burbona to his office, and returned to Hil in the hallway.

'What on earth's got into you?' he asked. 'You were borderline rude. In fact, actually you were rude.'

Hil looked at him obstinately for a moment before the expression broke. 'I'm sorry,' she said, 'I know I wasn't being particularly hospitable, I suppose – I just, I don't know. You've been talking about her and her background so much recently and then when I saw her looking so glamorous and elegant, I suddenly felt frumpy and plain and not particularly welcoming.'

Jemme's irritation melted away, 'You're so silly,' he said wrapping his arm around Hil's shoulder and squeezing her. He kissed the top of her head, 'You know I'll always think you're the most beautiful woman in any room.'

Hil sighed again, 'I'm sorry, I was being silly.'

'Yes you were! It's great to have a guest at the chateau, but only if both of us want him or her to be here.'

'I know, I know. I promise I'll make her feel welcome when she gets back.'

'Thank you, sweetheart.'

'Now, let's go to the kitchen and wait for her shall we? I'm sure you'd like a coffee and I expect you'll just about have time for one before she gets back.'

'That's more like it! Lead the way!'

Hil headed back to the kitchen. 'Hello Marguerite,' she said as soon as they had arrived. 'We've got a very special guest for lunch; I know it's last minute, and we should have warned you, but I would really appreciate it if you could look after her and cook one of your fantastic dishes for her.'

Jemme recognised that she was making amends, 'Thank you,' he said, squeezing her hand.

Marguerite seemed far less grateful and flew into a flurry of panic, 'Special guest, Madame? *Tiens*! I did not know there was a special guest! But it is already late in the morning – how will I cook a special lunch in time!'

'I'm sure you'll manage it. You made such a feast for us last night and this morning that you could easily just serve up some of that couldn't you?'

'Leftovers Madame?! *Leftovers*? But I cannot serve a special guest leftovers!' she threw up her hands in horror, 'Aude, *Aude!* Where is that girl? She is never here when I need her!'

'Calm down, Marguerite,' Jemme said kindly, 'You're getting into a flap and it's just not worth it. I'm sure that whatever you can put together will be wonderful. Besides, our guest will be expecting local home-cooked fare, not *haute cuisine*. In any case, it's just one person, it's not like you're entertaining royalty. Although I suppose it's not far off!' he added jokingly, then instantly wished he hadn't.

'Monsieur? Monsieur, what do you mean by that?' asked Marguerite, looking stricken.

'Nothing, nothing, I just mean that our guest is from rather aristocratic stock, that's all, but it's completely irrelevant.'

'*Aude!!*' shrieked Marguerite at the top of her voice, 'See – see?!' she said in a very high-pitched voice, 'now there is a real emergency, she abandons me!'

'Marguerite, calm down,' Hil soothed.

'But I cannot, Madame, I don't even know who this man is!'

'Well, it's not a man, she's a lady called Burbona and she's very gracious, so I'm sure that she will be generous with her praise and enjoy whatever you serve her. Like Jemme said, she hasn't come here expecting what she normally eats in Paris. She's come to eat proper food.'

Marguerite beamed at the compliment and calmed down a little, '*Bien*, I will show her what we can do out here,' she said determinedly.

'That's the spirit. Ah, I think I can hear her now,' said Hil, as the distinctive sound of high heels clipped down the stone-floored corridor.

Burbona entered the kitchen. 'I've finished telephoning,' she said, locking eyes with Jemme and ignoring everyone else. 'I'm ready whenever you like.'

'Burbona, I'd like you to meet Marguerite,' said Jemme. 'I suppose you could call her our *régisseuse*, but she's a great deal more than that. She's the glue that holds this whole place together, and we'd be completely lost without her.'

Marguerite blushed and smiled girlishly, which amused both Jemme and Hil. Burbona shot her a quick look, '*Enchanté*,' she said with a smile. There was a slight pause before Hil realised that she wasn't going to offer anything more. She jumped in, 'Why don't I show you the library, Burbona? It was one of the first rooms we completed, and it's got a couple of stories to tell.' She led the way out of the kitchen and Burbona followed. Pleased to see Hil was back to her old self, Jemme turned to follow them, he paused first, 'I'm sure whatever you cook will be wonderful, Marguerite,' he said.

'Ahh, Monsieur,' she replied happily, before widening her eyes, 'but she is so beautiful!'

'Burbona? Yes, I suppose she is rather attractive.'

'Attractive? Monsieur, la la! No wonder Madame Mafeze wanted to be here this weekend!'

'What do you mean?'

'Well, Madame does not come for many months, and now she comes at the same time as this beautiful lady? Monsieur, she wants to show that she is still the lady of the manor.'

'Well, I don't think that's the case, Marguerite, but I'm certainly pleased that everyone is here this weekend. I'll see you at lunch.' He trotted off to catch up with the others, puzzling over what Marguerite had said. It seemed to him to be a slightly odd observation to make.

He caught up with both ladies in the library, where Hil was doing an excellent job of recounting the room's past and Burbona was asking many questions. He breathed a sigh of relief that everything seemed to have smoothed over. 'Ah, Jemme, I've just been hearing the story of the American golfer!' said Burbona as he entered the room. 'It's remarkable how foolish some people can be.'

'I know, it beggars belief!' said Jemme, 'Can you imagine what would have happened to this place if he hadn't given up at such an early stage?'

'Ghastly,' said Burbona, shaking her head. 'I'm pleased that one of our national treasures has found such excellent custodians,' she smiled charmingly at both of them and Hil seemed to take the compliment well, without picking up on the slight barb.

'I think you should see the salon next,' said Hil. 'It's absolutely beautiful. Jemme has worked so hard on it and we've had some fabulous parties there.'

Jemme was pleased to note that everything was getting better and better, and he allowed Hil to lead the way to the salon, too. Burbona was very complimentary and Hil was positively beaming – things were going famously until Burbona's eyes lit on a mirror.

'What's this piece doing here?' she asked. She pointed towards the mirror, which, by contrast to its opulent surroundings was small. Its gold frame was rather chipped, but the intricate baroque pattern was still distinguishable. It was evidently an old piece and the glass had built up a delicate antique patina.

'Ah that mirror,' said Hil looking at it fondly, 'that's something of a family heirloom. It's been in my family for generations, and my parents gave it to us as a wedding present. I'll pass it on to my own children too.'

'It doesn't make sense where it is,' said Burbona. 'It clashes with everything around it and the style is all wrong.'

Hil looked a little taken aback. 'The style is wrong?' she asked.

'Yes, I'm glad you agree,' said Burbona. She peered closely at it. 'I don't even recognise the era at all, where has it come from?'

Hil visibly bristled, 'It's not about where it has come from or how much it's worth; it's about what it means to us. It's a very precious piece.'

Burbona shrugged, 'Well, if it's precious you can still keep it. It just doesn't look good there, that's all.'

'Oh? And where would you suggest?'

Burbona looked around the room for a while, 'Here,' she said, walking over to a small space low down on the opposite wall. Jemme followed her and looked at the space she had indicated. He took a few steps backwards and looked at it in context.

'Actually Hil, that does make sense,' he said. He looked at the space again. The mirror would be perfectly framed by the two pictures either side of it and the burnished gilt of their frames would complement its own. What's more, it would echo the shape of the small window above it and perhaps even catch some of its light.

'In fact, the more I look at it, the more I can't believe I didn't think of that in the first place,' he said.

'But –' began Hil.

'Oh, I'm sure it will be easy enough for Philby to move it. It's not like it requires specialist care -- he can just bang a new nail in the wall.'

Hil flared her nostrils at him.

'Come on, you know what I mean,' said Jemme. 'I'll ask him to do it this afternoon. If you really hate it we can change it back.'

Hil took a deep breath, and looked like she was saving something up to say to him later. Burbona smiled sweetly at her and they moved on. Over the course of the next few rooms, Burbona came up with a number of other helpful suggestions which Jemme jumped on and Hil became increasingly resentful of. Her natural aversion to confrontation and a deeply ingrained sense of politeness prevented her from dismissing them out of hand, but she felt she had made her feelings pretty clear on each one, and was exceedingly irritated that Jemme appeared not to have picked up on her feelings whatsoever.

Even though she wasn't in the least bit hungry, by lunchtime she was looking forward to some of Marguerite's food and a change in conversation. Burbona led the way back to the kitchen and Hil followed, vexed that she had lost the upper hand. Her spirits lifted when they entered the kitchen and she saw how much effort Marguerite had made. She could only imagine how hard she had been working since they last saw – and how hard she must have been working Aude too.

'I knew you would magic something up for us!' she said.

'But we must make our guest welcome,' said Marguerite, with her finest airs and graces on. 'Ah, Madame, welcome back. Lunch is ready,' she said as Burbona entered the room. Marguerite pulled out a chair and Burbona sat down. Jemme joined her the table and looked in slight amazement at all the dishes which had materialised since they were last there, 'How ever did you manage all of this?' he asked.

Marguerite was obviously relishing her success, 'It was nothing, Monsieur,' she said proudly.

'Well I hope we can do it justice,' said Jemme, reaching for one of the serving forks.

'Monsieur,' said Marguerite, intercepting him, 'I shall serve you.'

'Oh, right. OK, thank you.'

'But not before I have served our guest,' said Marguerite rather grandly, turning to Burbona. 'Madame, what would you like?' she asked brandishing a large spoon expectantly. Burbona glanced quickly over the dishes in front of her without paying them much attention.

'Is there any salad?' she asked.

'Salad…Madame?' asked Marguerite.

'Yes – maybe with some tomatoes and perhaps some sliced cucumber or something.'

'But Madame isn't interested in some of this ragout, or stewed rabbit?' said Marguerite, gesturing to two particularly tasty looking dishes. Burbona peered at them quickly and wrinkled her nose, 'No, no – I really don't think so. Just some salad please.'

Marguerite hovered for a moment looking as if she didn't know what to do. She had clearly spent all morning working towards this point, and looked as if the rug was being pulled out from under her feet.

'I'm sure it won't be too much trouble,' Burbona prompted, looking expectantly at Marguerite.

'No, no, no trouble at all,' said Marguerite, looking crestfallen and turning away. She put on some oven gloves and opened the oven door. Looking up at the table she evidently thought better of it, and shut the door again.

Hil took in her injured expression and suddenly became protective. Her resentment towards Burbona rose again and she hoped she would leave soon.

Chapter Thirty

The afternoon did not endear Burbona any further to Hil. Trailing round the chateau behind them, she resented the fact she was being made to feel like a third wheel. Jemme would excitedly start explaining a curio or piece of furniture to Burbona, who seemed to have something to say about each of them. She had variously studied the artist, attended the sale or even knew someone who had a matching piece. Hil began to wish she had paid more attention in recent years, so that she could join in the conversation. In fact, she was having a job just keeping up with them: not only were they striding ahead but they were talking so fast on such esoteric subjects, it was difficult to follow the conversation at all or even get a word in edgeways. Eventually there was a lull in conversation and she decided to seize the opportunity.

'We're thinking of working on the calligraphy gallery and Crusader rooms next – we have some friends who know quite a lot about the subject – '

'Excellent! What a good idea!' said Burbona, giving Hil a sugary smile. 'I'll be able to help you out on both rooms. In fact, there is a private sale of mediaeval armour in just a few weeks; I believe there are some very interesting pieces coming up. I'll secure you an invitation.'

'Mediaeval armour?' said Jemme looking interested.

'Yes. Weapons, some shields – that sort of thing. I believe there might be some other pieces too, but I've been so busy I haven't had the chance to look into it yet.'

'That sounds amazing – excellent, just what we need. I'm surprised though, I've been looking out for something like that for a long time and haven't come across anything. Neither has DD, and he's usually very good at that kind of thing.'

'Oh well, it's a private sale,' said Burbona dismissively.

Jemme looked at her, hungry for more information.

'It's not even really a widely-known sale, which is why you might not have heard of it. Old families selling off various pieces, you know.'

Jemme smiled, satisfied. Hil glanced at him and could read his thoughts instantly. She could see how gratified he felt at the thought of having penetrated the inner circle of France's elite. Since the first time he had met her, Jemme had talked about Burbona's connections and his suspicions that she would be a route in. Now not only had he been proved right, he had also obtained exactly what he had wanted. Hil wasn't surprised he was looking so smug but also wasn't especially pleased.

'We would be interested in attending, thank you,' she said politely to Burbona.

'Excellent. It's at the gentleman's house, so it will be a very private affair, but I'll make sure you get sent the address. I'll probably drive over and talk to him about it next week, so I'll have a look through what's on offer and pre-select some pieces which will work well in the room.'

'That's very kind of you,' said Jemme.

'Not at all – you don't want to waste your time looking through things that wouldn't be any good for the chateau.'

'But we don't know what we want yet,' said Hil, 'and besides, we don't even know what the room's going to look like. I mean, it's very kind of you, but –'

'Sweetheart, honestly, Burbona's an expert at these kind of things,' Jemme said. 'You'll have to trust me, she knows what we want better than we do ourselves,' he beamed at Burbona.

'If you would like just to come to the sale, that's fine.'

'No,' said Jemme quickly, sensing a precious opportunity slipping away, 'we'd love your expertise, thank you,' he shot Hil a look.

'Yes, thank you,' she added.

'My pleasure,' Burbona smiled, 'but you said you also had a friend who was an expert. I'm sure he will be very useful in the room's development. What is it he does.'

'He, he works in a library,' mumbled Hil.

'A noble profession,' said Burbona. She paused, 'I should really introduce you to Professor Laveda de La Durie. He's a great friend over at the Sorbonne. He's been an academic there for years and there isn't much he doesn't know about palaeography and different script systems. He will be very useful for the calligraphy room.'

'He sounds perfect!' gushed Jemme.

'But I think I remember you saying you had a friend too?' Burbona asked Hil.

'No, no, it's fine. I'm sure your professor will be a great help,' she said with as much grace as she could muster.

By the time they had finished their tour of the chateau, Hil felt flat and tired. Burbona and Jemme on the other hand were fired up and full of ideas. They had already decided on more rooms than there were in the chateau and, going by how long it had taken them to complete the small amount they had so far, it was going to take the rest of their lives to finish what Burbona and Jemme had planned.

Eventually their guest left, having been entreated by Jemme to stay the night and having bid a polite goodbye by Hil.

Hil felt a small sense of relief, but mostly she just felt an overwhelming sadness. She had not enjoyed Burbona's visit at all. It had made her feel distant and disconnected from Jemme, and just brought attention to the widening gulf between them she had been trying to ignore for so long. She made her way to the kitchen where Marguerite greeted her affectionately, settled her down at the table, and presented her with all the desserts that hadn't been touched at lunchtime.

'There are more, Madame – I just didn't have the chance to show them to you,' Marguerite said, whipping something which wobbled out of the fridge. Hil smiled and reached for a spoon, glad to forget the events of the day for an hour.

✻   ✻   ✻   ✻

Back in Paris, it seemed that forgetting about the trip was the very last thing Jemme wanted. He talked about all of his new plans with an enthusiasm Hil only ever saw when he was discussing the chateau. His face lit up as he described the furnishings that he was going to buy, and the history he was going to create. Hil sat and listened as he mapped out a plan of sales, auctions, trips, meetings with academics, museum visits and interviews with artists that sprawled and spread as far into the future as she could imagine. She couldn't see any time for them as a couple in the plan, and she certainly couldn't see any time for them as a family.

'What do you think, sweetheart?' asked Jemme, concluding one particularly lengthy monologue, about the Silk Route as a metaphor for the chateau.

'I think it sounds like you've got it all figured out,' said Hil.

'I think I do!' said Jemme, failing to grasp any hidden meaning in her words. 'I just can't wait to get started on it all – it feels like a whole new beginning!'

'Mmmm,' said Hil sadly. Jemme lent over and kissed her forehead.

'It's exciting, isn't it?!'

'Mmm,' said Hil, even more sadly than before.

Jemme's enthusiasm remained undimmed for the rest of the week. He was exceptionally busy at work, yet even when he got home very late each evening, he still seemed full of vim and energy. Hil, by contrast was withdrawing into herself again. She desperately wanted to be a part of things, and for them to work on the chateau together, but she found it impossible to engage with his plans. Names and dates washed over her, and sometimes she struggled to understand why an area, era or historical figure was worthy of inclusion at all. She had understood the project at the beginning – why it was important to Jemme and why it was important in its own right. Now, she felt like she understood Jemme less and understood the whole project less as a result – or perhaps it was even the other way around. The very concept of the chateau and its developments was beginning to feel increasingly Quixotic.

One evening Hil had fallen asleep long before Jemme came home. She woke slightly when he joined her in bed – just enough to smile when he put his arm around her. She fell back to sleep, feeling comforted and a great deal more relaxed. Suddenly the slumbering silence in the room was pierced by a trilling telephone. Both Jemme and Hil were jolted awake. Jemme jumped and sat bolt upright. He blinked in confusion and then grabbed the receiver.

Hil watched him in alarm, fearing bad news. She listened to his half of the conversation, holding her breath. Gradually her alarm turned to disbelief: although Jemme had initially sounded worried, now he was laughing and having a chat as if it was the most natural thing in the world. He was thanking whoever was on the other end of the phone profusely, and exclaiming that he didn't know how he or she kept doing it. Hil wasn't sure who it was or what it was that they kept doing, but she suddenly started to feel grumpy. She turned over and pulled the covers over her head, trying to go back to sleep. It wasn't particularly easy with Jemme chattering away in the background, and when he had finally hung up she emerged from the covers,

'Who was that?' she asked crossly. 'It had better be something pretty important for them to have called halfway through the night.'

'It was Burbona,' said Jemme.

'What did she want that was so important it couldn't wait until the morning?!'

Jemme smiled and shook his head, 'She's come through for us once again,' he said.

'Once again? What do you mean?'

'She's acquired a very special piece that I didn't even know was for sale. I can't believe she remembered,' Jemme said, shaking his head again.

'Remembered what? What's she acquired?'

'Well, the second time we met each other, we were talking about sculpture, and I told her that Carrier-Belleuse was my favourite sculptor.'

'I didn't know that,' said Hil.

'Yes,' said Jemme dismissively, apparently having convinced himself of the fact. 'Well, anyway, Burbona has gone and found an actual, genuine Carrier-Belleuse sculpture – *la Liseuse*. I didn't even know that it was for sale, I expect she knew about some exclusive private sale we would never have heard about though. In fact, knowing Burbona, I wouldn't be surprised if it wasn't for sale at all and she sweet-talked someone into selling it!' he chuckled to himself. 'Well, I am going to sleep soundly now!' he said, kissing Hil on the forehead and turning off the light.

Burbona arranged for the statue to be delivered to the Paris flat 'so that they could start enjoying it straight away'. Hil had to admit that it was a thing of beauty. Cast from bronze, she stood at about two feet high and had a look of quiet contemplation on her face as she gazed at the book she held. A gilt patina and ivory inlays picked out certain details, and her face had been so exquisitely formed it was hard not to believe that it would be warm to the touch. Hil positioned her next to her favourite reading chair, and often found herself staring at *la Liseuse* instead of reading. She found she brought a restful presence to the flat, and quickly became very fond of her. She started to hope that she would stay in Paris and not make the journey into the countryside. As the weeks wore on, she began to spend more and more time with *la Liseuse*. Jemme continued to work late at the bank, and Hil felt as if she only ever saw him in between sales and auctions. Almost every time she saw him, he had a new tale of paintings bought or rugs lost. In the vast periods of time between these brief encounters, still she found herself alone with *la Liseuse*. She made an effort and went along to the private viewing Burbona had organised, but found it hard to muster enthusiasm about the array of mediaeval weapons on offer, and by the end of the evening wished she had stayed at home with *la Liseuse*. From Jemme's point of view, the evening was a roaring success. He bought every single piece Burbona had pre-selected.

'I can't believe how astute her choices were!' he said to Hil for about the fifth time on the way home. 'It's as if she could *see* the room before we've even designed it. All of this is going to be absolutely fantastic – it's such a wealth of treasures! It's going to take no time at all to complete the room! I've never gone about it this way before, but it makes perfect sense! Instead of starting off with an empty room and then spending ages trying to find exactly the right pieces to fill it, why not start off with all the pieces?! It's so good to have someone else's ideas and perspective – it's completely revitalising this whole project!'

'I'm pleased,' said Hil. 'All that stuff isn't coming to the flat is it?'

'No, no – I'll get it sent straight to the chateau. The sooner it gets there the better! I can't believe how quickly we'll finish this room!'

Hil didn't reply, but tried to smile as genuinely as she could. She looked at Jemme and wished she could share his happiness. She couldn't understand when or why happiness became something only one of them could experience. They used to be so close that enjoyment of anything was impossible if it wasn't mutual. Perhaps all couples grow somewhat apart as they grew older, she reasoned. Yet, when she considered her own parents, she struggled to reconcile the idea with their own happy marriage. They had always been close and shared everything with each other. It was a marriage based on mutual trust, respect, interests and beliefs, and it was the standard by which she set all her own relationships. She had always pictured that that would be the way she and Jemme would be. She imagined that in their dotage they would be as close as they had been when they were first married, but with a lifetime's worth of happy memories and learned wisdom. Whenever she reasoned with herself that she was being idealistic, the spectre of her parents' marriage loomed before her eyes and reminded her that it was something she could hope for.

After the success of the armour sale, Hil noticed that Jemme was delegating more and more responsibility to Burbona. He trusted her judgement and taste absolutely, and sometimes seemed hesitant to make decisions without checking with her first. As Hil sat at home reading alongside *la Liseuse*, he visited the Quai de Louvre with Burbona, trawled through Sotheby's catalogues and toured the Hôtels Particuliers. It felt as if their fortunes had become divided; as Jemme's life was filled with excitement and new beginnings, Hil's was becoming emptier by the day. The more one seemed to flourish, the more the other seemed to suffer. Hil went back to staying in Paris at the weekend, and Burbona began to go to the chateau with increased regularity. Hil tried to think of the chateau as just a separate element of Jemme's life that she wasn't a part of anymore. It made her feel better about everything else for a while, before she realised that it was the most important element of Jemme's life. It wasn't merely a hobby or interest, it was who he was, and he could no more be separated from it than a breeze could be from the wind. As time went by, she realised that Burbona was an important part of that element of his life and so was now a part of their lives whether she liked it or not. It seemed Jemme had also been thinking about how large a part Burbona was now playing at the chateau.

'Sweetheart, I wanted to ask your opinion on something,' he said to Hil one evening.

'What's that?' asked Hil, closing her book.

'It's Burbona.'

'What about her?

'Well, I'm starting to feel awkward about her role.'

'Oh?' said Hil, looking interested.

'Yes, she's just been doing so much for us and she has so much responsibility within the chateau. She's so involved in everything that, to be honest, I couldn't imagine how I would continue the project without her.'

'Well you managed perfectly well before,' said Hil tartly, realising that they were not having the conversation she had thought.

'I know, but it's on a completely different level now – look how much progress we've made: the whole Crusader room is finished, the Calligraphy room will be finished in a couple of weeks, and several of the noble rooms are well on their way. I couldn't have done any of it without her, she's been indispensable. It's not just her input though, it's all the work she's doing elsewhere – arranging private viewings, finding sales, working her connections, everything like that.'

'Well, it doesn't sound much like there's a problem.'

'It's not exactly a problem, you're right. In a way things have never been better. It's just that I feel very indebted to her. She's doing so much work for me – for us – and she's not getting anything in return.'

'I wouldn't be so sure about that,' said Hil. 'I think she's enjoying it every bit as much as you are. It's not like she has an actual job that you're distracting her from.'

'What do you mean?' asked Jemme, furrowing his eyebrows.

'I just think she has a rather blessed life, that's all, so you don't need to worry too much about her. Think about it – she doesn't have any real responsibility at all. She gets to waft around fancy restaurants and beautiful houses, chatting to her wealthy friends about things that interest her. Now she gets to go to auctions and antique houses and spend someone else's money – it's not exactly like it's a hardship.'

'Hil, you're being quite mean – I'm really surprised.'

Hil paused for a moment; she honestly couldn't tell if she was being mean or not. She'd felt quite bitter when she'd spoken about Burbona, and wasn't ready to switch from that to contrition quite yet.

'You barely know her,' said Jemme.

'I don't know – I think I have the measure of her quite well,' said Hil.

'What's wrong with you – you're never like this!'

'I'm not being like anything!'

'You are, you're being...' Jemme searched for the word – 'spiteful.' He paused. 'And you're never like that. You don't know anything about Burbona – everything you've just said is based on pure speculation and your assumptions. You have no idea what she might have had to go through, or anything about her life at all.'

Hil pursed her lips but didn't say anything. She exhaled through her nose loudly and felt a hot ball of anger inside her chest.

'It's not fair of you to completely assassinate her character like that, just because you're jealous,' said Jemme.

The ball of anger exploded and Hil slammed her book down. She shot Jemme a glare and marched out of the room. Jemme shook his head in disbelief. He couldn't believe that jealousy could make his wife behave so differently to usual, and was cross with Hil for being so childish. He resolved not to give it another thought, and instead turn his attention to the real problem: how to make things right with Burbona. The next time they saw each other, a solution presented itself – albeit for the short term only. As they discussed future rooms, and Jemme indulged in another of his lengthy speeches about the philosophy behind the chateau, Burbona suddenly chipped in, 'When was the last time you went to Venice?'

Jemme stopped, surprised, 'Venice? Goodness, it's been a while; let me think…
I don't think I've been since I started this whole project.'

'That's what I was worried about.'

'Worried? What do you mean.'

'That it wouldn't be fresh in your mind. It's such a perfect exemplar for the
chateau and I think we could learn a great deal from it.'

'An exemplar?'

'Just listening to you talk about the passage of influence from East to West
made me realise that it was so glaringly obvious, we should have both thought of
it before. Can you think of one single place that encapsulates what you're trying
to do as much as Venice? It's a crucible of cultural influence and a hotbed of
artistic innovation. It should have been the first place we looked to for inspiration
and ideas.'

Jemme thought for a moment longer. 'You're right, of course, I can't
believe that we didn't think to look to Venice before. It's so obvious. A
childhood visit there was one of the most formative experiences of my life,
and where the whole philosophy behind the chateau was born. I suppose since
then I've always been trying to get back to that moment of understanding and
clarity.'

'In that case, we shouldn't waste any time!' said Burbona. 'I can book it pretty
much straight away, if that would suit you.'

Jemme laughed, 'You're so impulsive!'

Burbona shrugged, 'I don't see any point in waiting. If it's what we both want
to do, why not seize the moment?'

'Well, I'm sorry to be boring, but I have certain responsibilities at the bank – I
can't just up and leave I'm afraid, although believe me, sometimes I wish I could.
But anyway, regardless of when, I'll be the one booking it. You're coming as my
guest, and I refuse to let you pay for a single thing.'

Burbona flashed Jemme a winning smile, 'Thank you.'

'It's just a small way of saying thank you for all your hard work. We need to
talk about this properly at some point, but for now let me spoil you a little in
Italy!'

'I shan't protest too much about that!' said Burbona.

Jemme consulted with DD, and decided that the best time to go would be in
about three weeks. That would allow time to finish work on several key accounts
and ensure that the transition over to DD was as smooth as possible. Hil had not
taken the news particularly well, and had complained that Jemme had never been
able to find time to take her on holiday, and muttered about having thought
Venice was 'their' place.

'You're being ridiculous, Hil. It's a city – how can it belong to two particular people?'

'I mean that I thought it was special to us,' said Hil sulkily.

'Yes, it is, but just because I've been to one place with you, does that mean I'm not allowed to go there with anyone else? That doesn't make any sense at all.'

Hil looked hurt and told him that if he didn't understand now then he was never going to understand, and Jemme just felt exasperated. It was obvious, he thought, that Hil was jealous again, and it was making her impossible.

He spent the next few weeks tying up loose ends at work, and planning the Venice trip. He wanted to thank Burbona, obviously, and also to explore ideas for the chateau, but he also found himself wanting to impress her. Burbona had the upper hand in so much that they did in Paris, but a foreign country was a great leveller. It would give him the chance to demonstrate that his knowledge of restaurants, hotels and cafes was equal to hers, not to mention his understanding of the local art and history of the place. He wasn't quite sure why he wanted to impress her, he just felt the impulse to. He was so used to being in control in all his relationships, whether business or personal; having someone regularly best him was invigorating and revitalising, but he wasn't going to give up the opportunity to redress the balance if it presented itself. He soon realised that Burbona wasn't used to relinquishing control either. Once the flights had been booked, the next obstacle to present itself was a tussle over hotels. Burbona favoured the Hotel Danieli for its famous afternoon cakes and views over the Adriatic, whilst Jemme wanted to stay at the Gritti Palace, former private residence of the Doge, Andrea Gritti. They reached a slight impasse, before Burbona graciously backed down, 'I probably shouldn't be eating cake anyway,' she laughed, 'and besides, I've been there many times before already and it would be nice to go somewhere different.' Jemme was delighted and booked the best suite in the hotel.

'I hope you don't mind sharing,' he said, 'it's just that this room is so wonderful and the singles aren't anywhere near as spectacular. We'll have a very large room each and then there's a gorgeous sitting room that connects them, so it basically feels like two separate rooms anyway.'

'Not at all,' said Burbona, 'I'm looking forward to seeing it all. It will be nice to see a city from someone else's point of view as well. I'm looking forward to handing over all responsibility for restaurants and cafes to you.'

'Excellent,' said Jemme, feeling victorious.

'Of course, we're there to work as well, so if you don't mind, I'll make some suggestions on that front, but otherwise I cede everything to you.'

'Perfect.' Jemme paused. 'On that note, I still want to talk to you about this whole set up.'

'Which set up?'

'The fact that you're doing so much work for me – for Hil and me, for essentially nothing in return.'

'I wouldn't say nothing,' said Burbona, 'I'm enjoying myself hugely, and you're taking me to Venice!'

'I know, it just seems such a trifling recompense considering everything you've done. I was saying to Hil that I don't even know how I could continue with the project without you. I really want you to continue to be a part of how it develops, but I don't think I could ask you to make such a commitment of your time and energies, without setting out some kind of agreement.'

Burbona fixed a steady gaze on him, 'What were you thinking of?'

'Well this is where it gets a little tricky, and I've been feeling rather awkward about the whole thing. In any other circumstance, I would offer to pay you, but I –' Jemme flushed slightly, 'I'm just worried that you'll be insulted by that and it would change the dynamic. I love working with you as an equal, and you're one of the few people I actually have that relationship with. If I started trying to pay you then I might feel as if you were my employee, and it would make things strange. Also, I don't want you to think that I think you're only doing all of this because you want to get something out of it. I know that you believe in the project, and you're the last person in the world I would expect to be mercenary,' he ground to a halt, realising that he was rambling. Burbona's clear stare had unnerved him, as it often did. She paused for a moment.

'You're correct, I am not doing any of this for financial returns, and I do believe in this project. However, you are correct again that the situation needs redressing. I believe that the longer I work *with* you, the more it will feel as if I am working *for* you, and so the greater your unease about the situation. Here is what I propose: pay me a retainer. We can work out the amount at another point. I think far from making things awkward, it will make things awkward if you do not. It is the only way of ensuring that we both feel we are giving and taking equally from this partnership. I don't mind how much it is, I'm not particularly in need of the money, but it should not feel like a token amount, otherwise the whole idea is undermined.' She finished, and continued to look at Jemme. He was slightly taken aback at first; he had forgotten how direct and in control Burbona could be. Whilst he had felt stumbling and awkward bringing the matter up, she had been calm, measured and clear sighted. He was impressed. The more he considered what she was suggesting, the more he was impressed by that too. It was a simple, elegant solution and it made perfect sense. She was right. If he paid her a retainer, he wouldn't feel like he was insulting her at all. He would feel like he was giving her the recognition she deserved. Moreover, far from estranging them, it would make them more equal. She would feel more able to make suggestions and recommendations, and he would feel that he could criticise her and maybe even reject her proposals. He had not needed or wanted to do either so far, but he was sure if the situation had arisen he would have felt he could do neither, whilst she was doing him a favour.

Satisfied with the resolution, he focussed his energies on looking forward to Venice.

Chapter Thirty-One

Some three weeks later, Jemme and Burbona sat in a private departures lounge at Charles de Gaulle airport. Jemme had spared no expense when it came to the flights, and the staff – some of whom recognised him – were treating them like royalty. It was an auspicious start, and one smooth flight later they found themselves in a water taxi speeding down the Canal Grande to the Gritti Palace. The sun blazed down on them and the breeze from the canal was refreshing. Jemme looked around him as their driver threaded his way past gondolas, working vessels and pleasure craft. Burbona had been right – it was too long since he was last in Venice, and he had allowed himself to forget how utterly enchanting it was. He had a stab of longing for Hil. They had had such a wonderful time here together, and she was right, it had been a special place for them. He suddenly found himself missing her, and felt guilty that he hadn't brought her on this trip. He didn't think she would have wanted to come, but it seemed unfair to have gone without her to somewhere he knew she loved, and to be staying in the same room even.

'Here we are,' said Burbona, interrupting his train of thought. He looked up at the hotel in front of him and smiled. It was every bit as beautiful as he remembered. The driver had killed the motor and the boat bobbed around next to the private jetty whilst he fiddled with the rope. Now they were stationary he felt the full strength of the sunshine again, and he enjoyed a moment of pure serenity. It was good to be out of Paris.

As soon as they arrived in the reception, he knew that hotel had been the right decision. The building was filled with beautiful antiques and shimmering Murano glass. Intriguing fixtures and architectural details bore testimony to its past at the cross roads of eastern-western interaction, and he could feel inspiration begin to prick the edges of his mind. He knew he was going to come back from this trip filled with ideas. The suite was even better than he remembered. There was a slightly awkward moment when he saw that the staff had set out a bottle of champagne and two glasses, and he realised that they had probably misunderstood the situation. Burbona either didn't notice, or expertly smoothed things over by pointing out the view of the Santa Maria del Giglio square.

As the week unfolded, Jemme found himself retracing many of the holidays he and Hil had taken to Venice. Every restaurant they ate in, he had eaten in with Hil before; the shortcuts they took between galleries were ones he and Hil had discovered together; the cafes he recommended were ones he had whiled away the hours in with Hil, people watching and talking about life. There were a few moments when he felt guilty – he was taking someone else to all of their places. It was like he was violating a special unspoken agreement. There were even moments when he wondered if this trip itself was appropriate. He remonstrated with himself – he was being irrational. Yes, these places held special memories for him and Hil, but that didn't make them their exclusive domain. Over the course of several trips, they had discovered the best places to eat, drink, walk, shop and sit, so naturally these would be the ones he would return to – it made no sense to go to an inferior restaurant when he knew there was a better one just around the corner. As for the trip itself, now he was paying Burbona a retainer, the question of appropriateness was moot. There were no grey areas – it was a work trip; and work they did. They visited every forgotten corner of the city, retraced historical routes, sketched interesting features, and carefully copied passages from antiquarian books in the library. The research felt rigorously academic, and Jemme thoroughly enjoyed himself. *The Professor would be proud of me*, he thought.

He wasn't quite sure how he was going to put all this research into action at the chateau; he just knew that it was going to be useful. He knew that he was going to have a Silk Route section of the chateau, that was a given. He could already see how parts of it would pan out, and he was collecting embellishments for it, mentally, but also literally. He had known for a long time that the Ottoman Empire would feature heavily, as would the Byzantine, so he began to scout out examples of their influence. He didn't have to look too hard. Everywhere he turned, buildings sagged under onion domes, and glazed tiles glinted under the Italian sun. Inlaid metalwork, ceramics, lacquer-ware, enamelled glass and beautiful miniatures were threaded through the ancient houses of the city, channelling the best the East had to offer into this Western hub of commerce and diplomacy. Before his eyes he could see the passage of influence from the East into the work of some of the West's most celebrated artists – Bellini, Tiepolo and Carpaccio.

Over an al fresco lunch in St Mark's Square, Burbona pulled an auction catalogue from her handbag.

'I've been meaning to show you this for ages,' she said, 'and being here has just reminded me.' She flicked the catalogue open to a page which had the corner turned down. 'Look,' she turned it round and passed it to Jemme.

He looked at the page, two-thirds of which was taken up with a photograph of an oil painting, and the rest with text describing it. Immediately Jemme recognised the setting. He lowered the catalogue and looked around himself. 'Isn't that remarkable,' he said.

'How timeless it is?' asked Burbona.

Jemme nodded and looked back at the painting again. It was dated to the seventeenth century, but it could have been painted yesterday, so accurately did it portray the scene around him. It was a beautiful composition, and showed St Mark's Square in all its glory. An assembled crowd watched a theatrical production in the middle of the square. Jemme studied them closely; they were all exotically dressed in different national costumes – from thick Chinese silks to tall Ottoman hats. Jemme realised that like him, and Burbona, they were tourists in a foreign city too. Once they had finished with their merchandise, they were making the most of being in a new place. He found the parity between their two situations, separated by hundreds of years, oddly moving.

'When's the sale?' he asked.

'It's actually already happened, but I'm sure if we really wanted the painting it wouldn't be too difficult to track it down. I actually had another idea though.'

'What was that?'

'I thought it might be fun to commission someone to recreate this painting directly onto the walls of one of the rooms.'

Jemme thought for a moment, 'That would be fun – it would be really different.'

'Exactly. It would be a nod to the Italian fresco tradition too. If Venice epitomises the chateau philosophy, then this painting epitomises Venice.'

'But where would we put it? Could it be at one end of the Silk Route?'

Burbona looked at him for a moment, 'In the Venetian room.'

'The Venetian room?'

'Of course. We've seen and learned far too much on this one trip to scatter around other rooms. Venice definitely deserves its own room.'

'That's a brilliant idea! We'll come back with so much from this trip that it won't take us very long to complete at all.'

'Precisely, and now we know we're going to be creating a room, we can specifically choose select pieces to suit it, rather than buying pieces we like and storing them until we can work out how to fit them into another room. We can get everything shipped directly from here to the chateau.'

'*Salute*,' said Jemme, raising his water glass, 'this trip just keeps getting better!'

'Cin cin,' replied Burbona, picking up her glass and returning the toast.

They sat and chatted until the sun was fading over St Mark's Square, and the café was beginning to fill up with the dinner-time crowd.

'I think we'd better move on!' said Jemme, just after the waiter had been over for the third or fourth time to pointedly ask if they would be ordering anything soon. They found a small bar with outdoor seats facing on to the canal. It was the first place they had been that Jemme hadn't already visited with Hil. As they sat and watched reflected light dance on the canal water, Jemme marvelled again at the fact that they had effectively planned a whole room over the space of one afternoon. He couldn't believe that Burbona had been able to help him realise such ideas and he felt alive. He was working, and thinking, at the speed he had been hoping for, for years. It was exhausting, but also exhilarating. He wasn't used to being able to think in this way out loud. Before, he would talk to Hil, but in recent years she had become more of a sounding board before losing interest all together. To be able to exchange rapid-fire ideas with someone else was novel, and meant that he was working twice as fast as he was used to. He liked the way that Burbona thought; she understood his philosophy completely and deftly wove different strands together into the form of a room. The Venetian room was about as perfect an idea as Jemme could have hoped for, for the chateau. It would be a panegyric to one of the greatest cities in the world, it would record its importance at the intersection of East and West, showing the interplay of culture and the influence of learning. Furthermore, it would allow Jemme to continue artistic traditions. Artistic techniques redolent of Venice would be used by craftsmen to complete the room: trompe l'oeil, glass-blowing and mosaic laying.

The room would be filled with references and symbolism. He liked the idea that a visitor would have to stare at the walls for some time to unlock their meaning, if at all. He liked the thought that everyone would notice different details, and bring fresh meaning and context to the room, just like a gallery. The trompe l'oeil, for example, was to recreate the fabulous red velvet curtains of La Fenice. Some would see the reference to Venice's most famous opera house, and think of the city's great associations with Vivaldi and Verdi. Others would admire the refined artistic technique of trompe l'oeil, and think of the richly baroque history of artisans and master craftsmen. He liked the fact that everyone would come away having seen something new, or innovative or different, perhaps having even learned something. It was beginning to feel like his own little museum.

As the week drew to a close, not only had he all but finished his ideas for the Silk Route and planned the Venetian room in its entirety, he had also sketched out the plans for a further room. Inspired by the beautiful churches, chapel and religious paintings, he had begun to consider early Christianity. He had always found the spread of the religion fascinating, and been drawn by the way it acted as a conduit for book learning and brought new cultural and artistic influences with it. He had studied its continuing effect on the canon of Western art, through the Renaissance to the exquisite chiaroscuro of Carravagio, and eventually the glassy colours of Georges Rouault. However, he had never considered that the development and spread of Christianity could be directly relevant to the chateau. Burbona had first planted the idea by talking about Santa Sabina in Rome. She had been describing the beautifully carved wooden doors which stood at its entrance, and it had made Jemme think about how faith often drove cultural practice, as well as artistic style and academic learning. It was something he thought might be worth exploring in one of the rooms, and he broached the subject with Burbona.

'Well, why not explore it with specific reference to Christianity?'

'I could do, I suppose. I'm just rather hesitant to make anything within the chateau overly religious.'

'It doesn't have to be. It won't be a direct examination of the religion, more the way it acted as a channel for different cultural influences. Besides, think how beautiful some of the early Christian artefacts are – wouldn't they be a marvellous addition to the chateau? They would enrich the collection so much.'

'That's very true, I suppose it would be good to have some diversity in the collection.'

'But that's the beauty of it – it's all linked back in to the same theme.'

'What do you mean?'

'It's all examining the relationship between the East and West.'

'The East? You mean that we should be including artefacts from the Eastern Orthodox church – icons and other Eastern treasures?'

Burbona shook her head and her small, diamond drop earrings caught the light, 'No, much before that – during the very birth of Christianity itself. Think about where it came from.'

Jemme paused, 'Rome?'

Burbona shook her head again, 'No. Think! You're just saying that because we've just been talking about Rome.'

Jemme paused again; he didn't know what Burbona was driving at.

Burbona sighed with impatience at his confusion, 'The Levant!'

'The Levant?' Jemme repeated slowly.

'Yes! I meant much before Rome, I meant at the very, very beginnings. Where was the crucible, the very birthplace of the whole religion?'

'The Levant! Of course!'

'Exactly. It's a fascinating period from both a Western and an Eastern point of view, but it's even more fascinating in terms of the interaction between them.'

'You're right! It's something that has influenced and shaped Western society so much and it has roots in the East!'

Burbona nodded as if it was obvious.

'It's a great idea. There's so much we can include in the room as well! It's such a good demonstration of the passage of influence.'

Burbona nodded again.

'Do you know what? I'm going to recreate the doors of Santa Sabina as the entrance to this room. It's the thought that opened up this whole room, and so it should be the door that opens it too. Brava, Burbona!'

Burbona smiled and looked gratified.

With the week finally over, they flew back to Paris filled with ideas, just as Jemme had hoped they would. He was positively buzzing when he arrived home.

'Hello,' said Hil, morosely. Instantly his mood came crashing down.

'Hello sweetheart, you don't sound too cheerful,' he said, trying his hardest not to lose his high. 'What's the matter?'

Hil looked at him dolefully, 'I've been on my own for a week.'

'Well I'm sure you haven't been completely on your own! I'm sure it was a great opportunity to catch up with all your friends!'

'I didn't feel like going out.'

'Well then I'm sure it was nice to have the house to yourself.'

Hil stared at him, 'I often have the house to myself.'

'Well,' began Jemme, starting to feel a bit desperate, 'you could always have gone to the chateau, they would have loved to see you!'

Hil's stare turned into a glower.

'Right, I'll just go and unpack...' Jemme said, slinking off to the bedroom. He realised that now was not the time to start telling her all about his great plans. Sighing slightly, he realised that it probably wasn't the time to give her the souvenir he had brought back either.

✻   ✻   ✻   ✻

Back at work, DD had managed affairs so smoothly in Jemme's absence that he had barely any backlog at all to contend with. It left him free to jump onto the phone straight away, and begin coordinating deliveries of Venetian acquisitions, artists and decorators. After a few hours he put the now-hot telephone receiver down and felt a surge of adrenaline. Things were moving so fast and his dream was beginning to take life before his eyes. He couldn't decide which part of his plans he was most excited about. He expected that when everything was finished he would be able to choose a favourite, but for now the best part would be going to the chateau and finding dozens of artists and craftsmen at work. Just at that moment, DD came through with a list of antiquarian books he had acquired for the Vigne-Verte library in Jemme's absence, and Jemme felt his cup truly was full.

He headed into the countryside tingling with excitement that weekend. He wished Hil could have come too; it felt like months since they'd spent time together – the last time she visited the chateau in fact. It was probably for the best, he thought; he was going to be so preoccupied with all the works at the chateau that she might feel a little abandoned. *Perhaps if she came down when the place was buzzing with energy it might prove to be infectious*, he mused, as he turned off the road to the top of the driveway. Down at the bottom he was surprised, but also encouraged to see several cars he didn't recognise parked outside the main entrance. He drew up next to a mud-spattered vehicle with local plates and went inside. He all but bumped into Marguerite who was bustling through the Halle d'Honneur.

'Ah, Marguerite, excuse me!' he said, greeting his housekeeper.

'Oh!! Monsieur, oh, la, la, la – it is so busy here!' she said, retying her apron. 'I am running all over the place, like a *mouche!*'

'Like a fly?' laughed Jemme, 'Why are you so busy?'

Marguerite looked at Jemme, 'Men!' she said dramatically. 'They are everywhere! Not only your fancy foreign artist ones, but great lumbering local ones Philby has brought up from the village! They're bringing mud into the house, they're eating faster than I can cook, and they're cluttering up the place!'

Jemme bit the inside of his cheek to stop himself from laughing, 'I'm afraid I'm to blame for a great deal of that, Marguerite, I went on a bit of a binge this week and organised as much as possible to happen as soon as possible.'

'Binge, Monsieur? No, no it is not your fault. It is the fault of these *oafs!*' she shouted, as one particularly large man clumped past, thick with plaster dust which was dropping off him onto the floor as he walked. He noticed Marguerite staring daggers at him, and scuttled off with very little agility in the opposite direction.

'You see!' said Marguerite pointing accusingly at the deposits of plaster. 'I polished this floor because I knew you were coming! Now look at it!'

'I'm sorry Marguerite. There are going to be lots of different people coming in and out over the next few months. It might be better to leave the cleaning for a while.'

Marguerite looked like she had just sucked on a lemon.

'*Leave* it, Monsieur?'

'Well, not completely, I just meant that it doesn't have to look like a hotel all the time. It's such a pity when you've worked so hard, only for it all to be undone like this.' He gestured at the plasterer's trail. 'When the whole chateau's finished, we'll need someone with your exacting standards to keep it looking as good as any stately home, but until then I'm sure you'll be busy feeding all these new mouths.'

Marguerite looked placated – Jemme's flattery had worked well.

'Is Madame Mafeze here?' she asked, suddenly looking hopeful.

'I'm afraid not, not this time. I'm hoping that Burbona will come down either this weekend or next weekend though.'

Marguerite looked as if she had just put the lemon back into her mouth, 'Oh,' she said. Jemme went upstairs to unpack, puzzling over the look on Marguerite's face when he had mentioned Burbona. *I hope she's not jealous of her too*, he thought to himself.

After he'd dropped his bag in his room, Jemme made his way along the corridor and down the smaller set of stairs at the end. Instead of the grand stairs which would lead him back to the Halle d'Honneur, these took him down to the end of another corridor which would lead him to the kitchen in one direction and another entrance to the chateau in the other. He passed along the corridor until he had reached the hallway in front of the entrance. This was much more of a workman's entrance, and despite the fact it had been refurbished and boasted some period features, it was nowhere near as grand as the main entrance. Nonetheless, it was very useful for accessing this wing of the chateau, and the stone staircase which curled back on itself was perfect for all the rooms which would be in this eastern side. He made his way up to the first floor, where he had planned the room examining the birth of Christianity. He made note of the smooth painted walls on the way out – they were a blank canvas begging to be decorated with something. He wondered whether it should be some kind of narrative, which prepared visitors for the room they were about to see. He played with the idea a little as he climbed the steps. The birth of Christianity room would be the first room visitors would see on this side of the chateau and he liked the idea that the journey could begin at this side entrance, as soon as they stepped inside. Climbing the stairs would whisk them through history until they arrived at the gates of Santa Sabina. There was poetry in the idea, and he resolved to share it with Burbona next time he saw her. He would tell the Professor, too – he'd been neglecting him somewhat recently and he was sure the Professor would have some interesting ideas about filling up the walls.

When he reached the room at the top, he found that the doorway had already been extended and the doorframe refitted. Two large pieces of walnut had been cut to size and rested up against the wall either side of the door. A man was sketching onto one of the doors with a pencil, which had been thoroughly chewed at one end. He was engrossed in what he was doing and didn't hear Jemme approach. Jemme stood behind him for a moment before gently tapping him on the shoulder to alert him to his presence.

The man jumped and spun round. He had almond-shaped eyes which were a dark, almost indigo colour. He had a mop of curled, grey hair and Jemme could just make out another pencil sticking out through one curl, where it had been tucked behind his ear.

'Sorry, I didn't mean to startle you,' Jemme said, 'I'm Mr Mafeze.'

'*Ah, bonjour, Monsieur*,' said the man in very accented French. He extended his hand, tucking his pencil behind his other ear as he did so. 'Hussam,' he said offering his hand.

Jemme shook it, and was surprised at how calloused and leathery it felt. 'Hussam,' he repeated, 'that definitely doesn't sound like a French name!'

'Neither does Mafeze,' the man laughed, 'you're Turkish, Monsieur?'

'I am, but I've been living in France for a lifetime now.'

'I lived in Turkey for a while too. I have lived in most of the countries of the Holy Land. My work has taken me all over.'

He turned to face the door again and scrutinised his sketches.

'Well in that case, we have a great deal in common,' said Jemme, 'and I'm pleased that you're the one carving this door for us; it seems even more appropriate given your background.'

The man smiled, 'Yes, I heard of what you are doing here. I'm glad to be a part of it. My craft hasn't changed much since the original door would have been carved, probably in the sixth century, and I enjoy meeting someone who appreciates the continuity of that tradition.'

Jemme looked at the sketches with him for a while and noticed that he had taped a photograph of the doors to the edge of the door he was sketching on. 'What's your method?' he asked the carver.

'At the moment I'm just blocking out the different figures. You see how many elements there are to the composition?' he fished one of the pencils out and used it to point at the photo. Jemme nodded.

'Well, when you're carving, it's very easy to become sucked into the details. You're focussing on such fine chisel work that you don't notice its place within the whole piece. You're working away at your seraphim, and suddenly you realise it's sprawled out of the space it was meant to stay in, and there's no room for your cherubim.'

Jemme looked at the rough outlines and realised that the proportions of the space were much more important than the crude detailing that had been drawn on. 'I see, he said, flicking his eyes between the photo and the wood.

'It's even more important when you're carving across two pieces like this. You don't want to find that everything has shifted a quarter of an inch down on one half, by mistake. That way they won't match up when you close them. You see?'

Jemme noticed the faint grid of lines on the other piece of wood for the first time, 'I see,' he said again. 'How long to do you think it will take you to finish both pieces?'

'The man puffed his cheeks out and exhaled slowly, 'It's hard to say to be honest. I'll spend at least a day sketching before I even pick up a chisel. My mother was a dress-maker all her life, *measure twice, cut once*, she'd always say. The same's true in carpentry – I'll draw it all out in increasing detail, because once I've started carving into it, one small mistake can't be undone and can ruin the whole thing.'

'Of course, please, take as long as you like. I'm a big advocate of thorough preparation!'

'Once I've carved the top couple of lines, I'll have much more of an idea of how long it will take and I'll let you know. I won't know this piece of wood until then.'

'Won't know it?' asked Jemme.

The man chewed the end of his pencil slowly as he studied the photograph. He removed it and added a few lines to the right hand side of the door before turning to Jemme,

'Yes, won't know it. Each piece of wood is different you see – even if it's the same type. If I'd already carved something from this particular tree I would already know how it was going to behave and how much pressure I would need to apply, and whether it was going to chip or splinter. I don't know anything about it and how long it's been stored for, or whether it was seasoned, or how many wet summers it lived through. All of those things will change how I need to handle it, but as I don't know any of them, I'll have to find out for myself by treating it very carefully when I first start carving it. Once I understand it a little more I can speed up.'

'Well that all makes perfect sense,' said Jemme, 'I'd better leave you to it. If you need anything else, please do not hesitate to ask Marguerite. I'm guessing you've been fed already?'

The man patted his belly and looked slightly terrified, 'Yes, there's no danger of me going hungry whilst I'm here,' he said.

Jemme laughed, 'Marguerite can be rather frightening when she's wielding a soup ladle,' he agreed. 'I look forward to coming and seeing how you're progressing later on,' he said.

'I look forward to showing you,' said Hussam. Jemme wished him goodbye and went back to the spiral stairs. He had enjoyed chatting with him and learning a little more; it had been exactly the kind of conversation he had imagined himself having. He climbed up to the next floor and walked along the corridor a little way, to the room which he had designated the Venetian room. Although there were no artists waiting there to greet him, he was pleased to see that the room had been primed for them and the smell of paint from the freshly white-washed walls still lingered. In one corner of the room, a stack of dustsheets had been neatly piled up and a stepladder leaned up against the wall next to them. Someone, presumably Philby, had run an extension cord into the room, and a large free-standing spotlight stood ready to be turned on. Jemme looked at the size of the bulb – it looked big enough to blind someone, and he hoped that Philby wasn't being over zealous.

He made his way down the corridor to the other end, noting the blank walls again as he did so. At the end he opened a door out into the grand staircase again and made his way back to the Halle d'Honneur. He decided to go and peek at the library. Having just seen several rooms in their early stages, it would be nice to see one which had been completed so perfectly. It gave him something to aspire to. He flicked the lights on, only intending to stay for a few seconds, before noticing a small packet on his desk. He made his way over, and opened it with a bone-handled letter knife he kept in one of the desk's drawers. Inside were the carefully wrapped books which had been on DD's list. He must have given special instructions that they were not to be put away, but left out for Jemme to choose. It was the first time he had actually seen them, and gently lifting the top one up to his face, he took a long sniff of its spine. It smelled of old leather and must. He exhaled slowly and a smile spread across his face – these books harboured the mould and memories of centuries. He carefully explored each one, gently probing their dog-eared corners, torn fly-leafs and missing book-plates. Each imperfection told a story, and he lost himself in their mystery. His train of thought was interrupted by Marguerite's shadow, looming over him.

'Monsieur! Whatever are you doing in the library at this time of night!'

'I've just been deciding where these new books should go,' said Jemme.

'New? They don't look very new!'

Jemme laughed, 'Well you'd better not let DD hear you say that. He spent quite a long time finding them all.'

'Oh they're *those* books. Yes, Monsieur Dietz was very specific that I shouldn't handle them,' Marguerite wrinkled up her nose and peered at them, 'although I can't see why, it's not like I would damage their appearance!' she hooted with laughter. 'Anyway, it's far too late, Monsieur, and you haven't eaten yet,' she ushered him out of the library and turned the light off behind them. After a very large supper, Jemme suddenly found himself feeling very tired. There was just one more thing he wanted to see before he went to bed though, and, after wishing Marguerite goodnight and entreating her to allow Aude to finish the mountain of washing up tomorrow, he headed back towards the main entrance hall. Just before he reached the hall, he turned and opened a heavy wooden door. It was a pointed shape and sat in a stone frame, with a large iron ring for a handle. It swung open with a pleasing creak and Jemme flicked the lights on. He stared at the space in front of him and smiled to himself. He had made the right decision: it was perfect. It might have seemed an odd choice for such an important feature, but he was confident it was the right one.

Stretching out in front of him was one of the chateau's oldest features: a stone staircase which ran down to the building's original level. The stairs were wide, but shallow and two channels, feet-width apart, had been worn smooth over the centuries. The walls either side were bare, and it was here that Jemme planned to recreate the Silk Route. He had already chosen a small group of artists, and prepared some very rough sketches to show them. They would be arriving tomorrow, and he was excited about meeting them and getting started. He almost felt slightly nervous at the same time; this was such an important feature and concept and they might see it in a different way to him. He was originally thinking of dedicating one of the larger display rooms to the Silk Route, but when he thought about it, it didn't make sense ideologically. The person who was looking at it also had to be making a journey. To represent the route in a static context undermined its importance. The symbolism of going from one level to another worked perfectly, and he enjoyed the fact that the whole route would not be seen by someone standing at either the bottom or the top of the stairs. Just like in the room upstairs, dustsheets, lighting and various pieces of artistic equipment had been left in preparation. *Everything had moved so quickly over the past week and everyone had been so organised*, he thought to himself as he went back up the main stairs to bed. If things continued at this pace he would be finished before he knew it.

* * * *

The next day he rose early, and blinked in confusion at his surroundings until they came into focus and he remembered that he was in his bedroom at the chateau. He felt a rush of excitement, kicked the covers off and jumped out of bed. After a lightning-quick shower, he took the grand stairs two at a time and presented himself in the kitchen for his morning coffee. Poor Aude was still standing over the sink, working on a pile of dishes which looked even larger than it had last night.

'Good morning, Marguerite. Goodness, that seems to have grown!' he said, nodding towards the sink.

Aude turned round, '*Bonjour, Monsieur,*' she said shyly, her face red from the steam.

'Monsieur, that is just from breakfast!' Marguerite said. 'The girl had finished everything from last night and we had five minutes of a clean kitchen before they all descended for feeding again!'

'I take it they're still hungry?'

'I wouldn't be surprised if they ate those dirty old books of yours!'

Jemme laughed, 'Well it will all be worth it in the end, I promise.'

Marguerite looked placated, then stood over him until he had finished a large plate of fluffy scrambled eggs on thick slabs of toast. Eventually she was satisfied, refilled his coffee mug for him and let him leave. Sipping his coffee as he went, Jemme made his way back to the Venetian room as fast as his full belly would allow him. He could hear the bustle of activity before he made his way down the corridor, and his excitement rose. As he neared the room he could hear the unmistakable twang of American accents, intercut with good-natured laughter.

'Mornin'!' rang out one of the American voices once Jemme had arrived at the door.

'Ah, Mr Mafeze?' said another.

'Yes, good morning all!' said Jemme, going round and introducing himself to the quartet in the room. They each shook his hand powerfully and grinned, giving their names, which all appeared to have been shortened to one syllable.

'Thank you again so much for coming so far,' said Jemme, 'and at such short notice too.'

'It's a great commission; we're pleased to be working on it,' shrugged a high-foreheaded man, who had introduced himself as Marv.

'Yeah, thanks for putting us up! It's a real pleasure to get to stay in a genuine French *sha-tow*,' drawled a tall man – Tim, as far as Jemme could remember.

'Well, it's a pleasure to have you, I'm so pleased that we could find artists of your calibre so quickly, and persuade them to fly over from New York too!'

'Aw, Mr Mafeze, you'll make us blush,' teased the third American.

'Well there's not much I wouldn't do if Burbona asked me nicely!' said the fourth. 'Flying to France didn't seem to be too much of a sacrifice!'

His friends murmured their agreement. 'A real class act, that Burbona,' said Marv.

'Remind me how you met?' asked Jemme, not sure if he actually knew.

'About five years ago we worked on a loft apartment in New York – real nice place, bigger than you've ever seen. Client seemed to have an endless budget too, so we stayed there months and got to run wild with our imagination. Some of the best work we've ever produced, eh fellas?'

The other three nodded their agreement, 'Best work we've ever produced,' repeated Marv.

'Anyways,' Tim continued, 'this guy had some fancy friends who were always dropping by. Came from all over the world. Burbona was one of 'em, and – well, once you meet a lady like that, you don't forget her in a hurry.'

The others nodded. 'You don't forget her in a hurry,' agreed Marv.

'Then,' Tim continued, 'must have been about a year and a half later, we get this call to do a casino in Vegas. Completely different job, but client let us run away with the project again and I don't think I'm boasting when I say we did a darn fine job, eh fellas?'

'Darn fine job,' repeated Marv.

'Then, just as we've nearly finished, this French lady swishes up to us, looking a million dollars and straight away we realise it's Burbona! She says her hellos, and I says "we got to stop bumping into each other like this" – being all funny, and so I give her my card, hopin' we'd see her again one day.'

'Think we all was!' said the fourth American.

'Then, out of the blue, she calls a week ago and tells us about this special project she's working on. I guess lots of stuff happens at the right time – she just happened to see us working on two of our greatest pieces, and we just happen to be in between jobs when she calls. All came together nicely.'

Jemme smiled to himself. Hearing of coincidences like that, and examples of providence at work, always made him think of his grandmother.

'But you didn't want to hear that whole story,' said the third American, 'you want to talk about what we're going to do – what you want us to do, I should say.'

'Please,' said Tim, gesturing to the bottom step of the ladder, 'have a seat and tell us about this room.'

Perched on his tiny rung, Jemme detailed his plans for the room, describing some of the philosophy behind it at the same time. The four men listened carefully and allowed him to talk uninterrupted until he had completely finished.

'Sounds good to me,' said number three.

'Like what you're thinking,' said four.

'It's great,' agreed Tim, 'and you'd struggle to find a better trompe l'oeil artist than Marv here. Only thing I'm wondering about is the floor and the ceiling.'

Jemme paused, 'What about them?'

'Well, you've got big plans for the walls, what about the ceiling?'

'I wasn't going to do anything to it,' said Jemme, 'it's just been painted, so it's nice and fresh.'

'Yeah, but it's white.'

'Yes, it is,' agreed Jemme.

'Way I see it, you're creatin' an experience in here, not just a room, right?'

'Right.'

'So, you're going to all the trouble to get one of the world's best trompe l'oeil artists to create a real illusion on the walls right? I mean, you won't believe this thing when you see it! You're going to try and open those curtains every day! But, then you're going to go and break the illusion with a plain old ceiling. Bam! Straight away someone sees that and they're taken right back to being in a room.'

'I suppose that makes sense,' said Jemme. 'I want someone to feel they step into this room, and instantly they're in a different world.'

'Yeah, exactly,' enthused either three or four.

'What do you suggest?' asked Jemme.

Tim shrugged, 'If there's one thing Vegas taught us, it's go wild!'

'Go wild,' repeated Marv.

'You're in good hands, Mr Mafeze,'

'I can see that! Now that you're here, can I ask you to think of some ideas of your own? I'll be thinking too, but it would be great to get your input.'

'Sure thing, Mr Mafeze,' they chorused.

Jemme made his way down the spiral staircase below to check on the artist. Just as he had said, he was still in the drawing stages, although now the blocks on the second door were starting to look a little more angelic. Jemme talked about Turkey with him for a while, and then left him to his devices and went back to the Silk Route stairway. As he passed through the Halle d'Honneur, a sunbeam sliced through the just-open shutters and lit up the marble floor. He decided to go out to the garden instead and have a walk in the sunshine. The garden was developing faster than the house, and it was always pleasant to spend time wandering through the lime-tree bower, the orchard, and by the lakeside. The sculpture garden was blooming too, with new stone and marble works shooting up every time Jemme returned.

He made a half loop around the grounds, and took a small detour to look at the vegetable patch. He had been enjoying the solitude and so, when he found someone else sitting cross-legged at the edge of the marrow bed, he jumped. The figure looked up at him and they stared at each other for a while. Jemme recognised the odd-looking fellow but was struggling to place him. Without breaking his stare, the man reached one hand behind him and pulled a large jar of honey towards himself. He looked down at the jar and slowly unscrewed it, produced a spoon from one pocket and methodically scooped out one heaped spoonful of the thick-set honey.

'Ah, hello, Noury,' said Jemme, suddenly realising who he was.

Noury made sure he had licked the spoon clean before he replied.

'Hello,' he said, staring straight at Jemme again.

In all the excitement about the new wave of works, Jemme had completely forgotten about the mystery of who this man was, and how he had appeared suddenly at the chateau, or more to the point, why.

'Can I ask....what exactly it is you're doing by the marrows?'

'Attempting headstand,' replied Noury

'Of course,' replied Jemme, wondering why he had bothered asking at all. He contemplated the crossed-figured mystery before him. He didn't appear to be in any hurry to leave, and Jemme realised that whilst he was living under his roof and eating his food he might as well put Noury to good use. He looked at the honey pot again and remembered what the other staff had said about him never eating anything else. Well, whilst he was living under his roof at least.

'Noury, can you paint?' he asked.

Noury stared at him expressionless for a while, 'I am an artist,' he said.

'Of course,' said Jemme. He paused, 'Well, I think I have just the task for you. Would you be interested in painting a special one off piece?'

'I am an artist,' said Noury again.

'Of course,' said Jemme.

Noury pulled the honey jar towards him again. 'Well, this is going to be an interesting episode,' thought Jemme to himself.

Chapter Thirty-Two

Later that afternoon, Jemme had managed to put all thoughts of Noury behind him as he welcomed the Silk Route artists to the chateau. They were a motley assortment of individuals, who seemed to be a product of the route itself. They came from various stops along the ancient road – modern-day Azerbaijan, Russia and Turkmenistan; each one seemed to embody an odd assortment of influences, so that Jemme wasn't quite sure who was from where. He greeted them all warmly, and quickly discovered that they spoke varying levels of English and French. Mahmout, the Azerbaijani, was easily the most talkative of the group and seemed to speak the most amount of English. He wore a sateen shirt with buttonholes along the entire length of the sleeve slits, which looked distinctly Azerbaijani, and a small taqiyah perched on top of his head, which did not.

'Thank you all so much for coming,' Jemme said, 'I know some of you have come a long way and it's really appreciated. Being able to assemble the world's best craftsmen for this project is a privilege, and I'm looking forward to working with every one of you.' He paused and Mahmout bowed his head, as if on behalf of all of them.

'I've prepared some sketches,' Jemme continued, producing some papers and unfurling them. He handed them around the small group, who scrutinised them and nodded. Thoughtful and deliberate in their reactions, they couldn't have been more different to the Americans, but Jemme was just as excited to have them on board.

'I don't know if you're all familiar with the history of the Silk Road?' he asked.

Mahout bowed his head again, 'It is an important part of all our histories,' he said gravely.

'Good. Well, a friend of mine, a professor in fact, is rather an expert on the subject, and I've consulted with him very closely to make sure everything is as historically accurate as possible. I've got quite a good idea of how I want it to look, which is what I hope you can see in these sketches. The Professor will be dropping in from time to time to see how things are going and to contribute anything he thinks might be worthwhile. I hope that is alright with all of you.'

Mahmout nodded on their behalf for a third time, 'It is important to be correct,' he said.

'This picture – Dubrovnik?' said one of the group who had been staring closely at the sketch Jemme had handed him. His English was heavily accented, and he had a voluminous beard. Jemme tried to remember where he said he was from. He could have sworn he said Russia, but the man was wearing a jacket of thick Chinese silks, and looked almost Mongolian.

'Dubrovnik?' he asked again.

Jemme laughed, 'Actually, yes it is; and to be honest, I'm rather flattered that you recognised it! It's an important stop along the route – very important in fact – and I want to recognise that by painting it directly on the wall. All the major stops will be referenced in some way. This is just a sketch, but it's meant to show Dubrovnik – or Ragusa, as it would have been then, in its seventeenth century form. The Professor has discovered an old painting which we're going to use as an exemplar – he's sending me a print which you can use as a guide.'

The bearded man nodded slowly.

'It is important to be precise,' said Mahmout.

There was silence.

'I recognise,' said the bearded man, pointing to Jemme's sketch. Jemme couldn't tell through all his facial hair, but he thought the man might have been smiling.

'I'm pleased!' he replied, grateful for a snatched moment of levity, in an otherwise very dour situation.

Still, I'm glad they're all taking it seriously, he thought to himself as he made his way back upstairs, having explained his vision for the staircase thoroughly. He packed his bag and headed back to Paris with a heavy heart. It pained him to leave the chateau when everything was just starting. It felt like going to a concert hall, seeing the orchestra come in and take their bow, but then leaving before they played a single note. He resented the deep sense of obligation he felt in going back and realised it was duty, more than a desire to return, that pulled him away.

Back in Paris he managed to bury himself in work and bide his time until the weekend approached again. Hil hadn't wanted to hear about the chateau, and his clients were being difficult. He was beginning to wish that he hadn't come back at all. The only thing that cheered him all week was DD's find – a pair of beautiful columns from a sixteenth century French church. They had turned up at a salvage yard about 50 km north of Paris, and with his incredible sense for such things, DD had divined that they would work well within the birth of Christianity room. Jemme had seen a photo of them, and already knew they would be perfect for the room, even as it stood completely empty. A telephone conversation with the Professor on Friday evening, before he headed off for the chateau, also brightened his mood.

'I just wanted to see how everything was coming along,' Professor Johnston said, down a crackling line.

'Well, thank you,' replied Jemme, suddenly feeling chirpier, 'How are you? It's all too rare I see you these days!'

'I know, I wish it was more often too – I'm trying to get over to Paris as soon as I can, but things are a bit difficult. Although tenure there is finishing soon, I've still got so much work to do. I'm so busy here at Oxford though that I can't imagine when I'll get a moment to leave.'

'Don't feel any pressure on my behalf,' said Jemme. 'I know how difficult the life of the academic can be – it sounds like you're being pulled in all directions at once, and I'd hate to start dragging you in another.'

'Oh, I can tell you, it would be a welcome relief,' said the Professor wearily, 'so much of it is petty bureaucracy about funding. It's always good to come and see you and just talk. You have no idea what a pleasure it is to be able to talk about one's specialist subject unencumbered by politics and obligations to publish.'

'I can imagine,' said Jemme sympathetically. 'Well, you know that you're always welcome, whenever you need a break from it all.'

'I'll try my hardest to come over as soon as I can,' said the Professor. 'In the meantime, why don't you provide me with a moment's escapism, and tell me all about how things are at the chateau.'

Jemme smiled to himself, the Professor probably didn't realise how much it would be escapism for him too. He told the Professor about the various characters who were now working on the chateau. He described the bonhomie of the Americans, the dourness of the Silk Road troupe, the enigma of Noury ... and the Professor variously chuckled and listened intently.

'It sounds like you're building quite a cast there,' he said eventually, sighing with laughter.

'Yes, I suppose I am,' agreed Jemme, suddenly feeling pricked by a sense of responsibility as he realised that he was filling the chateau with people for whose welfare he was responsible. Marguerite and Philby had been working away there for so long that they felt like part of the family, but suddenly there were new people coming and going. 'Do you think I should be spending more time at the chateau?' he asked the Professor suddenly.

'Well if I was in your position I would be spending *all* my time at the chateau!' said the Professor good-naturedly, 'but you've got other commitments, so I think you spend as much time as you can. Why do you ask?'

'I was just thinking about how much is going on there at the moment. Perhaps I need to show my face a bit more as everyone's employer – in what other job would you show up and just be expected to get on with it for weeks on end with no feedback?'

'If they're professionals, they'll be used to working in this way,' said the Professor. 'Besides, it's not like they're your employees at the bank – they're artists. It's completely different!'

Jemme smiled, 'I suppose you're right.'

'On a more serious note though, I think if anything you should be worried about heading down there as manager more often. It concerns me that you don't have a project manager. What if someone starts going off-design? It could be a whole week before you discovered it, which would put you two weeks behind – one week to undo everything and then one week to get you back to where you were meant to be before.'

'I know, it's something that worries me, too. It's far too late at this stage to involve a project manager and besides, this is such a personal project, I could never explain it properly to someone; it's developing and evolving in my head the whole time. What if it was the manager who went in the wrong direction and took everyone else with him?'

'A fair point.'

'I'd just never find anyone who understood me or the project well enough for me to trust them with it.'

'I suppose Hil isn't interested in taking a more hands-on approach?'

Jemme hooted with laughter, 'Couldn't be less interested. Although...' he paused, 'Burbona on the other hand...' he thought for a moment. 'Yes, this might work very well indeed.'

'What might?'

'Burbona – I could ask her to take a more "hands-on" approach. She understands both me and the project so well, and she's the perfect person for it too, so knowledgeable and well connected. I might ask her if she'd mind popping down during the week occasionally, just to keep an eye on everything.'

'Does she not work during the week?'

'Yes, well, no, not exactly. Like I said, she's very well connected, and so she's sort of mistress of her own destiny I suppose.'

'Ah, the French aristo sort – I know her type well,' said the Professor. The conversation turned into a general discussion about the nature of the French aristocracy, and by the time Jemme wished the Professor goodnight he had a large smile on his face. He had thoroughly enjoyed the conversation and was feeling greatly refreshed. He was also pleased with his decision to utilise Burbona more. He could imagine her keeping the staff in line too; she certainly didn't suffer fools gladly. Hil and Marguerite, and for that matter pretty much every female who had met her, had complained that she was too abrasive. Jemme didn't think so at all; she just knew her own mind. Besides, it was probably exactly what was needed as a counterbalance to all the artistic types in the chateau.

Thankfully, the weekend was looming on the horizon before too long, and Jemme was making his way out of Paris before the streetlights had even been turned on. Marguerite was still waiting to greet him but, otherwise, all of the comfortable routines they had fallen into had been shattered by all the new arrivals. The chateau was a cacophony of new noises, the drive clogged up with unrecognised cars and the rooms filled with unknown smells. Paint, plaster, white spirits and a faint smell of sweat mixed to create an unfamiliar musk which hung about the place. Jemme loved the changes; it was invigorating and exciting. He couldn't wait to rush off and see what had been finished.

As he explored, he felt like he was seeing different rooms. With a week's worth of work, the doors of the Santa Sabina church gallery were taking on the shapes and forms of prophets and angels. The wood face had morphed and changed, and delicate features began to protrude from its grainy surface. Ilg had a friendly greeting for Jemme,

'Hello!' he said warmly, putting down the fine chisel he had been working with.

'Hello,' replied Jemme, shaking his hand. 'That looks like delicate work,' he added, nodding to the chisel.

'That? Oh, that's nothing. Compared to some of the tools I'm using for this piece that's practically a sledgehammer.' He unbuckled his leather tool-belt and laid it out on the surface in front of him.

'Here,' he said, pulling one teak handled piece from a pouch into which it fitted snugly. He showed it to Jemme.

'What is it?' he asked looking at the unfamiliar object.

'It's a chisel too.'

Jemme looked at it. Although it was the same length as a chisel, and its top bore the same mallet dents, its tip was as fine as a toothpick.

'It's very small for a chisel,' Jemme said eventually.

'That's what I was saying about making the other one look large and clumsy! This is one of the finest pieces I own, and it's for very delicate work. I've been using it for the facial features of the angels here. It's a job that requires much precision. If I tap the top of the chisel just a fraction too hard then suddenly there's an angel with one eye larger than the other, or I've knocked the nose off the Madonna.'

Jemme raised his eyebrows, 'That's quite some pressure to work under!'

Ilg chuckled, 'I suppose so. I just have to make sure that I don't drink any coffee before I start carving.

Jemme smiled, 'Rather you than me,' he said, and left Ilg to continue uninterrupted. He headed off to the kitchen, marvelling at the amount of care he was taking over the piece and how much of his attention it demanded. Not for the first time he felt lucky to have such an expert working for him. Stopping in the kitchen to say his hellos to everyone, he made his way down to the Silk Road staircase. The corridor was completely silent, and so he assumed that the artists had finished work for the day. However, as he neared the top of the stairs he could see the light from the spotlights Philby had set up for them. He found the assembled group of artists at work in complete silence. Each was deeply absorbed in what they were doing, and didn't hear him approach. Even after he coughed gently, Jemme failed to gain anyone's attention. He went up to Mahmout and placed a hand on his shoulder. Far from being startled, Mahmout turned around and looked at him with the same distant expression that Jemme was starting to recognise in his artists.

'Hello, everyone,' Jemme said, looking around. Gradually a few faces turned to look at him and he saw the same far-off expression confront him in each one of them.

'How is everything coming along?' he asked, as jovially as he could.

'Well,' said Mahmout. 'We are all working on our individual pieces,' he stated, matter-of-factly.

'Good, good,' said Jemme, trying to muster enough charisma for all of them. One of the artists still hadn't turned round, and had his back to the rest. Jemme tried to remember which one he was and went over to him.

'Sorry to interrupt,' he said, behind the man's shoulder.

The man turned around very slowly and blinked at Jemme. Jemme recognised his huge beard straight away, but the man was apparently not enjoying the same enlightenment. He looked at Jemme utterly blankly, then blinked at him again. Eventually a look of understanding spread across his face and he smiled, showing yellowing teeth. He stepped to one side to reveal what he had been working on,

'Dubrovnik,' he said simply.

Now it was Jemme's turn to blink, and he stared delighted at the image in front of him. The bearded artist had faithfully copied the painting, transposing every detail, every trick of light onto the walls of the chateau. Here, recognisable in an instant, was Dubrovnik with its winding streets of white washed houses, each topped with a warm terracotta roof. A chalybeous sea was bulwarked with a turreted sea wall which slithered around the town, binding in the isthmus just as Jemme remembered. It was a beautiful representation of the town, and a timeless one too. The image could have been from any point in the town's history, from its high point as trading post on the Adriatic to rival Venice, through to its capture by the Napoleonic army. The painting seemed to be drenched in sunlight, and it made Jemme yearn to be back on Croatian soil. He had passed a wonderful few weeks in Dubrovnik with Hil many years ago, and remembered spending a whole day in the Franciscan monastic library, poring over the handwritten documents, incunabulae and beautifully illustrated psalters. The Dominican library, too, had been a veritable treasure trove of rare documents and illuminated manuscripts. He remembered seeing an ancient chalice, brought back from Jerusalem as a prized object, and thinking about how interconnected the history of the East and the West had always been. It had fuelled his desire to begin the chateau project and now seeing this picture in front of him was fuelling his desire to return to Dubrovnik.

He realised he was slipping into the same trance-like state as his artists, and shook himself out of it. He thanked the bearded man for his work, and told him that he would send over something new for him to work on as soon as he received it from the Professor. He looked over the work the others were doing and murmured his thanks and praise. As he turned to go back upstairs, he saw Noury sitting, cross-legged, at the top of the stairs, staring down at him. A jar of honey sat next to him.

'Hello, Noury,' said Jemme, climbing the stairs and feeling very self-conscious under Noury's unrelenting stare. He reached the top.

'Supper?' he asked, nodding towards the jar. Noury narrowed his eyes and drew the jar in closer to himslf protectively, never letting his stare falter for a second.

Jemme felt like rolling his eyes, but managed not to. 'So, what have you been up to this week, Noury?' he asked with forced jollity.

'Preparing to paint,' said Noury.

'I see. Only preparing?'

'I am an artist,' said Noury. 'Preparation is an important part of painting.'

'Of course. And how long do you think you'll need to prepare for?'

Noury shrugged, 'You cannot rush art.'

'I wouldn't dream of it,' said Jemme.

Noury looked appeased, apparently oblivious to Jemme's frustration and sarcasm.

Jemme took a deep breath, 'Are you sufficiently far into the planning process that you can tell me what artistic delight I should prepare myself for?'

Noury eyed Jemme suspiciously and slowly unscrewed the lid of his honey jar. He dipped his finger in and looked up at Jemme.

'Animals,' he said.

Jemme paused. This had slightly taken him aback. He scrutinised Noury, who was sucking honey off his finger.

'Animals?' he asked eventually with trepidation.

Noury nodded as if he was talking to someone simple. 'Ani-mals,' he repeated slowly.

'I see,' said Jemme equally slowly, 'and.... where will I find these...animals?'

Noury removed his finger from his mouth and used it to point over his shoulder behind him.

Jemme looked confused. He was sitting at the top of the stairs; there was nothing behind him. He looked again. Nothing, that was, except the door.

'Are you planning on painting these animals on the back of the door, Noury?' he asked.

Noury sighed and gave Jemme a look as if that should have been obvious.

'I see,' said Jemme, sensing a losing battle. 'And these animals, are they going to be any animals in particular?'

Noury sighed even more loudly and Jemme decided to back off, I can always ask one of the others to paint over the door, he thought to himself. Still, it hadn't exactly been what he'd had in mind when he told Noury he had a special project for him.

After supper, Jemme headed up to the Venetian room, and instantly felt his spirits lifted by the genial Americans. The room was coming along beautifully, and the trompe l'oeil work could have rivalled some of the finest Jemme had seen in Venice. Despite their wisecracking and boisterousness, the Americans were no less dedicated than any of the other artists, and it was a pleasure to watch them apply themselves to their work with diligence, patience and sheer focus. They could be as absorbed by their work as the Silk Road artists, but they could also become a great deal more impassioned by it than the very serious Silk Route assembly. Once they had finished walking Jemme around the room showing him their progress, they sat him down and produced some of the plans they had been working on.

'Y'remember you said we could come up with some ideas for the ceilin', Mr Mafeze?' asked Tim.

'Yes, absolutely,' nodded Jemme.

'Well, we've been brainstormin' and sketchin', and we've come up with some ideas for you to have a look at.'

'Excellent! You must have worked very hard this week!'

Tim shrugged, 'Don't feel so much like work.'

'Besides, it's not like we've got anything else to do.'

'What do you mean?'

'Don't get me wrong, Mr Mafeze. We love being here; it's a real privilege to stay in real French chateau. I just mean it's not like it's Vegas, that's all – boy were there some distractions there!' he whistled and the other men laughed. 'Truth be told, we could probably have finished that project a fortnight early if we'd been more focused! I don't think we've ever been as productive as we're being here, and it's mighty relaxing too.'

One of the others nodded, 'I can't remember the last time I had so much fresh air!'

The rest nodded their agreement.

'Anyways, the plan!' said Tim, summoning them all back to the matter in hand. He produced a furl of papers from the pile of jackets in the corner of the room and peeled them off, handing them to Jemme one by one.

'They're not so pretty on the eyes as if an architect had done them, but it's just to give you an idea.'

'These are incredible!' said Jemme, looking at the first piece of paper, which bore a plan of the room, as if the walls had been unboxed and set out in one long line. They were perfect miniatures of the art he was seeing come to life before his eyes, but rendered in tiny detail.

'These are just as good as any architect's drawing I've ever seen!' he said. 'Where did you learn to paint like this?' he looked up and saw the men looking at him in slight confusion. One had a pencil tucked behind his ear, one had a smear of vermilion paint on the bridge of his nose and each one of them was wearing paint-spattered overalls.

'Well, we are artists,' said Tim eventually.

Jemme looked at him, then planted his face in his hands, 'I'm sorry, that was a stupid question,' he groaned.

The others all burst out into laughter, and Tim slapped him on the back.

'You're alright, Mr Mafeze,' he said.

Jemme smiled, it was good to feel like one of the gang, and as the manager of so many people in all the different areas of his life, it was a feeling he enjoyed all too rarely.

'But what do you think of the actual pictures – I mean, what they're showing you?' asked Tim.

Jemme looked at the pieces of paper he had been handed. He had been so taken by the draughtsmanship that he hadn't registered what they were depicting. He held them closer to his face and drank in their details. He could recognise the deep crimson swags of La Fenice's velvet curtains, and he could see the painting of St Mark's Square too. However, he could also see fine gold supports in the corners, holding up a ceiling which had been laid out on the next page. It showed a central balustrade encircling a cupola. Plants spilled over the side and trailed downwards.

'It looks so…real,' Jemme said eventually.

Hank, the third American artist, smiled, 'We reckon it will look pretty impressive when it's on the ceiling.'

'Yes, I can imagine it will make quite the impact! It's such a skilled piece of work, even in miniature form like this. The angles and perspective are so accurate.'

Tim shrugged, 'Marv here is a darned fine artist.'

Marv blushed.

'He most certainly is. He's part mathematician, part artist – it would challenge an engineer to work out some of these angles!'

'So you like it?'

'Like it? Definitely. Love it in fact; I knew you would come up with some great ideas. I like these too,' he said, pointing to the golden supports which appeared to hold the balustraded ceiling up at the edge of each corner, 'They've been done just as brilliantly as the ceiling – is this your work as well, Marv?'

'Ah, those!' he said and smiled slightly, 'those are actually real.'

'Real? What do you mean?'

'Well, part of them are. They're going to be real gilded supports. They'll look as if they're holding everything up, but only a small part of them will be real. The rest, all this embellishment here will be pure trompe l'oeil.'

Jemme looked at the drawing again, 'You're too good,' he laughed eventually, 'I can't tell what's real and what's not.'

'Hopefully it will be like that when you're in the room too,' said Tim. 'That's the feeling we really want. That's the true sense of being in Venice at its height. They loved stuff like this –' he indicated the picture. 'Trompe l'oeil is all about messing around with your eyes and your understanding. The Venetians were masters; I've studied them for years. Just when you think you've seen something for what it is, you move to a different angle and realise that there really is something sticking out of it!' he smiled, apparently enjoying talking about his passion. Jemme thought back to his last trip to Venice, and remembered seeing a church with large, carved stone panels on the outside. One of them appeared to show a lion jumping out of the panel onto the tiled wall surrounding it. It was a compelling image and when he had moved closer to it and run his finger across the lion, he had discovered that it was actually raised proud of the rest of the panel, further distorting the perspective and tricking the eye.

'That's made me remember something I saw recently,' he said. 'This is a great feature and a nice touch too. Thank you everyone.'

The Americans beamed back at him.

'We're not done yet though, Mr Marfeze!' said Tim.

Jemme rustled through the papers and saw there was one he hadn't paid any attention to.

'This one's the floor,' Tim explained leaning over and pointing out the various features to Jemme.

'It's called pietra dura,' he explained, 'Florence is the place that's really famous for it, but they used it all over Venice.'

'Yes, I recognise it. In fact, we had a very similar thing in the centre of my childhood home in Istanbul.'

'Ah, well then, you won't need me to explain how it's made, that's disappointing!' Hank said good-naturedly.

'To be honest I don't really know much about how it's made. I just know what it looks like. I know it's often associated with Italy, but you find it all over Asia.'

'Do you?' asked Tim, 'I can't say I've ever been to Asia.'

'Oh yes, although it's often called *parchin kari* there – it went as far East as the court of the Mughals and there are some great examples at the Taj Mahal.'

'Well, you learn something new every day. Moog-uls eh?'

Jemme smiled, 'I'm really pleased with everything you're doing, and even more pleased with everything you have planned, thank you all,' he said, getting up to leave. A chorus of cheerful 'Goodbye, Mr Mafeze' followed him out of the door, and he went back down the stairs with a wide smile across his face. It was a pleasure to know that there were people like that working on his dream.

He spent the rest of the weekend trying not to be infuriated by Noury's grandstanding and posturing about the 'important task' he was working on, and chatting with the other artists about future plans. He was delighted with the Venetian room and how it was developing, but it was almost too good. The walls were so sumptuously decorated that he was hesitant to put anything else in the room in case it distracted from them. He knew that there were some pieces which he'd vaguely earmarked for the room, and so he took his morning cup of coffee down to one of the storage rooms. It was filled with pieces which he'd had shipped directly to the chateau, and it was like wandering through a repository of memories. There were reminders of sales he'd been to, auctions won and countries visited. He'd forgotten many of the pieces, and it was a thrill to rediscover them.

Gently picking his way across the room to the back wall, he found everything he and Burbona had bought together whilst they'd been in Venice. He slowly worked his way through it, trying to recall what their plans had been for each piece. Just as he remembered, very little had been for the Venice room itself. Most were for inclusion in other rooms. However, he did come across one small box which he unpacked to find two, very carefully wrapped, candlesticks of finest Murano glass. They were beautiful and delicate. He held one up and looked at the way that the tiny bumps and fissures in the hand-blown glass broke up the light which shone through. These were small enough not to threaten the rest of the room; in fact, they would probably complement it rather well. He looked around. Nothing else was immediately obvious, but he knew that at some point he would want there to be somewhere to sit in the room. It would have to be just right, and it might take him a while to find, but he resolved to get DD on the case as soon as he got back to Paris.

The months passed, and although Burbona was a semi-regular visitor, much to the chagrin of many staff members, Hil hadn't set foot in the chateau in a very long time. Occasionally Jemme would offer or implore her to come down for the weekend, but she was disinterested and detached. She seemed unmoved by the amount of work which had gone on, or the ever-increasing list of rooms which were nearly finished. Sometimes Jemme would feel embarrassed by her absence, especially when he was having to explain to the staff again that she wouldn't be coming. Mostly, however, he just felt sad. This had started out as such as journey for both of them, but it was becoming more and more just about Jemme. He missed Hil's input, her sense of fun, and just having her around.

However, in the interim, he was very grateful to have Burbona around. It was nice to have someone who knew what was needed and knew how to get it too. He felt like some of the pressure had been removed for him, and he began to look forward to her visits and their Paris meetings more and more. She had been a life-saver one evening when he was entertaining at the chateau. He had invited some potential clients to spend the weekend, hoping to impress them with the project. Business connections were often on such a personal basis, and he wanted to show himself as a man of big visions with the capability of realising those ambitions. He had assumed that Hil would come, but during a rather busy week he hadn't actually got round to asking her, and when he finally did, a few days beforehand, she told him that she already had plans. Despite his emphasis on the importance of the deal and how important her being there was, she would not budge. Jemme knew that he couldn't really complain as he had left it until the last minute, but he was still annoyed. If Hil's plans were so important they couldn't be changed, then she would surely have mentioned them before, he reasoned.

There had been a moment when he wondered whether he should cancel the whole thing. He couldn't bear turning up and facing the expectant, 'Where's your wife?' questions. However, with impeccable timing, Burbona had called to inform him that she had just bought a marble statue for the chateau and was sending the invoice to DD. Jemme didn't even flinch when she mentioned the price, just thanked her for her hard work. He shared his concerns about the weekend,

'As it happens, I'm free this weekend. I can come and take Hil's place,' she said. Jemme thanked her profusely. He knew how many social commitments she usually had, and expected that she wasn't actually free that weekend, but would be cancelling on several other people to help him out. For a moment he wondered if it was a bit odd to take Burbona with him instead, and if the men would wonder if she was his mistress. He half thought about cancelling again, but then realised that Burbona would charm them senseless within about five minutes. If they mistakenly thought she was his mistress, then it would probably make them respect him even more.

The weekend had turned out better than Jemme could have hoped and he had received phone calls all round the next day, with everyone keen to tell him how much they had enjoyed themselves. He felt a little guilty, but couldn't help thinking that it had probably gone even better than if Hil had been there.

Chapter Thirty-Three

The months continued to roll past, and Hil continued to refuse to come to the chateau. Jemme had been trying to convince himself otherwise, but even he had to admit to himself that their relationship was flagging. He knew that they needed a holiday together, but he couldn't spend any time away from the chateau; it wasn't even through selfishness, he was responsible for so many people there that it was his duty to return every weekend. He still loved Hil profoundly and he couldn't imagine not being her husband, but their lives were growing increasingly separate. He wished he could stitch them back together somehow, but they wanted such different things. Hil still hadn't given up on the idea of having children, but it was a burning longing, which seemed to sap her energy and spirit, leaving her listless and sad. For his part, Jemme couldn't see a future that didn't involve developing the chateau. He tried to be as sensitive as possible about it when he was around Hil, and was careful not to mention it too much, but it meant they barely had anything to talk about. He had, however, stopped referring to Burbona as 'replacing' Hil on weekends to the chateau, after one particularly testy exchange.

Although his relationship with Hil was at a low ebb, his work in the chateau was going from strength to strength. The list of completed rooms was lengthening and the roster of artists was widening. Due to the efficiency of the Americans, he had been able to tick the Venetian room off as completed. It joined the Calligraphy room, the Crusader room and a host of other ante-rooms and corridors. There were many others which were due to be finished soon, and even more which were either in progress or due to start soon. Every time he returned to the chateau, it looked a little bit more like it had in his dream. He loved the spontaneity of it, and the fluidity of ideas which came from working with so many creative people. It was a joy to be able to experience an idea grow to fill a whole room. The Americans had been particularly good on this front. They had completed the Venetian room ahead of schedule, and had two weeks before they had to leave to start work on their next commission. They told Jemme that they would love to stick around and work on another room for him, and he had been delighted to have their expertise at his disposal. However, he couldn't think what he would like them to work on. He tried to think ahead to which rooms would require sumptuously painted walls and would make the most of their talents. However, there were so many other things taking up his time and attention that he couldn't focus. The short time frame only compounded the situation ; he didn't want to ask them to start something they wouldn't be able to finish in two weeks. In the end if was the artists themselves who provided the solution.

'Why don't you give us a room you don't have any plans for?' asked Tim. 'Not one of the fancy ones, and maybe one that's out of the way. We'll do something we think you'll like and then, if you don't, well – we'll paint over the top of it again before we leave and you're back to where you started.'

'It sounds like I can't lose!' said Jemme, looking at their smiling faces.

'We'll do ya proud, Mr Mafeze!' said Hank, clapping him on the shoulder with a hefty hand.

'I'm sure you will,' said Jemme. He had trusted them completely and left them to their own devices for the two weeks, without even so much as checking on their progress. It was a relief to know that he could focus on other things for a fortnight and at the end of it there would be a whole new room waiting for him. It was like a bonus treat at the end of an already satisfying meal. He realised how sorry he would be to see the American artists go.

Several weekends later, he headed down to the chateau, realising that he was going to be wishing them goodbye as they headed off for their next project. They were waiting for him outside, alongside Marguerite and Philby.

'It's all ready for you, Mr Mafeze,' said Tim. 'We think you're going to like it!

'I'm sure I will,' said Jemme, greeting everyone and following them all inside.

'Sorry, Marguerite, not this time,' he said as he noticed Marguerite's customary hopeful check of the passenger seat, to see if Hil had come along too. She looked disappointed, and trooped in after them. The Americans had entered into the spirit of things and insisted on blindfolding Jemme as they led him along the corridor. He soon smelled fresh paint and realised they had arrived in the room.

'Ya ready?' Hank said.

'Absolutely!' Jemme replied, and he felt Marv remove the blindfold.

He blinked as his eyes adjusted to the light, and looked around him. He took in the looks of anticipation on the artists around him and suddenly burst into laughter. There was a pause and then the others joined in.

'So you like it, Mr Mafeze?'

'Yes, I do. It's…. fun,' he said.

'It was a bit of a gamble,' admitted Hank 'but after something serious we wanted to give you something to lighten things up a bit, y'know. Anyway, it will be something to remember us by – unless you paint over it that is.'

'I definitely won't be painting over it,' said Jemme. He smiled again and looked around him. There, painted onto the walls, was a perfect recreation of Noah's Ark, surrounded by pairs of animals, ready to slink their way in to the boat. Compared to everything else underway in the chateau, it seemed completely incongruous, but also had a child-like naivety to it. The animals could have been from the page of any storybook, and the Ark looked as if it was filled with promise of adventure. They were right, it did provide light relief.

'I can tell I'm going to enjoy seeking refuge in here,' said Jemme. 'When it's getting hectic and complicated in the other rooms, I can just slope off to my own Noah's Ark room.'

'Pleased you like it, Mr Mafeze,' beamed four faces all around him.

'It's not just completely random though,' added Hank, 'we wanted it to have some connection with everything else you're doing here. It's a story that took place in the East to start with – 'least, that's how I understand it anyway. Also, we were talking to that guy who's been working on the door for ages.'

'Ilg?'

'Yeah that's the one – real nice guy, real professional. He was telling us that he was working on a room about the start of Christianity, and we thought, hey, what better story than this one.'

Jemme smiled again, 'I love it; it really will be something to remember you by.'

'Well, we've loved working here. We'll be sure to give you a call next time we're in France.'

'Are you not staying the weekend?'

'Wish we could, Mr Mafeze, but we've got to head off. Philby's driving us to the station so we can catch the last train to the airport. We just wanted to stick around and show you this.'

'I'm sad you're off,' said Jemme, 'but this has been a fantastic note to leave on. If I ever hear of anyone needing world-class trompe l'oeil artists, I'll be sure to send them your way.'

They each pumped his hand vigorously, flashed him another smile, and with that they were off. Jemme stood in the room for a moment longer after they had left, taking everything in. He hadn't been lying; he really did love the room. It was filled with light and had a happy atmosphere. He could fully imagine seeking shelter in here when he wanted some respite from artistic temperaments. He was just turning to leave when he saw a figure looming in the doorway. He jumped, then realised who it was.

'Ah, hello Noury.'

Noury narrowed his eyes, but didn't say anything.

'What brings you up here?' Jemme asked.

Noury continued to look at him through his narrowed eyes, and then stared past him to the long wall opposite which bore most of the Noah's Ark scene.

'I said I was doing animals.'

'Animals? What – oh, yes, of course, your *special* project,' said Jemme.

Noury continued to stare at the Ark, 'Now there are two sets of animals,' he said slowly and deliberately.

'Well, yes, I suppose there are, but it doesn't really matter. There will be repetitions of lots of things by the time the chateau is finished. It's just the way things are.'

'But I was doing animals first,' said Noury, still not looking at Jemme.

'Yes, I know, and I will make sure everyone knows that,' said Jemme generously. 'Besides, I didn't even know what was going on here, I only saw this for the first time about twenty minutes ago.'

Noury continued to stare sulkily ahead, and Jemme realised he was going to have to offer something more,

'How are your animals coming along Noury?'

'They are finished.'

'Finished? Marvellous! Can I see them?'

Noury turned his head slowly and eyed Jemme suspiciously, raising one eyebrow as he took him in.

'Yes,' he said eventually and turned to lead the way down to the Silk Road staircase.

Jemme followed him, not knowing whether to be amused or exasperated. Eventually they reached the top of the stairs. The other artists must have finished for the day, because all the lights were off. Noury opened the door and flicked them on. Jemme couldn't believe how much work had been completed since his last visit, and stared down the staircase, mouth almost ajar as he took it all in.

'Here's the Yellow River,' he exclaimed, 'the Himalayas and Tibet, the Khyber Pass. Oh my God,' he added, 'here's Palmyra and Antioch leading to Ragusa and Venice. This is amazing,' he murmured to himself. Noury must have heard, because he slammed the door in irritation.

'You're looking in the wrong direction!' he said.

'Oh. I see,' said Jemme, turning round and being confronted by the closed door.

'My painting is on the back of this door,' explained Noury impatiently.

'The back of the door? Ah, yes, of course,' said Jemme, going down a couple of steps backwards, so he could take everything in. It was taking all his will power not to turn around and look at the magnificent staircase, which was coming to life exactly as he had wanted it to. Instead he tried to make sense of what Noury was confronting him with.

'I see the animals,' he said eventually, squinting at the slightly blurred shapes on the back of the door. He was not entirely surprised to find that, despite his claims to the contrary, Noury was not actually at all gifted artistically. In fact, it was almost a struggle not to laugh at how abysmal the animals were. He couldn't even work out what they were all meant to be.

'So, these animals, Noury... do they represent anything? Are they doing anything?'

Noury narrowed his eyes into familiar slits and stared at Jemme.

'They are the animals of the Silk Route,' he said.

'Aha,' said Jemme, realising that there was, in fact, a connection with the surroundings, albeit a tenuous one. 'And when you say "the animals of the Silk Route'..." he said hesitantly.

Noury looked at him scornfully, 'There were many animals on the Silk Route,' he said.

'Yes, yes, I suppose there were.'

'There were different animals in different places.'

'Well yes, I suppose there were.'

'This,' said Noury, gesturing grandly to the piece behind him, 'shows the direction of the animals from East to West.'

'I see. So, you're saying that this is a depiction of the animals one might encounter as one journeyed along the Silk Route from East to West?'

Noury sighed loudly, and said something which sounded like, 'Pah!' Evidently he thought Jemme's questions too stupid to answer.

'Good, well, I'm glad we got that one sorted. I suppose this is a rather novel interpretation,' said Jemme. He went back to the top of the stairs, and crouched down so that he could look at this odd procession of assorted animals. The proportioning was different on each one, meaning that a crudely drawn elephant was smaller than something Jemme presumed was a donkey. Having just looked at the American's masterful animal work, this compared very poorly. He stared at the door a little longer, desperately trying to think of something to say.

'I like this camel,' he said eventually, pointing at a quadruped and hoping that it was, in fact, meant to be a camel.

'Yes,' Noury said, as if Jemme liking it was obvious.

'What is this part?' asked Jemme eventually, pointing to a meandering black line.

'That is the Silk Route.'

'Of course. Are these-?' Jemme began.

'The major stops, yes,' Noury finished for him, impatiently.

'Of course,' Jemme looked at them a little longer, trying to decipher Noury's scratchy handwriting. He concentrated hard on the line, and the animals meant to be walking along it.

'Noury,' he began with slight trepidation.

Noury glowered at him.

'It's just... I'm presuming that this animal here represents the start of the Silk Route in the East?'

'Yes,' said Noury.

'And this one here is the end of the Silk Route in the West?'

'Yes!'

'I see. It's just – and I don't really know how to put this – but, well, they don't correspond to the places you've marked here.'

'Correspond?' said Noury sounding outraged.

'Well you've painted the animals going from East to West and then the Route going from West to East. It's not a big issue though, I'm sure it won't take very long to fix,' Jemme said.

'Fix?!' said Noury, sounding even more outraged. 'Fix?!' he repeated.

'Well, I just know that an artiste of your calibre will want to leave everything absolutely perfectly, so I thought it was worth pointing out,' said Jemme. It was too late though; the damage had been done.

Noury flung the door back open, nearly knocking Jemme down the stairs in the process. He flounced out, muttering 'fix' in disbelief.

Jemme sighed and shut the door gently behind Noury, and giggled when he saw the strange animals and the back to front Silk Route. It was a bizarre piece both in execution and concept. He decided to leave it as it was for now; it would make a good story. He looked around at the rest of the staircase and had soon forgotten about Noury. The Silk Road was almost finished and it looked even better than he had imagined. The cities painted onto the wall had been an inspired touch, and he had Professor Johnston to thank for that. They provided context, each one grounding a stop on the route in a different geographical place and historical era. They documented the flourishing, and sometimes decline, of major mercantile stops along the route, proving a much-needed visualisation for the room. He slowly made his way down the staircase, looking at the walls on either side of himself as he did so. By the time he had reached the bottom he was even more pleased. He had intended the staircase to capture the experience of crossing the Silk Route, rather than being something merely decorative. With their depiction of the cities, and their mural-work, the artists had managed to execute that sense perfectly. As he made his way down the stairs, Jemme could sense the transition from Western images, styles and decoration, through to the distinctively Eastern. He turned around at the bottom and walked back up again, experiencing the passage from East to West as he did so. Once he had reached the top, he was once again confronted with Noury's painting, and he smiled to himself. *How did he manage to flip it around and how did he not even notice?* he thought to himself. He turned the light off and shut the door behind him, neatly drawing a line under the episode.

Back upstairs he came across Ilg in the birth of Christianity gallery.

'Burning the midnight oil?' asked Jemme, greeting him.

'Ah, hello,' said Ilg, tucking the fine-tipped chisel back into his belt and shaking his hand. 'I'm almost finished. I thought we were meant to be signing off on this, this weekend?'

'Were we? Who told you that?'

'A very Germanic-sounding man who calls from Paris to check how we're doing every so often.'

'Ah, DD. Yes that sounds very like him; he's quite fond of deadlines! In truth, I don't really mind when you finish, I'd rather you did the work to the best of your abilities, but I can't tell him things like that without panicking him.'

Ilg laughed, 'I know his type, Monsieur. Still, it is good to have deadlines to give everyone something to work towards. I probably would have finished this weekend anyway, and I wanted to show it to you before I left.'

Jemme joined him on his side of the workbench so that he could look at everything the right way up.

'It's been such a pleasure watching this come to life,' he said. 'It's difficult to believe that this has gone from a completely plain piece of wood to something filled with so much life and detail. The American artists were commenting on what a professional job you've done, and I have to agree.'

'Thank you,' said Ilg sincerely.

'It looks like you've almost finished though – is there much more to do?'

'I'm just honing some of the details on some of the faces, then I'm going to rub linseed oil into the whole piece. It will need to stand for a couple of days for everything to soak in before it's hung.

'It's beautiful,' said Jemme, taking a closer look at the doors. He found it hard to believe that Ilg could tease any more detail out of the wood, but he didn't doubt his ability for a second.

He left for Paris feeling a wonderful sense of completion. The chateau was growing into something more beautiful by the day. On the way back home, he pulled in to the antique shop he and Hil had stopped at so many times, and where they had bought her klavier, the very first piece in the chateau's story. He had been tipped off that there was a piece there which would be of interest, and he was keen to go and have a look. He parked up outside, and heard the bell jangle as he opened the door. Immediately the distinctive smell of an antique shop hit him, a characteristic smell of beeswax, worn leather and musty books. No matter where the shop was, and, to an extent, what the items for sale were, the smell was always the same. Jemme took a deep and satisfying inhale and made his way towards the back of the shop, where he knew the office was located. He tried to be disciplined and stare straight ahead, blanking out everything either side of him with fixed tunnel vision, but he couldn't help himself. He was drawn to Baroque clocks and Regency tables like a magpie, and kept stopping, lovingly looking at individual pieces and imagining them in one of his homes.

Just as he was fingering a Belle Époque letter knife, the owner came shuffling out to inspect the source of the bell ringing. He greeted Jemme like an old friend and asked eagerly after the *jolie madame* he used to come to the shop with. After exchanging pleasantries, the old man took him into the office.

'I was so sure you would like this that I took it off the floor and kept it to one side for you,' he said, ushering Jemme in.

'That was very kind of you,' said Jemme, 'especially when I haven't been here in a while.'

The old man shrugged in a very Gallic way, 'You have been a good customer over the years, Monsieur. Here,' he said, pulling a tatty dustsheet off a small object.

As soon as Jemme saw it, he already knew he was going to buy it, regardless of the cost.

'It is similar to the one you bought from me five years ago,' said the owner, 'but look at these beautiful fluted legs.'

Jemme had to agree; the cabinet was beautiful in form and the unusual legs only enhanced that. It also bore a fair resemblance to the last cabinet he had bought at this shop, which he had treasured for years. He couldn't even remember how he had first begun collecting pieces such as these, and didn't know what he planned to do with the collection either. The piece before him was classic. Made of ebony, it had been intricately decorated with delicate mother of pearl and ivory inlays, which picked out glistening patterns in sharp contrast to the dark wood. This piece stood at about two feet tall, and comprised of three drawers with thin gold handles. The fluted legs ended in clawed feet, concealing concealed tiny casters.

'What do you think?' asked the owner.

'I love it!' said Jemme. 'It will fit in with the others so well.'

'Ah, I am pleased. I remembered how pretty the last piece was, and so I thought of you straight away.'

Jemme carefully looked over the cabinet, and gently opened its drawers. He could see how carefully the whole thing had been put together and how expertly the joints had been dovetailed together.

'Do you know much about it?'

'Sadly, no. This one has come from a house clearance sale, so I don't know much of its provenance. I should guess that it was Venetian though, maybe from the late eighteenth century. It's very difficult to tell with these pieces, they're such a mix of styles and influences.'

'That's exactly why I like them,' said Jemme happily. He bought the piece on the spot and helped the owner wrap it up for transport. With his bag removed, it sat snugly in the boot of his car, and he was pleased he wouldn't have to wait for a delivery. As he drove back, he reflected on what a successful weekend it had been. He also tried to work out where the new piece would go, but still couldn't quite decide. It would be a beautiful addition to the Paris flat, but he had so many pieces like that there already. It was a very distinctive style, and one which encapsulated a history of East/West interaction. With its heavy Levantine and also Venetian influences, it was hard to look at a mother-of-pearl inlaid piece like this without thinking of the Silk Route. Jemme had grown up with similar pieces around him at home, and gradually bought pieces in similar styles until one day he took stock and realised that he had started a collection. Like so many of his pieces, he didn't actually know what to do with it, and, to some extent, why he had bought it in the first place. He knew that he would find a place for them eventually and it saddened him that he had to keep them stored away until that place presented itself.

Two pieces had already made their way out of the collection and into the Venetian room. Since the artists had finished, all Jemme had had to furnish the room with had been the two Murano glass candlesticks. He knew he needed something else, but it had to strike the perfect balance between functionality, decoration and unobtrusiveness. One day, browsing through the mother of pearl inlaid collection, he came across two flat, dustsheet encased pieces he had all but forgotten about. Whisking the sheets off he had been flooded with a sense of recognition, as two exquisite folding *dagobert* chairs were revealed. Portable yet luxurious, they were beloved by the Ottomans and their travelling court. The chairs' small diamond-shaped pieces of ivory swirled out into complex patterns, neatly defined by rare tortoiseshell inlays. To look at, they seemed to be of solid, sturdy construction, but a cleverly designed panel could be removed, allowing the chairs to fold in the middle, effectively flattening them so that they could be transported in the caravan which would have toured between the major mercantile centres of the empire. They were perfect for the Venetian room, and he had installed them straight away, fancying that the room now looked as if it was ready for the finest of Venetian ambassadors.

Aside from this pair of escapees, the collection sat in storage, unbothered by dust or sunlight, biding its time until the story could begin again. Once the new cabinet had been installed in the Paris flat and he had seen that there really was no room for it, he sadly sent it off to storage, to languish with the rest of the collection. He did not forget it though, and thought hard about how he could utilise it in the chateau. However, it was difficult to find a place for it, or indeed the assemblage as a whole. Whilst it represented an intermingling of cultural influence and contained many fine individual pieces too, he didn't want to have a room dedicated entirely to this style of furniture. It didn't fit within his decorative philosophy; a plain room containing only furniture would be more like a display showroom than anything else. It was not what he wanted to achieve with the chateau, and besides, it would be dull. He couldn't even think what he could put on the walls or the floor, and it would be too much like the museum rooms he despised, displaying beautiful objects in sanitised rooms, devoid of context. The whole impetus behind the chateau had been moving away from such rooms. He resolved to think on it further; he knew that the answer would present itself at some point. Who knew, perhaps Grandma would even exert her Sufi influence on the situation.

※　※　※　※

As the chateau bloomed, and the number of artists working on it multiplied, Jemme continued to find that the demands on his time were becoming almost unmanageable. There were artists such as Walid, who could re-glaze a window or re-gild the fittings unsupervised and produce a piece of work of the highest possible quality in the shortest possible time. However, there were also artists who seemed to create more work than they produced. Jemme's early exposure to artistic temperament had taught him the value of being firm from the offset. He could identify who was going to cause him trouble at a very early stage, and would then keep a tight reign on them for the duration of their work. Philby was an indispensable aid in this; he had never suffered fools gladly and he had absolutely no time at all for artistic sensibilities. Philby was his eyes and ears in the chateau when he was away. However, there were incidents which even Philby had not been able to avoid and which Jemme was powerless to resolve from his desk in Paris.

There had been one in particular which tried his patience. Aboudi had been a young cabinet maker from Syria. He was a pleasant young man, whose craftsmanship was impeccable, but whose over-riding ambition, perhaps even obsession, was to learn to drive a car. He was unrelenting in his eagerness to master this particular skill, and would hector the other artists, Philby and even the unassuming Aude to show him how to navigate up and down the drive. Jemme had even heard that when visitors came to the house, without fail, Aboudi would sidle up to them at some point and ask if he could accompany them, if they were driving into the village. Unsurprisingly, most of them made a hasty excuse, but some were not quick enough thinking on their feet. Those who reluctantly agreed to drive him into the village were first surprised to find that he didn't want to be left there, and in fact, had no interest in actually being in the village at all. Instead, he just wanted to go along for the drive. Returning him to the chateau some twenty minutes later, they would always look exhausted and more than a little stressed. According to Philby, he harangued these reluctant chauffeurs incessantly with questions and requests – *What does this button do? When are you going to change gear? How fast are you driving now? Can I sound the horn?* The latter was usually accompanied by a sudden lunging at and vigorous sounding of, said horn, much to the alarm of the driver and anyone else on the road. All, however, were accompanied by Aboudi compulsively opening and closing the glove compartment, or pushing buttons to operate electric windows and the sun-roof. He was like a small child, overcome with glee to be sitting in a moving vehicle.

After several months of inveigling himself into other people's cars, and asking a mountain of questions, it appeared that Aboudi felt confident that he had acquired all the skills necessary to take to the road. He'd mastered the theory, and now he felt ready to gain some practice! Unfortunately, his favoured mode of transport for his first solo drive was a very large green tractor, which Philby had just finished using and had left sitting with the keys in the ignition whilst he tended to something else. Aboudi saw his opportunity and seized it. It must have been a proud moment for him when he turned the key, carefully released the clutch, and felt the tractor move him forward at ten miles an hour. So far, so good, and Aboudi was enjoying himself as he trundled around the tree-lined alleys. Apparently this bolstered his confidence so much that he decided to experiment with faster speeds. For a few short minutes he was delirious with happiness, a tiny figure perched like a bird atop the huge rumbling tractor as he rolled along, the wind in his hair. Proceeding through the international forest, Aboudi opened it up full-throttle, but quickly realised that he was headed towards the lake. This was not a good moment for him to also realise that he had managed to wedge the throttle firmly down. The machine was old and temperamental and only Philby knew how to control it once it was running. This novice would have been out of his depth in the most driver-friendly of shiny new vehicles, but he had never stood a chance with this rickety pile of nuts and bolts.

It wouldn't have mattered if he'd known where the brake was, but he'd only been concerned with starting the tractor – he hadn't given a thought to how he would stop it. With a border of trees on either side of him, he couldn't veer off to either side, and the inevitability of rushing closer towards the lake resulted in a high, extended shriek of panic from Aboudi, which whistled through the trees, and brought everyone running from the chateau and nearby workshops.

Philby's recounting of the tale had him shouting, 'Brake! Brake!' then finally, 'Brake, you idiot!' However, Jemme very much doubted that Philby had been so restrained and suspected that he was being given a highly edited version. For his part, Aboudi still trundled relentlessly towards the lake, a look of frozen horror on his face. One of the more practical artists ran in front of the tractor, urging Aboudi to jump off, but was forced to leap out of the way at the last moment, just as Aboudi, still clinging to the steering wheel, drove straight into the lake. Both man and tractor sank immediately, and a stunned silence descended on all. Philby waited for Aboudi to resurface so he could give him what he described as 'a piece of his mind' (although Jemme suspected this was highly edited as well.) A few moments passed, during which everyone stared expectantly at the lake. After about a minute, a nasty sense that something might not be right descended, as Aboudi failed to materialise. Suddenly the assembled crowd of artists and household staff began to fear that he might be trapped under the tractor. The artists looked around in horror, not so much at Aboudi's fate, but the idea that they might be called upon for heroics. Marguerite was just striding to the lake, rolling her sleeves up when, to everyone's relief, Aboudi surfaced, coughing and spluttering. The optimism was short-lived when it became apparent that he couldn't swim and so Marguerite ended up in the lake after all, hauling him towards the edge, where she gave him a stern telling off. From what Jemme could gather, Philby was lining up behind her to take his turn, and by the end of it poor Aboudi was highly unlikely to so much as look at a car again.

Whilst Jemme was relieved that everyone was alright, and even thought that the story would be amusing when he looked back at it in the future, for now the episode represented a lot of wasted time and paperwork. He had to deal with the insurance claim on the tractor, and answer all manner of questions about who had been driving it and who would have access to it. He was already spreading himself very thinly as it was, and he just didn't have the capacity to expend any further time or attention on anything new.

However, no matter how much time the chateau took up, and no matter how exasperating dealing with its development was, he didn't regret it for a moment. Every time he returned, it had transformed into the chateau of his dreams a little bit more, and he was spurred on. He could not rest until he had completely transformed it into the place he had been seeing since he was five years old. Meeting the artists, hearing their stories and watching their work had been part of that joy. He had been fascinated by Caroline, a renowned specialist in the drapery business, who had been secured to work on the chateau's soft furnishings. She had inherited the business from her parents, and it had a long-standing reputation as a successful family concern. Caroline herself was extremely agreeable and Jemme had liked her a lot. Her company had received numerous prestigious commissions too, and she had worked on both the Ritz and the Elysée Palace. Whilst at the chateau, she had produced exquisite curtains, bed covers and tablecloths in Egyptian cotton, thick Irish linen, and the finest damasks and silks, and Jemme had been very happy with her work. In the course of discussions with her one day, he happened to mention the bourgeoning economy of Turkmenistan, something which had recently been a hotly-discussed topic at the bank. Caroline, who had a good head for business, obviously gave some thought to the comment, and a few weekends later mentioned that she had lined up her next job.

'Do you remember talking to me about Turkmenistan?' she asked.

Jemme concentrated, and remembered their conversation of several weeks earlier, 'Oh yes'

'Well', she continued, 'I looked into it a little further and it turns out that it's not just Turkmenistan; there are many states in that part of the world which have recently gained independence and are opening up to capitalism.'

'Yes, there are,' Jemme agreed, wondering where this could be leading.

'Well, I contacted the office of the president or prime minister in each country.'

'I see,' said Jemme, wondering what she was planning.

'I sent them some samples of my work, and said that I wanted to discuss replicating the success of my family's work on the Elysée Palace in their country.'

'Really?' said Jemme admiringly. 'That was rather enterprising of you'.

'Wasn't it?' she said, smiling. 'And guess what? An Uzbek minister saw my samples, was impressed, and offered me a job. I leave on Saturday!'

Sure enough, that Saturday Jemme saw her off and wished her luck in Uzbekistan. She promised she would return at some point to work on the remaining furnishings, but since the Uzbekistan project was to involve the refurbishment of several buildings, Jemme expected her to be away for a year or more. So, it was with some surprise that he bumped into her in Paris just a few months later. He greeted her warmly and, assuming she was there on a buying trip, asked if she had time for a quick cup of coffee.

'So how's life in Uzbekistan?' he had asked over an espresso in a nearby café.

'It isn't,' she replied, 'I left. And to be honest, I feel pretty lucky to have got out at all!'

She elaborated and revealed an extraordinary story. For the first week or so, things went well enough. She had plenty of work to do, and was brimming with ideas for the various projects. However, not speaking the language was a handicap; only one man in the building spoke a little French. This meant that she was totally reliant on him to communicate with anybody, which soon became tiring. She would have to find him, in a vast labyrinth of a building, in order to make the simplest request.

'I couldn't even have a cup of coffee without finding this man, and asking him to ask someone in the kitchen – who then asked another person – it was like Chinese whispers. It became tedious very quickly.'

It transpired that for her to make her own coffee would have been a grave faux pas. With a strictly enforced hierarchy, and a vast complement of staff filling each office, there was a very defined allocation of duties. However, this meant that even the simplest task became a rigmarole of poor communication and misinterpreted hand signals. It was difficult for her not to feel homesick,

'I toughed it out for a month,' she said, 'but I felt so isolated – I was suddenly so dependent on other people, after having lived a highly independent lifestyle in Paris. I mean, here I can walk into a café and have a coffee with you, then sit and talk freely, without struggling to make myself understood, or to interpret what is being said...you wouldn't believe how I missed that.'

'What happened next?' Jemme asked.

'I just couldn't stand it any more. I wanted to see my parents, my friends, my family. Talking on the phone was useless – the connection failed every few of minutes. Everything just became too frustrating. Finally, I said I wanted to leave.'

'Well it sounds like you made the right decision, if it was making you so miserable.'

'You would think wouldn't you? But when I tried to go, things became even worse.'

'How?'

'They offered me more money.'

'How is that worse?' asked Jemme.

'For me it was. The President is a hugely wealthy man, and to him everyone has a price. He just thought he needed to find mine.'

'I can't imagine you could be bought easily, Caroline,' said Jemme, smiling. He knew that she was plucky enough for this story to have a happy ending.

'He wasn't too happy when he found that out,' she said, 'and there were some rather insidious threats about my exit visa.'

'They actually threatened you?'

'I didn't understand exactly what they were saying, but I certainly understood the gist of it.'

'That's horrible, you must have been so worried.'

'I was, a little. I realised I was going to have to be smart. The President is not too difficult to figure out. His wealth is the driving force behind everything he does. He loves beautiful furnishings like the ones I was creating, but only because that proves he has the money to pay for them. It all feeds his ego, so I realised that in order to leave I would have to feed his ego too.'

'And so what did you do?'

'I offered to sell him my business.'

Jemme looked surprised, 'But your family built it up over years.'

'Given the choice between being semi-incarcerated in Uzbekistan and the family business, I know what they'd choose for me.'

'But how did you know he would even be interested?'

'Think about it: he's a vain man. In a country only just opening up to Western trade, buying a prestigious Western business is a real symbol of status. I laid it on rather thick about my work for the Elysée Palace, and I think that really appealed to him. He saw it as an equaliser with other world leaders.'

'It's certainly very bold of you,' said Jemme, wondering at this slight French woman trying to call the bluff of the President of Uzbekistan.'

'Not really, besides I was feeling a little desperate by this point. You haven't even heard the best bit though.'

'Go on,' Jemme said, a smile twitching at the corners of his mouth.

'He was so taken with the idea of owning a reputable French company, and associating himself with European interests, that it seemed to cloud his judgement slightly.'

'How's that?'

'A company like mine – there are no assets. We own some machines and have a small storage room of fabrics. The value is in our experience and our ability to command high fees for projects, based on our reputation. The President didn't have the first idea how to realise any of that value, and didn't understand that there was nothing to stop my staff leaving and joining me in a different company. He likes to think he's a major player and I was very happy to flatter that, but I knew that he didn't have a clue, especially regarding what the company was worth.'

'I suppose you told him…' Jemme laughed.

'Too right I did,' she said. 'He must be the first president to pay ten million dollars for a few industrial sewing machines and a couple of bales of silk.'

'Ten million?' Jemme said, staggered, looking at Caroline with renewed respect. 'How much do you think it was actually worth?' he asked.

'Truth be told, I don't know myself,' she said, 'I suspect it was less than a tenth of that, but more importantly it was worth my freedom, and I was flying back to Paris within two days, a very wealthy woman.'

Jemme shook his head, 'Ten million,' he murmured again.

'I know,' said Caroline, smiling. 'I think I can afford to get these,' she said nodding to the espressos, and settling the bill.

Jemme shook her hand warmly when they were back outside, and wished her well. He doubted she would end up coming back to the chateau, but he was delighted he had had the chance to meet her and hear her incredible story. It just added to the rich texture of the chateau. Now, whenever anyone asked about the draperies and soft furnishings, he would be able to tell them about Caroline and her game of cat and mouse with the President of Uzbekistan.

❃ ❃ ❃ ❃

As the chateau continued to develop, so did the stories around its creation. The Sicilian room reminded Jemme of the time he himself had played artist. After the success of the Venetian room and realising that he wanted to reference the Palatine Chapel somewhere in the chateau, he had decided on a having a Sicilian room.

He had visited the Palatine Chapel or *Cappella Palatina* in Palermo a number of times, and on every occasion had been struck by the wonderful mingling of influences to be found there. Christian and Arabic art covered the walls, depicting scenes of hunting in the Orient, feasting and life in the harem. They sat next to scenes of Norman life at court, with all its pomp and ceremony. The distinctive work of individual artists was also visible within the mix of works, and the whole combined into something beautiful; the work of myriad cultures and eras sitting harmoniously under one ceiling. The ceiling itself was spectacular; dating from the tenth century, when the Arabs had built a stunning honeycombed construction of wooden stalactites. In the twelfth century, the Normans had added their own unique paschal candelabrum, intricately carved with acanthus leaves.

Jemme had been struck by the parallel between the construction of this iconic Sicilian building, and his recreation of it many centuries later. Just as work had originally been conducted by artists and craftsmen shipped over to Italy from North Africa, now he found himself drafting in artists from all over the world to recreate his own version. The Cappella had been abandoned by the Arabs, who had originally used it for their emirs, then taken up by the Normans, who had conquered Europe, and turned the building into a glittering palace. Jemme felt that this too reflected the chateau's history, falling from beauty into a period of steep decline and then salvaged and regenerated into something magnificent.

However, whilst the Cappella had benefited from each culture leaving their mark, the same could not be said of the Sicilian gallery, and Jemme had been disappointed with the work here. Whilst the different styles complemented each other in the Cappella, in the chateau they clashed hideously, looking as if they had been commissioned by someone who lacked both historical understanding and taste.

Jemme realised that the artist hadn't been completely to blame. He had followed his instructions closely, depicting angels, ancient emirs, and even architectural vestiges of the Norman era. Technically the pieces were also competent, they just did not work in the room. They jarred and detracted from each other, but Jemme couldn't work out why. He pondered the problem for a while, and considered guiding the room towards narrative rather than recreation. Sicily was an important place of both artistic and cultural influence, between Italy, Central Europe and the East, and he wanted to reference that somewhere in the chateau.

He decided that perhaps this room needed a larger amount of both Eastern and European art to demonstrate the context of the Cappella's decoration. He realised that focusing on the narrative freed him to include anything he liked, and so decided to commission a painting of the Bosphorous on the ceiling, flowing from East to West and right through the city of his birth, where the two cultures met and his fascination with both had begun.

He commissioned the painting onto a canvas which could be finished off-site, and then applied to the ceiling directly. He saw it as being slightly similar to Noury's animal route; the river would be depicted underneath a trail of landmarks and important cultural and historical reference points. He was relieved to have found Bertrand, who lived reasonably locally and seemed to be up to the job. A large man, with a ruddy face, more akin to a farmer's than an artist's, Bertrand was a gruff Frenchman who seemed to think the whole project was complete folly, and very much implied that he was doing Jemme a favour by even considering the commission.

Jemme carefully explained exactly what he wanted, outlining the boats that should sit on the river and the landmarks that should sit on its banks. Whenever he stopped to check that Bertrand was following his ideas, he was met with a terse, 'If that's what you want.'

He provided him with a large book on the history of Turkish sailing, showing him the era he wanted to reference in the style of boat depicted.

Bertrand gave a cursory glance at the line drawing illustration, and then a barely perceptible Gallic shrug.

'If that's what you want,' he repeated, and Jemme began to wonder if he even spoke English or had just memorised those words in an effort to 'get by'. Then he surprised him.

'Mosques, boats, trading of merchants should go here,' he said pointing to the rough sketch. 'And then there should be castle turrets here, and churches on the hills of Romania and Bulgaria here, with Russian Orthodox churches here, and the port of Odessa, here,' he said, pointing again,

'Yes, yes,' said Jemme, delighted at this turn of events and that Bertrand seemed to understand his idea so clearly.

'If that's what you want,' Bertrand said once again, looking as if it was far from being what *he* wanted. He left Bertrand to work on the canvas. It was so huge that he would have to winch it into place somehow, and Jemme was pleased that he wouldn't have to be involved in the whole affair. The staircase leading up to Bertrand's studio was particularly rickety and Jemme wasn't quite sure how he would manage it at all.

A month or so later, he visited him to check on progress. A clamorous welcome awaited; he couldn't decide which noise he found more disagreeable: the sound of Bertrand's children squabbling and squealing or the sound of Bertrand's wife shrieking at them. No one seemed to have heard him arrive in the din, so he made his own way to find Bertrand.

'I hope that's not too distracting?' he said, struggling to make himself heard over the commotion.

'What's not?' Bertrand replied, apparently oblivious to the deafening racket. Jemme realised that, like the others, he must become so involved in his art that he was blinded to everything else whilst he was working. *Or, perhaps he's just completely deaf*, he mused to himself. The mosques had been nicely finished and the boats looked like they had come straight out of the pages in the book Jemme had leant him.

'This is all great, Bertrand, thank you.' He looked more closely, 'I'm not quite sure about these people,' he said eventually, indicating the figures painted, 'I mean, they look good. I'm just not sure about their clothes.'

'What do you mean?' asked Bertrand a trifle defensively.

'They might not be right for this period of history – they look a bit... contemporary.'

'Do they now?' he said, bristling.

'It's not a major criticism and I'm sure it's just because I was too vague in my instructions,' said Jemme quickly, 'Why don't I send over a book of costumes to give you something to work from.'

'You do that,' he said as Jemme left, climbing down the rickety stairs. Bertrand leaned over the banister, which seemed too unstable to support his weight, and watched Jemme attempt to negotiate his way through the throng of screeching children to leave.

After several months, Bertrand had finished. Once again, Jemme climbed the rickety stairs, which had seemed to become more precarious with each visit. He wasn't too sorry that this would be the last time that he would encounter the gaggle of noisy children, and the danger of the staircase.

He greeted Bertrand and inspected the canvas. He had obviously consulted the book he'd sent over, and the costumes were exactly right. The buildings were authentic enough too. However, something wasn't quite right.

'What don't you like?' asked Bertrand immediately, apparently sensing Jemme's unease.

'I think you've done it very well,' said Jemme.

'But that doesn't mean you're happy with it. What's the problem?'

'It's difficult to explain, I can't quite put my finger on it. I just don't think it's as I imagined it would look.'

'But everything is exactly as you asked for.'

'Yes, I know and it's very good, technically.'

Bertrand continued to stare at Jemme, who struggled to find the words to describe his dissatisfaction. 'I think, it's just that it looks as if you only finished painting it yesterday,' he said eventually.

'I did only finish painting it yesterday,' Bertrand replied, fairly.

'I know, I know, I just…. I suppose I wanted it to feel a little older, I wanted it to show ancient cities, but also look like an old painting in itself.

'Monsieur, I can paint old things but I cannot make my painting look old,' said Bertrand firmly.

Jemme hesitated.

'Can, you, Monsieur, make a new painting look old?' said Bertrand, looking at Jemme as if he was being utterly unreasonable.

'Well, I suppose… do you mind?' asked Jemme, indicating the pot of paint brushes and still-wet palette.

Bertrand had obviously intended it to be a rhetorical question and was too taken aback to protest. 'Monsieur,' he said with a mock grand gesture, indicating the painting tools to him.

For the very first time since Jemme embarked on the chateau project, he picked up the paintbrush and tried his hand at creating his vision. He fiddled with a dry brush to dislodge some piece of oil paint, instantly making that small section of the painting seem a little older. He flicked small dots of grey and brown paint at the edges of the canvas and smudged them together. It was a fairly crude effort, but it was effective and stopped the canvas from looking so bright, clean and brand new.

Bertrand shrugged, 'If that is what you want,' he said. He continued to work on the canvas until it looked a little bit more aged and slightly more as Jemme had envisioned. He still wasn't completely happy with it, but whenever he saw it he felt a sense of pride that he had been able to change the way it looked and make his own small artistic contribution to the chateau.

Chapter Thirty-Four

Jemme stared around the dining room of La Tour d'Argent. He was struggling to find something to say, when eventually his eye lit upon the duck press at the side of the room.

'Have I ever told you about how they make their famous *canard pressé*?' he piped up.

'Several times,' said Hil.

'Oh.'

He looked around the room, desperate to find something else to restart the conversation, but the truth was that both of them were desperately bored. It was difficult not to remember when he had been to the same restaurant for the first time with Burbona, and how thrilled he had been to hear about this exclusive dish. In fact it had been Burbona herself who had secured this booking for them. It had been Hil's birthday the weekend before, and she had insisted she hadn't wanted to make a fuss. However, Jemme had thought that a night of being spoiled in one Paris's finest restaurants would lift her spirits and help restore some of the vitality he had fallen in love with so many years ago.

It seemed that he was wrong, and he thought that if anything Hil looked even sadder than before.

He looked around the room again, struggling for inspiration, but only succeeded in catching the waiter's eye. Resigning himself to the inevitable, he asked for the bill.

'Thank you for such a nice meal,' said Hil as they stood up to leave.

'You are more than welcome, my love,' said Jemme, helping her on with her coat. 'You could have had much more if you liked though – I told you, it's my treat: anything on the menu!'

'I wasn't really that hungry,' said Hil quietly.

Jemme smiled at her, but had to stop himself from rolling his eyes, *suit yourself* he thought, then checked himself. He made an extra effort in the taxi home and found himself keeping the conversation going with forced small talk. By the time they got home he was tired out, and not entirely sure that the evening had been a success. Still, relative to how everything else had been between him and Hil recently, he supposed it wasn't a complete disaster, which was the main thing.

'Thank you again,' said Hil when they were back inside the flat. She leaned upwards and gave him a small kiss on the cheek.

'My pleasure, darling. Happy birthday again.'

Hil smiled at him, 'I think I'm going to go straight to bed if you don't mind, I'm very tired.'

'No, of course not,' said Jemme, trying to stop himself from sounding exasperated again. He wished Hil a goodnight, settled himself in his favourite reading chair and lost himself in a history book. As contentment washed over him, he started to feel truly relaxed for the first time all evening.

✳   ✳   ✳   ✳

That weekend, back at the chateau he sketched out a mirror he had seen in the restaurant, and gave it to a talented young craftsman who had just finished working on another task and was looking like he might be at a loose end. Jemme explained exactly how the mirror had looked, and suggested using an old mirror from the store room but constructing a new frame, cut as in his sketch and gilded. The craftsman looked at the sketch enthusiastically, and assured Jemme that it would be finished by the following afternoon.

'Well I suppose it wasn't a completely wasted restaurant trip after all,' thought Jemme to himself.

He toured the rest of the house, taking in everything that had been completed since his last visit. Most of the artists were finishing up for the day, and they chatted amiably with him as they packed away their tools, firmly screwing lids back on to pots and carefully wrapping paintbrushes in damp oil cloths so that they didn't harden overnight. There were some familiar faces, but a host of new ones too. Some he knew he would never see again. They were either local handymen called in for a quick mending job or specialists who would finish a specific piece of work and then fly off to the next job in another stately home or *hôtel particulier*. Nevertheless he made the effort to introduce himself to every one of them and ask them questions about their work, both for him and in general. It was important to know at least a little about the people who were helping construct his childhood dream, and they were part of the chateau's story after all.

As he made his way up the spiral staircase, he was pleased to see that the Santa Sabina doors had been hung. He paused to take them in. Monsieur Ilg had done a beautiful job, right down to the tiniest detail. They were a completely faithful reconstruction too – he thought he might even have difficulty distinguishing them from the real thing. He made a mental note to stash a photograph of the doors' Roman counterpart somewhere in the room, so that he could show guests who admired them. Walking along the corridor, he took in several of the embellishments and ornamentations he had requested. He had been determined from the beginning to make every part of the chateau decorative. He wanted to elevate every last inch from the functional to the meaningful. The corridors were narrative passages that linked the story in one room to the story in another. When the project was finished, a visitor would be able to walk from the Assyrian Empire through to the Babylonian to the Phoenician. On another floor, a visitor could wander through the Napoleonic wars, branching off into decorative rooms from all the baroque European palaces of that era.

This particular corridor was coming together nicely. In addition to the decorative flourishes, there were also several glass display cases – *vitrines* as the glazier who had made them had called them. They weren't complete yet, but they gave him a good feel for how the corridor would look. One had been filled with an assortment of ornaments and trinkets, just so that it didn't sit empty, and the other had been more carefully curated. It contained a collection of antique hunting daggers, of varying ages, decoration and provenance. There was an ornate knife from Spain, used to deliver the fatal *estocada* in a bullfight, and a silver knife with a brass hilt from Tudor England. With its fine decoration and filigree work it had obviously been the property of a noble, and Jemme liked to imagine that it had belonged to Henry VIII himself, used on wild boar hunts in the grounds of Hever Castle, or one of Jemme's other favourite places to visit whenever he was in England. There were Bedouin and Berber knives, Finnish knives and a particularly rare Faroese knife too. It had taken him years to amass the collection, although it had started from a much smaller collection his father had gifted him. He had treated the assemblage as seriously as if it was in a museum, carefully cataloguing it and displaying it as professionally and properly as he knew how. It made a fine addition to the corridor, and he had already commissioned a dozen similar *vitrines* to be made. He was looking forward to filling each one with another of his collections.

Passing to the end of the corridor, he made his way down the other staircase at the end. As he ambled towards the kitchen, he couldn't resist taking a small detour and peeking at the Silk Route staircase. It had been finished for a couple of weeks now, but the thrill he felt when he saw it was just as sharp as when it had been freshly completed. He felt the twinge of excitement again as he opened the door and peered in. Of all the rooms completed so far, this one had captured the sprit of the project the most, and made visual its whole philosophy. The grand rooms were great successes in their own right, but this staircase was the perfect example of decoration as narrative. He felt a sense of complete satisfaction as he stared at the work in front of him: it was just as it was meant to have been. He closed the door softly and went to the kitchen, where Marguerite was scolding several new kitchen maids. He caught the look of relief on Aude's face – she looked pleased to be out of the firing line for once. He paused and smiled slightly at the scene of organised chaos in front of him. Pots bubbled and rattled on the stovetop, the windows were steamed up, and every surface was heaped with dishes and pans. Four young girls ran around the kitchen frantically as Marguerite trilled orders at them, occasionally brandishing a bread knife dramatically. Her eyes suddenly lit upon Jemme,

'Monsieur!' she squeaked, 'I did not see you there!' She looked up and noticed the bread knife still in her hand. She put it down on the counter, 'Ah these girls make more work than they save, Monsieur!'

'I don't know, Marguerite, it looks like they're doing a pretty good job to me,' said Jemme generously. One of the girls looked up and gave him a shy smile.

'Oh, Monsieur, *hi*, you will encourage them,' said Marguerite, noticing the look and shooing the girl away. 'It is just the same as it is for you, Monsieur,' she said sternly, 'It is just like when you are managing all of these terrible artists you insist on dragging into this chateau.'

Jemme smiled and conceded defeat, 'Well I can't argue with you on certain individuals, Marguerite, we've certainly had our fair share of characters so far,' he said, settling down and letting Marguerite heap *bouef bourguignon* onto his plate.

Marguerite fussed around him, telling him about one particular craftsman she seemed to have taken exception to – a Monsieur Pontiac. The name didn't sound familiar to Jemme, and he couldn't quite get out of Marguerite exactly what it was that this fellow did, only that he seemed to be obsessed with some sort of box. Jemme resolved to seek him out the following morning, out of curiosity if nothing else.

Sure enough, after a hearty breakfast, he began his usual morning rounds, taking in progress and greeting all of the artists and craftsmen. It was a pleasant morning, sunny but crisp, and so he decided to start in the garden. Philby wasn't around, so Xelifon showed him some of his newest projects, as well the progress of some he had been working on for years. Xelifon's easy comfortable manner could not have been further from when he had first arrived at the chateau, and Jemme marvelled at how much he had progressed and developed in his time at Vigne-Verte. The same could be said of his projects, which had positively flourished. If all work on the gardens suddenly stopped, Jemme would still be pleased with them. The sculptures and statuary had seasoned in nicely, with the gleaming white edges slightly dulled, which stopped the marble from jarring so harshly with its surroundings. DD had been a terrific help in sourcing all of the artwork, and Philby had been incredibly savvy when installing it. He knew exactly how everything needed to be treated: whether sunk into a foundation ditch or installed onto a stone platform. Even though some pieces had been there for two years, there was no chance of them subsiding or sinking.

After returning to the house and wrapping his hands around a fresh cup of coffee to warm them, he decided to seek out Monsieur Pontiac. After wandering around the corridors for a while and encountering a clutch of unfamiliar faces, he suddenly realised that he didn't know what Pontiac looked like; he only knew him by reputation. As it turned out, that was definitely enough. Rounding one corner he saw a bald pate at the end of the corridor. The head was looking upwards and surveying a small piece of gilded plasterwork. The man looked about the right height to be Pontiac, from what Jemme had heard, and his area of interest seemed to match up, too. However, the single fact which identified him the most clearly was the large, completely square box over which he stood protectively. Jemme had heard that Pontiac was very particular about this box, and never let it out of his sight. He imagined that it contained the tools of his trade and wasn't especially surprised that Pontiac guarded it closely. Furthermore, given his experience with artistic sensibilities so far, he fully expected that Pontiac was a little eccentric in his guardianship. However, although Jemme didn't think anything was particularly out of the ordinary, Pontiac seemed to be the subject of much gossip and hilarity with the rest of the staff.

Jemme approached him and introduced himself.

'*Ah Monsieur*,' said Pontiac, extending a hand, 'I have been wondering when I would meet you. It is very strange to have been living in the house of a man I have never met.'

Jemme laughed, 'Yes, I can imagine it is. I used to find it strange to have so many people I had never met living in my house when I was far away in Paris, but I got used to it years ago.'

'*Ah, bon*?' said Pontiac thoughtfully, and shook his head slightly, 'A very strange position for a man to find himself in.'

'Indeed,' said Jemme. So far, so normal, he thought to himself.

'Well Monsieur Pontiac, I understand you're our resident gold-leafing expert.'

Pontiac shrugged. Jemme smiled to himself. In any other scenario he would have interpreted that shrug as a sign of modesty and a reluctant – even awkward – acceptance of praise. However, he had worked with artists for long enough now to know that in this case it was a pure recognition of fact. If he had told Pontiac that he understood he, Monsieur Pontiac, was the best gold-leafer in all the world, then he would have expected a similar reaction.

'I would love to hear a little bit more about your method,' he said.

Pontiac's expression clouded.

'Tell me a little bit more about how it all works,' Jemme said, 'I don't know much about gold leafing and I would certainly like to hear what it is that makes you such a master of the art.'

'B-b-but Monsieur, I cannot,' Pontiac stammered.

'Cannot? Whatever do you mean?' asked Jemme jovially, expecting him to have jumped at the chance to show off his skills.

'My methods, Monsieur… you must understand….' Pontiac looked pained.

'I would like to understand, that's why I'm asking!'

'*Non, non, non,*' Pontiac shook his head sadly.

Jemme eyed him suspiciously; he was rapidly beginning to suspect that Pontiac might not be the phlegmatic, well-grounded individual he had hoped. He didn't really understand what Pontiac was complaining about either; he hadn't really made much sense.

'Well, never mind,' he said, trying to keep the conversation light. 'Why don't you show me some of your tools? I'd love to see them.' He gestured towards the case. Pontiac stiffened, a flicker of panic passing across his eyes. Jemme's finger lingered.

'You do keep them in here don't you?' he asked, pointing at the box again. Pontiac leapt into action, and in one swift movement moved Jemme's hand out of the way and inserted himself between Jemme and the box. Jemme was surprised for a second before a sense of resignation sunk in. *Oh good, another one*, he thought to himself.

'*Non, Monsieur,*' said Pontiac firmly.

'*Non?*' asked Jemme.

'*Non,*' confirmed Pontiac.

'*Non* – I mean, no, I want to know what you are saying *non* to,' said Jemme.

Pontiac paused. 'My tools and my methods are the most valuable things I own, Monsieur,' he said very carefully.

'I understand that,' said Jemme, 'but I was just interested in seeing them, not touching them.'

Pontiac took a slow breath and tutted at the same time. He shook his head.

Jemme began to feel himself becoming irritated. 'Very well. I would like to know a little about your methods, though. It's important that I know at least something about everyone who works on the chateau for me.'

'Monsieur, I am the best gold leafer you will find to work on your chateau,' said Pontiac. 'That is enough for you to know.'

Jemme could sense he had a losing battle on his hands, and decided that he couldn't be bothered to argue it out.

'Well I hope so, Monsieur Pontiac,' he said, 'because I would be extremely disappointed if you didn't live up to your reputation.'

'You will not be, Monsieur,' said Pontiac firmly.

Jemme got the sense he was being dismissed, 'Well, I'm very busy, I must be off,' he said, trying to leave with the upper hand.

Pontiac nodded, 'Thank you for coming over,' he said solemnly.

Jemme felt irritated that Pontiac had had the last word. As he made his way back up the corridor, a sense of mischief crept in. *It would be tremendous fun to try and sneak a look into Pontiac's box when he wasn't looking,* Jemme thought to himself. He could make a sport of it. He resolved to have glimpsed its mysterious contents by the end of the weekend.

Having spent a whole day in the same building as Pontiac, he revised that to one month. Pontiac turned out to be one of the most secretive people he had ever come across. Over the course of a whole weekend, despite his most prodigious efforts, Jemme did not see Pontiac working once. Even when he sneaked up the end of the corridor and peeked around the corner, he still failed to catch the gold-leafer in the act. However, Pontiac was most certainly working. In fact, his output was remarkable for both its volume and extremely high quality. Finding completed pieces around the chateau was like striking lucky in a treasure hunt. Jemme felt as if he was uncovering a hidden, gilded jewel every time he stumbled across some of Pontiac's handiwork. They were scattered high and low throughout the whole chateau, too. Pontiac didn't seem to be following any kind of brief, but rather gilding anything which he had deemed to be drab or lacking in extravagant embellishment. His work was not confined merely to plaster either. No matter whether working with stone, wood or metal, it seemed he was able to apply his secret methods to any material, deftly finding every nook, cranny and crevice and gently folding precious gold leaf into each one. His work was consistently excellent, too. In fact it was beyond excellent; it was expert. Jemme could only imagine at the type of tools which were hidden in his box – stippling and soft paintbrushes, hammers, blades – sharp and blunt, tweezers and all manner of small instruments for pushing the leafing into the tiny fissures in antique wooden frames and the small whorls in stone slabs. He imagined it would take a working lifetime to build up the perfect collection of tools, and it was no wonder that Pontiac guarded it so ferociously. Jemme supposed the same was true of knowledge and techniques, and he grudgingly admitted to himself that he understood why Pontiac was so protective of this too. However, it didn't stop him wanting to see the gilder in action. If anything, his curiosity had been heightened. He was intrigued to watch such a master in action; he wanted to know exactly how everything was done. What did Pontiac do differently to leave a satin shine on some pieces of gilding and a glossy sheen on others? Jemme wondered if it was a difference in the materials used, the technique applied or a varnish painted on afterwards? The science of it all appealed to him and he longed to have a go himself, but he knew that Pontiac would be in no hurry to coach him.

He reluctantly left him to his own devices, but didn't stop trying to catch him at work. For the rest of his time he made his rounds, meeting artists and checking on work and progress. There were a couple of major pieces coming up, and he wanted to ensure that all loose ends had been tied up before they began. He knew that they were going to be challenging, technically, practically and imaginatively, but they were key dream-rooms and he had been itching to start on them. For the moment he was content to let everything else finish up, and would begin work on them properly on the next visit. It was nice to have a plan, however fluid it might be, and it was reassuring to feel that there was some structure to the project. Banking had trained him to be mistrustful of unknowns, and he had done his best to ensure that no eventuality had been left unexplored. No matter how vague, he had some sort of plan for every single piece in his collection, from the smallest artefact to the largest piece of furniture. However, one thing was bothering him: every time he thought of his collection of ivory and mother-of-pearl chests, he drew a complete blank. He couldn't come up with a single idea, and that in itself bothered him too.

He thought about the chests all the way back to Paris, and by the time he had arrived home, he still hadn't come up with any ideas. Hil was already asleep, but he never wanted to go straight to bed after a long car journey and so he settled himself in his favourite reading chair. However, the lack of solution made him restless. He got up and paced around the sitting room, pulling books off the shelf at random and flicking through them looking for inspiration. He desperately tried to force himself to see something in the photos, illustrations and sketches they contained, but nothing inspired him. Sighing, he pulled a large photobook down from the top shelf and settled into the chair again. It was a coffee-table-style book, filled with photos from the Winter Palace at St Petersburg. He had never really liked the book – the photographs were poor and their reproduction in this book just as bad. They utterly failed to capture the splendour of palace rooms and the richness of colour. Idly he leafed through to a photograph of the Malachite Room. The production qualities were so low that the splendid green he remembered so vividly looked muddy and almost black in the picture. He remembered that he had relegated this book to the top shelf with good reason, and was about to snap it shut when the picture in front of him caught his eye. Although it looked nothing like the Malachite Room, the dark colours, marbled with a sharply contrasting white, stirred a vague recognition. He stared at the picture, straining to see what he wanted to. Gradually it started to move and change before his eyes. The muddy green of the malachite turned completely to black, and its veins became whiter and whiter until they shone in brilliant contrast. They writhed and twisted and looped back on themselves until they started to form shapes. There were complicated geometric patterns, made up of tiny diamonds; there were birds; there were flowers. Suddenly he could place his sense of recognition exactly. The black background and gleaming white details were directly from his cabinets. The scenes and patterns depicted on their familiar surfaces had been unwrapped and spread out across the inside of the room he was looking at. He closed the book and allowed the vision to develop inside his mind. Many of the chests and cabinets would have been marriage pieces – commissioned as gifts for a newly-wed bride and groom. The careful inlays of ivory told a story of love and family unions. Each piece was laden with symbols, and deeply personal to its owner. Unwoven and spread across a ceiling, they create a dark cavern of stories, each one brightly picked out like stars in a night sky.

He kept his eyes closed, and sat back in the chair. A deep sense of relaxation took over as he studied the room in his vision. He already knew it was how the room must look; he just didn't know how he could recreate it. The swirling patterns of ivory were hypnotic, and as he concentrated on them they spun themselves around, untangling and reforming into new shapes. The blackness became darker and the gleaming white faded.

He felt his arm drop from the rest on the side of the chair and jerked awake. He realised he must have drifted off, and sleepily rose from his seat. His joints were stiff and his neck ached. He was glad he hadn't slept in the seat any longer, and looked forward to sinking into bed. Trying not to wake Hil, he slipped in next to her. Bleary-eyed, he gently leaned forward and kissed her on the forehead before falling back to sleep again. Hil woke just enough to smile, her eyes tightly shut. For a moment it had been just like they were their old selves again.

❖ ❖ ❖ ❖

The next morning, he woke to find that Hil had already left. He sleepily pulled his watch from the bedside table and realised that he had slept far later than he intended. No wonder Hil was already out of the flat. He dressed as quickly as he could, and realised he would have to have breakfast at the bank. On Mondays he enjoyed getting up a little earlier, settling in a café and poring over the papers with a couple of espressos and a croissant. By the time he arrived at work, he would be alert and fully up to speed with the weekend's international news. However, today, even after the brisk walk there, he still felt half asleep by the time he reached the bank. As always, DD had the perfect coffee waiting for him. Exactly the right temperature and with a pleasing bitterness; today he was especially grateful for it.

'Fantastic, DD, thank you.'

DD inclined his head.

'I overslept a little actually – so that was very much appreciated,' Jemme explained.

DD inclined his head again, 'I trust all is well,' he said.

'Oh, everything's fine – I was just puzzling over something to do with the chateau, and I dozed off in the sitting room by mistake.'

'I hope a conclusion was reached,' DD said as he cleared away the espresso cup and its tiny saucer.

'Not exactly, to tell you the truth. In fact, quite the opposite. It was more the beginning of the problem than the end.'

DD looked at Jemme impassively, patiently waiting for him to continue with the story.

'I've been thinking about the ebony and mother of pearl pieces,' Jemme began. 'They're sitting in storage at the moment, which I hate, but no matter how hard I've tried, I just haven't been able to think of what I can do with them.'

'A conundrum indeed,' said DD.

'Exactly. Well, I'm not sure I quite know how I need to do this, but I know I want to use them as decoration in the chateau, rather than as stand-alone pieces.'

DD raised one eyebrow a fraction as he waited patiently for Jemme to talk him through his reasoning.

'I got the idea when I was looking at a picture of the Malachite Room in St Petersburg. I want to achieve the same effect in the chateau.'

'With malachite, Sir?' asked DD, perfectly reasonably.

'Well, no. This is where I'm coming unstuck. I want to achieve the same effect, but using the pieces of furniture.'

DD waited, betraying nothing.

'In that room, the visitor is completely immersed into an entire world of malachite – it's all you can see, everywhere you turn. I want to create that experience, but with ebony and mother-of-pearl instead.'

There was a long pause.

'Using the pieces of furniture themselves, Sir?' DD eventually asked.

'Precisely,' said Jemme. 'It's crucial to the whole room that I actually use the pieces. I don't want to recreate them by copying their patterns onto the walls in paint, or anything like that. I want to use the pieces themselves.'

'I see,' said DD.

'Well, do you also see how difficult it is all going to be?' asked Jemme, a little desperately.

'Difficult, perhaps,' said DD in level tones, 'but certainly not impossible.'

'I admire your optimism,' Jemme laughed, 'I just wished I shared it.'

'The form of the piece is the most immediate problem,' said DD thoughtfully.

'Exactly!' Jemme agreed emphatically. 'I want to flatten very solid, three-dimensional objects and cover four walls with them.'

'Difficult, but not impossible,' DD repeated. 'The first thing you will need is a very good cabinet maker. I will sort this out and arrange for you to meet him next weekend at the chateau.'

'Thank you, DD, I knew I could count on you for help,' said Jemme. He thought a cabinet maker was a slightly odd choice – he already had the pieces after all, and didn't want new ones made, but he trusted DD completely. Now that his capable second-in-command had taken responsibility for the problem, Jemme felt freed up to concentrate on the business of the day. The only thing stopping him from giving the stack of papers in front of him his full attention was the twinge of hunger in his stomach. As if he had read his mind, DD suddenly appeared with a tray bearing another espresso, a crisp linen napkin and a very large, golden pain-au-chocolat.

'DD, you're a marvel,' Jemme said gratefully. 'I didn't even realise you'd left the room. I'll never know how you manage to do that.'

'It is my job, Sir,' said DD simply. With one efficient hand movement, he moved the stack of papers to one side, keeping their bookmarks and tabs exactly in place, and placed the tray down in front of Jemme.

※　※　※　※

Jemme buried himself in his work for the rest of the day, and tried to put thoughts of the Malachite Room at the back of his mind. He had plenty of other things to occupy him, and throughout that week any spare time he had to think was taken up by the prospect of the next big projects, which were due to start on the upcoming weekend. After much consideration he had decided to push one back by a couple of weeks, so he could dedicate all of his energies to ensuring that the other got off the ground properly. It had taken so much energy, effort and planning that he couldn't bear for something to be overlooked at the very beginning, and to undo months of hard work. Moreover, this was to be a dream room, directly from his imagination, and he wanted it to be perfect.

He had already started to think of the room as the *Salon d'Anadalousie* project, and it was to look exactly as it had when he had first seen it in childhood. It would be a paean to Andalucía's colourful cultural history. The place itself was integral to the chateau's expositional aims. It demonstrated a great zenith in Eastern culture and achievement, but in the context of close contact and cooperation with the West.

It had long fascinated him, and one whole bookcase back in Paris was filled with volumes covering various important epochs, from the beginning of the Arabic settlement through to the conquest of Ferdinand and Isabella.

He had started off with a couple of synoptic books, but as he had traced the fortunes of the region, its victories and its defeats, so the books on the shelves had grown, running onto the shelf below and then the one below that, until it was full. It was hard to tell which era of the region's long history he found the most interesting, or which aspect he found the most thrilling. The story had begun in 711 with the greatest victory of the Umayyad Caliphate. Routing the Visisgothic rulers, the army which had set out from North Africa, and which included African Berber troops as well as Arabs, had occupied the entire Iberian Peninsula within two years. The newly conquered territory became known as al-Andalus. He loved the poetry and romance of the name, and he loved thinking of this beautiful, sun-drenched place as being one of the main channels through which Arab culture penetrated into Western Europe. He had visited many times and, as he wandered its fragrant streets, he imagined this being the place through which the works of the Greek doctors and philosophers made their way north, to be translated into Latin. He thought of the ideas of Averroes and other great Andalusian thinkers being studied and readapted by Spanish Christians. He could imagine the music of the Arabs being adopted by the Christians in Spain, and how it would have sounded when strange new sounds rang out through the city and across the lemon groves.

All these strange new cultures, from learning to music to agriculture put down permanent roots: the canals which irrigated the countryside were used in the cultivation of exotic fruits such as oranges, apricots, peaches and pomegranates. The glazed pottery made in Arab Spain was imitated in France, Holland and Italy, while the pointed arches and tracery in the Muslim monuments in Spain had a deep effect on the Gothic architecture of Western Europe. It was a beautiful, elegant example of the fusion of foreign cultures.

The room itself would look exactly as it had in his dream, but he would embellish it with references to different periods in Andalucía's history. However, although he still saw the room of his dream clearly, he had quickly realised that it was unfettered by the rules of gravity, and any practical constraints whatsoever. In his dream, he had seen a thick forest of marble columns, each of which was a different, rich, luxurious colour. He remembered craning his head back as far as he could and being able to see a splendid golden capital on the top of each column, as if it were a magnificent crown. However, whereas the room of his dream had been able to support colossal marble columns, it turned out the room of his chateau could not. He knew he would not be able to include anywhere near the same number of pillars, and so he had reduced it down to a small sample – just enough to give the same forest-like experience he wanted to recreate. However, since then he had had to halve the number of pillars again, and even now, with a doubly-reinforced floor, the weight was looking perilous. The pillars had been commissioned and completed months beforehand, and were on their way to the chateau, due to arrive in time for the weekend's work. He hated the idea that they couldn't all be used. It wasn't only the wasted hours and materials, but knowing that the pillars existed somewhere that wasn't in the room would detract from the room. Jemme knew that it would always feel incomplete when he surveyed the marble forest, and thought about the solitary pillars dotted around the rest of the chateau without any context. Even worse, they might be relegated to storage, just like his precious ebony and mother-of-pearl furniture.

He roused himself from his daydreaming and forced himself to concentrate on work again. It wasn't easy; there were so many things occupying his thoughts. In addition to the columns, he was thinking about the mihrab for the room. He knew that it was essential he constructed one, but he didn't know how it should look. It had to evoke the glories of Andalucía in its heyday, represent it as a centre of cultural exchange, and yet also be historically accurate. He had enlisted the Professor's help and Professor Johnston seemed to be on the case, but Jemme hadn't heard from him in a while. Just as he managed to banish all thoughts of the chateau, he remembered the furniture and the Malachite Room again. *This is hopeless*, he thought to himself, and decided that another espresso break was in order.

✳ ✳ ✳ ✳

That weekend, Jemme arrived at the chateau with a slight feeling of nerves stirring at the bottom of his stomach. He was excited about the new projects, but he also knew there was a lot at stake. If something went wrong because of his calculations, not only would a large amount of work be destroyed, but it could be extremely dangerous.

By the time he had done the usual rounds, and eaten a hearty supper, his nerves had given way to anticipation and he couldn't wait until the morning to begin everything. Everyone seemed to have finished for the evening, so he wandered around having a look at the work which had been completed. It was all coming along nicely – there were no unpleasant surprises and everyone seemed to be working to schedule. He made his way up the staircase to the Santa Sabina doors to finish off. There was something that drew him to the doors every time he came back to the chateau. He found that looking at them was strangely restful. They were a product of hard work and skill – good old fashioned labour; there had been no cheating and no shortcuts. Just as he had planned to, he had brought a photograph of the actual doors with him, which he planned to stash in the room somewhere, so that he could show visitors. He pulled the photograph from its envelope and studied it carefully. There before him were his doors again. Every single detail and every expression had been reproduced exactly. He smiled to himself, and felt thoroughly pleased. For the first time he held the photograph up to the door and compared them. He looked between them and shook his head. Ilg had done a fantastic job, and all the time he had spent carefully planning and lining up the images had definitely been worth it. Jemme scrutinised every single attribute of the doors in the photos and then identified its wooden counterpart in front of him.

He picked out saints, cherubim and archangels with a broad smile across his face. As he was looking at a group of three angels, his face suddenly puckered in confusion. He looked at the door and then back to the paper again. His brow wrinkled and he slowly compared door and paper once more. There was a pause, 'Hmph,' he said aloud. He turned some more lights on and had another look. There was no mistaking it: the photograph showed a trio of angels in Rome and what he was looking at in France was very much a duo. He wondered where on earth the other could have got to, and chuckled to himself at the absurdness of the thought – it wasn't as if it would have just flown off.

The whole affair seemed bizarre to him. Ilg had spent so long on the doors that he found it hard to believe that he could simply overlook the extra figure. Perhaps he had begun to carve it, made some mistake and decided that it would be easier simply to chisel it off. Jemme didn't think that seemed likely either – he remembered Ilg describing his seamstress mother – *measure twice, cut once,* she had taught him. He puffed out his cheeks – *What a mysterious note to end the evening on,* he thought to himself and decided to turn in for the evening.

The following morning he woke up and blinked a few times as the room came into focus. As always, it took him a few moments to recognise where he was, and take in his surroundings. As soon as he remembered he was in the chateau, he sat straight up and a smile spread across his face. He yawned extravagantly and got out of bed. Having dressed, he happily plodded downstairs to the kitchen. As much as he was looking forward to the day, he didn't plan on facing it until he'd had at least one coffee. Marguerite had anticipated him, and the silver coffee pot was already sitting on the table, a gentle curl of steam emitting from its spout. Jemme settled himself in with a couple of thick *tartines* and slowly thought his way through the day. He needed to check in with Philby, review the work which was already underway, officially begin the Andalusian room, and meet the carpenter DD said would help him with the furniture problem. In addition to this, he had hundreds of small jobs and admin tasks to finish up.

Gulping down the last of his coffee and pouring another, he decided that he would go and see the grounds team first. He found Philby, who gave him a terse review of everything since they had last met, but then had to leave to help with a delivery of paving slabs which had just arrived. Jemme soon found Xelifon.

'Hello, Xelifon,' he said cheerfully.

A smile unfurled slowly across Xelifon's face, '*Bonjour, Monsieur,*' he said quietly.

'Philby's had to rush off before he'd finished telling me about everything that's been happening this week. I wonder if you might be able to finish off?'

Xelifon smiled again and nodded slowly. He paused and thought, 'The trees, Monsieur, are not well,' he said carefully.

'Not well?'

Xelifon shook his head, 'They are diseased, Monsieur,' he said sadly.

'Diseased? I didn't know a tree could have a disease!'

'*Oui, Monsieur.* Any living thing can have a disease. One tree may catch the disease from another.'

Jemme looked concerned, 'Is this a serious problem? How many of the trees are affected?'

Xelifon shrugged slightly, 'It is just the elm trees, Monsieur – Dutch Elm Disease. We have found the bad trees and Monsieur Philby has removed them. It is over.'

'Oh, well… good work,' said Jemme. Xelifon looked so sad at the fate of the trees that it was making Jemme feel guilty.

'What about this great big one here?' Jemme asked, trying to change the subject. He pointed at the tree towering over the bothy.

Xelifon looked even sadder, 'Monsieur, that tree is dead,' he said sorrowfully.

'Oh,' said Jemme. He squinted up and realised that it didn't have any leaves and many of its upper branches were missing. He wished he'd seen that before he'd pointed it out.

'Well, I suppose we'd better get this one down as soon as possible,' he said, 'We don't want a great beast like that falling on your hut eh?' he added, trying to cheer Xelifon up.

Xelifon eyed him balefully, 'No, Monsieur, that tree is big, but it is not heavy.'

'Eh?'

'It has been dead for a long time. It is completely hollow in the middle. If it fell there would be no damage.'

'Big but not heavy,' Jemme repeated.

'*Oui, Monsieur.*'

'I think you might have just given me an idea, Xelifon,' said Jemme.

Xelifon looked up at the old tree with a fondness that could have been directed at a doddering uncle, and Jemme decided it was time to leave.

Back at the chateau, he made his way around the artists as quickly as he could. He found Pontiac standing next to an exquisite piece of gold leafing, which he must have just finished. He had already managed to put all of his tools back into his box and, in fact, was looking at the gilding with all the cool detachment of one who had just happened to be passing. I'll catch you soon, thought Jemme to himself as he greeted him.

The pillars weren't arriving until eleven, and he had been so efficient in his rounds that he had finished by half ten. He was just wondering what to do next when Aude's friend Florence came trotting up to him.

'*Monsieur, Monsieur,*' she said, out of breath.

'Good morning, Florence,' said Jemme, what can I help you with?'

Florence tried to smooth her hair down, but she was looking rather dishevelled and slightly panicked. 'Madame Marguerite,' she paused for breath, 'she says I must find you immediately.' She paused again. 'There is a man here for you, Monsieur.'

'A man? Do you know who he is?'

Florence took in another big breath and gained a small amount of composure, 'He is an *ébéniste* – cabinet maker – Monsieur,' she said eventually.

'Oh good, what excellent timing. Thank you for coming to find me,' he took in her panicked look again, which had not disappeared now the message had been delivered.

'Tell Marguerite I was very pleased,' he added.

A look of relief spread across Florence's face and she headed off back to the kitchen. Jemme watched her go, half-walking and half-running, and smiled to himself. Marguerite certainly keeps them all in line, he thought to himself. He headed off to the grand staircase to meet his guest, who he assumed was waiting for him in the hall.

He had guessed correctly, and as he descended down the sweeping staircase, a very small bespectacled man came into view. He had snowy white hair, neatly clipped, and wore a pale grey suit. By the time Jemme had reached the bottom of the staircase and made his way over, he realised that the man was a good three heads shorter than him. The man smiled broadly when he saw Jemme and offered him a powerful handshake, which took Jemme slightly by surprise.

'Monsieur, delighted to meet you,' he said. 'Jako Le Selmelif,' he added, pumping Jemme's hand again.

'It's a pleasure to meet you too, Monsieur Le Selmelif,' Jemme returned.

'I am so pleased to hear of all the work that has been going on here, and even more pleased to finally see it!' said Le Selmelif warmly.

'Ah, do you live locally, Monsieur?' Jemme asked, 'You'll have to forgive me, my second-in-command back in Paris usually finds everyone who'll be working here, so I'm afraid I don't know much about your background.'

'You are a busy man, Monsieur, I imagine – I would not expect you to know,' said Le Selmelif cheerfully. 'I do not live very locally; I actually live further north and west, towards the coast. I have heard of the work you are doing though!'

'Really? I had no idea that word had spread any further than the village!'

'*Ben, oui, Monsieur*! The community of artists and craftsman in this part of the country is spread out, but it is very small. We are all used to travelling very far to work on our projects and news travels very quickly about exciting new projects too. I have always known about the existence of this chateau, and it has saddened me that it has been looked after so poorly – I am very pleased that it is finally getting some attention.'

'Well, I am even more pleased to have you involved, if that is the case!' said Jemme, 'I like anyone who works here to have some kind of personal connection with what's going on, no matter how small.'

'A good philosophy, Monsieur.'

'I'm pleased you think so. How much do you know about what I need you to do?'

'The German gentleman who called me gave me an outline. You have a selection of antique furniture you would like to distribute and curate, no?'

To Jemme's relief, Le Selmelif repeated this as if it was the most natural request in the world. If he thought it was complete folly, he was certainly keeping it to himself, which made things a little easier.

'I'll take you there now,' said Jemme. As he walked Le Selmelif to the room he had in mind, they chatted amiably about Le Selmelif's background. Jemme was impressed. He was highly qualified, and had served his apprenticeship under a prestigious master carpenter. He seemed modest about his experience and the projects he had worked on, and was entirely focussed on the task in hand. Jemme showed him to the room, pointed out any unusual dimensions, nooks and crannies he thought worth mentioning, and left Le Selmelif to his own devices. On the other side of the chateau he was fairly certain that the marble columns would be arriving, and he didn't want to miss anything.

Chapter Thirty-Five

Jemme watched the men unload the marble columns from the truck. There were five burly individuals in all, and each one looked as if he could have lifted two men Jemme's size. However, it took three of them to offload each column and even then the strain was obvious on their faces. Jemme looked on nervously. He winced every time he saw one of the movers grimace: it didn't bode well for the floor.

As the protective dustsheet slipped from one of the columns he caught a glimpse of the glossy aubergine colour beneath, marbled with fat white veins. He smiled excitedly, completely forgetting about his misgivings.

He craned his neck eagerly, trying to see the other columns, but they had been too carefully wrapped. He moved towards the back of the van and peered inside at all of the dustsheet-clad columns, leaning up against the back wall. Even though it was a pale imitation, he could still imagine how spectacular the forest of pillars would look when they had been installed. He continued to gaze at the cloth-swaddled pillars, hoping to catch a flash of what was underneath the covers. Eventually one of the movers, obviously not knowing who Jemme was, gruffly told him to stop getting in the way. Reluctantly he slunk off.

He headed back to the kitchen to think about what he would spend the rest of the morning doing. He was impatient to get started on the two new rooms, but he knew he would have to wait until everything was ready. Idly his mind returned to the problem of the pillars again. He pulled a piece of scrap paper towards him and sketched out some calculations on it. He tried to remember how many pillars he had seen in the back of the van, and how much he had been told each one would weigh. He paused as he jotted the numbers down. It had been a while since he'd had to think about downward pressure and high forces, and he wished he had a structural engineer on hand he could consult. It was sometimes lonely being the one in charge of everything with no executive team to back him up. He felt his mind wander to Hil – if she'd been here, at least she could have provided moral support. He stopped himself from indulging in that thought, and refocused on the figures, but it was no good. Even if they reinforced the floor several times, he still felt that the strain would be too great.

He slowly folded up the piece of paper and put it in his pocket. Perhaps he would have to consult with an engineer back in Paris, after all. He had prided himself so much on doing everything by himself, but this involved people's safety. If he couldn't come up with a solution by the end of the weekend, he would definitely consult an engineer, he promised himself.

With that, he decided to do another quick tour of the chateau to see if there were any new craftsmen he hadn't met yesterday. Walking along the corridor on the third floor he came across Monsieur Pontiac, putting a brush back into his mysterious box. He heard Jemme coming and snapped the lid shut quickly.

'Monsieur,' he said brusquely, nodding at Jemme.

Jemme was momentarily irritated that he had so narrowly missed catching Pontiac at work, but when he saw how beautifully Pontiac had gilded the cornice in front of him, he grudgingly congratulated him. Pontiac accepted his praise, with about as much enthusiasm as Jemme had offered it. There was an awkward pause.

'Anything interesting in the box at the moment, Monsieur?' asked Jemme bluntly.

Pontiac blanched, 'Interesting…Monsieur?' he asked cautiously.

Jemme sighed, 'Yes, interesting – you know, anything out of the ordinary, anything particularly noteworthy.'

Pontiac shrugged, 'It depends on who thinks it will be interesting, Monsieur,' said Pontiac.

Jemme could feel the frustration rising – *I was only trying to pass some time*, he thought to himself. He was about to leave without bothering to say another word when Pontiac casually mentioned that he had just bought some 'precious' supplies.

It was enough to hook Jemme. 'Precious supplies?' he repeated.

'*Oui, Monsieur*,' repeated Pontiac, 'precious metals to be exact.'

'For the gilding?' asked Jemme.

Pontiac sighed loudly, 'Yes for the gilding, Monsieur!' he said as if he was talking to someone slow. 'I have five types of gold here, two types of bronze leaf, copper and white gold. It is all hand-beaten,' he added proudly. He paused for a moment and then turned to Jemme, narrowing his eyes, 'It is very *expensive,* Monsieur,' he added deliberately.

Jemme suppressed a smile – surely Pontiac didn't imagine that he, Jemme, might steal his gold leaf? He couldn't resist the opportunity to tease him a little, 'Tell me, Monsieur,' he said, with a deliberately false-looking casualness, 'how do you protect your box when you are sleeping…?'

Pontiac looked alarmed, 'The box is with me at all times!' he squeaked.

'Yes, but how do you make sure that, when you are fast asleep, no one breaks into it?' asked Jemme, trying to look as if that was exactly what he was planning on doing.

Pontiac's forehead began to look clammy. He gulped loudly, took a deep breath and then began firmly, 'Monsieur. This box goes with me everywhere I go. It is with me at all times – *at all times, Monsieur*! I need to go to the *sanitaire* – I take my box with me. I stop to take *un café* – I take my box with me. I must sleep – I take my box with me!' he practically shouted the last sentence. 'I decide that I will –' he began again.

'Yes, yes,' Jemme interrupted, 'You will take your box with you. I understand. Well, I'm glad we cleared that one up. You are doing a very good job of the gilding, Monsieur Pontiac. Keep it up.' With that he wandered off down the corridor. He had grown tired of the game, and had decided that he had had enough of artistic temperaments for the morning.

He estimated that the movers would be at least another half hour unloading the columns and moving them into the storage room, so he made his way down to the ground floor, where he knew there was some flooring work going on. The parquet was badly damaged, and in places was beyond repair. He had decided that in certain rooms it should be dug up completely and replaced with high-quality granite. It would be far more durable and, Jemme felt, would add a certain grandeur to a couple of the noble rooms. He had forgotten about this particular project until that morning, and he couldn't remember much about it, even now – he didn't even remember whom he had engaged to work on it.

He arrived at the first room, and could see that work had already begun in earnest. The rotten floorboards had been completely dug up, and glassy granite tiles were already beginning to spread out from the doorway like a black puddle. A man was hard at work; leaning on all fours facing away from the doorway, he was smearing grout carefully along the edge of the outermost tile. His elbows rested on a scrap of cardboard, which was also protecting the tile's surface from the grout.

Jemme knocked on the open door, 'Hello!'

The man unfolded himself slowly and stood up. Jemme tried not to look surprised – he was well over six and a half feet tall, perhaps even larger.

'Monsieur Mafeze!' he greeted Jemme as if they were long-standing acquaintances.

Jemme took in his face; he was obviously from the Middle East, but he couldn't be sure if he was Turkish. He had a thick, dark moustache and pale green eyes which looked kindly back at Jemme.

'Husam Mustafy,' he prompted, holding out his hand to shake Jemme's. 'From the Blue Mosque.'

'Of course!' Jemme pumped his hand enthusiastically, 'I'm so sorry Husam, I recognised you of course, I was just trying to place you.'

Husam smiled, 'Well I am impressed you recognised me at least. It was a while ago, and it sounds like you have had many people working on this project.'

'Well that's true enough, but regardless, it is good to see you. Have you come straight from Istanbul, or were you in France already?'

'I have come from Istanbul – I left two and a half weeks ago.

Jemme looked momentarily confused.

'How long it since you were last in Istanbul?' asked Husam.

Jemme forgot his consternation as a wave of nostalgia swept over him. They reminisced about Istanbul and Turkey, and a crystal-clear memory of the time he had met Husam came back to Jemme. Husam had been working on the astonishing blue-tiled interior of the mosque. He was undertaking some restoration and repairs, and Jemme had been fascinated by his work. They had begun chatting and he had told Jemme a story he had never forgotten about the mosque. He learned that Sultan Ahmed had commissioned the architect, Mehmed Aga, to build him a mosque to rival the Sofia, which was the largest and most renowned mosque in the whole land. The Sultan stipulated that he wanted a minaret of gold – *altin* in Turkish. However, Mehmed understood the Sultan as saying *alti* meaning 'six'. On completion, Mehmed realised his mistake – instead of giving the Sultan four golden minarets, he'd given him six minarets, not one of which was gold.

Mehmed must have been distraught to realise he had misinterpreted the Sultan's instructions, Husam mused. No doubt he wondered how the Sultan would react, and it must have occurred to him that he could lose his head. Yet, when the Sultan saw the mosque, he was overjoyed. Most mosques had four minarets. No previous Sultan had a mosque with six – he was delighted to be the first!

Jemme had been charmed by this story, and impressed by Husam's application to his work. Although they had met when the chateau project had been in its infancy, he had taken Husam's details in case any suitable work ever arose. They had continued to chat for an hour or so, and Jemme had been impressed by the breadth of Husam's knowledge of Islamic art and traditional craft.

It was many years later that he had passed on the details to DD and asked him to liaise with Husam about the flooring. However, so much had happened since then, that he had completely forgotten. He was delighted to have such a man working for him, and even more pleased to have such a welcome memory from his past. As they discussed the floor, the mosque and Turkey, Jemme tried to vicariously absorb the sunshine and smells of his childhood home. He completely forgot about the pillars and listened, rapt, to Husam's talk of date stalls, orange trees and large Turkish feasts back at home with his family. Jemme asked him if his family were craftsman too.

'Most of them,' Husam replied, 'but my brother owns a bicycle shop. That's where I got my own bicycle. It's my pride and joy – did you see it on the way in?'

'See it? It's here in France?!'

'Of course it is.'

'You brought it with you?'

'Well it would have been difficult not to.'

Both men looked at each other in confusion. Eventually Jemme spoke, 'Husam, how exactly did you get here?'

'I cycled.'

'On a bicycle?!' Jemme said incredulously.

'Yes,' replied Husam, as if it was the most matter of fact thing in the whole world.

'All the way from Istanbul?!' Jemme said, his voice getting even higher.

'Well yes,' said Husam, calmly.

'But, how – *why*?!' asked Jemme.

Husam shrugged, 'My brother sells the best bicycles in Istanbul. Mine is very old but it still works very well. I have it, so why not use it?'

'Well, yes – but…' Jemme trailed off. Husam looked at him with an open expression, and Jemme took in his calm demeanour. He felt a growing sense of respect – instead of being the act of a mad artist, it felt like this was the most simple and honest act of a genuine man. He paused and thought, 'Husam, how are you planning on getting back to Istanbul?'

'I will cycle,' said Husam plainly. 'I would not want to come all the way here and leave my bicycle behind,' he said as if it was an obvious point.

'No….no, I suppose not,' said Jemme, smiling. He felt a renewed affinity with Husam; he was obviously a man of great strength and integrity. He chatted with him a little more about the work he was going to be undertaking, and Husam answered each of his questions thoroughly and intelligently with a calm assurance.

After they had discussed the floor, and reminisced about Istanbul some more, Jemme decided to get out of his way and leave Husam to do what he had cycled so many hundreds of miles to do.

He wandered back to the kitchen and out of the back door, so he could walk through the grounds to the front entrance. He looped around until he reached the driveway, enjoying the satisfying crunch of gravel underfoot. Once at the front he saw that the delivery had been fully unloaded, and so he went back in through the main entrance to check with Philby that everything had been in order.

He found a small knot of people gathered around the columns, talking animatedly. The columns themselves looked as if they had been scattered around – some were propped up against the walls, some were stacked on the floor. If they hadn't been so heavy, Jemme might have thought they had been blown in by the wind. He went over to the small group and greeted Philby, Le Selmelif and several of the artists. The conversation seemed to be rather animated.

'Monsieur, you must trust me, my brother is a civil engineer!' one of them was saying.

'But I myself have studied pressures and load-bearing structures,' another was saying.

'Yes – of wood!' the third artist interrupted, 'You are no more qualified to talk about this than the rest of us!'

'What's going on, Philby?' asked Jemme, joining the group.

Philby looked up, 'These marbles are too heavy,' he said simply.

'Too heavy? For what?'

'Everything, Monsieur!' one of the artists answered dramatically.

'There is some truth in what he is saying,' said Le Selmelif gently to Jemme 'These columns – beautiful as they are, are extremely heavy. In fact, we are all a little worried about them – some more than others,' he added in confidential tones cocking his head towards the dramatic artist. 'Monsieur Philby and I were even a little concerned about resting all the columns up against the walls here – it is a huge amount of pressure, especially for an old building.'

'We put them like this,' said Philby, gesturing around. 'It's fine for down here, but it will be difficult to get them upstairs.'

'Thank you for your help,' Jemme said to Philby and Le Selmelif, and then turned to smile at the rest of the group.

'I really do appreciate your input, but I would hate to distract you from your work,' he said. They gradually dispersed, leaving just Philby and Le Selmelif.

'Do you think it will be a major issue?' he asked the two.

'Monsieur, even if you have reinforced the floor I would still be extremely cautious,' replied Le Selmelif.

Philby nodded his assent.

'In an old building the joists are almost always timber, and you can never be sure what kind of condition they're in. It may be that they will be absolutely fine, but of course it may be that they just will not support the weight. If it was me and I knew that there was any risk of the latter, I wouldn't be prepared to gamble on the former.'

'Thank you,' said Jemme, 'I really value your opinion – Philby, do you have anything to add?'

Philby paused, 'I agree,' he said eventually, 'it was hard enough getting them in here – I don't fancy their chances upstairs.'

'Do either of you have any suggestions?' asked Jemme, trying not to sound desperate.

'Perhaps only use a few?' suggested Le Selmelif.

Jemme felt a flicker of panic at the idea, 'No, no, I can't do that – it's all of them together, or it's none of them at all. I'm trying to create a forest of marble columns and so volume is everything.'

'Well then, Monsieur, we will just have to start thinking about how to make these pillars lighter!' said Le Selmelif cheerfully.

Philby snorted softly. Jemme, however, wasn't discouraged. In fact, quite the opposite.

'Yes, there might be something in that!' he said, suddenly feeling excited again. 'Stay here, I need to check something.'

He rushed straight back out of the front door again and looped back towards the kitchen, retracing his steps from earlier. About half-way round, he could see the bothy and veered off, jogging towards it. He stopped when it was about twenty feet away and stared, not at the bothy but at the damaged tree next to it. He recalled Xelifon saying that it was completely hollow on the inside, yet, from the outside it looked as solid and as strong as any tree in the grounds. He looked at it once again before turning round and heading back to the house. Philby and Le Selmelif were exactly where he had left them, waiting patiently for his return.

'I think I've solved it,' he said, a broad grin across his face, 'we'll hollow the pillars out.'

* * * *

There was a pause whilst Philby and Le Selmelif looked at him. Philby looked resigned, but Le Selmelif looked intrigued.

'*Hollow*? Monsieur?' Le Selmelif asked, as if he might have misheard.

'Yes!' said Jemme jubilantly. I don't know why I didn't think of it before. It's all an illusion you see.'

'An "illusion", Monsieur?' Le Selmelif asked politely.

'Precisely,' Jemme nodded enthusiastically. 'You see, in a real palace these columns would be supporting the ceiling, wouldn't they?'

'Yes,' replied Le Selmelif, with the air of someone who was wondering where this could possibly be leading.

'Exactly! So their purpose would be functional. They would need to be solid and heavy – supportive, if you will. The decorative element is a nice addition, but not necessary.'

'I suppose,' said Le Selmelif.

'Here, though,' Jemme continued, 'it's completely the other way around. We don't need them to *actually* hold up the ceiling – it's already up! Instead, we want them to be purely decorative. Therefore their weight isn't at all important. What matters most is how they look, and if we can reduce their weight then we can fit in as many as we like. The more the better!'

Le Selmelif nodded slowly, but Philby remained impassive, utterly inured to Jemme's flashes of inspiration.

'The idea came to me when I was outside,' Jemme said. 'There's a tree out there that's completely hollow, but I only knew that because Xelifon told me. As far as I, or anyone else, was concerned, it was a very dense, very heavy, very real tree. It's the same with these columns: we just need to find a way to hollow them out and the whole problem will be solved. As long as they look like columns, it doesn't matter if they'll crumble under the slightest pressure, or support a hundred tons,' He paused to see if the others had followed his train of thought.

Philby continued to look impassive, whilst Le Selmelif looked deep in thought. Eventually he laughed,

'I think it might work!' he said.

'It sounds utterly preposterous, but I like how daring the idea is. If you can find the right masons, then I don't see why it wouldn't work. In fact, I don't even think you would need particularly skilled stone cutters; even an apprentice could do it!'

Jemme beamed. 'Philby what do you think?' he asked.

'Do I need to find these stone cutters?' Philby asked.

'Oh goodness, no – don't worry about that! Jemme said, 'I can sort something out, or DD will be able to help.'

'I'm sure I could find someone too, Monsieur,' said Le Selmelif.

'Well there you go,' said Jemme, turning back to Philby. 'We appear to have it covered.'

Philby shrugged, his way of telling them that if he didn't need to do anything further then they could do whatever they liked.

✳   ✳   ✳   ✳

Precisely one week later, Jemme found himself in conference with Philby and Le Selmelif yet again. They both appeared to be managing different elements of the project. Le Selmelif had helped find the craftsmen, and was overseeing the work. Philby's role seemed to be to eye the new artists with suspicion and make sure they didn't break anything. Both men appeared to be playing their part with incredible flair.

Le Selmelif gave Jemme an update, and showed him the empty room which had been temporarily turned into a marble carving workshop. There was a thick layer of purple dust-powder on one of the workbenches, and an aubergine pillar stood propped up against the wall next to it.

'Look,' said Philby, 'this one's been finished.'

'It's been completely emptied?' asked Jemme.

'Yes, it's like a chocolate Easter egg,' said Le Selmelif. 'See how glossy and perfect it looks on the outside?'

Jemme nodded.

'Well, it is no more than an inch thick all the way around.'

'Marvellous,' said Jemme looking at it closely. 'It's definitely this one here?' he asked, scrutinising it again.

'Yes – in fact, I can show you how light it is,' said Le Selmelif. He sized up the column … and then obviously thought it better of it.

'Well, I'm a little shorter than most men,' he chuckled, 'but if I was a bit stronger then I would be able to lift it up by myself.'

'That's incredible,' said Jemme, thinking back to the three men it had taken to lift each single pillar off the truck. He wished he had thought of this scheme before. Apart from anything else, it would have saved several tons of marble.

He looked at the other columns, which were all at various stages of being emptied.

'Do you have any idea how they do it?' he asked Le Selmelif.

Le Selmelif shrugged, 'It is not particularly technical, but it is quite a skilled task, and one which requires a fair amount of strength too. It is just a matter of chiselling the marble in exactly the right place with exactly the right amount of force. If you come down tomorrow I will ask one of them to show you.'

'Thank you, I would like that. Thank you also for all your help with this,' Jemme said warmly.

Le Selmelif smiled, 'It is my pleasure, Monsieur. It is very enjoyable to be involved in a project such as this. Now, do you have a spare half hour?'

'Of course.'

'*Bon.* I would like to show you something.'

He led Jemme up to the room being saved for the ivory and mother-of-pearl furniture. A piece from the collection stood in the middle of the room, and next to it was a modern piece of furniture of the same shape. It looked like it had been made cheaply and from substandard materials. The fascia – if it could even be called that – had been levered off, exposing the unfinished edges of the drawers inside.

Jemme shuddered slightly at the ugliness of the piece, especially when compared with the beautiful antique next to it.

'What is that doing here?' he asked.

'Oh that, don't worry about that Monsieur, it's just a *maquette* – a mock-up, if you will. I have been doing some thinking.'

'Oh?'

'Yes, I was inspired by your problem-solving last week to tackle this room in an entirely different way.'

'Oh really?'

Le Selmelif nodded enthusiastically, 'It was fascinating to see you approach the problem of the pillars in such a different way. I thought the same fresh thinking could be applied here. Instead of seeing them as pieces of functional furniture, I needed to start looking at them as beautiful pieces of decoration. Tell me, Monsieur – what is your favourite feature about the pieces in the collection?'

'The inlays,' said Jemme straight away.

'Precisely. It is not the drawers or the hinges or the shelves. You are never going to use these for their original function, you just want to admire them for their decoration.'

'Yes, I suppose that's true.'

'I also remembered you talking about the Malachite Room, and how immersive it is.'

'Yes, that's really what I want to achieve here.'

'*Oui.* So, what we shall do is take apart the furniture!'

'Take it apart?' Jemme repeated.

'Yes – much like I have done with this modern piece here. We will build a simple frame on each walls as a support, and then we can very carefully mount the front-pieces of each piece of furniture onto the walls. I have already been sketching how it could work,' He gestured to a pile of papers on the desk behind him. 'The shapes these inlays make and the stories they tell are so beautiful that they deserve to be shown together.'

'But,' Jemme began, 'and just to make sure I've got this absolutely clear: you would destroy the furniture to make this room?'

Le Selmelif shook his head, 'No, Monsieur, no I would never destroy something this old or this beautiful. I will remove the most decorative elements with the greatest amount of care, and we shall put the remaining structure in storage. That way if you change your mind at any point, we shall be able simply to "remake" the pieces.'

Jemme didn't say anything, but he didn't look completely convinced either. Le Selmelif obviously sensed this.

'Look, it's a big decision,' he said, 'and I would never ask you to do something you were not comfortable with, so you should definitely think about it some more. If it would help, I can show you the sketches,' He grabbed the stack of papers and placed them in Jemme's hands one by one, showing him the drawings on each one.

'They're all arranged differently;' he explained as he put the last one down, 'but they each show different configurations of the decorative pieces on the walls.

Some are arranged thematically, some by date, some by shape. There's potential to be even more creative with lay-out, I just wanted to give you an idea.'

'Well, thank you – you've certainly given me several ideas,' said Jemme.

'I've been doing a great deal of thinking about this,' said Le Selmelif, so if you have any questions, don't hesitate to ask. I look forward to hearing what you think. Don't forget – they're in storage anyway, so you don't stand to lose anything!'

'Well, I suppose…' Jemme began.

'And remember the lesson of the pillars!' Le Selmelif added.

Chapter Thirty-Six

That evening Jemme left the chateau far later than he had meant to. He had been planning on getting back in time to have dinner with Hil, and catch up with her. It had been another week in which he had felt that they were ships passing each other in the night. He hadn't even seen her to suggest they eat together – he had left her a note on the kitchen table: *Shall we have supper together on Sunday?* It felt funny to be asking his wife such a thing, and extremely strange to be doing it in such a way, but he had no idea when they would next be in the apartment together. Sure enough, the next time he was home, he recognised Hil's handwriting – *yes*, she had written on the bottom of the note.

He smiled to himself, then realised that this was the first contact he had had with her in a whole week. His smile fell, and he sighed softly. Sadly he folded the paper up into four neat squares and slipped it in his pocket. By that evening he had forgotten about it, and it wasn't until Saturday when he found himself wearing the same trousers that he rediscovered it. At the time he had felt slightly guilty, and resolved to leave in good time the following day. However, by Sunday he had become so involved in all the work going on that he couldn't bear to tear himself away. As he looked over Le Selmelif's sketches, and reached into his pocket, he discovered the note yet again, its sharp corners pricked his conscience and urged him home. 'Just another hour,' he told himself, 'then I'll definitely go.' However, one hour had turned into two which had turned into three and a half. By the time he finally left the chateau it was long past dinner time, and by the time he actually arrived back at the flat, he knew Hil would have been asleep for at least an hour. He hadn't felt too guilty about it, reasoning with himself that she hadn't left a particularly enthusiastic response and that she might well have forgotten herself.

As soon as he stepped through the front door he realised that she had done anything but forget, and all the guilt he had reasoned away washed over him. He took in everything in the dining room, and imagined the scene which must have occurred several hours earlier. The table was spread with a beautiful linen cloth. Jemme recognised it straight away – the garlands on it had been hand-embroidered by Hil's great grandmother, and the piece was a family heirloom as well as being one of Hil's most treasured possessions. He also recognised their wedding porcelain on the table, set for two. A cut crystal decanter and two glasses were souvenirs from the first trip they had ever taken together, and the vase containing the bunch of fresh flowers was a replica of a piece she had once admired in the British Museum on a trip to London. Jemme had commissioned someone to make an exact copy for her, with her name stamped into the bottom, and he remembered at the time she had said it was the most romantic thing anyone had ever done for her.

It was a table which had been laid with care, and was heavy with memories. Hil had obviously invested a great deal in this meal, and he winced as he took in the long blown-out candles and the silver napkin rings. He made his way to the kitchen, where he found a solitary plate sitting on the counter, wrapped in tin foil. There was a note on top of it – *I waited, but you never came.* It was short but incredibly poignant. Jemme knew that it didn't just refer to this missed meal, but all the times Hil had found herself eating alone, and probably all the times she had found herself ringing around her friends desperately looking for a theatre or concert partner, too. He took the plate back through to the dining room and sat down heavily. He peeled back the foil and sighed again when he saw what care had gone into the food. He was hungry and so ate more hurriedly than such a meal deserved. Even in the short time he was sitting there, he saw how miserable it was to be sitting alone surrounded by things intended for two. He hoped Hil hadn't waited too long for him. Of course she would have done, he admitted to himself eventually. He felt wretched, especially when he saw that Hil had pulled out an old photo album and carefully placed it on the table, no doubt with the intention that the two of them would go through it together and reminisce. He flipped it open and flicked through the pages. Two happy, young faces stared back at him in front of the monuments of the world. Relaxed and smiling, the couple he saw in front of him were desperately in love. He remembered the time when they shared absolutely everything together. Nothing was too trifling or too small, every decision was taken together and every problem solved together. They had almost ceased to exist as individual entities, living only in the context of a partnership. *How did everything change so much*? he thought to himself as he stared at the photos. He snapped the album shut and made his way to bed … before he had too much time to think about the answer.

He slept lightly, but still found that Hil was gone by the time he awoke. He spent every free moment at work the next day trying to work out how he could make it up to her. By the end of the day he realised that the most important thing was that he was just there. He looked at the time, and realised that she would be home in half and hour. He slipped the lid on his pen and clicked it into place decisively.

'DD, I'm heading off early this evening,' he called out towards the door as he put his jacket on. DD appeared in the room without saying a word.

'Don't forward any calls to me, unless it's really important. In fact – don't forward any calls to me at all. Nothing's so important it can't wait until tomorrow morning.'

There was a slight twitch of one of DD's eyebrows, but otherwise he didn't register any sign of the unusualness of the situation.

'Of course, Sir,' he said calmly.

'Thank you, I'll see you tomorrow,' Jemme flashed him a smile and DD solemnly bowed his head in reply.

Downstairs, it felt strange to be leaving with all the secretaries and junior members of staff. A couple saw him and checked their watches with alarm. Jemme was only interested in getting home as quickly as possible.

He made it back to the flat before Hil and frantically looked around, wondering what he could do that would be a significant gesture. He knew that Hil would have spent hours planning the meal, and anything he could scrabble together in ten minutes would have looked slapdash at best. He heard a key in the lock and realised he wouldn't have time to do anything at all.

Hil started when she saw him, 'You're...here,' she said eventually.

Jemme walked towards her, 'Yes, yes I am, sweetheart, and I'm *so* sorry I wasn't last night.' He wrapped his arms around her and tried to embrace her but she felt stiff and awkward. Reluctantly he released her and made his way to the settee. 'Why don't you sit with me?' he asked, indicating the space next to him.

Hil sat down wordlessly and looked at him. Her expression was completely blank, as if she didn't know what to make of this turn of events.

Jemme took a deep breath, 'Look, I know I can't make this up to you and I know how upset you must be, but I want you to know how genuinely sorry I am about last night, I can only imagine how disappointed you must have been.'

Hil smiled sadly and sighed, 'No, not disappointed, just...' she trailed off and looked at him, shaking her head slowly.

'I had no idea that you would go to so much effort. If I'd known, of course I would have rushed back.'

Hil shook her head again, 'No, no you wouldn't.'

'Of course I would!'

'No, I mean you wouldn't have any idea. You have no idea how much effort I put in and how important that meal was to me.'

'But I didn't know!' said Jemme pleadingly.

'That's the whole point,' said Hil. She didn't seem angry, or even that sad, just – well Jemme couldn't put his finger on what exactly.

'Resigned,' said Hil, 'that's the word I was looking for. I wasn't disappointed, just resigned.'

Jemme blinked. That had been the word he was looking for, to describe how she was looking now. He felt a fresh stab of guilt.

'Resigned?' he asked tentatively.

'Yes, resigned to the fact that this is how my life would be.'

Jemme stared at her, a horrible feeling of foreboding rising in him. He swallowed, 'What do you mean "would be",' he asked slowly.

Hil raised her eyebrows and shook her head again, 'I mean that last night was confirmation that my life would be one endless string of missed dinners and nights of wondering where you were. At least, that's what it would be like if everything continued as it is now.'

Jemme swallowed again. He wasn't sure what she meant exactly, but he really didn't like where this conversation was going.

'Hil, listen, I'm sorry things have got to this stage. I should have listened to you a long time ago and talked to you about what was wrong. But I want to make it right now. I want you to be happy – whatever you want to change about the situation as it is now, we can change. Whatever it is which is making you unhappy, we can change right now.'

Hil looked at Jemme then looked away. She was still shaking her head.

'This is who you are – I can't ask you to change. I knew how passionate you were about your interests and chasing your dreams when I first met you. I can't ask you to change everything about yourself.'

'Then what?' asked Jemme desperately, 'what can I change?!'

They looked into each other's eyes for what seemed like an age, and Jemme finally allowed himself to understand. The truth he had kept hidden at the back of his mind for so long slipped free.

He took her hand, 'Hil,' he said solemnly, 'would your life be happier if you were no longer married to me?'

As soon as the words had escaped his mouth, he realised that everything had changed forever. No matter what happened between them, even if they resolved everything, the shape of their relationship had been altered. It would always be a dark mark, lingering in the narrative of who they were.

Hil had continued to stare into his eyes. She squeezed his hand and shut her eyes tightly. Her face crumpled and she began to sob. Without opening her eyes again, she nodded her head.

Jemme sat rooted to the spot. He felt as if the room was closing in on him. He held onto Hil's hand as tightly as he could, and tried to breathe.

✳   ✳   ✳   ✳

Although they spent the entire evening talking, neither one tried to change the other's mind. There was no blame and no recrimination, they just talked. Jemme couldn't remember the last time he had felt this close to Hil. It was as if finally admitting the inadmissible had released them both. Jemme knew that he would have to contend with crushing sadness at some point soon, but for now he was enjoying Hil's company too much to care. They talked themselves hoarse and then they sat in a comfortable, contemplative silence.

The rest of the week seemed to slip by in a dreamlike blur. Jemme made very little contact with anyone at the chateau, and left the bank on time every day. He channelled all of his energy into dealing with the one area of his life which was about to change. He did everything he could to make the change as comfortable for both of them as possible. Hil was very nervous of the divorce process – she didn't even like using the word. She was worried that it would be long and drawn-out, and would drive them into hostility and exhaustion. Jemme promised her he would ensure it was as painless and amicable as possible. It made him feel better to be able to have at least some control over such a dramatic change.

He was glad he was able to rely on DD's support and discretion. Despite never having been married – or indeed, as far as Jemme knew, never having been involved in any sort of romantic relationship – DD seemed to know the best divorce lawyer in Paris. He was also able to secure an appointment with her at the end of the week, despite her extensive waiting list.

He passed on the news to Hil, who flinched slightly, 'The end of the week? It's all happening so quickly!'

'I thought that's what you wanted?'

Hil took a deep breath and smiled, 'You're right, it's not a good idea to put it off; we might as well get started on everything straight away.'

'Her name is Béatrice Photier,' said Jemme, 'I thought you'd be more comfortable around a female lawyer,' he added.

'Thank you,' Hil exhaled slowly and paused. 'So far, this isn't that bad!'

Jemme returned her smile, 'We'll get through it together,' he said reassuringly. It wasn't until later on he realised that it was a strange thing to say to someone he was about to divorce.

That Friday afternoon, he made his way to Béatrice Photier's office on a particularly grand street, well known for its historic connections to the legal profession. Her office was in a beautiful marble-clad building. They waited in the smart reception to be called in. Hil looked around her approvingly,

'This is an impressive place; she must be good.'

Jemme smiled, but didn't say anything. He had met too many people who put on a good show, and experience had taught him to reserve judgement until he had the measure of someone.

A short while later, the telephone rang, and the receptionist who answered it informed them that Madame Photier was ready to see them. She showed them up to the tall double doors.

Labour *of* Love

Béatrice Photier was sitting behind a large antique desk, in an extravagantly decorated room. Thick damask curtains hung either side of the floor to ceiling window, and oil paintings depicting dramatic battle scenes hung from the wall. A large mantelpiece bore an array of silverware, as did a long, elegant sideboard. Béatrice herself wore a tight bun, very high on her head, and a ruffled blouse. She was expensively dressed, with small diamond earrings which caught the light as she moved her head. Hil had taken in every detail within an instant, Jemme, however, had not noticed a single thing, except the smell. It had hit him as soon as the door had opened – a musty, deeply unpleasant odour. It was so thick on the air, he could feel his eyes begin to water. He tried his hardest not to grimace, and wondered how Hil could look so normal. He realised he had been holding his breath and took the shortest possible breath in. It hit him again, and he gulped in distaste. He wondered what on earth it was coming from and looked around the room.

Hil made her way towards the desk and introduced herself. Béatrice Photier stood up and seemed to lose her balance – *I'm not surprised with that smell*, thought Jemme to himself; *it nearly knocked me off my feet too*. He realised he was being rude and introduced himself too.

'*Monsieur Mafeze, enchanté*,' said Béatrice and shook his hand.

'Please, take a seat,' she said and gestured at the seats in front of the desk. Jemme noticed again that she looked a little unstable on her feet, but thought nothing of it. He was about to sit down when something on the chair moved. He jumped and looked around in alarm,

'Ah, Frédéderic! There you are! Come to Maman,' Béatrice cooed. A large black cat jumped onto her lap and she stroked the top of his head.

'Oh, I'm sorry, I didn't see him,' said Jemme.

'It is not you, Monsieur; my cats like to hide in my office!' said Béatrice and chuckled to herself.

'Cats?' asked Hil.

'*Oui, Madame!*' she chortled in strange, high-pitched way, 'They love to hide. I expect you probably haven't seen a single one except Frédéderic.'

Jemme was fast getting the measure of Béatrice Photier, but Hil was much more indulgent.

'No, actually I hadn't,' she said, sounding genuinely interested.

Béatrice made the same strange laughing noise, then leant backwards and shook the thick curtain behind her,

'*Cou-cou*,' she called. A small, fluffy ginger tom ran out, then settled himself on the carpet next to the desk, licking his paws.

'That is Mathieu,' she said, 'he loves the curtain.'

Jemme's heart began to sink.

By the time she had pointed out five more cats she seemed to be sharing her office with, his expectations had plummeted, although at least he had worked out where the smell was coming from.

'Anyway, you did not come here to play with my cats!' said Béatrice abruptly. 'To business.'

Jemme sat up – things were starting to look more promising.

'Would you like anything to drink before we begin?' Béatrice asked.

'Thank you, I'd really like some water,' said Jemme, convinced he could taste the smell in his mouth.

Béatrice laughed, 'Come, Monsieur, I'm sure you want something stronger than that! You are here to talk about divorce after all!' She turned to Hil, 'You don't want to mess around with water, do you Madame? What will you have?'

'Um... some tea?' ventured Hil, wondering if that was the right answer. It appeared not to be, as Béatrice looked at them both in disbelief for a moment before calling through to the receptionist,

'Yes, a water for the gentleman, some tea for the lady, and a *proper* drink for me,' she said pointedly.

Jemme sank back down in his seat again – it was definitely not looking promising.

Sure enough, when the receptionist brought in the tray, the third glass was a large brandy balloon, filled with a good inch of rich, amber-coloured liquid.

'*Santé,*' said Béatrice cheerfully when she had received her drink.

Hil awkwardly half-raised her tea and mumbled something. Jemme stared straight ahead. They both watched Béatrice take a large swig of her drink, which she drank as if it was water.

'Well, I think we're all ready,' she said, 'let's talk about how this is all going to work out.'

'The most important thing is that this remains amicable throughout,' said Jemme, 'it's the highest priority for both of us.'

Béatrice hooted and took another large swig of her drink.

'Monsieur, this is France! There is no such thing as an amicable divorce!'

Hil looked concerned, 'It really is very important to both of us, Madame Photier; it's been all we've talked about since we made the decision.'

'Sure, it's important to you now, but give it a year and then tell me you still want things to be amicable. Trust me – by this time next year you'll wish you'd never laid eyes on each other.' She chuckled and muttered 'amicable divorce!' to herself as she scratched another cat which had climbed onto her lap.

'No, no, that's not we want at all,' said Hil, sounding distressed. She paused for a moment, 'What do you mean in a year?' she asked, 'We want to get everything sorted within a couple of months at the most.'

Béatrice laughed again. She seemed to be genuinely enjoying herself, 'Madame, in all my career I have never heard of a divorce being finalised in a matter of months. It is ludicrous – you might be waiting that long just for a court date.'

'Court?' said Hil sounding even more upset, 'We really don't want this to go through a court. We just want to sort it out between ourselves.'

Béatrice chuckled and looked Hil up and down as if she had been sent solely for Béatrice's amusement.

'I can tell that neither of you has been divorced before! *Of course* you will be going to court! Two or three times at least, probably more. Divorce is not a simple process you know. That's why you need a good lawyer. Don't worry, I know exactly how the system works.'

'I bet you do,' said Jemme. He had heard enough. He stood up and offered his hand. Béatrice looked startled and retuned his handshake limply.

'Thank you for your time,' he said firmly, 'I'm sure you will understand that we will need to discuss this between ourselves.'

He strode purposefully towards the door. Hil gathered her things and followed him, looking just as perplexed as Béatrice. Jemme nearly tripped over a cat on the way out,

'Be careful of Édith!' shrieked Béatrice from across the room, and 'My consultations are not for free, Monsieur!' just as Jemme was shutting the door.

'I bet they're not,' he said, once the door was firmly shut behind him. He breathed a sigh of relief, and turned to see Hil looking at him with an expression of dismay.

'Come on,' he said, 'I saw a nice looking café on the way here. Let's head over there and debrief.'

He left the building as quickly as possible and Hil had to trot to keep up with him on the way to the café. They found a quiet table in the corner and sat down in the comfortable seats.

'Ahh that's more like it,' he said.

Hil was fiddling with the small posy in the middle of the table. She looked up and caught his eye, and they both burst into giggles.

'Well that was one of the strangest episodes I've had in a while,' she said. 'I didn't really question it at the time, but on the way here, I was just thinking about all her cats and the fact she was clearly drunk, and I realised how silly it all was.'

Just then the waiter arrived and Jemme ordered an espresso,

'Are you sure you wouldn't like a *proper* drink?' Hil mimicked and they both giggled again.

'I couldn't believe it when she shook that cat out from the curtain!' said Jemme.

They chatted and laughed about the whole affair until their drinks arrived. Hil looked thoughtful as she sipped her tea.

'What I don't understand though, is how DD could have got it so wrong. Didn't you say she was meant to be the best divorce lawyer in Paris? I've never known him to make anything but impeccable choices.'

'I know, I was wondering about that too, but having met her I think I understand the whole situation a little more.'

'Which situation?'

'What it's like to divorce in France. In fairness to DD, I think she does have a reputation as the best and I know he had to work some magic to get us a meeting at such short notice. I also think that her reputation has been bolstered by all the wealthy French men she's helped.'

'How?'

'It's a perfect set-up – she wants the process to drag on for as long as possible so she can get paid as much as possible. Rich French men who are divorcing their wives can tell their wives they're sorting the divorce, and then escape for an hour or two and drink cognac with Béatrice. She'll do everything she can to prolong it – court cases, paperwork and so on.'

'But I don't understand. I mean I can understand why it would be in her interest to make everything last as long as possible, but why would her clients want that?'

'Like I said, I'm willing to bet that the overwhelming majority of her clients are men and they come from the upper, upper echelons of Parisian society. No matter how high her fees are, they won't be as big as the alimony these wives will be demanding. The longer the men have to put off paying, the better for them; so they tell all their friends that she's the best.'

'I see, that's what they mean by "best". Oh poor DD, he would have acted in such good faith as well.'

'I know, he'll be mortified. It is quite amusing though.'

Hil smiled.

'The thing is Hil, although I don't think everyone here is as bad as her, I really think this is what divorce in France is going to be like.'

Hil's smiled faded, 'That is just not what I want,' she said seriously.

'I know, me neither, but I feel like it's inevitable if we stay here. I was thinking about it on the way over, and I have a suggestion. It's simple. We just won't get divorced here. There's no reason to; if we do it properly elsewhere then it's just as valid anywhere in the world.'

'Did you have anywhere in particular in mind?'

'Yes, England. It's easy to get to, we both feel at home there and there's a lawyer – Duncan, who has worked on my corporate affairs there for years. It's not his area of expertise, but I trust him and he'll make sure everything's OK for us.'

Hil looked reassured, 'Well if you trust Duncan, I trust Duncan. I think that sounds like a good plan.'

✳   ✳   ✳   ✳

Jemme set everything in motion as quickly as he could. He booked them both flights, and arranged a meeting with Duncan for the following weekend. He realised that it would be the first time he had been absent from the chateau for two consecutive weekends in years. He tried to put it to the back of his mind; he only called for the briefest of reports and only when he was at the bank.

In many ways, the week that followed was one of the easiest of Jemme's life. With very little of his attention focussed on the chateau, and finishing work early every day, he suddenly found that he had more leisure time than he had ever experienced before. He filled it all with Hil. Things between them were easy and relaxed, and they enjoyed the comfortable dynamic of two people who had known each other for years. They went for coffees together, they walked in the Jardin du Luxembourg; they even went for dinner a couple of times. It was as if they were both subconsciously paying tribute to a wonderful marriage, which had just ceased to function.

By the time they flew to London, Jemme was feeling optimistic. They took a car from the airport to Duncan's offices in Mayfair. The building was modern and glass, and had nothing of the grandeur of Béatrice's office. They were shown straight in to see Duncan, who greeted Jemme with a vigorous handshake,

'Great to see you,' he said, cheerfully.

'And you must be Mrs Mafeze,' he said, pumping Hil's hand with equal enthusiasm, 'It's so nice to finally meet you, although I wish it could be under different circumstances.'

Hil smiled, 'It's nice to see you too, Monsieur,' she said, not noticing the French tic slip out.

'Oh please, Duncan,' he replied, 'do sit down, I'm sure Charles will bring in some tea in a minute.'

They sat, and Hil quickly looked around the room. The contrast couldn't be greater. The office was large and bright, with simple clean lines. It was filled with light, and completely minimalist, save for a few pieces of statement furniture. Duncan himself had fair skin and neatly cut dark hair. He wore a very plain blue shirt, with cufflinks that Hil had forgotten in an instant. He was a man who obviously wasn't concerned with putting on a show, which was a good sign.

A few moments later there was a soft tap on the door, and a man appeared with a tea tray.

'Excellent, thanks Charles,' said Duncan, taking the tray and pouring them both a cup of tea. 'Now, let's get straight to it, I know you're not sticking around for very long.'

Jemme took his tea wordlessly and gave Duncan his full attention.

'I've spoken to a few colleagues and I see no reason why we can't get this sorted as quickly as possible – if we all get our act together I'm hoping it can be wrapped up in a few weeks.'

'The whole thing?' asked Jemme.

Duncan paused to drink some tea and nodded. 'Yes, but you'll have to meet every deadline I give you.'

'Of course,' Hil nodded, impressed with his obvious efficiency.

'Good stuff. The first thing I'm going to need is from you, Mrs Mafeze. I'm sure you're not going to like doing this, but I'm afraid I need a list of financial demands. It's not a pleasant task, but if you focus you should be able to complete it in a day or so. I'll be on hand to help if you need it. If Jemme agrees to everything then that speeds things up. All we need to do is fix a meeting with judge to finalise everything.'

'Will we have to go to court?' asked Hil.

'It won't be anything as formal as that – it's more of a meeting in a room. It will just be you, Jemme and I, a barrister and the judge. In most divorce cases, each of the couple has their own lawyer and they fight it out. If things are amicable then it's so much easier.'

'So it is possible to keep everything friendly throughout?'

'If the two of you can sit in a room together and have this conversation with me, then you can have a friendly divorce,' said Duncan, 'although I don't know if that's a term that gets used much in the legal world!'

Jemme laughed, 'We really appreciate your help in all this.'

'Honestly, it's a pleasure to have a quick break from corporate law. This should all be very straightforward. I mean, it's not a simple process at all – there's lots of paperwork and complicated applications, but that's why you've hired a lawyer. I'll sort all of that out for you. There's no reason why you'll have to stay in England whilst I work on it either. You might as well go back to Paris and get on with your lives. I'll call you as soon as we have a date sorted with the judge and the barrister, and if I have any questions.'

'Duncan, this is music to my ears, I knew I could rely on you.'

Duncan didn't even register the compliment, 'Just doing my job,' he said breezily.

They descended into a brief summary of Jemme's other business, and then exchanged small talk about Paris. Duncan was charming and polite to Hil, and by the time they left the office they were filled with confidence.

'It's so good to have some structure and reassurance,' said Hil. 'I mean, I don't really know how I'm going to cope afterwards, but if I can trust someone to take me step by step up to a certain point, then I can relax for a while.'

'I know what you mean,' said Jemme. 'When I think about what life's going to be like afterwards…well it actually doesn't bear thinking about.' He looked at Hil sadly.

'I know,' she said softly.

Jemme flew back to Paris at the end of the weekend, but Hil ended up changing her flights and staying in London for a few more days. It was a city she had always loved, and she said she needed a few days away from Paris to think about things. Once he was on the plane home, Jemme realised that she probably wanted to write up her financial demands as far away from him as possible. He knew her too well and knew she wouldn't be able to bear doing it when he was around.

He thought the flat would feel empty without Hil, but he realised guiltily that their lives had overlapped so little of late that it didn't feel any different at all. With Hil gone he threw himself back into work, staying late into the night at the bank, and dedicating the rest of his time to chateau work. He wrestled with the decision about the mother of pearl and ivory room for a while, but eventually rang Le Selmelif and gave his permission. Although, in principle, altering the pieces was against his chateau-decorating philosophy, so was leaving them languishing in storage, and he trusted Le Selmelif not to damage them, just to change them. He followed progress carefully for the first few days, and called for regular updates, but was soon satisfied that Le Selmelif knew exactly what he was doing. He also told Jemme that he had found him two very skilled stonecutters who could work on the pillars in the Andalusian Room. Combined with the three DD had also found, it was more than enough to make a team. Jemme authorised them to start work straight away, although he was a little sad he wouldn't be able to oversee the 'emptying' of the pillars himself.

Later that week he received a phone call from Duncan, telling him he had secured an appointment with the judge and the barrister for just over a week's time. It was impressive work, and Jemme was pleased with how focussed Duncan had been. DD brought him his midmorning espresso and he thought to himself about how quintessentially French their first foray had been. Although he had lived in France for almost all his adult life, there were some aspects of the culture and way of doing things he could just never get used too. He thought on it some more as he sipped the rich, bitter liquid. Suddenly, the sobering realisation that his marriage would be finished within the fortnight dawned on him. It was accompanied by a pain that was almost physical. He leaned forward in his chair and clutched at his stomach. He hadn't been exaggerating when he had told Hil he didn't know how he would cope. Even thinking about it now intensified his feeling of nausea. The odd sensation in his gut sharpened, and he winced in pain.

Just at that moment DD arrived.

'Is everything alright, Sir?' he asked. His calm voice was exactly what Jemme need to hear to quell the rising sense of panic. He took a deep breath as quietly as he could, sat up and forced a smile.

'Everything's absolutely fine, thank you – the coffee was a bit hot, that's all.'

'My apologies, Sir,' said DD looking concerned. He picked up the small cup; his expression remained exactly the same, even though he had obviously registered the fact that it was stone cold. 'I will fetch you another,' he said in the same even tones.

By the time he returned, Jemme had managed to pull himself together a little. DD set the tray down and Jemme saw that he had somehow managed to procure a large *viennoiserie,* which he recognised as being from one of his favourite pastry shops. It was a good twenty minute's walk away, and the mystery of how he had got it from shop to plate in just over five minutes was enough to dull the pain Jemme was still experiencing in his stomach.

'I'll need some flights booked to London,' he said in as business-like a manner of possible. 'Duncan has arranged a hearing with the judge for next Thursday.'

'That is good news, I shall organise them this morning,' said DD. 'Will I be buying Mrs Mafeze's flights too?'

The pain returned and Jemme winced. He swallowed hard and tried to steady his voice, 'I'll let you know. Just do mine for now.' The truth was, he had no idea where Hil was – she could be in London still or she could be staying with a friend in Paris. He didn't even know how he would go about contacting her.

That afternoon, he telephoned Duncan to confirm that he had booked his flight and ask if there was any paperwork he needed to bring with him.

'No. Leave all that to me, you just make sure you get there on time. Mrs Mafeze says she'll see you there.'

'You've spoken to her?'

'Yes, I've been helping her draft the financial document which I posted to you yesterday. She knows which date it is and she'll be there.'

'Oh…. good.'

A few days later, the documents arrived from Duncan's office. Jemme knew exactly what they were and so he didn't open them straight away. They sat unopened on the dining room table for a couple of days, and then on his desk in the office, too. He had decided not to go to the chateau that weekend, although he felt like he didn't really have a good reason. Hil wasn't around, so it wasn't like he would be spending time with her. However, he felt that that he was duty-bound to focus all his attentions on the matter in hand, until it was finished. It was irrational, but he almost felt as if going to the chateau halfway through their divorce would be a betrayal of Hil. Instead he spent the weekend alone, reading through well-thumbed history books and browsing auction catalogues, pausing every now and then to glance up at the still-sealed envelope from London, which had made its way back to the dining room table.

By the time he found himself in the airport it had still not been opened, and he had made sure it was at the very bottom of his briefcase so he wouldn't have to see it. He took a car to the address Duncan had given him, which was also in Mayfair. Once there he gave his name to the receptionist, who knew exactly who he was and walked him down a long corridor, stopping to knock at one of the doors. She showed him in and he saw that Duncan and Hil were already seated at the same table, with the judge on a table facing them. There was another man at the table with Duncan and Hil he didn't recognise. Both the man and Duncan rose when he came in and went over to shake his hand.

'Jemme, this is Jeremy, whom I told you about on the phone.'

'Of course, pleased to meet you,' said Jemme, shaking his hand. He had completely forgotten he would be there. He vaguely remembered Duncan saying something about a barrister being present, and him being called Jeremy, but that was about it. He greeted Duncan and sat down next to Hil in the seat Jeremy had just vacated. He realised that everyone had gone silent and looked up. They were all staring at him – Duncan slid his eyes to the seat at the end of the table and raised his eyebrows at him. Jemme looked back in disquiet; he didn't know what Duncan was trying to tell him. He looked around and caught the judge's eye.

'Mr Mafeze,' he said, 'it is highly irregular for both parties to be seated next to each other. I believe your solicitor is trying to get you to move.'

'Oh, I see,' said Jemme, feeling slightly embarrassed. He moved to the seat furthest from Hil. 'My apologies, I didn't realise you weren't allowed to sit next to each other.'

The judge looked amused, 'You are allowed to sit next to each other, Mr Mafeze, it's just highly irregular. In my many years of divorce hearings I have never come across two people who would voluntarily sit next to each other. Usually the two lawyers sit between them like a barrier – even that's not enough for some people.'

Jemme wanted to look over at Hil, to see if she was blushing as much as he felt he was. He hadn't even had the chance to say hello to her, but he didn't want to do something else that was 'highly irregular'.

'Well, I see no point delaying, let's proceed,' said the judge, 'I take it you have both completed your period of reconciliation?'

Jemme felt a twinge of anxiety – this was the first he had heard of it.

'They have, your honour,' said Jeremy on their behalf. Jemme resisted the urge to look conspiratorially at Hil.

'And you have read and agree with the financial request documents?' asked the judge looking at Jemme.

Jemme thought guiltily about the envelope still lying unopened at the bottom of his briefcase. He had no idea what it said, and he didn't really want to know. All he knew was that he trusted Hil.

'Yes,' he said.

'You agree to *all* of it Mr Mafeze?' asked the judge sounding surprised. He peered at Jemme over the top of his glasses.

'Yes. Definitely. In fact, if anything it's not enough!' said Jemme, desperately trying to avoid thinking about the pages in the envelope which divvied up their property and their marriage into two separate lots.

'Not enough?' repeated the judge.

'I mean – can I add more? Is that possible, is that something people do?' asked Jemme trying to do everything he could to shut the image of the envelope out of his mind. 'I'll do it – I'll add ten per cent. Fifteen even!' Jemme said wildly.

'That will do, Mr Mafeze,' said the judge. Jemme sank down in his seat. He felt hollow and numb, and suddenly wanted to do anything he could to be out of the room. Just then Hil leaned forward and tried to catch his gaze across the two lawyers, the solicitor and barrister.

'What are you doing?' she mouthed at him.

Jemme didn't answer. It was the first time he had properly seen her since he had entered the room, and all he could do was look at her. He hoped he had spent enough time telling her how beautiful she was during their marriage. She was wearing a new fitted jacket and had put her hair up in a different way, which exposed her long slender neck. They looked into each other's eyes and Jemme experienced a moment of calm.

'A most generous offer I'm sure,' he heard the judge say dryly.

He looked up, 'Well I love her, your honour,' he said looking up but still seeing Hil in his mind.

The judge lowered the copy of the financial request he had been looking at, 'Could you say that again?' he asked.

'I said I love her,' said Jemme.

'Indeed,' said the judge. He looked at Hil, 'Mrs Mafeze, what say you – were you aware of this?'

Hil looked up and nodded, 'Yes your honour, it is no secret, I love him too.' Jeremy sunk his head into his hands, but Duncan leapt to his feet,

'Regardless of how they feel about each other, your honour, both of my clients have verified that this marriage has become untenable. They have both requested that the decree nisi be expedited and the divorce finalised as quickly as possible.'

He turned round and looked at both of them meaningfully, before turning back to the judge,

'Mr and Mrs Mafeze will both confirm that this is their request, your honour,' he said.

Silence followed, so he turned around again to prompt each of them. Hil sighed softly and pulled herself out of her reverie. She looked at Jemme again and nodded slowly,

'It's the right thing to do,' she said to him, 'we both know it.'

She turned back to the judge, 'Your honour, I do love my husband, but he has been decorating a chateau in the countryside for over ten years. It is more than just decoration though, he is building something quite remarkable –'

'That's enough Mrs Mafeze, I don't want to hear the whole story, and I certainly don't want to hear about your decoration woes! Mr Mafeze, can you confirm what your solicitor has said?'

Jemme looked at Hil one more time. She smiled at him and nodded again.

'Yes, your honour,' he said quietly.

'Well, in that case I grant you your divorce. You can get on with your wallpapering or whatever you're doing, Mr Mafeze, and you won't need to go anywhere near it, Mrs Mafeze.'

He began to talk to both lawyers about the paperwork, but Hil caught Jemme's eye one last time. She gestured to the door. He nodded.

'Excuse us,' he said as they both stood up, turned around and walked out of the room.

'Strangest couple…' he heard the judge say as the door shut behind them. 'I've been in court for thirty years, I've never seen a divorce on the ground of love and decoration before.'

They walked back down the long corridor and out onto the street.

'I don't suppose they have finished up all our paperwork yet, so I think we have at least an hour of being married left,' said Jemme, 'Shall we go for a coffee one last time as Mr and Mrs Mafeze?' He offered Hil his arm and they walked down the street together. She looked up at him and smiled,

'Marriage is a funny business, isn't it?' she said.

Chapter Thirty-Seven

Jemme stayed in London until the weekend to make sure that everything had been finished up neatly. He apologised to Duncan for leaving the room so abruptly, and thanked him for his hard work. He had also thanked him for helping Hil through the financial documents.

When they had had their coffee Hil had raised this subject too, and told him that he hadn't needed to be so generous. He had waved her comment away,

'To be honest, I hadn't actually read them,' he added.

'Oh, then you won't have seen,' Hil replied.

'Seen what?'

'My property request.'

'Property?' Jemme hadn't wanted to think that far ahead, he hadn't wanted to come to terms with the fact that they wouldn't be living in the Paris flat together.

'Of course, you must have your own place,' he had said. 'But it's fine, I agree to whatever you want. I want to make sure you're set up properly.'

'Thank you, but it's not that. I've been doing nothing but looking for the past week, and I've actually found somewhere already,' she had paused, 'It's here in London.'

Now, flying back to Paris alone, Jemme turned the conversation over in his head again. Hil was right, of course; she knew that the next few months were going to be painful, and she had wanted a clean landscape in which to deal with them. Paris was heaving with memories and mutual friends, and there was every chance they would bump into each other in their favourite pastry shops, restaurants and parks.

'I know there will come a time when that's fine. In fact I hope there's a time when we specifically arrange it, but it's not now, and if we ever want to get to that point, we need to be complete separate for a while,' she had said.

Jemme knew it was sensible, and he was impressed by Hil's ability to think so clearly. However, it didn't help sooth the sense of dread which was mounting as they neared Paris. He didn't want to have to go back to the flat, and be surrounded by Hil's things. He also didn't want to pack them away. The flat had been hers as long as it had been his. He had taken an early flight, and by the time he arrived there would be an entire day ahead of him completely empty of plans.

He tried not to think about it, and focussed his attention on the newspaper an air stewardess had just handed him. It was no good. The words all jumbled into each other as he thought of Hil's clothes hanging in the wardrobe, her pictures on the walls and her books on the shelves.

By the time they landed at Charles de Gaulle, he was about ready to board any other flight out again, just so he wouldn't have to deal with it. He suddenly had a better idea. He flagged a taxi outside the airport and jumped in. They drove right up to the flat, but he instead of going in he went through the door that led to the underground garage. He made his way down to the first level, found his car, threw his suitcase in the boot, jumped in and didn't stop driving until he reached the chateau. He focussed on the road directly ahead the whole time. He didn't let himself look at all the antique shops and cafes he and Hil used to visit together, he saw only the grey tarmac ahead.

He made good time and it wasn't even noon when he arrived at the chateau. It had only been about three weeks since his last visit, but it felt like years. He was pleased there were cars he didn't recognise in the drive; it meant there were new people to meet. He parked up and got out. He paused for a moment and looked around him. The grounds were a perfect tableau which could have been from any era of the chateau's history. They were tranquil but beautiful. He stared at the glassy lake, which was catching the sunlight in a way that made it look silver. He took in a deep breath of the sweet, fresh air and exhaled slowly. A figure moving in the middle distance caught his eye. As it neared Jemme he realised it was Xelifon.

'*Bonjour, Monsieur,*' he said when he had reached him.

Jemme saw his familiar, lop-sided smile and retuned it with a broad one of his own, 'Xelifon, I can't tell you how good it is to see you.'

Xelifon looked shy and blushed a little.

'I've had the strangest few weeks of my life and it's so good to be home. Shall we go inside?'

Jemme stepped into the grand entrance hall, and experienced the same sense of soothing familiarity which had washed over him as he turned into the top of the driveway. He looked around – there was evidence of activity everywhere, from piles of dustsheets to stacks of paint cans.

'It's so good to be back,' he said to Xelifon again. 'Where is everyone?'

Xelifon looked at the ground and shook his head, 'Monsieur, I stay in the garden. Inside the house – I do not know…' he trailed off then looked up. 'Would you like to see the garden, Monsieur? The seedlings are ready to be planted, and today the saplings are arriving,' he smiled and Jemme couldn't resist the look of pure joy on his face.

'Of course,' he said, 'I'd love to see.'

He took one more look around the entrance hall, nodded approvingly to himself and followed Xelifon back out to the garden. Xelifon had been working on a pretty bower that covered a wrought iron bench, and he pointed out where the new saplings were to be planted. He took Jemme on a tour of the lake, where the sedge had bedded in, and pointed out everything new to him. They walked all the way to the far side of the grounds, right up to the perimeter fence. In a small copse, Xelifon showed Jemme a new potting shed, completely hidden by trees. He proudly opened it up and began to show Jemme around. It was tiny, but neat and organised inside. There was a small set of shelves, with a line of terracotta pots on each shelf. Green shoots poked their way out of each one, and a thin white planter was labelled with the name of the pot's contents in both French and Latin. The same careful handwriting could be seen labelling each drawer, with names of tools at the bottom and seed types at the top. Jemme looked around, impressed.

'Who works in here, Xelifon?' he asked.

Xelifon looked straight at him and smiled broadly, 'Only me, Monsieur,' he said.

They walked back around the perimeter of the grounds, finishing off at the bothy, where they encountered Philby. Jemme greeted him warmly and Philby responded in his usual gruff fashion.

'Xelifon has been showing me all the progress in the grounds, as well as his new shed.'

Philby nodded. 'The spring is early. It is a good time to be potting,' he said plainly.

'Apparently so,' said Jemme. 'Philby, do you have time for a quick catch-up on everything I've missed? I've seen everything that's going on in the grounds, but it would be nice to get an overview of the house.'

Philby nodded. There was a pause and Xelifon shyly spoke up, 'Messieurs, should I stay?'

'No, you don't need to if you don't want to, thank you, Xelifon. I'm sure you'd much rather be back in the garden!'

Xelifon smiled at both of them and left. Jemme sat down on a rickety three-legged stool, 'It feels like such a long time since I've been here,' he said. 'I know we've spoken on the phone, but you are my eyes and ears here and I just want to know that everything has been OK.'

Philby leaned backwards onto a stack of compost sacks. He scratched his ear with his little finger.

'Everything has been fine. This is a good set of people. Even your artists.'

'Really?'

Philby shrugged, 'I have been watching them. They are honest. They work hard.'

Jemme smiled, 'Well that's a great relief to hear. Are you sure they've all been fine?'

'The man with the gold. He was a nuisance. When he went you were left with good men. No dramas. No difficulties. The man with the bicycle – he is a good man. The men cutting the stone – they know what they are doing. Good workers.'

Jemme was relieved. He knew how low Philby's tolerance of drama or hysteria was, so if he was satisfied then everything must be going well. They talked for a while, and Jemme caught up on everything that had happened in his absence. Philby seemed to like Husam.

'He is honest. He is strong. He works hard,' he said simply. Jemme knew that this was just about the highest praise Philby could give. He wasn't surprised that Philby had warmed to him, he would have expected as much.

'Has he finished all the tiling?' asked Jemme.

Philby nodded, 'He finished a while ago. He has been working on small jobs since then. Useful to have around – he is a *very* strong man.'

'I can imagine. I'd like to be able to offer him work if he wants it. Could we find a job for him?'

'As long as he wants to stick around, we'll be able to find work for him,' said Philby. He chuckled, 'He fixed the roof last week.'

'The roof? Was there a problem with it?'

Philby nodded, 'Few tiles slipped off the oldest part – the slanted area round the back,' he jerked his thumb back towards the house.

Jemme thought for a moment, 'The Louis XIII roof?' he asked. It was the oldest original part of the roof, but the slate tiles were brittle and their holdings loose. They were liable to dislodge in the smallest breeze.

Philby nodded, 'He did the whole thing. Cut the tiles himself, then said he might as well hang them. I didn't have a problem with that, so I was going to organise some scaffolding. Thought it would take a couple of days to organise and set up. Before I'd even made the phone call, Aude comes running out, all over-excited to tell me there's someone on the roof. I get there and see him up there, nimble as you like, hanging his tiles.'

Philby chuckled again and shook his head.

'But that roof is so steep!' said Jemme in alarm, 'Not to mention high! I've seen what's happened to the tiles when they fall off – they smash into tiny pieces. That could easily have been him.'

Philby shrugged, 'Didn't seem to bother him. For such a big man he's dainty on his feet.'

'Even so…' said Jemme, thinking it over and trying to picture it. He thought of the steep roof, 'actually, wait – how did he even get up there?' He imagined the roof from the outside. In other places there were small ladders leading between different sections, and it was possible to walk across, although it was dizzyingly high and a safety harness would be essential. This section, however, had no access points that he knew of. It had been a problem in the past when they had lost tiles, and they had concluded that the only way to replace them was by setting up scaffolding.

Philby shrugged, 'Climbed out I guess.'

'Climbed out?! From where?'

'There's a window on the top floor,' said Philby.

Jemme tried to picture the building from the outside again. Philby was right, and he knew the one he meant. It was the only possible way Husam could have got onto the roof, but the window was tiny, only about a foot square. The idea of such a large man hauling himself through it and up onto the roof above was ludicrous, especially when Jemme realised that Husam would have been carrying the delicate slate tiles the whole time.

'Like I said,' Philby said, 'hard worker.'

Jemme certainly couldn't argue with that. They chatted for a little while longer until Jemme realised he wanted Philby to do him a favour. Although Philby must have known all about it, Jemme was hugely appreciative that he hadn't mentioned the divorce once, or asked about Hil. He knew that the same could not be expected of all the chateau staff, and there was one in particular who would have plenty of questions and sorrowful exclamations. He didn't quite feel ready to face them.

'Philby, I was wondering if you would mind doing one more thing for me?' Philby raised his eyebrows, ready to listen. Jemme paused; he didn't know the best way to broach such a delicate subject. He decided not to skirt around it. Philby only ever spoke plainly, so he would do the same. He took a deep breath,

'I really don't want to have to talk about the divorce. It's too fresh. I know Marguerite is going to bring it up and I know that it won't just be once either. Could you speak to her before I see her and ask her not to mention it?'

Philby, shrugged, 'Of course. I will do it now – if we are finished.'

'Yes, thank you. I think I'll just sit here for a while and give you a head-start.'

Philby stood upright and turned to leave the bothy. When he reached the door, he turned and looked back at Jemme. He paused for a moment, as if he was searching for something to say, but his mouth stayed tightly shut. He looked at Jemme, who understood perfectly.

'I know. Thank you.'

Philby nodded and left. Jemme knew that was the last time the subject would be raised between them. He waited for a while, then walked back towards the chateau, stopping at the car to get his suitcase. Peering through the main door to check, he saw that the entrance hall was empty and slipped upstairs to his bedroom. He unpacked his case, throwing the envelope and anything related to the divorce straight into the bottom drawer of his dresser. Once he had finished he sat down on the bed for a moment and thought. Jemme wondered if he had given Philby enough time to talk to Marguerite. It was definitely lunchtime. He paused for a few moments then hunger got the better of him. If it came to it, he could tell Marguerite himself.

He made his way down to the kitchen, grateful for the waft of delicious smells that greeted him when he reached the top of the passageway. The kitchen was a cosy familiar fug of steamed up windows, piled up dishes in the sink and clattering pans on the hob. The air was thick with something sweet, and Jemme could definitely make out the smell of nutmeg too. As usual, Marguerite was in the centre of the room, overseeing everything like the conductor of a chaotic orchestra. She turned and saw him,

'Monsieur!' she shrieked, rushing over. She wiped her hand on her apron, and tried to smooth her hair down, 'You have been gone so long! You forget about us all here at the chateau *hè*?' she chastised.

'Of course not! How could I forget about all this?! Jemme asked, gesturing around the room. 'I'm sorry it's been so long. I've missed this place; I've missed all of you! I've had a lot to sort out in Paris and London recently.'

Marguerite's face fell, and two bright spots appeared in her cheeks. She wiped her hands nervously on her apron again and looked at the floor, then she opened and shut her mouth about half a dozen times and mumbled something. Despite the fact Jemme would have given anything not to be reminded about the divorce, he couldn't help but be amused by the scene in front of him. He had never witnessed someone struggle so hard to contain themselves when they were so obviously desperate to talk about something; he decided to put her out of her misery and change the subject,

'I hear that everyone's been working away very hard,' he said, 'Philby seemed to think that this was the least problematic group we've had here for a while! It's quite a change to come back and not be told any dramatic stories.'

Marguerite looked up, 'No dramatic stories, Monsieur? Just because Monsieur Philby does not tell you, does not mean that there has been no drama!' she said, being overly dramatic herself. 'Tsk, what does he know, being out there amongst the trees all day? He has no idea what it is like being trapped inside with this *asile des fous*!'

Jemme smiled; this was exactly the tonic he needed. He could switch off for a moment and let Marguerite rant. 'Oh really?' he said encouragingly.

'*Oui, Monsieur*! You have no idea! There is one man – he is a *géant*. I have never seen a man so tall and I have never met a man so mad! Do you know how he got here, do you know how he arrived at this chateau?'

'No, how did he get here Marguerite?' asked Jemme, doing his best to spur her on.

'By bicycle! Monsieur – all the way from Turkey!' Marguerite revealed. 'He is a complete lunatic!'

Jemme thought of the gentle, focussed Husam, and wondered whether there was anyone who could less justify being called a lunatic.

'Well that is unusual,' he said.

'Unusual? Monsieur, it is only the beginning! Not only did he cycle his way here, but now he is here he is doing everything he can to get himself killed! He is dancing around on the rooftops like a crazy person!'

'Ah, yes, Philby did mention something about that.'

'Well I bet he didn't tell you the whole story – a great big man like that, do you know how he got onto the roof in the first place?'

'No, Marguerite,' said Jemme innocently, the corners of his mouth twitching slightly.

'He heaved himself out through the tiniest window in the whole chateau! All of him! Every last inch of that massive man squeezed through a tiny window like a cat flap, and do you know what for?' she didn't give Jemme a chance to answer, 'To hang a couple of tiles!' she concluded in exasperation.

'Goodness me,' said Jemme. 'That certainly sounds dramatic.'

Marguerite got her breath back. 'That is just one small thing,' she said.

'You mean there's more?'

'Oh, Monsieur, everywhere I look there are men doing the strangest things. Do you know what they are doing upstairs, to your beautiful pillars?'

Jemme lied, and shook his head.

'Well, I don't even know what they are doing, but I don't like it. Every time I go up there, there are chunks of marble all over the place. I think they are destroying your columns, but I don't know which ones, because every time I count there are the same number. But – the dust Monsieur, there is marble dust everywhere.'

She leant back against the counter, looking exhausted by all her exclamations.

Jemme was thoroughly amused, 'Well I'm glad I've got you to keep me filled in, Marguerite. What is it that smells so delicious?

Marguerite perked up, 'Ah, Monsieur, sit down, I shall fetch you some lunch. I did not know you were coming, so it is nothing special.'

'I'm sure it will be delicious,' said Jemme, 'To be honest, I'm so hungry that even bread and butter would be a feast.'

'Monsieur, we can do better than that,' said Marguerite, ladling a persimmon-coloured liquid from the largest pan into a bowl. 'There were some beautiful squashes at the market yesterday. This one has been roasted and then turned into a thick soup with some spices.'

'I thought I could smell nutmeg,' Jemme said.

'*Oui*, nutmeg and a few others. When you've finished that there is a game pie.'

'That sounds wonderful! You're far too modest, Marguerite, it's a feast fit for a king!'

'Ouf! You are a flatterer, Monsieur!' said Marguerite, fussing around Jemme and sorting his lunch out for him. Just as he'd suspected, it was delicious. Sitting in the snug kitchen eating a home-cooked meal whilst someone looked after him was wonderfully comforting. It was exactly what he needed, and as he ate the last few crumbs of his pie, he tried to work out if he could come up with a future life plan which meant he never had to leave the kitchen. Marguerite produced a lemon meringue pie from nowhere, and he wondered if he could run the bank from this very table, without ever going back and facing Paris. He allowed himself to indulge in his fantasy until he had finished his pudding, then, sighing, he put down his fork and realised that he couldn't put it off forever. He could, however, put it off for the rest of the afternoon, and so he thanked Marguerite and headed off to inspect the work.

So much had been going on, he didn't know where to start. There were small improvements everywhere – evidence of Pontiac's gilding talents, the new glass display cases, carpets fitted, pictures hung and busts mounted on pedestals. He came across them everywhere he turned, and he knew that there were large-scale improvements too. Looking for Le Selmelif, though not really expecting to find him, he was delighted to bump into him on the second floor at the top of the corridor.

'Monsieur, what a pleasure to see you!' said Jemme.

Le Selmelif laughed and shook his hand, 'Exactly what I was about to say to you! I didn't know you would be here this weekend.'

'I know, it was a bit of a last-minute decision, so I'm only half expecting to find everyone here.'

'I think you'll be pleasantly surprised in that case – it's a full house as far as I'm aware.'

'Well that's good news. Philby has been telling me how diligently everyone's been working.'

'I think everyone just wants to get the job done,' said Le Selmelif. 'Talking of which – I've been making good progress since your phone call. Would you like to come and have a look?'

'I'd love to.'

Le Selmelif lead the way back down the corridor again, 'Everyone's been working together so well, it's been a real team effort. I thought it would take me at least a week to build the frame for the room, but a couple of the stone cutters pitched in and we'd finished it all in about three days – taking the measurements, cutting the wood, the whole thing.'

'That's just the kind of thing I need to hear at the moment,' said Jemme. An expression of concern flickered across Le Selmelif's face. He had obviously heard the news, but within a fraction of a second decided not to bring it up. He smiled widely at Jemme, 'It's so rewarding when everyone in a team works together like that,' he said, sweeping the conversation along.

He opened the door, 'Welcome back,' he said as they went in. 'I know if doesn't look like much at the moment – it's in the awkward "in between" stage, but it's coming along nicely and I hope it gives you an idea of how it will look.'

Jemme looked around him. Each wall was clad in a latticed wooden frame about three inches thick. It had been expertly finished, and if he hadn't known what it was intended for he might almost have thought it was some strange modern art installation piece. Le Selmelif had already begun mounting the frontispieces on one wall, working from the bottom up. He had only attached four so far, but it was enough for Jemme to see how the patterns of mother-of-pearl seemed to swirl from one piece onto the next.

Le Selmelif wandered over to the wall with him, 'The biggest job was probably planning the positioning,' he said. 'I probably know that furniture collection by heart! I've looked at it over and over again. I've measured each piece and calculated how large each front will be too. It took me a while but I've mapped out the whole room, so that each piece tessellates and the patterns work together.'

'I'm impressed,' said Jemme.

'To tell you the truth, I rather enjoyed it. It was like a huge riddle that tested both my mathematical skills and my artistic intelligence. Every time I thought I had worked out how to fit them all by pattern, I would realise that they wouldn't physically fit on the wall in that configuration, or, even worse they would fit, but would leave a huge gap. You can't imagine how happy I was when I finally cracked it.'

Jemme smiled at him, 'It's always satisfying to solve a good puzzle.' He squatted down to look at the pieces on the wall. It had been a while since he'd seen the collection, but he recognised one piece straight away – it had once formed the top of a small coffee table he had bought at the Quai de Louvre some five years ago. He looked at the others trying to recall what their original form had been.

'How did you find removing the decorative panels?' he asked Le Selmelif.

'Difficult,' replied Le Selmelif, 'although I was expecting that. I think it will take a while to go through the whole collection. It's worth spending time on it though. I want to make sure it's done properly and nothing's damaged, rather than just wrenching it off.'

'Absolutely,' Jemme nodded. He was looking at the visible edges of the pieces on the wall. There was not a single mark on them, no chisel scrapes, or accidental gouges. They were pristine.

'How did you do it?' he asked Le Selmelif.

'It's been different for each piece so far,' he replied. 'Some just need very gentle teasing to loosen the joints, some need other parts and panels removed first. It's been a learning experience so far. I'll tell you something though, they are well-made pieces of furniture. People knew what they were doing back then, Monsieur; it's not like this cheap modern rubbish.'

They chatted about the death of craftsmanship for a while, and Jemme was able to lose himself in one of his pet subjects.

Le Selmelif walked him to the Andalusian room, where all the men at work greeted him like an old friend.

'You won't have had the chance to meet him yet, but this is Mr Mafeze,' said Le Selmelif, introducing Jemme to everyone. They came forward one by one and shook his hand.

'Did you like the frame in the *Nacre et Ivoire* room?' one of them asked.

Jemme looked at Le Selmelif questioningly.

'There are so many rooms in progress at the moment that it became confusing,' said Le Selmelif. 'We took to calling that room *Nacre et Ivoire*. This one is the *Salon d'Andalousie*.'

Jemme smiled, 'I like it, they're good names. I was very impressed by the work that's been going on there,' he said and looked around him, 'I'm equally impressed by the work that's been going on in here too!'

There was not a trace of the marble dust Marguerite had complained about, and every one of the pillars had been erected. They soared upwards in a gorgeous array of glossy colours. They ended rather abruptly, and the walls of the room were still a stark white, but it was well on the way to feeling like the forest of marble he had wanted to create. He reached out and stroked the surface of the pillar next to him. It was a deep aubergine colour, but he was nervous of its fragility and only brushed it with his fingertips.

'Go ahead, push it!' laughed one of the stonecutters. 'We've installed them all properly; they're just as secure as if they were solid. Look!' he pushed at one of them.

'Go on, try it,' said another man.

Jemme looked at their expectant faces. He wanted to show them that he had faith in their work, but also didn't want to topple a pillar onto any of them. He prodded at one cautiously. The hard surface pushed back against his finger. He pushed a little harder and it still didn't yield. He pushed harder still, this time with his entire hand. The pillar remained completely upright and unmovable.

'Excellent work, gentlemen,' said Jemme approvingly. 'How did you find the whole process?' he asked. He had been curious about how it would all work, and part of him had hoped that they took their time so he could see them at work.

The men looked around at each other. One of them spoke up, 'Honestly, Monsieur – it was the strangest brief we've ever received,' he shrugged. A few of them laughed in agreement. 'The first pillar took us a few days,' he said. 'We'd never done anything like this before and we had to work slowly whilst we learned where the stress points were and experimented with the best methods. This is quality marble, and the last thing we wanted was to crack or split it.'

The others nodded in agreement.

'Once we'd got that first pillar sorted, then we sped up a little,' he continued, 'and it got faster with each one we worked on.'

'We were in pairs by the end,' said another man, 'two to each pillar – one to start working on it from each end. You put a lot of force on the stone when you hit it with a chisel and it's vulnerable to cracks. If you're hitting it from both ends at the same time, then some of the force cancels itself out. You've got to get into a good working rhythm with your partner though; it's a team effort.'

'It seems everyone has been working together very well recently.'

The men nodded their agreement.

'One thing I'm curious about,' said Jemme, 'what have you done with all the marble you removed?'

'We've kept it all – it's in ton sacks in one of the workrooms.'

'Is there much of it?' asked Jemme.

One of the men laughed, 'Oh yes, just a bit.'

'I wonder what on earth I can do with it,' thought Jemme out loud. He turned to the man who had mentioned it, 'Like you said, it's good quality marble and it seems a waste to send it to landfill,' he said.

The men exchanged glances. Le Selmelif spoke up, 'Actually, we have a plan for it which we wanted to discuss with you.'

'Go on.'

'It's funny you mention team work, because there's one person we've been working very closely with who's not actually here.'

'Really?' Jemme asked, trying to think who it could be.

Le Selmelif nodded, 'Your English professor,' he said. 'He's been researching a piece for this room for you.'

'Of course – the mihrab!' Jemme said. With everything that had happened, he'd completely forgotten.

'Well he rung up to ask some questions about the dimensions of the room and we got on very well. We've been speaking a great deal since. You'll have noticed that the columns are missing something,' said Le Selmelif.

'Yes, I hadn't got as far as thinking about the capitals,' said Jemme. 'In fact, I don't know where to start with them. I think I'll need the Professor's help on that too.'

'He's already started working on it. We all have,' Le Selmelif said, 'We didn't know what you had in mind, and everyone wanted to make as much progress on the room as possible. I discussed it with the Professor, and he said that you'd mentioned it might be a problem a long time ago.'

'Did I?' said Jemme.

'He said it was only in passing, but you said you didn't know what the *chapiteaux* should look like. So, we pooled all of our ideas. These people have worked with marble all over the world;' he said, gesturing at the men in the room, 'they've seen pretty much every type of capital formation there is.'

'My background is in reconstruction,' one of the men said, 'I spent years developing a typological record for my work.'

'I've never heard of such a record,' said Jemme, 'what is it?'

'It's a way of classifying styles according to their characteristics. It's useful when you're trying to date something and have nothing to work from, except the way it looks. Every time I see or study a new type of column or capital, I add it to my record.'

'It's been an invaluable resource,' said Le Selmelif. 'Everyone else has contributed sketches and designs too, and the Professor has been doing his research and giving us advice down the phone. We've come up with a final series of designs for you to look at.'

'I don't know what to say,' said Jemme. He was touched by their hard work and thoughtfulness. 'Thank you,' he said eventually, 'I had no idea you were working on this.'

One of the men shrugged, 'We all just want to get the job done,' he said.

Jemme smiled at him, it was good to know that he had people on his side.

'Would you like to look at the designs?' asked Le Selmelif.

Jemme nodded, 'I'd love to.'

One of the men produced a large sketch book, and handed it to Jemme. He opened it and looked carefully at the first page. It had clearly been drawn by an excellent draughtsman, and its design was brilliant too. It instantly evoked the grandeur of Andalusia in its heyday. He looked at it admiringly for a moment longer, before turning to the next page. This capital was completely different, yet still managed to be evocative of the same era. He liked it just as much, and was trying to decide between the two when he turned the page and saw yet another that he also liked. He continued looking through the sketch book until he had seen all seven designs. He shut it. 'Let's do all of them,' he said decisively.

The men looked at each other and murmured their agreement that this was a good idea.

'I think that is a very diplomatic move, Monsieur,' said Le Selmelif. 'It's been a team effort, but there's been some good-natured rivalry. If you'd picked a clear favourite it might have put *un pavé dans la mer*, as we say.'

Jemme laughed, 'Well I'm equally pleased with all of them, and I'm very happy that you were working on such a thing. Thank you all again. I'm not quite sure how we should go about actually making these things though. I suppose we'll have to consult a civil engineer or something along those lines. It won't do to have heavy solid capitals on top of these hollow columns.'

'We've already thought of that too, Monsieur,' said one of the men.

'Really?' asked Jemme, sounding genuinely surprised.

The man nodded, 'Yes, and I think our suggestion will help stop your excess marble from going to landfill,' he said, seeming gratified by the look of intense curiosity on Jemme's face.

'The excess marble is in different sized chunks at the moment. Some pieces are as small as pebbles and some are as big as a melon. We use an industrial grinder to grind them all down to a fine powder. Then, we gradually stir in a little bit of water and a lot of a special binder. It's a mix I've been experimenting with for years, but it's all natural and mostly gum. The whole thing will turn into stucco – you're able to pour it, but you have to work quickly because it will set rock hard. We'll prepare moulds of each of these capital types, then all we need do is pour the stucco in and wait for it to set. Of course, we'll need to tidy it up a bit when it comes out, but other than that it will be ready straight away.'

'That's brilliant,' said Jemme.

The man beamed proudly, 'It won't weigh nearly so much as a real marble capital would, but you won't be able to tell the difference. The marble dust will give it the same sparkle. Plus, it will take a fraction of the time – we'll be able to make seven at a time.'

'Also, it will be a fraction of the cost,' said another of the stonecutters. 'It would be very expensive to commission all of these capitals. With these intricate designs it would probably cost you more than the pillars did. You already have the material you're going to use, and anyone can pour the mix into the moulds; you're not going to have to hire a master craftsman.'

Jemme shook his head, 'Gentlemen, I am beyond impressed. Thank you again. It's rare to find myself in this situation, but I really am speechless.'

Everyone looked around in a congratulatory fashion.

'Just trying to get the job done,' said one of the men cheerfully.

The rest of the afternoon flew past. Jemme was able to inspect most of the other work, and also to thank Husam for his nimble footwork on the roof – although Husam didn't appear to think it was worth mentioning. Marguerite fussed around Jemme at every possible opportunity, and everyone generally went out of their way to be nice to him.

By the time he finally tore himself away he felt restored, and was buoyed up for the journey back to Paris. Marguerite insisted on tucking tin foil parcels and boxes into the car, answering 'You *must* eat, Monsieur!' whenever he protested. Almost everyone came out to wave him off, and he reached the top of the driveway with renewed spirit. Night was falling as he began the drive back, but he welcomed it. The darkness blanketed all the memories he would have to drive past; he wouldn't have to block them out like he had on the journey down. As he reached the outskirts of Paris he felt his resolve waver slightly. He looked at the seat next to him and saw a box he knew contained a freshly cooked pie. He smiled; although he had objected, the gesture had meant a great deal to him. He took a deep breath, focussed himself and drove the familiar route back to the flat. Once inside he headed straight for bed, pausing only to drop off all his provisions in the kitchen.

The following morning, he tried to use the same tunnel vision when he was leaving the flat. He didn't want to have to look at anything, he just wanted to get out and get to the bank as quickly as possible. The bank was his space. Whilst he dreaded facing the familiarity of the flat, he found the familiarity of the bank calming. As he hurried towards it, the sight of its brass handrail and stone steps soothed him. DD greeted him in exactly the same way he always had, and Jemme sat down behind the desk he knew like the back of his hand. He realised that routine was going to help carry him through this difficult period, but he didn't think that alone would be enough. DD appeared with his coffee and the morning's files. He placed them silently down and turned to leave.

'I trust everything went according to plan, Sir?' he asked with a deliberate casualness.

'Thank you, DD; it went as well as it possibly could have done in the circumstances.'

DD nodded and went to put the tray back in the kitchen. 'Poor DD,' thought Jemme to himself, 'he's so fond of Hil and he must be dying to ask more.' However, DD was the model of discretion, and Jemme knew he could rely on him to steer clear of the subject. He applied himself to the day's work with vigour and worked into the evening. When he reached a natural stopping point, he tried to catch up with some admin, but soon he had to admit to himself that he was procrastinating. He got his coat and slowly left the building. For the first time since he had moved to the city, he didn't know where to go. He was hungry but didn't want to go to a restaurant alone, and couldn't bear the idea of sitting in an empty flat eating food from the chateau. All the museums and galleries were long closed and the streets were quiet. He wandered aimlessly for a while; stopping to look at views he had seen a thousand times before. He tried to black out his growing hunger, but then realised that most restaurants would have stopped serving anyway. There was nothing for it; he was going to have to go back.

The flat was cold and it seemed quieter than usual. He went into the kitchen and heated up some of Marguerite's soup. Its bright colour cheered him for a moment, but when he went and sat in the dining room, the quietness returned. He was conscious of every tiny noise he made echoing around the room. Looking at the bowl in front of him, he sighed. Somehow its contents looked sadly out of context. He thought back to yesterday when he had been eating the same meal but surrounded by cheerful noise, lively conversation and genuine fondness

When he finished eating, he found he wasn't tired. He sat listlessly, looking at his empty bowl. It was clear he needed something or someone to distract him, but he hadn't spoken to any friends since he had been back and didn't want to have to answer any questions about the divorce. There must be someone who wasn't connected to Hil in any way and wouldn't think to ask him about it. For a moment he considered phoning DD, but he wasn't exactly the best conversationalist and would assume it was a work call. He sighed, then suddenly inspiration struck – Burbona! She had still been working for him and he had continued to pay her retainer, but it had been a while since their paths had crossed. She was exactly who he needed to talk to, someone interesting, full of life and ideas. He knew she was unlikely to be at home, but he picked up the phone and called her anyway. After only a couple of rings he was surprised to hear her sultry voice.

'Burbona!' he said, delightedly.

'Jemme?'

'Yes! It's been such a long time since we last spoke, I just wanted to give you a call to say hello.'

'You're right, it does feel like a long time. How nice to hear from you,' she said.

'I'm surprised to find you at home.'

'I was meant to be out at dinner with the Vice-Chancellor of the Sorbonne, but he's cancelled on me.'

'Oh I'm sorry to hear that,' said Jemme, amused by her name-dropping.

'These academics…anyway, how is everything at the chateau? I have so many ideas that I want to discuss with you. So many sales have come and gone too – you've missed out some fabulous auctions, too.'

'I know, I know. I can't wait to get back into the swing of it. Any particular stories?'

Burbona yawned, 'Just the usual. There have been some exciting paintings coming onto the market recently, and the bidding battles were extremely tough. They were much more dramatic than I had anticipated and I came up against some hard opposition.'

'Really?' asked Jemme, eager for auction gossip. 'What happened? Who won?'

'I did, of course,' said Burbona. 'I was bidding on behalf of a friend of mine. We should go on the hunt together soon – what are you doing next weekend? There's a sale of French silverware I think you might like.'

'Actually, I think I'll be heading down to the chateau. Like I said, I want to get back into everything as much as possible.'

'Well then, I'll come down to the chateau. I haven't been for a while.'

Jemme smiled, he had forgotten quite how forthright she was.

'Of course, when would you like to come? We can drive down together on the Friday if you would like, but then you'll be stuck without your car.'

'Not a problem, I'll stay the whole weekend and drive back with you as well.'

'Right,' said Jemme, amused.

They chatted for a while longer; Burbona gave Jemme news of Parisian society, auctions she had been to and her ideas for the chateau. He was happy just to listen and by the time he hung up felt as if he had been able to escape for an hour or so.

The next day he made his way out of the flat as quickly as he could again. He settled into his chair at the bank and prepared for an uninterrupted day of work, wondering if he could eke it out a little longer than yesterday. Deep in thought, he was very surprised when DD knocked on the door and told him he had a visitor. He hadn't even had time to wonder who it could be when Burbona breezed past DD into his office.

'We've got lots of decisions to make before this weekend,' she said, 'so I thought we should begin.'

Chapter Thirty-Eight

For the rest of the week, Jemme didn't have the opportunity to feel sorry for himself. Burbona had turned the full force of her attention on what she referred to as 'the chateau project.' Since she had first turned up in his office on the Tuesday, she had become a regular visitor. She never rang ahead, and never let DD show her in either; she simply breezed past him as if she had been working there for years. Jemme knew that this irritated DD, even if he didn't show it.

For his part, Jemme was merely amused, and he welcomed Burbona's visits, even if they were often at inopportune times. She would always turn up looking extremely glamorous, bearing news of an exciting sale or talking about a glitzy event she had just attended, full of the intelligentsia and nobility. It was a welcome distraction, and Jemme didn't mind when she called him at home in the evenings either. Talking with her and thinking about the chateau expanded to fill the empty hours he had been dreading. As Friday approached, he breathed a sigh of relief and congratulated himself of having survived the first difficult week.

He was just finishing up his paperwork, and leaving everything on his desk ready for Monday, when Burbona swept in.

'Good evening,' she greeted him. She was holding a very expensive-looking crocodile skin holdall.

'Hello Burbona, I'm just finishing up here – I won't be long, then we can get going.'

'Oh I'm sure this can wait,' she glanced over at his desk. 'You're just moving paperwork around and I know you have someone to do that for you. Dietz will do it, won't you?' she said, turning to DD, who had just appeared.

'If you would like,' said DD, looking straight at Jemme.

'Of course he would like,' said Burbona. 'Now come on,' she said, taking Jemme's jacket from its hanger on the hat-stand, 'let's go.'

'If you could, DD, that would be great,' said Jemme behind him as he was leaving the room. He meekly followed Burbona to his own car, and on the drive to the chateau realised how much she'd just bossed both of them around. If it was anyone else and in any other context he would have been outraged. As it was, he was merely amused and grateful for the diversion. She certainly kept things interesting.

As they turned down the driveway, Jemme saw the warm rectangle of light shining at the windows of the chateau. It was a welcoming sight.

'Well it's nice to be back after so long,' said Burbona, interrupting his thoughts.

'I'm pleased you think so. I'm sure you'll notice a great deal of change since your last visit.'

'And I'm sure *you'll* notice a great deal of change after this visit!'

Jemme laughed.

They pulled up, and he saw that Marguerite and Philby were waiting for them. Marguerite was beaming at the car, a look which only broadened when Jemme got out.

'*Bienvenu, Monsieur, bienvenu*! Oh you are looking healthy – I knew I was right to give you those pies!'

'Good to see you, Marguerite – you definitely made sure I didn't go hungry over this past week!' He moved round to the other side of the car and opened the door for Burbona. When Marguerite saw his passenger her smile fell, and she looked as if she had just taken an particularly long suck on a lemon.

'Madame,' she said nodding her greeting at Burbona. 'It has been a while since you were last here,' she said matter-of-factly.

'Yes,' said Burbona as she got out of the car and looked around, taking the chateau and grounds in. Her eyes fell on Philby, and she shot him a winning smile.

'My bags are in the back,' she said before turning and entering the chateau. Jemme followed her in.

He showed her to her room and then took her on a tour of the chateau, introducing her to anyone who was still at work, and showing her all the progress since her last visit. Although she seemed impressed on the whole, she teased him about not having installed nearly enough antiques or paintings yet. 'It looks like I've arrived just in time,' she said.

Their tour gave Jemme the chance to see what the work of the past week had produced, and he was happy to see that everyone was still working well together, even if the change was much less dramatic than it had seemed on his last visit. Burbona charmed everyone she met, with one notable exception. Jemme was disappointed to see that Le Selmelif clearly didn't like her, especially as Jemme himself had really taken a shine to Le Selmelif. He recalled that Burbona had put quite a few noses out of joint when she had been a more regular visitor in the past, but over time he must have underplayed it in his memory. Now he thought about it, he remembered that the female members of staff in particular had found her difficult to get along with as, of course, had Hil. At the time he had put it down to jealousy and he thought that were was still probably a lot of truth in that. Whenever one of his craftsmen seemed to be cold towards her, he had attributed it to a culture clash. He was surprised at

Le Selmelif though. Although he had grown up not too far from the chateau and had lived in the *département* all his life, he had a worldly air about him and had always seemed very open minded. Jemme was grateful at least that he had hidden his dislike reasonably well.

'Would you like to see any more?' he asked Burbona, 'You've seen the major changes, but there are plenty of smaller ones I can show you, and I can talk you through my plans for the rooms too.'

Burbona glanced at her slender gold-faced watch, 'What time did your lady say dinner would be ready?' she asked.

'Marguerite?' Jemme glanced at his own watch. 'Oh you're right, it will be any minute now. Maybe we should head down,' he turned and started making his way down the corridor.

'Wait a minute,' said Burbona, who hadn't followed him, 'I might have forgotten my way around a little, but we haven't seen anything on this side of the chateau yet. As far as I recall, if we head this way, then take the stairs down two floors, we'll find ourselves finishing up right by the *Salle à Manger*.'

'Um… yes, you're right,' he said. 'That reminds me of something. Would you mind if I left you here to look at these displays for one moment whilst I attend to something?' He gestured to the showcases filled with ornamental knives. As soon as Burbona turned to look at them, he went back in the direction he had been heading before. Once he had turned the corner he dashed his way down to the kitchen, where, as he had suspected, Marguerite had set the table for two.

'Ouf, Monsieur, why are you running around like that! Never mind; it is good you are here. Dinner is nearly ready and I hope it will be up to *Madame*'s standards,' she said pointedly.

'I'm sure it will be great,' said Jemme hurriedly, 'Marguerite, listen, would you mind moving us to the *Salle à Manger*?'

'The *Salle à Manger*, Monsieur?'

'Yes, I think Burbona expects… well, I mean I know that she… Listen, it's just going to be a lot easier if we can eat in the *Salle à Manger*, and we'll both be coming downstairs very soon.'

Marguerite shrugged, 'Of course, Monsieur, it is no problem, especially if the kitchen is not grand enough for Madame.'

'I'm sure it's not like that at all,' said Jemme, although he knew that that was exactly what it was like. 'Thanks for your help, Marguerite,' he said as he dashed back upstairs. He found Burbona still looking at the display case.

'A nice collection,' she said, nodding her approval. 'I like this case too; we should get more of them.'

'Good idea,' said Jemme, 'I think dinner is ready. Shall we?' he indicated the way down to the end of corridor, the route Burbona had suggested.

They made their way downstairs, with Jemme stopping to point out anything they passed en route which he thought might be of interest. Eventually they reached the dining room, where Marguerite, to her credit, had set everything for them. Jemme knew that the room was seldom used; it had been a long time since he had entertained clients there. The shutters were closed during the day and most of the furniture protected by dustsheets. In the time it had taken Jemme to retrieve Burbona, Marguerite had managed to make it look as is the room had been waiting for them all evening. An arrangement of flowers sat on the table and tall tapers burned in the silver candelabra. She had even set the table with the formal dinnerware, which they never used in the kitchen.

They made their way to the table and, for a fraction of a second, Jemme had begun to sit down when he realised that Burbona was waiting expectantly by her chair. He went to pull it out for her and hoped she hadn't noticed.

'I don't suppose this room has changed much since you were last here,' remarked Jemme, trying to smooth over his momentary lapse in chivalry.

Burbona looked around, 'No, I don't think so.' Her eyes rested on the long wall opposite, 'Ah, I'm pleased to see that the mirror is still where I suggested.'

Jemme winced as he remembered the icy confrontation between Hil and Burbona over where the mirror should hang. It was on Burbona's first visit and Hil hadn't changed her opinion of Burbona much since then. Jemme didn't really know how to respond. He felt duty bound to defend Hil in some way, but it would come across as a little odd, especially over something so small. He smiled a little awkwardly and then wondered if Burbona knew about the divorce. She hadn't brought it up, but then she also hadn't asked about Hil at all. It was true that they weren't the greatest of friends, but if she wasn't going to feign politeness and enquire after her health, it seemed odd that Burbona hadn't even asked if Hil would be joining them. She must know, Jemme reasoned with himself, she's someone that makes it her business to know these things. He smiled again slightly awkwardly, and was relieved to see Marguerite coming in with a large dish. Jemme's heart softened a little when he saw it. Although Marguerite always served directly from the pot whenever they ate in the kitchen, she had transferred everything into the nicest tureen they had in the chateau. Jemme was touched that she had made the effort, especially as he knew it was all for him, so that he could put on a good show.

Aude had followed Marguerite in, and she set down a plate warmer, lighting the four small candles it held. She replaced the grill on top of them and Marguerite put the tureen down. Instead of the usual oven gloves, she had a crisp white linen napkin, which she used to lift the lid. A small puff of steam escaped, carrying with it sweet, herby aromas.

'Marguerite, that smells wonderful, what is it?'

'*Coq au vin, Monsieur.*'

'I was hoping it might be!' Jemme turned to Burbona, 'I always tell Marguerite that she makes the best *coq au vin* in all of France. Wait until you've tasted it, I'll bet you'll agree.'

Burbona smiled tightly, 'I always forget how different food is in the country,' she said.

Marguerite visibly bristled, but she still served Burbona in the sweetest manner possible. Jemme could just imagine her getting back to the kitchen and shrieking all the things '*Madame*' had said at Aude.

'That's enough,' said Burbona, after Marguerite had barely served her two ladlefuls. She paused for a moment,

'You are sure – there is plenty here!'

'Yes, quite sure thank you.'

Marguerite raised her eyebrows, but didn't say anything. She moved on to the other side of the table and served Jemme until he couldn't see the plate anymore. He laughed,

'Marguerite, that's definitely enough, thank you! If you give me all of this, how will I come back for seconds!' He smiled at her affectionately.

Burbona started talking about the candlesticks, and Marguerite disappeared into the kitchen. *That's the quietest I've ever heard her!* Jemme thought to himself. He turned his full attention to Burbona,

'I'm sorry, I was miles away.'

Burbona tossed her hair to one side and laughed, 'I was admiring these pieces, and saying that this place could do with some more silverware, unless you're keeping some hidden that I don't know about.'

Jemme laughed, 'No, no Aladdin's cave of silver here I'm afraid. I thought I'd built up quite a collection over the years, but it is a little lost in a place this size.'

'Leave it to me,' said Burbona decisively. 'Silver is very fashionable at the moment and there are always lots of sales going on. I'll be able to give your collection a bit of a boost in no time.' She smiled at Jemme, who felt awkward again.

'You also don't have much carved woodwork as far as I can see.'

'Carved woodwork? No I suppose not. Not in its own right at least. Lots of our pieces feature carved decoration, but it's not something I've sought out on its own.'

'Well you should; it's also something that's very fashionable at the moment, so there is a great deal about. It's only just starting to become popular though, so the prices haven't gone up too much as yet. If we move quickly, we could pick up some real investment pieces. Don't worry, I can organise everything.'

Jemme put down his fork and smiled at her, 'Burbona, what would I do without you?'

Burbona smiled again and shook her glossy hair slightly, just enough to catch the candlelight.

'This place can feel like such an island,' said Jemme. 'More than that in fact, it's a bubble. It's my retreat from Paris, and if I don't watch what I'm doing I can be completely cut off from everything here – it's its own fully functioning, tiny world, I swear I'd never need leave at some points. Anyway, I'm glad I've got you to connect me back to the real world and everything that's going on.'

Burbona smiled, 'Sometimes it's good to forget the real world,' she said, looking straight at Jemme. She had barely touched her supper.

* * * *

The weekend had a very different tone to other chateau weekends. Jemme was used to losing himself in the hectic pace of all the work that was going on. He worked to his own schedule and drifted around the house, drinking coffee and chatting with the artists. Now he felt like he had a guest to entertain. He couldn't wander from one room to another at will and take a walk by himself in the grounds. It was nice to have a change of pace though, and he loved the feeling that he was showing off the chateau. Burbona seemed impressed with all the developments, and had a comment to make on each one. From anyone else, Jemme would have found it irritating, but he genuinely valued Burbona's contributions. Every improvement she suggested, no matter how slight, was well-judged.

'You have to remember that this is a work in progress,' she told Jemme. 'Even if it looks like a room is finished, there are always additions that can be made.'

Jemme agreed wholeheartedly, 'There is just so much work to finish I can't imagine ever feeling like the end is in sight!' he said.

Burbona smiled, 'Of course it is. We will get there eventually.' She looked directly at Jemme as she said it. He blinked innocently.

'The key is to increase your pace of acquisitions,' she continued, before he had a chance to consider the ambiguous nature of her comment. 'When I first met you, you were barely out of the auction house. Now it looks like you haven't bought anything in ages. The more antiques, paintings and *objets* in this place, the better. It will start to look finished in no time. Luckily for you, this is my speciality! I will start on it as soon as we get back to Paris.'

Aside from Burbona's suggestions, Jemme was pleased to see that work was still progressing at the same sure and steady pace. Highly decorated frontispieces were gradually creeping their way up the walls in the *Nacre et Ivoire* room, and for the first time Jemme could really imagine how the room was going to look when it was finished. Le Selmelif filled him in on the new techniques he had developed when separating the pieces from their original forms. Jemme listened with interest, but he could tell that Burbona was underwhelmed. Whether it was the room itself or the fact that Le Selmelif was not impressed by her, she obviously did not want to be there. She paced around whilst Jemme talked to Le Selmelif, and glanced disinterestedly at the surroundings. When there was a small pause in the conversation she jumped in.

'You know, I think there could be real potential to do something with this room,' she said brightly.

'We are already *doing something* with this room, Madame,' Le Selmelif replied.

'Yes, yes, I know,' said Burbona, waving her hand dismissively, 'I meant *after* all this carpentry is finished.'

Le Selmelif raised his eyebrows and bit his lip, but didn't say anything. Jemme's mouth twitched slightly. He realised he should probably say something, and defend Le Selmelif, but he was too amused by Burbona's boldness and her ability to enrage. It seemed to be matched only by her ability to flatter, both of which she employed in turn to get exactly what she wanted. Jemme couldn't help admiring her for it. Le Selmelif obviously did not.

'Well, let's see how we get on with this "carpentry" first shall we, Madame, then perhaps you can make your suggestions.'

'I think we've finished in this room,' Burbona said to Jemme. 'There's really nothing more to see.'

They left the room, with Jemme nodding his thanks to Le Selmelif. Back outside Jemme was keen to show Burbona the room that was fast becoming his favourite. He took her along to the *Salon d'Andalousie* to show her the columns and the nascent forest of marble. Some of the stonecutters were in the room and he was able to introduce them. Burbona dazzled them with a winning smile, and they seemed keen to talk to her about their work. She chatted with them with charm and ease and cooed over their achievements, looking over every now and then to smile at Jemme. She laughed when she heard the story of the pillars being emptied, 'How ingenious!' she beamed at the man who had relayed the details to her. He looked pleased with himself, and told her about the plans for the capitals.

'Marvellous!' she said. 'I'm sure my friends in Paris will be amused to hear of pieces of masonry being made like chocolates in a mould!' she laughed.

'Talking of the capitals, how are they coming along?' asked Jemme.

'Well, Monsieur,' replied another of the men. '…in some ways. In other ways we have discovered some difficulties.'

'How so?'

'Well, we've only worked on one design so far. It took us much longer to cast the mould than we had imagined. It might be because we chose the most complicated one, though.'

'Well, it's always good to start off with the hardest option,' said Jemme, 'you face all the challenges at the beginning and there aren't any unpleasant surprises later.'

'That was what we thought as well. We were pleased with the mould though; it looks exactly like we wanted it to.'

'How did you make it?'

'We couldn't cast it on site. You'd need a powerful kiln and that would involve installing a transformer and all sorts of electrical complications. There's a pottery not far from here and they let us use their kiln when they had finished for the day on Wednesday. Anyway, like I said, it looks good. The marble mix went well too – it created stucco of just the right consistency and it went into the mould beautifully.'

'That's great,' said Jemme.

The man nodded, 'We were pleased too. The best part is probably the chips though. We mixed in marble chips of just the right size to add to the sparkle of the mixture. It went better than we could have imagined, and the finished piece is so lifelike you'd have trouble telling it apart from the real thing.'

'But this is all wonderful news!' said Jemme, 'it sounds like everything's gone better than any of us could have possibly hoped.'

'In some ways, Monsieur,' said the man.

'Well, what on earth is the problem?' asked Jemme.

'It's the weight, Monsieur. Even though it weighs nothing compared to a real marble piece, it is still heavy. We've just made one as a sample, but when you multiply that by the number of pillars in this room...well, we're starting to worry about the strain on the floor.'

'Couldn't you just change the mix?' asked Jemme, 'Perhaps you could use less powder in it?'

The man shook his head, 'I wish it was as easy as that. The proportions in the mix are exact though – it's a science as much as an art. It only works when everything is in exactly the right ratios – too much powder and it's too stiff to pour, too little and it never sets. We just want to be certain, having gone to all this trouble with the pillars.'

'Of course, you were right to bring it up – I appreciate your diligence. Did you say you had made a sample already?'

The man nodded, 'Yes, it's in one of the workshops – would you like to see it?'

They all made their way down to the rooms which had been serving as *ateliers* since the project began. The largest one was filled with ton sacks, which were themselves filled with marble dust.

'Wow, you weren't joking – there's loads of this stuff!' said Jemme looking around him.

One of the men laughed, 'We could create the same number of pillars again with all of this, and still have some left over!'

'So you won't use it all in the moulds?'

The men all laughed.

'For all of the capitals we will only use a tiny amount from just one of these bags!' one of them said.

Jemme grimaced slightly as he took in just how much that would leave over, 'I thought you told me you had a solution for getting rid of it!' he joked.

'Well, the capitals are only the beginning. This is an ambitious project. We've heard all about your plans from the Professor and everyone here. It sounds like the place will be filled with marble by the end.'

'Well, I don't know about filled….' Jemme said.

'You'll be needing a lot though, for all these museum rooms,' said another. 'The Professor's described some of the rooms to us; it sounds like marble will feature pretty heavily. The pieces all sound like they will need high levels of expertise, and will take a great deal of time too. Why not use the same process we're using for the capitals?'

Jemme looked interested.

'You have the material already and we can either make the pieces for you ourselves whenever you need them in the future, or train someone else how to do it, it's up to you.'

'That's very generous of you.'

The man shrugged, 'Of course, I hope you'll call on us, but failing that we just want to make sure the job gets done properly, even if it's not us doing it.'

'You wouldn't have to use it for every piece of marble work,' said another of the men. 'If it was going to be a feature piece, then you could make that out of the real thing. If you were going to be making lots of identical pieces, especially ones that were just to accent walls or corners, then it's ideal.'

Jemme smiled, 'You really have provided me with a solution! I love it!'

The men looked pleased, 'I'm sure you'll want to see what the results are first – that's why we came down here in the first place!'

'Yes, I have a tendency to get very sidetracked in the chateau,' Jemme laughed.

One of the men moved a pile of dustsheets, '*Voila!*' he said, gesturing at the floor, 'your first faux-marble, marble capital!'

Jemme squatted down to look at it. He took in the intricate detail – it looked like it had been expertly carved with the finest of chisels. As he moved around and looked at it, the chips sparkled and glinted, just the way real marble did.

'I really can't believe it's not proper marble,' he said at last.

Burbona hadn't squatted down, but she had peered over at it and made her approval known.

'Excellent work, gentlemen,' she said, flashing a smile that caused one of the men to blush.

'We're pleased with it too,' another of them told Jemme. 'It turned out even better than we had hoped. We thought it would only work when it was on top of a pillar and no one was looking at it for too long, but even on close inspection it's still OK.'

'It's more than OK; it's brilliant! I can't believe you've managed to solve so many problems for me. It's such a relief to know that everything is finally sorted with the *Salon d'Andalousie*. Once we have all the rest of the capitals then we can move straight on to decorating it. We'll have it finished, months before I'd imagined, maybe even a year!'

He had run away with himself a little and only just noticed the looks on the men's faces.

'What's the problem?' he asked, 'I thought you'd be as excited as I am.'

'But, Monsieur,' said one of the men, 'you forget. The reason we are down in the *atelier* at all is because we were all worried about the weight of the capitals.'

Jemme felt stupid, 'Of course, my apologies – I told you, I have a tendency to get sidetracked!' he squatted down again and looked at the capital. 'Do you know how much it actually weighs?' he asked eventually.

'Truthfully, no – we haven't long finished it. One man could lift it without much trouble. It's more the combined weight of all of them we are worried about.'

'Of course,' Jemme looked at the capital again, trying to estimate its weight and trying desperately to run through the maths in his mind. It was no use, he realised that he wouldn't be able to rely on his own arithmetic. 'I think we'll have to consult an expert on this one, just to make sure. Much as I'd like to be able to solve this particular riddle myself I think I need a civil engineer.' He stood up, 'I'm sure someone back in Paris will be able to recommend me a good person, so hopefully we'll be able to sort all of this out as quickly as possible.'

'Don't you worry about a thing, I know just the person,' Burbona beamed at all of them. 'He owes me a favour, so he can make himself available straight away. I'll ask him to drive down in the next couple of days, so by our next visit everything will be sorted.' She turned and smiled at Jemme again, 'Aren't you lucky to have me?' she said playfully.

Chapter Thirty-Nine

Over the next week, Burbona was an ever-present feature at the bank. She never announced her visits. Jemme just knew that, inevitably, she would sweep in at some point during the day. She certainly caused a distraction when she breezed through the main office on the third floor. Occasionally she would flash a smile at a junior clerk, who would blush furiously and quickly look away, trying desperately to pretend he hadn't been watching. In fact she was pretty much the only individual who came even close to flustering DD, but for entirely different reasons. Although he remained impeccably composed, Jemme knew that Burbona's unannounced visits irked DD. He knew too that his own willingness to drop everything, and veer dramatically away from the schedule DD had planned, caused his second in command to feel the closest he ever came to consternation.

However, Jemme did not mind any of this, as Burbona was distracting him too. Every day that successfully went past was one day he moved further away from the divorce. At first the time in front of him had seemed dauntingly huge, and he had no idea how he could begin to tackle it. However, now, every tiny diversion progressed him forwards just a little. He realised that he only needed to survive another week and a half and he would have made it through the first month. A busy week and a chateau weekend would really help with that.

Burbona had been more animated than ever over the past week. After her comments on the chateau's lack of silverware, she had taken it upon herself to bolster the collection. Each time she arrived at the office, she had news of some more pieces she had acquired, either at auction or from one of her seemingly limitless dealer friends. Jemme noticed that she hadn't discussed any of them with him first, but he barely minded. They were small pieces after all, and he was grateful that she was working under her own initiative and helping advance the project. Each piece was being sent directly to the chateau, and he was excited by the fact he had new things to look forward to.

There was another matter driving Burbona's animation too: the appointment of an architect. She had talked rapturously of Roberto, his illustrious career and the regard in which he was held by the artistic community. By the end of the week Jemme was beginning to wonder how they had managed to secure this man's services at all, and was feeling heavily indebted to Burbona, and of course the estimable Roberto. He was surprised, but delighted, that Roberto had agreed to come to the chateau that very weekend to look at the marble columns and to decide whether the floor could support them.

'Isn't it going to be a bit… beneath him?' asked Jemme slightly nervously. He didn't want a feted architect feeling insulted as soon as he turned up at the chateau.

Burbona waved her hand, 'Not at all. In fact, I have never met such a talented man with so much humility. Besides, he is very curious to see everything that's going on – I have been telling him all about the project. He already feels as if he knows it.'

'And I already feel as if I know him,' smiled Jemme. 'I'm looking forward to meeting him this weekend a great deal; thank you again for organising everything.'

Burbona smiled, 'I think we are both looking forward to it.' She continued to speak excitedly about how honoured they were and how wonderful the weekend was going to be. Jemme was happy to sit back and listen to her, his mind far from the divorce.

The following day Jemme tried to focus on the spreadsheet in front of him, but his mind kept wandering. He was trying to imagine what Hil's new house looked like and how she had filled it. He wondered if it felt like half a home, just like the Paris flat did for him. He was reluctant to admit to himself that it probably didn't. Whereas the flat felt like something essential had been wrenched out of it, and only the shell was left, Hil was starting with a clean slate. She was free to start with fresh memories, rather than live with painful ones. His thoughts were interrupted by the telephone ringing -- a well-timed distraction. He knew it would either be DD, ringing to ask if he would accept an outside call, or Burbona ringing directly through to his office. He picked up the phone expecting to hear one of two voices and was surprised to hear someone completely different,

'Hello,' said a cheerful English voice.

'Professor! How nice to hear from you,' said Jemme warmly.

'Yes, I'm sorry, it has been a while. I've been rather sucked into university life recently.'

'Oh really? Is there anything exciting going on?'

The Professor sighed, 'Quite the opposite in fact. Well, some people seem to think it's pretty exciting, but I want to stay out of it as much as possible: they've announced a new fellowship and two readerships and the politics and in-fighting it kicked off was unbelievable! So much plotting and scheming! Of course, these people have studied every plot, scheme and coup in history, so they shouldn't be underestimated.'

Jemme laughed.

'Anyway, I became involved slightly by accident and it seemed to take up all of my time for a while. It's nice to come out of that little bubble, and I'm looking forward to getting involved with the chateau again.'

'Your involvement is always very welcome. I'm looking forward to seeing you a great deal and catching up. When do you think you'll next be able to come over – are you in England at the moment?'

'Yes, I'm stuck in rainy Oxford and I'm dying to get out! In fact, as luck would have it, there's a conference at the Sorbonne this Friday. It doesn't look particularly interesting, but I'm sure I can make a case for going, and ask the university to pay for my flights out there. I'll slink off to the chateau as soon as I arrive. The subjects they'll be discussing are so tired and hackneyed that I can definitely sound like I went.'

'I've never heard you be so devious!'

'To be honest, at this point I feel like they've taken a lot out of me, and if I can cadge some free flights as repayment then I'm going to.'

'Well I can't argue with that, especially if it means I'm going to be able to see you the day after tomorrow.'

'Rather exciting eh?' said the Professor with renewed vim. 'I'll bet you've made some changes to the place since I was last there, I'm sure I'll hardly recognise it!'

'I don't know if I'd go that far,' Jemme laughed. 'Do you really think you'll be able to come this weekend?'

'Don't see any reason why not. I want to get away, so if they make a fuss about the flights, I'll just get 'em myself. Either way, I'll see you on Friday. Can you give me a lift down?'

'Of course, we'll wait until you've arrived and all drive down together.'

'Smashing, see you then!' said the Professor and hung up without asking who 'we' was.

Jemme replaced the handset and sighed happily. The news that he would be seeing the Professor had cheered him a great deal. It was a wonderful surprise – he certainly hadn't expected to see him so soon. He was looking forward to chatting with him about all the different rooms, and getting his opinion on the developments. Although Burbona had a wonderful eye for aesthetics and a shrewd understanding of the historical impulse behind many of the rooms, the Professor was an academic heavyweight with a deep scholarly understanding of the subjects about which Jemme was the most passionate.

He realised Burbona and the Professor had never actually met. He was sure that they would get along well, and she would charm him in the same way she seemed to charm almost everyone else. The weekend was shaping up to be a very fulfilling one.

＊　＊　＊　＊

On Thursday Burbona arrived at the office half an hour after Jemme. She was on her way to a brunch meeting, and could only stay long enough to drop off some auction catalogues. Before Jemme had had the chance to tell her the good news about the Professor, she was shooting out her *ciao* and was on her way out of the door again. No sooner had the door closed behind her than it opened again, and DD appeared with Jemme's morning espresso.

'Ah, you've just missed Burbona,' said Jemme. 'You must have passed her on the way in.'

'A great shame,' said DD, inclining his head slightly. 'Will she be back?'

'I shouldn't think so,' said Jemme. 'She was in a bit of a hurry, and besides we're spending all weekend together.'

'A great shame,' DD repeated, although Jemme could have sworn he detected a faint glint in his eye.

Jemme sat and talked over the day's business with DD. He tried to focus, but it wasn't until he subtly slipped the auction catalogue under a sheaf of papers and removed the temptation that he could give DD his undivided attention.

That evening as he sat at home, he flicked through the catalogue in his favourite reading chair. Burbona had circled several pieces and there were some notes next to a couple in her elegant, looped handwriting. Once again, Jemme couldn't fault her taste. He looked at the auction dates and was excited to realise that he'd actually be able to go. It had been a while since he'd experienced the thrill of an auction, and it was exactly what he needed.

He reached the end of the catalogue and turned straight back to the beginning again. There was something soothing about rhythmically flipping the pages over, and he was able to lose himself amongst the statues, paintings and pieces of furniture for a while. He concentrated hard on each one, trying to recall anything he might know about the artist, craftsman or period in question. Occasionally he would draw a complete blank, and he made a mental note to bring the subject up with the Professor to see if he could share some wisdom.

He shut the catalogue and decided to pack his weekend bag before he went to bed so he wouldn't have to worry about it in the morning. Opening the wardrobe, he realised he needn't have worried. A few solitary work shirts hung forlornly in the cavernous space. It was a wardrobe intended for two people's clothes, and he remembered how crammed it used to be. Hil's special dresses hanging in protective bags, and her other clothes, filled far more than her fair share of it. He used to tease her about it and feign exasperation when he couldn't find any spare hangers. Now, almost all his casual clothes were at the chateau. He kept a couple of spare suits at work and all that seemed to leave were the few shirts he was looking at now. They were swinging slightly on their hangers from when he had opened the door. There was something slightly pathetic about the sight and he shut the door quickly – no need to really pack at all, he thought to himself.

The following morning, after he brushed his teeth, he popped his toothbrush into a sponge bag with his razor. He looked at the two lone items before he zipped it up. *If I could buy spares of each then I wouldn't have to pack anything at all*, he thought to himself. He closed the bag and sighed, unsure if the thought had cheered or upset him. On the way to work, he tried to banish the image of the empty wardrobe from his mind and focus on the upcoming weekend. He was thoroughly looking forward to seeing the Professor; it felt like such a long time since he had been able to while away the hours listening to him with fascination or deep in engrossing conversation. He was proud of everything they had achieved at the chateau and was looking forward to showing it off as well. His mind turned towards the other event of the weekend: meeting Roberto. He wondered if he would look anything like Jemme imagined he would. Burbona had described him at such length, and in such detail, that he had already developed a picture of him in his mind so clear it could have been a photo. In fact, he was expecting a man of such superlative intelligence, suaveness and accomplishment that he almost felt intimidated.

Throughout the day, whenever he had an idle moment, his mind drifted to Roberto, wondering if he would bear any likeness to his mental portrait. He wondered if he would be impressed with all the work they had completed, and if he would be willing to give suggestions about future developments. The day seemed to crawl past; the work he was doing was uninspiring and he found it difficult to engage with it on any level. He realised that he was scared of being left with his own thoughts, and so headed out for a long lunch break. Even though it was quite a walk, he made his way to the little Turkish café where he had often met the Professor. It was as lively as ever and he was greeted like an old friend, despite the fact it had been a very long time since his last visit. He treated himself to *Beğendili Tavuk* – chicken with creamy, pureed aubergine, which had been a childhood favourite, then lingered over a thick, sludgy Turkish coffee at the end.

After promising to return soon, he made his way back to the office, much comforted. Glancing at his watch, he realised that the Professor would be getting ready to board his flight in London around now, and he was further cheered. Back at the office he was finally able to focus, and the afternoon mercifully began to slip by. He was interrupted by the sound of his door opening. He looked up to see Burbona entering and he almost did a double take. Even by her standards she was looking exceptionally glamorous, dressed in a way that flattered her every feature. Jemme could only imagine the disruption she had caused when she had made her way across the office this time.

'Good afternoon, Burbona. You look nice,' he said.

Burbona shrugged nonchalantly, as if she had pulled an old sack on, rather than looking as if she had just stepped straight off one of the catwalks of Paris Fashion Week.

'Are you ready?' she asked Jemme. 'We should make an early start.'

'I'm pretty much ready to go whenever,' said Jemme. 'I'm afraid we'll have to make a bit of a detour though.'

Burbona raised one eyebrow questioningly.

'The Professor should have landed by now, but knowing him, it will take an eternity for him to find his bags and get out, so I'm in no great rush to head over to the airport.'

'Airport?'

Jemme nodded, 'Charles de Gaulle.'

Burbona shook her head, 'Professor?'

'I'm sorry,' said Jemme, leaning back in his chair and rubbing his eyes tiredly. 'I forgot that I hadn't told you – I only found out myself on Wednesday, and then I barely saw you yesterday. Professor Johnston is flying over, he'll be joining us for the weekend.' He stopped rubbing his eye and looked at Burbona excitedly. She didn't look as instantly pleased as he had expected. In fact her nostrils had flared slightly.

'The weekend?' she asked.

'Yes, it's all very last minute, but luckily enough he'll be able to stay for the whole weekend.'

'Luckily?' Burbona repeated as if was a question. She narrowed her eyes slightly, 'Professor Johnston?' she said disinterestedly.

'Yes, you haven't actually met yet; he's been away at Oxford for a while. He's an old friend though; he's been involved in the chateau since the early days and I really value his input. He's such an expert on everything I really care about.'

'I see,' said Burbona, her eyes still slightly narrowed. Jemme didn't understand why she didn't seem pleased.

'Look, Burbona, I'm sorry if the weekend's not going to be exactly as you planned,' he offered, wondering as he did so why he was apologising for inviting an old friend to his own home.

There was a pause, then Burbona flashed her most charming smile.

'Silly!' she laughed as she flicked her hair. 'Why are you sorry? It will be delightful. The more experts at any one time in the chateau, the better for the whole project,' she gushed, smoothing everything over. Jemme felt relieved, and decided he must have been imagining her initial displeasure.

'Well, we don't want to keep Professor Johnston waiting at the airport, do we?' she asked, looking around for his suit jacket. She found it hanging on the hat stand by the filing cabinet, and unhooked it.

'Shall we?' she asked, looking at Jemme.

He smiled, 'Of course, let me just finish up a few little things.'

'Oh, come on,' Burbona pouted, teasing him.

Jemme laughed, 'Alright, alright, I'll come now.' He took his jacket from Burbona and followed her down to his car, bidding DD a meek goodbye on the way out.

They were caught in the rush hour traffic on the way to the airport, and by the time they arrived, Jemme realised that even the Professor couldn't still be finding his way to the arrivals hall. He hoped he hadn't been waiting too long. They parked up and wandered in. Jemme looked up at the boards and saw that the flight had landed on time. He scanned the seating area and saw a figure in the distance. He wandered over and soon recognised the Professor. He laughed to himself. The Professor's attaché case was as over-stuffed as ever and two crumpled paper coffee cups had also been shoved into the top, dribbling coffee dregs down the papers that were sticking out. The Professor himself was looking slightly dishevelled, with a creased jacket and a chin swathed in grey stubble. Jemme saw his suitcase and smiled. He wouldn't have expected anything less. It looked about a hundred years old, and in places was held together with nothing but tape. Jemme wondered how it had made it through the flight in one piece.

'I don't see him,' said Burbona who had caught up with him. She looked around, her eyes completely passing over the shabby figure in front of them.

'He's right here,' said Jemme. 'Professor!' he called.

The Professor looked up from the small book he had been scrutinising, and broke out into a broad smile.

'Jemme!' he said and stood up, knocking over his suitcase in the process. It clattered to the ground, causing several security guards to look up.

Jemme laughed, but noticed that Burbona looked slightly horrified.

'It's so good to see you,' said the Professor, pumping his hand warmly, 'and my goodness it's good to be out of Oxford!'

'Well it's wonderful to have you here, welcome back,' said Jemme. 'I'd like you to meet Burbona too,' he said, 'she's been helping a great deal at the chateau – she seems to know half of Paris and pretty much everyone in the antiques business.'

'Jolly good,' said the Professor, offering his hand and starting ever so slightly when he looked at Burbona properly.

For her part, Burbona looked faintly disgusted and bemused by the individual in front of her. As soon as the Professor had offered his hand, however, she flashed a winning smile,

'*Enchanté*, Professor. I've heard so much about you,' she said, full of charm, as she shook his hand.

'Well it's very nice to meet you too,' said the Professor. 'I'm looking forward to getting back to the chateau immensely,' he added cheerfully.

'In that case, shall we?' asked Jemme moving to pick up the Professor's case.

'Oh, I wouldn't touch that thing if I were you,' the Professor laughed. 'It will probably fall apart as soon as you pick it up. I'll take it,' he said. He looked at the handle, obviously thought better of it, grabbed the case by both sides and stuffed it under his arm. Jemme grinned at Burbona, who returned his smile with a very thin, pursed one of her own.

On the way to the car, the Professor chatted animatedly about everything he had been working on recently, as well as talking disparagingly about the conference he was evading. Jemme hung on his every word, variously laughing, exclaiming his outrage and sympathising in disbelief. Burbona barely got a word in edgeways, and when Jemme caught sight of her out of the corner of his eye, he thought it looked like she was pouting. When they reached the car, Jemme opened the boot for the Professor who paused before throwing his suitcase in.

'Jemme, listen…. I want you to know…. I was really sorry to hear about you and Hil. Really sorry.'

Jemme swallowed hard. He hadn't been expecting to be reminded of everything so abruptly.

'I didn't want to bring it up, because I thought it might all be a bit – you know….' said the Professor, 'but I wanted to make sure you knew that I was…. Well, you know.'

'I know, Professor, thank you,' said Jemme.

The Professor nodded, slightly awkwardly. Jemme shut the boot and the Professor paused again,

'I wasn't sure whether I should tell you this or not, but, well, I've seen her very recently.'

Jemme felt his heart jump, 'Really?' he said, trying not to let his voice shake.

'Yes, well she's in London now.'

Jemme nodded eagerly, not wanting to ask for more information, but hoping the Professor would give it to him anyway.

'I heard she was there, and the last time I was down I looked her up, just to say hello, you know.'

Jemme smiled, despite the pang of sadness he felt. He knew that the Professor had always been fond of Hil, and he was pleased he had made the effort to keep in touch. Hil would certainly have appreciated the visit. He looked at the Professor and saw a living, tangible link with Hil. He wanted to ask him everything – how she had looked, how she was doing, what she was doing, but he summoned every ounce of self-control he could.

'I know she would have been pleased to see you,' he said quietly.

The Professor nodded sadly, and that was the end of the matter.

Burbona meanwhile had pointedly gone and sat in the car. Jemme had actually hoped that the Professor could sit in the passenger seat so that he could continue talking to him on the drive down, but he realised he couldn't very well ask Burbona to move. As it turned out, he ended up talking to the Professor for most of the journey anyway, leaning back behind him whenever the car stopped. Burbona stayed silent for most of the journey, and whenever Jemme caught sight of her, he was increasingly sure that she was pouting. He wondered if he had done anything to offend her, and tried to include her in the conversation a few times, but her replies were brief and she sounded uninterested.

By the time they arrived at the chateau, Jemme had become so involved in everything he wanted to show the Professor, and all the different things he wanted to ask him about and hear his opinion on, that he had all but forgotten about Roberto's visit. They pulled into the driveway and the Professor stopped talking for a moment as he took in the scene in front of them.

'It really does look marvellous when it's all lit up like that, doesn't it?' he asked.

Jemme nodded, 'It's one of the most heartening, welcoming sights in the whole world.'

As they pulled up in front of the main entrance they saw that Marguerite was waiting for them.

'And there's another!' said the Professor cheerfully, getting out of the car. 'Marguerite! How lovely to see you! What a long time it's been.'

'*Professeur*!' Marguerite trilled, 'I was not expecting you!'

'Well it's all been a bit last minute, but I'm very glad to be here.'

'We are so pleased to have you!' Marguerite said, wreathed in smiles. 'Madame,' she said suddenly and very seriously, turning and nodding her head as she saw Burbona get out of the car. Burbona offered her a tight smile that had disappeared within a fraction of a second.

Marguerite turned back to the Professor, 'Come, come, let's get you inside – you must be hungry after your long journey,' she said warmly. She trotted after the Professor as he retrieved his case, and threw up her hands in horror when she saw what he had been carrying his possessions around in. 'We will have to sort this out immediately!' she scolded him.

The Professor grinned, 'Well, as long as you're feeding me, I don't really care what you do with it!'

Marguerite fussed around him, before suddenly stopping, 'Ah! Monsieur! I almost forgot! There is a visitor here for you, a monsieur from Paris.'

Burbona suddenly stiffened in attention. She let out a sharp sigh of frustration, 'I knew this would happen. We would have been here first if we hadn't gone via the airport. I hope you have looked after him,' she said sharply, turning to Marguerite, who visibly bristled.

'*Bien sur*,' she said curtly. 'You have no need to question our hospitality here, Madame.'

'I'm sure you've done a wonderful job,' said Jemme, trying to smooth over everything. 'We're all looking forward to meeting him.'

Burbona looked mildly placated, and led the way into the main entrance hall. She looked around, as if wondering where Marguerite could have put Roberto. She didn't need to look long, as the man himself soon appeared.

'Burbona!' he said, walking towards her with outstretched arms.

'Roberto!' she purred, her earlier irritation completely forgotten. He embraced her and they kissed on both cheeks.

'What a pleasure to see you again,' said Roberto.

'What a pleasure it is to have you here!' returned Burbona, flicking her glossy hair and smiling at him. 'How was your journey here?'

'It was fine, easy enough to find and the place is just as you described.'

'Well you are very welcome,' she said, giving him a lingering look.

Jemme was standing on the edges of their conversation, wondering if he should introduce himself at some point, or if Burbona was going to. He had quite wanted to be the one to welcome this man into his home. Thankfully at that moment Burbona finally broke her gaze off and turned to Jemme.

'You must meet Roberto,' she said, beckoning him over. 'Roberto, this is Jemme Mafeze,' she said, presenting him.

The men shook hands and Jemme took the opportunity to study him up close. On the whole he matched up to how Jemme had imagined. He was tall, slim and tanned with dark, slicked-back hair. He had dark eyes and sharp cheekbones, and Jemme could see why Burbona had talked so much about his good looks. She had been careful not to say that she found him attractive, more that he was considered desperately good looking by all the Parisian socialites. From the way he carried himself and his general manner, it was very apparent that Roberto was a confident man.

'I'm delighted to meet you,' he said, shaking Jemme's hand and revealing slightly nicotine-stained teeth.

'Likewise,' said Jemme, 'I've heard so much about you, I really appreciate you making the journey down here.'

'I have been looking forward to seeing this chateau of yours ever since Burbona first started telling me about it,' said Roberto. His voice was smooth and rich, but Jemme could detect a slight accent. He couldn't quite place it – it was almost as if he had Italianate inflections on some words. Jemme suspected that Roberto was cut from the same cloth as Burbona – a mix of old aristocratic stock from across Europe. He wouldn't be surprised to find out that he too had a string of surnames, which tied him into most of the old families across France and further afield. It was no bad thing, and these connections had been working well to Jemme's advantage so far.

He noticed the Professor still standing around, and brought him into the conversation,

'I'd like you to meet Professor Johnston,' he said. 'He is a key figure in this project as well as an old and trusted friend.'

'I was just about to introduce him myself,' said Burbona quickly.

'Professor,' said Roberto offering his hand. As the two men shook hands, Jemme wondered if there was any way they could have looked more different. The Professor was unkempt and wearing a beaten-up old jacket that was probably bought at the same time as his suitcase. As he reached his arm forward his sleeve pulled back to reveal his watch, with its scuffed face and the two mismatched parts of the strap. Roberto on the other hand was meticulously groomed and unshakeably urbane. Every detail about his dress and appearance had been precisely and expensively observed. Jemme smiled to himself. The best part, and certainly the thing which endeared him to Jemme the most, was the fact that he knew all these facts would be completely lost on the Professor.

'Oh, so you're an architect!' he heard the Professor exclaim delightedly whilst talking to Roberto. He smiled, while Burbona's lips thinned.

'Well, now we're all here, why don't we get started with a small tour? We'll have time to take in the most recent work before heading for supper I'm sure. Professor, I'm dying to show you one room in particular,' Jemme said, turning to Professor Johnston.

'Actually, I think Roberto will be most interested in starting with the noble rooms,' said Burbona. 'I thought we could start with the *Salon* and work our way around until we end up in the *Salle à Manger* for supper.'

Jemme shrugged, not wanting to make a scene. 'Whatever you like,' he said, although he was secretly a little irked. He had been really looking forward to showing the Professor the *Salon d'Anadalousie*. There was nothing new about the noble rooms, and the Professor himself would have seen them hundreds of times. He realised that they were probably more impressive in the conventional sense and reasoned that this was probably why Burbona wanted to show them to Roberto. She led the way and he meekly fell in line behind her, trying to remember all the questions he wanted to ask the Professor.

Burbona ended up doing most of the talking, and showed Roberto around with ease and familiarity as if it had been her own home. She was the perfect hostess; charming, witty and interesting, telling little anecdotes or giving the background stories to particular pieces she knew would interest him. Jemme began to feel a little redundant, and wondered if Roberto had been underwhelmed by him; he certainly didn't feel as if he was being particularly impressive. The sight of the *klavier* which Hil had chosen so many years ago, and which he had declared to be the first official piece for the new chateau made him wince. It was strange to hear someone else telling the story of the chateau's development and colouring it with their own choice of stories. For him, it was the deeply personal connections to pieces, and the memory of times in which they were bought, which were the most important. After she had finished telling Roberto how Jemme had acquired the magnificent carpet in the *Salon*, Burbona excused herself and disappeared for five minutes.

'This is a beautiful room,' said Roberto, turning to Jemme, 'and you have obviously taken a great deal of care in its restoration.'

'Thank you,' said Jemme, grateful for the chance to finally talk to Roberto. 'There wasn't much here at all when we started.'

'So I understand,' said Roberto.

'In fact, to be honest, there wasn't much of anything in the chateau when we started. Most of the grand reception rooms were completely empty, and in places the fixtures had actually been ripped out.' Jemme launched into the story of the chateau's narrow escape from life at the centre of a golf course and Roberto listened, aghast.

'Such waste!' he said, shaking his head, once Jemme had finished.

'I'll say,' agreed the Professor.

Just then Burbona reappeared, 'Everything alright?' Jemme murmured to her.

'Absolutely fine,' she said brightly. 'I just wanted to find your kitchen woman and make sure everything was alright with supper.'

'Marguerite?' asked Jemme.

'Yes, that's her name,' said Burbona, although Jemme was pretty sure she had known that already.

'I'm sure she has everything under control,' he said, well aware of how unwelcome Burbona's intrusion would have been.

'Well, I just wanted to go and check,' said Burbona, unabashed, 'I half-thought she might do something like seat us at that little table in the staff kitchen.'

Jemme found himself wincing yet again. He knew how offended Marguerite would have been, and just hoped that Burbona had been a little more tactful than he suspected she was.

'Do I understand that you are converting part of the house into a museum?' Roberto asked.

'Well,' Jemme paused, 'that's not really my intention, but I suppose on the surface it does look a bit like that. For me this is the most exciting part of the whole chateau, and where the Professor has really helped. I'll take you there tomorrow and you'll be able to see. We've divided one floor up into a series of rooms of equal proportion, and then dedicated each one to a particular era of civilisation. It's a little bit like a museum, except the rooms aren't empty galleries filled with artefacts, they're much more immersive than that. We've tried to create the feeling of actually being in that era, when an individual stands in the room.'

'It sounds fascinating,' said Roberto. 'I'm looking forward to seeing them.'

'Shall we move on?' said Burbona. 'We should just have time to make our way leisurely to the dining room before dinner is served.'

'Excellent idea!' said the Professor jovially, 'I'm famished.'

'I'm sure we will follow you,' said Roberto to Burbona, with a smile she readily returned. She led them once again, this time pausing slightly for effect before throwing open the double doors of the dining room.

'What a magnificent room,' said Roberto, looking at Burbona then Jemme.

'It's looking marvellous,' said the Professor enthusiastically. 'Certainly much better than it does when it's covered with dust sheets.'

Jemme laughed, 'That's true enough. It's so nice to be getting some use out of this room. This was one of the first rooms we completed in the chateau,' he explained to Roberto, 'and at the time we thought we were going to use it a great deal for entertaining. In fact we did at the beginning, but things never work out quite as you intend, and now I'm afraid it spends much of its life under dust sheets, just as the Professor says.'

'A great pity,' said Roberto graciously. 'I'm pleased to be able to see it now though, and just like Professor Johnston says, it is looking *marvellous*.'

Jemme laughed. The word sounded completely different when Roberto said it.

Dinner itself was a pleasant but slightly strange affair. Every member of the party seemed to want the conversation to go in a different direction. Burbona wanted to talk to Roberto about mutual acquaintances in Paris, and parties they had both been to. Roberto wanted to talk to Jemme about the previous projects he had worked on, and Jemme wanted to talk to the Professor about the mihrab in the Andalucían room. For his part, the Professor seemed happy to chat to anyone, but specifically wanted to talk to Marguerite, whenever she appeared, about the exact ingredients in each dish she was serving.

'*Professeur!* Why are you so interested in my cooking all of a sudden, eh?' she chided as the Professor peered into the serving dish she was trying to carry past him.

'I'm sorry Marguerite, it's just that I've been in eating in university cafeterias for the past few months. I'm so excited about eating something with some flavour!'

* * * *

After he woke the next morning, Jemme gradually made his way down to the kitchen for his morning cup of coffee. He was still partly asleep, and had completely forgotten that he had guests. He arrived in the kitchen, looked around and yawned. Marguerite was busy rushing around, and hadn't even noticed him come in; Aude had looked up nervously and smiled at him, then busied herself at the chopping board again, where she seemed to be creating a fruit platter big enough for the entire village.

'Monsieur!' Marguerite finally turned around and saw him.

'Morning, Marguerite,' said Jemme sleepily, 'is there any coffee in the pot?'

'Tsk, tsk,' she said, ushering him away from the counter, 'you should not be in here. You should be next door!'

'Next door? What's happening next door?'

'Monsieur! You should be in the *salle à manger* – that's where they all are. They'll be wondering where you have got to!'

'They?' Jemme paused. 'Oh of course, the others,' he said, feeling as absent minded as the Professor. 'I'll go through now. I must say, it feels very formal to be eating breakfast in the *salle à manger*, Marguerite.'

'Well, I don't think Madame will appreciate eating in the kitchen too much,' said Marguerite pointedly, with her hands on her hips.

Jemme thought she was probably right, but thought it wiser not to say so. He looked thirstily at the coffee pot, but realised he would have to do his hosting duty before he was going to be able to have his morning espresso. Making his way through to the much grander surroundings of the *salle à manger*, he found that his guests were already assembled. Burbona and Roberto were deep in what looked like a very intense conversation and the Professor was ambling around the room, occasionally picking up small ornaments to inspect them on a much closer basis.

'Good morning, everyone,' Jemme said, 'I'm sorry to have kept you waiting.'

'Hello!' said the Professor enthusiastically, 'not to worry at all, I've been enjoying looking at all these new bits!' he gestured vaguely around the room.

Burbona looked reluctant to break off her conversation with Roberto, but eventually looked up, 'I'm sure we've all been able to find something to do,' she said, looking Jemme in the eye.

'I'm pleased to hear it,' said Jemme, not completely certain he knew what she was talking about. 'I hope you're all hungry. I think we're in for quite a large breakfast if what I saw in the kitchen is anything to go by!'

The Professor's ears pricked up, 'Well that sounds promising,' he said, moving straight to the table and seating himself expectantly.

'It's always good to eat a hearty breakfast,' he told a disinterested Roberto. 'Especially when there's lots of thinking to be done!' he added to an equally impassive Burbona.

He seemed completely blind to their lack of shared enthusiasm, and looked excitedly at the entrance from the kitchen, waiting for breakfast to materialise.

He looked so much like the spaniel one of Hil's friends owned that Jemme couldn't help smiling. He remembered the look the dog used to get whenever he was about to be fed – the Professor was replicating it perfectly.

Soon enough, Marguerite appeared, bearing two large trays. Aude trotted behind her carrying the fruit platter Jemme had seen her preparing – it was so large she had difficulty in carrying it with both hands. Marguerite set all the food down, and even on the large table it seemed that she was having trouble finding space for all the dishes and plates. Jemme's eyes were drawn straight away to the large platter that bore four or five different types of glossy, flaky pastries. Marguerite saw him eying it up,

'*Chausson aux Pommes, Monsieur*,' she said, pointing at one, 'made with apples from the orchard.'

'You didn't make these pastries yourself, did you Marguerite?!' asked the Professor.

'*Ben oui, Professeur*,' said Marguerite in confusion, 'you do not expect me to serve pastries I have bought from a shop?'

'Fair enough,' the Professor shrugged.

Marguerite continued to set down bowls of eggs, plates of ham and several loaves of puffy brioche, accompanied by small dishes of homemade jam and a large pat of golden-yellow butter. She had barely laid the last item down when the Professor began heaping things onto his plate.

'Madame, what can I get for you?' she said, wielding a spoon and looking at Burbona.

Burbona looked at the spread in front of her and wrinkled her nose ever so slightly, 'I'm not really in the mood for *tartines*,' she said, 'I think I'll pass.'

There was a pause and Jemme looked up anxiously, hoping Marguerite had not taken offence. 'Don't worry, Marguerite, I can serve myself,' he said.

'Very well. Then I wish the rest of you a *bon appetit*,' she said, looking menacingly at Burbona. She swept out of the room with Aude in tow. Burbona looked after her for a brief moment then turned to Roberto again as if nothing had happened and continued her conversation.

'What a spread!' said the Professor, also as if nothing had happened.

Jemme slowly sipped a coffee, which he had finally been able to pour for himself, and looked around the table wondering if he had imagined the whole thing.

Once he had eaten a little himself, he began to chat with the Professor,

'We should start thinking about doing some research again. It is a while since we last discussed everything, and I know you've had other priorities.'

'Not at all!' said the Professor, 'I welcomed the distraction. I haven't been able to do as much as I would have liked, but I certainly haven't forgotten about everything. I've been doing some work on how the cupola and the mihrab might have looked and I've brought my notes with me.'

'That's fantastic news! I can't believe you found time. It sounded like everything at the university had been taking up your every waking minute.'

The Professor waved his hand, 'It's all nonsense. Like I said, anything to take my mind off it! Now,' he began, 'you recall that the problem with the mihrab was that we knew there should be one, but we had no idea what it should look like or how to go about finding out.'

Jemme laughed, 'I recall.'

'Well, I managed to lose myself in a rather large wing of the history faculty's library, poring over manuscripts and sketches.'

'That sounds like an agreeable way to pass an afternoon,' said Jemme, enviously.

'Quite. Well, after getting incredibly side-tracked, I started talking to the librarian, who is a good friend of mine. He told me about a blue-leafed Qur'an they held in the rare books section and showed it to me. It was very beautifully illustrated and made me decide to look to Kairouan for inspiration.'

'Kairouan?'

'Now, it's a suburb of modern-day Tunis, but it's a wonderfully historic city and contains a beautiful mosque – the Great Mosque of Sidi-Uqba. It's an absolute masterpiece. Most of the features have come from even earlier buildings, so it's a fantastic place for getting ideas.'

'How old is it then?'

'Well, it's a bit of a mix, because it's been developed over such a long period and contains so many pieces from different eras. It's often thought of as representing the height of Islamic civilisation though. You would love it – I know you've been thinking about columns and pillars recently and this will really impress you! There are over four hundred of them!'

'Four hundred?!' said Jemme, instantly starting to worry that the Andalucían room was far too small and unambitious in scale.

'Yep, four hundred and fourteen, to be precise,' said the Professor happily, 'although – and this is an interesting fact – it used to be forbidden to count them.'

'Forbidden?'

'Yes, with blinding as the punishment for whoever dared. I suppose it was to prevent people from trying to quantify their impressiveness, or remove some of their mystery – most of them came from the ruins of Carthage you know. They're an impressive sight even now, a mix of granite and marble and porphyry – the stone with the large crystals.'

'Yes, I know it,' said Jemme.

'Well anyway, they were all very impressive and you should really go and see them in person. In the meantime, I've compiled some copies of sketches I found in the library and its archives. I thought you could give them to your architect chap here,' he indicated Roberto, 'and he could either copy them directly or perhaps amalgamate them all into a new design.'

'That sounds brilliant,' said Jemme. 'Do you have them here?'

'Yes, although not down here – I have everything upstairs.'

'Would you mind getting it before we head over? It would be nice to have a look when we're doing a tour of the room. I haven't decided who we're going to ask to complete the work yet, but I certainly would appreciate Roberto's input.'

At the sound of his name, Roberto broke off from his conversation with Burbona and looked up.

'Monsieur?' he asked.

'I was saying that I'd like your opinion on quite a few things when we're in the *Salon d'Andalousie*, if that's alright.'

Roberto bowed his head, 'But of course, that is why I am here, Monsieur. I am looking forward to talking with you about the project a great deal more. My apologies, I was just entranced by something Burbona was telling me.'

'What was that then?' asked Professor Johnston innocently.

Burbona smiled sweetly, 'I'm afraid it was about a mutual acquaintance Professor, I'm sure it wouldn't interest you in the slightest.'

'Ah, right – well in that case I'll pop off and grab those notes before we get started.'

'Thanks Professor, I really appreciate it.'

'It's no bother,' the Professor shrugged, and grabbed a pastry from the platter for the journey back to his room.

Whilst he was gone, Jemme finally had the chance to talk with Roberto, who told him about some of his previous projects. Roberto seemed to work mostly with glass and steel, and specialised in making imposing modern edifices in city centres. It couldn't have been more different to everything Jemme was working on. Roberto's installations demanded attention and dominated the space they occupied. Jemme wanted the work he commissioned to blend seamlessly into its surroundings. It should create atmosphere and in some cases, set a particular scene, but if one single piece stood out above the others, then something had gone wrong. Still, the work Roberto had completed was technically accomplished. Jemme knew a few of the high-rise office blocks he had mentioned. They weren't to his taste, but they were noticeable. The two he was thinking of had been completed as a pair in Frankfurt, a few years ago. He knew the bank that had commissioned them and knew that they would have been extremely rigorous in their selection of an architect. Moreover, if Roberto was capable of calculating the weights and stresses on such tall and complex buildings, then the Andalucían columns would be no challenge to him.

Soon enough the Professor returned with a notebook and some pieces of paper he was holding, loose, in the other hand.

'Brilliant pastries!' he enthused, grabbing another with the notebook hand.

Burbona wrinkled her nose very slightly again, but no one apart from Jemme seemed to notice. She shot the Professor a winning smile when he looked at her, and so Jemme quickly decided he must have imagined it.

'If everyone has had enough, then I suppose we should get started,' he said.

They all followed him to the room, with Burbona pointing out small features to Roberto along the way.

'It's all just as you described. I'm impressed,' said Roberto.

'Thank you,' said Jemme and Burbona at the same time.

Chapter Forty

Once they were in the *Salon d'Andalousie*, Jemme noticed a change in Roberto. He almost visibly changed from houseguest to architect. His expression altered completely and he almost seemed to grow in stature. He wandered around the room, asking Jemme very specific questions – Jemme was pleased he wasn't able to answer all of them straight away; it gave him confidence that he was dealing with an expert. For her part, Burbona watched Roberto at work with a look of pure admiration on her face.

'I told you he was good,' she said to Jemme when Roberto had paused for a moment, earning her a smile from the architect.

'So where are these pillars that you've been talking about so much?' asked the Professor.

'Well they couldn't very well be in this room! That's half the problem! I'll take you to see them in a moment. This room is all in pieces I'm afraid. It's a bit of an empty shell at the moment, but I wanted to show you what it was like first and then show you everything I want to put in it. With your advice, that is,' he said looking at Roberto, who nodded.

They looked around the room for a little longer, before Jemme decided it was time to take them down to the would-be forest of marble, which was currently still lying flat in the workshop. He couldn't resist stopping on the way.

'I hope you don't mind – I just haven't had the chance to visit this room yet, and I really want to see all the developments since my last visit.'

'Of course,' said Roberto. Burbona smiled.

'Which room is this?' asked the Professor.

'The *Nacre et Ivoire* room – do you remember me telling you about it?'

'Ah yes! Well I'm very interested to see what's happened to that beautiful furniture collection of yours.'

Jemme opened the door and almost stopped in his tracks. The Professor managed to walk straight into him regardless.

'Goodness!' said Professor Johnston, recovering and looking around.

Jemme stepped into the room properly and slowly looked around, taking in everything. A broad smile spread across his face. It was exactly as he had wanted it, and exactly as he had imagined it.

'I see what you mean about the Malachite Room,' said the Professor approvingly. 'It really captures that essence, but still manages to look like something completely different.'

Jemme nodded, 'It's everything I could have hoped for,' he said. When he had opened the door, it had felt just like stepping into another, tiny world. Instantly he was surrounded by nothing but jet black and twinkling mother-of-pearl. It was a new landscape; its walls traced stories through the patterns in slivers of ivory, but they provided a beautiful plane, onto which the visitor could project his own stories and imaginings. The room felt completely separate from the rest of the chateau. There was no natural light and no reference points to the real world. It was a place for dreams.

'That carpenter of yours has done a nice job with the woodwork,' said Burbona prosaically.

'Le Selmelif?! He's done more than that. He's given me exactly what I wanted.' Jemme smiled again. Le Selmelif had only told him he was over halfway through; he hadn't told him that he had finished the whole room, and this was a wonderful surprise.

'She's right,' said the Professor, 'he's finished everything beautifully. I don't think I've ever met him have I?'

Jemme shook his head, 'I don't think so, but I'm sure you will. I'd love him to take on a bigger role in the chateau – even more so now. I hope he's available.'

'I'm sure he will be,' said Burbona tartly.

Jemme looked around him approvingly one more time and led the way downstairs to look at the columns. They were just as beautiful as he remembered, and he was filled with renewed excitement about how they would look when he saw their rich aubergine, and emerald colours.

Roberto looked very serious again and began to inspect them closely, asking him numerous questions. Jemme told him the story of emptying the pillars to lighten them, which drew a loud guffaw from the Professor and caused Roberto to furrow his brow even further and talk at length about material density and downward pressure.

Whilst he was working, Jemme removed a dustsheet to show the Professor something else, 'These are the capitals I was telling you about,' he said.

The Professor squatted down to scrutinise them. 'These are great!' he said. 'Are they really made from this strange marble mix you were talking about?'

Jemme nodded, 'It's hard to tell, isn't it – they look so much like the real thing.'

'Don't they?!' said the Professor, leaning up very close to one and moving his head from side to side. Still squatting down, he looked rather comical. 'They even glint like the real thing,' he said to Jemme.

'I know. They're going to look really good on top of the columns. I can just imagine looking up at them as you enter the room.'

'Ah, that reminds me – talking of looking up, have you thought about how you're going to do the ceiling?'

'Honestly, no. This room is becoming so complicated, and I just haven't been able to get that far yet. It's going to have to be just right though, however it ends up.'

'Well, we can talk about that too when we look through these,' said the Professor, waving his bundle of papers at Jemme. 'I've brought all sorts of things I thought would interest you, and it's good to look at all these things at the same time.'

Later that day, Jemme sat over yet another meal in the *salle à manger*. Just as with breakfast, it felt oddly formal to be eating lunch there, especially with the Professor, whom he normally met in the most unremarkable of cafes. Roberto arrived after they had all been sitting for a while.

'My apologies,' he said to Jemme, 'I wanted to complete the work before I arrived.'

'Have you finished already?' asked Jemme.

Roberto nodded, 'It is not a difficult problem to solve, but I needed to sit down and go through the calculations a few times to make sure I was satisfied.' He launched straight into a lengthy explanation that Jemme tried to follow. He was very dry in the way he described everything though, and his conversation was dense with facts. However, Jemme understood the gist of it, which was that everything would be fine if they did something simple to the floor near the supporting wall. That was all he really needed to hear.

'Thank you, Roberto,' he said, feeling excited about the prospect of work on the room beginning to gather momentum again. Burbona beamed at both of them.

'Are you in the mood for looking at some of these sketches?' asked the Professor.

'More so than ever,' Jemme nodded.

As Marguerite brought out a tureen big enough to swim in, and began to pile the table up with dishes again, Jemme and the Professor pored over the sketches, notes and photographs the Professor had amassed. Jemme particularly enjoyed looking at the sketches. He had always loved travel writing, and some of these pictures had originally been published in books that had become famous and well-established. For many people, these second-hand reports would have been their first exposure to new and exciting places, and completely different worlds.

'Look, I've made some notes here,' said the Professor, indicating some scrawl on one of the photocopies, next to a small sketch. 'I've made a list of the Qur'anic extracts used in the mihrabs in both Kairouan and Madinat al-Zahrab too. I thought you might like to use the same when you commission the piece.'

'Yes, that will be a nice reference, thank you.' Jemme peered at the Professor's notes some more, 'What does that say?' he asked.

'That just says *24 carat gold,*' said the Professor. I was looking at the lists of materials used in various mosques. There's always some kind of documentation in the historical record. I think you'll have to include it somewhere for the accuracy, if not the look.'

'Of course.'

'In fact, I bet I can find you someone. A friend of the faculty in fact.'

'Really?'

'Yes, they're always in touch with conservation experts – it goes hand-in-hand with academia really. There's someone I've met a few times, he's called Hardouin Mansart – he's a fantastic gilder. He's worked on Les Invalides, and right down to a couple of the tiny brooches in the Louvre. I can see if he's free?'

'That's very good of you Professor, thank you.'

The Professor shrugged.

'I know a great many gilders back in Paris,' Burbona stepped in. 'Perhaps I should introduce you to a couple, too, so that you're able to choose the best one?'

Jemme thought for a moment, 'To be honest Burbona, I probably don't need you to bother. If the Professor's friend is an academic already, that's good enough for me. I'll let you know if he's not free though. Maybe you could help then?'

Burbona pouted for a second then smiled widely, 'Of course!' she said brightly, flicking her hair over her shoulder.

'Now,' said the Professor, looking back at his notes, 'I thought this would interest you,' he flicked through a couple of pages until he found another photocopy. 'The original of this no longer survives,' he said, 'and I actually don't know much about the provenance of this panel either, but I thought you would like its subject matter.'

Jemme looked at it closely, 'I don't see what it is.'

'Here,' said the Professor, turning it around so Jemme was looking at it the right way up. 'It's a single carved marble panel. It shows the Caliph in discussions with his representatives from different academic fields. I thought it was a nice representation of what you were doing here.'

Jemme looked at it again and picked out the figure of the Caliph. He imagined him discussing philosophy, science and astronomy at the height of Andalucía's power. Known for its excellence as a centre of learning, it would have attracted the finest scholars and poets as well as jesters and entertainers. Jemme looked around himself at the small group gathered in the room with him – an architect and a university professor. It was modest by comparison, but he indulged himself for a moment by drawing a few parallels with the Caliph and his scholars.

'We should commission a replica of this piece, for certain,' he said. 'It will take pride of place in the room when it's finished.'

Burbona looked up, despite the fact it had seemed that she was fully engrossed in conversation with Roberto.

'I know someone who can do that for you,' she said quickly, before the Professor had had the chance.

'Thank you, Burbona,' said Jemme and turned back to the notebook.

By the end of the weekend, Jemme felt alive with enthusiasm for the new room. He was delighted with progress so far, and thrilled to be working with the Professor once again. He had enjoyed meeting Roberto, and was grateful for his input regarding the columns, but he couldn't help feeling they hadn't really clicked. Whereas Burbona was instantly warm and engaging, he had found it difficult to get a handle on Roberto. He wondered vaguely whether their paths would ever cross again.

Although the Professor had to fly back to England on the Sunday, they remained in close telephone contact throughout the week. The Professor was continuing his research and had offered to have some ideas sketched out and completed for Jemme by the next weekend.

'That's the beauty of undergraduates,' the Professor had said, 'they're always keen to help their Professor out!'

Meanwhile, Burbona's visits to his office during the week continued undiminished. At one point, he was actually on the phone to the Professor when she arrived. He noticed that she looked put out, and he thought about how he had found her slightly different over the weekend. She was usually so easy to get along with, but she didn't seem completely settled around the Professor, and at times he thought she was almost icy towards him. He didn't know what was different – perhaps it was Roberto's presence, and the fact she was anxious to make a good impression in front of someone she obviously respected a great deal.

The next time she arrived in his office, she came bearing a small mock-up of what the carved marble panel would look like, and his observations were soon forgotten in his excitement.

'I thought you'd like to see,' she said, 'it's just an artist's model from plaster-of-paris, but it's what he'll be working from, and it will give you an idea of how it will look.'

'I love it!' said Jemme enthusiastically, 'thank you for showing it to me, I'm excited about seeing the real thing now!'

'I thought you would like it,' said Burbona, 'but that's not everything. I've done some looking around, and I think I've found something you can get really excited about!'

Jemme looked intrigued and Burbona teased him for a while longer before producing an auction catalogue.

'This sale isn't official yet – even this catalogue itself is just a printer's mock up, but I heard a rumour about this piece and I thought it was worth tracking down. Look,' she opened the marked page to reveal a large photograph of a tapestry.

'They haven't got as far as filling in the text yet, but this is a sixteenth century Belgian tapestry. Look at the scene it shows.'

Jemme looked at the photograph of scholarly figures surrounding one central character. 'He's the Caliph!' he said excitedly.

'Exactly,' beamed Burbona. 'I don't know if this was created after someone saw that precise panel,' she indicated the model Jemme was holding, 'or, if it was something similar, but it's perfectly possible and it would make a nice story if that is how it happened.'

'Burbona, I don't know what to say. This is such a find!'

Burbona smiled back at him. Jemme genuinely didn't know how to express himself. Mostly he felt guilty. He had been quick to judge Burbona, but this showed she had obviously been paying attention all weekend and listening carefully. She had picked up on the fact that the panel represented something special to him, and had decided to go one stage further.

'All I know is that the sale will be in Flanders,' she said, 'but I will keep you updated with details when I receive them.'

'Thank you,' I really appreciate it.

She smiled at him and sat down in the seat on the other side of the desk.

'What are you working on?' she asked, looking at the mass of papers spread out in front of him.

'A couple of different things actually. Partly I'm doing some actual work,' he indicated a stack of bound reports. 'We're assessing the feasibility of an acquisition for a client. It's not at a particularly interesting stage though, so it's quite difficult to concentrate. It means I'm spending most of my time on this,' he indicated the sketches and scribbled notes laid out in front of him and paused. 'To be honest, for the next few months I just want to keep myself as busy as possible,' he added in a moment of candour.

Burbona smiled, 'I'm sure I can help with that.'

Jemme realised that she still hadn't made any reference to the divorce.

'Anyway, since we visited the chateau and the Andalucían room is back on track, I'm filled with more energy than ever to plough on with the project. I just want to spend every free second I have either at the chateau, or thinking about the chateau.' As he said it, he realised it sounded slightly obsessive, but it was exactly as he felt.

'It was amazing to see so much work completed when I was back, but it was one of the first times I think I haven't seen artists *at work* there.'

'I'm sure it was just a matter of timing,' said Burbona. 'It's always better to go when they've finished anyway.'

'I don't agree – I want to be there as everything's taking shape around me. I want to feel like I can see things developing in front of my eyes. I've been trying to think of new rooms to work on, and which can be started before I even visit this weekend. I don't want to wait,' he paused and bit his lip to stop himself from getting too carried away. He was starting to think about how much he had sacrificed for the chateau project, and it made him realise he had to dedicate even more of his time and energies to it than ever before.

Chapty Forty-One

Whenever he had an idle moment, Jemme found himself dwelling on all he had sacrificed for the chateau. It was the last thing in the world he wanted to allow himself to think, and whenever the thought niggled its way out of his subconscious, he tried to quash it as quickly as possible, usually by busying himself with chateau work. He couldn't help thinking about Hil and all he had lost. He realised that she would probably still have time to meet someone else and start a family, and he thought about how much their paths had diverged. In many ways he wanted that life for himself; it would certainly be easier. The chateau was all-consuming though – it was like a vocation, even when other opportunities tempted him, he still found it calling to him. The more he forced himself to focus on chateau work and to ignore anything else, the more obsessive he became. His ideas for new rooms became wilder and wilder. Although the dream was still the driving impulse that ran through the centre of the project, he found himself spinning off into increasingly erratic tangents.

One afternoon was spent desperately trying to avoid thinking about Hil, after a phone call in which the Professor mentioned that he'd seen her. He had heard that she had been taking riding lessons at a stable just outside London, and he recalled how much she loved horses and riding. At one point he had promised her a stable in the grounds of the chateau, but work on the international forest and statue installation had taken over, and the idea somehow never went anywhere. He kept imagining her riding through the countryside, but would instantly chide himself; it was no good thinking about such things. He managed to push the romanticised image to the back of his mind, and focus on the chateau yet again. However, he obviously hadn't been as successful at distracting himself as he had thought; by the end of the day he had designed a new room focussed purely on horses and equitation. He had decided to call it the *Musée du Cheval d'Alep*; it would tell the story of the three progenitors from whom all thoroughbreds could trace their lineage. It would also contain artefact and display pieces.

He was so pleased with the idea that he failed to see what had influenced it. Instead he had decided that the horse was a beautiful symbol for Aleppo's influence throughout the world. With a long history of tolerating foreigners, and its reputation for cultural and artistic innovation, he was surprised that this was the first time he had thought to reference Aleppo in the chateau's narrative so far. The more he considered it, the more pleased he was with the idea. He started to become obsessed with it; convincing himself of how perfect and apt it was, and using the noise to drown out thoughts of Hil.

He researched the story furiously, and commissioned an artist to paint large portraits of each of the original thoroughbreds – the Darley Arabian, Byerly Turk and Godolphin Arabian. He focussed especially on the Darley Arabian and his journey to England with the merchant, Thomas Darley. He discovered a scientific study which linked ninety-five per cent of all English thoroughbreds back to this one stallion; it was exactly the validation he needed, and it spurred him on to continue with his research. He began to enlarge the scope of the room and look at other famous horses of history – from the Trojan horse to Marengo, Napoleon's grey Arab mount in battle.

The region near the chateau was famous for its *attelage* and so he asked DD to buy him as many pieces of bridlery and *cravaches* as possible, feeling satisfied that had made another excellent decision. If Hil had been around, she would have been concerned about how compulsive he was being, and his sudden obsession with a single room. The fact that she was not, was the root cause of this troubling behaviour though, and so Jemme could continue, completely unchecked. DD had noticed the change in him, but was too discreet to express his concern verbally; instead, he tried to steer Jemme towards bank work, and refocus his attention. It was little use – it just meant that Jemme read late into the night once he was at home, rather than doing it at work. For her part, Burbona didn't seem to have noticed any difference. Instead, she was thrilled by the renewed zeal for auctions and sales, and the energy with which Jemme was targeting acquisitions. She never stopped to ask why the project was taking this slightly bizarre turn, she just spread her net of influence further, and telephoned Jemme more frequently with news of various friends who had 'just the piece he was looking for.'

Jemme's drive was unstoppable. He did not allow himself a moment's rest, mentally as well as physically. He refused to admit to himself that he was tired, instead increasing the pace with which he went about his tasks. One afternoon he headed for his favourite Turkish café. Sitting at the table, surrounded by warm Turkish chatter and the spice-laden atmosphere, he felt himself begin to relax, and his mind flooded with the nostalgia of childhood. As soon as he had let his guard down, exhaustion began to creep in too, so he distracted himself straight away by sketching out plans for a new room on the back of one of the paper menus. Wistful thoughts of his grandmother translated themselves into plans for a room that celebrated Sufism and the whirling Dervishes. Likewise, memories of the beautiful coastlines of the Levant suddenly turned into plans to commemorate the most famous sea-faring people of the region's history – the Phoenicians.

By the time he next went to the chateau, he was so filled with ideas that he didn't think he would have a moment's free time to do anything other than work on the chateau for the foreseeable future, which suited him perfectly. He had arranged to drive Burbona down to the chateau for the weekend, and yet again she arrived in his office long before he was ready to go. He looked up from his paperwork slightly wearily, but was soon caught up in her enthusiasm for some recent acquisitions. She put a pile of catalogues directly on top of the spreadsheet he had been working on, and started flipping them open to book-marked pages, showing him recent purchases.

'I didn't check any of them with you, I'm afraid – they were all quite low value and I didn't want to miss out on any of them by waiting.'

'That's fine, I trust you,' said Jemme, too excited by the prospect of new things waiting for him at the chateau to notice some of the guide prices.

'Let's go,' said Burbona decisively, unhooking Jemme's jacket and looking at him expectantly.

Jemme looked down at the partially covered spreadsheet, but he lacked the enthusiasm to do anything with it. He shrugged, 'Why not.'

Burbona led the way to the car, and talked about all the things she was hoping to achieve this weekend. She talked about pieces to be installed, pictures to be hung, and measurements to be taken. Jemme was too pleased by the diversion to notice that she seemed to have been on a bit of a spending spree of late. They reached the car, and Burbona waited expectantly by the passenger seat, until Jemme opened the door for her.

'Roberto will be meeting us down there a little later,' she said matter-of-factly as she got into the car.

'Oh – I, I didn't know Roberto would be joining us again,' said Jemme.

'Well of course,' said Burbona, looking disconcerted momentarily, 'we need him too much for him to miss a weekend. He would have come down with us, but he had a dinner engagement.'

'I…. I see,' said Jemme, wondering how he felt about the news.

Burbona picked up on his hesitation, 'Don't worry,' she said, waving her hand airily, 'I already telephoned your housekeeper and told her we would need an extra room made up.'

'Marguerite?' said Jemme, hoping that Burbona had been a little more tactful than she had been last weekend.

'Oh, is that her name?' said Burbona dismissively, and started telling a story about a drinks party she had been to recently with a gallery director at the Louvre.

'I was telling him about everything we've been working on,' she said, 'He would like to come down and have a tour at some point, so I said I'd set something up.'

The thrill of excitement Jemme felt when he heard the news made him completely forget any misgivings he might have felt about the Roberto news.

He wondered if Burbona's Louvre friend would also think of the project as being like a museum. It would certainly be flattering if he did.

'That would be excellent, Burbona, I would enjoy it very much. The sooner he could visit the better, I'd love to meet him. Could I leave it to you to arrange for whenever he's next free?'

Burbona gave a small shrug, 'Of course. I will call him as soon as I'm back in Paris.'

As the suburbs slipped past them and turned into countryside, Jemme imagined himself talking to the Louvre director about some of his favourite subjects. He hoped he would be impressed with the chateau's emphasis on the immersive and experiential rather than staid and sanitised displays, and he longed to hear what the man thought.

He sat back and relaxed as he listened to Burbona tell little amusing stories from the same drinks party, until they reached the chateau. The nights were becoming shorter, and although the lights weren't yet on to welcome them down the driveway, a beautiful dusk settled over the grounds. Jemme felt a soothing sensation pass over him as they drove down. It was as if he knew that he would stop having to try so hard. At the chateau he would be looked after and effortlessly busy. All the worries which he had been expending so much energy keeping at bay would naturally slip away, in this little world he had created.

He was pleased to see both Marguerite and Philby waiting for him on the steps down from the main entrance. Marguerite waved cheerfully as the car emerged into view.

'*Bienvenu, Monsieur!*' she squealed as soon as he stepped out.

'Well that's quite the welcome, anyone would think I hadn't seen you for weeks,' said Jemme with a smile.

'We are always pleased to see you, Monsieur,' said Marguerite happily. 'Madame,' she added, politely to Burbona who had just stepped out of the car looking slightly irritated that Jemme had forgotten to open the door for her. She nodded in greeting to Marguerite, and flashed a quick smile at Philby.

'My things are on the back seat,' she said.

'Tsk, Monsieur,' said Marguerite, looking at Jemme more closely. 'You are looking so tired!'

'Am I?' said Jemme.

Marguerite gave him the once over and shook her head, 'You are looking much, *much* too tired. I hope you are looking after yourself properly in Paris,' she said with genuine concern.

'I'm fine, Marguerite, honestly,' said Jemme. He could hear the weariness in his own voice, even though he felt better than he had in a whole week.

'Are you eating properly?' Marguerite probed. 'I will send you back with some good food,' she decided before he had had the chance to answer.

'Really, Marguerite,' began Jemme; just then he caught Burbona's eye and saw how impatient she looked.

'Shall we?' she asked, indicating the main entrance.

'We'd better get inside, Marguerite,' smiled Jemme.

'*Mais oui,*' Marguerite answered as if it had been obvious. 'I don't want you getting cold – you feel it even more when you're tired.'

Jemme laughed, 'I'm not tired,' he tried to protest. He turned to give Philby a hand with the luggage, but the gardener waved him away circumspectly.

'It's fine. I have them. You rest.'

Jemme shrugged, wondering if he really was looking as exhausted as everyone was making out. He certainly hadn't expected Philby to comment on it.

'Just leave it in my room,' said Burbona to Philby, indicating the case.

Marguerite's lips pursed slightly, 'Would you like me to show you to *your* room, Madame?' she asked pointedly, emphasising the word.

'No thank you, I know where it is. When will supper be ready?'

'Supper will be ready in about ten minutes,' Marguerite said to Jemme, as if Burbona hadn't asked anything.

'That sounds marvellous,' said Jemme, craving the cosiness of the kitchen, but fully expecting it to be in the formal surroundings of the *salle à manger*. He knew that Burbona would have specifically stated this to Marguerite as one of her requirements when she rang up about the room, and could only imagine how indignant Marguerite must have felt.

As it turned out, Roberto wasn't too far behind them, and was able to join them for the evening meal. However, it felt like a slightly stiff affair. Although Burbona was as easy and engaging as ever, supper had a completely different feel to the meals Jemme usually enjoyed the most in the chateau. Without the Professor acting as a genial foil, Jemme felt almost as if he was at a social engagement back in Paris. Although what Roberto was saying was relatively interesting, he spoke so dispassionately that Jemme found it difficult to concentrate. He kept finding his mind had wandered onto what he was eating, and wondering what Marguerite was going to bring out next. When the Professor had been here, he had felt fired up with enthusiasm; they frequently talked over the top of each other in their haste to express themselves. When Jemme was with the Professor, the niceties of polished high society completely disappeared, which is much how he preferred things. Here, with all the formalities and etiquette, he felt weighed down by an unnecessary sense of occasion.

He felt less and less included in the conversation, and when the meal finally finished he was suddenly tired. For the first time in a while, he longed to be on his own.

'If you don't mind, I think I might turn in for the night,' he said to his two guests. 'I'd like to be up early tomorrow.'

'Of course,' said Roberto politely.

'Yes, there's lots to get through,' said Burbona. 'Let's meet back here for breakfast at about eight o'clock, so we can start at nine.'

'Fine,' said Jemme, almost too tired to be irritated. He didn't usually mind when Burbona acted as if the chateau was her own home; it was far easier than being around a faltering or nervous guest. Having just felt like a guest at a dinner party she had organised though, he was in no mood to indulge her.

'There's nothing so formal as a sit-down breakfast usually, Roberto,' said Jemme. 'Last weekend was a bit of an exception. Usually I just make my way down to the kitchen whenever I get up, and Marguerite sorts me out with something. It's probably easiest if we all do that and then meet afterwards at nine, let's say in the hall?'

Roberto opened his mouth to say something, but Burbona interjected, 'I'm sure Roberto would like something a little more substantial to start the day,' she said smoothly. 'Let's meet at eight and we can discuss the day's work over breakfast. Don't worry about anything – I'll arrange it with the cook and make sure we get something that everyone will enjoy.'

Jemme paused. He realised it would be difficult to say anything without it turning into a scene.

'Very well,' he said, 'I shall see you both at eight. I'm sure Marguerite will make us something delicious.'

'Don't worry, I'll make sure of it,' said Burbona, flashing a smile at him.

Not for the first time, Jemme felt as if she had dismissed him. He said his goodnights and went up to his room. He was annoyed by the way in which the evening had played out. Chateau evenings were precious – a respite he looked forward to throughout the week, and he found himself feeling protective of them. He hadn't really enjoyed himself at supper, and he was irked by the way Burbona had acted. It sometimes felt like such a power struggle with her. Every time he said one thing that he thought would firmly establish himself as in charge of the situation, she would undercut him. She would say something so sweetly, or with such charm, that he didn't necessarily notice at first, which was even more galling; regardless, she would deftly manoeuvre herself back into the position of power, inevitably having the last word in the process. Jemme took a deep breath and exhaled slowly, trying to dispel the irritation that had built up. 'It's just because she's a strong personality,' he said to himself. 'Think how much less you would like her if she wasn't.' Suddenly, and from absolutely nowhere, he found himself thinking about Hil and how considerate of other people's feelings she had always been. Whenever she had been talking to someone – anyone at all – she would make sure that they felt as if they were the most important person in the room. The memory blind-sided Jemme. He hadn't expected it, and it pierced through his mind with a pain that was almost physical. He tried to suppress it as quickly as possible, and ran the last few paces to his room. As soon as he was safely inside with the door shut, he pulled out his notebooks and began furiously planning the *Cheval d'Alep* room, making even longer lists of notable historical horses to include, key display items and decoration ideas. After about half an hour's frantic scribbling and sketching, he could feel himself start to relax a little, and within about another five minutes he had fallen asleep in his chair.

He slept deeply and woke up the next morning in exactly the same position, stiff and unrefreshed. If anything, he felt even more tired than he had the night before. He knew that the only way to counter it was with activity, so he shook himself properly awake and forced himself out of the chair, ignoring his aching limbs and pretending that he couldn't feel his puffy face.

He showered and dressed as briskly as possible. Then, out of habit, he made his way straight down to the kitchen.

'Good morning, Marguerite,' he said with forced jollity.

'Monsieur, what are you doing in here?!' Marguerite said, looking slightly frantic.

'Eh?' said Jemme, stretching a little as he looked around for the coffee pot.

'You are meant to be having your breakfast next door – Madame had very *specific* demands!'

'What, I – oh yes of course, I'd forgotten. Are they there already?' he asked, glancing up at the large round kitchen clock.

'No, you are up early, Monsieur. They will not be taking their seats for another quarter of an hour,' Marguerite said, slightly facetiously.

'Well, I think that gives me enough time for a coffee in here with you,' Jemme said. 'Better make it a large one,' he said, trying to suppress his yawn with a smile.

Marguerite poured him a coffee and brought it over to him at the table. She put it down in front of him and sighed,

'Monsieur, this will not do – you look exhausted, *épuisé*!'

'I'm fine, Marguerite, honestly,' said Jemme, forcing a smile as far across his face as he could. 'At least, I will be when I've had this,' he joked, looking at the coffee.

Marguerite furrowed her brow, '*Heh*, you need some rest,' she looked at him fondly. 'When you come to the country it should be a time for relaxation, not work.'

'It doesn't feel like work to me,' said Jemme.

'It might not *feel* like work, Monsieur, but it will still wear you out in the same way,' she scolded. 'Paris is such a big dirty city, everyone is rushing around so fast and working too hard,' Marguerite continued, warming to her theme, 'when you come here it is different – there is no need to be rushing around all over the place. Have some fresh air, some good food – these are the important things, Monsieur.'

'I know, Marguerite, you're right, thank you. I'll take it easy this weekend, honestly,' he knew her intentions were good and he didn't want to hurt her feelings, but taking it easy was the last thing he felt like doing. In fact, quite the reverse. Whilst last weekend had been productive in many ways and it had been wonderful to spend some time with the Professor, it had lacked a sense of activity and action. He hadn't seen any artists at work, or talked to any craftsmen. It was impossible to feel that the project was moving forward if he couldn't see motion and movement all around him. There should be a good number of artists starting new projects over this weekend, and he was looking forward to meeting them all individually. It felt like a long time since he had learnt anything new about artistic techniques or artisanal skills, and he knew that this was exactly what he needed.

'Well, I should imagine that the others will be there now,' he said quickly draining the rest of his coffee and standing up before Marguerite could raise any further protests.

He made his way into the dining room, just as Burbona and Roberto were arriving. Roberto was as sharply dressed and impeccably groomed as ever, and Burbona was laughing at something he had just said.

'Ah, good morning,' she said happily when she saw Jemme. 'Roberto was just telling me the funniest story,' she added, laying a hand on Roberto's arm.

'Oh really?' said Jemme, trying to sound interested, but finding it very difficult to imagine Roberto being even remotely amusing.

'Go on,' Burbona encouraged.

'I don't know if I could tell it twice,' said Roberto, sounding hesitant.

'Oh, I couldn't ask you to – maybe later on,' said Jemme, relieved. He noticed Roberto was standing stiffly behind his chair,

'Why don't you take a seat, I'm sure Marguerite will be in, in a moment, with everything.'

Roberto politely inclined his head, drew the chair out and sat down, all in a very measured and precise way. Jemme puzzled over him for a moment as he was sitting down – *Doesn't he ever take a moment off?* he thought to himself. It must be so tiring to be so relentlessly formal. Marguerite's words were still ringing in his ears – this place was so different to Paris in every single way. Surely Roberto could sense that, and see that he didn't need to comport himself in such a way. Just then Roberto looked up, and so Jemme quickly flicked his eyes away.

'I trust you slept well,' said Roberto.

'Yes, very well thank you,' Jemme lied.

'Were you comfortable in the room Marguerite made up?'

'Very much so,' said Roberto. Marguerite appeared with the first of the breakfast dishes. It would have been a fitting moment to thank her, but Jemme noticed that like Burbona, Roberto barely seemed to notice that she was there. He moved innately to one side when she was dishing something onto his plate, without even looking up to see her. It was the practiced movement of someone who had been served his entire life.

'Thank you, Marguerite,' said Jemme loudly as she poured him another coffee. The other two had already become locked in conversation, and so his efforts were wasted. He took a sip of coffee as he watched them – today was not going to be another day like last night, so as soon as there was a pause, he interjected,

'I thought we could talk over everything that's planned for today,' he said.

'Burbona was kind enough to go over everything with me last night,' said Roberto.

Jemme felt irritated again. Burbona didn't know everything that he had planned – he had only decided some things over his first coffee. Besides, even if she did, they were *his* plans. He took another sip of coffee and forced himself to exhale slowly and quietly again – his tiredness was making him petty and he didn't want to seem ungracious in front of his guests.

He smiled at Burbona, 'That was helpful of you,' he said with all the good grace he could muster. 'Perhaps it would be useful if we discussed everything together too.'

'Of course,' Burbona smiled, and tossed her hair.

It was just as well they did discuss everything, as it turned out their plans for the day were wildly different. Jemme's consisted of him meeting each artist and discussing their briefs. He wanted to make sure they understood what he needed, and also get to know them a little bit more; they were working in his home after all. Any time not spent with artists would be spent planning the next rooms. Burbona would be on hand to give her opinions and get a good feel for the context of her acquisitions when she was back in Paris. He wasn't quite sure where Roberto fitted in to everything; in fact, he wasn't quite sure why Roberto was there at all, but he imagined that he would tag along and perhaps contribute if a structural issue arose.

For her part, Burbona seemed to see the day as a tour of the chateau, led by her, in which she pointed out to Roberto various rooms and features she would like him to work on. She didn't even mention meeting any of the artists; in fact, she seemed to see them as something of an inconvenience, as if they might be cluttering up the place whilst she was conducting her grand tour.

Jemme didn't really know how to respond, or how to reconcile their different ideas.

'I think it's important we don't get ahead of ourselves,' he said as diplomatically as possible. It seemed Burbona had very big plans for Roberto, and he wanted to discuss this in private with her, or at least have some time to think about it before they started talking about his future role with Roberto himself.

'There's no harm in planning a little, though,' said Burbona assuredly. 'It's good that we already have the first thing lined up for Roberto, but we should plan the next project before he's actually finished the mihrab.'

'The mihrab?' said Jemme in surprise.

'Yes, for the Andalusian room,' said Burbona.

'I know where it's going to be, I just –' Jemme began. The mihrab had become a bit of a special project for him, and he hadn't even considered Roberto for its execution – he didn't even know what the man was like with his hands.

Burbona mistook his hesitation for forgetfulness, 'We were all talking about it last weekend,' she prompted, 'when your English friend was here. He is doing some research at the moment, then he'll give Roberto the final designs.'

'Well, that's not exactly how....' Jemme trailed off. He didn't really know what to say. He decided that now was not the time though. By the time the Professor had finished his research, he would have had the chance to straighten things out with Burbona.

He smiled at Roberto, 'Your input will be very welcome,' he said.

Breakfast was approached in much the same manner as dinner had been the night before. Jemme was used to grabbing something quickly in the kitchen, and getting started with the day, but the others were treating this as an important a dining occasion, like any other. No manners or fastidiousness were spared, meaning that it took the three of them about five times as long as it took just Jemme on his own. By the time they had finally finished, he was itching to get on and start work. He led them to the room he had decided would serve for the *Cheval d'Alep*. On the way there, Burbona told Roberto about everything she had bought for the room already, and everything she was planning on buying from upcoming sales. He made impressed noises.

'You are so fortunate to have someone as accomplished as Burbona working on your behalf in the bidding room,' he told Jemme.

'Yes, I know, I am,' said Jemme, smiling at Burbona in genuine appreciation. She looked as if she was ready to purr.

'It is a long time since I was last in an auction;' said Roberto, 'it is not something I enjoy.'

'Oh really?' said Jemme, 'I have to say I love it. I wish I had more time to attend. Like you said though, Burbona is a worthy substitute when I can't. Do you not enjoy the bidding, or have you just never found an auction of pieces you're interested in?'

'Oh, it is not that, Monsieur. I love antiques. I spend a great deal of time in antique shops and that is very pleasurable indeed. It is the atmosphere in the auction house I cannot stand. It is so cut-throat – there is far too much adrenaline for me. I can't stand the tension in the big sales, and when it all reaches a crescendo towards the end of bidding, the people are so hungry – they're like animals!' he almost shuddered.

'Fair enough,' Jemme laughed, thinking to himself that that exact energy was what he enjoyed most about an auction. Roberto was much too sensitive a soul, he decided.

They reached the room destined to be the *Musée du Cheval d'Alep* and Jemme was pleased to find that the artist he had engaged was waiting for him. She introduced herself, and he introduced her to Burbona and Roberto, who were polite but disinterested. The artist herself seemed excited about the project though, which was all Jemme really cared about anyway. She liked the idea of painting directly onto the walls, and had already begun marking off different sections with masking tape. They discussed the four different thoroughbreds for a while, and Jemme gave her some notes and photocopies. She had already done a fair amount of research herself, and by the time they wished her a goodbye and left her to her devices, he felt confident that they shared the same vision of the finished room.

As they made their way to the next room, he barely heard Roberto's polite stream of questions. He was mentally running through the list of famous horses from history he had devised, and wondering if he could include more. He started to think about other noteworthy horses and equestrian organisations. There was the Swiss Polo School, the Haras du Pin, the Spanish School in Vienna, the Nevzerov Haute École of Russia and that was without even thinking that hard. If the artist did a good job of the thoroughbreds, he would ask her to stay on and complete some more paintings.

He tuned in to hear Roberto asking about his acquisitions.

'I'm sorry, would you mind saying that again?' he asked Roberto.

'I was curious about how you acquired most of your pieces,' said Roberto. 'Would you say the majority came from auctions?'

Jemme paused for a moment and thought, 'It's a bit of a mix really,' he said, 'and that's where having someone like Burbona is such an asset. She's very good at finding interesting pieces coming up for auctions. To be honest, sometimes she seems to find them so ahead of time that I could swear she knows something is for sale before the auctioneer himself does,' He smiled at Burbona who flashed him a smile in return and tossed her silky hair.

'The collection isn't all auction driven though,' Jemme continued, 'we get many pieces from sales. Sometimes an old chateau has fallen out of family ownership and various pieces are being sold off.' Roberto nodded with interest, but looked pained.

'It is always a great pity when an old family loses their ancestral seat,' he said sombrely.

'Yes, I suppose it is, although I have to say that I have benefited tremendously from such a set of circumstances in the past.'

Roberto looked conflicted,

'Of course, it's not all from family homes,' said Jemme. 'Sometimes we've bought directly from museums.'

'Museums, Monsieur?' asked Roberto, sounding pained.

'Yes, museums and art galleries, you know.'

Roberto made a small sound in his throat, 'And is this common?' he asked, sounding horrified by the idea that the nation's treasures might be being sold off outside his control.

'Reasonably common;' said Jemme, ignoring the tremulous look in his face, 'sometimes museums want to raise some cash quickly for a restoration project, or sometimes it's just for a new acquisition. They'll sell off a piece which might have been in storage for years, or fallen out of fashion, or just have become irrelevant to their collection. It's really no big deal, it happens all the time.'

Roberto didn't look convinced. In fact, he looked extremely uncomfortable with the idea. Jemme was starting to get irritated with him. He had encountered this attitude amongst the old aristocracy before; it was as if they alone could be the custodians of France's past, and they became extremely nervous when anyone else took on any form of guardianship. Jemme was pleased that Burbona hadn't shared this attitude. He probably wouldn't have been able to work with her if she had; he certainly wouldn't have liked her. Thankfully, just as he was struggling to think of something to say to Roberto that wouldn't be confrontational, Burbona herself came the rescue.

'Absolutely, Roberto, it's a fabulous resource for any collector, and it happens all the time,' she said breezily. Roberto looked slightly relieved. 'Anyway that reminds me,' she said, turning to Jemme. 'I've acquired a beautiful piece for the room by that very method.'

'For the *Cheval d'Alep*?' asked Jemme, his irritation forgotten.

'Yes, just last week actually. It was from a small museum in the 9th Arrondissement. To be honest, I'd never even heard of it until I heard that they were selling off a few of their pieces.'

'Well don't tease me, what it is it?!' Jemme asked, starting to feel like he was salivating.

Burnona laughed then gave him a coy smile, 'I would never deliberately tease you,' she said. 'The piece is a small bronze sculpture of Charles Martel in battle. The horse has been beautifully rendered, and it's very obvious from its features that it's a thoroughbred.'

'Wonderful!' enthused Jemme. 'How big would you say it was?'

Burbona was far too refined to gesture with her hands, 'I will send you all the specifications,' she said instead. 'It is not big enough to be a main feature of the room, more of a side installation.'

Jemme, sighed, satisfied, 'Charles Martel,' he repeated out loud. 'He's a historical figure I'd like to know a great deal more about.'

Roberto blanched, 'But he is an incredibly important figure in French history, Monsieur. Every schoolchild knows of him.'

'Yes, I'm aware of his importance,' said Jemme, his satisfaction giving way to his irritation again, 'I was just saying I'd like to know a little bit more about him, that's all.'

Burbona leapt in to smooth things over, and within a few moments they were all laughing at an anecdote she had just recounted. However, when he found himself alone later that evening, he thought back over his interactions with Roberto that day. It would be too strong to say that he disliked the man, but he certainly hadn't warmed to him. It was difficult to get any sort of handle on him; in fact, on the whole, he felt that Roberto was just a little too polished. He paid too much attention to his dress, his manners, his position in society, at the cost of having any sort of personality. If he had betrayed some flaws, no matter how slight, Jemme would have found him a much more genuine individual and would have enjoyed spending time with him a great deal more. He had no idea what Roberto thought of him, but if his reactions during the day were anything to go by, they seemed to suggest he thought he was some kind of cultural thug, intent on destroying the old order, and undermining France's decorous past.

The rest of the day was spent looking at new rooms and meeting artists. Jemme was able to put his coolness towards Roberto to one side as he discussed different techniques with the craftsmen, and listened, fascinated, to their descriptions of different tools and what they did. He felt energised and refreshed by the time they went for dinner, although his energy began to dissipate slightly as Roberto launched into a very lengthy tale about a skyscraper he had designed. Jemme wished he had had an ally around the dinner table. He would have loved to catch someone's eye and make an exasperated face. Instead, however, Burbona hung on Roberto's every word, telling him how clever he was to make the decisions he had, and asking him detailed questions about what seemed to be the most boring parts of the story.

Jemme was glad when they finally finished dinner and he could excuse himself. He left them discussing another of Roberto's clever decisions, and made his way to the library. Several years ago the Professor had sent him a bundle of books; at the time he must have been more interested in their bindings than their contents as he had put them straight onto the shelves. He remembered a discussion with the Professor about Frankish history when he had sent them though, and he wondered if the books were on the subject. He opened the large doors to the library and slipped inside. Once the lights were on and the room's splendour revealed, he felt a warm happiness slip over him. It was an astonishingly satisfying feeling to know that he had created this room from nothing, and to know also that there wasn't a single thing he would change about it. It was exactly as he wanted it and exactly as he enjoyed it. Full of memories and personal touches, it also fitted perfectly with the chateau's age and status. Everything felt as if it had been waiting for him, and he happily made his way to the bookcase he had remembered filling with the Professor's shipment. He recognised the books straight away, and, as he gently removed them from the shelves, he paused for a moment to take in the quality of the bindings again.

He settled down in his chair, and carefully opened the first. It showed a map of the Carolingian Empire on the title page, and the contents page listed chapters on the rule of Pepin the Short and the Treaty of Verdun. He thought for a moment, and realised that these events were all a little too late. Closing the fragile book as gently as possible, he turned to the next. This was evidently by the same author, as the title page featured another map, set with the same typeface. It showed the Merovingian Empire and the contents page described chapters on Clovis I and Brunhilda. It was an era Jemme knew little about, but the briefest of investigations revealed it to be too early. He momentarily became sidetracked as he read about Dagobert I, King of Neustria, Burgundy and all the Franks. He was the first Frankish king to be buried in the basilica of St Denis and united several kingdoms under his rule, to become the most respected sovereign in the West. One of the things that fascinated Jemme the most was a description of his throne. Cast in bronze, the base was formed by a *curule* seat, just as those used in the Roman Republic. The arms and the back had been added later by Charles the Bald. The throne in its entirety was then used by French leaders and rulers, even until the time of Napoleon, who was seated in it when he created the Légion d'Honneur. Rather than the seat's illustrious provenance, it was its shape that intrigued Jemme. It was just like those he remembered from childhood, which he had always assumed were traditional Turkish seats. The more he thought about it, the more he thought he could remember them being referred to as *Dagobert* seats. It was a fascinating example of different cultural influences, stretching back as far as the Roman period.

He rallied himself and tried to focus. Reluctantly closing the second book he turned to the last one, hoping that this would contain something on Charles Martel. As soon as he opened the first page and saw the map of the Frankish kingdom, he knew that he had struck lucky. Scanning through the contents page, he made his way right to the back of the book, and settled down to read about Charles Martel. As he read through the chapter, several facts and dates came back to him and he realised he knew a great deal more than he had initially thought.

One thing he had not known anything about though, was the battle of Tours-Poitiers. He read, fascinated, about this epic clash between Charles Martel's army and Arabic troops, and wondered at the decisiveness of the battle. He couldn't believe that he hadn't come into contact with the event before; it pulled on so many threads that fascinated him, and tied them all together. The experienced

Arab forces were led northwards by one of their most skilled and most renowned commanders, Abdul Rahman Al Ghafiqi. The previous Emir of Cordoba had attempted to drive his troops into Northern Europe, sweeping up territory as he went. However, he had been stopped at Toulouse by Odo the Great, Duke of Aquitaine. As the new Emir, Abdul Rahman al Ghafiqi had rallied his troops, and focussed his attention northwards again, pushing upwards in an attempt to conquer everything north of the Pyrenees. Combined with the force of Berber horsemen, he advanced towards Tours. He appeared to have every advantage – experience, power and timing. However, he had reckoned without the tactics of Charles Martel. Instead of attacking the riders, his troops attacked the horses, with devastating effect. Horses fell, shedding riders into the paths of oncoming cavalry. Those who struggled to their feet were ill equipped for battle on the ground, with the wrong armour and weaponry.

Jemme had always enjoyed military history, and this was a particularly fine example of a tactical victory. It was after this battle that Charles earned his epithet of 'hammer' or *martel,* and the more he read on the battle, the more he wondered at how different the development of European history could have been. If it had not have been for Charles' merciless hammering of his enemies, the Umayyad forces would have expanded their territories throughout western and northern Europe, perhaps even reaching as far as Great Britain. The book he was reading was rather old, and the language of the author full of heroic dash and derring-do. Jemme realised that he should probably read some more modern interpretations once he was back in Paris for some balance, but it was difficult not to get swept up in the author's enthusiasm and see the event as a defining clash between Eastern and Western forces. Regardless, he was delighted that the battle was going to be referenced in the *Cheval d'Alep* room. It was a fine way to commemorate a heroic figure of French history, as well as pointing to the importance of horses in battle.

He closed the book, and gently returned all three of them to the shelf again. *The Professor will be pleased to hear I've actually read them,* he thought to himself, and wondered what the Professor's insight into the battle would be. He stretched out behind the desk and pondered what to do with himself. He wasn't tired enough for bed yet, and he wanted to keep himself occupied until he was pretty much ready to fall asleep. Much as he loved the library, it wasn't a particularly comfortable room, and he longed to relax somewhere a little cosier. Normally he would have gone to the kitchen, but he didn't want to risk running into Burbona and Roberto, and getting caught up in yet another skyscraper story. The gallery rooms weren't really good places to go and sit, neither were the formal reception rooms. He wanted somewhere full of warm lighting and soft cushions – a little like the majlis of his childhood. He wondered what the nearest equivalent would be, and realised that there wasn't one. If he wanted a majlis, then he was going to have to build a majlis. With all thoughts of relaxation gone, he pulled a sheet of paper and a pencil from one of the desk's drawers and began planning a new room. He worked until tiredness finally set in and he was only able to drag himself to bed, knowing that he would fall into a deep and dreamless sleep.

The rest of the weekend passed in a similar manner. Jemme's energy and enthusiasm was raised when he began to talk with new artists, and then tempered when he found himself alone with Burbona and Roberto. Whenever he found himself on his own, he would plan new rooms with fervour and not stop until he was on the verge of falling asleep. In this way he was able to avoid facing his thoughts, and to ensure that there was no space for memories, however faded, to surface.

By the time he finally returned to Paris his exhaustion was compounded, yet a nervous energy coursed through him; he relied on it to get him through the day, yet he cursed it at night. He worked longer and later into the night every evening, waiting until sleep would finally take hold. At one point he caught sight of himself in the mirror in the corridor. He was paler than he had ever been, and his cheeks had taken on an unhealthy, hollowed look. He shuddered to himself, and resolved to take the mirror down and replace it with a painting.

His hard work was being rewarded by progress at the chateau though, and by the next weekend the progress felt as if it was equivalent to three weeks' work. He was mildly irritated to find that Roberto was joining them again, and outright annoyed to find that Burbona had commissioned him to work on a few pieces without even consulting Jemme. There was also a great deal more talk about Roberto working on the mihrab, which Jemme wasn't especially enthusiastic about. However, a trip to the *Musée du Cheval d'Alep* soon helped him forget his misgivings. With the paintings on the walls completed, the museum had begun to come to life. Better still, Burbona's statue had arrived and been installed. It was even better than he had imagined, and the perfect fit for the room. As soon as anyone walked in they would be able to tell exactly what the room was dedicated to, even at this early stage. The artist herself wasn't there, so he couldn't thank her in person, but he made a note to get in touch and see if she was free to work on further murals in the room.

He was delighted to discover that the room he had started to design last week had progressed so much as well. He had given DD a list of everything he needed for the room, and he must have organised it all during the week – it was already beginning to take shape. In fact, it didn't look how he had imagined at all. Instead of the homely yet smart majlis of the Levant, he appeared to have recreated what looked like the interior of a Bedouin tent. The carpets had been laid on top of each other on the floor, with a low cushion running around the edge of the room. The colours and patterns of the carpet were also redolent of the Maghreb, and it reminded Jemme of his travels in the region. Although it hadn't been what he had imagined, it actually still created exactly the atmosphere he had wanted. In fact, it anything it was even cosier and more comfortable than he had imagined. He pictured it filled with interesting books and highly decorated, and was pleased to think that it would be a little sanctuary for him.

He sat down and tested the cushion. It was very soft and comfortable, although not quite right. He wriggled around a little and realised what was missing. He would have to recreate some sort of *moukhada* or backrest. He remembered this from his childhood home – it would be some sort of Levantine/Maghrebi seating fusion. He was confident that if he sketched it out, either Marguerite would be able to create it herself or find someone locally who could. He looked at the walls; they were a stark white and not at all conducive to the cosiness of the room. He wondered what sort of decoration would be the most fitting and suddenly remembered a trip to the royal palace of Morocco. It was a deeply buried memory, but the colours of the carpets must have freed it and allowed it to float to the forefront of his mind. He could suddenly picture the beautiful *lambris* of the palace. The image was as clear in his mind as if he had only seen it yesterday. He recalled the brilliant colours that picked out a pattern of foliage, and the glaze which added a further layer of texture to the faience. He wondered if he would be able to recreate such a thing – the hot-fired clays of North Africa might not fare too well in the damp of Northern France. He stared at the wall and tried to imagine how it would look. It didn't take him long to arrive at the solution: he would recreate the patterns and the imagery, but he would do so in pietra dura. It would be far more durable, and also add another level of cultural influence. Satisfied, he looked around himself, picturing other innovations. He paused as he looked at the ceiling; he wasn't quite sure how he could finish it so that it would be in keeping with the room. He looked down at the carpets again, and thought just how much they reminded him of the floor of a nomadic tent. *A tented ceiling!* he suddenly thought to himself. It would be an excellent way of completing the room, and would give it exactly the feeling of escapism he had been hoping for.

He left the room and went to join the others. In a strange way, he was pleased that Burbona hadn't been helping him with this particular room. It made the whole thing much more of a private project, which was exactly what he wanted. He found Burbona and Roberto back in the Andalusian room, looking up at the ceiling.

'*Bonjour*,' said Roberto politely, when he heard Jemme come in.

'Hello, sorry to leave you two, I was just having a quick look at some of the other rooms.'

'Not at all, we have just been looking at a couple of the other rooms as well. Burbona was explaining some of the structural problems which you are likely to encounter in the next phase of the project. I was attempting to offer any insight which experience has brought.'

'Right,' said Jemme.

'It was wonderful insight;' gushed Burbona, 'we are very lucky to be able to draw on it.'

'You are too kind,' said Roberto. 'Working on a modern skyscraper and an old chateau are of course very different,' he pointed out – rather needlessly, Jemme thought. 'Of course,' he continued, 'there are also many similarities.' He launched into a detailed comparison of different building techniques, which seemed to have very little in common with each other and bored Jemme rigid. He struggled to pay attention, and instead looked around the room as subtly as possible. Now that everything had been installed, it was very nearly finished and he couldn't have been more pleased with how it had turned out. The Professor had sent over some further sketches, and the design for the mihrab was complete. All he needed to do was find the right person to work on it, and the room would be finished.

He suddenly realised that Roberto had stopped talking and was looking at him expectantly. He hadn't a clue what the architect had just asked him, but would hazard a guess that it had something to do with skyscrapers and Roberto's own role in their construction.

'Oh yes, very impressive indeed,' he said, nodding. It seemed to have been just what Roberto had been looking for, as he ploughed onwards with his story. Jemme drifted off again and began to imagine what else he could include in the majlis room. He thought of a couple of busts he had recently acquired at auction – they were dressed in traditional North African costume and had been completed by Orientalist sculptors. They would be perfect for the room, and he was confident that he could acquire some similar pieces to go with them. He pictured the bookcases he was planning on installing, and wondered what he could fill them with. There was a small collection of manuscripts in storage back in Paris, which he hadn't thought about in years. They were scientific and Qur'anic, and as well as being interesting examples about the transfer of knowledge, they also contained wonderful miniatures and pieces of manuscript art. It was terrible to think of them languishing in storage; this would be a good opportunity to display them, but also to focus on building the collection again. Miniatures and illuminated texts were underrepresented in his general manuscript collection, and it was something he had been meaning to address for a while. The Persian miniature tradition in particular was something that deserved a great deal more attention in the chateau project. Together with influences from China, it had shaped the art and book culture of the Ottoman Empire. He thought of the beautiful marbled paper, or *ebru* he recalled being produced in the workshops near to his father's business, and remembered the skills of bookbinding and calligraphy – *cilt* and *hat* – being just as important as *tezhip* – illumination. This room would honour this rich heritage; through the newly bolstered collection he would also be able to reference the *Nakkashane* – the special studios the artists worked in. He was delighted with this new direction and had just decided to call this new room the Manuscripts and Miniatures museum when he realised that Roberto had stopped talking again, only this time both Roberto and Burbona were looking expectantly at him.

He paused, struggling to remember anything he had heard them talking about. For a moment, he thought about telling Roberto how impressive he was again, but he realised it would be much more difficult to fob off Burbona.

'I'm sorry, could you repeat that?' he said eventually.

'Roberto was just saying that with his skills and experience so far, he really is the only person you should consider to work on the mihrab for this room,' said Burbona. 'I wholeheartedly agree. We're lucky that he's even offered – to have an architect of his prowess work on such a small project for us is an honour indeed,' she paused to smile in a syrupy way at Roberto. 'However,' she continued, looking directly at Jemme, 'I know this project is very close to your heart, so I wanted to make sure you were happy before we asked Roberto if he would be able to work on it for us.'

'I, um,' Jemme began. He was annoyed – Burbona had put him in an awkward position – he suspected on purpose. She had already asked him in private if Roberto could work on the project, and because he had been non-committal she was asking him in front of Roberto.

'Oh, I'm sorry – would you like someone else to work on the project?' she asked innocently. 'I didn't realise you had been talking with other people.'

Jemme tried to smile, 'No, no I haven't,' he was forced to admit. He took a small breath. 'Roberto, would you consider the task?' he said, irritated that he had to frame it as a favour.

'Monsieur, I would be honoured,' said Roberto graciously, 'I know that this project is close to your heart, so I will treat it with the utmost care and dedication.'

Jemme forced a smile again, 'I'm sure you will, thank you.'

'Well,' said Burbona brightly, 'I'm glad that's all sorted. Shall we continue with our tour?'

Jemme seethed for the rest of the day. Even the sight of some newly completed work wasn't enough to distract him from the feeling of having been manipulated. As soon as supper was over, he retired to the soon-to-be Manuscripts and Miniatures room. It was proving itself a refuge already.

Chapter Forty-Two

Nestled in the cushions of the Manuscripts and Miniatures Room, Jemme suddenly began to find his mind wandering. He hadn't taken anything to read, and he was soon staring at the space around him, searching for distraction, desperate to keep thoughts of Hil and his loss at bay. He didn't have to search for too long. His eyes soon lit on a space perfect for a bookcase. He imagined the shelves he would commission – light walnut with mother-of-pearl and ivory inlays. They could house the precious manuscripts on shelves at the bottom, with space at the top available for displaying open books. He was pleased with the idea, and soon his mind started wandering back to thoughts of the workshops producing their beautiful marbled papers, the bookbinders with their special tools and pots of natural paste, and, of course, the calligraphers.

He had long been fascinated by calligraphy: the skill and patience it required and the elegance of its long swooping minims. In its most complex form, letters could wrap themselves around each other, interlocking and twisting around, until they had hidden the sacred or religious message they expressed, and the viewer could understand nothing more than a beautiful piece of art. It had been an important foundation of applied, expressive and decorative art in the Levant, and he thought it deserved recognition and reference in the chateau too. What's more, he thought he knew the perfect site for it. The side entrance to the chateau led straight onto a landing with a small staircase leading to the corridor, which eventually ran to his office and a larger spiral staircase descending to the sous-sol. It meant that the ceiling was unusually high, and much larger then the small landing it covered. The broad, curved coving was like an opening book, inviting lines of calligraphy to flow across it. It was positioned perfectly as well; an expression of high art, learning and book culture to greet the visitor.

He wondered if he would be able to find anyone in France for the job. He was sure that there were plenty of capable calligraphers and illustrators, but he was not sure that he would find someone with the deep understanding of the Arabic language that only comes from growing up surrounded by its complex curves. He decided to enquire at the University of Damascus; historically it had been associated with the production of the world's finest calligraphy, and now it was associated with its study and conservation. He was confident he would be able to find someone he could consult with closely on both the text and script which should be used, and he hoped they would be able to start working on it straight away.

A small wave of relief rippled through him after he had made the decision, almost as if it had been something that had been bothering him for a long time, and suddenly and without warning, he fell asleep. He woke up a couple of hours later, still sitting upright on the soft cushions. The seat was so comfortable that he didn't feel stiff or sore, and he mistook this for feeling rested and so began to plan the next room and run through all the practicalities of the projects, mentally running through the artists he would need, the equipment they would need and how many rooms could be decorated concurrently. His mind fizzed with ideological and logistical problems, making him feel awake and recharged. It was a strange kind of vigour though, a sham veneer that tricked him into feeling as if everything was fine and masked a deeper exhaustion and malaise. This thin, ersatz energy soon ran dry, and he was irritated to find that he woke up a couple of hours later, having fallen asleep again. Disorientated, and with no sense of the time or how long he had slept for, he forced himself to get up from this cosy, protective room and make his way through the dark and silent house to his own bedroom.

Back in Paris he wasted no time in finding a calligrapher. For once the Professor didn't seem to have any contacts, and, rather than rely on DD to telephone, he decided he might as well do it himself.

He found a number for the most relevant sounding department and called them up, introducing himself, explaining a little about the project and describing exactly what he was looking for. As he had suspected, it was exactly the right institution. The person he spoke to was helpful, interested and eager to hear more. He soon recommended a professor who would be able to give advice on the commission and complete it. He wasn't in the department that day as he was conducting some restoration work elsewhere – which Jemme took to be a very good sign, but the person Jemme spoke to took his details and assured him that he would get the professor to call him the next morning.

He was true to his word, and the next morning Jemme had only just finished his morning briefing with DD when the phone rang.

'Good morning, could I speak with Mr Mafeze?' said someone in heavily accented French. The accent sounded familiar – it wasn't quite Turkish, but it sounded a lot like those he had heard in his youth, in towns towards the border with Syria.

'Speaking,' he replied in French.

The voice on the end of the phone began a faltering introduction.

'I don't mean to interrupt,' began Jemme, trying to put him out of his misery, 'but do you speak Turkish,'

There was a pause; the man had obviously recognised the word 'Turkish.'

'*Türk?*' he asked hopefully.

'*Evet,*' Jemme replied trying to sound as encouraging as possible.

The man's voice relaxed and he unleashed a string of Turkish, still heavily accented, but this time fluent and unhesitating. He introduced himself as Professor Char Mathoranic of the University of Damascus.

'What a relief!' he said. 'My colleague passed on your details and asked me to call you, but it was a French telephone number – I've never really spoken French, and I was worried that if I couldn't introduce myself properly then I wouldn't be able to discuss this idea with you.'

'It's always difficult in another language,' said Jemme, 'I certainly found that when I first moved to Paris.'

'You, yourself are not French. You sound like a Pacha,' said Prof. Mathoranic. 'I was intrigued when I saw your name.'

Jemme laughed, 'No, I'm not French, although I have lived here for a long time now. I grew up in Istanbul.'

'Ah, the Pearl of the Levant;' the professor sighed wistfully, 'it is a city close to my heart. My sister has lived there for some twenty years and my eldest daughter has recently moved there too.'

They discussed the city for a while, and Jemme felt the prick of nostalgia even more keenly as he heard precious memories being described in his own tongue. Eventually conversation moved towards the project and the chateau in general.

'It sounds most interesting,' said Professor Mathoranic, 'I would be very keen to become involved, even if it was just offering you general advice about the Levantine elements – although it sounds like you're pretty well covered on that front!'

They arranged for Professor Mathoranic to fly to the chateau at the first possible opportunity. Jemme was disappointed that it couldn't be that weekend, but he was delighted that the professor would be there the weekend after that.

He returned to his work for the day, but the nostalgia the professor had stirred in him was distracting. He kept finding himself daydreaming of Turkey, and of the colour and smells of his childhood. He yearned for the constancy yet excitement he remembered; life was filled with fresh, exciting new discoveries, but all of it was underpinned by the surety of Grandmother's steadfast presence. It was not the first time that he had experienced such a sensation. The last time it had occurred, he had found himself half-planning rooms themed around Turkey, and wistfully trying to recreate the essence of all that he loved about the country and its culture. Now that he was experiencing the same sensation again, he found himself returning to the same rooms, wondering how he had managed to become so distracted. His banking work forgotten for the morning, he began to plan with fervour. He thought of Grandmother and how he had always felt so calm and confident in her presence, emotions he knew were transferred directly from her. He thought of sitting quietly in the corner, watching her Sufi friends gathering in their magnificent robes before transcending into an ecstatic state, both mystical for those experiencing it and mystifying for those watching it. It was a special and sacred event, but there was also an element of theatre to it. Although not as intense as participating in it, watching it was an experience in itself.

He sketched idly on a piece of paper, wondering how he could recreate the same sensation he had felt as a child. The experience was so dynamic – the sound of the instruments, the movement of the dervishes, the swirl of their clothes. He didn't know how he could recreate the thrill of movement in an empty room. As he continued scribbling and erasing, snapshot memories of childhood floated free from his subconscious – the tang of salt on his tongue after a bowlful of olives, the sparkle of the Bosphorous under the afternoon sun, and the stickiness of his fingers after a large square of Turkish delight. They had all been forgotten for years, irrelevant to his current life and his future. By denying himself grief over the loss of the future he had planned, it was as if he had instead started to mourn the childhood he had long lost. He didn't stop to question this though, nor did he consider it strange that he should suddenly remember how the orange groves near his school smelled. Rather, he did the only thing he knew how; translating these emotions and memories into plans for new rooms. As he sketched and scribbled, he shielded himself from anything uncomfortable or unpleasant. All he could think about – all he would let himself think about – was the chateau.

✣ ✣ ✣ ✣

As the week progressed, his plans for the weekend became more and more ambitious. Burbona came to see him several times, and by the middle of the week, he had already accepted Roberto's presence that weekend as an inevitability. There was a great deal of work already under way at the chateau, and he was looking forward to reviewing it by the time of his visit. The tented ceiling would be finished by then, and the bookcases would be near completion. He had already commissioned several smaller projects, and was looking forward to meeting with the artists before they started on Saturday. Burbona had bought a couple of small paintings at auction; they had already been delivered to the chateau and he was planning on viewing them before discussing hanging. They were quite expensive and he was a little bit uncomfortable with the thought of having spent that much blindly, but he trusted her and was keen not to let anything slow the momentum.

He spent his days going through the motions with his banking work, but he found it difficult to muster any enthusiasm for it. He kept daydreaming of childhood and Turkey. He would work on planning new rooms late into the night, until exhaustion took over and forced him to sleep. His sleep was either deep and oblivious or filled with fractured dreams, confusing in their imagery and unsatisfying in their conclusions. There was certainly nothing as rich or vivid as the childhood dream that had shaped his life.

By Friday he had designed a room he was calling *The Theatre of the Whirling Dervishes*. It was to feature a continuous mural, covering all four walls, which would depict the dervishes in full flow, watched by onlookers and their accompanying musicians. The viewer could stand in the middle of the room, and, as they turned, the room would afford them a panoramic view of the scene; it would be as if they were looking in on it, yet at the same time feel that they were at the centre of it. He was considering hanging real instruments from the walls too, adding texture, and connecting the painted scene to those he had experienced. He had already found an artist who could start work immediately, and was planning on meeting her on Saturday as well.

Amidst this most recent swirl of nostalgia, he had also found himself revisiting plans for a Phoenician room. It was something he had considered before, but he had never completed the plans, and they had been half-forgotten. Now he had returned to them, he wondered how he could ever have abandoned such an idea. The civilisation and the period were crucial to the narrative he was trying to create, and the area he was elegising. He had soon discovered that the task was much greater than he had first realised and would require a great deal of research. Initially he was disappointed that he wouldn't be able to start work on the room straight away, but now he was relishing getting his teeth into a more academic, research-heavy project. He was planning on calling on Professor Johnston's expertise, and was hoping to consult Professor Mathoranic when he came to the chateau too. For now, he found himself reading late into the night and occasionally at lunchtime too, gradually developing a more detailed picture of this sea-faring people, and the room he was going to design to honour them.

On Friday evening he drove Burbona down to the chateau, in what was starting to become their regular routine, except that this time Roberto also joined them. Burbona sat in the passenger seat, so that she could command the attention of both Jemme and Roberto, Jemme assumed. For most of the journey, she and Roberto exchanged stories of recent society events they had attended, which Jemme found exceedingly dull. Occasionally Burbona would break off to promise to introduce Jemme to a certain person, or emphasise the interest of another person in the project, but on the whole, Jemme was disinterested in the whole conversation. When Roberto began talking about a recent convention he had attended on modern innovations in skyscraper construction, what little interest he had had evaporated completely. He spent the rest of the journey thinking about the Phoenician room, his new special project, and trying to forget the fact that Roberto had muscled in on his other special project – the mihrab. It was a relief when they finally pulled into the chateau, and he realised he wouldn't have to feign interest in any of Roberto's exclamations on 'clean lines' and 'glass spaces.'

His relief, however, was short-lived when her discovered that this was to be the principle topic of conversation over dinner too. Roberto was obviously invigorated by this conference and talked at length about the modern approach to building, denouncing decoration and advocating emptiness of space, neutrality of furnishings and modernity of materials. It was everything that Jemme hated and was trying to move away from in the chateau. Roberto was talking as if glass, concrete and steel were the only materials which could ever be considered when undertaking any building project, regardless of context. It reminded Jemme of the museums and galleries he despised, which stripped objects of a *milieu* and thus eroded part of their meaning and relevance. After listening to Burbona gush over Roberto as if he was some revolutionary thinker, he was irked into saying something.

'Don't you think you're creating a very sterile environment?' he asked.

Roberto looked up, apparently surprised to be challenged.

'Not at all, Monsieur, I am doing the opposite of that – I am creating a free environment. With glass structures I do not create a building, I enclose a space. It does not force structure on people, it liberates them.'

'But it's so....' Jemme struggled to think of a word that would not be offensive and in the end gave up, 'uninspiring,' he concluded.

'Not at all, Monsieur,' repeated Roberto, as politely as ever. 'A glass space, filled with light is the most inspirational, free place a person can be. In fussy old buildings, which are over-decorated and filled with paintings and pieces of furniture, there is no space for individual thought; a person is forced to experience the same as the creator. He is coerced into feeling and reacting in the same way as the decorator, even if he does not know it. In an empty space, every person is able to experience something different, to see the space in a different way and observe its shadows and light in a different way. It is the modern way and the future, Monsieur. Soon people will understand that the relics of our past are what hold us and society back.'

'Bravo,' said Burbona, looking admiringly at Roberto after his little speech.

Jemme felt deeply irritated. Firstly, he resented the fact that Roberto seemed so quick to criticise the chateau, yet he was ready to praise it when he thought he could profit from it. Secondly, Jemme marvelled at the man's hypocrisy. He criticised an old regime and way of thinking that was tying France to its past, when really he was a product of that old world, and would be lost without it. In fact, Jemme had never met anyone who was so invested in the old way of thinking, acting and socialising. However, the thing which aggravated Jemme the most was the fact that this was a topic Roberto clearly felt strongly about, and yet the man delivered his opinions in exactly the same dispassionate, measured way he used when discussing something as mundane as the fish which had been served for supper. Jemme's apathy towards him grew, as did his protectiveness over his new project.

The next day, Jemme rose early; he had already told the other two he wouldn't be joining them for breakfast, and relished the opportunity to grab a quick coffee and begin his morning rounds. There were a few artists starting that morning, and he wanted to have a quick chat with them before they started; he knew that if he had waited for Roberto and Burbona then the artists themselves would have been waiting around for half the morning, and work wouldn't have started until the afternoon. After exchanging morning pleasantries with Marguerite, he made his way to the hallway on the third floor. It was close to a number of rooms he had vaguely earmarked for the ancient Levantine civilisations, and he had an idea of how he wanted the hallway. Luckily the artist, or rather artists, were already there, waiting for him.

'Good morning, gentlemen,' said Jemme cheerfully and introduced himself.

The two men introduced themselves in thickly accented French. Jemme pumped their hands,

'I have to say I was only expecting one of you,' he said.

'This is my cousin, Boris,' said the man who had introduced himself as Yuri. 'He hears of this piece and is very keen to join. We telephone your office and the man there says yes – he says we will make the piece finish faster.'

'Ah, DD, yes – he likes efficiency,' Jemme smiled. 'Well, you're both very welcome, I just wanted to come and introduce myself, see if the commission had been properly explained and if you had any questions.'

The two men looked at each other for a moment. Yuri was obviously the designated speaker, but he looked as if he had to think carefully before he spoke every time, as if he was trying to plan ahead all the words he would need. He saw Jemme looking at him expectantly,

'I'm sorry,' he said at length, 'it is difficult – my French…'

'Don't worry,' said Jemme, 'it's always hard in another language. Where are you two from by the way?'

They both appeared to have understood this and answered 'Russia' in unison. 'Well, I'm afraid I don't speak much Russian, but you are extremely welcome in that case, seeing as you are so far from home. Do you know the battle I'm asking you to paint?'

They both looked at him and nodded a few moments later, when they'd obviously had time to translate what he'd asked them.

'We know this battle very well,' said Boris, 'we are excited to paint it. We understand battle very well.'

'Yes, I'm sure,' said Jemme, not sure if they were talking about this one specifically. 'Well, if you know this battle then that's the most important thing, I really want you to show the drama of the battle at its height.'

'*Drama?*' repeated Yuri to his cousin, who responded with a single word in Russian.

'Oh, yes – "drama". We do much "drama."'

Great, well... then I suppose I'll leave you to it,' said Jemme, realising he wouldn't be able to communicate his ideas much further.

Yuri nodded slowly and looked around the space, 'We paint here, here, here, here,' he said, indicating the four walls.

'Yes, yes please – I want it to go all the way around.'

He nodded slowly again, 'What about here?' he pointed upwards at the ceiling.

'Oh, well I suppose, yes, if you could that would be brilliant.'

'What?'

'Um, well, why don't I just leave it to you?' said Jemme.

The men paused then nodded again, 'OK, we do.'

Jemme thanked them and went off to the next room, wondering what he would find when he came back to the hallway. Despite their slightly stilted conversation, something told him that he could be confident in the men. There was a solemnity to them that suggested they would portray the heat and devastation of battle very well. In fact, there was something about them that made Jemme think it might be something they had experienced already.

He made his way down three flights of stairs to the next room, which he was looking forward to starting this weekend. On the way he had to pass by the library, and remembered that a small amount of restoration work had been carried out that week on one of the bookcases that had started to show the first signs of dry rot. He popped in quickly to give everything a quick review. He couldn't remember which one it had been, and as he looked around it was impossible to tell. *Well, I suppose that answers my question about how well they finished it,* he thought to himself. He wandered round the bookcases a little longer, stopping in front of one for no particular reason. He gazed through its glass frontage, pleased with the beautiful collection of bindings in front of him. Eventually his eyes rested on the gold lettering running up a navy blue cloth-covered spine.

A History of Hever Castle he read. He hadn't seen or thought about this book for some years, and without thinking he opened the case and pulled the book out. He ran his hand over its spine, feeling the small depression where each letter had been hand-pressed in. As he did so, he thought about Hever Castle. It was a pretty thirteenth century castle in Kent, which had at one point passed into the hands of Thomas Boleyn, whose daughter, Anne, was raised there before going on to marry Henry VIII. However, it wasn't necessarily the castle or its history that appealed to Jemme. For him, its thick stone walls were filled with happy memories of times with Hil. They had often visited it when they had been in London. It was an easy day trip, and felt like a wonderfully refreshing burst of countryside. Hil in particular had loved it, and after a couple of happy trips, it had become their special place, with certain traditions built around it, such as the little tea shop they always went to afterwards, and the jar of local honey Hil always brought back.

He smiled, lost in a warm brume of memories. He opened the book, and a postcard fell out of the first page. He picked it up and looked at it. It showed the castle from the east side with the grounds laid out behind it and sun just beginning to set. He knew the view but didn't recognise the postcard, and wondered how it had made its way into the book. Curious, he turned it over and immediately recognised Hil's looped handwriting:

For my darling Jemme, I bought this on our last wonderful trip to Hever – I had such a happy time with you and wanted you to remember it whenever you look at this book, and to look forward to our next trip there together. Always yours, love H x

Jemme felt a hard lump forming in his throat. He had no idea how long the note had sat in the book, but it was like a message from the past. It was a window into a happier time when Hil had obviously looked forward to and believed in a future filled with similarly happy day trips. The lump in his throat was quickly followed by a rising sense of panic in the pit of his stomach. Jemme knew he couldn't allow himself to revisit those memories, or think about how different things were from the happy optimism encapsulated by the note. He stuffed the postcard back in the book and shut the bookcase quickly. Pacing around the library for a while, he tried to focus on something else, but nostalgia for their castle trips was flooding, unbidden, into his consciousness. He desperately tried to distract himself, by thinking about anything else, but to no avail. His pacing increased, as did the strength of the memories, and he began to accept the inevitable but to subvert it as much as possible. Allowing himself to think of Hever Castle, but focussing instead on its history seemed to work. He tried as hard as he could to remember every piece of information he had ever absorbed about its construction, its previous owners, its features and grounds. Eventually, even that ran dry and his mind rested on an image of Hil sitting on a picnic rug in the grounds one sunny June afternoon. He tried to banish it, but he couldn't think of a single other fact and he was reluctant to get the book out again and face its note. *A room!* he suddenly thought to himself – it should have a room! Why not! I should commemorate this quintessentially English castle in my French chateau. Sitting down at the desk, Jemme grabbed some paper and began planning the room. Eventually the sense of panic subsided, the lump in his throat dissolved and he found himself fully absorbed in the meditative task of planning another room for the chateau.

Inevitably, he lost himself in the task, and by the time he finally put down his pencil, satisfied, the dangerous memory had been buried again and its potency dissipated. He looked at the sketches in front of him and was pleased to see a room taking shape across the pages. Glancing down at his watch, he realised that it was much later than he had realised, Roberto and Burbona would be waiting for him. He made his way over to the next room on his list, assuming they would have gone straight there, but he arrived to find only the artist waiting in the room. Realising he couldn't very well leave, he stopped and introduced himself.

This room was to be dedicated to Sufism and the Dervishes and so he had asked DD to be very particular in his choice of artist. The project was very personal to him, and so he wanted to make sure the artist understood exactly how he wanted it to look, and, ideally, have some experience of the subject matter themselves. DD had found him a talented young French artist who had spent three years in Turkey studying traditional art, and who specialised in murals. He combined everything Jemme was looking for, and he was pleased to meet him.

Dominique introduced himself and returned Jemme's handshake.

'I hear you studied in Turkey?' said Jemme,

'Yes, for several years – it's a country that will always hold a special place in my heart though, and I hope to go back soon.'

'Whereabouts were you?'

'Oh, I moved all over, I started off in Istanbul, but I spent quite a few months in Konya and then travelled through the countryside around Lake Abant for a while too.'

'Lake Abant!' Jemme cried, 'We used to take childhood holidays there all the time!'

Dominique smiled fondly at the memories the place obviously invoked, 'What a wonderful place that must have been to grow up. My childhood was spent in Paris, and I would have given anything for water that blue and sun that warm!'

Jemme groaned, 'What are you doing to me?! I was feeling nostalgic enough when I was just thinking about this room! Now it's even worse!'

'Sorry,' Dominique laughed and they lapsed into talking about their various experiences of Turkey, until Jemme remembered his two guests.

'I'm so sorry, I hate to be rude, but I have to go and collect a couple of people – I'll be back as quickly as possible, and then we can talk about the room.'

'Of course, please, take your time.'

Jemme dashed back to the *salle à manger*. He had no idea where Roberto and Burbona were, but this was a good place to start. He was very surprised to find them still sitting over breakfast, deep in conversation; they must have been there for hours, but each was so involved in what the other was saying they didn't even notice him come in. Jemme paused for a moment, feeling slightly awkward. Neither of them looked up.

'Good morning!' he said loudly.

They both looked up, seeming surprised to see him.

'Good morning,' said Burbona with her usual demure air.

'Ah, Monsieur, good morning,' said Roberto. 'We have just finished breakfast.'

'So I see – it seems we have all let time run away with us a little today; it's actually nearly lunchtime!'

Roberto glanced down at his watch and looked genuinely surprised, 'It is much later than I realised,' he admitted, 'I hope we have not kept you waiting; Burbona is such an entertaining and engaging hostess that time with her simply flies past.'

Burbona positively glowed at the compliment, but Jemme found himself feeling irritated by Roberto's measured delivery and dispassion again.

'Well, if you're ready, let's move on shall we?' he said decisively, 'There's someone who's waiting for me, and whom I'd like you to meet.'

He led them to the Whirling Dervishes room and introduced them to Dominique, before giving them a very brief overview of what he planned to do with the room.

'The Dervishes,' repeated Roberto, sounding slightly unsure.

'Yes – have you ever heard of them?' asked Jemme.

There was a slight flicker of doubt across Roberto's face; he paused, 'I am perhaps not as familiar as I would like to be with their history,' he conceded.

Jemme felt a surge of triumphalism. Roberto obviously prided himself on being a learned, cultured individual and it was oddly satisfying to know that he had discovered a chink in this. He took great pleasure in describing the Dervishes to Roberto who nodded thoughtfully, as if being reminded of something he already knew, rather than hearing it for the first time.

At one point, the artist added in a few facts which Jemme knew would have really needled Roberto, despite how innocently it was intended. For her part Burbona acted as if she was well-read on the subject, but Jemme knew she would never have let slip if she was not. Eventually the conversation moved on to the room itself, and Jemme discussed with Dominique exactly how he wanted everything. Dominique seemed to understand very well, and Jemme felt confident in leaving him to start the room.

'Do you know,' said Burbona as they were leaving, 'I've never known where the word "Dervish" comes from.'

'Ah, well I can help you with that,' said Jemme. 'It's from the Persian *Da*, meaning door, so it translates literally as "One who opens the door."'

'Of course,' said Burbona, 'that makes perfect sense.' She sounded every bit the expert, but Jemme had a sneaking sense it was the very first time she had come into contact with the subject matter, and he wondered how many other topics she feigned knowledge on. He trusted her on so many things, and often took her wisdom and judgement at face value without stopping to question its authority. His thoughts were interrupted by Burbona herself.

'I thought we might look at the paintings I bought,' she announced. 'We can decide where to hang them.'

'Yes, that's a good idea,' said Roberto, 'I'm very much looking forward to seeing your latest acquisition.'

Jemme paused, 'I was intending to…' Burbona shot him one of her looks and a smile at the same time. 'Well never mind,' he said, 'let's go and have a look, I'm sure it won't take long and we can come back here later.' He was rewarded with an even wider smile from Burbona, who instantly took charge of the situation and led them to the room where the paintings were in storage.

'Oh,' she said when they arrived, 'they're still wrapped. I really thought they would have unwrapped them for me – I told them I wanted to view them today. Still,' she sighed, 'I suppose you can't expect the gardener to act as a gallery attendant.'

She smiled at Roberto, who laughed.

'I'm sure Philby would have done it if you'd asked him,' Jemme said defensively.

Burbona didn't reply, but looked pointedly at the two paintings, wrapped up in their protective packaging. Jemme refused to take the hint.

'I'll unwrap them for you,' said Roberto. Jemme wondered if Roberto thought he sounded heroic. He watched the architect begin to unwrap the anonymous paintings, and remembered how much they had cost. He stared intently as the layers began to fall away, wondering what they would reveal. He thought again about how much he trusted Burbona on everything, and how that had led her to make this expensive purchase without consulting him. Roberto could be unwrapping anything at all, Jemme genuinely had no idea what to expect.

Eventually Roberto set one painting gently down and stepped back to admire it.

'Isn't it wonderful?' Burbona trilled.

'It is beautiful,' Roberto said, staring at Burbona.

Jemme couldn't even see and had to move around Roberto who was still looking fixedly at Burbona, rather than the painting.

Eventually his eyes rested on the object and his heart sank. He hated it. It was an insipid watercolour in an overly ornate frame. The still life was dull, and the overall composition uninspiring. He stared at it, trying to find one redeeming feature.

'Isn't it wonderful?' said Burbona again, noticing his silence.

Jemme paused; he didn't really know what to say. His disappointment was giving way to anger over how much the horrible piece had cost him.

'Who's it by?' he asked eventually.

Burbona named an artist he had never heard of, and some of his contemporaries he had also never heard of. His anger at the purchase was rising, but he consoled himself that perhaps the second piece would redeem things.

'Well?' Burbona prompted.

'Let's see the second one,' he replied as diplomatically as possible.

'Oh, they're a matching pair,' said Burbona airily, 'although Roberto can unwrap that one too if you wanted to see them together.'

Any hope of redeeming the situation vanished. All Jemme could think was that he would have to look at this wretched painting twice. He had no idea how Burbona could have thought it was worth that much, and he was furious when he thought of how many other beautiful pieces he could have bought instead. He was certain that neither painting would find their way onto the walls of the chateau.

'Would you like it unwrapped?' asked Roberto.

'No, I think I've seen enough. Thank you for showing them to me; shall we head back?' he said.

Burbona looked slightly put out for a moment, but that soon disappeared under the praise Roberto showered on her. As they made their way back to where they had left off, he praised her exquisite taste, her nous in the auction room and her steely determination. If he hadn't been so angry Jemme would have wanted to laugh.

* * * *

His displeasure was soon soothed by what he had decided would be the Phoenician room. The yearning for his homeland had found him focussing on the peoples, history and culture of the Levant, and this room had grown from being a mere nod to the Phoenicians to an elegy to the sea-faring peoples of the Northern Mediterranean.

The Phoenicians had occupied the East Levantine coast from as far north as Antioc, all the way down to Ashkelon, incorporating Emesa, Laodiciea and Mahara. They were primarily seafarers, but this did not stop them from erecting large fortified buildings such as at Homs and Hamma. A notable people from a historical point of view, nevertheless their impact and influence on the artistic world was not particularly long-lasting. Jemme had been struggling to find quintessentially Phoenician motifs and decoration he could feature in the room. However, despite his close consultation with the Professor, he had found that the majority of their artistic endeavours had been adopted and adapted from the Assyrians before them, as well as a small amount of mutual exchange with the Ancient Greeks and Romans.

He thus had very little to work with when planning the room, but it hadn't deterred him; he saw it as an opportunity to showcase the record of an entire civilisation in one room. Every surviving fragment of history could be referenced within these walls. It was an exciting prospect, but it was fairly obvious that this enthusiasm wasn't shared by Burbona or Roberto, who both looked around at the entirely empty room and appeared slightly underwhelmed.

Roberto was having even less success pretending that he knew anything about the Phoenicians than he had with the Dervishes.

'And what did they do?' he asked Jemme, after Jemme had just finished a potted history.

'I'm sorry, what do you mean *do*?' asked Jemme.

'Well, you yourself have said that they have left no artistic legacy, and it seems that very few people have heard of them, so I am surprised that you want to dedicate a whole room to them.'

'Just because a people didn't leave a great trace in the historical record doesn't mean they haven't had a big influence on history,' said Jemme. 'They were great traders and travelled all the world – it's hard to describe the amount they enabled influence between different cultures.'

Roberto didn't respond, so Jemme decided to carry on.

'They traded tin and Iberian silver with the British, dye and textiles with the North Africans, and wine and gold with Egypt.' He looked at Roberto who remained placid. Not a single shred Jemme's passion or enthusiasm had rubbed off onto him.

'I see,' said Roberto politely.

Jemme sighed quietly.

'I expect you'll be able to tell us how they got their name as well,' said Burbona playfully. Again, Jemme found it impossible to tell if she was humouring him, covering up her own lack of knowledge or even teasing him.

'Actually I do,' he said, 'but I don't want to bore you if you're not interested.'

'Don't be silly,' said Burbona smiling at him. 'We'd love to hear, wouldn't we Roberto?'

'Yes, please do tell us,' said Roberto, looking at Burbona rather than Jemme.

'Well,' said Jemme, taking a deep breath, unsure if this addition was actually welcome, 'it all comes from the same source as their power as traders. The trade in powdered Tyrian Purple dye with the Ancient Greeks was what lead to their great success, so the Greeks named them after the same substance: *phoinikèia* meaning "purple". I suppose it shows you just how long purple has been loved by royalty and the upper classes.' Jemme looked around at his audience. Neither of them seemed to have paid any particular attention to what he'd just said.

'Anyway, that's where the name comes from...' he ventured. Burbona smiled at him, but he didn't feel particularly encouraged; in fact, he suddenly felt very defensive about the room. It had huge personal significance for him, and he suddenly felt like he didn't want to share it at all. He pointed out a couple of things he wanted to do, neither of which elicited much of a response, and then moved them on quickly to the next project. The morning rounds soon turned into a tour of work Burbona thought should be given to Roberto, and by lunchtime he had begun to feel slightly disillusioned by the whole thing. It felt like they were on completely separate tours and Roberto and Burbona were seeing something very different to him.

Talk over lunch seemed to focus on Roberto's upcoming projects again; Jemme wasn't too happy about the way in which Roberto's presence seemed to have been accepted into the chateau's future, without any question. He couldn't remember a single time he'd actually sought out Roberto's opinion or hoped to engage him on a project. Rather it seemed that he was trying to fit him in wherever possible, and he had no idea why he was doing him the favour. For her part, Burbona was spending lunchtime discussing the paintings she had bought, which only rankled with Jemme further. He had already decided that as soon as he arrived in Paris, he would ask DD to secure a valuation for them, and would then try and put them back on the market. They were too lifeless, simply too ugly to have in his home, but too valuable to relegate to storage. He wondered if he should raise the matter with Burbona. If they proved to be worth less than she had paid, then his faith in her purchasing ability was significantly undermined. However, he was prepared to give her the benefit of the doubt. They *could* be valuable, just not to his taste. As he silently ate his lunch, he turned this thought over in his mind; he realised that this outcome was even worse. If Burbona didn't know his tastes and requirements by now, then it was a significant matter. He looked up at her, talking to Roberto, and wondered what he should do.

He decided that he would start to steer the two of them away from projects which had personal significance for him. He was perfectly capable of completing these on his own, and, in fact, that's exactly what he had been doing for quite some time, until Burbona came along. After lunch, instead of returning to the Phoenician room and discussing his mosaicking plans, he took them to meet a couple of the artists he had working on smaller projects. He knew that both of them would enjoy the opportunity to be in charge, and it would give him some more time to think about his grand Phoenician plans.

He found the afternoon tour frustrating and ponderous. If he had been on his own, he would have flitted between different rooms, chatting to artists at will, and stopping and starting at his own pace. In fact, he needn't have been on his own, just with the right person, such as the Professor, or even Burbona. However, he was constantly aware of his responsibility towards the others, and the duty to act as host at all times. Everything took much, much longer than usual, and even when they were visiting the rooms it also felt much less productive. He felt like he was a museum guide instead of the overseer of a sprawling and complex project.

Eventually the frustration overtook his patience. 'I tell you what,' he said, 'I've got a couple of things I really need to see to, which I'm sure would bore you. Why don't you use the time to have a look around the house and even the grounds too – I'd love to hear your thoughts, Roberto; and Burbona, I'm sure you'll be a wonderful guide.'

Each of them seemed flattered by this proposal, and they soon headed off, leaving him on his own. He headed straight to the kitchen, had a quick chat with Marguerite (who asked if 'the Paris People' would be back next weekend) grabbed a coffee and headed back to the second floor. He was hoping to look at the space he was planning on creating the Hever Castle room in, but he bumped into a curious looking individual on the way. He positively jumped when he heard Jemme behind him,

'I'm sorry, I didn't mean to make you jump, I'm Jemme Mafeze,' he said stretching out a hand.

The man slowly pushed his glasses up to the top of his long nose and blinked a couple of times. He was carrying a small chisel in each hand, but stuffed one in his pocket and returned Jemme's handshake.

'Sandro,' he said, in an accent that was unmistakably Italian.

'Well, I'm pleased to meet you, Sandro. You'll have to forgive me though; I have so many people coming and going on this project that I'm not quite sure if I can place you.'

Sandro looked a little nervous and fiddled with the chisel in his pocket. Jemme judged him to be in his early twenties, and wondered if this was the first time he had been away from home.

'I am a marble artist,' said Sandro falteringly.

'Ah, I see, well that's very good to hear; I am a great devotee of marble work, so I'm very pleased to meet you,' Jemme said encouragingly.

Sandro smiled broadly, revealing an extremely large gap between his two front teeth, 'I have been working on the pietra dura here.'

'Excellent, as I said, I love anything to do with marble – I would very much like to see some of your work.'

'Of course, I will show you some I've only just completed,' said Sandro, who was beginning to look a great deal more relaxed. He led Jemme to one of the bathrooms leading off the corridor. It was one of a number of rooms Jemme didn't have specific plans for, but wanted to be decorated in some way nonetheless.

'Here,' said Sandro, pointing to a very skilled piece of pietra dura work. The pieces were very small, but tessellated perfectly, almost as if they had been painted on. Sandro had picked out a repeating pattern in brilliant scarlet and green. Jemme traced its course around the wall.

'I'm impressed,' he said, 'where did you learn your craft? You seem very young to have developed such a skill.'

Sandro smiled, 'I'm Italian; this is in my blood!'

Jemme laughed, 'Well, I suppose that's true enough. I remember the first time I saw anything like this; I was only boy, and it was on a school trip to Venice. It stayed with me for a very long time.'

'Ah, Venice has the best pietra dura work in all the world! I grew up not far from Venice, and so I have been surrounded by inspiration since childhood.'

'That must have been wonderful.'

Sandro nodded happily, 'It was also where I learned to work with alabaster.'

'Alabaster? That's rather unusual – I'm sure we'll want some alabaster work at some point during this project, so it would be good to know that we have an expert on hand.'

Sandro looked shy again, 'I don't know about expert,' he said.

Jemme chatted with him for a little longer, but was suddenly hit by a wall of tiredness. It had been happening to him with increasing frequency recently, but he had trained himself to ignore it and to drink however much coffee was necessary instead. He excused himself and headed back to the kitchen.

'Monsieur!' Marguerite greeted him, 'I was not expecting to see you, and on your own again too, how nice!' she beamed at him, raising the wooden spoon from the bowl she was stirring in greeting.

'Hello, Marguerite. It's only a flying visit I'm afraid – how's everything in the kitchen?'

Marguerite returned the spoon to the bowl and continued mixing, '*Ah, bon, Monsieur,*' she said with a shrug, 'I am making you a cake to take back to Paris.'

'Oh, well that's very nice of you – it will be good to have all my lunches and suppers for next week sorted,' said Jemme.

Marguerite just about managed to splutter out, 'But you cannot eat cake for *diner*, Monsieur,' before Jemme assured her that he had been joking.

Marguerite eyed him suspiciously as she continued to stir.

'I've just met another artist,' said Jemme, keen to change the conversation.

'*Ah oui,*' said Marguerite, adding handfuls of cherries and almonds to the cake mix.

'Yes, a young Italian called Sandro – have you come across him?'

Marguerite shook her head sadly, 'Ah, this Sandro. Yes, I have met him. He is very strange with his nose and his teeth. He is a good boy though, and talented too. The other artists –' she sighed, 'they do not like him, Monsieur.'

'Really? Why on earth not? I couldn't see anything objectionable about him.'

Marguerite shrugged widely as she stirred in another stream of cherries, 'I do not know, Monsieur, but they laugh at him a great deal. Perhaps it is the way he looks.'

'But he doesn't look that odd,' said Jemme, saddened to find that there was squabbling between the artists.

'Like I say, I do not know why. Myself, I like him, but the others are constantly mocking him – even down to the way he mixes his glue. Maybe they are all friends and he is in on the joke, but maybe they are jealous of him.'

Jemme didn't know what to say; he suspected it was the latter. 'Well, would you mind keeping an eye on him?' he asked, 'I just want to make sure he's OK.'

'Of course,' said Marguerite, spooning the batter out into a tin she had prepared. '*Tiens!*' she muttered to herself, 'I knew I hadn't made it big enough!'

Jemme poured himself a coffee and headed back upstairs, taking one last look at the cake before he went, and thinking that it would be big enough to share with the whole arrondissement.

✻ ✻ ✻ ✻

Having the rest of the afternoon to himself felt like an unbridled luxury, and Jemme indulged in wandering around exactly as he pleased, spending a long time with individual artists and craftsmen, and swooping off onto tangents whenever enthusiasm ran away with him. It was a thoroughly pleasant afternoon, and even the prospect of another dull dinner did little to dampen his mood. Although it felt uncharitable, he couldn't help but wish that Roberto wasn't there. When he had Burbona to himself, he hugely enjoyed her company. They could talk for hours and he enjoyed asking her opinions, arguing with her on certain points and eventually drawing up plans together. However, everything felt different with Roberto there. He swallowed up all of Burbona's attention, and she somehow seemed less lively and vivacious when she was around him; she almost seemed to get swept into his tedium.

He revisited the empty Phoenician room a couple of times, trying to imagine how it would look when it was finished and how he could present all the fragments of decoration in a cohesive way. It was a puzzle he was relishing, and he realised that the only thing for it would be to continue his research on the Phoenicians and see if he could find a common thread or a fresh new angle. His mind buzzing, he was reluctant to interrupt the flow of everything to go for dinner, especially when he knew it would probably last for several hours. Feeling rather guilty, he told

Roberto and Burbona that he had a headache and was going straight to bed, then popped into the kitchen to tell Marguerite that he would be eating alone a bit later on, and to be discreet about the matter. Even as he said the words, he wondered why he was bothering, when he knew full well he was talking to the least discreet woman in Northern France. He had underestimated her on this matter though. She smiled broadly, and looked delighted to be involved in the conspiracy.

'Ahhh, Monsieur, I do not blame you,' she said.

Jemme blushed, embarrassed that she had seen straight through him.

'Well, I'll see you later then,' he mumbled and headed over to the library.

There were several bookcases loosely classified as 'Ancient Civilisation' and of those several shelves were exclusively dedicated to the Phoenicians. He pulled out a couple of well-read volumes he knew would act as a good starting point, as well as several with interesting titles which he didn't know as well. The books jumped around in their chronology, and he was soon feeling a little lost. He started to make notes of key dates, and knit together a narrative to serve as the foundation for the room.

The civilisation lasted from around 1200 BC to 539 BC, which were the first two dates he wrote at the top. He marvelled that something that had lasted for so long could have left such little evidence, and wondered again how he could fill the room. As he read, he made notes, detailing the sixth century decline, following the conquest by Cyrus the Great in 539. The Phoenician kingdom was carved up and the Phoenicians themselves gradually migrated to Carthage, were executed after rebelling, or simply intermixed with the Persians. In 65 BC, their culture was incorporated into the Roman Empire, but by then its power had dwindled and its influence diminished.

However, at its apogee it was a thriving civilisation of world-class mariners and astute traders, and it was this energy that he wanted to capture in the room. He sketched out a rough map of what the kingdom would have looked like. It ran down the East Levantine coast. He looked at the map and reflected on what it would have been like to live within the borders he had recreated on the piece of paper. A member of such a mobile society would probably pass through these towns frequently on their way back and forth from the coast. He thought about everything they would see – the industrious towns and their exotic riches. As he imagined the journey, he realised that there was no better way to document this whole civilisation. He began to sketch on a new piece of paper, creating the narrative that would bind the room together.

He decided that the story of the journey would be told over a series of panels. The first would show Byblos, the ancient capital and starting point of many long voyages. However, Antioc would also have been an important city in launching sea journeys, and so he drew the outline of the castle of Tutush Radwan d'Antioc, of whom he had just read a couple of gripping paragraphs.

He also decided to include a couple of the end points of the Phoenicians' journeys, and so outlined the Balearic island of Ibiza on another panel. He was searching for other destinations to include when he became sidetracked by an anecdote in one of the books he hadn't read before. It related to the Phoenicians' constant exploration for metals for trade and export. Tin mines in particular were potentially lucrative, and as a sea faring people, the Phoenicians were able to travel widely, both to discover them and to commandeer their mining. Southern Ireland and the Breton kingdom were rich in tin, and one of the biggest sources of the world at that time. The writer postulated that the Phoenician sailors, starved and exhausted by the time they rounded the north of France, would have caught sight of the land they had been trying to reach and raise the shout of the 'The bre! The bre!' There was no 'p' in the Phoenician language, just like Assyrian, Arabic and Hebrew, so 'the prairies' translated as 'the bre', and this might be shouted, in a similar way to the 'land ahoy!' of European sailors. Having sighted the land, the writer believed that the next shout that might have gone up could have been 'The tin! The tin!', meaning that the sailors would have been talking about the *bre* of *tin*, or, to put it another way, *Brittany.* Jemme wasn't sure how much truth there was in the story and he was pretty sure the Professor would have picked it apart in minutes. Nonetheless, he was amused by it, and decided to represent Ireland through some lush grass, in reference to the story.

He stood up and searched through the shelves for more books until, by a stroke of serendipity, he came across a very slim volume entitled *The Ships and Sea-faring Crafts of the Ancient Mediterranean Maritime Peoples.* He took it over to his desk and leafed through it. He found some sketches of the Phoenician's long boats with their curved bow and stern and billowing sails. These could be included across all the panels he decided, as he sketched them in. He flicked through the rest of the book, but there was nothing further of interest, so he picked up another from the pile; this one focussed mainly on Carthage. He tracked the city's rise, which seemed unstoppable. It continued to grow both in terms of power and wealth, and stirred Rome to take decisive action. The Romans countered in what became known as the Punic Wars. He knew little of this period, except for the fact that Hannibal's crossing of the Alps has become emblematic of the war. As he skimmed through the chapters, he decided that Carthage would have to be represented, as would Hannibal himself.

As he continued to read through the books next to him, the stack of notes he was making grew too. There was certainly no danger of the room being empty. In fact, he was beginning to wonder whether the room he had chosen was too small. He finished reading another interesting chapter on the cedar wood from which the boats were made, and which was so emblematic of that region and wrote *cedar?* at the bottom of one page. He didn't have time to wonder how he could incorporate it, because he suddenly flicked the page and discovered a chapter on Agenor, the powerful king of Phoenicia. His entry into the body of classical mythology seemed a good demonstration of the close links between Greece and Phoenicia, and how they were mutually influenced by each others' cultures and figureheads. *Agenor,* he wrote at the top of a new sheet of paper, quickly followed by *flowers,* as he read further down the paragraph. He decided to depict Agenor with a bouquet of flowers, representing the myth of his daughter Europa: the Greek God Zeus fell in love with her as he saw her gathering flowers one day. He transformed himself into a white bull and carried her away to Crete. Once there, he revealed his true identity and made her the first Queen of Crete. Jemme vaguely remembered the story from childhood, and felt that it fitted well with the room. The last note he scribbled read *Pegasus?* He had been interested to discover that, although the legend of Pegasus was usually associated with the Greeks, it played a role in Phoenician culture too, further illustrating the connections between the two civilisations. Some academics believe that the Phoenicians saw Pegasus as emblematic of a ship, a sky-borne equivalent, and a bridled horse was often used as the figurehead on their ships. He was hoping that he would be able to find a Pegasus figure carved from cedar wood, which would nicely tie two different themes together.

By the time he finally put down his pencil, he had filled nearly ten pages, and emptied two whole shelves in one of the bookcases. He rubbed his eyes, and was suddenly aware that he was hungry. He glanced at his watch and saw that it was nearly ten thirty. He wondered if Burbona and Roberto had finished eating, and if it was safe to sneak into the kitchen. Based on previous experience, he fully suspected that they were still sitting over dinner, and Roberto was still telling the same story, which probably featured both himself and a tall building he had designed. He was anxious to avoid getting involved at any cost, but his stomach was trying to persuade him to abandon caution and to head straight for the kitchen. He made his way there as carefully as he could, thankfully not bumping into anyone en route.

'Monsieur!' Marguerite greeted him delightedly, 'I have been waiting for you! It is so late – you must be so hungry!'

'I am, rather,' said Jemme quietly, wishing Marguerite wasn't being so loud herself. 'Did everyone else enjoy their supper?' he asked casually.

'I could not tell you, Monsieur. Madame, she barely eats anything, and I do not think she enjoys it anyway. Even if she did she would not tell me. And that Monsieur, well, I do not know what to make of him!'

Jemme smiled, Marguerite's candour was always refreshing. He paused, 'And...are they still eating?'

'*Mais non*! They went to bed some time ago.'

'Oh I see,' said Jemme, relieved, although he couldn't help thinking it was a little strange. He had been expecting them to linger for hours.

'I have cooked you something special though, Monsieur – this has been cooking all day,' said Marguerite, waving Jemme over to the stove. She lifted the heavy cast iron lid from a pot and a sweet, yet deliciously meaty aroma escaped.

'A special lamb stew;' she said to Jemme, 'my own mother's secret recipe.'

'It smells wonderful, Marguerite, I'm honoured to be on the receiving end of a family recipe.'

He sat down as she served him a large bowlful, with some fondant potatoes she had been keeping warm in the oven.

'What has been keeping you so long in the library anyway?'

'I've been planning another room?'

'Another?!'

'Yes, this is a new idea – it's for the Phoenicians.'

'I have never heard of them, Monsieur. I am not much of a historian,' said Marguerite, reminding Jemme how much he valued her openness and forthrightness. He could never imagine Roberto admitting his ignorance so happily. Nor could he imagine Roberto listening with such openness and eagerness as he explained the history.

Jemme gave another potted history, which Marguerite seemed fascinated by. She listened closely and, when he had finished, declared that, 'They sound like an excellent group, Monsieur,' and that she was '… glad you are putting them in the chateau!'

'Well, thank you, Marguerite, so am I – the problem now is just *how* I put them in the chateau. I think it's going to take a lot of thought to make everything look right.'

'I'm sure you will manage it, Monsieur, with all your professor friends and all these architects,' Marguerite said.

'Your confidence is much appreciated!' laughed Jemme.

Marguerite shrugged, 'I have seen what you have done with some of these other rooms; they way they have been transformed – it is magical.'

'Magical,' Jemme repeated. Hearing the word brought him great happiness; it was exactly what he was hoping to achieve with the chateau, and exactly the feeling he had experienced when he had wandered around his dream palace. He kept turning the word over in his mind on the way back to Paris, feeling validated and inspired by it.

* * * *

Later that week, he sat with the Professor in his office. Marguerite's enormous cake sat between them and, although Jemme had been offering it to his visitors with superlative generosity, he had still made only a small dent in it. The

Professor had eagerly managed three slices, but his pace was slowing, and he was now eying it with no small amount of regret. Jemme had been delighted that he had managed to snatch another quick visit with the Professor; he was only passing through, but it had been long enough for them to catch up, and plan a couple of rooms.

Jemme had given him an overview of the Phoenician room. He had not been surprised when the Professor had looked sceptical about the idea ('So little documented art!') nor when he had laughed at the story of how Brittany acquired its name ('What a lot of tosh!'). However, when Jemme talked him through all of his ideas and described the panels to him, the Professor warmed to the idea.

'You're obviously enthused by it,' he said, 'and I agree, you really need to reference the Phoenicians somewhere in this project, but I'm still not sure that there's enough to fill a room.'

Jemme told him about all the different cities he planned to depict, and the boats, as well as elements of classical mythology to show the interaction with the ancient Greeks.

The Professor stroked his chin thoughtfully, 'That all sounds rather good actually. Have you thought about how you will execute it all?'

'What do you mean?'

'Materials, technique, that kind of thing.'

'No, not really to be honest. I only got as far as deciding that cedar should be in there somewhere.'

The Professor looked thoughtful again, 'What about mosaics?'

'Mosaics?'

'Yes, it would be historically accurate, and I think it would add a nice texture to the story you're telling.'

'It would definitely look good. I just had no idea it was a technique they used.'

The Professor nodded, 'Everyone thinks of mosaics as being Roman, but it was an art form used by a huge number of people over a very broad area too. You'll notice how different the end result looks when you get into researching it a little more, and I'd be happy to help. I'm afraid though – ' the Professor stood up and started to fiddle with his attaché case, 'I have to be off. I'm sorry it was so fleeting, but let's talk more about this room and keep in touch about this calligraphy fellow too. I'm interested to see how that will all pan out.'

'I will, thank you,' said Jemme. He looked at his desk then at the Professor, 'Slice of cake for the road?' he added hopefully.

The Professor blanched, 'I just don't think I can,' he said sorrowfully.

Jemme saw far less of Burbona than he had been expecting that week. He spoke with her a couple of times briefly on the phone but it sounded like she had been spending the majority of her time with Roberto 'planning rooms' as she put it. It made Jemme slightly nervous, but every time he tried to ask just what they were planning, and how Roberto was involved, she swept his concerns aside,

'Silly,' she said breezily on one occasion. 'Of course I will ask you if it is something important! I am just making sure that we make the most of Roberto's expertise; it would be such a pity to waste access to so much talent.'

Jemme made a rather unenthusiastic noise in response.

'I have some more news that will cheer you up!' she said brightly.

'Oh really?'

'Yes, I have some more paintings for you!'

'Great, when are they up for sale?'

'Silly,' Burbona repeated with her tinkling laugh, 'they have already been up for sale and I have already won them!'

There was a pause as Jemme tried not to sigh too audibly.

'I thought we discussed this. I thought I made it clear that I wanted to be involved before the buying.'

'Of course and you will be; these were not very expensive pieces, but I knew you would like them so I wanted to make sure you had them.'

Jemme refused to be swayed, 'How much were they?' he asked

'Oh, not very much at all.'

'But if I asked you for an actual number..?'

'Oh numbers, details, I can't remember just off the top of my head. I care much more about the art and you having beautiful art too – I thought you felt the same. When did you start caring about things like cost?' she asked, sounding as if even mentioning the word was distasteful.'

'Of course I care about the art, Burbona, I just would feel more comfortable if... well, never mind, perhaps it will be easier if we discuss this in person when we next see each other.'

'As you wish,' she said languorously, before telling him how much progress Roberto had made on the mihrab, and how *lucky* they both were to have a man of such *talent* working on everything for them.

Jemme made the same mildly unenthusiastic noises and then made his excuses before hanging up – it was the first time he had ended a conversation early with Burbona, but she had irritated him and he wanted to get back to work.

He barely heard from her for the rest of the week, but was still surprised when DD passed on the message that she would meet him at the chateau on Friday evening, instead of travelling down with him. The news that he had also been spared a car journey with Roberto cheered him immensely and made him forget this slightly unusual development.

As it happened, he thoroughly enjoyed the opportunity to travel to the chateau in silence. It gave him time to think over the different rooms and everything he had planned. Although his mind was racing the whole time, he found the experience strangely relaxing. By the time he reached the chateau, he felt refreshed and ready to get on with work. Marguerite and Philby were waiting for him and greeted him warmly,

'You are the first, Monsieur!' Marguerite congratulated him, 'Your friends from Paris have not arrived yet,' she said, looking very happy.

'Oh really? I thought they would have been here by now. Well, it's probably for the best – it will give me time to look over a few things before they arrive.'

'Will you be eating all together?' asked Marguerite.

Jemme looked tempted to say otherwise, but sighed, 'I suppose I'd better. It will have to be a very quick tour.'

'Well, many of the artists are waiting inside for you to see their work, so it should be very easy,' said Marguerite.

'Excellent.'

Jemme thanked Philby, who was carrying his bags for him, and headed straight in. The first room stop was the Whirling Dervishes room.

'Monsieur Mafeze, it is good to see you again,' said Dominique. 'I've been enjoying working on this room a great deal. I hope you like it,' he said, stepping to one side.

Jemme looked around. He was in a sea of colour and movement.

'It's so lifelike and realistic!' he said. He moved closer to the walls and scrutinised them, 'I can't believe the level of detail either.'

Dominique shrugged, 'Of course.'

Jemme took a step back and slowly turned around, 'This is exactly what I wanted to create – a feeling of total immersion. I really feel as if I could be back at one of my grandmother's meetings, watching everything unfold. Thank you.' He stopped looking at the room for long enough to give Dominique an earnest smile.

He spent a while longer in the room, chatting to the artist and praising his work, before moving on to the next. Just as Marguerite had said, the artists were waiting – in this case both of them.

'Good evening, gentlemen,' he greeted the Russian pair.

'Hello,' replied the nominated speaker. 'Battle is finished,' he said, slightly ominously.

Again, Jemme looked around him and took in the scene. Again, it was exactly as he had imagined – if not a little better. There, all around him, was the frenzied action of a battle at its peak. It had been depicted in such a lifelike way he could almost hear the clash of spear on shield and see the steam of the horse's nostrils as they champed at the bit, racing forward and pulling their chariots behind them. He took in not just these details, but the wider scene the mural was depicting. It was all perfectly recreated – he was looking out onto a faithful representation of the battle of Qadesh.

He realised that the two were silently watching him, waiting for a reaction.

'I'm very impressed,' he said to them, 'thank you.'

The more vocal one nodded, which the other interpreted as a good sign and nodded too.

'We know battle well,' said the man again.

'Yes, I can see that you do; this is how I always imagined that it would look when I read about it,' said Jemme. He looked over the mural again and admired a couple more features; the artists had painted the characteristic lightweight chariots of both sides, and a couple of well-recorded manoeuvres by both the Hittite forces under Muwatilli and the Egyptians under Ramesses. In addition to the towns and rivers, each soldier had been beautifully painted, as had their weaponry, the horses and their carriages – both upright and fallen.

Jemme nodded his approval again, 'This is excellent, thank you.'

'Sky too?' asked the man.

'Sky?'

The man pointed upwards. Jemme suddenly remembered that he had told them they could decorate the ceiling however they liked. They had painted the sky directly on the ceiling, a common decorative device in chateaux of this age, and one Jemme usually enjoyed. However, he was almost shocked by this particular example. Perhaps a stormy sky was fitting for a battle scene, but this was so dramatic it was difficult to look at for any length without feeling its imposing presence. It felt as if suffering and war imbued the entire sky. Even the clouds seemed to be shot through with battle. Jemme could only wonder at the tormented scenes the pair were used to documenting, and what they had actually meant by 'we know battle.' Perhaps this painted example was not the first battle they had experienced.

He thanked them again, pleased that he had already seen two completed rooms within the first hour of arriving at the chateau. He realised that Burbona and Roberto would be arriving soon, so he should probably head back. They still weren't there, but it gave him a chance for a slightly longer catch-up with Marguerite.

'How is everyone doing?' he asked. 'I know that you know everything that goes on around here.' Marguerite beamed, even though it hadn't necessarily been a compliment 'It's always good to know whether the staff are happy, and if everyone's getting along,' Jemme continued.

Marguerite shrugged, 'Everything is well, Monsieur, even with these artists. Monsieur Philby is happy. Xelifon – well, this place is the best thing that has ever happened to him. The work he has done in the gardens is *formidable*! Aude and Florence and the other girls do well, even though sometimes I think they are quite stupid. As for the rest, well, there are so many coming and going it is difficult to keep track of them – I have not seen many big dramas recently. The only thing that puzzles me is this young Italian, Sandro.'

'Sandro – is he the marble artist? The one with the gap between his teeth?'

'Yes, Monsieur, that is him. I told you that the others all tease him, but I hope he does not take it too much to heart.'

'I hope so too. I shall have a word with him. What is it that's puzzling you though?'

'It is his sheets, Monsieur – I have made a bed up for him in the artist's quarters, yet every time I change the bed for him, it has not been slept in.'

'That is strange. Perhaps he goes into the village at night to sleep? Maybe he has friends there, or relatives?'

Marguerite shook her head, 'I do not think so; I think this is the first time he has left Italy.'

'Well, I'll bring it up when I talk to him in that case.'

Just then they both heard the sound of a car coming down the driveway.

'Ah that will be *Madame*,' said Marguerite. 'I expect she will want some kind of welcome committee,' she added sourly and wiped her hands on her apron before heading towards the main entranceway. 'Are you coming too, Monsieur? I know that she will be pleased if you do.'

Chapter Forty-Three

Jemme heaved himself up from the table and went out to greet Burbona. On the walk to the entranceway, he puzzled over the mystery of Sandro. He wondered why the man was not sleeping in his bed, and where he was going at night. He didn't mind – he was free to come and go as he pleased, but he was concerned with his welfare; it was yet another reminder of how much responsibility this project put on his shoulders. Not only was he responsible for a piece of French history, he was also charged with all those who worked on the project. Some of them warranted little concern; the gnarled builders from the local village would turn up for a couple of hours a day, and then return to their homes. They had known Philby, Marguerite and some of the other domestic staff for years, and the chateau had been an ever-present backdrop as they lived and worked in the surrounding areas. The work, environment and people came naturally to them. However, for others the transition was strange and jarring. Some of the artists and craftsmen had travelled considerable distances, from Russia, the Levant and even Asia. For many, this was the first time they had left their homelands, and for some the first time they had left home as well. Jemme could only imagine how bewildering it was for some of them to find themselves in the cold, damp climes of northern Europe, working in different media, on different subject matter, in a building unlike any they'd ever seen before. He decided that the mystery of Sandro's whereabouts would be solved by the end of the weekend, and he wouldn't go back to Paris until he was satisfied that all was well. He would also ask Marguerite to keep a watchful eye on the rest of the artists, and notify him immediately if there was cause for concern – a task he knew she would relish.

He reached the front door, and found himself taking a deep breath before he opened it for Burbona. *How things change*, he thought to himself. *There was a time when I would have been excited about her arrival.* He reasoned that it was probably the fact that he knew she would be with Roberto. He swung open the large door, and saw a low-slung sports car he didn't recognise near the bottom of the driveway. *I wonder if that's Burbona's*, he thought to himself, realising that he had never once seen her drive; she always seemed to be chauffeured by someone else. He was therefore not at all surprised when the door on the driver's side opened, Roberto got out and straight away went around to open the door on the passenger's side. *She has him well trained*, Jemme thought to himself, and smiled. He looked on with enjoyment as Roberto opened the door, helped Burbona out, and immediately went round to the boot to take her luggage out.

Burbona flicked her hair and smoothed out her dress. She spotted Jemme at the top of the steps and made her way over to him, nimbly crunching over the gravel in her pin-point heels as if it was the easiest thing in the world.

'Jemme! How nice to see you,' she purred. She glanced behind her, where Roberto was struggling with her cases.

'I missed you on the journey down,' she said, leaning in confidentially, 'I was not nearly as comfortable in this little roadster of Roberto's.'

'Well, it's nice to see you too,' said Jemme, smiling in spite of himself. Roberto finally reached the top of the steps and put the baggage down. His cravat was askance and his shirt had worked its way loose. He looked thoroughly flustered, and Jemme realised that this was probably the first time he had carried his own luggage.

'Monsieur,' said Roberto, extending a hand and trying to tuck his shirt in as surreptitiously as possible with the other.

Once the formalities were over, Jemme let the visitors go to their rooms and gratefully retreated to continue with the rest of his rounds. He had noticed that it was a nice sunny morning when he had let Burbona and Roberto in, so he decided to do a quick tour of the grounds and catch up with Philby. He wandered back out through the front door and looped around to the back of the chateau, wanting to take in the herb gardens and vegetable patches that Xelifon had planted so many years ago.

He was delighted to see them flourishing. Thick bushy leaves sprouted up in regular intervals along Xelifon's neat furrows, and Jemme imagined the radishes and carrots fattening up under the earth. He saw delicate yellow courgette flowers curling around the thick spiky stems that supported them, and remembered how he had once thought they were a pretty, but useless addition to the plant. Marguerite and Xelifon had been quick to educate him, though. Xelifon had picked the entire crop, and Marguerite had filled them with goat's cheese and lightly fried them for him. It had been a simple and delicious supper, and he had remembered the deep sense of satisfaction it had given him. Now he noticed that the crop was nearly ready again, and he looked forward to eating the delicacies soon.

He wandered around the patch, looking at how fertile and purposeful everything was, and experienced the same sense of satisfaction again. It felt wholesome and honest; the success of every civilisation he had studied and showcased in the chateau had been measured by their ability to cultivate the land they lived on. He rubbed the stalk of a rosemary plant between his thumb and forefinger, and took in its sweet smell. Smiling, he took one more look around himself and continued on his way. Although it was a roundabout route, he really wanted to walk through the international forest. Along the way he passed statues that looked as if they had been there for hundreds of years, and huge trees that stood nobly as if they had been there for longer than the chateau. It was all testament to Xelifon's skill and ability to weave together a harmonious landscape – *another way of telling a story*, Jemme thought to himself. He felt so relaxed and peaceful in the gardens that he lost track of time, and it was only the pangs of hunger he suddenly felt that reminded him he had better get on with his day.

He didn't find Philby in the gatehouse, and he wasn't in the potting shed either. He retraced his steps to the gatehouse one more time to see if he could find Xelifon. Just as he was wondering where they both were, he saw Philby approaching from the other side of the lawn. He was walking more rapidly than usual, and even from a distance, Jemme could see that he looked angry.

'Good morning, Philby,' said Jemme cheerfully when he arrived.

'Monsieur,' grunted Philby and nodded his head.

'What's the matter?'

Philby puffed out his veined cheeks and exhaled in frustration. 'One of the men.'

'Really, which one?'

'Jean-Claude,' said Philby, making an impatient clicking nose just after he said the name.

'I've never heard of Jean-Claude. Is he one of the artists?' Jemme asked, remembering how short Philby's temper was, when it came to them.

Philby shook his head, 'Maintenance,' he said gruffly.

Jemme was distracted by another figure trotting across the lawn towards the gatehouse. As it got a little closer, he realised it was Xelifon. Although he was nowhere near as dour as Philby, it was clear that he was little agitated too.

'Good morning, Xelifon,' said Jemme as he entered the small shelter.

'Monsieur,' Xelifon said and broke into a wide smile, which Jemme readily returned, appreciating his insuppressibly sunny disposition.

'Yes?' Philby almost barked at Xelifon.

'It is fixed,' he replied with an encouraging smile, obviously intended to calm Philby down.

Philby harrumphed and shook his head. 'How?' he asked eventually.

Xelifon faltered, 'It was the repair you made.'

'He did nothing else?'

Xelifon paused again and smiled sadly. He shook his head.

Philby harrumphed again.

'What's going on?' asked Jemme.

Xelifon looked to Philby, who made the same irritated clicking noise again.

'Jean-Claude,' he began, and then made the noise one more time for good measure, 'is not good at his job.'

Jemme smiled to himself. Philby was nothing if not to the point.

'I'm still not sure who this Jean-Claude is,' said Jemme.

Philby had exhaled with impatience again at the man's name, so Xelifon shyly spoke up.

'He fixes things, Monsieur,' he said. They both saw Philby shake his head in rebuttal.

'Not very well though, Monsieur,' Xelifon added.

'I see. I haven't ever met this Jean-Claude, but I'm guessing he's a sort of handyman?'

'*Oui, Monsieur,*' Xelifon nodded. 'He has been here for several months.'

'Where did he come from?' Jemme asked, 'It doesn't sound like he's a friend of yours, Philby.'

Philby looked particularly sour at the idea. 'Cousin of one of the builders from a while back,' he said. 'Needed him to fix some things I don't have time for. Ends up making more work than he saves.'

'How so?'

'Doesn't do a thing – everything gets worse and takes longer to fix. Does do something, I spend even longer repairing the damage.'

'Goodness, he doesn't sound like good news. Has he been here full time?'

Philby gave a single, curt nod.

'Well, what has he been doing with himself all that time?'

Xelifon giggled shyly. 'He enjoys talking to the *Mademoiselles,* Monsieur.'

Philby looked thunderous. 'Stops them from doing their jobs, too.'

'Does he favour any *Mademoiselles* in particular?' asked Jemme, tickled by the whole scenario.

'Oh no, Monsieur, he likes them all,' said Xelifon earnestly.

'Does he now?' said Jemme wryly.

'*Oui,*' Xelifon said, nodding to make his point. 'Aude, Florence and many of the girls who come in to clean and help with the cooking,' he paused, then shook his head slowly, suddenly looking a little sorrowful, '… they do not like him though.'

'Oh no?'

'*Non,* Monsieur. Madame Marguerite chases him out of the kitchen and calls him a bad man.'

'Well we can't have that. It's not nice for him to be harassing people all over the place. I should talk to this Jean-Claude, I don't want him treating my staff like that. Did you say he wasn't much good at repairing things either, Philby?' Jemme asked, then immediately regretted it – Philby looked like he was about to explode.

'*Non,*' he replied eventually.

'What sort of things has he been fixing? Or rather, *not* fixing?' Jemme corrected himself hurriedly to placate Philby.

'Easy jobs. Loose hinges on doors,' Philby said.

'I see,' said Jemme, wondering how this Lothario was bungling simple tasks to such a degree that it created even more work for Philby.

'What sort of things is he doing?' Jemme asked.

'Just now, there was a leaking pipe,' said Philby, gesturing over to the direction he had come from. 'Very easy to fix. Xelifon could do it. Instead of stopping the leak, he made it worse. There was so much water, the whole section collapsed. It was only because I was walking past at the time and noticed that we stopped it going inside.'

'You mean it was going to flood the inside of the chateau?'

Philby nodded.

Jemme winced. In all likeliness it would have discoloured some paint in one of the workshops or unfinished rooms, but there was always the potential that it could have been worse.

'Out of curiosity, where was this?' he asked Philby.

'Library.'

Jemme couldn't help his jaw dropping slightly. He had invested a considerable amount of time and money in controlling the humidity levels in the library. He was terrified of moisture getting into the room, and was very strict about who was allowed to even enter. The thought of water suddenly gushing into this sanctum was too much to stomach.

'I think I should speak with this Jean-Claude right away,' he said.

Philby looked somewhat placated and Jemme was even able to encourage him to talk about the upkeep of the lake.

He made his way back to the chateau, intending to find the loathsome Jean-Claude after a spot of lunch. He ambled along to the kitchen, planning to pick up some bread and cheese and maybe a drop of coffee. Marguerite was in the middle of doing something complicated at the stove, and he suddenly remembered that he had guests. He had been so immersed in his own little world that he had been blissfully oblivious to their presence. Now he remembered, it suddenly felt like a wearisome burden. He sighed,

'Hello, Marguerite. Don't worry – I'm heading next door. Have they been waiting long?'

'I haven't been in the room since I laid the table,' said Marguerite, looking stressed as she quickly moved things from one pan to another. 'I told them it would be ready about ten minutes ago,' she said, looking up at the large kitchen clock, 'so, *oui,* I assume. They can wait though, Monsieur, it is your house,' she said, suddenly looking a little brighter. 'Why don't you have a little coffee out here first – look, I made you a fresh pot.'

The stress vanished from her face as she fussed over him, 'Take as long as you like, Monsieur,' she cooed, 'this food will not spoil – it is important to be rested,' she added, looking as if she was thoroughly enjoying herself.

Jemme sipped his coffee and looked around the kitchen. He noticed the local paper on the table and flipped it open, scanning through for any interesting happenings or news. Every time he set it down and looked set to go through to the *salle à manger*, Marguerite would swoop over and refill his cup, pointing to the 'highly interesting' story about a big marrow on page seventeen or something of a similar ilk.

Eventually, Jemme felt he couldn't leave them any longer.

'Look, Marguerite, I like relaxing and reading the paper as much as the next person, but I'm worried that I'm being rude. I really think I should head through.'

Marguerite shrugged, as if she hadn't been doing anything to try and stop him.

Jemme drained his coffee and put his cup down. He headed through to the dining room with a suitably apologetic look prepared on his face. He was extremely surprised to find that the dining room was empty, although the table was ready and waiting. He looked around, but they weren't anywhere in the room. None of the chairs looked like they had been moved, and he wondered if they'd even been in the room at all. He looked around one more time, feeling a little silly – almost as if he expected them to pop out from behind a curtain. When they didn't materialise, he sat down, perplexed. He wondered where they could be. It wasn't as if they had huge amounts of responsibility for a certain section of the chateau and so wouldn't be able to tear themselves away. What's more, Marguerite had definitely told them what time lunch would be ready, so it wasn't as if they didn't know. If anything, they were the ones being rude – as she had pointed out, they were *his* guests.

The more he thought about it, the more he couldn't even imagine what they were up to, and he began to question why they had even come. He was sure Roberto must have other places where he could drone on about skyscrapers and modernism, and people would actually be interested and perhaps even commission him to work on something. He seemed to have little genuine interest in this project, despite how much Burbona tried to persuade him to the contrary. Only the day before yesterday, she had called Jemme at the office and waxed lyrical about Roberto's 'passion' for the chateau and how 'indispensable' he was for the project's realisation. He imagined them wandering around together, Roberto pointing at things he wanted to concrete over, and Burbona fawning over the ingenuity of the idea, then promising to put in a good word with Jemme. He shuddered slightly, and wondered if it was a possibility, and if he needed to pull Burbona up on asking his permission before commissioning and acquiring again.

His train of thought was interrupted by the arrival of his two guests. Roberto was reeling off some statistics on pressure exerted on the foundations of high-rise buildings, and Burbona was uttering little gasps in all the appropriate places. Although he rose to greet them, neither of them seemed to notice him until they reached the table. Roberto nodded a hello, and Burbona flashed him her usual winning smile before they both seated themselves and continued their conversation. Neither of them so much as acknowledged the fact that they were over forty minutes late. Jemme listened to Roberto finish his rambling anecdote, with seething resentment. He was so outraged; it rendered him completely speechless. It didn't seem to make any difference -- both of them continued as if he wasn't there anyway.

He ate his lunch as quickly as he could, before standing up abruptly, 'Well, I need to get going, I have lots to do,' he said.

Roberto nodded again, and Burbona flashed the same smile before they went straight back to their conversation again.

Jemme stormed out to the kitchen.

Marguerite was trying to forge some kind of order from the chaos of pots, pans and chopping boards.

'Monsieur, you ate quickly,' she said looking up in surprise.

Jemme looked at the mess around her, and remembered how much work she had put into the meal. He felt a pang of guilt and tried to put his bad temper aside.

'Only because it was so delicious!' he said. He pulled himself together, and tried to forget about the vexatious pair he had left behind in the dining room.

'Marguerite,' he said, 'tell me about this Jean-Claude character. He seems to have caused Philby a lot of bother, and I'm not sure I like the sound of him. What do you think?'

'*Oof,* Monsieur, he is no good at all,' she shook her head. 'I do not even know what he is supposed to be doing here, but whatever it is, he does not do it. He is always making a nuisance of himself in the kitchen – I have to chase him out the whole time. I was even thinking of using the broom one day!'

'Why would he even be in the kitchen?' Jemme asked.

Marguerite shrugged, 'He chases the girls, and he avoids work. They are two very good reasons for coming to the kitchen, Monsieur.'

'That's true enough I suppose. They're two very good reasons why I'm questioning his employment, too.'

'I could give you many more reasons to do that Monsieur. It is not good, him chasing my girls like this. They do not like his attentions, and although those girls cause me nothing but trouble, I will not have anyone bothering them!'

Marguerite puffed out her chest in defiance, like a particularly belligerent mother hen.

'Well if two of my longest serving and most trusted employees think I need to get rid of him, then that is good enough for me. Where can I find him?'

Marguerite shrugged broadly, 'If I could tell you that, I wouldn't be telling you that you needed to fire him,' she said, then chortled.

'Yes, I suppose that's true enough,' said Jemme.

'I do not think you even need to bother doing it yourself,' said Marguerite, 'Monsieur Philby would be very happy to do it for you.'

'Judging by his reaction this morning, I think you're probably right,' said Jemme, deciding that he would delegate the pleasure to his groundsman.

He glanced at his watch and realised that it was well into the afternoon, and he had barely started. Thanking Marguerite again for a delicious lunch, he headed off to explore the rest of the works.

❖   ❖   ❖   ❖

Jemme knew that the calligrapher would be waiting for him, so his first stop would be under the piece of ceiling he had dedicated to showcasing different calligraphic styles. He remembered their conversation in Turkish on the phone, and was looking forward to meeting the man. When he got there, he found him sitting on one of marble steps leading up to the landing.

'Adid?' said Jemme, extending his hand.

Adid stood up, revealing himself to be much shorter than Jemme had imagined. He was therefore surprised at the strength with which Adid pumped his hand, and also the depth of his voice.

'Mr Mafeze, it is a pleasure to meet you.'

'I'm so sorry to keep you waiting.'

Adid shook his head, 'It is not a problem at all. I have enjoyed being able to study the space, and gain an understanding of how everything will look in context. I have begun the plans, look,' he said and sat back down on the step, unfurling the papers he carried in one hand and smoothing them flat on the landing.

Jemme sat next to him and looked as Adid traced the swirls and loops on the plans with his finger.

'This ceiling will show the evolution of the Arabic script in a series of *cartouches*,' he said. 'They will run around the edges up here,' he gestured to the line where the ceiling and wall met, 'and each will be decorated in a slightly different way. I thought we could start with Kufic here, by the door, and end up with modern Arabic script on the other side of the door, so it will have completed a full loop. Although the decoration will be different, I want to use gold and blues in every one.'

He paused to see if Jemme was taking it in, 'What do you think?' he asked.

'It sounds like you have it all worked out,' said Jemme, impressed. 'I wish everyone was as easy to work with as you!'

Adid shrugged, 'I assume this is how everyone works.'

Jemme sighed, 'If only it was!' He looked at Adid's drawings. He couldn't fault the general concept and, now he scrutinised the details, he found them to be excellent as well. Adid was clearly a talented calligrapher, and each type of script was a beautiful example of its style. He stared at them for a while longer, mesmerised by their beautiful curves and swirls.

'Do you have all the equipment you need?' he asked eventually.

'My own paints, drawing and gilding equipment, yes. The only thing I will need is some scaffolding and some old sheeting to cover up this beautiful marble – I wouldn't want it to be damaged in any way.'

'Right, well I can organise that for you, no problem,' said Jemme, secretly thinking that the scaffolding would have to be very high in order for Adid to be able to reach the ceiling.

'I can map these out whilst it's all set up,' said Adid, 'then I can start straight away.'

'This is all music to my ears,' said Jemme, 'I'll organise it for you right away.' He shook Adid's hand warmly, and headed off to ask Philby to get everything up and running.

At the same time, he asked him if he would be able to give Jean-Claude the boot, and was amused by the small smile of satisfaction that cracked the normally serious groundsman's face.

On the way back from seeing Philby, he wandered through the vegetable patch again, as he had found it so pleasing before. He stopped by the same rosemary bush and surveyed everything around him. Realising he was at the edge of a small herb garden, he stopped to pick a few sprigs of mint and thyme. His mind began to wander, and he remembered something he had read once about herb gardens in England during the Elizabethan age. He recalled reading about knot gardens, in which herbs and small bushes were planted in an intricate pattern, which would be followed by the ladies of the house as a form of exercise. Imagining the Tudor ladies in all their finery picking their way through a maze less than a foot high, Jemme wondered if it felt at all pointless to them when they could see where they were going at all times. Then he tried to remember where he had read about the gardens, or where he might even have seen one.

Gradually it dawned on him – it had been on one of his trips to Hever Castle with Hil. He had misremembered: he hadn't actually read about it, she had told him.

The familiar feeling of loss stirred in his belly. He didn't feel it as keenly as he had before, but it still sat there heavily, and he wondered if he would always carry it with him. Then, as always, his mind raced into planning something else, so he wouldn't have to dwell on it for too long.

He wandered away from the herb garden and through the orchard to the flat piece of lawn behind it. At one point he had considered putting a tennis court there, but as he had received fewer and fewer guests at the chateau and begun to focus on work more and more, he had slowly realised it wasn't worth the effort: he would have no one to play with. The patch of land, he realised, would be perfect for a maze. He had already begun work on Hever Castle inside, so why not reference it somewhere outside too? It would be a fantastic project for Xelifon to work on and Jemme knew he would plant the hedges in exactly the right way, so it would look like it was an old feature.

Jemme wandered back to the house, pleased with his plan. Thoughts of England were weighing heavily on his mind. He wondered how Hil was doing in London and then tried to distract himself by wondering if there were any other English castles or palaces he should reference elsewhere in the chateau. There was certainly enough space. He tried to think of anywhere he had visited that had had a lasting impact on him and would be relevant to the chateau project. Realising that he might as well celebrate the fact he still had a library, he decided to go and browse through the – mercifully dry – shelves for inspiration.

At first he didn't find anything. There was wealth of material on the Tudors and the transition from the mediaeval to the early modern period, but this had already been well documented all over the chateau. Likewise, the spread of the Renaissance across Europe had been exhaustively showcased.

He wondered if he had anything from a little later on and tried to rattle through English history in his head, trying to remember what had happened after this period of intense development. There was the monarchy, lost and restored, the imperial march of colonialism and the heavy coal-stained spread of industrialisation. It was all fascinating, but he didn't know where any of it could fit in. He thought some more about the industrial revolution and the empire it drove. It was a fascinating parallel for so many empires which had unfurled before, and which he had carefully referenced elsewhere. The British Empire should definitely be showcased, he realised. Tea, oranges, silk, silver and spices flooded from the exotic East to smoke-choked London, and would have elicited the same sense of awe and wonder as they had when they travelled towards the West on the old silk route. He thought of Queen Victoria, sitting at the centre of an expanding modern network, filled with new technologies, innovations and cultural exchanges. It was exactly what he needed to reference – it would give him an exciting segue into America too and the developments occurring in that part of the so-called New World.

His mind fizzed with ideas as he pulled books he had barely read before from the shelves. These would be the most modern rooms he had included in the chateau so far. They would be the easiest to research and could be the most detailed in decoration too. He could use the newest and most advanced decorating techniques of the age in each one, and even feature some of the technologies driving this new global culture, such as the telephone and the electric light bulb?

He began to think of America and all the decorative possibilities it opened up… he could even examine the White House itself. As a building, its neoclassical style demonstrated a range of different styles; even including grand French chateaus very similar to the very one he was currently sitting in. The house itself had always been a showcase for the nation's most accomplished designers, most modern techniques, and most innovative styles. Every redecoration had been carefully and painstakingly documented, providing an invaluable resource for Jemme – it was like having a step-by-step guide written specially for him.

He jotted down notes on a new piece of paper; the scope seemed limitless… he could even take the decorations as far as the Kennedy renovations in the 1960s. As he flicked through the book he realised that it didn't deal exclusively with the White House, but rather it gave a potted overview of American interior decoration. If this book could give such excellent detail, then he could only imagine what tasty extras he could glean from specialist books, and there must be huge numbers available.

He skimmed the pages, trying to pick up on anything useful or valuable for his notes. The small section on the Kennedys was fascinating. It described the team of decorators, collectors and designers the First Lady assembled around her. Jemme was intrigued by each of these characters. Several of them seemed to have European provenance, or had worked on Royal Palaces that were referenced elsewhere in the museum. It wove the idea of a White House room into the chateau's narrative even more tightly. He started making a list of names he wanted to read up on. *Stéphane Boudin* was the first name he wrote down; then, as he read a little further, he wrote *Maison Jansen* next to Boudin's name. Jemme recognised the name straight away; it was still one of the most prestigious interior design firms in Paris. Boudin had apparently been president of the atelier and hand-selected by Jansen himself. Jemme continued to read, and soon he had added *Henry Francis du Pont (Winterhur Museum)* to the list, then *Dorothy-Mae Parish*. They all seemed to be important characters, and Jemme was amused to read about the power struggles and political feuds that had emerged between the designers and decorators during the renovations. It all sounded very familiar. So too did the work which had been conducted during the Kennedy restoration. He hadn't realised how extensive it had been, and how significant in terms of restoring vital parts of the building's history.

The work had initially begun to counter the installation of modern fabrications and casual reproductions of period pieces during the era before. Furthermore, many of the rooms were not decorated in a way befitting the stately heritage or office of the building. The project had involved sourcing period pieces, fine paintings and antique fabrications, all meticulously researched and expertly installed. Moreover, different periods of the early Republic and of world history were selected as a theme for each room: Federal style for the Green Room, French Empire for the Blue Room, American Empire for the Red Room, Louis XVI for the Yellow Oval Room, and Victorian for the President's study.

He ran over the parallels in his mind. The motivation behind the work, its execution, even the creation of individual rooms dedicated to different eras, was all so similar to what he was doing. Wandering through the corridors of power and opening individual doors, each one would lead to another world. It was precisely what he had been trying to achieve over the course of a lifetime. He decided to research the room some more when he got back to Paris. Unsure what form it would take, and even how many rooms it would span, he was nevertheless looking forward to working on something fresh and different. He might even be able to visit some of the very workshops that had produced the furnishings for the White House. Finally, he noticed one more name before he shut the book and he added it to the bottom of the list – *Zuber & Cie.*

Back outside the library, he realised that he was still behind with his day, and he would have to move quickly if he wanted to get anything achieved before supper. He went to the kitchen to ask Marguerite what time everything would be ready, and found that it was the usual whirl of bustle, with Marguerite at the centre of the chaos, conducting operations.

'Ah, Monsieur!' she said when she saw him, 'Have you had a good afternoon?'

'Very good thank you, Marguerite. I've made quite a few useful decisions.'

'*Ah bon*, and that Jean-Claude – ' Jemme saw Aude look up in slight alarm at the name, as if the man himself might just have appeared. 'You have fired him, no?'

Aude's eyebrows shot up, and a look of eagerness spread across her face.

'Actually, I told Philby he could have that pleasure, but he will certainly be gone by Monday – if Philby can find him, that is.'

'If Monsieur Philby has such a message to deliver, then I'm sure he will be able to find him,' Marguerite chuckled to herself. '*Tsk*, don't just stand there with that stupid smile on your face child, get back to work!' she said to Aude.

Aude didn't seem to mind the scolding at all, and happily returned to stirring the pot on the stove with the same broad smile on her face.

'Marguerite, I was just wondering how long I had until supper?'

Marguerite surveyed the kitchen, 'About an hour and a half, Monsieur, but we can make it earlier or later if you would like?'

'No, that sounds perfect – just enough time for me to get something done, I'll see you then,' he said, leaving the kitchen and heading for the second floor.

He'd been looking forward to seeing the progress of one room in particular. Although he realised he had left it too late to talk to the artist, he was hoping to see some of his work, and perhaps talk with him the next day. On his way he passed the Manuscripts and Miniatures room and put his head around the door quickly. He was deeply satisfied with what he saw – it was a well accomplished room and put him in the right mindset for the next room. Further down the corridor, he came to it: the Persian room. Whereas many of the rooms he had been working on recently were new additions and arose from the chateau's own story, this was a room directly from his dream. He had a very clear picture in his mind of how he wanted it to look, but he knew it would be very complicated to realise. The room would be rich in terms of its decoration, fixtures, fittings and overall texture. Sourcing everything so that it was just right would be a challenge in itself. However, so too would be the architecture of the room. Jemme wanted at least two cupola installed, possibly three. He had no idea how this could be achieved, but he imagined it would involve either raising the current ceiling or installing them under the current ceiling level, lowering the height of the room. He didn't necessarily have a problem with this. His dream had been filled with shifting dimensions and spaces, and he was attempting to recreate an unexpected or unusual experience. However, he didn't know what would need to happen in terms of structural support and reinforcing the floor. His experience with the Cordovan columns had made him realise how far-reaching the implications could be. He knew that this was exactly the kind of thing that Roberto could help with, and that it made sense to ask him, especially when the man seemed to be cluttering up the chateau every weekend. However, by chance he had never mentioned the room to Burbona, and now he had taken the conscious decision not to mention it to Roberto either. He would probably get an architect in Paris to look over the plans, and ask some local builders to follow them. In the meantime, he had engaged ceramicists, gilders and tilers to work on the room. The ceramicist was the one who Jemme had been hoping to meet that weekend; she had been to look at the space available and sketch out some plans for him. By the time he reached the room, as he suspected, she was long gone. However, it gave him the opportunity to look around and try to reconfigure the rich colours and textures of his dream within the empty white space before him. It was too small, too limited to be able to adequately pay homage to the might of the Persian Empire. However, it was so influential, that even if it had not been in the original dream room he would have had to include it in the chateau somewhere.

For him, Persia played a large role in the story of interaction between East and West and, ever since the very earliest times, there had been cultural interaction between Persia and her western neighbours. He had situated this room on the same corridor as the Babylonian room as it had been the Persians who, in 539 BC, had put an end to the later Babylonian Empire. Under their leader Cyrus, they had deposed the cruel Babylonian government and ushered in more humane and clement era. It was just one episode in a long tradition of shifting influence and cultural adaptation. When Persia herself was invaded by the Arabs over a thousand years later, her citizens resisted the Arabic language, but gradually converted to Islam. With an artistic and literary tradition of its own, open to influences from the Far East, Persia was to make an immense contribution to Islamic culture.

Jemme had already begun to reference some of these contributions elsewhere, in the Manuscripts and Miniatures room. One of the first things he had learned about this civilisation had been from his grandmother, who told him of Persia's important contribution to literature. Not only were they responsible for the transmission of certain rediscovered Greek texts to the Arab world, but they also provided fables and legends. Some of the tales were of Indian origin and reached Persia from the East, together with the game of chess, in the middle of the sixth century. Under Persian influence a far more florid literary style was to develop, with colourful imagery in contrast to the austere tradition of the early desert writers. The Arab historians were to take the Persians as their models, while the Persians, accepting and reworking the rules of Arabic poetry, produced poetic works of extraordinary beauty both in Persian and Arabic.

This had long fascinated Jemme, and he had been collecting manuscript art since he had started his first adult job. The collection and the tradition itself were too important to be contained within this one room, so he was pleased that there was another dedicated just to this. It had been this skill, and this culture of book production, which had led the Persians to excel in another field: calligraphy. During the eighth and ninth century, Persia was producing some of the most remarkable calligraphy in the Eastern and Western worlds and some of the finest Qu'rans, many of which remained superlative, over one thousand years later. Much like with the manuscript art, Jemme had felt that the calligraphy could not be represented in only one room. He had commissioned the piece that Adid was working on, and was certain that he would make a feature of calligraphy elsewhere in the chateau as well.

One thing that he knew would be included in this room would be the thing that the Persians were perhaps most famous for: the carpet. He hadn't yet found the perfect piece for the room, and didn't yet know which era and even which region he would source it from. Although it wasn't common knowledge, the most famous types of Persian carpets were named after the different cities from which they originated: the Ghum, the Ardabile, the Okrah, the Tabreze, the Ispahan and the Tehran. Artisans were so highly skilled in some of these cities that production was relatively low, and examples of their types extremely rare.

He knew that Ardabile had produced so few carpets in its heyday that every single one had a luxury status, and was a covetable item. He had only ever seen one come up for auction in all the time he had been living in Paris, and it had sold for an eye-watering amount. In fact the only other example of an Ardabile carpet in existence that he actually knew about was a large piece in the Victoria and Albert Museum in London, one of their most prized acquisitions.

Jemme knew that the Arabs were followed by other conquerors of Persia, the Seljuks in the eleventh century and the Mongols in the thirteenth century. However disruptive these invasions were in certain respects, they were unexpectedly fruitful from an artistic point of view. It was above all the Mongols who introduced Far Eastern elements into Persian art, preparing the way for the first great age of Persian miniature painting. They adopted the motifs and colours and, as time went by, these became ever richer and more sophisticated.

As different dynasties came to power, the Persian artists received constant encouragement. For more than three centuries, their paintings retained a striking originality and affected the pictorial art of their neighbours. In Europe, Persian influence arrived late. It was not until the seventeenth century that the fashion of the Persian carpet replaced that of the Turkish one, and it was only in the late eighteenth century that Europeans became properly acquainted with Persian literature and painting. By the middle of the nineteenth century, however, Persian influence was clearly perceptible, not only in the world of some of the 'orientalist' painters, but also in the many new schools of design.

Jemme had studied Persian history his whole life, and never once tired of it. It had influenced many aspects of the chateau, and he was excited about the prospect of this new room. He had decided that it would specifically reference two different Persian dynasties: the Sassanid and Safavid. He had described exactly what he had wanted in great detail to the ceramicist, and had been delighted that she appeared to understand precisely. With DD's help, he had already acquired some seventeenth and eighteenth century tiles. The job of the ceramicist would be to create some new tiles for the room, which were sympathetic to the old ones and yet were stand alone pieces in their own right. He didn't want reproductions or something that looked like a pastiche, but rather something sensitive and almost syncretic in its function. It was a very specific brief, but she had seemed excited by it, and had been eager to start work straight away. She had already been to look at the original tiles back in Paris, although he hadn't had the chance to meet her then either, and she was at work on some designs at the moment. Part of the challenge would be to mix the striking but very distinctive indigo dye with which they would be painted. It would have to be completely organic, preferably even made with plant materials sourced from that part of the world. Harsh modern dyes with a chemical base would be too obvious and too jarring.

Again, she had seemed to understand this straight away, and described to him some restoration jobs she had worked on in the past in museums and private houses, which had required very similar skills. Jemme was looking forward to meeting her the next day and hearing about her progress.

There wasn't much more he could do in the room at the moment, so he headed back downstairs, pleased that it was taking direction, if only in his mind. He went via the calligraphy staircase, and was pleased to see that the scaffolding was set up, ready for Adid to begin work. Crossing the Halle d'Honneur, he made his way back up the stairs again, wanting to take in one more room before he headed to supper. This room had all been completed remotely, from his desk in Paris. He had chosen the room, hired the artists, sent over the furnishings, purchased the pieces and commissioned the work, all from the same seat. It was probably the only room so far which had been completed from start to finish without him seeing a single part of it. He made his way down the corridor, counting the doors as he did so – he had asked for it to be the third room on the left. Finding the correct door, he opened it and entered the room.

It took him a few moments to take everything in. It hadn't been exactly as he imagined, but as he studied the room, he realised that that didn't matter: it included everything he had asked for, and it all came together perfectly. This room wasn't a dream room, but had been inspired by one. When he had been cataloguing part of his collection, he had assembled several pieces that could be loosely categorised as Abbasid in theme. He wanted to create a small gallery to house them all together; as a collection they had a greater significance than as individual pieces. He studied his surroundings: it was the perfect middle ground. If it had gone too much in one direction, it would have felt as if he was stepping into ninth-century Baghdad; too much in another direction, as if it was a twelfth century scientific library, and too much in yet another, as if he was wandering into the reading room of the Bibliothèque Nationale. He imagined that everyone entering the room would see it in a different way and take something different away with them, depending on their experiences and perceptions.

For him, it was the perfect mix of library, museum gallery, cultural homage and chateau room. It was less formal than a gallery and was almost cosy – it was certainly an inviting place of repose. It was filled with books of a scientific nature, and statues of great sages from history. The carpet was pure silk, and several armchairs softened the room, inviting the visitor to stay and read through centuries of acquired knowledge.

If all the different references, manuscripts and statues were considered, this room covered the period from 750 all the way to 1254 when Al-Musta'sim, the last Abbasid Caliph of Baghdad, was deposed by Hulagu Khan. Jemme looked at the delicate silk carpet on the floor, and remembered the story of invading

Mongol forces wrapping Al-Musta'sim in a rug and trampling him to death with their horses, allegedly so as to avoid spilling holy blood. This had finished a dynasty of almost five centuries. The gruesome ordeal certainly seemed far removed from the peaceful sanctuary he had created here.

A small oil painting of Harun al Rashid hung on the wall facing Jemme. Although the portrait was modest, al Rashid was certainly a focal figure of the room. Perhaps the most famous of all the Caliphs, Harun al Rashid oversaw a flourishing in culture, science and learning, which included the foundation of the Bayt al-Hikma library, the 'House of Wisdom'. During his rule, excellent diplomatic relations, specifically with the West, were cultivated and upheld. The Frankish scholar Einhard and the Benedictine Nokter of St. Gall both refer to envoys travelling between the courts of Haroun and Charlemagne and amicable discussions being held regarding Christian access to the Holy Land. Jemme remembered seeing Haroun al Rashid in his dream room, surrounded by the gifts of diplomacy: Spanish horses, Frisian cloaks and hunting dogs, sent by Charlemagne. In later years, when he had experienced the dream, he had seen Charlemagne receiving the exchange gifts, a different treasure every time he had had the dream: silks, a brass candelabrum, perfume, balsam, ivory chessmen, a giant tent with curtains of every colour, an elephant, and a water clock which struck the hour by dropping bronze balls into a bowl, as small mechanised knights signified the hour by emerging and retreating from little doors.

Although Haroun al-Rashid was the conceptual focus, perhaps the most obvious physical focus was the biggest treasure in the room: a beautiful astrolabe. This coincided with a map of the world from the ninth century, which filled the ceiling of the room. It had been a significant acquisition, and he had Burbona to thank. She had been instrumental in setting up meetings, forging introductions and eventually negotiating the purchase from the Rothschild Museum. The piece represented an extraordinary advancement in scientific technology: as well as locating and predicting the sun, moon, planets and stars, it could be used to determine local time, survey triangulation and to cast horoscopes. It was emblematic of the Golden Age of Islam and embodied its broad output of learning and innovation. The piece was extraordinarily valuable, not just historically, but also in cold financial terms too. By rights it should have been in a safe, or at least a locked room. There was something thrilling about its unprotectedness, almost nakedness. The realisation that he could reach out and touch it if he wanted to was compelling, especially as it had spent the last one hundred and fifty years of its life behind glass.

Jemme realised that he had probably been about an hour and a half, and he should make his way back to the dining room. He gave the Abbasid room one final look, and a satisfied nod of approval, then closed the door behind him and retraced his steps. The room had also set an excellent precedent for completing future rooms from Paris, especially those which were fairly straightforward.

By the time he reached the kitchen, he realised that he was late again. His whole day had been put out by waiting for Burbona and Roberto at lunchtime, which was irritating. Nonetheless, it had still been productive and enjoyable, so he found it hard to be bad-tempered. He planned to take a shortcut through the kitchen to get to the dining room, but was waylaid by Marguerite en route.

'Monsieur, there you are!' she said, waving a spatula around to emphasise the finding.

Jemme knew her well enough to know that she was about to reveal something dramatic.

'Monsieur, I have solved the mystery of Sandro!' she said with a flourish and some more spatula waving.

'Sandro...? Oh, *Sandro*,' said Jemme, remembering the plight of the bullied Italian who didn't appear to be sleeping in his own bed.

'Yes, *Sandro*,' said Marguerite significantly.

Jemme didn't want to deny her the pleasure of the big reveal, so he let her rattle through each of her individual suspicions, and how she had tested them.

Eventually she got to the point, '*Le placard*! Monsieur! *Le placard*!'

'The *placard*? The cupboard?'

'*Oui, Monsieur*! He has been sleeping in the cupboard!'

'Are you sure? That just seems so...bizarre.'

'Yes, I am quite sure, Monsieur – I investigated it thoroughly.'

'I'm sure you did. I just... well, like I said, it seems very odd.' He thought about it some more. It was certainly odd, but not impossible. Sandro was rather short and the built-in cupboards in some of the original rooms were rather spacious. In fact, compared to the rooms in tiny modern Parisian *appartements*, the cupboards were voluminous. Jemme stopped thinking about whether or not Sandro would have fitted in the cupboard, and realised that the real question was why he was in there in the first place.

'Is he alright, Marguerite?'

Marguerite shrugged and her face softened, 'I do not know, Monsieur. He seems so young compared to the others and he is far too sensitive for their coarse humour. I don't think they mean harm, but he takes everything they say to heart, and at night he has been crawling into the cupboard with his eiderdown and pillow like a *petit animal*, hiding in his burrow,' she looked saddened. 'Italy is a long way from here when someone is feeling like that, Monsieur,' she said.

Jemme winced, he felt extremely guilty; he didn't like the thought of anyone feeling like that at the chateau, and he knew the burden of responsibility was firmly on his shoulders.

'What do you think we can do to make it better? What can I do? Should I speak to the others?'

Marguerite sighed, 'I think that might make it worse, Monsieur. You are the employer of all of them – they might resent him for getting them all in trouble.'

'Yes, I suppose you're right. I can't just do nothing though,' he said feeling a little helpless.

'Listen, I will help, Monsieur. It is much easier for me to talk to them. Now that we know what is going on I can keep an eye on him, and if it hasn't got any better then you can step in.'

'Are you sure, Marguerite? It's very kind of you to offer, but I really feel like I should do something.'

'Trust me, it is better this way. I know that you would do anything you could. *Ça va très bien, Monsieur.*'

'I don't know what I would do without you, Marguerite,' he said, smiling at her appreciatively. 'I suppose I'd better go through, I don't want to keep the others waiting – are they there?'

Marguerite shrugged, 'I have not been through, I was waiting for you, but they must be there – I should think they will have been there for fifteen minutes or so.'

Jemme scuttled through to greet his guests and apologise for not having spent any time with them during the day. He couldn't believe it when he entered an empty dining room for the second time that day. He looked around again, but yet again saw that there was no sign they'd even been in the room. This time he found it difficult to fight off the bad temper that descended on him. He couldn't imagine where on earth they could be and what they could be up to – in his house no less.

He paced around the room, then sat down at the table. He felt restless and irritated, so got up and paced around the room again. Starting to feel like a fool, or at least, like he was being taken for one, he was on the verge of heading back into the kitchen when he heard their footsteps across the Halle d'Honneur. The clicking noise of Burbona's spiky heels was unmistakable, and Jemme noted that she didn't seem to be in any particular hurry.

He had no choice but to sit and wait whilst the footsteps gradually got louder and his guests deigned to make their appearance in their own time. Just as before, they were talking between themselves as they entered the room.

'Good evening,' said Jemme pointedly.

Once again, Roberto nodded a greeting entirely free of charisma.

'Jemme, how good to see you – we missed you this afternoon,' said Burbona with a radiant smile. Jemme didn't believe her for a moment.

'What have you been up to?' he asked.

Burbona sat straight down and continued speaking, whilst Jemme noticed Roberto hover stiffly behind his chair until he was sure everyone else was seated.

'Oh, there has been so much to do!' she said. 'We have covered so much I'm feeling exhausted!' she laughed.

'Do? What do you mean *do*? I don't understand exactly what it is the two of you have been *doing* here.'

Burbona evidently noticed the edge in Jemme's voice, and realised that he was not in the mood for playfulness. She shifted her focus onto Jemme and gave him her full attention,

'You are such a tease,' she purred, 'you know we have been working as hard as you!'

Jemme opened his mouth to say something to the contrary, but she quickly interjected,

'I think when you see our plans you'll be very pleased indeed.' She exchanged smiles with Roberto and looked back at Jemme.

'Plans?' asked Jemme.

'Yes, you don't need to worry about a thing, we've taken care of it all from beginning to end.'

'It?' asked Jemme, his mouth starting to feel dry. He remembered Burbona's purchase of the paintings. She had planned the whole thing herself without consulting him at any stage, and it had ended up costing him a great deal of money and leaving him deeply dissatisfied.

Burbona raised her perfectly shaped eyebrows at him questioningly.

'What do you mean "…we've taken care of it?"' asked Jemme as slowly as he could.

'I meant that we have devised the concept, planned its completion and commissioned the work – you haven't had to worry about a thing! We've completed the whole process for you, without you even having to be involved.'

Jemme counted to five and forced himself to unclench his jaw and exhale slowly.

'You're speechless,' Burbona observed correctly. She turned to Roberto with a big smile. 'I told you it would be a wonderful surprise.'

Roberto looked as impassive as ever, and merely inclined his head.

Jemme didn't know how to react. He was so furious that he had almost transcended through his anger to serenity.

With extreme control, he turned back to Burbona, 'Please tell me more about these plans,' he said, in as measured a manner as possible.

Burbona needed no further encouragement, 'I simply *knew* you would be delighted,' she said and tossed her hair. 'We've been working on this for weeks, and not just here – back in Paris as well. It all started when we were thinking about how underused Roberto is here. We're so lucky to have someone of his stature working here, and we have been using him for such menial tasks. A less magnanimous man would have left a long time ago, I'm sure.'

Jemme could feel his jaw clench again. *We haven't been using him for any tasks at all*, he thought to himself. He took another deep breath, 'Go on,' he said to Burbona.

'Well we were thinking about where Roberto's skills really lie. It would be criminal to have someone of his finesse and renown here, and not to reference his own work somewhere in the chateau.'

Jemme winced at the idea – he wanted to reference the achievements of the Umayyad dynasty, the Golden Age of Islam, the art of the Venetians and the cultural flourishing of the Silk Route, not the meaningless glass structures of a man he barely liked.

'I see,' he said.

'Roberto is such an *accomplished* architect,' said Burbona, positively dripping honey from the word, 'but this project does not make the most of his skills. The rooms are too old and the materials too traditional.'

This time, Jemme couldn't contain his frustration, 'Burbona, it's a chateau! What do you expect?!'

Burbona smiled away his outburst, 'Of course, and it's one of the most beautiful chateaus I have visited in this whole region. I think your plans are ambitious and exciting, which is why I agreed to work with you. However, I'm sure you would admit that they are quite limiting.'

Jemme gulped, 'Limiting?' he asked.

'Yes, absolutely,' Burbona nodded in agreement. 'For all that it looks back, this chateau doesn't really look forward.'

'Forward? Well, I –' Jemme didn't even know what to say.

'Well, that's where Roberto and I can help you. We looked at all the available space and considered which areas would lend themselves well to more forward -looking decoration.' She paused and smiled at Roberto again. He had been listening intently and evidently thought that this was the moment to step in.

'Many of these rooms would not suit a modernist approach,' he said with a very serious expression. 'Their ceilings are too low and their shapes are not clean enough.'

'Not "'clean" enough?'

Roberto nodded sombrely, 'Yes, Monsieur, there are unwanted angles, wobbling walls and a pronounced lack of symmetry.'

'But that's the whole point of a building this age! That's where all the character comes from!' The only thing tempering Jemme's anger was his utter exasperation at what he was hearing.

'These "quirks", Monsieur, impose unwanted character on the space enclosed within the room. They interfere with it, and hinder the architectural vision.'

'I see,' said Jemme, who couldn't disagree more.

'However, there is potential in one part of this chateau.'

'Well, that's good to hear. I was starting to worry it was a lost cause.'

'Not at all. The *sous-sol* is full of open space, and with careful planning and skilful workmanship there is the opportunity to create something magnificent there.'

'In the *sous-sol*?' Jemme couldn't believe what he was hearing.

'Yes, absolutely. The first stage is to remove all the dividing walls.' Roberto pulled out a small leather-bound notebook which was filled with calculations and neat sketches. He carefully made his way through to a particular page. 'Here,' he said, turning it around to face Jemme.

'What is this?'

'This is a sketch of a section of the *sous-sol* with all the internal walls removed.'

'But it's just an empty rectangle.'

'Exactly,' said Roberto significantly.

'I see. What is the next step?' Jemme asked disinterestedly.

'The next step is to clad everything in marble,' Roberto said, finally starting to sound animated.

'Everything?'

'Absolutely. We will have not just marble walls and flooring but also a marble ceiling too.

'Right. Then what?'

'Then we will install windows, to light this space.'

'Windows? In the *sous-sol*?'

'I have gone over the blueprints and, with some small excavation work, there will be space for windows, right at the top of the wall.'

'I told you we had covered everything,' said Burbona, looking pleased.

'Well, it certainly seems as if you have covered everything in marble,' said Jemme. 'Is there anything more to this plan?'

'More?' asked Roberto.

'Well, once you've lined this room with marble and installed some windows, then what are you going to put in it?'

'Put in it?' Roberto asked, looking aghast.

'Well yes, you're not just going to leave it as an empty room are you? It sounds like Ramases' tomb!'

'Monsieur, it is not an empty room, it is a *space*,' said Roberto, sounding pained. 'To put anything in it – any furniture, any ornamentation – would destroy it completely.'

Jemme tried hard not to roll his eyes. He was getting fed up with listening to this.

Burbona could see that he wasn't thrilled with the plan, and evidently thought that he hadn't understood it properly.

'Think about when you go into a grand modern building – like a skyscraper,' she said. 'You always enter into a grand and empty foyer don't you?'

'Yes,' said Jemme, thinking about how much he hated these imposing, posturing spaces.

'Well, they set the tone for the whole building,' said Burbona triumphantly. 'It will be a fabulous way of setting the tone for the whole chateau.'

'But it will be underground.'

'It will be the perfect antidote to all the other rooms here,' said Roberto.

'What do you mean antidote?'

'All of the rooms so far are very cluttered, very…busy. They are beautiful in their own way, but they are overwhelming for the visitor – they trap him in that environment – it is very intense. The visitor will almost forget that he is in the chateau at all.'

Jemme had heard enough. There were many aspects of this plan which angered and infuriated him, and he would think them through individually at a later date. For now though there was one overriding and pressing concern,

'Do you even understand what I'm trying to do here?!' he said.

Roberto looked taken aback, 'To do here?'

'Yes! Here in the chateau, with this whole project?'

'Well, of course, yes. I understand that. I am just providing you with a way of making it more complete.'

'More complete?' Jemme took another breath. For the first time in their acquaintance, he thought that Burbona looked almost flustered. She flashed a smile, flicked her hair and attempted to smooth things over. Jemme was not in the mood.

'I'm sorry, Burbona,' he said, interrupting her just as she started, 'I just feel as if Roberto has fundamentally misunderstood the whole purpose of this entire project. I *want* to impose on the visitor. I *want* them to feel as if they've left the chateau and entered a tiny room each time they open a door, that's the point – that's everything I've been trying to achieve since I started this. I don't want to strip anything back – in fact, if anything I want to put more in. Do you understand that?!' he looked at Roberto, almost beseechingly.

Roberto looked lost and turned to Burbona for help. She smiled uncertainly for a moment, and then looked as if she'd decided to take charge of the situation.

'Jemme,' she purred, 'I think you're just surprised, that's all. I know how much you like to be involved in decisions, but that's why you've been working too hard. That's why I'm here, to help you with everything. I told you, you didn't need to worry about a thing, we've done it all for you.'

'But that's the point – you've done it all!'

'Come now,' said Burbona, chiding him with a look that suggested he was being an obstinate child. 'I know it's different to everything else here, but that's the beauty of it. It will be such a perfect foil for the other rooms that each will seem more beautiful as a result.'

Jemme was slightly appeased, but only until Roberto opened his mouth again.

'This is exactly what I was trying to say: the noise of the rooms upstairs will only make the tranquillity of this room more welcome, more necessary even.'

Jemme could feel the heat of temper rising within him. He didn't want to make a scene, but he desperately wanted to impress on Roberto just how wrong he was.

Once again, Burbona stepped in, 'Why don't you look at the plans?' she asked. 'I'm sure you'll feel differently once you've seen everything all mapped out.'

She took the notebook from Roberto, and strode confidently around the table to Jemme, pulling out a chair and sitting down next to him.

'Look,' she said, leafing through it to show him the notes. It was a small notebook and Roberto's handwriting was even tinier. Coupled with the extremely large ring Burbona was wearing on the hand she was using to turn the pages, Jemme couldn't see a thing.

'Can I see?' he asked, putting out a hand.

He noticed a flicker of reluctance cross Burbona's face, although she quickly smiled, 'Of course,' and handed it over.

Jemme looked through, trying to read Roberto's notes and see if there was any further detail in the diagrams when he looked at them up close. If anything, they looked even plainer and less interesting. There were a few rectangles and arrows, labelling where light would enter the room. It looked like the marginalia one would expect to find next to an actual diagram – the scribbled notes that give dimensions and the boring, practical details, certainly not the actual picture itself.

Jemme sighed loudly. There was no rescuing this situation and no way he was going to proceed with these plans. Idly, he flicked to the next page. Two neat columns of figures filled the page. He scrutinised them for a while – they didn't look like measurements and he didn't understand what they were referring to. He scanned them again and his eye came to rest at the total at the bottom of the page. It was an extremely large number, but it didn't show any units or reference points.

'What is this?' he asked, tapping the number with one finger.

'I told you we'd taken care of everything,' said Burbona brightly, 'we've covered absolutely everything, including costing the whole project for you.'

'Well that was good of you,' said Jemme.

'I knew you'd think so,' said Burbona, oblivious to his tone. 'I know it's quite high, but we wanted to source the very best materials – '

'Wait, this number here refers to Francs?!'

'Yes, of course.'

Jemme gulped hard and looked at the figure again. It was eye-poppingly high... he even blinked, but when he opened his eyes it was exactly the same.

'Burbona, do you realise that this is more than I have spent on any single item in this entire chateau! All the precious books and carpets, all the antiques, even the custom made pieces in the different rooms – not one cost as much as this!' He paused and thought for a moment. It was definitely true, he had never spent such a huge amount on just one piece. In fact, the second largest amount he had spent had also involved Burbona and the purchase of the ill-fated pair of paintings.

'As I said, I know it seems like a lot, but we wanted to source the very best materials –'

'Even if you were sourcing pure gold, I don't imagine it would cost this much.'

Burbona was starting to look unsettled, 'Look,' she said, 'I would never bring substandard or poor quality materials onto this project. I know that you only want the best, and so do I. More importantly, Roberto is a highly accomplished architect – he will only work with the best.'

'More importantly?'

Just as she was starting to get a little worked up, Burbona tried to diffuse the situation again,

'Of course it's not more important,' she said in a soothing voice, 'no one is more important on this project than you. However, we are extremely fortunate to have an incredibly sought-after architect at our disposal, and one who is the toast of Paris. It is a huge shame that we have been wasting his talents. Now that we finally have the opportunity for him to do the thing he does best, do we really want to provide him with shoddy materials?'

'We don't want to provide him with anything!' Jemme almost shouted, 'I haven't agreed to any of this. If you two want to cook up this plan in your own time then that's fine, that's your business. If you want to have any chance of seeing it put into action though, then it becomes my business and I *must* be involved from the very beginning!'

Although he was the centre of discussion, Burbona and Jemme were talking as if Roberto wasn't there, and for all he was contributing he might as well not be.

'Also, the thing that Roberto does best is not the thing that I want in this chateau! It is completely wrong for the period, the building and all its surroundings and the fact that neither of you can see that is almost as upsetting as the fact you've come up with this plan behind my back.' He finally looked over at Roberto. The architect was sitting up straight, still full of the air of stiffness and formality that Jemme resented, despite the heated nature of the situation.

He shifted uncomfortably, as he realised he would have to get involved in the conversation, 'Monsieur Mafeze, I can assure you that I investigated the marble available very thoroughly in order to find the best and most fitting example for this project. I'm afraid that this is just how much marble of this calibre costs.'

'So this astronomical bill is *just* for the marble? Nothing else? None of the cutting or installation or conditioning?'

Roberto looked even more uncomfortable. 'I'm afraid that that is just the cost,' he repeated limply.

'Roberto, you must have *seen* the rest of the chateau. You must have seen that there is marble everywhere! I know *exactly* how much it costs and how much it's worth.'

Roberto shifted again and exchanged a furtive look with Burbona.

Chapter Forty-Four

For the rest of the week in Paris, Jemme seethed over the lower gallery *sous sol*. Every element of it was injurious to him, from the concept to the fact he hadn't been consulted on the planning to the nature of the planning itself – he didn't know which was more insulting. That he hated the idea, he already knew. There was absolutely no possibility that such a room could exist in his life's work. Such an empty expanse would be like wilfully creating a void in his dream. What he didn't know was how he felt about the business of the marble. Either Roberto was exceptionally gullible and was being taken for a ride by an unscrupulous supplier, or Roberto thought that he, Jemme, was gullible and was chancing his luck. He didn't know which was worse, working with someone foolish or working with someone who thought *he* was. Either way, he knew that the weekend Roberto had just spent in the chateau would be his last.

He leaned back in his chair. The day's work was spread out in front of him on his desk, but the only thing he focussed on was the gleam of the telephone's plastic receiver. It looked so inviting, and he was surprised to find that he was relishing the task ahead of him. During his career at the bank he had had to fire many people, and he had always dreaded it. Even when the person in question deserved it, he still felt awful during the actual conversation. He thought about it a little more, and realised that that was because nobody he had fired so far had actually wronged him. They might have made a costly mistake, committed some sort of transgression, or just been useless at their job, but they had never tried to cheat him personally, in the way that he was starting to suspect Roberto had. The only thing stopping him from picking up the receiver straight away was the fact that he had not yet decided how he wanted the conversation to go. He didn't want Roberto to think he had put one over on him, but he still wasn't convinced that Roberto was trying anything underhand. For one thing, the man was just too dull to attempt anything as remotely intriguing. The other difficulty was the fact that he had never really hired Roberto in the first place. He had just turned up one day, and then proved impossible to shift. He occasionally paid him for some of his work on the chateau, but it certainly wasn't a regular salary like Burbona received. In fact, Jemme still didn't know why Roberto even visited the chateau at all. He was so clearly disdainful of it, and he appeared to draw no enjoyment from his time there; his only pleasure appeared to be regaling Burbona with his stories of architecture, for which she seemed to have an insatiable appetite.

Jemme paused, his hand ready to pick up the phone. A thought suddenly struck him: *What if he made Burbona fire him*? There was something pleasing about the idea. It would be a way of getting rid of Roberto without actually having to talk to him, and of clipping Burbona's wings slightly in the process too – letting her know that he was not happy with the way she had acted.

He picked up the phone. Just as he was about to dial Burbona's number, he stopped himself. As much as she would hate having to fire Roberto, he also didn't want to miss out on the opportunity himself. He flicked through his address book with one hand until he found the number he wanted,

'Good afternoon,' a well-spoken voice answered the other line.

'Hello, Roberto, it's Jemme Mafeze.'

'Ah, Monsieur Mafeze, hello – I have been hoping to hear from you.'

'Have you?'

'Yes, I –' Roberto faltered for a moment, sounding nervous, 'I was hoping to clear up anything unresolved from that unfortunate issue of the marble.'

'Well, I'm glad you brought that up, Roberto. That's exactly what I was calling about too. I was wondering if you would be free to meet – perhaps later on this evening.'

'Yes, I could make myself free.'

'Good, some things need to be settled face to face, and, like you said, I have some unresolved issues I'd like to discuss.'

'Pleased to hear it,' said Roberto, sounding a good deal brighter and suggesting a time and place. Jemme agreed.

'Well, I look forward to it,' said Roberto.

'Yes, me too,' said Jemme, enjoying feeling a little villainous.

He returned to his work, only stopping when DD came in to give him news on Zuber & Cie. Jemme had scribbled the company's name down when researching ideas for American rooms in the chateau, and DD had been trying to contact them.

'Any success?' Jemme asked him.

'Yes, a great deal. The company are very easy to find, and are extremely well regarded. Everyone I have spoken with there has been well informed and helpful.'

'Well, that's a good start. What about their work?'

'They are still producing wood-blocked wallpapers, and I believe they are amongst the last to do so. The piece you were interested in is one of their most famous. It is called *Vue de l'Amérique du Nord* and was originally designed in

1834. They still own some of the original wood blocks, and have created replicas of the blocks that were lost or are too damaged to use. They would like to have several further consultations, but it is likely that they would be able to create the paper again for you within your specified dimensions. Once we have discussed it a little more, I will ask them for some quotes; it's a very labour-intensive and expert process and so I suspect it will be a high-budget endeavour.'

The smile that had spread across Jemme's face was so broad that for a moment he didn't speak.

'DD, you are a marvel. I don't think you could have given me better news, thank you. I would be very keen to commission this piece, so do tell your contact that we can have as many consultations as necessary and start as soon as he likes.'

DD nodded, then moved on to some banking matters. A couple of deals had gone much better than expected, which only improved Jemme's mood. Once DD had left, he sat back in his chair and the smile reappeared across his face. Then, he remembered that he was shortly going to be firing Roberto, and the smile widened.

He finished the rest of the day's work in good spirits, and then made his way to the place Roberto had suggested. As expected, it was staid, formal and stuffy. It felt like a relic from a past, long forgotten by all but a few French families who clung to it religiously. He shook his head; he couldn't believe that Roberto was a product of this society, yet still espoused modernism and portrayed himself as so forward-looking.

Jemme found the man himself in one of the dining rooms. He went over towards him, but was stopped in his tracks by a man in the establishment's green and gold uniform. This fellow seemed very agitated by the fact that Jemme hadn't signed in, and took him back over to the door, before fussing around with a guests and member's book. Jemme wasn't in the least fazed. It was exactly what he would have expected from a place like this. He also wasn't at all surprised when Roberto strode over and made a show of getting him in.

'This gentleman is with me,' he announced rather grandly to the uniformed man. Jemme smiled graciously, knowing that Roberto would soon be looking a little less smug.

Roberto ushered Jemme in as if it was his own home, 'Please, take a seat.'

'Thank you,' said Jemme, sitting down in an extremely uncomfortable straight-backed chair.

'I was very pleased to hear from you,' began Roberto, as soon as Jemme had sat down. 'I felt that matters were somewhat unresolved, when we last met.'

'Did you?'

'Oh yes, most definitely. I don't like to leave things unresolved.'

'Neither do I,' said Jemme, looking him directly in the eye.

Roberto looked momentarily confused, 'Well, yes,' he continued, 'as long as there is no confusion.'

'I can assure you, Roberto, there is no confusion at my end,' Jemme began.

'Good, good,' said Roberto, visibly relaxing. He opened his mouth to speak again, but Jemme continued.

'There is no confusion. I do not want you at the chateau any more.'

Roberto's already open mouth stayed open in surprise.

'Let me be absolutely clear, so that there is no confusion at your end either,' said Jemme. 'You will no longer be coming to chateau either in a professional or personal capacity. You will no longer be consulted on projects, even here in Paris, and you will no longer be required to contribute your own ideas. Thank you for your help until this point, but it is no longer required. Send me your bill and we'll call it quits.'

Roberto's mouth had formed a surprised 'o' shape. He remained that way for a few moments after Jemme had finished speaking, then evidently realised and shut it. He tried to muster all his dignity.

'I must say that I'm extremely surprised.'

'Really?'

'Most surprised,' repeated Roberto, 'and unable to think of anything which would have elicited such a response from you.'

'Really,' Jemme repeated, drawing the word out slightly, to emphasis his disbelief.

'Is this all because of the lower gallery *sous-sol* project?'

'It's not all because of it, no. However, the incident of the marble is what has finally made up my mind.'

'The incident?' Roberto asked.

'Roberto,' Jemme said, staring at him fixedly, 'I am not a fool. I know exactly what's going on, and I'm not happy. I suspect I know what's going on with Burbona too.'

Roberto returned his stare and for a moment the two men seemed to be sizing each other up. Jemme was unflinching and Roberto seemed to back down first.

'I see,' he nodded eventually. 'Well, in that case, I won't argue with you. I can see your mind has been made up.' He rose and offered Jemme his hand. 'I wish you good luck with the rest of your project.'

'Likewise,' said Jemme. He shook Roberto's hand. 'We won't be seeing each other again,' he said firmly, before turning and leaving.

On the way down, he replayed the conversation in his head. He had been hoping to flush Roberto out, and he was trying to decide if he had or not. He couldn't work out if Roberto's acceptance of his banishment was an admission of guilt.

Either way, he felt good about the outcome. It was a relief to know that he wouldn't have to put up with Roberto any longer, and that he could return his focus to the project again.

He felt much lighter on his way home, and took the time to take in his surroundings. Although it was a well-heeled and stuffy part of the city, it was also a beautiful one. He rarely came this way, and he wandered home slowly taking in the ornate window surrounds, highly decorative lintels and fine plasterwork on the outside of the buildings. It was obviously designed to signify the wealth and importance of the occupant, and Jemme wondered how Roberto managed to square this with the love of empty spaces he espoused.

By the time he was back in familiar terrain it was late, but Jemme was still able to catch one of his favourite cafes before they closed for the evening. Although it wasn't actually a Turkish café, Jemme had been going there for years and the owner knew him well. He was able to make him a mint tea which would rival many Jemme had drunk back in Istanbul – made with fresh mint and sweetened with honey, not sugar. He sipped it slowly and thought about how much he was looking forward to his next chateau visit. Plans were taking shapes for the Victorian and American rooms, and his mind was filled with ideas for everything in between. There were so many corridors, staircases and even rooms not yet decorated, and designing modern rooms felt fun. Change was refreshing, he thought to himself as he drained his brass cup. The mint leaves beneath were suddenly exposed, and he prodded at them thoughtfully with a spoon whilst he wondered what else he could change about his life.

By the time he finally got home, it was extremely late. He was therefore very surprised that the phone should ring within moments of him closing the front door behind him.

'Hello?' he said, concerned, as he picked up the receiver.

'I've been trying to call you all evening!' said an agitated voice at the end of the line. Jemme recognised Burbona's voice, but only just. The polish was gone and her tone was harsh.

'Hello Burbona, what's the matter? Is everything alright?'

'Is everything alright?!!' repeated Burbona as if was a ridiculous question. Jemme couldn't believe how grating her voice sounded. She usually spoke in a very honeyed way, particularly if she wanted something. Now her voice was harsh and clipped, and reminded Jemme of so many of the upper class French people he'd met and disliked since he moved to Paris.

'I was just wondering, because you're calling so late at night.'

'Well I tried to call you earlier but you didn't answer,' she snapped back at him.

'Yes… you said,' said Jemme, not liking her tone or this new side to her. 'I'm sorry if it was an emergency, I was out. With Roberto in fact.'

'Oh, I know exactly who you were out with.'

Jemme didn't really know what to say. He had been in such a good mood when he had arrived home, and he was not particularly happy about this turn of events. He also didn't understand why Burbona sounded so accusatory, and wondered what he could have done to vex her.

'Look, Burbona, I don't mean to be rude, but it's very late – what's this all about?'

'How could you?' said Burbona, drawing out the question.

'How could I what?'

'I think you know exactly what.'

'Look – I really have no idea what you're talking about and I would also really like to go to bed. Can this wait until tomorrow or is it an emergency?'

'All that hard work!' Burbona said. 'All for you! And you go and ruin everything because you're too proud,' she paused, 'or maybe it's because you just don't understand how business in France works.'

Jemme paused, slightly taken aback. Before he had a chance to reply, Burbona had leapt in again. 'Both. I expect it's both. Too proud *and* a poor understanding of French business.'

'Burbona, I have been running a very successful investment bank here for years and years. I think I understand how French business works. What's more, if you talk to anyone who actually knows me, they'll tell you that I am certainly not proud. Now, unless you get to the point, I'm going to hang up. I'm not going to sacrifice sleep to stand around and be insulted.'

It was the most confrontational he'd ever been with her, and it actually felt quite good. A memory of sitting in front of the café musing about change and how refreshing it was flicked through his mind. Perhaps there should be further changes, he thought to himself.

'Well, it appears that neither of us like having our time wasted. I know exactly what you've done – you've fired Roberto.'

'Oh,' said Jemme, wrinkling his nose. 'That's what this it about. Yes, I did. A couple of hours ago in fact.'

'Do you have any idea how crass that is?!' said Burbona, sounding even angrier. 'You cannot just *fire* Roberto! Do you have any idea how lucky you are – you were – to have one of Paris's most celebrated architects working for you? How lucky you were that I set that up for you?'

'I'm sure that, in certain circles, Roberto is very much admired and I'm sure that there will always be people to praise even his plainest skyscrapers, but I will never be one of those people,' said Jemme, determined to keep his cool. 'I very much hope that you can see how wrong he was for this whole project, otherwise I will be forced to question your judgement.'

'Question *my* judgement?!' Burbona repeated, sounding absolutely livid. 'I don't understand how you could even say something like that! Do you know how lucky you are to have me working for you on this project? Do you know how many other people approach me, how many people seek me out because of my taste and experience?!'

'I'm grateful for a lot of your input; you know that. However, Roberto was not right for this project, he won't be working on it any more, and that is the end of that. If you would like to talk some more about this tomorrow, then I suggest you call me when you've calmed down.'

There was a silence. For a moment, Jemme genuinely thought that Burbona was trying to compose herself at the other end of the line. However, when she finally spoke, he realised that it was because she was so outraged she hadn't even been able to speak.

'I have *never* come across someone who was so ungrateful for everything that they were being offered. I have never met anyone who was so unaware of how fortunate they were. To sack Roberto is unforgivable. This will tarnish my reputation as well as his. However, to deliberately ruin my plans is just spiteful.'

'Your plans? What plans have I apparently ruined?'

'You've scrapped the entire *sous-sol* project!' Burbona practically shrieked.

'Well, yes, of course I have. It was utterly ridiculous – surely you can see that!'

'See that? I set the whole thing up! What I see is you deliberately ruining an opportunity for me – something I had worked hard on.'

'How does it affect you in any way if this project goes ahead?' asked Jemme.

'Because I set the whole thing up!' Burbona repeated, managing to sound furious and exasperated at the same time. 'This is what I mean – no understanding of the way things are conducted in France.'

'Burbona, I assure you that I have every understanding of how things are conducted in France,' Jemme said coldly. He thought quickly – everything was suddenly falling into place: her fury at the project being cancelled, her and Roberto working on the whole thing together, the vast expense of the marble.

'Burbona,' Jemme began, slowly and very deliberately, 'do I understand that you were to benefit financially or otherwise if this project was executed?'

'Well of course I would – I organised everything, I sourced all the materials and commissioned the design! You don't think that I would do all of this and not expect anything in return?'

Jemme didn't reply. He didn't know how he felt. A small part of him had been hoping that his fears wouldn't be confirmed, that it had all been a misunderstanding and they could go back to how everything had been before, at the beginning. However, another part of him was almost relieved. It felt like confirmation of something that had been building up for a long time.

He sighed out loud – he couldn't deny that there was another part of him that felt very, very hurt.

'Burbona, what you are getting in return was a wage,' he said, hoping he didn't betray any sadness in his voice. He had always felt that there was something more, that she was there because she believed in what he was doing and wanted to be a part of it.

'A wage? You pay me nothing! This is how all business works in France, and you are naïve if you think otherwise.'

'Well I do think otherwise. I do not work with bribes and backhanders. I never have and it hasn't done me the slightest bit of damage so far. I have always been honest, transparent and conscientious in all my business dealings, and I have absolutely no intention to change now. I had thought that you were the same, and I'm disappointed to find out that we have such different viewpoints.' As he said it, Jemme tried to remember various purchases and commissions Burbona had made and given. He wondered if she had been creaming a commission on all of them too.

'Don't try and act like this is a moral issue,' said Burbona contemptuously, 'this is just how business is in France. I have invested a great deal of time in this, and I am very unhappy that I will not be getting any kind of reward for it.'

Jemme was at a loss for a reply. He couldn't believe how brazen she was being about the whole affair. Roberto had at least had the decency to be cagey and non-committal. Jemme wondered if he had actually managed to flush Roberto out in the end. It wouldn't surprise him at all if Roberto had run straight to Burbona after their meeting, to warn her. However, instead of being contrite and guilty, he couldn't believe how angry she was that he had thwarted her plans. He wondered how much Roberto would be earning for the whole thing as well.

'Burbona, I really don't know what to say. I'm not happy that it has come to this, but if you genuinely believe that there is nothing wrong with what you have done, and if you genuinely believe that that monstrosity of a room is what I wanted, then there is no way that we can continue to work together.'

'So you are firing me as well?!' said Burbona.

'Well, do you think that both of those things are alright?'

'I *cannot* believe this! I *cannot* believe that you are so...' she trailed off in her indignation. 'Fine, you will not see me again – there are plenty more like you.'

'I'm sure there are,' said Jemme and put down the phone.

He stared down blankly at the telephone for a moment, and struggled to piece together his thoughts. Manoeuvring himself around the desk, he sat down heavily in his morocco swivel chair. He leaned back and uttered a protracted sigh, and turned to face out of the window. Down in the street below, which was silent and empty, a couple of revellers returned home from the night's exertions in the city, giggling and stumbling over the pavement under the orange glow of the street lamps. Jemme was somewhat shaken, but he felt triumphant. He felt that he could now persevere with his work on the chateau without the doubts and suspicions that had been plaguing his mind of late. A flicker of a smile passed across his lips as he watched the partygoers disappear beyond the trees at the other end of the avenue. Their voices faded, leaving the scene beyond the glass panes still and silent. Jemme's brow then furrowed and the corners of his mouth drooped. Darker thoughts had stirred within his mind, and the satisfaction he had felt in disposing of the services of Burbona gave way to an acute feeling of longing, because he found himself thinking only of Hil. He could not explain it, but his eyes glistened as images of their wedding day crowded into his mind, images of her smile and her sparkling eyes and of the sorrowful look upon her face that fateful night he missed their dinner. There was all of the time they had lost; he had sacrificed his love for her to his love for the work on the chateau. Suddenly, the matter of Burbona seemed utterly trivial in comparison. With the feeling that he could bear it no longer, Jemme swivelled back to face the desk and, without pausing to give the matter much consideration, lifted the receiver and dialled Hil's number, still clear in his heart. He put the receiver to his ear, his heart in his mouth. It rang several times, but Hil did not answer. His resolve was waning when, on the seventh ring, a voice answered.

'Hello?'

Jemme immediately recognised Hil's voice. She sounded tired and surprised, though he supposed that was natural, given the late hour in which he found himself calling her.

'Hello?' she repeated, for Jemme had not yet worked out what to say to her. He cleared his throat and began.

'Hello Hil, it's Jemme here,' he said sheepishly. Hil remained silent. Jemme awkwardly cleared his throat once more.

'I... Is now a good time to talk?'

Hil sighed on the other end of the line. 'What is it, Jemme?' she asked wearily.

'I just wanted to see if we could talk for a few minutes.'

'About what?' asked Hil. 'What is there left to say?'

'I...'

Jemme's voice faltered. He didn't know how to answer this question.

'I just want to talk to you is all,' he replied.

Hil sighed once more. 'Fine,' she said quietly, 'talk.'

'I just had to let go of Burbona, and earlier I had to fire Roberto as well.'

Hil paused for a moment.

'Surely you'll be happy with that?' she replied.

'What makes you think that?' he asked.

'I know what you're like. I'm sure you relished the moment,' she said with uncharacteristic spite.

'I didn't relish it,' he said. 'I did what had to be done. Roberto was no good for our project and Burbona was a charlatan. They couldn't stay. I didn't fire them for the sake of deriving pleasure from the experience.'

Hil remained silent on the other end of the line.

'And, well, the whole situation just got me to thinking,' continued Jemme, uncertain about what his next words would be, yet feeling compelled to speak them just the same, fearful that Hil would hang up on him at any moment. 'I was thinking about us, and...'

'There is no "us,"' replied Hil blankly.

'Hil, please, don't be like this.'

'How should I be?' she asked in frustration. 'You call me in the middle of the night to tell me that you've just fired two people? After this long silence? After everything that happened between us? What do you want, Jemme?'

'I just want to talk. I want to talk about us.'

'Well that will be a short conversation because, as I just said, there is no "us."'

'But *could* there be?' asked Jemme. 'Could there be an "us" again?'

Hil did not respond.

'I was just thinking back to our wedding day, Hil, about all the good times we had. I know now that it's my fault that our relationship fell apart.'

Hil cleared her throat.

'I know now,' he continued, 'that it was my obsession with the chateau that ruined our marriage. I've even neglected my banking work because of it. I have been working like a man possessed to get this project just right, and in the process I've alienated most of my employees and my friends and, worst of all, I have alienated you.'

There was a brief silence.

'I'm glad you finally realise that,' she replied with a touch of warmth.

Sensing her slight change in tone, he knew it was now or never.

'I've been immersed in this project for how ever many years now, and I feel like it's taken over my life. I've fallen victim to interior design!'

Hil could not stop herself from giggling.

'It's true!' cried Jemme. 'I've fallen victim to parquet, to marble, to mosaics, to frescos, to murals, to gilding! I have let my other responsibilities and passions fall by the wayside.'

'You can do more than two things at once, Jemme,' replied Hil. 'The chateau doesn't have to consume your life. You can live a balanced life, and still care about the house.'

'I know I should be able to,' replied Jemme, 'but it just seems to be so much more exciting than my life as a banker. Banking is the most boring and stupid profession there is. There are only ever two decisions to be made as a banker. Invest or divest. That's it! That's all I end up doing when I speak to London, New York, Frankfurt and Tokyo in the morning. With the chateau, I have already had to make over forty thousand different decisions! Can you imagine how much more exciting a life that is for me?'

'I'm sure it is,' sighed Hil, 'and I can see why you've been sucked into the whole project, but there comes a time when you have to stop and say, "Enough is enough." That time is now, Jemme. You need to find balance in your life again.'

'I know you're right,' he replied. 'It's difficult though, because I just feel as though I'm surrounded by people who are taking advantage of me, of my passion for the house. I feel that if I take my eye off the ball even for a second, then someone will try to screw me over. I need someone in my life whom I can trust.'

'That's the banker in you talking,' returned Hil. 'You're not lacking people you can trust. You just have to make the leap and trust them.'

'The problem is that I can't afford to let anyone mess up the project now. Not at this stage.'

'You have to make *some* compromises, Jemme. I don't particularly want to rake up the past, but just look at what happened between you and me. That was all because you couldn't find balance in your life. Do you really want to carry on living that way?'

Jemme paused.

'No, I don't,' he said softly. 'Hil, I want to get back to the way we were. Do you think we could do that?'

'I don't know,' she replied hesitantly. 'I just think that the same thing would happen all over again. You might start out with good intentions, but sooner or later you'd slip back into your old ways and I'd be pushed to one side.'

'It wouldn't be that way,' he declared. 'Just meet me halfway. That's all I'm asking. You know I can't give up on the chateau now.'

'I would never ask you to do that, Jemme.'

'Having said that, I could scale back my trips to the house. I could give Le Selmelif and Philby a little extra authority so that they can make certain decisions on my behalf. That way I would only have to go down there every other weekend. That would give us so much more time to spend together. What do you think?'

'Jemme,' she replied, 'I'm not convinced. You're very good at talking the talk, but I'm not sure you'd be able to cope with delegating so much responsibility away from yourself. It's just not how you operate.'

'But I want to *try*,' he said. 'I want to try to do this because I want to try to be the man you deserve. You're more important to me than that old pile of bricks, as much as I love it.'

'I want to believe you, Jemme, but there's still so much left to do with the chateau. Will you ever be finished with it? You will always find something to tweak, something to change. You will never be able to stand back and say, "This is enough."'

'Probably not, Hil, but that doesn't mean it has to take up all of my time any more. It's true, there is still a great deal more to be done. I want to decorate the house with depictions of all sorts of places and historical events. I want to represent Napoleon's life and conquests, the discovery of North America, the construction of the palaces in St. Petersburg, the lives of Mozart and Beethoven in Vienna. I want to build a Roman bath. I even want to decorate my bathrooms with beautiful editions of the works of the greatest authors in history, so that you'll always have something good to read when you go to the toilet.'

Hil could not help herself. She laughed. Jemme smiled.

'But I want you to participate in all of this with me. I want you to have a voice in this. I want to do this together. So, what do you say? Can you give our love another chance? Can you meet me in the middle?'

There was a long pause at the other end of the line, and Jemme's facial muscles tensed.

'Jemme,' she finally responded, 'I still love you. I've always loved you. If you can promise me that you'll devote more time to us and, moreover, that you'll *want* to do that out of love for me, not merely out of fear of losing me, then yes. We can give it another shot.'

Tears welled in Jemme's eyes. An involuntary sob escaped his lips.

'Thank you, Hil,' he said, his voice breaking. 'Thank you.'

Hil began to well up in response to Jemme's display of emotion.

'I've always loved you, and I always will,' she wept.

'I'm catching the first train to meet you in the morning,' he said.

'That would be lovely,' she replied, struggling to compose herself. 'I'll see you in the morning, then.'

'Yes, you will. Everything will be different, you'll see.'

They said their goodbyes, and he hung up the phone. He turned back around to face out at the dark avenue beyond the window. He noticed his own face in the reflection in the window and laughed, wiping away his tears.

You did it, he said to himself.

JAMES EDEN

During his career, James Eden was responsible for hiring more than 2,000 employees around the world, covering the U.S., Europe, the Near East and Asia. Of these employees, several dozen were hired to help him and his family achieve a lifelong ambition – to restore and decorate to the highest possible standard an old chateau in rural France. His experiences with these employees, and the strain this ambitious project placed on his relationships with family members, inspired him to pen this, his second novel. Now retired, he devotes much of his time to writing.